"Sullivan presents 50 outstanding selections."

—Publishers Weekly

"The collection is a buff's delight. This book offers pure fun, in large dollops." *—Chicago Sun-Times*

"This fat and beautifully packaged anthology is a major book. It will become a reading staple for mystery fans everywhere." *—Ed Gorman*

"There's no better book for the mystery lover to pick up on a rainy night, or a clear moonlight night, or a stormy night, or a cold night, or—well—let's face it, this book filled from cover to cover with *Ellery Queen* mysteries is good for any kind of night." *—The Macon Beacon*

"This treat, edited by Eleanor Sullivan, brings together a who's who of mystery from the pages of the leading magazine in the field." *—Richmond Times-Dispatch*

FIFTY
BEST
MYSTERIES

Edited by

Eleanor Sullivan

CARROLL & GRAF PUBLISHERS
NEW YORK

Fɪꜰᴛʏ Bᴇꜱᴛ Mʏꜱᴛᴇʀɪᴇꜱ

Carroll & Graf Publishers
An Imprint of Avalon Publishing Group Inc.
245 West 17th Street
New York, NY 10011

Originally published by Carroll & Graf as *Fifty Years of the Best from Ellery Queen's Mystery Magazine* in 1991.

First Carroll & Graf paperback edition 1992
Second paperback edition 2004

Library of Congress Cataloging-in-Publication Data is available.

ISBN: 0-7867-1347-X

Printed in the United States of America
Distributed by Publishers Group West

CONTENTS

Acknowledgments   ix
Introduction   1
The Forties

THE CLUE OF THE RED WIG
  by John Dickson Carr   5
LOST STAR by C. Daly King   28
THE BLOOMSBURY WONDER
  by Thomas Burke   40
DRESSING-UP by W. R. Burnett   63
MALICE DOMESTIC by Philip MacDonald   73
I CAN FIND MY WAY OUT by Ngaio Marsh   88
THE FOURTH DEGREE by Hugh Pentecost   109
MIDNIGHT ADVENTURE by Michael Arlen   123
A STUDY IN WHITE by Nicholas Blake   135
THE PHANTOM GUEST
  by Frederick Irving Anderson   150

The Fifties

AS SIMPLE AS ABC by Ellery Queen   173
MONEY TO BURN by Margery Allingham   188
THE GENTLEST OF THE BROTHERS
  by David Alexander   197
ONE-WAY STREET by Anthony Armstrong   210

MURDER AT THE DOG SHOW
  by Mignon G. Eberhart   218
ALWAYS TRUST A COP by Octavus Roy Cohen   228
THE WITHERED HEART by Jean Potts   243
THE GIRL WHO MARRIED A MONSTER
  by Anthony Boucher   253
BETWEEN EIGHT AND EIGHT by C. S. Forester   268
KNOWING WHAT I KNOW NOW
  by Barry Perowne   279

The Sixties

CHANGE OF CLIMATE by Ursula Curtiss   297
LIFE IN OUR TIME by Robert Bloch   306
THE SPECIAL GIFT by Celia Fremlin   313
A NEAT AND TIDY JOB
  by George Harmon Coxe   322
RUN—IF YOU CAN by Charlotte Armstrong   336
LINE OF COMMUNICATION by Andrew Garve   345
DANGER AT DEERFAWN by Dorothy B. Hughes   354
THE MAN WHO UNDERSTOOD WOMEN
  by A. H. Z. Carr   367
REVOLVER by Avram Davidson   376
THE ETERNAL CHASE by Anthony Gilbert   387

The Seventies

REASONS UNKNOWN by Stanley Ellin   407
THREE WAYS TO ROB A BANK
  by Harold R. Daniels   418
THE PERFECT SERVANT by Helen Nielsen   427
THE MARKED MAN by David Ely   439
FLOWERS THAT BLOOM IN THE SPRING
  by Julian Symons   448
A NICE PLACE TO STAY by Nedra Tyre   462
PAUL BRODERICK'S MAN by Thomas Walsh   471

WHEN NOTHING MATTERS
   by Florence V. Mayberry   483
THIS IS DEATH by Donald E. Westlake   492
WOODROW WILSON'S NECKTIE
   by Patricia Highsmith   503

The Eighties

THE JACKAL AND THE TIGER
   by Michael Gilbert   517
THE FIX by Robert Twohy   536
ONE MOMENT OF MADNESS
   by Edward D. Hoch   546
LOOPY by Ruth Rendell   558
THE PLATEAU by Clark Howard   568
THE BUTCHERS by Peter Lovesey   585
BURNING BRIDGES by James Powell   596
A GOOD TURN by Robert Barnard   607
CLAP HANDS, THERE GOES CHARLIE
   by George Baxt   614
BIG BOY, LITTLE BOY by Simon Brett   624

ACKNOWLEDGMENTS

Grateful acknowledgment is made to the following for their permission to use their copyrighted material. Every reasonable effort has been made to trace the ownership of all copyrighted material included in this volume. Any errors which may have occurred are inadvertent and will be corrected in subsequent editions, provided proper notification is sent to the publisher.

The Forties: The Phantom Guest by Frederick Irving Anderson, copyright 1941 by American Mercury, Inc.; *Midnight Adventure* by Michael Arlen, copyright 1938 by Michael Arlen, reprinted by permission of Watkins, Loomis Agency, Inc.; *A Study In White* by Nicholas Blake, copyright 1949 by American Mercury, Inc., reprinted by permission of The Peters Fraser & Dunlop Group Ltd.; *The Bloomsbury Wonder* by Thomas Burke, reprinted by permission of John Hawkins & Associates; *Dressing-Up* by W. R. Burnett, copyright 1930 by Harper & Bros., reprinted by permission of Scott Meredith Literary Agency, Inc.; *The Clue of the Red Wig* by John Dickson Carr, copyright 1948 by John Dickson Carr, reprinted by permission of Harold Ober Associates, Inc.; *Lost Star* by C. Daly King, copyright 1944 by C. Daly King, reprinted by permission of Blanche C. Gregory, Inc.; *Malice Domestic* by Philip MacDonald, copyright 1946 by American Mercury, Inc., from SOMETHING TO HIDE, reprinted by permission of Doubleday, a division of Bantam, Doubleday, Dell Publishing Group, Inc.; *I Can Find My Way Out* by Ngaio Marsh, copyright 1946 by American Mercury, Inc., reprinted by permission of Harold

and Tidy Job by George Harmon Coxe, copyright © 1960 by Davis Publications, Inc., renewed © 1988 by Elizabeth Coxe, reprinted by permission of Brandt & Brandt Literary Agents, Inc.; *Change of Climate* by Ursula Curtiss, copyright © 1967 by Ursula Curtiss, reprinted by permission of Brandt & Brandt Literary Agents, Inc.; *Revolver* by Avram Davidson, copyright © 1962 by Davis Publications, Inc., reprinted by permission of Richard D. Grant, Literary Agent; *The Special Gift* by Celia Fremlin, copyright © 1967 by Davis Publications, Inc., reprinted by permission of the author; *Line of Communication* by Andrew Garve, copyright © 1967 by Andrew Garve, reprinted by permission of Curtis Brown Ltd.; *The Eternal Chase* by Anthony Gilbert, copyright © 1965 by Davis Publications, Inc., reprinted by permission of Curtis Brown Ltd.; *Danger at Deerfawn* by Dorothy B. Hughes, copyright © 1964 by Davis Publications, Inc., reprinted by permission of Blanche C. Gregory, Inc.

The Seventies: Three Ways to Rob a Bank by Harold R. Daniels, copyright © 1972 by Davis Publications, Inc.; *Reasons Unknown* by Stanley Ellin, copyright © 1978 by Stanley Ellin, reprinted by permission of Curtis Brown Ltd.; *The Marked Man* by David Ely, copyright © 1979 by Davis Publications, Inc., reprinted by permission of Roberta Pryor, Inc.; *Woodrow Wilson's Necktie* by Patricia Highsmith, copyright © 1972 by Patricia Highsmith, reprinted by permission of Diogenes Verlag Ag.; *When Nothing Matters* by Florence V. Mayberry, copyright © 1979 by Davis Publications, Inc., reprinted by permission of the author; *The Perfect Servant* by Helen Nielsen, copyright © 1971 by Davis Publications, Inc., reprinted by permission of Ann Elmo Agency, Inc.; *Flowers that Bloom in the Spring* by Julian Symons, copyright © 1971 by Davis Publications, Inc., reprinted by permission of Curtis Brown Ltd., London; *A Nice Place to Stay* by Nedra Tyre, copyright © 1970 by Davis Publications, Inc., reprinted by permission of Scott Meredith Literary Agency, Inc.; *Paul Broderick's Man* by Thomas Walsh, copyright © 1979 by Davis Publications, Inc., reprinted by permission of Thomas

INTRODUCTION

Exactly one hundred years after the publication of "The Murders in the Rue Morgue," which along with Edgar Allan Poe's two subsequent tales featuring C. Auguste Dupin set down the general principles of the pure detective story forever, the need for a magazine devoted to short detective fiction was so great that the busily writing Ellery Queen nevertheless took on the formidable commitment of editing, hands on, a mystery magazine under his name.

"This first issue is frankly experimental," he wrote in the Introduction to Issue 1 in 1941. "Our belief that a large public exists which impatiently awaits such publication can only be confirmed by that public. For the present therefore we plan to publish *Ellery Queen's Mystery Magazine* quarterly. Our ultimate purpose is to publish a new volume each month. That, however, depends upon the reception accorded this and future volumes. The more wholehearted and widespread your response, the more quickly regular monthly publications will be scheduled."

By 1946, *EQMM* had achieved monthularity and the 1962 *Reader's Encyclopedia of American Literature* (Crowell), under its lengthy tribute to Ellery Queen, said: "In 1941 they [Frederic Dannay and Manfred B. Lee, who collaborated as Ellery Queen] began to edit *Ellery Queen's Mystery Magazine,* the finest periodical of its kind. They stated, 'Queen has waged unceasing battle on two fronts: to raise the sights of mystery writers generally to the target of a genuine and respected literary form and to encourage good writing among our colleagues by offering a practical market not otherwise available among American magazines, as well as to develop new writers seeking expression in the genre.'

"Queen has achieved victory on both these fronts; he has given the detective story a respectable place in serious writing. Queen's magazine often carries mystery stories by well-known authors both current and past and has made it seem as if every writer of note in history produced at least one such story."

One can be unnerved at the prospect of selecting stories for any anthology, and choosing the fifty best published in *EQMM*'s first fifty years of publication—fifty stories from some eight thousand, only ten from the hundreds published each of the first five decades—was clearly an enormous challenge, given the fact that the editors have tried to provide the very best stories they could find in every single issue of the magazine published over those fifty years.

We took the task by decades and decided to go after—of those stories to which rights were available and had not been well and duly anthologized already—solid and entertaining stories by regular and significant contributors, stories that reflected the time in which they were written and the best work being produced in that decade. There are authors not included here who ought to be—yet all fifty of the authors who are here should be. They and the stories they wrote elicited the wholehearted and widespread response Ellery Queen openly hoped for when he ventured the editorship of *EQMM* and wrote that first Introduction.

Reflecting the times in which they are written, as most fiction does, the detective/crime/suspense story underwent many changes in the hundred years between "The Murders in the Rue Morgue" and the first publication of *EQMM,* and it has undergone many more in the turbulent years since. (In the past year alone, there has been much conjecture about what will happen with the spy story. What to do? Set them back in time, which would dampen their air of immediacy? Transfer the emphasis to industrial espionage?) Both the straight detective and the private-eye story demand the most innovative imitation if they are not to be stale, and a strong sense of reality in concept and character if they are to be acceptable to contemporary readers.

But this is being managed with such alacrity by a host of mystery writers on both sides of the Atlantic *and* the Pacific, north *and* south of the Equator, investing their imagination and talent in the short form as well as the long, that I'm in awe of the task facing the editor asked to choose the best from the next fifty years of *EQMM.*

—Eleanor Sullivan

The Forties

THE CLUE OF THE RED WIG

by JOHN DICKSON CARR

They usually put the paper to press at two a.m. MacGrath, the news editor, who was not feeling well after the Christmas celebrations, went home early to his own bed and left things at the office to young Patterson. MacGrath was sleeping a shivering sleep when the telephone at his bedside rang.

MacGrath made unearthly noises, like a ghost roused before midnight. But he answered the phone.

"Hazel Loring?" he repeated. "What about her?"

"She's dead," answered Patterson. "Murdered, it's pretty certain. Do you know Victoria Square?"

"No."

"It's a quiet little residential square in Bayswater. Hazel Loring lived there. In the middle of the square there's a garden reserved for the use of residents. About eleven o'clock a policeman on his rounds found Hazel Loring dead in the garden with practically no clothes on—"

"What?" shouted MacGrath; and the sleep was struck from his eyes.

"Well, only a brassiere and a pair of step-ins. She was sitting on a bench, dead as Cleopatra, with the rest of her clothes folded up on the bench beside her."

"In *this* weather?"

"Yes. The policeman saw her go into the garden an hour before. Cause of death was a fractured skull, from several blows with a walking stick whose handle was loaded with lead. Signs of a struggle behind the bench."

"Right!" said MacGrath. "Splash it on the front page. Every woman in the land will want to know what happened to Hazel Loring!"

Everybody knew the name of Hazel Loring, the face of Hazel Loring, the opinions of Hazel Loring. "Smile and Grow Fit" was the title of her weekly column in the *Daily Banner,* a deadly rival of MacGrath's own *Daily Record.* "Smile and Grow Fit" was also the title of the booklets, sold by the thousand, in which she explained to housewives how they might keep slim without anguish. She was no grim taskmistress of health. She did not sternly order them to eat a dry biscuit, and like it.

"I've devised these exercises on the advice of a doctor," she wrote. "Just three minutes each morning; and don't bother any more about it. If you like chocolates, in heaven's name eat chocolates. Only mind you do my exercises: and then eat what you like."

Her chatty, intimate manner warmed their hearts. She became more than an adviser on health. She counselled them about love and hats and husbands. Everybody had seen pictures of the strong, square, pleasant face, showing fine teeth in a smile, and with a dimple at each corner of the mouth. She was slim, with a good figure, and intensely active. She was well dressed, but not offensively so. Her brown hair was bobbed, her brown eyes grave. Her age might have been thirty-five. Thousands felt that they knew her personally, and wrote to tell her so.

Yet somebody killed her, half-dressed, in a public garden on a bitter December night.

If truth must be told, even in MacGrath, hard-boiled as he was, the first reaction was a twinge of pity. His wife was even more emphatic.

"Poor woman!" said Mrs. MacGrath from the opposite bed. "Poor woman!"

"Ho? Is that how it strikes you?" asked MacGrath, his news-sense instantly on the alert.

"Of course it is. Of all the brutal, senseless—!"

"Then that's how we'll play the story. I think I'm getting an inspiration. But Hazel Loring. Oh Lord!"

The next day he carried his inspiration to Houston, the managing editor.

The offices of the *Daily Record* occupy a huge modernistic building, a sort of chromium-plated goldfish bowl. Fleet Street was buzzing with gossip. The murder of Hazel Loring, though they could not yet call it a murder, was considered so important that they held a conference in the managing editor's office. Here, in a cubist-designed room with bright curtains, the stately Houston sat behind a desk topped with black glass, and drew down the corners of his mouth.

"Impossible," Houston said. "We can't do it. Dignity."

"All right. *Be* dignified," said MacGrath. "But don't pass up a thing like this. Now see here, J. H. This is a woman's crime; it oozes feminine interest. It's good for a daily story. Our-Correspondent-Watches-Police; Developments-Day-By-Day. So, with half the women in England crying for news of their favorite, what do we do? Why, we put a woman to cover it."

Houston passed a hand over his thin, high forehead.

"A woman doing police reporting?"

"Why not? She can be dignified, can't she? Womanly and kind, with a touch of sadness? Man, they'll eat it up!"

Houston hunched up his shoulders. "She'd have to be tough," he pointed out. "Covering a war is one thing; covering a murder is another. I don't know who I could assign to it."

"What about that French girl? Jacqueline Dubois. Only been with us a week. Came over when things there went to blazes. But I'll tell you something, J. H. She had the reputation of being the smartest news-hawk in Paris; Richart of *L'Oeil* recommended her in superlatives, and I think he's right."

"She speaks English?"

"She's half English. Her mother was a Cockney. She speaks English all right."

"And she will be—er—dignified?"

"Absolutely. I guarantee it, J. H."

"Get her," said Houston.

Nevertheless, he was uneasy until he actually set eyes on Jacqueline Dubois. Then he drew a breath of relief, and almost beamed.

MacGrath, on the other hand, was jarred. In recommending this girl MacGrath had been acting on a hunch; he knew little about her beyond Richart's word. And, at his first sight of Jacqueline, he had a panicky feeling that Richart must have been indulging in a deplorable Gallic sense of humour.

Jacqueline entered the office so timidly that Houston rose to draw out a chair for her. She was a golden blonde, small and plump, with one of those fair skins which flush easily, and those dark blue eyes which are either wide open or modestly lowered. Her mouth expressed confusion, but anxiety to please. Her fur coat was good but unobtrusive; from her plain grey dress to her tan stockings and shoes she was trim and yet retiring. She kept her big eyes fixed on Houston except when he looked directly at her. In a soft, sweet voice she hesitantly asked what was wanted.

While MacGrath stood in despair, Houston told her.

"And that's the idea, Miss Dubois. Your purpose is to—"

"To pester the police," groaned MacGrath.

"To print," said Houston sternly, "all desirable news which will be of interest to our public. Would you like the assignment?"

Jacqueline raised her limpid blue eyes.

"Would I like it?" she breathed. "Hot ziggety damn!"

Houston sat back with a start. She was covered in confusion, modesty struggling with gratitude.

"I thank you on my knees," she went on, clasping her hands together. "Miss Loring. The poor lady who has so unfortunately kicked the ghost. I had wished to cover that story, yes; but, blimey, I never thought I should get it. Oh, you are a dear. Would you like me to kiss you?"

"Good heavens, no!" said Houston.

But Jacqueline was not listening. She was utterly absorbed. The toe of her shoe tapped the carpet. Her eyes were turned inwards, a pucker of concentration between the brows; and, as she reflected, she nodded to herself.

"I am handicap," she confessed. "I am new to England and I do not know the ropes yet. If I get you a scoop, I must get it funny-ways. Who is the head of your whole police department?"

"The Assistant Commissioner for the Criminal Investigation Department," said MacGrath.

"Good!" said Jacqueline briskly. "I make love to him."

Houston gave her a long, slow look.

"No, no, no!" he said.

"Yes, yes, yes!" said Jacqueline, continuing to nod briskly.

"But you can't do that, Miss Dubois!"

"I do not understand," complained Jacqueline, breaking off to look at him with shy astonishment. "You do not wish me to do it? Why?"

"To explain that fully, Miss Dubois, might take a long time. I can sum up by saying that it would hardly be in accord with the policy of this newspaper. Besides, there are—er—practical considerations. In the first place, you'd never get near him. In the second place, even if you did you wouldn't get any story."

A twinkle appeared in Jacqueline's limpid eyes.

"Ha, ha, ha," she said. "That is what they tell me when I make eyes at Mornay, the *juge d'instruction*. He has whiskers this long"—her gesture indicated a beard of improbable dimensions—"but I get from him the official photographs of De La Rive shooting at all the gendarmes in the rue Jean Goujoun, and I scoop the town! Still, if you do not wish it?"

"Definitely not."

Jacqueline sighed. "Orright," she conceded. "Then I must find out the name of the policeman in charge of the case, and make love to *him*. Also, please, I should like a newspaper photographer to go with me all the time."

"A photographer? Why?"

"First because it is practical. I have got some fine pictures when I work for *L'Oeil*. Once I get a picture of the Comtesse de la Tour St. Sulpice, which is a kleptomaniac, pinching a necklace out of Paulier's in the rue de la Paix."

"Is that so?"

"Oo la la, what a sensation!" She gurgled delightedly. "Then too it is useful if you can get a picture of a police officer doing something he should not. You tell him you will publish the picture unless he gives you a story."

Houston had been listening under a kind of hypnosis. Jacqueline seemed to be surrounded by a rose-leaf cloud of innocence, like a figure on a valentine. He could not have been more startled if the Mona Lisa had suddenly leaned out of her frame and put out her tongue at him. He found his voice.

"We begin with vamping and pass on to blackmail," he said. "MacGrath, I can't do it. Young woman, you're fired! You'd ruin this paper in a week."

"If she's fired," roared MacGrath, "I resign. Splendor of saints, here's a newspaperman at last!"

"Do you want the Home Office to put us out of business?"

"We've got subeditors to read her copy, haven't we? I tell you, J. H., if—"

"Then there is another thing," pursued Jacqueline timidly. "One of your photographers is called Henry Ashwin. He is a good fellow, though I think he drink too much visky-soda. He is the photographer I want, please."

"Ashwin? Why Ashwin?"

"I find out he is making the goo-goo eyes at Hazel Loring's maidservant. Yes! That is something the others pass up, eh? So I give him visky-soda and I talk to him. Already I get much information, you see."

"Before you were assigned to the story?"

Jacqueline raised her eyebrows.

"But yes, yes, yes! Of course. Listen! This Miss Loring, her age is thirty-five. In private life she is very bad-tempered. Henry Ashwin thinks she is what you call a phony, somehow, but he is not sure about what. Also she is good-goody, what you call a prude. Is she married? No! But she has a fiancé, a lawyer which is called Edward Hoyt; and he hang about her for five years and still it is no soap. Why does she not marry him, eh?"

"Well?"

"I find out," answered Jacqueline simply. "Now I tell you something the police have not told you."

"Go on," muttered Houston, still hypnotized.

"This is what her maid say to Henry Ashwin, and Henry Ashwin say to me. When Miss Loring is found sitting on the bench in that garden, wearing only the brassiere and the step-ins and her shoes, the other clothes are folded up on the bench beside her."

MacGrath was instantly alert. "We know that. It's in all the papers."

"Yes! *But,*" said Jacqueline, "there are other things too. Folded up in the clothes (so) there is a red wig and a pair of dark spectacles."

Houston and MacGrath stared at each other, wondering whether this might be some obscure French metaphor. But Jacqueline left them in no doubt.

"A red wig," she insisted, tapping her golden hair. "And the smoky spectacles you look through." She cupped her hands over her eyes in mimicry. "Why should Miss Loring have them, eh? Blimey, but that is not all! It is certain she undressed herself, and was not undressed by anybody. Her maid tells Henry Ashwin that Miss Loring has a special way of folding stockings, like . . . ah, zut! . . . would you like me to take off mine and show you?"

"No, no!"

"Orright. I only ask. But it is special. Also the way of folding the dress. So she take her own dress off, and she have a wig and spectacles. Please, will you let me find out why?" Her big blue eyes turned reproachfully on Houston. "You say you will fire me, and that is not nice. I know I am a goofy little beasel; that is what they all say in Paris; but if you will please be a nice man and give me a chance I will get you that story, cross my heart. Yes?"

Houston had the darkest misgivings. But he was a journalist.

"Hop to it," he said.

Inspector Adam Bell, Criminal Investigation Department, stood in the prim little front parlor of number 22 Victoria Square. He looked alternately out of the window, towards the garden in the center, and then back to the white-faced man opposite him.

Sedate and dun-colored was Victoria Square, Bayswater, in the bleak winter afternoon. The house fronts were sealed up. In the garden, surrounded by teeth of spiked iron railings, the branches of trees showed black and knotted against a muddy twilight; its gravel paths wound between iron benches and skeleton bushes, on grass hard with frost.

Inspector Bell, in the white, antiseptic front parlor of the dead woman's house, faced Hazel Loring's fiancé. Inspector Bell was a young and very serious-minded product of Hendon, but his sympathetic manner had already done much.

"And you can't tell me anything more, Mr. Hoyt?"

"Nothing!" said Edward Hoyt, and fingered his black tie. "I wanted to take her to a concert last night, but she refused, and I went alone. I —er— don't read the sensational press. So I knew nothing about this business until Hazel's secretary, Miss Alice Farmer, telephoned me this morning."

Inspector Bell shared Hoyt's views about the sensational press: the house was triple-guarded against reporters, though a hundred eyes came to stop and stare in the square.

Edward Hoyt suddenly sat down beside the small fire in the white grate. He was a long, lean, pleasant-faced man of just past forty, with big knuckly hands and a patient manner. He had certainly, Bell reflected, been a patient suitor. His eyes in the firelight were faintly bloodshot, and he turned them often towards a sofa on which lay a neat wig, a pair of dark spectacles, and a heavy blackthorn walking stick.

"It's fantastic and degrading," he went on, "and I still don't believe it. Can't *you* tell me anything, Inspector? Anything at all?"

Bell was noncommittal.

"You've heard the evidence, sir. Miss Farmer, her secretary, testifies that at a few minutes before ten last night Miss Loring left the house, refusing to say where she was going." He paused. "It wasn't the first time Miss Loring had gone out like that: always about ten o'clock, and usually staying out two or three hours."

Hoyt did not comment.

"From here," said Bell, "she must have gone straight across to the garden—"

"But why, in heaven's name," Hoyt burst out, "the *garden?*"

Bell ignored this. "A policeman on his rounds heard someone fumbling at the gate of the garden. He flashed his light, and saw Miss Loring opening the gate with a key. He questioned her, but she explained that she lived in the square and had a right to use the garden, even on a blacked-out December night.

"The constable let her go. But he was worried. About an hour later, his beat brought him round to the garden again. The gate was still open: he heard it creak. He went in, and found Miss Loring sitting on a bench . . . there . . . at the first turn of the gravel path, about fifteen feet from the gate."

Bell paused.

He visualized the scene, sharp in its loneliness. The gate squeaking in a raw wind; the brief, probing light on icy flesh and white silk underclothing; the head hanging down over the back of the bench; and the high-heeled shoes with button-fastenings undone.

"The rest of her clothing—fur coat, dress, suspender-belt, and stockings —lay beside her: folded in such a way that her maid, Henrietta Simms, swears she took off the clothes herself. Her handbag was untouched. The key to the garden gate, with a large cardboard label attached, lay on the path."

Each time Bell made a statement, Edward Hoyt nodded at the fire.

Bell went over to the sofa and picked up the walking stick. It was top-heavy, because its nickel-plated head contained half a pound of lead.

"She'd been killed," Bell went on, "behind that bench. The ground was hard, but there were prints of those high heels of hers all over the place. There'd been a struggle: she wasn't any weakling."

"No," agreed Hoyt.

"Her skull was fractured over the left temple with this stick." Bell weighed it in his hand. "No doubt about this as the weapon. Microscopic traces of blood, and a hair, on the handle: though the wound hardly bled at all outwardly. Our laboratory identifies—"

He broke off apologetically.

"I beg your pardon, sir. I'm not trying to give you the third degree with this. I only brought it along to see whether anybody could identify it."

Hoyt spoke with old-fashioned courtesy.

"And I beg *your* pardon, Inspector. It is a pleasure to deal with a gentleman." He got to his feet, and drew the back of his hand across his mouth. "I'm glad there was no blood," he added. "I'm glad she wasn't—knocked about."

"Yes."

"But is that reasonable, Inspector? A fatal injury, with so little blood?"

"Oh yes. It's the rupture of brain-tissues that counts. A friend of mine got concussion from being struck by the door of a railway carriage and never knew there was anything wrong with him until he collapsed." Bell's tone changed; he spoke sharply. "Now, sir, I've spoken my piece. Have you anything to tell me?"

"Nothing. Except—"

"Well?"

Hoyt hesitated. "I'd been a bit worried about her. She hasn't been looking at all well lately. I'm afraid she had a tendency to overeat." There was the ghost of a smile on his face, contradicted by the bloodshot eyes. "But she said, 'So long as I do my exercises every morning, as thousands of my followers are doing'—she was very proud of her position, Inspector—"

This was hardly what Bell wanted.

"I mean, do you know any reason why anybody should have wanted to kill her?"

"None. I swear!"

"Or why she should have undressed herself in order to get killed?"

Hoyt's mouth tightened. But he was prevented from answering by the entrance of a soft, quiet, but quick-moving woman in horn-rimmed spectacles. Miss Alice Farmer, the perfect secretary, resembled the old-time notion of a schoolmistress. Her face, though not unattractive, was suggestive of a buttered bun; her brown hair was dressed untidily; she wore paper cuffs and flat-heeled shoes.

Miss Farmer had many times shown her devotion to Hazel Loring during six years' service. Now her eyelids looked pink and sanded, and occasionally she reached under the spectacles to dab at them with the tip of a handkerchief.

"Ghouls!" she said, gripping the handkerchief hard. "Ghouls! Inspector, I—I know poor Hazel's body has been taken away. But didn't you give orders that *none* of those horrible reporters was to be admitted to the square over there?"

"Yes, of course. Why?"

"Well," said Miss Farmer, putting out her chin bravely, "they're there now. You can see them from my window upstairs. Two of them. One is a man taking pictures; and the other, if you please, is a *woman*. How any *decent* woman could lower herself to write for the—" She stopped, and her face grew scarlet. "I mean *report,* of course; not write *nice* things; that's altogether different. Oh, dear. You do see what I mean, don't you?"

Inspector Bell saw only that his orders had been disobeyed. He stiffened.

"You're sure they're reporters?"

"Just *look* for yourself!"

Bell's pleasant face grew sinister. He drew a deep breath. He picked up his overcoat and his bowler hat from a chair.

"Excuse me just one moment," he said formally. "I'll attend to them."

By the time he left the house, Bell was running. The garden gate, on the west side of the square, was almost opposite Hazel Loring's house. The iron bench—once green, but now of a rust color—itself faced due west, where the gravel path curved in front of it.

Round it prowled a small golden-haired figure in a fur coat, and a large untidy figure with a mackintosh and a camera. Inspector Bell "Oi'd" at them; then he squared himself in front of them and began to talk.

Henry Ashwin, the photographer, took it stolidly. All he did was to pull his hat farther on a pair of large projecting ears, and shrug his shoulders in an apologetic way. But Jacqueline, between indignation and utter astonishment, was struck dumb. She sincerely felt that she was helping in the investigation, and she could not understand what this man was going on about.

"You must not be such a grimy camel!" she cried, reasoning with him kindly. "You do not understand at all. I am Dubois of the *Record.* This is Mr. Ashwin of the *Record.*"

"I know Mr. Ashwin," said Bell grimly. "Now, for the last time, madam: will you get out of here, or must you be taken out by main force?"

"But you do not mean that!"

Bell stared at her.

"What makes you think so?"

"And you should not talk so to the Press. It is not nice and you get yourself into trouble. Henry, I do not like this man. Kick him out of here and then we get on with our work."

"Ashwin," said Bell, "is this girl completely off her head?"

Ashwin intervened in a protesting rumble. "Sorry, Inspector; I'll fix it. Look here, Jackie, things aren't the same here as they are in France. That's what I've been trying to tell you. In England, reporters aren't allowed to—"

"You will not do it?"

"I can't, Jackie!"

"Now I am mad," said Jackie, folding her arms with an air of cold grandeur. "Blimey, now I am good and mad; and just for that I do not tell you anything about the clue I have discovered."

"Clue?" said Bell sharply.

"Ha, *now* you are interested, eh?" cried Jacqueline, wagging her head. Her tone changed: it became timid and pleading. "Please, I like to be nice, and I like you to be nice too. I could help you if you would let me. I think I know what happen here last night. As soon as I hear about Miss Loring's shoes being unbuttoned, and hear about the wig and spectacles—"

Bell whirled round on her.

"How do you know her shoes were unbuttoned? And about any wig and spectacles? That wasn't given out to the Press!"

Twilight was deepening over the spiky trees of the garden. Not a gleam showed in Victoria Square except the hooded sidelights of a taxi, which circled the square with its engine clanking noisily. Jacqueline opened her handbag, and drew out a large oblong of glazed paper.

It was a photograph of Hazel Loring's body, taken from in front and some dozen feet away. The shadows were behind it, so that every detail showed with crude realism: the upright posture but limp arms, the head thrown back, the slim muscular legs and shoes whose open fastenings were visible at a glance.

"Where," Bell shouted, "did you get this?"

"*I* got it, Inspector," Ashwin admitted. "I climbed over the fence this morning, before they'd moved anything. If I'd used a flashbulb your men would have spotted me straightaway; but there was a good strong sun up to ten o'clock, so I just took a snap and hared off."

Ashwin's little eyes blinked out of the shadow of his shabby hat. It had grown so dark in the garden that little more could be seen of him except the shift and shine of his eyes, and the fact that he needed a shave. If ordinarily he might have been something of a swaggerer, he was subdued now. He also had found Jacqueline a handful.

"I wasn't even going to use the picture, I swear!" he went on, and stated his real grievance. "This girl pinched it from me, when I wasn't even going to show—"

"Shoes!" insisted Jacqueline.

Bell swung round again. "What about the shoes?"

"They is clues," said Jacqueline simply. "You must not ask me how I get my information. The wig and the spectacles I learn about from Miss Loring's maid, in a way. But I do not mind telling you what will solve your case for you, strike me pink."

Bell hesitated.

"If this is some sort of game," he snapped, "there's going to be a lot of trouble in store for certain people I could mention. Now, I warn you! But if you've got anything to tell me, let's hear it."

Jacqueline was complacent.

"You do not see that the shoes show what has happen here?"

"Frankly, I don't."

"Ah! That is why you need a woman to detect for you when a woman is murdered. Now I show you. You see in the picture that the shoes have very high heels. Yes?"

"Yes."

"And they fasten only with one strap and one button across the . . . the . . . ah, zut!"

"Instep?"

"I am spikking the English very well, thank you," said Jacqueline, drawing herself up coldly. "I do not need your help to be pure. And I have already think to say instep. But you still do not tumble? No?" She sidled closer. Coaxing and honey-sweet, her voice caressed him out of the twilight. "If I tell you, then you do something for me? You will be a nice man and let me print what I like?"

"I most certainly will not."

"Orright. Then I will not tell you."

Adam Bell's wrath boiled clear to the top. Never in his career had he met anyone quite like this. It is true that his career had not been a long one; but then Jacqueline's could not have been so very long either. Now he meant to have no more nonsense. He would put her in her place, and with no uncertain adjectives.

He had opened his mouth to do this, when there was a flicker of a shrouded light across the square. The door of number 22 opened and closed.

Bell had a sharp premonition of disaster as soon as he heard the flat-heeled footsteps rapping and ringing on frosty pavements. A squat little figure, coatless and with wisps of hair flying, hurried across the street into the garden.

When the figure came closer, Bell saw that tears were trickling down Miss Alice Farmer's face.

"It's all your fault," she said accusingly to Bell. "Oh dear, if only you hadn't left! If only you'd stayed with him!"

"Easy now. What is it? Steady, Miss Farmer!"

"Your sergeant's phoned for the ambulance; and he says they may pull him through, but oh dear, if they don't I don't know what I shall do. Oh dear, it's even more dreadful than—"

Then she pulled herself together.

"I'm sorry. It's poor Mr. Hoyt. He's taken poison. You'd better come over to the house at once."

Adam Bell was not able to interview Hoyt until the following day. That morning's edition of the *Daily Record* was in Bell's pocket: he wondered what the Assistant Commissioner would have to say about Jacqueline Dubois's story.

A nurse conducted him to a small private room, where Edward Hoyt lay propped up among the pillows of a white iron bed. Alice Farmer sat in a squeaky rocking chair by the window, looking out at the snowflakes that had begun to thicken over Kensington Gardens.

"Rather a foolish thing to do, wasn't it, sir?" Bell asked quietly.

"I recognize that, Inspector."

"Why did you do it?"

"Can't you guess?"

Hoyt even managed a sour smile. His hands, snake-veined, lay listless on the coverlet; his gaze wandered over the ceiling without curiosity. Yesterday he had seemed in his middle forties: now he looked ten years older.

"The curious thing is," he went on, frowning, "that I had no intention of doing it. That's a fact, Inspector. I hadn't realized—by George, I hadn't!—how terrible and irresistible a mere *impulse* can be."

He paused, as though to get his breath.

"I went upstairs," he said, "to have a look at Hazel's room. That's all. It honestly is all. I glanced into the bathroom. I saw the medicine cabinet open, and a bottle of morphine tablets inside. Before I had any notion of what I meant, I had filled a glass of water, and swallowed seven or eight of the tablets as fast as I could get them down. At that time, I admit, I didn't want to live any longer."

"No, sir?"

"No. But I have changed my mind now. I am sorry: it was, as you say, a very foolish thing to do."

Always the gentleman, thought Inspector Bell.

From the direction of the window came a sharp, almost malignant squeak from the rocking chair. Alice Farmer glanced over her shoulder, and back again quickly. The snow shed shifting lights into the warm, close room.

"Of course I realize," Bell said awkwardly, "that as Miss Loring's fiancé—"

"It is not quite accurate to call me her fiancé," returned Hoyt, with detached calmness.

His tone made Inspector Bell sit up sharply.

"Meaning, sir?"

"Hazel never intended to get married, to me or anybody else."

"How do you know that?"

"She told me so. But I kept on patiently waiting. I have always had a fancy for the senseless role of the *preux chevalier*. God knows I'm cured of that now." Hoyt closed his eyes, and opened them again. "You see that I am being frank."

"You mean she didn't love you?"

Hoyt smiled faintly. "I doubt if Hazel was ever in love with anybody. No: I wasn't referring to that."

"Well?"

"I think she was married already. One moment!" The weak voice sharpened and grew firm. "I have absolutely no evidence for saying that. It's a guess. An impression. A—well, Inspector, I haven't known Hazel Loring for five years without learning something about her beyond those famous eyebrows and dimples. I knew her moods. And her heart. And her mind: which was, after all, a second-rate mind. Lord forgive me, what am I saying?"

He broke off, looking still more ill. There was another squeak from the rocking chair as Alice Farmer got up to pour him a glass of water from the bedside table.

Hoyt thanked her with a grateful nod; and she hardly glanced at him. But to Inspector Bell, watching every turn of lip or hand, that glance meant much. Bell thought to himself, with a rush of realization: if Hazel Loring wasn't in love with Edward Hoyt, I know who else is.

Miss Farmer fluttered back to her chair.

"I tell you that," pursued Hoyt, setting down the glass, "because I want to see this mess cleared up. If Hazel *had* a husband tucked away somewhere in secret, she could hardly divorce him. She had set herself up in too pious a position before the world."

Drawing up the collar of his overcoat, Bell went out of the nursing-home into the falling snow. Jacqueline Dubois, wearing a fur coat and a hat with an outrageous veil, was waiting for him at the foot of the steps.

Inspector Bell took one look at her, and then began to run.

His excuse for this was a bus, which would set him down beside a hotel in a side street only a few yards away from Victoria Square. The bus was already some distance away, and lumbering fast. Bell sprinted hard after it, sprang aboard, and climbed up to a deserted top deck. He had no sooner settled back than Jacqueline, flushed and panting, was beside him.

The girl was almost in tears.

"You are not genteel!" she wailed. "I have twist my ankle. Would you like it that I should hurt myself bad?"

"Candidly," said Bell, "yes."

"You do not like me at *all?*"

"No. Remember, I've read your story in the *Record* this morning."

"You do not like it? But, *chéri,* I wrote it to please you!"

"In the course of that story," said Bell, "you four times described me as 'handsome.' How I'm going to dare show my face back at Scotland Yard again I don't know. What is more important, you headlined—"

"You are not angry?"

"Oh, no. Not at all."

"Besides, I have a clue."

Despite everything, Bell suddenly found himself chuckling. Rules were rules; but still, he reflected, he had been behaving like a good deal of a stuffed shirt. This girl need give him no trouble. And in her way Jacqueline was rather attractive.

"Not again?" he said.

"No, no, no! It is the same clue. You will not let me explain. You will not let me explain how I know that Miss Loring was not killed in the garden at all, but that the assassin kill her somewhere else and carry her to the garden afterwards."

The bus lurched round a snow-rutted curve.

Bell, taking two tickets from the conductor, almost dropped both of them.

"Is this," he demanded, "another stunt?"

"It is the truth! I know it by the shoes. The shoes have very high heels, and their straps are not buttoned."

"Well?"

"She could not have walked in them. Yes, I tell you so! She could not have walked a step in them. It is impossible. Either the shoes fall off, or *she* fall off.

"Listen! You say to yourself, 'Miss Loring has entered the garden; she has started to undress herself.' So? Then why does she take off her stockings and put her shoes back on? You say, 'While she is like this, the assassin catch her; there is a struggle; she is hit; the assassin pick her up and put her on the bench.' I say, no, no, no! She could not have walked in those shoes. It is jolly sure she could not have *fight* in them. They would just fall off, and then there would be marks on her feet. And there were no marks, eh?"

"Go on," said Bell, after a pause.

"It jumps to the eyes that the assassin has put the shoes on Miss Loring after she is dead."

"But—"

"Now I tell you something else. What is it that puzzle you so much, *chéri?* What is the big headache? It is the reason why Miss Loring should have undress herself in the open with the weather freezing zero. Yes? But she did not.

"She has gone first to the garden. Then she has left the garden, and gone somewhere else which is indoors; and there she has undressed herself. There the assassin catch her and kill her. Then he take her back to the garden in the blackout, to make you think she was killed there. He is just starting to dress her fully when he is interrupted, and has to run. Yes?"

Their bus had gone clanking up Gloucester Terrace, and was turning into Hargreaves Street, which led to Victoria Square. Already Bell could see the square ahead. Bell smote his hand against the top of the seat in front of them.

"By all the—" he burst out, and stopped. "I wonder if it could be?"

"I do not wonder," said Jacqueline. "I am sure it is true. For any woman to take off her clothes outdoors in such weather is not practical; and even if I am a goofy little beasel I see that straightaway, gorblimey!"

"Just a minute. What about the heel marks of the struggle in the earth behind the bench?"

"They is phony," returned Jacqueline calmly. "I do not think there be any marks with the ground so hard. The assassin has made them too."

Stopping with a jolt, the bus threw them against the bench ahead. They climbed down to the pavement beside the quiet hotel only a few steps from Victoria Square. Though Jacqueline was dancing round him, Bell would not be hurried either mentally or physically.

"It's nonsense," he decided.

"You are a nasty man and I do not like you. Why is it nonsense?"

"Well, where did the woman go? You say Miss Loring went somewhere and 'undressed.' Where? Apparently she didn't go back home. Where could any woman go at that hour of the night in order to undr—?"

He checked himself, and raised his eyes. A raw wind shouted down Hargreaves Street, whipping the snow to powder. The grimy red-brick building in front of them had two entrances. Across the top of one was blazoned in gilt letters the name of the hotel. On the glass doors of the other were smaller letters in white enamel, but they were letters which made Bell jump. They said:

LADIES' AND GENTLEMEN'S
TURKISH BATHS.
OPEN DAY AND NIGHT.

The woman behind the counter was scandalized. When she first caught a glimpse of them, coming down in the automatic lift into the warm, dim basement-foyer, she threw up the flap of the counter and ran out.

"You, sir!" she cried. "You can't come in here!"

"I am a police officer—," Bell began.

The woman hesitated only a second. "Sorry, sir, but you still aren't allowed here. This is Wednesday. It's Ladies' Day. Didn't you see the notice upstairs?"

"*I* can come in?" cooed Jacqueline.

"Yes, madam, of course."

" 'Ow much?" asked Jacqueline, opening her handbag.

Taking hold of Jacqueline's arm in a grip that made her squeal, Bell drove the other woman before him until she retreated behind the counter.

First he showed his warrant card. Then he drew out a large close up photograph of Hazel Loring's face.

"Did you ever see this lady before?"

"I—I don't know. There are so many people here. What do you want?"

On the counter lay a tray of pens and pencils. With a coloured pencil Bell drew on the photograph a crude representation of an auburn wig. To this he added a pair of dark spectacles.

"Did you ever see *this* lady before?"

"I did and all!" admitted the woman. "Of course I did. She was always coming here at night. If you'd just tell me what you—"

"Was she here on Monday night?"

The attendant, who seemed less frightened than anxious that Bell should not get beyond the doors at the left, admitted this too.

"Yes, she was. She came in about a quarter past ten, a little later than usual. I noticed because she looked awfully groggy; sick like; and her hands were shaky and she didn't leave any valuables here at the desk."

"What time did she leave?"

"I don't know. I—I don't remember." A puzzled look, a kind of spasm, flickered across the attendant's face. "Here's Mrs. Bradford," she added. "She'll give you what-for if you don't get out of here!"

It was very warm and faintly damp in the tiled basement. A dim humming noise throbbed beyond it. Soft lights shone on the counter, on the wall of steel boxes behind it; and, towards the left, on leather-covered swing doors studded with brass nailheads.

One of these doors was pushed open. A stocky, medium-sized woman, with dark hair drawn behind her ears and eyebrows that met over the top of her nose, first jerked back as though for flight, and then stood solidly. Her face was impassive and rather sinister. She wore a white duck coat and skirt; her bare feet were thrust into beach sandals.

"Mrs. Bradford—," the attendant began.

Mrs. Bradford gave the newcomers a long, slow look. Emotion, harsh and pressed to bursting, filled that foyer as thickly as the damp. Voices, faint laughter, made a ghostly background beyond.

"You'd better come in here," she told them. Opening a door which led into a small office, she nodded at them to precede her. When they were inside, she closed and locked the door. Then she flopped down in an office-chair and presently began to cry.

"I knew I couldn't get away with it," she said.

"So that's it," Bell muttered ten minutes later. "Hoyt told me that Miss Loring was fond of overeating."

Mrs. Bradford uttered a contemptuous snort. She was sitting forward, her elbows carelessly on her knees; she seemed to feel better now that she had been given a cigarette.

"Overeating!" she growled. "She'd have been as big as a barrage-balloon if she hadn't nearly killed herself with more Turkish baths than any human being ought to take. Yes, and keeping a medicine cabinet full of slimming drugs that were downright dangerous. I warned her. But, oh, no! She wouldn't listen. She was making too much money out of this slimming campaign of hers."

"You knew her?"

"I've known Hazel Loring for twenty years. We were kids together in the north. She was always the lady. Not like me. And she was clever: I give her that."

Bell was putting many facts together now.

"Then the simple-exercises-and-keep-fit campaign—?"

"It was all," said Mrs. Bradford, wagging her head and blowing out smoke contemptuously, "a fake. Mind, her exercises maybe did do some people good. There's some women could hypnotize themselves into believing anything. And, if they thought it kept 'em slim . . . why, perhaps it did. But not little Hazel. That's why she had to sneak over here in a damn silly disguise, like a film star or something. She was desperately frightened somebody'd spot her."

"And yet," said Bell, "somebody murdered her. It was you, I suppose?"

The cigarette dropped out of Mrs. Bradford's hand.

"Murdered!" she whispered; and missed the cigarette altogether when she tried to stamp it out with her foot. Then her voice rose to a screech. "Man, what's the matter with you? Are you clean daft? Murdered?"

"Sh-h!"

"*Murdered?*" said Mrs. Bradford. "She fell down and died in the steamroom. I had to get her out of here on the q.t., or the scandal would have ruined us."

"She died from concussion of the brain."

Mrs. Bradford's eyes seemed to turn inwards.

"Ah? So that was it! I noticed she'd got a kind of red mark on her temple, half under the wig. I supposed she had hit her head on the edge of the marble bench when she collapsed—"

"No," said Bell. "She was beaten to death with a lead-loaded walking stick. The laboratory can prove that."

Distant fans whirred and hummed: the air was astir. Mrs. Bradford slid up from her chair, with a lithe motion for a woman so stocky, and began to back away.

"Don't you try to bluff a woman that's always been honest," she said, in a thin unnatural voice. "It was an accident, I tell you! Either heart failure, or hitting her head when she fell. It's happened before, when people can't stand the heat. And now you come and tell me—"

"Just a moment," said Bell quietly.

The tone of his voice made Mrs. Bradford pause, her hand half-lifted as though to take an oath.

"Now tell me," Bell continued, "did you see Miss Loring arrive here on Monday night?"

"Yes."

"How did she look? Ill, for instance?"

"Very ill. Lucy at the desk can tell you that. All shaky and funny. That's why I kept an eye on her."

"What happened then? No, I'm not accusing you of lying! Just tell me what happened."

Mrs. Bradford stared at him.

"Well . . . she went to one of the booths, and took off her clothes, and wrapped herself up in that cotton robe they wear, and went on to the hot rooms. I'm manager here: I don't act as masseuse usually, but I did it for her so that nobody shouldn't discover about the wig. I was nervous because she looked so ill. Afterwards I went up to the steam room, and there she was lying on the floor. Alone. Dead. I thought: Holy mother, I knew something would happen, and now—!"

"Go on."

"Well, what could I do? I couldn't carry her down to where her clothes were, because there were ten or a dozen other women here and they'd know what had happened."

"Go on."

"I had to get rid of her. I *had* to! I ran down and rolled her clothes and handbag up into a bundle and ran back up to the steam room. But I couldn't dress her there, because somebody might have walked in any minute. Don't you see?"

"Go on."

Mrs. Bradford moistened her lips. "Upstairs there's a door that leads out into an alley by the hotel. I slung her over my shoulder, and carried her out into the blackout wrapped in that cotton robe.

"I knew where to put her, too. Beside her handbag there'd been a big key, with a cardboard label saying it was the key to the garden in Victoria Square. I got her into the garden and sat her down on the first bench I came to. Then I started to dress her properly so nobody shouldn't know she'd ever been at the baths. I'd just got the underclothes on, and slipped the shoes on her feet so they'd be handy, when I heard a noise. I slipped back a little; and it's a good thing I did, for there was a great big blazing light—"

"Did I not say it?" murmured Jacqueline softly. "Did I not say the policeman has come in and interrupted her?"

"So I hopped it," concluded Mrs. Bradford, wiping her eyes. "I still had the cotton robe in my hand; but I forgot the wig and spectacles." Her face grew harsh and ugly. "That's what I did. I admit it. But that's all I did. She wasn't murdered in these baths!"

"As a matter of fact," replied Bell calmly, "I don't think she was. For all practical purposes, I think she was dead before she got here."

It was not easy to frighten Jacqueline Dubois. Only her imagination could do this. Her imagination conjured up wild visions of a dead woman in a red wig, the face already bloodless, walking into the foyer and confronting the attendant with blind black spectacles. It unnerved her. Even the humming of the fans unnerved her.

She cried out at Bell, but he silenced her.

"Queer thing," Bell mused. "I was telling Mr. Hoyt yesterday about a friend of mine. He was struck by the door of a railway carriage. He got up, brushed himself, assured everybody he wasn't hurt, went home, and collapsed an hour later with concussion of the brain. Such cases are common enough. You'll find plenty of them in Taylor's *Medical Jurisprudence*. That's what happened to Hazel Loring, in my opinion."

"You mean . . ."

"Mind!" Bell held hard to his caution. "Mind, I don't promise anything. Whether they'll want to hold you as accessory after the fact, Mrs. Bradford, I can't say. But, just between ourselves, I don't think you've got a lot to worry about.

"As I read it, Hazel Loring met the murderer in the garden at ten o'clock. There was a fight. The murderer struck her down and left her for dead. She got to her feet, thought she was all right, and came over here to the baths. In the steam room she collapsed and died. And you, finding the key to the garden, carried her body straight back to the real scene of the crime."

Bell drew a deep breath and his forehead wrinkled in thought.

"Talk about the wheel revolving!" he added. "All we want now is the murderer."

Edward Hoyt, released from the nursing home on Friday morning, took a taxi to Victoria Square under a bright, watery sun which was turning the snow to slush.

The exposure of Hazel Loring's racket, appearing in Thursday's *Daily Record,* was both a revelation and a revolution. It was a real scoop for the paper.

MacGrath, the news editor, danced the saraband. Henry Ashwin, the photographer, swallowed three quick whiskies and went out to find Jacqueline. Sir Claude Champion, owner of the *Daily Banner,* swallowed aspirins and vowed vengeance. All over the country it made wives pause in the very act of the patent exercises. Yet nobody was satisfied. Through the excitement ran a bitter flavor: however much of a fake the dead woman might have been, still she was dead by a brutal attack and her murderer still walked and talked in the town.

Edward Hoyt's face seemed to express this as he went up the steps of number 22. The door was opened for him by Alice Farmer, whose face brightened with joy. And this performance was watched with interest by Jacqueline Dubois and Henry Ashwin, the photographer, lurking behind the railings in the garden opposite.

"The point is," insisted Ashwin, giving her a sideways glance, "what is Bell doing? He now seems to think you're a kind of mascot—"

Jacqueline was not without modest pride.

"He think I am pretty good," she admitted. "I just try to give him ideas, that is all. But between you and me and the pikestaff, I do not know *what* he is doing. He is very mysterious."

"Beaten, eh? Shame on you!"

Jacqueline's color went up like a flag.

"I am not beaten either! But maybe perhaps I am wrong about him. First I think he is only a stupid Englishman, all dumb and polite, and now I think his mind may work funnier than I expect. He keep talking about lights."

"Lights?"

"Big lights. Oi! Look!"

She pointed. There was another visitor for number 22. Mrs. Eunice Bradford, almost unrecognizable in an oversmart outfit and a saucer hat, strode briskly along the street. The morning sun streamed full on the doorway; they saw Mrs. Bradford punching the doorbell with assurance. She was admitted by Miss Farmer.

"Got 'em taped," said the voice of Inspector Bell.

Jacqueline felt a shock. Bell, followed by Sergeant Rankin and a uniformed constable, was coming across the slush-marshy garden with the sun behind him.

"Don't sneak up like that, Inspector!" protested Ashwin. He nodded towards the house across the way. "So it's a gathering of the suspects, eh?"

"It is."

"And you're going to nab somebody over there?"

"I am."

Jacqueline began to shiver, though the air held an almost springlike thaw. Bell's expression was guileless.

"You can come along, if you like," he said to Jacqueline. "In fact, I might say you've got to come along. A good deal of my evidence depends on you, though you may not know it. I'll give you some poetic justice too. You've spent half your time in this business worming things out of people or pinching things from people. I've taken the liberty of pinching something from you."

"You go away!" said Jacqueline. "Please, what is this? I do not understand."

Bell opened the briefcase he was carrying. "You remember," he said, "how you solved your part of the problem by deducing something from the unbuttoned shoes in a photograph taken the morning after the murder?"

"Yes."

Bell drew a large glazed oblong of paper from the briefcase. It was the picture they had all seen: Hazel Loring's body on the bench, every detail sharp-etched with the shadows behind.

"Is this the same photograph?"

"Ah, zut! Of course it is."

Bell glanced inquiringly at Ashwin.

"You confirm that? This is the same photograph you took at about ten o'clock on Tuesday morning?"

Ashwin, with a face of hideous perplexity, merely nodded. Sergeant Rankin suddenly guffawed: a sharp sound which he covered up with a cough.

"Then it's very curious," said Bell. He held up the photograph. "It's the most curious thing we've come across yet. Look at it. Every shadow in this picture, as we see, falls straight behind bench and body. Yet the bench, as we've known from the start, faces due west and has its back to the east.

"Look at the bench now. See how the shadows fall in front of it along the path. In other words, this photograph couldn't possibly have been taken in the morning. It couldn't have been taken at any time during the day, because the sun was gone in the afternoon. That bright light and those dead-black shadows could have been made in only one way. The photograph must have been taken, after dark, by the glare of a flashbulb: which was the 'great big blazing light' Mrs. Bradford saw when she—"

Jacqueline screamed.

One face in the group altered and squeezed up as though it were crumpling like a wet paper mask. A pair of hands flung forward to grab the photograph from Bell and rend it in pieces; but Sergeant Rankin's arm was round the man's throat and the two of them went over backwards in a crashing cartwheel on the path.

Bell's voice remained level.

"Henry Ashwin, I arrest you for the murder of your wife, Hazel Loring. I have to warn you that anything you say will be taken down in writing and may be used as evidence against you at your trial."

To Jacqueline, that night, Bell was a little more communicative.

"There's nothing much to tell," he said off handedly. "Once I got Hoyt's tip, and we put the organization to work, it didn't take long to discover that one Hazel Ann Loring and one Henry Fielding Ashwin had been married at the Hampstead Registry Office in 1933." He grinned. "That's where the official police will always score over you amateurs."

Jacqueline was agog.

"He try the blackmail on her. Yes?"

"Yes, in a small way. A nasty bit of work is Ashwin. In the first place, he was a no-good who would take some explaining; in the second place, she couldn't afford to have the gaff blown about her racket. That was why Ashwin was pretending to make what you call goo-goo eyes at Hazel Loring's maid: he had to have some excuse for hanging round the house so constantly.

"But Hazel was getting fed up with it. She issued an ultimatum, and arranged to meet him in the garden. There was a wild, blind row: both of them, we know, had ugly tempers. Ashwin laid her out, and then ran. It wasn't a planned crime: he just ran.

"After he'd had a couple of drinks, he began to get scared. He'd left that stick behind. He didn't *think* they could trace it to him; but suppose they did? So he went back to the square—and must have thought he was losing his mind. For he saw Eunice Bradford bringing the body back.

"In any case, he thought it was a gift from heaven. If he could frame any evidence against her, Mrs. Bradford would swing for the crime as sure as eggs. He set his flashbulb and fired blindly for a picture. But in the dark his aim was bad; Mrs. Bradford had jumped back; and he didn't get her in the picture at all. He saw that when he developed the picture. Of course he'd never have shown that photograph to anyone. He'd have torn up the pictures and destroyed the negative. Only—"

Jacqueline nodded radiantly.

"I pinch it from him," she declared, with pride. "And then he have to stew up some explanation for it."

"Yes. Of course, I saw that the dim, paper-covered torch of the policeman who discovered the body could never have produced that 'great big blazing light' described by Mrs. Bradford. Then, once you looked closely at the photograph and noticed the fall of the shadows, that tore it. I gathered the obvious suspects in one house to throw Ashwin off his guard; and got him to confirm his previous story before police witnesses. That's all."

He chuckled.

"There's one good result from it, anyway," he added. "Edward Hoyt and Alice Farmer should be extremely comfortable with each other."

But Jacqueline was not listening. Her eyes were shining and absorbed. She put her hand with innocent fervor on his arm.

"If I had not pinch the picture," she said, "and if I had not deduce those things, maybe you would not have solved the case. Eh?"

"Maybe not."

"You do not think I am such a goofy little beasel. No?"

"No."

"In fact, day by day in every way I am becoming indispensable to you. Yes?"

The hair froze on Bell's head. "Hold on! Take it easy! I didn't say that!"

"But *I* say it," declared Jacqueline, with fiery earnestness. "I think we go well together, yes? I pinch things for you; and if you like you can be my Conscience and go gobble-gobble at me, but you do not be too mad when I help you. Then each day I get an exclusive inter—inter—"

"Interview," suggested Bell.

"Okay, if you say so, though my knowledge of English is formidable and you do not have to tell me. If I like you very much and am a good girl, will you let me help with the detecting when I ask to?"

Bell looked down at the flushed, lovely face.

"I will," he said, *"ou je serai l'oncle d'un singe!* My knowledge of French is formidable too."

LOST STAR

by C. DALY KING

Tarrant and I were sitting quietly enough, that evening, in his apartment in the East Thirties. It was only a day or so after the denouement of what he called the City of Evil episode—in fact, the bullet holes in his living-room walls had not yet been treated by the decorators—and I, for one, had had all the excitement I wanted for the moment.

The scene now, however, was as peaceful as anyone could have wished. Brihido, having served his usual excellent dinner, had cleared away; the tightly closed living-room windows reduced the city's clamor to a low drone only occasionally interrupted by the squawk of a distant taxi; the few, well-placed, mellow lights were pleasant to the eye in this luxuriously masculine room. Across from us the dial of the walnut radio cabinet glowed a dull yellow above the modulated music issuing from beneath it.

Tarrant was slowly turning the stem of his brandy pony. "You know, Jerry, knowledge is sometimes more important than money in getting the good things of life. This brandy costs less than some of the widely advertised brands but it comes from people who know what brandy is and are not trying to unload the tag ends of their product onto the gullible American market. Do you like it?"

I did, and said so. "If it's all the same, I'll have another pony. The brandy is fine but that music is too dopey for me. How about getting a dance orchestra?" Tarrant had tuned the instrument to a popular concert being broadcast from the Mall.

He smiled. "You're a Philistine, Jerry. You are listening to one of the most famous conductors in the world. However, I'll agree that I don't care for his program, myself. That's the trouble with these popular concerts; the musical appreciation of the audiences is so low that the selections have to be fairly uninteresting. This one is almost finished, though. Let's see what he will give us next; if it's no better, I'll turn it off."

But he didn't turn it off; we were destined to listen to most of that concert.

Tarrant was tipping the decanter over my empty glass and the music was entering a rather horrible, syrupy passage when it was abruptly cut off and an unexpected voice spoke distinctly from the radio.

"Trans-Radio Flash. Gloria Glammeris has been kidnapped! Her absence was discovered at nine-forty-two by Operative Huggins of the All-American Agency. This is Lou Vincent speaking for the Trans-Radio News Service. We will stand by and bring you further details as we receive them. Station WJEX."

The instrument was silent for a moment, then brought us smoothly the last two notes of the selection on the Mall, followed by a burst of applause.

I sat up in my chair with the brandy glass in my hand. "Good Lord, Tarrant, that *is* going pretty far for a publicity stunt, isn't it?"

He shook his head. "We don't know that it is a publicity stunt. Our friend, Peake, down at Headquarters is convinced it's not. Of course he has contact with the All-American people and they tell him that they view it seriously. After all, they're the biggest private detective agency in the country; they certainly can't be bribed into staging a fake crime, and when they send ten of their best men out to Hollywood, it looks like business. Just the threatening letter—yes, that might be a phony. But it seems that the thing has actually been pulled off, right under their noses."

The music had commenced again but we were paying no attention to it. I said, "Just the same, her new picture is about to open. And she's the biggest star the Kolossal outfit has. People with brass enough to call themselves Kolossal, and misspell it into the bargain, would do anything."

"All I know is what I've been told," was Tarrant's reply. "Peake says that All-American was hired by Ike Bronsky, Kolossal's president, that he flew east to confer personally with their head office and that they believe he would gladly give up half a year's publicity to get to the bottom of the matter and protect his star. It's true there will be plenty of publicity now; she has a tremendous following and she is certainly a lovely girl."

"Ho-ho! I had no idea you went for film stars. How long has this been going on?"

"Blast it, Jerry," declared Tarrant, "I'm no monk. I admire beauty in any form. And a girl with a face, a figure, and a voice like hers combines all the beauties of painting, sculpture, and music simultaneously. I've never met her but I would say she is no pretty Hollywood blank. Judging from her work, that girl has both talent and intelligence. I'll wager several millions of people are being bored with radio programs all over the country while they're waiting to—"

The music from the Mall was fading out and Tarrant interrupted himself to listen.

"Trans-Radio Flash," came the voice. "Further regarding the kidnapping of Gloria Glammeris. The crime was discovered at 6:42 Pacific Time, 9:42 Eastern Time, not by Operative Huggins, as previously announced, but by

Miss Jane Smith, Miss Glammeris's secretary. At that time Miss Smith went to Miss Glammeris's apartments on the second floor of her Beverly Hills home. Huggins had been on duty outside the door ever since a previous visit of Miss Smith two hours earlier and was still on duty. Miss Smith knocked on the door, opened it, and immediately cried out that Miss Glammeris was not there. Operative Huggins entered the room at once and a hurried search showed that the star had vanished.

"For the benefit of listeners who have not followed the case, I will say that two weeks ago Gloria Glammeris received a letter, which has not yet been traced, threatening her with kidnapping during the present week. As she is not now making a picture, she agreed under protest, but at the urgent request of her employers, Kolossal Films, to spend the week in her private apartments in her home. Today is the third day she has been in retirement, up to this evening in perfect safety. Two detectives of the All-American Agency have been constantly on duty within the house and eight others have been patrolling the grounds outside. In addition, two Special Officers of the Los Angeles Police Department have been stationed in the immediate vicinity. It is therefore out of the question that Miss Glammeris could have been removed from her home. A thorough search is now in progress and it is believed that her whereabouts will be discovered at any moment. A Trans-Radio man is now upon the premises and will give you an immediate bulletin of further developments. This is Lou Vincent of Trans-Radio News Service. This flash was brought to you through the facilities of Station WJEX."

Tarrant smiled, as the music welled up again from the cabinet. "I'm afraid it's a false alarm, Jerry. At first I thought it might be something to sharpen our wits on. But my guess is that Miss Glammeris has retired to one of her beautiful bathrooms to take a bath. Or perhaps she has gone downstairs to consult with her cook. I have no doubt we may very shortly expect a final bulletin in which she indignantly denies any intention of upsetting the detectives. . . . How about a highball, Jerry?"

"Yes, thanks. In which case," I went on, "this certainly isn't a stunt, for an anticlimax like that would be mighty poor publicity. The threat against her will remain, of course. Naturally she must be in the house; but keep it turned on, anyhow, and let's see where they found her."

Tarrant mixed himself a drink but had not yet resumed his seat when Mr. Lou Vincent was with us again.

"Trans-Radio Flash. Our last bulletin on the Glammeris kidnapping was delayed and we now have further details for you. The house and grounds have been thoroughly searched and Miss Glammeris has not been found. The circumstances as reported by our Trans-Radio man on the scene are most extraordinary. Here are the details.

"At four-thirty this afternoon, Pacific Time, Miss Glammeris was finishing a short conference with her secretary in her study on the second floor of her house. This room is not lavishly furnished; it contains a large desk, a couch, some portable book cases and several chairs. It has no windows but is ventilated by the air-conditioning system of the house. There are three doors; one to the main corridor, where Operative Huggins sat; one to a small lavatory which is little more than a cubbyhole and has no windows or other means of exit; the third opens into Miss Glammeris's sleeping apartments and has recently been cut through, since by way of the main corridor it is some distance between her bedroom and the study.

"At four-thirty Miss Glammeris concluded her conference in the study and Miss Smith came out. Before Miss Smith left, Huggins had distinctly heard the two women talking, one voice deep, the other high, through the corridor door left partially open by Miss Smith when she had come to the study for the conference a few minutes before.

"From that moment until six-forty-two, Pacific Time, Operative Huggins never left the immediate vicinity of the study-corridor door. No one passed through this door in either direction. At six-forty-two Huggins entered the study immediately behind Miss Smith and found the room empty. There is no place within the study or the adjoining small lavatory where Miss Glammeris could conceal herself, let alone be concealed by a kidnapper. The lavatory, as we said, is a mere blind alley from which no egress is possible. And the door from the study to the sleeping quarters was locked. This door can be locked from either side by means of two bolts embedded in the construction of the door itself, each bolt operated by turning a small handle above the doorknob on either side. It also appears that, although it is an interior door, it is weather-stripped on both sides. When Huggins and Miss Smith entered the study, this door was secured not only by one bolt but by both. In other words, it was not only locked from the side of the bedchamber, which could be done after Miss Glammeris had been taken through it, but was also locked from the inside, the study side. It is established that in the case of this particular door, the inner bolt cannot be operated after one has passed through and closed the door from the other side. Detective Huggins at once discovered that both bolts were shot by unlocking the door from the study side and by finding that it was still secured by the bolt on the bedroom side.

"Although bewildered by the situation, Huggins did not lose his head. He ran into the corridor, accompanied by Miss Smith, and locked the study-corridor door from the corridor side, retaining the key. He then ran downstairs to acquaint the other detective in the house with the disappearance and to draw the outside cordon closely about the walls. Needless to say, none of the outside guards had reported anything unusual during the preceding two hours.

"With two of the other detectives Huggins hurried upstairs again, where they found Miss Smith frantically searching her employer's bedroom, a search which disclosed nothing of any significance. The three detectives, followed by the secretary who was now becoming hysterical, hastily searched the whole house, after which they collected the servants together and put them through a severe questioning. All professed complete ignorance of what had occurred and, as Huggins could testify that none had so much as appeared in the upstairs corridor during the crucial time period, they were segregated in the kitchen while a more thorough search of the whole house went forward.

"This time the All-American operatives went through the rooms more slowly and carefully, from cellar to attic. All closets were opened, the refrigerators and furnaces searched, wardrobes if locked were burst apart, even the film star's forty trunks were each examined in turn. It is hard to believe that such a probing yielded no result—but that is the fact. Meantime, the cordon around the house had stood inactive but alert and the All-American man in charge felt he could no longer put off informing the Los Angeles Prosecutor's Office as to the situation. The Prosecutor's Office, called on the phone, insisted that both outside doors of Miss Glammeris's study be sealed at once and that no one should enter until the morning, when the Prosecutor should have flown back from Palm Springs and undertake the investigation personally.

"The secretary, Miss Jane Smith, has suffered a complete breakdown and has been removed to the Los Angeles Hospital. This is Lou Vincent, speaking for Trans-Radio News Service. This bulletin came to you through Station WJEX."

Whereupon the instrument resumed with its miserable music. Tarrant, who after the first few seconds had been rapidly jotting down notes on the back and face of an old envelope, looked up and gave his peculiar whistle. Brihido stood in the doorway.

" 'Hido, bring me some paper and that drafting board of yours. We have a little puzzle. Rather an old and hackneyed one, I fear; the sealed room trick again—it keeps turning up regularly every so often."

The valet brought in the materials and sidled up with a sly expression. "My help, mebbe," he grinned.

"Why, certainly, doctor," Tarrant answered. "Pull up a chair and I will sketch out the problem for you. See if you can solve it." The maneuver caused me no surprise, for I knew that the butler was a servant, not by class but by exigency; he did, in fact, hold a medical degree in the Philippines.

"Now," Tarrant was saying, "this room that I am diagramming won't be correct, for I've never seen it. It holds a desk, a couch, some chairs, some portable bookcases. No windows. We will put the three doors one on each of three different sides. Their exact location isn't as important as their condition . . . there they are. Now this door—call it A—leads to a corridor and is covered by a guard. This door, B, gives access to a small lavatory from which there is no other exit of any kind. Door C, bolted on both sides, opens into a bedroom."

"Door A, corridor," murmured Brihido. "Door B, lavatory; door C, bedroom. Yiss."

Tarrant then explained the other details, referring to the scribbles on his envelope. "We won't bother now about how Miss Glammeris was taken from the house," he concluded. "The question is: how was she removed from this room? Now, doctor, you've got it all; go ahead."

To me it seemed a somewhat difficult assignment but the Filipino tackled it without hesitation. He said, "First, door A: this covered by guard. Guard could be bribed, hit lady on head and take her out of room in two hours easy. Further difficulty to leave house but this not present problem. How about?"

"No good," smiled Tarrant. "This is a problem with the factors given. You can't change them upside down; you cannot assume that the guard is the kidnapper. Actually, there isn't a chance in the world that he is involved; he's an All-American operative, a carefully picked man. A poor solution, I'd say."

The butler agreed. "Not think so much, myself. Then, if guard honest, door A is out. Door B to lavatory also out: might as well be solid wall. Must go through door C to bedroom. And why not? No guard here, only question of locking door again from outside after lady is taken through. Quite possible for expert crime fella to lock doors from outside, I think."

I told him, "No," for this was one point I had got clearly. "These are bolts, not ordinary locks with a key. One on each side of the door and operated by turning a little handle, like the ones usually installed on bathroom doors. The bolts are inside the door itself, not on the outside."

"That's right," Tarrant confirmed. "Both bolts were shot and my conclusion is that neither could be operated from the wrong side of the door, especially since for some weird Hollywood reason the door is doubly weather-stripped, leaving no possible apertures around its circumference. Apart from my own conviction, the bolts were examined by the All-American men and they—"

The cabinet behind us said sharply, "Trans-Radio Flash. The Glammeris kidnapping. In some way not yet discovered Gloria Glammeris was taken from her guarded study and from her house at 6:42 this afternoon, Pacific Time. The house is still under guard, the study sealed for the Prosecutor's visit in the morning. Alarms have been sent to the police of five states. Air fields and docks are under observation at Los Angeles. The Mexican border patrol has been increased, the Canadian border is being closely watched. By morning the police of the whole country will be on the lookout for the kidnappers. Federal agents are cooperating. This bulletin by Trans-Radio News Service, through Station WJEX."

"Hah," observed Brihido. "Method of leaving house mebbe important, too. We go back to study. Door C could be taken off hinges mebbe and bolts not disturbed. Which side of this door, by the way, sit hinges? Study side or bedroom side? You know?"

"I don't know about the hinges, but it doesn't make any difference, doctor. I think it most unlikely that a door with even one bolt shot could be removed that way and fitted back into its place again, in anything but a most dilapidated old house, which Miss Glammeris's home certainly is not. . . . No, if you have selected door C as the means of her exit from the study, you are squarely up against the problem of relocking that door after she had been taken through. It cannot be done from the bedroom side after the door has been closed, and no one could have reentered the study past the guard at door A, to relock it from the inside. . . . So you give it up, doctor?"

Well, that seemed about the end of it to me. With both those doors disposed of, the only two possible exits from the room, the thing was simply insoluble. I was astonished to hear Brihido reply, "Oh, no; certainly not give up. In fact, see quite clearly now how was done. Please repeat all details of movements by guard and secretary. Only one way possible, I think."

After Tarrant had complied with the request, the valet continued, "Must be what you call publicity gag, like I read in paper when kidnap letter first published. At four-twenty-five lady sit in study with secretary. Door C to bedroom then unlocked both sides. At four-thirty she step through into bedroom and speak a few words with secretary still standing in study, so guard at door A can hear. Secretary is accomplice; then secretary close and bolt door C *on study side* and come out through door A. Lady bolt door C *on bedroom side* because that where she sit until discovery of empty study.

"At six-forty-two secretary come back and make believe finding lady gone from study. She yell, guard run in and guard himself *unlock door C from study side.* Secretary grin at this, mebbe, for he doing some of her work. Then they run into corridor, guard locks door A, puts key into pocket and hastens downstairs. So secretary runs to bedroom and tells lady now all right to go back in study; lady unlocks door, goes in study; secretary bolts door C *on bedroom side* and makes much useless search of that room. Meantime lady lies down under couch in study, in case guard should open door A and take another quick glance from corridor doorway. But he not even do that. Now study all nicely sealed up *with lady inside* and she stay there until Prosecutor come tomorrow morning. By then too late to stop headlines in papers all over country. Good trick, mebbe."

"Excellent, doctor!" said Tarrant. "Of course there's *another* theory—

No, I think you have the proper answer. So that's that; we can forget it now and listen to the music again."

Brihido smiled impishly. "For scientific fella necessary some proof before hypothesis become fact. Not any way in which we can check up on my theory?"

"Not without breaking the seals on the study, I'm afraid. And I could never persuade them to do that." Tarrant remained a moment in thought. "Well, perhaps there is a chance of proof. If your theory is correct, the secretary is an accomplice; therefore, she was pretending hysteria. It will be a little expensive but perhaps I can get some proof for you. You deserve it, after solving the problem."

He walked over to the telephone and slid the dial through its single revolution to call the operator. "Long distance, please. . . . Long distance: A person-to-person call. I want to speak either with Miss Jane Smith, a patient in the Los Angeles Hospital, or to the doctor who is attending her. Yes, I'll hold on. Thank you."

Someone must have left a key up in the central office, for Tarrant apparently could hear the call being put through. "St. Louis," he said to us; "ah, there's Kansas City. The hospital doctor won't have been fooled by a fake hysteria. Phoenix is on. . . . Now we're through to Los Angeles; I can hear them ringing the hospital."

He waited for almost a minute, then cut in with, "Hello. Hello, Los Angeles operator. . . . All right, get me the doctor who took care of her. It's important, operator, I must speak with him. This is a New York police call." I have noticed that Tarrant, for a truthful man, has a singular lack of hesitation about lying when he thinks it's necessary. This lie got him the man he wanted.

We heard him say. "Yes. . . . Yes. . . . When? . . . Well, about when? . . . Thanks. Yes, thanks, doctor. Good-bye."

He placed the receiver back in its cradle and turned around to us. "She faked the hysteria without any doubt. No objective symptoms at all when she got to the hospital. But she wasn't discharged; she was booked for the night. Sometime during the past hour she left without notifying anybody. Sneaked out."

Brihido was beaming with pleasure. "My theory correct—"

"Yes," Tarrant interrupted him seriously, "but there is that other possibility. How much of a chance do I dare take? Suppose the second theory *is* the real one! Suppose . . ."

Tarrant's tone, which had risen from sobriety to tenseness, convinced me that the affair had suddenly become vital. He was dialing the telephone now with quick, nervous tension in his fingers.

"Centre Street? Peake, Inspector Peake, I must speak with him immediately. Hurry!"

Tarrant tapped his foot rapidly against the floor beneath the telephone stand. Then, "Peake? This is Tarrant. Do you know the Glammeris kidnap details? . . . Good, good. Peake, the girl is in that sealed study and is probably dying, if not dead! You must get in touch with Los Angeles at once! Make them break in—tell them to take a doctor along with them! . . . What? Oh, blast it, man, of course I know how it was done! I'll tell you later. I can't get action out there but you can. You've *got* to persuade them. . . . Now, listen, Peake, listen to me! You remember that penthouse job? I warned you and you wouldn't believe me; you let a policeman be murdered, didn't you? *This girl is dying right in her own study while you fuss about proprieties!* By God, Peake, I'll have your name and address on the front page of every newspaper in New York City if you let her die while you delay! I mean it. Good-bye."

Tarrant strode over to the cellarette and splashed whiskey into a highball glass. "The hell with their stuffy, official courtesies," he muttered.

"But what the devil?" I demanded. "Why should she be dying? That's no kind of publicity to—"

"This doesn't look like publicity," was the reply. "Miss Glammeris went through door C both ways, just as Brihido said; he was right about her *movements.* But she didn't go by herself; she was dragged out and dragged back in again by the secretary. At four-thirty Miss Glammeris had already been assaulted and was on the bedroom side of door C. What the guard heard didn't amount to anything; a low voice and a higher one mumbling unintelligible words—it's nothing. Jane Smith did that; you don't have to be even a good mimic to get away with it, under the circumstances. If she shot Miss Glammeris or stabbed her, the girl is dead. But I doubt it. A shot would be heard, a knife would have to be disposed of. There are a good many drugs whose action would be as fatal if the victim gets no attention. And there was a bathroom in which to wash out the glass and dispose of any telltale drug remaining. Some of them work slowly, though; there may be a chance if they break in soon enough.

"Motive? How do I know what the motive was? Maybe the secretary has been stealing her employer's money and has to cover up; maybe Glammeris took a lover away from Jane Smith. There are dozens of motives, but motive doesn't enter the problem, because we have no information on it at all. The problem was a purely mechanical one—the question of what happened in and about the study."

"Wait, pliss," cried Brihido. "What you say not possible, pliss. If secretary drag lady into bedroom at four-thirty and return to study for exit through door A, then lady either dead or unconscious, because she raise no alarm. In this case *who lock door C from bedroom side?* Secretary could bolt door C only from study side."

"True," Tarrant admitted. "But where is the contradiction? When Jane

Smith came out of the study at four-thirty this afternoon, she had just bolted door C on the study side and of course it was then still unbolted on the bedroom side. I see nothing, however, that would have hindered her from visiting the bedroom at some time between four-thirty and six-forty-two and *at this later time* having bolted the door from the bedroom side, perhaps over the unconscious body of her employer. She would have had to do that, as indeed we know it *was* done—in order to prevent the guard, when he finally entered the study, from going through at once to the bedroom, as he tried to do when the alarm was first given. Miss Glammeris's body had to be quickly accessible for return to the study and may even have been in full view. But Jane Smith knew that the guard would have to inform the other detectives before anything else, and those few minutes were all she needed. The point is that in any event Miss Glammeris *must* now be in the study; given the present factors, *there is no other possibility in logic.* But there are two alternatives concerning her presence there; either it is a stunt with Jane Smith as accomplice or it is a crime with Jane Smith as criminal . . . and Jane Smith has run away."

Brihido had screwed up his face and was saying, "Yiss. Mebbe," when the telephone gave a series of quite angry buzzes. My friend lifted it from its cradle, said, "Tarrant speaking," and immediately a whole series of staccato barks issued from the instrument.

For a time Tarrant said nothing. He emitted an incredulous whistle and a moment later made clucking noises indicative of astonishment or chagrin, or both. Finally he spoke. "Well. . . . Well, I am sorry, old man. I offer my most sincere apologies. . . . Yes. If there is anything I can do beyond apologies, of course I'm at your service." He put down the receiver.

"It seems," he told us quietly, "that Peake got through directly to the house. At his insistence the police have unsealed the doors and entered the study." Tarrant paused. "There is no body in the study. There is no one there at all. The study is *empty.*"

"Eh?" I sounded blank, even to myself. After the way it had all been figured out so neatly, this pretty well stopped me.

'Hido sat back on his haunches and gave a very fair imitation of Tarrant's previous whistle. Then he started hissing. "But not possible. *Musst* be lady in study! No? Iss kidnap, then. But how thiss done?"

Tarrant motioned him to silence. He was murmuring, "We have overlooked something. Probably something so obvious that we can't see it." He took a pull at his highball and stared down at the rug between his feet. "And why not?" he asked finally. "Why not the very thing we started with?"

"How you mean?" 'Hido could hold himself in no longer.

"How about our original notion?" Tarrant reminded him. "The publicity stunt, the faked kidnapping?"

'Hido insisted, "No, not possible. Lady can get out of study, like I invent long ago. But not out of house. House been searched; lady not there, nor in study, either. Must be police mistake; you already say only one possibility in logic."

"With the factors given," Tarrant answered. "But with the factors changed, another possibility arises. Since this possibility has actually occurred, we must deduce a change in our assumed factors."

Tarrant paused, deep in thought.

Then, "There's one catch." My friend smiled wryly. He pulled a fat directory from his shelves and flipped the pages over to the G's. "Yes, here it is. 'Secretary: Jane Smith, 3030 St. Clair Street, Rockford, Ill., or c/o Kolossal Studios, Hollywood, Calif.' Hm. Well," he said suddenly, "we'll have one more try. It will be about the longest shot I've ever played—but here goes."

My first speech for some time: "Here goes what?"

"Some more nice person-to-person business for American Tel. and Tel. If Jane Smith *should* be in Rockford, Illinois—I'd better hurry."

And, indeed, five minutes later, when the operator called him back, he could hardly conceal the surprise in his voice.

"This is Miss Smith? . . . Trevis Tarrant speaking —a friend of Miss Glammeris's. You *are* Miss Smith and you have been in Rockford for a week? . . . Oh, you thought this was from Miss Glammeris because it was a long distance call to you personally? Well, young lady, you are going to receive a lot more long distance calls any minute now but they won't be from friends. If you want my advice, don't answer any more calls at all; just leave word that you are *not* there until Miss Glammeris reaches you. . . ."

Brihido gasped and I cried, "What the hell!", as he turned away from the phone.

Tarrant regarded us quizzically. He said, "Surely you see it now? If Jane Smith is in Rockford tonight, she wasn't in Hollywood this afternoon. Why not a vacation during Gloria's 'retirement' and 'kidnapping'? In other words, there never *was* a secretary—in Hollywood this afternoon, I mean. Miss Glammeris played both roles—that of herself earlier in the day and of her secretary from the four-thirty conference on. No trick at all for an actress of her ability. Remember, we were told that the guard, Operative Huggins, never saw the two women together. The part of Gloria in the afternoon was no more than an offstage voice.

"It's simple enough, once you nail down the vital fact. Gloria's movements were those we have been attributing to Jane Smith, because at that time she *was playing* Jane Smith. That's how she got out of the study. Then she faked the secretarial hysteria—*to get out of the house.* She was taken to a hospital; and skipped at the first opportunity. Probably right now she's registered at the Los Angeles Biltmore as Mrs. F. N. Trelawney or something, all done up in a pair of dark glasses and prepared to wait patiently a few days for a phony exchange of half a million dollars' ransom and the best publicity in film history."

"But in that case," I managed, "Peake—"

"—probably won't speak to me for a week. I hope. As to Gloria versus the public, I'm for Gloria. . . . I trust," he added pleasantly, "that she thanks me for it some day. She really *is* lovely, you know."

THE BLOOMSBURY WONDER
by *THOMAS BURKE*

I

As that September morning came to birth in trembling silver and took life in the hue of dusty gold, I swore.

I had risen somewhat early and was standing at the bathroom window of my Bloomsbury flat shaving. I first said something like "Ooch!" and then I said something more intense. The cause of these ejaculations was that I had given myself the peculiarly nasty kind of cut that you can only get from a safety razor, and the cause of the cut was a sudden movement of the right elbow, and the cause of that was something I had seen from my window.

Through that gracious gold, which seemed almost like a living presence blessing the continent of London, moved a man I knew. But a man I knew transformed into a man I did not know. He was not hurrying, which was his usual gait. He wasn't even walking. He was sailing. I never saw such a schoolgirl step in a man. I never saw such rapture in the lift of a head.

He was not tall, but he was so thin, and his clothes fitted so tightly, that he gave an illusion of height. He wore a black double-breasted overcoat, buttoned at the neck, black trousers and nondescript hat. He held his arms behind him, the right hand clasping the elbow of the left arm. His slender trunk was upright, and his head thrown back and lifted.

In the dusty sunlight he made a silhouette. I saw him in the flat only. And I realised then that I always had seen him in the flat; never all round him. The figure he cut in that sunlight made me want to see round him, though what I should find I did not know and could not guess. And to this day I don't know and can't guess.

II

In conventional society, I suppose, he would have been labelled a queer creature, this Stephen Trink; but the inner quarters of London hold so many queer creatures, and I have so wide an acquaintance among them, that Trink was just one of my crowd. I forget how I came to know him, but for about two years we had been seeing each other once or twice a week; sometimes oftener. I liked him almost at once, and the liking grew. Although I was always aware in his company of a slight unease, I took every opportunity of meeting him. He charmed me. The charm was not the open, easy charm of one's intimate friend, for we never reached that full contact. It was more spell than charm; the attraction of opposites, perhaps. His only marked characteristic was a deep melancholy, and now that I try to recall him I find that that is the one clear thing that I can recall. He was one of those men whom nobody ever really knows.

Stephen Trink would have been passed over in any company, and at my place always was. Only when I directed my friends' attention to him, did they recollect having met him and examine their recollection; and then they were baffled. I once asked five friends in turn what they thought of him, and I was given pictures of five totally different men, none of whom I had myself seen in Trink. Each of them, I noted, had to hesitate on my question, and stroke his hair, and say: " 'M . . . Trink. We-el, he's just an ordinary sort of chap—I mean—he's a—sort of—" Then, although he had been with us ten minutes ago, they would go on to draw a picture as from hazy memory. They seemed to be describing a man whom they weren't sure they had seen. Their very detail was the fumbling detail of men who are uncertain what they did see, and try to assure themselves by elaboration that they did at any rate see *something*. It was as though he had stood before the camera for his photograph, and the developed plate had come out blank.

In appearance, as I say, he was insignificant, and, with his lean, questing face and frail body, would have passed anywhere as an insipid clerk. He stressed his insipidity by certain physical habits. He had a trick of standing in little-girl attitudes—hands behind back, one foot crooked round the other—and of demurely dropping his eyes if you looked suddenly at him; and, when speaking to you, looking up at you as though you were his headmaster. He had, too, a smile that, though it sounds odd when used of a man, I can only describe as winsome. The mouth was sharp-cut, rather than firm, and drooped at the corners. The lower jaw was drawn back. His hair was honey-coloured and plastered down. His voice was thin, touched with the east wind; and it was strange to hear him saying the warm, generous things he did say about people in the sleety tone that goes with spite. To everything he said that tone seemed to add the words: *Isn't it disgusting?* His eyes, behind spectacles, were mild and pale blue. Only when the spectacles were removed did one perceive character; then, one could see that the eyes held curious experience and pain.

Wherever he might be, he never seemed to be wholly *there*. He had an air of seeming to be listening to some noise outside the room. He would sit about in attitudes that, since Rodin's Penseur, we have come to accept as attitudes of thought; but if you looked at his face you'd say it was empty. He was not thinking; he was brooding. Though indoors he was languid and lounge-y, and his movements were the movements of the sleepwalker, in the street his walk was agitated and precipitous. He seemed to be flying from pursuit. One other notable point about him was that, quiet, insignifi- cant, withdrawn as he was, he could be a most disturbing presence. Even when relaxed in an armchair he somehow sent spears and waves of discom- fort through the air, sucking and drying the spirit of the room and giving me that edge of unease.

What his trouble was—if his melancholy arose from a trouble —he never told me. Often, when I urged him, flippantly, to Cheer Up, he spoke of This Awful Burden, but I dismissed it as the usual expression of that intellectual weariness of living which we call "modern."

He had private means by which he could have lived in something more than comfort, but he seemed contented with three rooms in the forlorn quarter where Bloomsbury meets Marylebone—well-furnished rooms that one entered with surprise from the dinge of Fitzroy Square. He was a member of two of the more serious clubs, but used them scarcely twice a year. His time he employed in the Bloomsbury and Marylebone fashion— as an aimless intellectual. He occupied himself writing metallic studies for all sorts of hole-and-corner Reviews; and all the time he was doing it he affected to despise himself for doing it and to despise the breed with whom he mixed. He attended all their clique and coterie gatherings—teas, dinners, Bloomsbury salons, private views—and took part in all the frugal follies of the Cheyne Walk Bohemia. You saw him, as they say, everywhere. Yet, at all these affairs, though he looked younger than most of the crowd, he had always the attitude of the amused grownup overlooking the antics of the nursery. I can't think how even their pallid wits didn't perceive that em- bodied sneer at them and their doings.

Although not physically strong he had immense vitality, which he ex- hibited in long night walks through London. This was a habit which I shared with him and which, begun in childhood, gave me my peculiar and comprehensive knowledge of the hinterland of this continent of London. I believe that it was on one of these night wanderings that we first really met, though there must have been a perfunctory introduction in somebody's flat. Knowing that I was an early riser, he would sometimes, at the end of one of these rambles, knock me up at half-past seven for breakfast, and then go to sleep on my settee. Glad as I always was to have his company, he was a difficult guest. He had a disorderly mind and Japanese ideas of time. A "look-in" often meant that he would stay for four or five hours, and an arrangement to dine and spend the evening often meant that he would look-in for ten minutes and then abruptly disappear without a word about dinner. He had a habit of using in casual conversation what is called bad language—a certain sign of uneasy minds—and his talk was constantly agitated with purposeless use of "blasted" and "bloody" and "bastard." In all other matters he was gentle and thoughtful. He would not, as they say, do anything for anybody, but for a few people his time and labour and influence were available in full measure. He was so kind of spirit, so generous of affection, that sometimes I thought that his melancholy arose from a yearning to love and be loved. At other times this would be contradicted by his self-sufficiency.

And that, I think, is all I can tell you about him. He eludes me on paper as he eluded me in life. So with this light sketch I pass on to the real matter of this story—to his friends, the Roakes; for it was by his friendship with them that I was brought into contact with horror.

Another of our points in common was a wide range of friendships. Most men find their acquaintance among their own "sort" or their own "set," and never adventure beyond people of like education, like tastes, and like social circumstances. I have never been able to do that, nor Trink. We made our friends wherever we found them, and we found them in queer places. An assembly of all our friends at one meeting in our rooms would have surprised (and dismayed) those of them who knew us only as writers in such-and-such circumstances. I had, of course, a number of close friends among fellow-authors and among musicians, but my most intimate friend at that time, who knew more about me than any other creature, was an old disciple of Madame Blavatsky, who devoted his spare time to original research on the lost Atlantis. Trink's was a shopkeeper; a man who kept what is called a "general" shop at the northern end of Great Talleyrand Street.

Despite my own assorted friendships, I could never quite understand *this* friendship, for the man had no oddities, no character, no corner where he even grazed the amused observation of Trink. It may have been, of course —and this fact explains many ill-assorted friendships—that they liked the same kind of funny story, or walked at the same pace in the streets. I don't know. Friendships *are* bound by slender things like that. Or it may have been—and I think this is what it was—that they were bound by love. I am sure there was more in it than mere liking of each other's talk and company, for Trink, being what he was, could have found no pleasure in the pale copy-book talk of Horace Roake. I thought I could perceive on either side an essence or aura of devotion, and if the devotion were at all stronger on one side, it was on the side of the cultivated man of brains rather than the tired, brainless shopkeeper. I spent many evenings in their company, either at Trink's flat or in the shop parlour, and I noted their content in long silences, when they merely sat together and smoked, and their quick, voiceless greeting when they met. Trink seemed to be happier in Roake's shabby room than anywhere. *Why* was one of his mysteries.

Although the public spoke of Roake's shop as a General Shop, he did not himself recognise that style. There are traditions in these matters. In trade-lists there are no drapers, or milkmen, or greengrocers, or ironmongers. The man we style milkman styles himself dairyman, though he may never have seen a dairy. The greengrocer is a pea and potato salesman. The bookmaker is a commission agent. Drapers and ironmongers are haberdashers and deal-ers in hardware. The butcher is a purveyor of meat, the publican a licensed victualler. So Mr. Roake, who kept no pastas or Chianti, or bolognas or garlic, styled himself an Italian warehouseman. His shop stood, as I say, at the northern end of Great Talleyrand Street, between Woburn Place and Gray's Inn Road.

This is a district of long, meaningless streets and disinherited houses. Once, these houses were the homes of the prosperous; today they have only faded memories. They lie, these streets and houses, in an uneasy coma, oppressed by a miasma of the secondhand and the outmoded—secondhand shops, secondhand goods, secondhand lodgings, filled with secondhand fur-niture, and used by secondhand people breathing secondhand denatured air.

When Roake set up his shop here, he blunderingly chose the apt setting for himself and his family. They belonged there. They were typical of a thousand decent, hardworking, but stagnant families of our cities. For four generations the family had not moved its social level. A faint desire to rise they must have had, but rising means adventure, and they feared adventure. On the wife's side and the husband's side the strain was the same—luke-warm and lackadaisical. There they had stood, these many years, like root-less twigs in the waste patch between the stones and the pastures; and there, since the only alternative was risk and struggle, they were content to stand. Roake himself, if I saw him truly, had the instincts of the aristocrat hidden in the habits of the peasant. One of life's misfits. He had the fine feature and clean eye of that type, but though he looked like what is called a gen-tleman, nobody would have mistaken him for one. His refinement of fea-ture and manner came really, not from the breeding of pure strains, but from undernourishment in childhood. He had a mind of wide, if aimless, interests, and a certain rough culture acquired by miscellaneous reading.

His wife was largely of his sort, but without the culture. Her life had been a life of pain and trial, and it had taught her nothing. Her large, soft face was expressionless. The thousand experiences of life had left not even a fingerprint there, and she still received the disappointments and blows of fortune with indignation and querulous collapse.

There were two boys and a girl. The girl had something of her father's physical refinement. Her head and face were beautiful; so beautiful that people turned to glance at her as she passed in the streets. Her manners and voice were—well, dreadful. She would often respond to those admiring glances by putting out her tongue. She was wholly unconscious of her beauty, not because she was less vain than her sex, but because her beauty was not to her own taste. She admired and envied girls of florid complexion and large blue eyes and masses of hair and dimpled mouths—chocolate-box beauties —and her own beauty was a glorious gift thrown to the dogs. To see that grave dark head and those deep-pool Madonna eyes set against those sprawling manners and graceless talk gave one a shudder.

Of the two boys, one might say that they saw life as nothing but a programme of getting up, going to work, working, eating, going to bed. Only it wouldn't be true. They saw life no more than a three-months' old baby sees life. They were clods.

These were the people Trink had chosen as friends, and by all of them he was, not adored, for they were incapable of that, but liked to the fullest extent of their liking. He was their honoured guest, and on his side he gave them affection and respect. The two boys worked together in a boot and shoe factory, and the shop was run by Mr. and Mrs. Roake and the girl, Olive. Olive knew enough about the business to do her bit without any mental strain, and she had a flow of smiles and empty chatter that in such a shop was useful.

These General Shops—often spoken of as "little gold mines"—are usually set, like this one, in side streets. It is by their isolated setting that they flourish. The main streets are not their territory, and such a shop in a main street would certainly fail, for these streets hold branches of the multiple stores as well as shops devoted singly to this or that household necessity. Your successful General Shop, then, chooses a situation as far from competition as possible, but in the centre of a thicket of houses. In that situation it wins its prosperity from the housewife's slips of memory. She arrives home from her High Street shopping, and finds that she has forgotten salt or custard powder or bacon, and to save a mile walk she sends one of the children to the General Shop. It is for this that it exists; not for regular supply but as convenience in emergency. Unhampered by other shops and encircled by hundreds of forgetful households, the well-conducted General is certain of success, and many of these shops have a weekly turnover, made up of pennyworths of this and ounces of that, near two hundred pounds.

So the Roakes were doing well. Indeed, they were very comfortable and could have been more than comfortable; but they were so inept, and knew so little of the art of useful spending, that their profits showed little result in the home. If they could not be given the positive description of a happy family, at least they lived in that sluggish sympathy which characters only faintly aware of themselves give each other; and that was the feeling of the home—lymphatic and never *quite*. The wireless set worked, but it was never in perfect tone. The sitting-room fire would light, but only after it had been coaxed by those who knew its "ways." The hot water in the bathroom was never more than very warm. The flowers in the back garden were never completely and unmistakably blossoms. The shop door would shut, but only after three sharp pressures—the third a bad-tempered one. They bought expensive and warranted clocks, and the clocks took the note of the family, and were never "right." New and better pieces of furniture were frequently bought for the sitting room, but it never succeeded in looking furnished. If you saw the house, you could imagine the family; if you met the family, you could imagine the house.

Hardly a family, one would think, marked out for tragedy, or even for disaster; yet it was upon these lustreless, half-living people that a blind fury of annihilation rushed from nowhere and fell, whirling them from obscurity and fixing their names and habits in the scarlet immortality of the Talleyrand Street Shop Murder.

It was about the time when those gangs called "The Boys" were getting too cocksure of their invulnerability, and were extending their attentions from rival gangs and publicans to the general public, that the catastrophe came by which Stephen Trink lost his one close friend. Beginning with sub-Post Offices, the gangs passed to the little isolated shops. From all parts of London came reports of raids on these shops. The approach was almost a formula. "Give us a coupler quid. Come on," or "We want a fiver. Quick. Gonna 'and over or gonna 'ave yer place smashed up?" Given that alternative the little shopkeeper could do nothing but pay. He *might* have refused, and have had his place smashed up, and he might have been lucky enough to get the police along in time to catch two or three of the gang and get them six months or twelve months each. But that wouldn't have hurt *them,* since their brutal and perilous ways of life make them utterly fearless; and he would still be left with a smashed shop, pounds'-worth of damaged and unsaleable goods, the loss of three or four days' custom during repairs, and no hope of compensation from anybody. So, as a matter of common sense, he first paid up, and then reported the matter to the police; and serious citizens took up his grievance, and wrote to the papers and asked what we supported a police force for, etc., etc.

Then, sharply on top of a dozen of these shop raids, came the murder of the Roakes.

III

Marvellous and impenetrable is the potency of words. Hear the faint spirit-echo of *Shelley;* the cold Englishness of *Shakespeare;* the homespun strength of *John Bunyan.* And so it is with ideas; and so, particularly, with that idea for which sign and sound is MURDER.

Now, by long association, murder is linked in our minds with midnight, or at least, with dark; and these two conceptions of the cloaked side of nature combine in dreadfulness to make deeper dread. Again, poetic justice.

But harmonious combinations of dreadfulness, though they intensify each other, are dreadfulness only, and are therefore less potent to pluck at the heart than dreadfulness in discord with its setting; for there comes in the monstrous. Rape of womanhood is dreadful but understandable. Rape of childhood goes beyond the dreadful into depths that the mind recoils from sounding. Murder at midnight, though it will shock as it has shocked through centuries of civilisation, is a shock in its apt setting. But murder in sunlight is a thought that freezes and appals. It bares our souls to the satanic shudder of blood on primroses.

One can catch, then, the bitter savour of a certain moment of a sunny afternoon in Great Talleyrand Street. From the few horrified words of a neighbor I am able to reconstruct the whole scene.

IV

It was just after three o'clock of a September afternoon—a September of unusual heat; hotter than the summer had been. The heat made a blanket over the city, and in the side streets life was in arrest, bound in slumber and steam and dust. In Great Talleyrand Street carts and cars stood outside shops and houses as though they would never move again. Even the shops had half-closed their eyes. Errand boys and workless labourers lounged or lay near the shops, sharing jealously every yard of the shade afforded by the shopblinds. The faded Regency houses stewed and threw up a frowst. Through its dun length, from its beginning near Gray's Inn to its nebulous end somewhere in St. Pancras, the heat played in a fetid shimmer and shrouded either end in an illusion of infinity. The gritty odours of vegetable stalls, mixed with the acrid fumes of the cast-off-clothes shops, were drawn up in the sun's path to float in the air and fret the noses of the loungers. The ice-cream cart, zones with the Italian colours, made a cool centre for the idle young. A woman was offering chrysanthemums from a barrow piled high with that flower. Her barrow and her apron made a patch of living gold against the parched brown of the street.

Then, into this purring hour, came a figure and a voice. From the upper end of the street it came, crying one word; and the blunt syllables of that word went through the heat and dust, and struck the ears of those within hearing with the impact of cold iron. The street did not stir into life. It exploded.

Those nearest scrambled up, crying—not saying; such is the power of that word that it will always be answered with a cry—crying: "Where? Where?" "In there—there—three-ninety-two." And the man ran on to Tenterden Street, still crying, "Murder!" and those who had heard the word ran in a trail to number 392.

The shop, with its battling odours of bacon, cheese, paraffin, spice, biscuits, bread, pickles, was empty. The runners looked beyond it. A small door led from the shop to the back parlour. The upper half of the door was of glass, and this half was veiled by a soiled lace curtain. Its purpose was to screen the folk in the parlour—where they sat at intervals between trade rushes —from the eyes of customers, while those in the parlour could, by the greater light of the shop, see all comers. But since the curtain served a purely workaday office—the private sitting room was upstairs—it had been allowed to overserve its time, and frequent washings had left it with so many holes that its purpose was defeated. People in the shop could, by those holes, see straight and clearly into the parlour; could see the little desk with account books and bills, and could often see the cashbox and hear the rattle of accountancy. It was proved by experiment that a man on the threshold of the shop could, without peering, see what was going on in the shop parlour.

The leaders of the crowd looked hastily about the shop and behind the two small counters; then, through those holes, they had the first glimpse of what they had come to see.

The sun was at the back. It shone through the garden window, and made a blurred shaft of dancing motes across the worn carpet and across the bloody body of Horace Roake. He lay beside his desk. The back of his head was cleanly broken. By the door leading to the inner passage lay the body of Mrs. Roake. She lay with hands up, as though praying. Her head was flung violently back, disjointed. Of the two boys, who had been spending the last day of their holidays at home, the younger, Bert, lay in a corner by the window, almost in a sitting posture. His head hung horridly sideways, showing a dark suffusion under the left ear. The leaders looked and saw; then someone said, "The girl!" They pulled open the door leading to passage and kitchen. In the sun-flushed passage lay the twisted body of Olive Roake. Her head, too, was thrown back in contortion. One glance at the dark excoriations on her neck told them how she had met her death. Three glances told them of the dreadful group that must have made entrance here: one to kill with a knife, one with a blow, and one to strangle with the hands.

For some seconds those inside could not speak; but as the crowd from the street pushed into the shop, and those in the shop were pushed into the parlour, those inside turned to push them back; and one of them, finding voice, cried uselessly, as is the way in dark moments: "Why? Why all this —these nice people—just for a pound or two? It's—it's *unnecessary!*"

He was right, and this was felt more strongly when it was found that this thing had not been done for a pound or two. The desk was locked, and the cashbox and the two tills in the shop were intact. Clearly this was not haphazard killing for robbery. There was a grotesquerie about the scene that hinted at more than killing: an afterthought of the devilish. These people, who had led their ignoble but decent lives in ignoble back streets, were made still more ignoble in death. The battered head of Roake, the crumpled bulk of Mrs. Roake, the macabre mutilation of the gracious symmetry of youth and maidenhood, were more than death. Not only were they dead, but the peace that touches the most ugly and malign to dignity, the one moment of majesty that is granted at last to us all, was denied them. The temple of the Holy Ghost was riven and left in the derisive aspect of a dead cat in a gutter.

So they lay in the floating sunshine of that afternoon, and so the crowd stood and stared down at them until the police came. Who had done this thing? How did they do it in an open shop? How did they get away?

Then someone who knew the family cried, "Where's Artie?" And some went upstairs and some went into the little garden. But all that they found was an open bedroom window and signs of a flight. No Artie.

V

It was between three o'clock and half past of the day when I had given myself that nasty cut that Trink made one of his "drop-in" calls. I was accustomed to these calls. He would come in, potter about, turn over any new books or periodicals I had, make a few remarks about nothing, disturb the atmosphere generally, and then slide away. But this afternoon he didn't disturb the atmosphere. He seemed lighter and brighter than usual. Something of that morning mood that I had seen in him seemed to be still with him. Tired and pale he certainly was—the result of his night-walk, I guessed—but there was a serenity about him that was both new and pleasing. For almost the first time I felt fully at ease with him; no longer conscious of the something that I had never been able to name. In that quarter of an hour I seemed to be nearer to him and to know him better than I had ever known him. To put it into a crude colloquialism, he seemed *more human*. He stayed but a short time, not fidgeting, but sitting restfully on the settee in that complete ease that one knows after long physical exercise. I remarked on this. I told him that I had seen him from my window, bouncing through the square, and told him that the bouncing and his present mood proved that plenty of exercise was what he needed, and that he would probably find, as George Borrow found, that it was a potent agent for the conquest of accidie—or, I added, liver. He smiled; dismissed the diagnosis of his trouble, and soon afterwards went, or, rather, faded away, so that when I resumed work I was barely certain that he had been with me at all.

About an hour later I became aware that I was disturbed, and when, half-consciously and still at work, I located it as something coming from the street; a sound that came at first from below the afternoon din, then rose to its level and spilled over it. It was the cry of newspaper boys.

As my flat is three floors up (no lift) I did not send out for a paper, but I rang up a friend on the *Evening Mercury,* and asked what the big story was. He gave me the story so far as it had then come in.

After the first shock, my first thought was of what it would mean to Trink. Terrible as the fate of that family was, they meant little to me, and I could only feel for them the detached and fleeting pity that we feel at any reported disaster. For you will have noted, as a kink of human nature, that nobody ever does feel sympathy for a murdered man. All our interest—yes, and a perverse, half-guilty sympathy—is on the murderer. But for Trink, their friend, it would be a blow, and a keener blow since it came with such ghastly irony on top of his happy, swinging mood of that day. He had just, it seemed, found some respite from his customary gloom, only to be brutally flung back into it, and deeper. I thought at first of going round to him, and then I thought not. He would want no intruders.

Meantime, the papers were publishing rush extras, and as the news had withdrawn me from work, and I could not return to it, I went out and bought the three evening papers, and sat in a teashop reading them.

There was no doubt that the affair, following on the large publicity and discussion given to the shop-raids, had stirred the press and alarmed the public. I saw it on the faces of the home-going crowd and heard it reflected in the casual remarks of stranger to stranger in the teashop and around the buses. All that evening and night the word Murder beat and fluttered about the streets and alleys and suburban avenues, and wherever it brushed it left a smear of disquiet. Accustomed as London is to murder, and lightly, even flippantly as it takes all disturbances, the details of this one moved them, for clearly it was no ordinary murder of anger or revenge, or for the removal of inconvenient people for gain. How could these little people have offended? Who would want them out of the way? If it was the work of "The Boys," it might be anybody's turn next. If it wasn't the work of "The Boys," then, said the press, it must have been the work of wandering lunatics of gorilla's strength and ferocity. And if they were loose, nobody would be safe. Private houses and people in the streets would be wholly at the mercy of such fearless and furious creatures as these appeared to be. In the meantime they *were* loose; even now, perhaps, prowling about and contemplating another stroke; sitting by your side in train or bus, or marking your home or shop for their next visit. They were loose, and while they were loose they spread their dreadful essence as no artist or prophet can hope to spread *his*. Scores of mothers from the streets about Talleyrand Street, hearing the news and seizing on the press conjecture of wandering madmen, ran to schools in the district to meet their children. They were always aware of peril from the filth that hovers about playground gates; today they were made aware of a more material and annihilating peril. Through all the thousand little streets of the near and far suburbs went the howl of the newsboy, and its virulent accents went tingling through the nerves of happy households. To people sitting late in their gardens, veiled from the world, came at twilight a sudden trembling and sweeping of the veil as the wandering Chorus stained the summer night with: *Shawking Murd' 'n Blooms-bree—' Pur!' London Fam'ly Mur-der—' purr'!* It broke into the bedrooms of wakeful children, and into the study of the scholar, and into the sick room and across quiet supper tables and wherever it fell it left a wound. The press, having given the wound, went on to probe and exacerbate it with the minutiae of horror; ending with the disturbing advice to householders to see to their bolts and fastenings that night. It was the "splash" story of the day, and each paper had a narrative from neighbours and from those who were near the shop at the time of the crime's discovery. At late evening the story was this.

Artie Roake had been quickly found and interviewed. He frankly explained his absence by the regrettable fact that he had run away. Some information he was able to give, but none that in any way helped the search for the murderers.

As that day was the last day of his holidays, he had, he said, been taking things easy, and after the midday dinner had gone upstairs to lie down. He left his brother in the garden. His father and sister were in the shop-parlour, and his mother was in the shop. From two o'clock to five o'clock was a slack time with them. Most of the business came before twelve or from five o'clock to closing time; the afternoon brought mere straggles of custom. He remembered lying down on his bed, with coat and waistcoat off, and remembered nothing more until he suddenly awoke, and found himself, he said, all of a sweat. His head and hands were quite wet. He jumped up from the bed and stood uncertainly for a few moments, thinking he was going to be ill. And well he might have been ill, seeing what foul force was then sweeping through the air of that little house. Out of the sunlight something from the neglected corners of hell had come creeping upon it, to charge its rooms with poison and to fire it with the black lightning of sudden death. At the moment he awoke this creeping corruption must then have been in the house, and in its presence not the thickest and most wooden organism could have slept; for by some old sense of forest forefathers we are made aware of such presences. We can perceive evil in our neighbourhood through every channel of perception; can even *see* it through the skin. The potency of its vapours, then, must have worked upon the skin and the senses of this lad, as the potency of the unseen reptile works upon the nerves of birds, and he awoke because an alien and threatening presence had called him to awake. It must have been that, and not a cry or a blow, that awoke him, because he said that, during the few seconds when he stood half-awake and sweating, he heard his mother's voice in a conversational murmur. It was some seconds after *that* that the sweat froze on his face at the sound of his father's voice in three plodding syllables—"Oh . . . my . . . God!" —and then of a noise such as a coalman makes when he drops an empty sack on the pavement. And then, almost simultaneously with the sack sound, he heard a little squeak that ended in a gurgle; and overriding the gurgle an "Oh!" of surprise from his brother, and soft, choking tones of terror saying "No—no—no!" And then silence. And then he heard two sharp clicks, as of opening and shutting a door; and then a moment's pause; and then swift feet on the stairs. Had he had the courage to go down on his father's first cry, his courage, one may guess, would have been wasted. Hands would have been waiting for him, and he too would have ended on a gurgle. But if he had had the courage to wait before he fled until the figure or figures on the stairs had come high enough to give him one glimpse, he might have had the clue to one of the men that would have helped the police to the others. But he didn't wait. He bolted. He offered the reporters no feeble excuse of going to raise the alarm or get help. He said that those sounds and the sort of feeling in the house so affected him with their hint of some unseen horror that he didn't think of anybody or anything; only of getting out. Peering from his door, he said, just as the sound of the feet came, he could see part of the staircase, and the sunlight through the glazed door between shop-passage and garden threw a shadow, or it might have been two shadows, half-way up the stairs. He could hear heavy panting. In the moment of his looking, the shadow began to swell and to move. He saw no more. In awkward phrases (so one of the reports stated) he tried to say that he felt in that shadow something more than assault ending in killing; he felt something horrible. From later information I understood this. It *was* horrible; so horrible that even this vegetable soul had responded to it. So, driven by he knew not what, and made, for the first time in his life, to hurry, he turned from the house of dusty sunshine and death to the open world of sky and shops and people. He bolted through the upper window and over the backyard, and did not stop or call for help until he was four streets away; at which point the cry of Murder led to a pursuit and capture of him.

He made his confession sadly but without shame. He *knew*, he said, that it was all over; that he could be of no use; that they were all dead. But when they pressed him *how* he knew, he relapsed from that moment of assertion into his customary cowlike thickness, and they could get no more from him than a mechanical, "I dunno. I just knew."

He was detained by the police for further questioning, and it appeared later that the questioning had been severe. But though there was at first an edge of official and public suspicion of him, he was able to satisfy the police that he knew nothing, and was allowed to go home to an uncle's.

No weapons were found, no fingerprints, no useful footprints. Nor had any suspicious characters been seen hanging about; at least, none markedly suspicious to the district; for in these misty byways queer characters of a sort were a regular feature, and its houses were accustomed at all hours of day and night to receiving furtive strangers. Taking it, at first sight, as gang work, the police, it was said, were pursuing enquiries in that direction, which meant that for the next few days all known members of North London and West End gangs were rounded up and harried out of their wits by detentions, questionings, and shadowings. Already, at that early hour, reports had come in of the detention of unpleasant characters at points on the roads from London—Highgate, Ealing, Tooting. Communications had been made with all lunatic asylums in and near London, but none could report any absentees. All those on the police list who might have been concerned in it—the shop and till specialists—were being visited and questioned, and many, knowing that they would be visited anyway, were voluntarily coming in to give satisfactory accounts of themselves.

One bright "special" had put his mind to the case and lighted the darkness of the police with a possible culprit. He learned that Horace Roake was 55, and from his study of "our medical correspondent" he knew that 55 was the male climacteric, the age when men of formerly sober life — particularly quiet men of Roake's type—go off the rails into all sorts of jungles of unnamable adventure. Was it not worth asking, he said, whether Mr. Roake might not have been doing badly in business, and being at that age had . . . ? But a rival paper, in a later issue, took this torch and extinguished it by bank evidence that Roake was not doing badly in business, and by private police-surgeon information that neither Roake nor any other of the victims could possibly have died by suicide.

There, that evening, it was left. Next morning there were further details, but nothing pointing towards an arrest. From some of these details it was clear that the affair, if planned at all, had been most cunningly planned and timed, and swiftly done; for the people were seen alive a minute and a half before the cry of Murder had been raised. The more likely conjecture, though, was that it was the impulsive act of a wandering gang.

A woman volunteered that she had visited the shop just after three — about ten minutes after—and had been served by Mrs. Roake. Nobody else was in the shop. She left the shop and went a little way down the street to leave a message with a friend, and having left the message she repassed the Roakes' shop, and saw a man whom she did not closely notice standing at the counter rattling some coins and calling "Shop!" Her own home was twelve doors from the shop. She had scarcely opened and closed her door, was, indeed, still on the mat, setting down her shopping basket, when she heard the cry of Murder. In the immediate instant of silence following that cry she heard a church clock strike the quarter past three, which meant that only three minutes had passed from the time of her being served by Mrs. Roake, and one minute from the time of her seeing the man.

Another statement came from a man whose house backed on to the Roakes'. He was on a night shift at the docks, and went on at four o'clock. By daily use he knew exactly how to time himself to get there punctually from his home in Frostick Street; the time was fifty minutes; and he left home regularly at ten minutes past three. He was putting on his boots, he said, when, happening to glance through the window, he saw Mr. and Mrs. Roake in the shop parlour doing —well, as he put it, clearly without any intent of flippancy, carrying-on and canoodling. They must then have remembered that they were open to curious eyes, for they immediately moved away from the window into the darker part of the room. At half-past four the evening paper came into the docks, and he saw that the family had been discovered dead five minutes after he had seen this little husband-and-wife moment.

One of the morning papers gave me a particular irritation. There was a solemn youth named Osbert Freyne (recently down from Cambridge) who used to come into my place at odd times, though I never made him welcome. He used to sit and blither—talk one could not call it. I don't know why he continued to come, because I was always as rude to him as I can allow myself to be to anybody; but he did come and he did meet Trink, and he knew of Trink's acquaintance with the Roakes.

Well, one of the papers had an appendix to the Talleyrand "story"—an appendix by this solemn youth. Like most of his unbalanced kind, though he affected to despise modern writing, he wasn't above making money out of it when he could. The fellow had had a talk (or blither) with Trink, and had sold it to the paper as an interview with "an intimate friend of the unfortunate family." The result was that Trink had been visited and questioned by the police on the family's history and habits and their friends, and other journalists had followed the police, and altogether the poor fellow's miserable day had been made additionally miserable.

I knew what he must be feeling about it, for I myself began to be moved by it, though quite unwarrantably. I had scarcely any interest in those people, yet whenever I thought about the affair I suffered a distinct chill, as though I personally were in some way touched by it; an entirely unreasonable chill which I could not shake off because common sense could not reach it.

Among the first to be examined were the witnesses who were in the street at the time the alarm was given. This again brought nothing useful; indeed, the result was only confusion on confusion. Seventeen people who had been near the spot were asked—Who was the man who rushed from the shop crying Murder? None of them knew him. They were then asked —What sort of man was he? Not one could make a clear answer. Eleven were so surprised that they didn't look at him. The other six—who, if they had looked at him, hadn't seen him but wouldn't admit it—gave six different descriptions. One saw a tall firmly built man with a red face. One saw a short man in a mackintosh. One saw a man in shirt and trousers only— obviously a confusion with the fleeing boy, Artie. One saw a fat man in a gray suit and a bowler hat. One saw a medium-sized man in cloth cap and the strapped corduroys of the navy. One saw a black man.

It seemed fairly certain, though, that the man who cried Murder could not have been the murderer, for two witnesses had seen members of the family alive within less than two minutes of the murders; and one man could not have been responsible for that wholesale slaughter in that space of time. The man who ran out must have been the man who had been seen by the woman witness standing there and shouting "Shop!" and as that was only one minute before the alarm, clearly *he* could not have been the murderer. He had not come forward, but then, there might be many innocent explanations of that. He might have been a man of nervous type who had received such a shock from what he had seen that he wished to avoid all association with the matter. Or he might have been a quiet, shy fellow who would hate to be mixed up in any sensational public affair. Having given the alarm, and having no useful information to offer beyond what the crowd saw for themselves, he might have considered that he had done his duty.

Generally, it was felt that it must have been the work of a gang—either a gang of thieves who were disturbed by the alarm before they could get at the cash, or, as suggested, a gang of drunken or drugged Negroes—and the gang must have entered from the back, or someone in the street would have noted them. It was the Negro suggestion that caught the public, chiefly because it seemed obvious and because it afforded a pious opportunity of shaking what they liked to think was an un-English crime on to those who were un-English. In talk around the streets the police were criticized for not concentrating on the Negro quarter. It was all very well to say that all the Negroes questioned had accounted for their movements. If the public were in the police's place, the public would know what to do, and so on.

The evening papers of that day brought more news, but none of it led anywhere. More suspicious characters on the outskirts of London had been detained, and two men—one a soldier at Sheerness, the other a tramp at Gerard's Cross—had given themselves up for the murder, only to be thrown out an hour later. People in the neighborhood now began to remember strange and significant happenings centering on the Roakes, which they hadn't remembered the day before. Queer visitors, letters by every post, sudden outgoings, late home-comings—all the scores of commonplace family happenings which, when isolated and focussed and limelit by tragedy and publicity, assume an air of the sinister and portentous. If Mrs. Roake had gone out in a new hat the day before they would have seen *that* as a possible clue.

Day by day the story mounted, and all fact that was thin was fortified by flagrant conjecture and by "sidelights" and comparison with similar crimes. The police were following a clue at Bristol. A broken and stained bicycle pump had been found behind the mangle in the scullery and was being examined by the Home Office experts. Three of the leading yard men had left London for a destination unknown. The writer of an anonymous letter, received at Bow Street the day after the murders, was asked to communicate with any police station under a pledge of the fullest protection from all consequences. The Flying Squad had spent a whole day combing the road from Stoke Newington to Waltham Cross. Watch was being kept at Gravesend, Queenboro', Harwich, Grimsby, Hull, and Newcastle for two men, believed to be Norwegians. The police were anxious to get in touch with these men. Blandly and hopefully they invited these two men to visit the Yard. But despite these invitations, despite official rewards and newspaper rewards running into many hundreds of pounds, no outside help was secured, no "splits"—those ever-present helps in baffling crimes—came forward to give their pals away.

Then, at the end of the week, the Sunday papers had a plum. All these minor diversions were cancelled and the men called off. The new story was that the District Inspector, with a detachment of officers in an armoured police car, had left for Nottingham; and the story was given out with such a note of assurance that the thing appeared to be settled. And it was. Press and public waited eagerly on the result of this expedition. And they waited. After two days, as the result of waiting, the press was proudly silent on Nottingham. There was no report on the Nottingham expedition, but in its place a calm ignoring of it, as though it had never been. Nottingham was still on the map of England but it was out of the news. The public heard nothing. Not a word. Somewhere between London and Nottingham the Great Talleyrand Murder Mystery faded away; crept into the valley of undiscovered crimes, and died as mysteriously as the Roake family had died.

Thereafter public and press interest declined. From being a "splash" story it came to an ordinary column; then, from the main page it passed to the secondary news page; then it fell to half a column, and at the end of three weeks it had no space at all. The mystery that had been the subject of talk in offices, shops, trains, restaurants, and homes was forgotten. The best brains had been at work upon it and had failed; and although I, in common with other amateurs, had my theories about it, not one of them bore steady examination.

Today I know the solution, but I did not arrive at it by my own thought or by thought based on the experts' labours. We were all looking for madmen, or, if we dismissed madmen, then for some possible motive; and in looking for motives we were looking for the ordinary human motives that we could appreciate, and that appear again and again in murder. None of us thought of inventing a *new* motive; and that was where the solution lay. It was not the experts, but Stephen Trink, the dabbler, who showed me where to look; who took my eyes off a gang, and showed me how all this death and disaster and stretching of police wits could have been the work of two hands belonging to one man. He even pointed to the man.

VI

It was about a month after the affair had died down that I found among the morning mail on my tea tray a letter from Trink. It was dated from a hotel in the New Forest, and was an unusually long letter from one who scarcely ever addressed more than a postcard. And a queer letter. I read it in bed, and for some long time—an hour, I should think—I could not bring myself to get up and face the day. When at last I did, I found work impossible. All that day and night I was haunted by a spectre of forbidden knowledge, and I went perfunctorily about my occasions with a creeping of the flesh, as when one discovers a baby playing with a boiling kettle, or touches something furry in the dark. I knew then what it was that the boy Artie was trying to say.

But as the letter requires no editing or pointing, I give it *verbatim*.

"Dear T.B.,

"As we haven't met for some time I thought you might like a word from Stephen Trink. I've been down here for a week or so among the pines, seeking a little open-air massage for jangled nerves. You understand. It was a dreadful business, and I didn't want to see anybody, especially friends. I'm here doing nothing and seeing nothing—just breathing and drowsing.

"I suppose they've got no farther with it. Strange that the police, so astonishingly clever in making up really baffling and complicated cases, are so often beaten by a simple case. But you, as an artist, know how often a subtle piece of work which the public imagine to have been achieved by laborious and delicate process, was in fact done with perfect ease; and how often the simple piece of work has meant months of planning and revision. I don't know if you've thought about it at all, but it seems to me that they've been misled all along by the matter of time. They assumed that that little time, for such a business, must imply a gang. No sound reason why it should, though. As Samuel Nicks established an alibi by accomplishing the believed impossible—committing a crime at Gad's Hill, Kent, early one morning and being seen at York at seven o'clock the same evening, so this man deceived public opinion. The public of the seventeenth century held that it was not possible for a man to be in Kent in the morning and at York in the evening; all the horses in the kingdom couldn't carry him that distance in that time. Therefore, it hadn't been done, and Sam Nicks hadn't been in Kent that day. But it *was* done. And so here. Four murders by different means had been accomplished in a few seconds over a minute. Therefore, say the public (the experts, too), arguing from the general, it must have been the work of a gang. They were satisfied that no one man could do it, and if no one man could do it, then no one man *had* done it. But public opinion is always saying It Can't Be Done, and is always eating its words. You and I know that what any one man can *conceive,* some other man can *do.* I can imagine that this could be the work of one man, and I'm satisfied that it *was* the work of one man. It was done by the exception to the rule, and I'll show you how he could have done it, and how he got away. As to getting away, of course he got away by running away. If you say that a running man at such a moment would attract attention, well, we know that he did attract attention. He was clever enough to know that in successfully running away, it depends how you run. He covered his appearance and his running by drawing the whole street's attention to himself. He knew enough about things to know that his cry would blind everybody. They might be looking, but they wouldn't be seeing—as we know they weren't. All their senses would gather to reinforce the sense of hearing. As soon as he was round a corner he could slip his hat in his pocket and put on a cap. Nothing makes a sharper edge on the memory, or more effectually changes a man's appearance, than the hat. Then he could fling his coat over his arm, and go back and join the crowd.

"The affair had to the public, as we know, the air of being the work of a brilliant and invincible gang of schemers, who weren't playing by any means their first stroke: or else of a gang of crafty madmen. It was this that increased its horror. But it was no planned affair, and no gang affair. It was the work of a man momentarily careless of results. Being careless, he made no mistakes. As often happens, he, the inexpert, achieved casually what trained minds arrive at step by step.

"Now as to how. Really very simple. The core of the mystery is this: he was a man of unbelievable swiftness of act and motion. That's all.

"People don't seem to realise that taking human life is a very simple matter. They seem to think that it involves thought, planning, struggle, and mess. Nothing of the kind. It can be done as easily as the slaughter of a rabbit—more easily than the slaughter of a hen. A pressure with two fingers on a certain spot, or one sharp flick on a point at the back of the neck, and the business is done. It's part of the irony that plays about the creature, Man, that the neck, which supports his noblest part, should be his weakest part. You could do it without fuss in the club, on top of the bus, at

Lord's, or at the theatre, or in your own home or your victim's. You remember that morning when you were showing me your collection of Eastern weapons? Among them you had a case of Burmese poison darts. You took these out of their cylinder and showed them to me. I was leaning forward with my hands on your desk, and you were turning them about between finger and thumb. One minute movement of a minute muscle of your forefinger, and the point would have touched my hand, and Trink would have been out. Supposing you'd been not feeling very well—liverish—and my face or my voice had irritated you to the point of blind exasperation. A wonderful chance. Accidents often happen when things like that are being shown round. You may have seen the chance. If you did, only common good nature can have restrained you—supposing that you were irritated by me—as nothing but good nature restrains me from slapping a bald head in front of me at the theatre. One second would have done it, where shooting and throat-cutting not only take time but often cause disorder and fuss, besides involving extravagant use of means. One stroke of a finger directed by a firm wrist achieves the result without any stress or display. Many people are killed by four or five stabs of a knife, or by a piece of lead shot from an instrument that has to be loaded, and in which a lever has to be released, causing a loud bang. Unnecessary, and possibly wasted. Because no result can be achieved unless that piece of lead goes to a certain spot. And there's nothing that that piece of lead can do that four fingers can't do. You could have six friends in your room looking over your curios, and with merely the movement of the arm that an orchestral conductor makes in directing a three-four bar, you could, holding one of those Burmese darts, touch the hands of those friends. In five minutes you would have changed your warm gossipy room into a sepulchre. And yet people still think of murder as implying revolvers, knives, arsenic; and murderers still take five minutes over throttling from the front with both hands, when two seconds with the side of one hand will do it from the back. It is because of this that the unintelligent conceive murder as terrific, demanding time and energy; and still think that all murder must leave obvious traces of murder. Not at all. For every one murder that is known to be a murder, I am certain that six other people, who meet Accidental Death or are Found Drowned lose their lives by murder.

"This man, as I say, was swifter than most of us. He strolled into the shop. Calling 'Shop!' he went to the parlour door. There he met Roake. One movement. Mrs. Roake would turn. Another movement. The girl was coming through the door leading to the passage. Two steps and another movement. The boy comes through the garden to the shop. A fourth movement. One movement with a knife on the back of Roake's head. One pressure with the thumb to Mrs. Roake. One movement with both hands to the girl. One sharp touch on the boy's neck. And the foul thing was done in a matter of seconds. A movement overhead. The other boy stirring. He waits for him to come down. The boy doesn't come. He hears the noise of his flight. Then he makes his own by running full tilt into the faces of a score of people and crying his crime.

"That's all.

"Looking over this, I'm afraid it reads as though I'm writing with levity. But I'm not. I'm just analysing the situation and the probable attitude of the man. The whole thing is too frightful for me to treat it as seriously as I naturally feel about it; or, rather, in trying to treat it as a problem, I've forgotten that these poor people were my friends.

"Now as to why any man not a natural criminal or lunatic should have created this horror of destruction—this isn't going to be so easy. Here I'm on dangerous and delicate ground, and before I can present what looks to me like a reasonable explanation I must ask you to empty your mind of your reason and of all that knowledge of human nature on which people base their judgment of human motive and human behaviour. It should never be said that 'people don't do these things' or that such and such a thing is contrary to human nature; because people do anything and are always going contrary to our accepted notions of human nature. You must see it as clearly as one sees a new scientific idea—without reference to past knowledge or belief. It means trespassing into the forbidden, though I think you've peeped into more secret corners of the mind than the ordinary man. Or not peeped, perhaps. I think you've always known without peeping.

"It's difficult to put the presentation of it into assured and assuring phrasing. But I'll try.

"What I offer is this. This man had a motive for this wanton slaughter. But not a motive that would pass with common understanding. Neither hate nor lust nor the morbid vanity that sometimes leads stupid people to the committal of enormous crimes. Nothing of that sort. And he wasn't a madman without responsibility for his actions. He knew fully what he was doing and he did it deliberately. He committed more than a crime; he committed a sin. And meant to. Most men think that sin is the ultimate depth to which man can sink from his gods; but this man didn't sink. He rose, by sin, out of something fouler than sin. That something is the spirit of unexpressed, potential evil; something that corrodes not only the soul of man in whom it dwells, but the souls of men near him and the beautiful world about him. This evil doesn't always—indeed, seldom does—live in what we call wicked people. Almost always in the good. In comparison with such people the wicked are healthy. For these people, the germ-carriers, are more dangerous to the soul of the man than a million criminals or a thousand sinners. They can penetrate everywhere. We have no armour against their miasma. They do no evil, but they're little hives of evil. Just as some people can spread an infection without themselves taking the disease, so these good people can, without sinning, spread among the innocent the infection of sin. They lead stainless lives. Their talk is pure. Yet wherever they go they leave a grey trail that pollutes all that is noble and honest. They diffuse evil as some lonely places—themselves beautiful—diffuse evil. You must have met people of this sort—good people—and have been faintly conscious, after an hour of their company, of some emanation that makes you want to open spiritual windows. Happy for them, poor creatures, if they can discover and prove themselves before death for what they are. Some do. For those who don't, who only discover the foulness of their souls after death, God knows what awaits them.

"There's something in these people. Some awful essence of the world's beginnings. Some possession that can only be cast out in one way—a dreadful way. Where it began one cannot say. Perhaps strange sins, projected in the cold hearts of creatures centuries dead, projected but never given substance, take on a ghost-essence and wander through the hearts of men as cells of evil. And wander from heart to heart, poisoning as they go, until at last they come to life in a positive sin, and, having lived, can die. Nobody knows. But that's my explanation of these people—they're possessed. Possessed by some radioactive essence of evil, and before they can be saved they must sin. Just as poison is necessary to some physical natures and, denied it, they die, so sin may be necessary to these spiritual natures. They must express and release that clotted evil, and they can no more be cleansed of it before it's expressed than a man can be cleansed of a fever before it's reached its climacteric. Once expressed, it can be met and punished and pardoned; but abstract evil can't be met. Even God can't conquer Satan. There's nothing to conquer. Satan lives in these million wandering fragments of potential evil, and until that evil is crystallised in an act, all the powers of good are powerless.

"Let's suppose that this man was one of these, consciously possessed of this intangible essence of evil, conscious of it as a blight upon him and upon those about him; tortured by it like a man with a snake in his bosom, and for many years fighting its desire for expression and release until the fight became unbearable. There's only one way of escape for him—to sin and to sin deeply. Always he's haunted by the temptation to sin. His whole life's been clouded by visions and lures of unnamable sins, and by agonising combats to escape them. Always he fights this temptation, and so, continuing to shelter the evil, he gives it time to grow and to make his own emanations stronger. When his only real hope of conquering it lies in giving it life.

"And then at last he yields. There comes, one day, the eruptive, whirlwind moment of temptation, stronger than any he has known. All his powers of resistance go down in an avalanche. With a sigh of relief he yields. And suddenly, with the disappearance of resistance, and with the resolve to sin, he would find, I think, the serenity of resignation filling his whole being, and setting his pulse in tune with erring humanity. He would walk the streets with a lighter step than he has known since childhood. All his temptations would have been towards the foulest sin he could conceive, the lowest depth; and at last, driven by the importunate fiend, it's this sin that he commits. It may be that he was led farther than he meant to go. He may have intended to murder only one, but in committing the one murder, his fiend broke out in full power, and led him deeper and deeper into maniac slaughter. That's how it looks. But the thing was done, the sin committed, and in the satanic moment he frees himself forever from his fiend, not by binding it, but by releasing it. Like a long-embalmed body exposed to the air, it has one minute of life, and the next it crumbles into dust, and he is free.

"That's my theory. This man, without sin, would have died here and hereafter, for his soul didn't belong to him at all. Indeed, he was a man without a soul. Now he's a man with a stained soul which can be purified. He has seen himself as he is, on this earth, in time to prepare himself for his next stage. By that sin he can now, as a fulfilled and erring soul, work out his penance and his redemption.

"I guess I've said enough. You may dismiss this as a far-fetched and ludicrous fancy. But it isn't a fancy; it's a statement. You may say that no man could, under the most overwhelming temptation, do this appalling act of murdering, not an enemy, but a friend; or, having done it, could live under its burden. I can't argue with you as to what man can and can't do. I only see what is done. It's useless to tell me that this couldn't have happened. I can only say that it did.

"Whatever you may know as to the reactions of humanity to this or that situation, I know that, after years of torment, I'm now, for the first time, at peace.

"Yours,

"S.T."

DRESSING-UP

by W. R. BURNETT

When the store manager saw Blue and his girl, Birdy, coming in the front
door, he turned to Al, one of the clerks, and said:

"Look at this, Al. The stockyards're moving downtown."

Al laughed, then he put on his best professional manner, clasped his hands
in front of his stomach, inclined his head slightly, and walked up to Blue.

"What can I do for you, sir?"

Blue was short and stocky. His legs were thin, his waist small, but his
shoulders were wide enough for a man six feet tall. His face was red and
beefy, and his cheekbones were so prominent that they stuck out of his face.
He looked up at Al.

"I'm buying an outfit, see," he said. "I'm gonna shed these rags and climb
into something slick."

"Yes, sir," said Al. "How about one of our new spring models?"

"He wants a gray suit," said Birdy, adjusting her new fur neckpiece.

"Double-breasted," said Blue.

"Yes, sir," said Al.

"But first I want some silk underwear," said Blue. "I'm dressing from the
hide out."

The store manager came over and smiled.

"Take good care of this young man, won't you, Mr. Johnson?"

"Yes, sir," said Al.

"Warm, isn't it?" the store manager said to Birdy.

"Yeah, ain't it?" said Birdy, taking off her neckpiece and dangling it over
her arm like the women in the advertisements.

The store manager walked to the back of the shop and talked to the
cashier:

"There's a boy that's got a big hunk of money all of a sudden," he said,
"and he's gonna lose it the same way."

"Yeah?" said the cashier. "Well, I wish my rich uncle that I haven't got
would die. Take a look at that neckpiece his girl's wearing. He didn't get
that for five dollars."

Al spread out the silk underwear on the counter, and Blue looked through it. Birdy held up a lavender shirt.

"Here you are, Blue. Here's what you ought to get."

"Say . . . !" said Blue.

"Yes, sir," said Al; "we're selling lots of that. Just had an order for a dozen suits from Mr. Hibschmann out in Lake Forest."

"That's where the swells come from," said Birdy.

Blue looked at the lavender shirt and the lavender shorts and said: "All right. I'll take a dozen."

Al glanced up from his order book, caught the manager's eye, and winked. The manager came up to Blue, put his hand on his shoulder and said:

"My dear sir, since you seem to know real stuff when you see it, I'll let you in on something. We got a new shipment of cravats that we have only just begun to unpack. But if you'd like to look at them, I'll send down to the stockroom for them."

"Sure," said Blue.

"Thanks awfully," said Birdy.

"It's our very best stock. Handmade cravats of the best material obtainable."

"We want the best, don't we, Blue?" said Birdy.

"Sure," said Blue.

While the manager sent for the cravats, Blue bought a dozen silk shirts, some collars, a solid gold collar pin, some onyx cuff links, a set of military brushes, and two dozen pairs of socks. Al bent over his order book and wrote in the items swiftly, computing the possible amount of this windfall. In a few minutes a stock boy brought up the neckties and stood with his mouth open while Blue selected a dozen of the most expensive ties. The manager noticed him.

"Just leave the rest of the stock, please," he said, then he turned his back to Blue and whispered, "Get out of here!"

The stock boy went back to the basement, and the manager turned back to Blue, smiling.

"Those cravats retail at four dollars apiece," he said, "but because you're giving us such a nice order, I'll let you have them for three fifty."

"O.K.," said Blue.

"Them sure are swell ties, Blue," said Birdy, putting her arm through his. "Won't we be lit up though?"

"Sure," said Blue.

When the accessories had been selected, Blue began to try on the suits Al brought him. Blue strode up and down in front of the big triple mirror, puffed out his chest, struck attitudes, and studied his profile, which he had never seen before except in one Bertillon picture. Al stayed at his elbow, offering suggestions, helping him with the set of a coat, telling him how wonderful he looked; and the manager stayed in the background occasionally making a remark to Birdy whom he addressed as "Madam."

Blue, after a long consultation with Birdy, selected two of the most expensive suits: a blue serge single-breasted and a gray double-breasted. Then he bought a gray felt hat at twelve dollars, a small sailor at eight, and a panama at eighteen.

"Well," said Blue, "I guess you guys got about as much of my jack as you're gonna get."

"How about shoes?" Al put in.

"By God, I forgot," said Blue. "Hey, Birdy, I forgot shoes. Ain't that good? Look at this suitcase!"

He held up his foot. He was wearing big tan brogans, and there was a hole in the sole which went clear through the sock to the skin.

"Put your foot down, Blue," said Birdy. "Where you think you're at?"

Blue bought a pair of tan oxfords, a pair of black oxfords, and a pair of white and tan sport shoes.

"Now we're done," said Blue. "I guess I ought to look pretty Boul' Mich' now."

Al totaled up the bill. Birdy and the manager had a long conversation about the weather; and Blue stood before the triple mirror studying his profile.

Al hesitated before he told Blue the amount of the bill. He called for the manager to O.K. it, then he said:

"Cash or charge, sir?"

Blue took out his billfold which was stuffed with big bills.

"Cash," he said, "how much?"

"Four hundred and sixty-five dollars," said Al.

Blue gave him five one-hundred-dollar bills.

"Now," said Blue, "I want you to get that gray suit fixed up right away so's I can put it on. I'm gonna dress from the hide out, and you guys can throw my old duds in the sewer."

"Yes, sir," said Al. "I'll get our tailor right away. We got a dressing room on the second floor."

The cashier rang up the sale and gave the change to the manager.

"Are you going away for the summer?" asked the manager as he handed Blue his change.

"Yeah," said Blue; "me and the girlfriend are gonna see New York. It'll be our first trip."

"That'll be nice," said the manager. "Are you in business for yourself?"

Blue glanced at Birdy, and she shook her head slightly.

"I'm in the oil business," said Blue. "I got some wells. I'm from Oklahoma."

"That's interesting," said the manager.

When they were leaving the café Blue took out his billfold and gave the doorman a five-dollar bill. The doorman's eyes popped but he managed to bow and smile.

"Yes, sir, yes, sir," he said. "Do you want a cab?"

"Yeah," said Blue, hanging on to Birdy who was drunker than he was.

"Yeah, you're damn right we want a cab," said Birdy. "Do we look like the kind of people that walk?"

"That's right," said Blue.

"Yes, sir," said the doorman, and he went out into the middle of the street and blew his whistle.

Before the taxi came a small sedan drew up at the curb across the street, and two men got out.

"There he is," said one of them, pointing at Blue.

"Hello, Guido," shouted Blue. "Look at me. Ain't I Boul' Mich'?"

Guido ran across the street, took Blue by the arm, shook him several times, and said:

"You got to sober up, keed! Get it! You got to sober up. Somebody spilled something, see? Me and Bud's taking it on the lam. Saint Louie won't look bad to us."

"Yellow," said Blue.

"Sure," said Guido; "but I got a stake and I'm gonna spend some of it before I get bumped. Somebody wised Mike's boys up. They're looking for Pascal right now."

"What the hell!" said Blue, laughing. "Look at me, Guido. Ain't I Boul' Mich'? I got silk underwear under this suit. Look at Birdy."

"Look at me," said Birdy; "ain't I Boul' Mich'?"

"Say," said Guido, "you better ditch that tommy and put in with us. We got room in the heap."

"Not me," said Blue. "I ain't scairt of Mike Bova. I'll bump him next."

"All right," said Guido; "you'll have a swell funeral."

"Guido," called the other man, "let that bum go."

"So long, Blue," said Guido.

"So long," said Blue.

"Bye-bye, Guido," said Birdy.

Guido crossed the street, got into the driver's seat, slammed the door, and the sedan moved off. The taxi was waiting, and the doorman helped Birdy and Blue into it.

"Good night, sir," said the doorman.

Birdy was lying on the lounge flat on her back with her hands under her head and an empty drinking glass sitting upright on her stomach. Blue, in his shirtsleeves, his collar wilted and his tie untied, was sitting at the table reading a crumpled newspaper. There were three-inch headlines.

BOVA'S LIEUTENANT KILLED

SHOT DOWN AS HE LEFT

HIS OFFICE BY GUNMEN

"You hear me!" said Blue. "Funniest thing ever pulled. There I was waiting in a room across the street trying to read a magazine, and Pascal was sitting with his head against the wall sleeping. 'Christ,' I says, 'there's Pete now.' He was coming out of his office. We wasn't looking for him for two hours yet. So I jist set there. Hell, I couldn't move, see, 'cause he come sudden, see, and I was figuring he wouldn't be out for two hours yet. 'Pascal,' I says, 'there's Pete now.' But Pascal he jist opens his eyes like a fish and don't say nothing. Pete he stops and looks right up at the window where I'm sitting, see, and I wonder does this guy know something. Hell, I couldn't move. I wasn't ready, see? Well, so Pascal he slips and falls over and hits his head. This makes me laugh but still I couldn't move my trigger finger. Pete he holds out his hand like he's looking for rain, then I let him have it. I don't know. It was funny. I jist let him have it without knowing it, see, and before, I couldn't pull that trigger when I wanted to. When the old Thompson starts to bark, Pascal gets up and yells, 'What you smoking for, you bum? It ain't time yet.' Then he looks out the window and there's Pete on the sidewalk dead as yesterday's newspaper and an old woman is pointing up at us. We ditch the gun and beat it down the back stairs. That's all there was to it. There wasn't nobody in the alley, see, so we jist walked along slow, and pretty soon we come to a drugstore and went in to get some cigs 'cause we smoked all ours waiting for that guy to come out."

"Pour me a little drink, honey," said Birdy.

Blue got up, took a big flask out of his hip pocket, and poured Birdy another drink. Then he sat down, took out his billfold and extracted a couple of railroad tickets.

"Look at them, old kid," he said. "When we ride, we ride. Twentieth Century to New York. That's us, kid; and won't we give 'em a treat over in Brooklyn! Say, them Easterners think we're still shooting Indians. Hell, Chi makes that place look like a Y. M. C. A. Yeah, I used to know Ruby Welch, and he was big stuff from Brooklyn; but what did he do when Guido started gunning for him? He got himself put in the can as a vag. Yeah, we ought to go over big in New York, kid. What they need over there is guts. We can give 'em that, kid. When somebody needs somebody for the No. 1 caper, Blue's the guy for the job. I was born with a rod in my cradle and I'm the best there is. Yeah, when the Big Boy wanted Pete bumped who did he call on first? Old Blue, yes, sir, old Blue."

Blue got up, turned on the gramophone, and started to dance with a chair.

"Hey," he said, "come on, let's dance, Birdy. We're big shots now, Birdy; let's dance. Look at me! If I had my coat on I'd look like the Prince of Wales. Boul' Mich', kid; that's us; Boul' Mich'. We'll knock their eyes out on Fifth Avenue, kid; yes, sir. Let's dance."

"I'm getting sick," said Birdy.

Blue went over and looked down at her. Her face was pale and drawn; there were blue circles under her eyes.

"Getting sick, Birdy?"

"Yeah. I can't stand it like I used to when I was with The Madam. Put me to bed, honey."

Blue picked Birdy up and carried her into the bedroom. Birdy began to hiccup.

"Gimme glass of water," she said.

"You don't want water," Blue said; "you want a nice big slug."

"No, gimme glass of water."

She lay down on the bed and, before Blue could bring her a glass of water, she was asleep. He stood looking down at her, then he went back into the living room, took a long pull at his flask, and picked up the crumpled newspaper. But he had read the account of the killing of Big Pete so many times that he knew it by heart. He sat staring at the paper, then he threw it on the floor and sat rolling a cigarette between his palms.

It had begun to get light. He heard a milk wagon passing the house. He got up and went over to the window. The houses were still dark, and far off down the street a string of lighted elevated cars ran along the horizon, but the sky was gray and in the east some of the clouds were turning yellow. It was quiet. Blue began to notice how quiet it was.

"Birdy," he called.

But he heard her snoring, and turned back to the table.

The telephone rang, but when he answered it there was nobody on the line.

"What's the idea?" he said.

He sat down at the table, took out his billfold and counted his money; then he took out the railroad tickets and read everything printed on them. Again he noticed how quiet it was. He got up, put away his billfold, and went into the bedroom. Birdy was sleeping with her mouth open, flat on her back, with her arms spread out. Blue lay down beside her and tried to sleep, but he turned from side to side, and finally gave it up.

"I don't feel like sleeping," he thought. "I'm all het up about going East on The Century. Here I am, old Blue, riding The Century dressed up like John Barrymore and with a swell frail. Yeah, that's me. Boul' Mich' Blue."

He got up, put on his coat, and began to pose in front of the living-room mirror.

"Boul' Mich' Blue," he said.

Finally he sat down at the table and laid out a game of solitaire; but he had so many bad breaks with the cards that he began to cheat and then lost interest in the game.

"I know," he said, "what I need is food."

He got up and went to the refrigerator, but there wasn't anything in it except a few pieces of cold meat.

"Hell!" he said, "I guess I'll have to go down to Charley's."

He put on his new soft hat, but hesitated. If they was looking for Pascal, they was looking for him, too. Right now there wasn't nobody on the streets and it was a good time to bump a guy.

"Hell!" he said, buttoning his coat, "I got a streak of luck. It'll hold. Boul' Mich' Blue'll be on The Century tomorrow. Yeah bo! I ain't scairt of no Mike Bova."

When Blue came out of the apartment house the sun was just coming up. The alleys and areaways were still dark, but there was a pale yellow radiance in the streets. There was no one about; no sign of life. Not even a parked car.

"Hell!" said Blue; "safe as a tank-town."

A window across the street was raised, and Blue ducked without meaning to; but a fat woman put her head out of the window and stared into the street.

There was nobody in Charley's, not even a waiter. Behind the counter the big nickel coffee urns were sending up steam. Blue took out a fifty-cent piece and flung it on the counter. Wing, the counterman, looked in from the kitchen.

"Come on, Wing," said Blue, "snap it up."

"Didn't know you, kid," said Wing. "Ain't you dressed up, though? Must've struck it."

"I sure did," said Blue. "Give me a combination and some of that muddy water."

"Muddy water, hell," said Wing. "I jist made that Java."

Blue leaned on the counter and stared at himself in the mirror, while Wing went back to make his sandwich.

"Hey, Wing," Blue shouted, "did you know I was going East on The Century?"

"Are, hunh?" Wing shouted back. "You're on the big time now, ain't you, kid?"

"That's the word," said Blue.

Blue turned to look out into the street. He saw a man passing, and stared at him. The man was small and had a slouch hat pulled down over his face. Blue thought he recognized him and slid his gun out of the holster under his armpit and put it in his coat pocket. The man passed without looking in.

"I got the jumps," said Blue. "It's that rotten gin."

Wing came in with the sandwich, drew Blue a cup of coffee, then leaned his elbows on the counter and watched Blue eat.

"Well," said Wing, "I see where they got Big Pete."

"Yeah," said Blue.

"I knew they was gonna," said Wing. "I got inside dope."

"Yeah?" said Blue.

"It was coming to him."

"Yeah."

Blue finished his sandwich, lighted a cigarette, and sipped his coffee. It was broad daylight now, and trucks had begun to pass the restaurant.

"Going East, are you, kid?" said Wing.

"Yeah," said Blue. "I got in on a big cut and I don't have to worry none for some time. I jist took my dame down and dressed her up this afternoon. Is she hot? Me, I got silk underwear on."

He unbuttoned his shirt and showed Wing his lavender underwear.

"You're sure a dressed-up boy," said Wing. "I bet you paid ten bucks for that hat you got on."

"Twelve," said Blue. "It was the best they had. I paid eighteen for a panama. You like this suit?"

"It's red hot," said Wing; then with a twinge of envy, "If I wasn't going straight maybe I could wear rags like that."

"How long's your parole got to run?"

"Plenty long. And I got the dicks down on me. They thought I'd stool for 'em in this ward. But that ain't my way."

"Why don't you make a break for Canada?"

"Yeah," said Wing, "and get jerked back to stir."

Blue finished his coffee, paid his check, and gave Wing a dollar bill. Wing turned the bill over and over.

"Say," he said, "give me another buck and I'll put you onto something hot at Arlington."

Blue laughed and tossed Wing a silver dollar.

"Never mind the tip," he said. "I know lots of better ways to lose my dough. Why don't you lay off the ponies, Wing? You can't beat that racket."

"I got the itch," said Wing.

Blue looked into the mirror and adjusted his hat to the proper angle.

"Well," he said, "I'm leaving you. I'll send you a postcard from the Big Burg, Wing."

But Blue noticed that Wing had begun to get nervous; his face was twitching.

"Blue," said Wing, "for Christ's sake watch your step. I'm telling you straight, kid. One of Mike's boys was in here buzzing me about you jist 'fore she began to get light. I'm telling you straight, kid. It ain't my fight and I wasn't gonna peep. But you're a right guy, Blue."

Blue rubbed his hand over his face, then he said:

"It was The Wolf. I seen him go past."

"Yeah," said Wing.

"Jesus!" said Blue, "which way'd I better go?"

"I'd put you upstairs . . ." Wing began.

"No use," said Blue. "The Wolf seen me."

Wing drew himself a cup of coffee and drank it at a gulp.

"If they knew I'd peeped they'd bump me sure," said Wing.

Blue stood staring at the counter, then he pulled his hat down over his eyes, and slipped his right hand into the pocket where the gun was.

"Well," he said, "the alley's no good. It's blind my way. The side street won't get me no place. So all I got's the front way. Hell!" he went on, puffing out his chest, "I got a streak of luck, Wing. It'll hold."

Wing drew himself another coffee.

"Here's hoping," he said.

Blue went to the door and, putting his head out a little way, looked up and down. The street was deserted except for a truck which was coming toward him slowly. It was a Standard Oil truck.

"Wing," he said, "has any of Mike's boys got a hide-out anywhere around here?"

"Don't know of none."

"Well," said Blue, "here I go."

"So long," said Wing.

Blue stepped out of the restaurant, threw his shoulders back, and began to walk slowly toward Birdy's apartment. The Standard Oil truck passed him and went on. The street was quiet. At the end of the street he saw an elevated on its way toward the Loop.

"I wish I was on that baby," he said.

But the nearer he got to the apartment the surer he became that his luck would hold. Hell! it was the first break he'd had since he and Guido hijacked that big Detroit shipment. He had tickets on The Century. When a guy has tickets on The Century he uses them. And that wasn't all. He was a big shot now; the Big Boy had promised him a bonus; he had on silk underwear.

"Hell!" said Blue, "it ain't in the cards."

Across from Birdy's apartment he saw the same fat woman leaning out of the window. When he looked up she drew her head in hastily. Blue made a dash for the door, but across the street a Thompson gun began to spit. Blue stumbled, dropped his gun, and ran blindly out into the middle of the street; then he turned and ran blindly back toward the house. An iron fence caught him just below the belt and he doubled over it. Across the street a window was slammed.

MALICE DOMESTIC

by PHILIP MacDONALD

Carl Borden came out of Seaman's bookstore into the sundrenched, twisting little main street of El Morro Beach. He looked around to see if his wife were in view, and then, as she wasn't, walked to the bar entrance of Eagles' and went in. He was a big, loosely built, rambling sort of a man, with untidy blond hair and a small, somehow featureless face which was redeemed from indistinction by his eyes, which were unexpectedly large, vividly blue and always remarkably alive. He was a writer of some merit, mediocre sales, and—at least among the wordier critics—considerable reputation.

He sat on the first stool at the bar and nodded to the Real Estate man, Dockweiler, who had once been a Hollywood actor; to Dariev, the Russian who did the murals; then—vaguely—to some people in booths. He didn't smile at all, not even at the barman when he ordered his beer—and Dockweiler said to old Parry beside him, "Catch that Borden, will you! Wonder whatsa matter. . . ."

The barman, who was always called Hiho for some reason everyone had forgotten, brought Carl's drink and set it down before him and glanced at him and said, "Well, Mr. Borden—and how've you been keeping?"

Carl said, "Thanks, Hiho—oh, all right, I guess. . . ." He took a long swallow from the cold glass.

Hiho said, "And how's Mrs. Borden? Okay?"

"Fine!" Carl said, and then again, "Fine!" He put a dollar bill on the bar and Hiho picked it up and went back to the cash register.

Carl put his elbows on the bar and dropped his face into his hands; then sat quickly upright as Hiho returned with his change. He pocketed it and swallowed the rest of his beer and stood up. He nodded to Hiho without speaking and walked out into the street again.

His wife was standing by the car with her arms full of packages. He said, "Hey, Annette—hold it!" and quickened his pace to a lumbering trot.

She smiled at him. A brief, wide smile which was just a little on the toothy side. She looked slim and straight and cool and soignée, as she always did. She was a blond Norman woman of thirty-odd, and she had been married to Carl for nine years. They were regarded, by everyone who did not know them well, as an "ideal couple." But their few intimates, of late, had been vaguely unsure of this.

Carl opened the door of the car and took the parcels from Annette's arms and stowed them away in the back. She said, "Thank you, Carlo," and got into the seat beside him as he settled himself at the wheel. She said, "Please —go around by Beatons. I have a *big* package there."

He drove down to Las Ondas Road and parked, on the wrong side of the street, outside a white-fenced little building over which a sign announced, BEATON AND SON—NURSERIES.

He went into the shop, and the girl gave him a giant paper sack, stuffed overfull with a gallimaufry of purchases. He picked it up—and the bottom tore open and a shower of the miscellany sprayed to the floor.

Carl swore beneath his breath, and the girl said "Oh, drat!" and whipped around to help him. He put the things he had saved on the counter, then, stooping, retrieved a thick pamphlet called *The Rose-Grower's Handbook* and a carton labeled KILLWEED in white lettering above a red skull-and-crossbones design.

The girl had everything else. Apologizing profusely, she put the whole order into two fresh sacks. Carl put one under each arm and went out into the sunny street again, and saw Dr. Wingate walking along it, approaching the car. Carl called out, "Hi, Tom!" and smiled his first smile of the morning as the other turned and saw him.

"Hi yourself!" Wingate said. He was a man in the middle forties, a little dandiacal as to dress, and he wore—unusual in a medico—a small, neatly trimmed imperial which some people thought distinguished, others merely caprine. He turned to the car and raised his hat to Annette, wishing her good-morning a trifle formally. He opened the rear door for Carl and helped him put the two packages in with the others. He looked at Carl, and for a moment his gaze became sharply professional. He said, "How's the book going?" and Carl hesitated before he answered, "Fine! Tough sledding, of course—but it'll be all right, I think."

"Well—" said Wingate, "don't go cold on it. It's too good."

Carl shrugged. Annette said, impatiently, "We must get back, Carlo," and he got into the car and started the engine and waved to his friend.

He drove back through the town and then branched inland up into the hills and came in five minutes to the narrow, precipitous road which led up to his house, standing alone on its little bluff. It was a sprawling, gray-shingled building, with tall trees behind it and, in front, a lawn which surrounded a rose bed. Beside the lawn a graveled driveway, with traces of devil-grass and other weeds showing through its surface, ran down to the garage.

As he stopped the car, an enormous dog appeared around the corner of the house and bounded towards them. Annette got out first, and looked at the animal and said, "Hello," and put out her hand as if to fondle it.

The dog backed away. It stood with its head up and stared at her. It was a Giant Schnauser, as big as a Great Dane, and it was called G.B. because something about its bearded face and sardonic eye had always made Carl think of Shaw.

Annette looked at it; then, with a quick little movement of her head, at her husband. She said sharply, "The dog! Why does he look at me like that?"

Carl was getting out of the car. "Like what?" he said—and then it was upon him, its tail-stump wagging madly, its vast mouth open in a wet, white-and-scarlet smile.

"Hi there, G.B!" Carl said—and the creature rose up on its hind legs and put its forepaws on his shoulders and tried to lick his face. Its head was almost on a level with Carl's.

Annette said, "It is—peculiar. He does not like me lately." She was frowning.

Carl said, "Oh, that's your imagination," and the dog dropped upon all fours again and stood away while the packages were taken out of the car.

Carl carried most of them, Annette the rest. They stood in the kitchen, and Annette began to put her purchases away. Carl stood and watched her. His blue eyes were dark and troubled, and he looked like a Brobdingnagian and bewildered little boy who has found himself in trouble for some reason he cannot understand.

Annette wanted to get to the icebox, and he was in her way. She pushed at his arm, and said sharply, "Move! You are too big for this kitchen!"

But he put his long arms around her and pulled her close to him. He said, "Annette! What's the matter, darling? What is it? What have I done?"

She strained back against his arms —but he tightened their pressure and drew her closer still and buried his face in the cool, firm flesh of her throat.

"Carl!" she said. She sounded amazed.

He went on talking, against her neck. His voice sounded almost as if there were tears in it. He said, "Don't tell me there isn't something wrong! Just tell me what it *is!* Tell me what I've *done!* It's been going on for weeks now—maybe months. Ever since you came back from that trip. You've been—different. . . ."

His wife stood motionless. She said, slowly, "But, Carlo—that is what I have been feeling about you."

He raised his head and looked at her. He said, "It's almost as if you were —suspicious of me. And I don't know what it's about!"

She frowned. "I—," she said, "I—" and then stopped for a long moment.

She said, "Do you know what I think? I think we are two very stupid people." The lines were leaving her face, the color coming back to it.

"Two stupid people!" she said again. "People who are not so young as they were. People who do not see enough other people—and begin to imagine things. . . ."

She broke off as there drifted through the open window the sound of a car, old and laboring, coming up the hill. She said, "Ah!" and put her hands on Carl's shoulders and kissed him at the corner of his mouth. She said, "The mail—I will get it," and went quickly out of the side door.

He made no attempt to follow her, no suggestion that he should do the errand. Annette had always been very jealous about her letters, and seemed to be growing even more so.

He stood where he was, his big shoulders sagging, the smile with which he had met her smile slowly fading from his face. He shook his head. He drew in a deep breath. He shambled away, through the big living room and through that again into his study. He sat down in front of his typewriter and stared at it for a long time.

He began to work—at first slowly, but finally with a true and page-devouring frenzy. . . .

It was dusk, and he had already switched on his desk light, when there came a gentle sound behind him. He dragged himself back to the world which he did not control and turned in his chair and saw his wife just inside the door. She was very slim, almost boyish, in her gardening overalls. She said, "I do not want to interrupt, Carlo—just to know about dinner." Her face was in shadow, and she might have been smiling.

He stood up and threw his arms wide and stretched. "Any time you like," he said, and then, as she moved to leave the room, "Wait a minute!"

He crossed to her and took her by the shoulders and looked down at her. For a moment she was rigid; then suddenly she put her arms around his neck and moulded her slim strong softness against him and tilted her face up to his.

It was a long and passionate kiss—and it was only broken by the sound of a jarring, persistent thudding at the French windows.

Annette pulled abruptly away from her husband's clasp. She muttered something which sounded like, "Sacré chien! . . ." and went quickly out through the door behind her.

Except for the pool of light upon the desk, the room was very dark now, and after a moment Carl reached out and snapped on the switch of the overhead light. Slowly, he walked over to the windows and opened them and let in the big dog.

It stood close to him, its head more than level with his waist, and he stroked it and pulled gently at its ears. He shut the window then, and went out of the study and upstairs to his own room, the animal padding heavily beside him. He took a shower and changed his clothes, and when he had finished, could still hear his wife in her own room. He said, "Come on, G.B." and went downstairs again and out of the house.

He put the car away and shut the garage—and was still outside when Annette called him in to dinner.

This was, like all Annette's dinners, a complete and rounded work of art —and it was made all the more pleasant because, during it, she seemed almost her old self. She was bright, talkative, smiling—and although the dog lay directly in the way of her path to the kitchen and would not move for her, she made no complaint but walked around him.

As usual, they had coffee in the living room. After his second cup, Carl got up, and stretched. He snapped his fingers at G.B., who went and stood expectantly by the door. Carl stood over his wife, smiling down at her. He started to speak—but she was first, looking up at him in sudden concern.

She said, "Carlo—you do not look well! . . . You work, I think, too hard! . . . You should not go out, perhaps."

But Carl pooh-poohed her. "Feel fine!" he said and bent over and kissed her on the forehead and crossed to the door and was gone.

Whistling, and with G.B. bounding ahead of him, he walked down the steep slant of their own road and onto the gentler slopes of Paseo Street.

He had gone less than quarter of a mile when his long, measured stride faltered. He took a few uneven steps, then stopped altogether. He swayed. He put a hand up to his forehead and found it covered with clammy sweat. He wobbled to the edge of the road and sat down upon a grass bank. He dropped his face into both his hands. A vast, black bulk appeared out of the darkness and thrust a damp nose at him. He mumbled something and took his hands away from his face and clapped them to his stomach and bent his head lower, down between his knees, and began to vomit. . . .

Old Parry was sitting in his living room, a book on his knee, a glass on the table beside him. He heard a scratching at the porch door; then a series of short, deep, demanding barks. He stood up creakily and went to the door and pulled it open. He bowed and said, "I am honored, Mr. Shaw!"—and then had his high-pitched giggle cut off short as the enormous dog seized the edge of his jacket between its teeth and began to tug at it with gentle but imperious sharpness.

"Something the matter, boy?" said Parry—and went the way he was being told and in a moment found the sick man by the roadside.

Carl had stopped vomiting now, and was sitting straighter. But he was badly shaken and weak as a kitten. In answer to Parry's shocked inquiries he mumbled, ". . . all right now . . . sorry . . . just my stomach upset . . ." He tried to laugh—a ghastly little sound. "I'm not drunk," he said. "Be all right in a minute—don't bother yourself . . ."

But Parry did bother himself: he had seen Carl's face—pinched and drawn and of a strange, greenish pallor shining with an oily film. Somehow, he got the big man to his feet; somehow, under the watchful yellow eye of the Schnauser, managed to pilot him into the house and settle him, half-seated, half-sprawling upon a sofa.

"Thanks," Carl muttered. "Thanks . . . that's fine . . ." He sank back on the cushions and closed his eyes.

"Just a minute now—" said old Parry—and went out into his little hallway and busied himself at the telephone to such effect that in less than fifteen minutes, a car pulled up outside and Dr. Thomas Wingate, bag in hand, walked in upon them.

Carl protested. He was much better already, and his face was pale with a more normal pallor. He was embarrassed and shy. He was grateful to old Parry, and yet plainly annoyed by all this fuss. He sat up very straight, G.B. at his feet, and said firmly, "Look, I'm all right now! Just a touch of ptomaine or something." He looked from his host to the doctor. "Awfully good of you to take so much trouble, Parry. And thanks for turning out, Tom. But—"

"But nothing!" Wingate said, and sat down beside him and took hold of his wrist and felt the pulse. "What you been eating?"

Carl managed a grin. "Better dinner than you'll ever get," he said—and then, "Oh—I had lunch out, maybe *that* was it! Annette and I went to The Hickory Nut, and I had fried shrimps—a double order! Tom, I bet that's what it was!"

Wingate let go of his wrist. "Could be," he said. He looked at Carl's face again and stood up. "That's a trick tummy of yours anyway." He turned to Parry. "I'll just run him home," he said.

Carl got up too. He thanked Parry all over again, and followed Wingate to his car. They put G.B. in the back and he sat immediately behind Carl, breathing protectively down his neck.

Wingate slowed down almost to a crawl as they reached Carl's driveway. He said, with the abruptness of discomfort, "Look now, I know you pretty well, both as a patient and a fellow human being: this—call it 'attack'—may not have been caused by bad food at all. Or bad food may have been only a contributing factor. In other words, my friend, what everyone insists on calling 'nerves' may be at the bottom of it." They were in the driveway now, and he stopped the car. But he made no move to get out. He looked at Carl's face in the dimness and said, "Speaking purely as a doctor, Carl, have you been—worried at all lately?" He paused, but Carl said nothing. "You haven't seemed like yourself the past few weeks. . . ."

Carl opened the door on his side. "I don't know what the hell you're talking about," he said curtly.

As he stepped out of the car the front door of the house opened and Annette came out onto the porch. She peered through the darkness at the car. She called, "Who is there? Who is it?" Her voice was high-pitched, sharp.

"Only me, dear," Carl said. "Tom Wingate drove me home." He opened the rear door and G.B. jumped out, then followed his master and Wingate up the steps to the house.

Annette stood just inside the door as they entered. Her face was in shadow, but she seemed pale. She acknowledged Wingate's formal greeting with a stiff little bow, and Carl looked harassed and uncomfortable. He tried to stop Wingate from saying what had happened, but to no purpose. Annette was told the whole story, firmly, politely and incisively—and Annette was given instructions.

She was most distressed. She said that Carl had not looked well after dinner, and she had not wanted him to go out. She was extremely polite to Dr. Wingate, and repeated his instructions carefully and asked for reassurance that the attack had been nothing serious. But all the time she was rigid and unbending, with frost in her manner. Only when Wingate had gone—and that was very soon—did she thaw. It was a most complete thaw, however. She rushed at Carl and fussed over him and got him upstairs and nursed him and mothered him. And when he was comfortably in bed, she kissed him with all the old tenderness.

"Carlo, *mon pauvre!*" she said softly, and then, "I am sorry I was not nice to your doctor, *cheri*. But—but—*eh bien,* you know that I do not like him."

He patted her shoulder, and she kissed him again—and he was very soon asleep. . . .

It was ten days after this that he had the pains again. They struck late at night. He was in his study, working. It was after one, and Annette had been in bed since before midnight.

They were much worse this time. They were agonizing. They started with painful cramps in his thighs—and when he stood up to ease this there was a terrible burning in the pit of his stomach. And then a faintness came over him and he dropped back into his chair. He doubled up, his hands clutching desperately at his belly. Great beads of cold sweat burst out all over his head and neck. He began to retch. Desperately, he swung his chair around until his hanging head was over the big metal wastebasket. He vomited hideously, and for what seemed an eternity. . . .

At last, momentarily, the convulsions ceased. He tried to raise his head—and everything in the room swam before his eyes. Outside, G.B. scratched on the French windows, and a troubled whining came from his throat. Carl pulled a weak hand across his mouth and his fingers came away streaked with blood. He rested his forehead upon the table top and with tremendous effort reached out for the telephone and managed to pull it towards him. . . .

In exactly ten minutes, a car came to a squealing halt in the driveway—and Wingate jumped out of it and raced up the steps. The front door was unlocked, and he was halfway across the living room when Annette appeared at the top of the stairs. She was in a night gown and was fumbling to get her arms into a robe. She said, wildly, "What is it? What is the matter?"

Wingate snapped, "Where's Carl?"—and then heard a sound from the study and crossed to it in three strides and burst in.

Carl was on his hands and knees, near the door of the toilet. He raised a ghastly face to Wingate and tried to speak. The room was a shambles—and beside his master, near the leaf of the French window he had broken open, stood G.B.

Carl tried to stand and could not. "Steady now!" Wingate said. "Take it easy. . . ." He crossed quickly to the sick man and half-dragged, half-lifted him to a couch and began to work over him. G.B. stopped whining and lay down. Annette came into the room and stood at Wingate's shoulder. Her hair was in tight braids and her pallid face shone beneath a layer of cream. Her eyes were wide, their pupils dilated. A curious sound—perhaps a scream strangled at birth—had come from her as she entered, but now she seemed in control of herself, though her hands were shaking. She started to speak but Wingate cut her short, almost savagely.

"Hot water," he snapped. "Towels. Glass."

She ran out of the room—and was quickly back with the things he wanted; then stayed with him, an efficient and self-effacing helper, while for an hour and more he labored.

By three o'clock, though weak and languid and gaunt in the face, Carl was himself again and comfortable in his own bed. He smiled at Wingate, who closed his bag with a snap.

"Thanks, Tom . . ." he said—and then, "Sorry to be such a nuisance."

"You're okay." Wingate smiled back at him with tired eyes—and turned to Annette.

"You go to bed, Mrs. Borden," he said. "He'll sleep—he's exhausted." He turned towards the door, stopped with his fingers on the handle. "I'll call by at eight-thirty. If he wants anything—don't give it to him."

Annette moved towards him but he checked her. "Don't bother—I'll let myself out," he said—and was gone.

Very slowly, Annette moved back to the bed and stood beside it, looking down at her husband. The mask of cold cream over her face had broken into glistening patches which alternated with islands of dryness which showed the skin tight and drawn, its color a leaden gray.

Carl reached out and took her hand. He said, "Did I scare you, darling? . . . I'm awfully sorry!"

Stiffly, she bent over him. She kissed him. "Go to sleep," she said. "You will be all well in the morning. . . ."

And indeed he was, save for a great lassitude and a painful tenderness all around his stomach. He barely waked when Wingate came at eight-thirty, and was asleep again the instant he left five minutes later.

At twelve—like a child about to surprise a household—he got up and washed himself and dressed. He was a little tired when he finished—but less so than he had expected. He opened his door quietly, and quietly went downstairs. As he reached the study door, Annette came out of it. She was in her usual houseworking clothes, and carried a dustpan and broom. Under the gay bandanna which was tied around her head, her face seemed oddly thin and angular.

She gave a little exclamation at the sight of him. "Carlo!" she said. "You should not be up! You should have called me!"

He laughed at her tenderly. He pinched her cheek and then kissed it. "I'm fine," he said. "Sort of sore around the midsection—but that's nothing." He slid his arm around her waist and they went into the study together. She fussed over him, and was settling him in the big chair beside the desk when the telephone rang.

Carl reached out and picked it up and spoke into it. He said, "Hello? . . . Oh, hello, Tom. . . ."

"So you're up, huh?" said Wingate's voice over the wire. "How d'you feel?"

"Fine," said Carl. "Hungry, though. . . ."

"Eaten yet?" The voice on the telephone was suddenly sharp.

"No. But I—"

"Good. Don't. Not until you've seen me. I want to examine you—run a test or two—while that stomach's empty. Can you get down here to the office? That'd be better. Or do you want me to come up?" Wingate's voice wasn't sharp any more: it seemed even more casual than it normally was.

Carl said, "Sure I can come down. When?"

"Right away," said the telephone. "I'll fit you in. G'bye."

Carl hung up. He looked at his wife and smiled ruefully. "Can't eat yet," he said. "Tom Wingate wants to examine me first." He put his hands on the arms of the chair and levered himself to his feet.

Annette stood stock still. "I am coming too," she announced. "I will drive you."

"Oh, phooey!" Carl said. "You know you hate breaking off halfway through the chores." He patted her on the shoulder. "And I'm perfectly all right, darling. Really! Don't you think I've caused enough trouble already?"

"Oh, Carlo—you are foolish!" Her face was very white—and something about the way her mouth moved made it seem as if she were about to cry.

Carl put an arm around her shoulders. "You must be played out, sweet," he said.

"I am very well," she snapped. "I am not tired at all." And then, with effort, she managed to smile. "But perhaps I am," she said. "Do not mind because I am cross. Go and see your Doctor Wingate. . . ."

She hooked her arm in his and walked through the living room with him, and at the front door she kissed him.

"Take care of yourself, Carlo," she said. "And come back quickly." She shut the door behind him.

As he entered the garage, G.B. came racing up—and the moment Carl opened the car door, leapt neatly in to sit enormous in the seat beside the driver's. His tongue was hanging out and he was smiling all around it.

Carl laughed at him; then winced as the laughter hurt his sore stomach-muscles. He said, "All right, you bum," and got in behind the wheel and started the car and backed out.

He drove slowly, but in a very few minutes was parking outside Wingate's office. He left G.B. in charge of the car and walked around to the back door—entrance for the favored few.

Wingate was standing by his desk. The light was behind him and Carl couldn't see his face very well, but he seemed older than usual, and tired. Even the little beard looked grayer. He waved Carl to a chair and then came and stood over him, feeling his pulse and making him thrust out his tongue to be looked at.

Carl grinned at him. "Goddam professional this morning," he said.

But Wingate didn't answer the smile, or the gibe. He sat down in his swivel chair and stared at Carl and said, "You were pretty sick last night, my friend," and then, after Carl had thrown in a "You're telling me!", added sharply, "You're lucky not to be dead."

Carl's grin faded slowly—and he gave a startled "Huh?"

"You heard what I said." Wingate had taken a pencil from the desk and was rolling it around in his fingers. He was looking at the pencil and not at Carl.

He said, "By the way, there's some property of yours there," and pointed with the pencil to a bulky, cylindrical package, roughly wrapped in brown paper, which stood upon a side table. "Want to take it with you?"

Carl looked bewildered. "What? . . ." He stared uncomprehendingly. "What you talking about?"

"That's your wastebasket." Wingate still kept his eyes on the twirling pencil. "From your study. I took it with me last night. . . ."

"Why? . . . Oh—you mean to get it cleaned. . . ." Carl was floundering. He burst out, "What the hell *is* all this? What're you driving at, Tom?"

Wingate looked at him, and drew in a deep breath. He said, in a monotone, "You'll find out very soon. Where did you eat yesterday?"

"At home, of course. What's—"

"Be quiet a minute. So you ate at home. What was the last thing you had? Probably around midnight."

"Nothing. . . . Wait a second, though—I'd forgotten. I had a bowl of soup—Annette's onion soup. She brought it to me before she went to bed. But that couldn't—"

"Wait! So you had this soup, at about twelve. And around an hour later, you have cramps in the legs and stomach, faintness, nausea, acute pain in the intestines. And you vomit, copiously. A lot of it, but by no means all, was in that metal wastebasket. And the contents of the basket, analyzed, show you must have swallowed at least a grain and a half of arsenic. . . ."

He let his voice fade into silence, then stood up to face Carl, who had jumped to his feet. He put his hand on Carl's arm and pushed him back into his chair. He unconsciously repeated the very words he had used the night before. "Steady now!" he said. "Take it easy!"

Carl sat down. His pallor had increased. He pulled a shaking hand across his forehead and then tried to smile.

"Narrow squeak," he said—and after that, "Grain and a half, huh? That's quite a dose, isn't it?"

"Could be fatal," Wingate said. "And you had more, maybe."

Carl said, "How in hell d'you suppose I picked it up?" He wasn't looking at Wingate, but past him. "Vegetables or something? They spray 'em, don't they?"

"Not in that strength." Wingate went back to his own chair and sat in it. "And you had that other attack ten days ago. Same thing—but not so much." His voice was absolutely flat. "And you ate at home, both times."

Carl shot out of his chair again. His face was distorted, his blue eyes blazing.

"For God's sake!" he shouted. "Have you gone out of your mind! What are you hinting at?"

"I'm not hinting anything." Wingate's voice was still toneless. "I'm stating something. You have twice been poisoned with arsenic during the last ten days. The second time provably."

Carl flung his big body back into the chair again. He started to speak, but all that came from him was a muffled groan.

Wingate said, "You don't imagine I like doing this, do you? But you have to face it, man! Someone is feeding you arsenic. The odds against accident are two million to one."

Carl's hands gripped the arms of his chair until his knuckles shone white.

He said, hoarsely, "If I didn't know you so well, I'd break your neck!" His voice began to rise. "Can't you see the whole thing must have been some weird, terrible accident! Don't you *know* that what's in your mind is completely, utterly impossible!" He stopped abruptly. He was panting, as if he had been running.

Wingate sat motionless. His face was shaded by the hands which propped it. He spoke as if Carl had been silent.

"Arsenic's easy to get," he said. "Especially for gardeners—ant paste, Paris green, rose-spray, weed-killer—"

"God blast you!" Carl crashed his fist down upon the chair arm. "There *is* weed-killer in the house—but *I* told her to get it!"

He got to his feet and towered over Wingate. He said, "I'm going. And I'm not coming back. I don't think you're lying about the arsenic, but I know you're making a monstrous, evil mistake about how I got it—a mistake which oughtn't to be possible to a man of your intelligence!"

He started for the door, turned back. "And another thing," he said. "I can't stop you from thinking your foul thoughts—" his voice was shaking with suppressed passion—"but I *can* stop you from voicing them—and I will! If you so much as breathe a word of this to anyone—I'll half kill you, and then I'll ruin you! And don't forget that—because I mean it!"

He stood over the other man for a long moment—but Wingate did not move, did not so much as look at him—and at last Carl went back to the door and opened it and passed out of the room. He got out into the air again and made his way to the car. He was very white. He opened the car and slumped into the driving seat. He put his arms down on the wheel and rested his head upon them. He was breathing in long shuddering gasps. G.B. made a little whimpering sound and licked at his master's ear—and two women passing by looked at the tableau with curiosity.

Perhaps Carl felt their gaze, for he raised his head and saw them. He straightened in his seat, and pushed the dog's great head aside with a gentle hand.

He drove home very slowly. Annette heard the car and opened the front door as he climbed up the steps. She said at once, "What did he say, Carlo? Did he know what is the matter with you?" Her haggard, worn look seemed to have intensified.

Carl looked at her—and then he shook his head. He stepped through the door and sank into the nearest chair. He said, slowly, "No . . . No, he didn't. I don't think he knows much about it. . . ."

He said, "God, I'm tired! . . . Come and give me a kiss, darling."

She came and sat upon the arm of his chair and kissed him. She pulled his head against her breast and stroked his hair. He could not see her face as she spoke.

"But, *chéri,*" she said, "he must know *something.*"

Carl sighed. "Oh, he used a lot of medical jargon—all beginning with *gastro* . . . But I don't think he really knows any more than I do—which is that I happen to have a nervous stomach." He leaned back in the chair and looked up at her. "I tell you—maybe you're right about Tom Wingate. I don't mean as a man—but as a doctor. I think another time—well, I might go to that new man . . ."

Annette jumped up. "That is quite enough talk about doctors," she said. "And I, I am very bad! Here is my poor man here, white and weak because he has no food! Wait one little moment, Carlo. . . ."

She hurried off to the kitchen. She seemed to have shed her fatigue, her tenseness.

Carl sat where he was. He stared straight ahead with eyes which did not look as if they saw what was in front of them.

In a very little while Annette came back. She was carrying a small tray upon which were a spoon, a napkin and a bowl which steamed, gently and fragrantly.

She said, *"Voilà!—"* and set the tray on his knees and put the spoon in his hand and stood back to watch him.

He looked at her for a long unwavering moment—and when she said, "Hurry now and drink your soup!" he did not seem to hear.

He said, very suddenly, "Annette: do you love me?"—and kept on looking at her.

She stared. She said, after an instant, "But yes—but of *course,* Carlo!"

And then she laughed and said, "Do not be a baby! Take your soup—it is not very hot."

He looked at the spoon in his hand and seemed surprised to find it there. He set it down upon the tray and picked up the bowl and looked at his wife over the edge of it.

"Santé!" he said—and put the china to his lips and began to drink in great gulps. . . .

He did not have the pains that night.

A week went by and he did not have them—a week in which he had not spoken to, nor seen, nor heard any word of Dr. Thomas Wingate.

It was past eleven at night, and he was walking with G.B. up the last slope of Pasco Street. Behind him, old Parry called a last good-night, and he half-turned and waved a valedictory hand. He had been returning from a longer walk than usual and had met Parry at the mailbox; a meeting which had somehow led to drinks in Parry's house and a long talk upon Parry's favorite topic, which was that of the world's declining sanity.

He reached his own steep little road and shortened his stride for the climb and whistled for G.B., who came at once and padded beside him.

He was humming as he strode down the drive and up the steps. He opened the front door and let the dog ahead of him and then went in himself.

He said, *"Oh, my God!"*

He stood motionless for an instant which might have been a century.

Annette was lying on the floor, twisted into a strange and ugly shape—and all around her prostrate and distorted body the room was dreadfully befouled.

G.B. stared, then pushed through the half-open door to the kitchen. There was a thump as he lay down.

Carl dropped to his knees beside the prostrate woman. He raised her head and it lolled against his arm. Her eyes were closed and her stained and swollen mouth hung open. She was breathing, but lightly, weakly—and when he felt for her heart its beat was barely perceptible. . . .

Somehow, he was in the study, at the telephone . . . As if automatically, his shaking fingers dialed a number . . .

He was speaking to Wingate. "Tom!" he said, on a harsh high note. "Tom! This is Carl. Come at once! *Hurry!"*

His hand put back the phone. His feet took him out into the living room again. His knees bent themselves once more and once more he held his wife in his arms. . . .

He was still holding her when Wingate came.

Wingate examined her and shook his head. He made Carl get up—and took him into the study. He said, "You've got to face it, Carl . . . She's dead."

Carl was shaking all over—his hands, his body, his head, all of him.

Wingate said, "Sit there—and don't move!" and went out into the living room again.

He looked at the dead woman; at the foulness around her; at everything in the room. He was staring at the two coffee cups which stood on the top of the piano when G.B. came in from the kitchen, paced over to the study and disappeared.

Wingate picked up the cups, one after the other. They were small cups, and each held the heavy, pasty remains of Turkish coffee. He dipped a dampened fingertip into each cup in turn, each time touching the finger to his tongue. The second test gave him the reaction he wanted—and, his face clearing, he strode back to the study.

Carl had not moved, but his trembling had increased. The dog sat beside him, looking into his face.

Wingate put a hand on the shaking shoulder. Carl tried to speak—but his teeth started to chatter and no words came out of him.

Wingate said: "You know, don't you? She tried again . . . You wouldn't let *me* look after you—but the Fates did!"

Carl mumbled, "I—I—I d-don't understand . . ."

Wingate said, "She was overconfident. And something went wrong—some little thing to distract her attention." He lifted his shoulders. "And—well, she took the wrong cup."

Carl said, *"God! . . ."* He covered his face with his hands, the fingers digging into his temples. He said: "Tom—I almost wish it *had* been me!"

"Come on, now!" Wingate took him by the arm. "Stop thinking—just do what I tell you!"

He hauled Carl to his feet and led him out of the study and up the stairs and into his own room. G.B. came close behind them, and lay watchful while Wingate got Carl out of his clothes and into bed and finally slid a hypodermic needle into his arm.

"There!" he said. "You'll be asleep in five minutes. . . ."

He was turning away when Carl reached out and caught his hand and held it.

Carl said, "Don't go . . ." And then he said, "About what I said in your office—I'm sorry, Tom. . . ."

Wingate did not try to release his hand. "Forget it," he said. "I have."

And then he started talking—slowly, quietly, his casual voice a soothing monotone. He said, "All you have to do now is go to sleep . . . I'll see to everything else . . . In a little while, all this will just be a nightmare you've half-forgotten . . . And don't go worrying yourself about publicity and scandal and things like that, Carl . . . There won't be any . . . You see, I was *sure*— and in spite of what you said I told Chief Nichols . . . He and I will explain it all to the coroner . . ."

He let his voice trail off into silence—Carl Borden was asleep.

It was three weeks before Carl permitted himself to smile—and then he was not in El Morro Beach. He was in San Francisco—and Lorna was waiting for him.

When he smiled, he was driving up Market Street, G.B. erect beside him.

"Tell you something, boy," he murmured. "I nearly took too much that second time!"

The smile became a chuckle.

I CAN FIND MY WAY OUT

by NGAIO MARSH

At half-past six on the night in question, Anthony Gill, unable to eat, keep still, think, speak, or act coherently, walked from his rooms to the Jupiter Theatre. He knew that there would be nobody backstage, that there was nothing for him to do in the theatre, that he ought to stay quietly in his rooms and presently dress, dine, and arrive at, say, a quarter to eight. But it was as if something shoved him into his clothes, thrust him into the street and compelled him to hurry through the West End to the Jupiter. His mind was overlaid with a thin film of inertia. Odd lines from the play occurred to him, but without any particular significance. He found himself busily reiterating a completely irrelevant sentence: "She has a way of laughing that would make a man's heart turn over."

Piccadilly, Shaftesbury Avenue. "Here I go," he thought, turning into Hawke Street, "towards my play. It's one hour and twenty-nine minutes away. A step a second. It's rushing towards me. Tony's first play. Poor young Tony Gill. Never mind. Try again."

The Jupiter. Neon lights: I CAN FIND MY WAY OUT—*by Anthony Gill.* And in the entrance the bills and photographs. *Coralie Bourne with H. J. Bannington, Barry George and Canning Cumberland.*

Canning Cumberland. The film across his mind split and there was the Thing itself and he would have to think about it. How bad would Canning Cumberland be if he came down drunk? Brilliantly bad, they said. He would bring out all the tricks. Clever actor stuff, scoring off everybody, making a fool of the dramatic balance. "In Mr. Canning Cumberland's hands indifferent dialogue and unconvincing situations seemed almost real." What can you do with a drunken actor?

He stood in the entrance feeling his heart pound and his inside deflate and sicken.

Because, of course, it was a bad play. He was at this moment and for the first time really convinced of it. It was terrible. Only one virtue in it and that was not his doing. It had been suggested to him by Coralie Bourne: "I don't think the play you have sent me will do as it is but it has occurred to me—" It was a brilliant idea. He had rewritten the play round it and almost immediately and quite innocently he had begun to think of it as his own although he had said shyly to Coralie Bourne: "You should appear as joint author." She had quickly, overemphatically, refused. "It was nothing at all," she said. "If you're to become a dramatist you will learn to get ideas from everywhere. A single situation is nothing. Think of Shakespeare," she added lightly. "Entire plots! Don't be silly." She had said later, and still with the same hurried, nervous air: "Don't go talking to everyone about it. They will think there is more, instead of less, than meets the eye in my small suggestion. Please promise." He promised, thinking he'd made an error in taste when he suggested that Coralie Bourne, so famous an actress, should appear as joint author with an unknown youth. And how right she was, he thought, because, of course, it's going to be a ghastly flop. She'll be sorry she consented to play in it.

Standing in front of the theatre he contemplated nightmare possibilities. What did audiences do when a first play flopped? Did they clap a little, enough to let the curtain rise and quickly fall again on a discomforted group of players? How scanty must the applause be for them to let him off his own appearance? And they were to go on to the Chelsea Arts Ball. A hideous prospect. Thinking he would give anything in the world if he could stop his play, he turned into the foyer. There were lights in the offices and he paused, irresolute, before a board of photographs. Among them, much smaller than the leading players, was Dendra Gay with the eyes looking straight into his. *She had a way of laughing that would make a man's heart turn over.* "Well," he thought, "so I'm in love with her." He turned away from the photograph. A man came out of the office. "Mr. Gill? Telegrams for you."

Anthony took them and as he went out he heard the man call after him: "Very good luck for tonight, sir."

There were queues of people waiting in the side street for the early doors.

At six-thirty Coralie Bourne dialled Canning Cumberland's number and waited.

She heard his voice. "It's me," she said.

"O, God! darling, I've been thinking about you." He spoke rapidly, too loudly. "Coral, I've been thinking about Ben. You oughtn't to have given that situation to the boy."

"We've been over it a dozen times, Cann. Why not give it to Tony? Ben will never know." She waited and then said nervously, "Ben's gone, Cann. We'll never see him again."

"I've got a 'Thing' about it. After all, he's your husband."

"No, Cann, no."

"Suppose he turns up. It'd be like him to turn up."

"He won't turn up."

She heard him laugh. "I'm sick of all this," she thought suddenly. "I've had it once too often. I can't stand any more. . . . Cann," she said into the telephone. But he had hung up.

At twenty to seven, Barry George looked at himself in his bathroom mirror. "I've got a better appearance," he thought, "than Cann Cumberland. My head's a good shape, my eyes are bigger, and my jaw line's cleaner. I never let a show down. I don't drink. I'm a better actor." He turned his head a little, slewing his eyes to watch the effect. "In the big scene," he thought, "I'm the star. He's the feed. That's the way it's been produced and that's what the author wants. I ought to get the notices."

Past notices came up in his memory. He saw the print, the size of the paragraphs; a long paragraph about Canning Cumberland, a line tacked on the end of it. "Is it unkind to add that Mr. Barry George trotted in the wake of Mr. Cumberland's virtuosity with an air of breathless dependability?" And again: "It is a little hard on Mr. Barry George that he should be obliged to act as foil to this brilliant performance." Worst of all: "Mr. Barry George succeeded in looking tolerably unlike a stooge, an achievement that evidently exhausted his resources."

"Monstrous!" he said loudly to his own image, watching the fine glow of indignation in the eyes. Alcohol, he told himself, did two things to Cann Cumberland. He raised his finger. Nice, expressive hand. An actor's hand. Alcohol destroyed Cumberland's artistic integrity. It also invested him with devilish cunning. Drunk, he would burst the seams of a play, destroy its balance, ruin its form, and himself emerge blazing with a showmanship that the audience mistook for genius. "While I," he said aloud, "merely pay my author the compliment of faithful interpretation. Psha!"

He returned to his bedroom, completed his dressing and pulled his hat to the right angle. Once more he thrust his face close to the mirror and looked searchingly at its image. "By God!" he told himself, "he's done it once too often, old boy. Tonight we'll even the score, won't we? By God, we will."

Partly satisfied, and partly ashamed, for the scene, after all, had smacked a little of ham, he took his stick in one hand and a case holding his costume for the Arts Ball in the other, and went down to the theatre.

At ten minutes to seven, H. J. Bannington passed through the gallery queue on his way to the stage door alley, raising his hat and saying: "Thanks so much," to the gratified ladies who let him through. He heard them murmur his name. He walked briskly along the alley, greeted the stage-doorkeeper, passed under a dingy lamp, through an entry and so to the stage. Only working lights were up. The walls of an interior set rose dimly into shadow. Bob Reynolds, the stage manager, came out through the prompt-entrance. "Hello, old boy," he said, "I've changed the dressing rooms. You're third on the right: they've moved your things in. Suit you?"

"Better, at least, than a black hole the size of a W.C. but without its appointments," H.J. said acidly. "I suppose the great Mr. Cumberland still has the star-room?"

"Well, yes, old boy."

"And who pray, is next to him? In the room with the other gas fire?"

"We've put Barry George there, old boy. You know what he's like."

"Only too well, old boy, and the public, I fear, is beginning to find out." H.J. turned into the dressing-room passage. The stage manager returned to the set where he encountered his assistant. "What's biting *him?*" asked the assistant. "He wanted a dressing room with a fire." "Only natural," said the A.S.M. nastily. "He started life reading gas meters."

On the right and left of the passage, nearest the stage end, were two doors, each with its star in tarnished paint. The door on the left was open. H.J. looked in and was greeted with the smell of greasepaint, powder, wet-white, and flowers. A gas fire droned comfortably. Coralie Bourne's dresser was spreading out towels. "Good evening, Katie, my jewel," said H.J. "La Belle not down yet?" "We're on our way," she said.

H.J. hummed stylishly: *"Bella filia del amore,"* and returned to the passage. The star-room on the right was closed but he could hear Cumberland's dresser moving about inside. He went on to the next door, paused, read the card, "Mr. Barry George," warbled a high derisive note, turned in at the third door and switched on the light.

Definitely not a second lead's room. No fire. A wash basin, however, and opposite mirrors. A stack of telegrams had been placed on the dressing table. Still singing he reached for them, disclosing a number of bills that had been tactfully laid underneath and a letter, addressed in a flamboyant script.

His voice might have been mechanically produced and arbitrarily switched off, so abruptly did his song end in the middle of a roulade. He let the telegrams fall on the table, took up the letter and tore it open. His face, wretchedly pale, was reflected and endlessly rereflected in the mirrors.

At nine o'clock the telephone rang. Roderick Alleyn answered it. "This is Sloane 84405. No, you're on the wrong number. *No.*" He hung up and returned to his wife and guest. "That's the fifth time in two hours."

"Do let's ask for a new number."

"We might get next door to something worse."

The telephone rang again. "This is not 84406," Alleyn warned it. "No, I cannot take three large trunks to Victoria Station. No, I am not the Instant All Night Delivery. No."

"They're 84406," Mrs. Alleyn explained to Lord Michael Lamprey. "I suppose it's just faulty dialing, but you can't imagine how angry everyone gets. Why do you want to be a policeman?"

"It's a dull hard job, you know—" Alleyn began.

"Oh," Lord Mike said, stretching his legs and looking critically at his shoes, "I don't for a moment imagine I'll leap immediately into false whiskers and plainclothes. No, no. But I'm revoltingly healthy, sir. Strong as a horse. And I don't think I'm as stupid as you might feel inclined to imagine—"

The telephone rang.

"I say, do let me answer it," Mike suggested and did so.

"Hullo?" he said winningly. He listened, smiling at his hostess. "I'm afraid—," he began. "Here, wait a bit—Yes, but—" His expression became blank and complacent. "May I," he said presently, "repeat your order, sir? Can't be too sure, can we? Call at 11 Harrow Gardens, Sloane Square, for one suitcase to be delivered immediately at the Jupiter Theatre to Mr. Anthony Gill. Very good, sir. Thank you, sir. Collect. Quite."

He replaced the receiver and beamed at the Alleyns.

"What the devil have you been up to?" Alleyn said.

"He just simply wouldn't listen to reason. I tried to tell him."

"But it may be urgent," Mrs. Alleyn ejaculated.

"It couldn't be more urgent, really. It's a suitcase for Tony Gill at the Jupiter."

"Well, then—"

"I was at Eton with the chap," said Mike reminiscently. "He's four years older than I am so of course he was madly important while I was less than the dust. This'll larn him."

"I think you'd better put that order through at once," said Alleyn firmly.

"I rather thought of executing it myself, do you know, sir. It'd be a frightfully neat way of gate-crashing the show, wouldn't it? I did try to get a ticket but the house was sold out."

"If you're going to deliver this case you'd better get a bend on."

"It's clearly an occasion for dressing up though, isn't it? I say," said Mike modestly, "would you think it most frightful cheek if I—well I'd promise to come back and return everything. I mean—"

"Are you suggesting that my clothes look more like a vanman's than yours?"

"I thought you'd have things—"

"For Heaven's sake, Rory," said Mrs. Alleyn, "dress him up and let him go. The great thing is to get that wretched man's suitcase to him."

"I know," said Mike earnestly. "It's most frightfully sweet of you. That's how I feel about it."

Alleyn took him away and shoved him into an old and begrimed raincoat, a cloth cap and a muffler. "You wouldn't deceive a village idiot in a total eclipse," he said, "but out you go."

He watched Mike drive away and returned to his wife.

"What'll happen?" she asked.

"Knowing Mike, I should say he will end up in the front stalls and go on to supper with the leading lady. She, by the way, is Coralie Bourne. Very lovely and twenty years his senior so he'll probably fall in love with her." Alleyn reached for his tobacco jar and paused. "I wonder what's happened to her husband," he said.

"Who was he?"

"An extraordinary chap. Benjamin Vlasnoff. Violent temper. Looked like a bandit. Wrote two very good plays and got run in three times for common assault. She tried to divorce him but it didn't go through. I think he afterwards lit off to Russia." Alleyn yawned. "I believe she had a hell of a time with him," he said.

"All Night Delivery," said Mike in a hoarse voice, touching his cap. "Suitcase. One." "Here you are," said the woman who had answered the door. "Carry it carefully, now, it's not locked and the catch springs out."

"Fanks," said Mike. "Much obliged. Chilly, ain't it?"

He took the suitcase out to the car.

It was a fresh spring night. Sloane Square was threaded with mist and all the lamps had halos round them. It was the kind of night when individual sounds separate themselves from the conglomerate voice of London; hollow sirens spoke imperatively down on the river and a bugle rang out over in Chelsea Barracks; a night, Mike thought, for adventure.

He opened the rear door of the car and heaved the case in. The catch flew open, the lid dropped back and the contents fell out. "Damn!" said Mike and switched on the inside light.

Lying on the floor of the car was a false beard.

It was flaming red and bushy and was mounted on a chin-piece. With it was incorporated a stiffened mustache. There were wire hooks to attach the whole thing behind the ears. Mike laid it carefully on the seat. Next he picked up a wide black hat, then a vast overcoat with a fur collar, finally a pair of black gloves.

Mike whistled meditatively and thrust his hands into the pockets of Alleyn's mackintosh. His right-hand fingers closed on a card. He pulled it out. "Chief Detective-Inspector Alleyn," he read, "C.I.D. New Scotland Yard."

"Honestly," thought Mike exultantly, "this is a gift."

Ten minutes later a car pulled into the curb at the nearest parking place to the Jupiter Theatre. From it emerged a figure carrying a suitcase. It strode rapidly along Hawke Street and turned into the stage-door alley. As it passed under the dirty lamp it paused, and thus murkily lit, resembled an illustration from some Edwardian spy story. The face was completely shadowed, a black cavern from which there projected a square of scarlet beard, which was the only note of color.

The doorkeeper who was taking the air with a member of stage staff, moved forward, peering at the stranger.

"Was you wanting something?"

"I'm taking this case in for Mr. Gill."

"He's in front. You can leave it with me."

"I'm so sorry," said the voice behind the beard, "but I promised I'd leave it backstage myself."

"So you will be leaving it. Sorry, sir, but no one's admitted be'ind without a card."

"A card? Very well. Here is a card."

He held it out in his black-gloved hand. The stage-doorkeeper, unwillingly removing his gaze from the beard, took the card and examined it under the light. "Coo!" he said, "what's up, governor?"

"No matter. Say nothing of this."

The figure waved its hand and passed through the door. " 'Ere!" said the doorkeeper excitedly to the stagehand, "take a slant at this. That's a plain-clothes flattie, that was."

"*Plain*clothes!" said the stagehand. "Them!"

" 'E's disguised," said the doorkeeper. "That's what it is. 'E's disguised 'isself."

" 'E's bloody well lorst 'isself be'ind them whiskers if you arst me."

Out on the stage someone was saying in a pitched and beautifully articulate voice: *"I've always loathed the view from these windows. However if that's the sort of thing you admire. Turn off the lights, damn you. Look at it."*

"Watch it, now, watch it," whispered a voice so close to Mike that he jumped. "O.K.," said a second voice somewhere above his head. The lights on the set turned blue. "Kill that working light." "Working light gone."

Curtains in the set were wrenched aside and a window flung open. An actor appeared, leaning out quite close to Mike, seeming to look into his face and saying very distinctly: "God: it's frightful!" Mike backed away towards a passage, lit only from an open door. A great volume of sound broke out beyond the stage. "House lights," said the sharp voice. Mike turned into the passage. As he did so, someone came through the door. He found himself face to face with Coralie Bourne, beautifully dressed and heavily painted.

For a moment she stood quite still; then she made a curious gesture with her right hand, gave a small breathy sound and fell forward at his feet.

* * *

Anthony was tearing his program into long strips and dropping them on the floor of the O.P. box. On his right hand, above and below, was the audience; sometimes laughing, sometimes still, sometimes as one corporate being, raising its hands and striking them together. As now; when down on the stage, Canning Cumberland, using a strange voice, and inspired by some inward devil, flung back the window and said: "God: it's frightful!"

"Wrong! Wrong!" Anthony cried inwardly, hating Cumberland, hating Barry George because he let one speech of three words override him, hating the audience because they liked it. The curtain descended with a long sigh on the second act and a sound like heavy rain filled the theatre, swelled prodigiously and continued after the house lights welled up.

"They seem," said a voice behind him, "to be liking your play."

It was Gosset, who owned the Jupiter and had backed the show. Anthony turned on him stammering: "He's destroying it. It should be the other man's scene. He's stealing."

"My boy," said Gosset, "he's an actor."

"He's drunk. It's intolerable."

He felt Gosset's hand on his shoulder.

"People are watching us. You're on show. This is a big thing for you; a first play, and going enormously. Come and have a drink, old boy. I want to introduce you—"

Anthony got up and Gosset, with his arm across his shoulders, flashing smiles, patting him, led him to the back of the box.

"I'm sorry," Anthony said, "I can't. Please let me off. I'm going backstage."

"Much better not, old son." The hand tightened on his shoulder. "Listen, old son—" But Anthony had freed himself and slipped through the passdoor from the box to the stage.

At the foot of the breakneck stairs Dendra Gay stood waiting. "I thought you'd come," she said.

Anthony said: "He's drunk. He's murdering the play."

"It's only one scene, Tony. He finishes early in the next act. It's going colossally."

"But don't you understand—"

"I do. You *know* I do. But you're a success, Tony darling! You can hear it and smell it and feel it in your bones."

"Dendra—," he said uncertainly.

Someone came up and shook his hand and went on shaking it. Flats were being laced together with a slap of rope on canvas. A chandelier ascended into darkness. "Lights," said the stage manager, and the set was flooded with them. A distant voice began chanting. "Last act, please. Last act."

"Miss Bourne all right?" the stage manager suddenly demanded.

"She'll be all right. She's not on for ten minutes," said a woman's voice.

"What's the matter with Miss Bourne?" Anthony asked.

"Tony, I must go and so must you. Tony, it's going to be grand. *Please* think so. *Please.*"

"Dendra—," Tony began, but she had gone.

Beyond the curtain, horns and flutes announced the last act.

"Clear please."

The stagehands came off.

"House lights."

"House lights gone."

"Stand by."

And while Anthony still hesitated in the O.P. corner, the curtain rose. Canning Cumberland and H. J. Bannington opened the last act.

As Mike knelt by Coralie Bourne he heard someone enter the passage behind him. He turned and saw, silhouetted against the lighted stage, the actor who had looked at him through a window in the set. The silhouette seemed to repeat the gesture Coralie Bourne had used, and to flatten itself against the wall.

A woman in an apron came out of the open door.

"I say—here!" Mike said.

Three things happened almost simultaneously. The woman cried out and knelt beside him. The man disappeared through a door on the right.

The woman, holding Coralie Bourne in her arms, said violently: "Why have you come back?" Then the passage lights came on. Mike said: "Look here, I'm most frightfully sorry," and took off the broad black hat. The dresser gaped at him, Coralie Bourne made a crescendo sound in her throat and opened her eyes. "Katie?" she said.

"It's all right, my lamb. It's not him, dear. You're all right." The dresser jerked her head at Mike: "Get out of it," she said.

"Yes, of course, I'm most frightfully—" He backed out of the passage, colliding with a youth who said: "Five minutes, please." The dresser called out: "Tell them she's not well. Tell them to hold the curtain."

"No," said Coralie Bourne strongly. "I'm all right, Katie. Don't say anything. Katie, what was it?"

They disappeared into the room on the left.

Mike stood in the shadow of a stack of scenic flats by the entry into the passage. There was great activity on the stage. He caught a glimpse of Anthony Gill on the far side talking to a girl. The call-boy was speaking to the stage manager who now shouted into space: "Miss Bourne all right?" The dresser came into the passage and called: "She'll be all right. She's not on for ten minutes." The youth began chanting: "Last act, please." The stage manager gave a series of orders. A man with an eyeglass and a florid beard came from further down the passage and stood outside the set, bracing his figure and giving little tweaks to his clothes. There was a sound of horns and flutes. Canning Cumberland emerged from the room on the right and on his way to the stage, passed close to Mike, leaving a strong smell of alcohol behind him. The curtain rose.

Behind his shelter, Mike stealthily removed his beard and stuffed it into the pocket of his overcoat.

A group of stagehands stood nearby. One of them said in a hoarse whisper: " 'E's squiffy." "Garn, 'e's going good." "So 'e may be going good. And for why? *Becos* 'e's squiffy."

Ten minutes passed. Mike thought: "This affair has definitely not gone according to plan." He listened. Some kind of tension seemed to be building up on the stage. Canning Cumberland's voice rose on a loud but blurred note. A door in the set opened. "Don't bother to come," Cumberland said. "Good-bye. I can find my way out." The door slammed. Cumberland was standing near Mike. Then, very close, there was a loud explosion. The scenic flats vibrated, Mike's flesh leapt on his bones and Cumberland went into his dressing rooms. Mike heard the key turn in the door. The smell of alcohol mingled with the smell of gunpowder. A stagehand moved to a trestle table and laid a pistol on it. The actor with the eyeglass made an exit. He spoke for a moment to the stage manager, passed Mike, and disappeared in the passage.

Smells. There were all sorts of smells. Subconsciously, still listening to the play, he began to sort them out. Glue. Canvas. Greasepaint. The call-boy tapped on doors. "Mr. George, please." "Miss Bourne, please." They came out, Coralie Bourne with her dresser. Mike heard her turn a door handle and say something. An indistinguishable voice answered her. Then she and her dresser passed him. The others spoke to her and she nodded and then seemed to withdraw into herself, waiting with her head bent, ready to make her entrance. Presently she drew back, walked swiftly to the door in the set, flung it open and swept on, followed a minute later by Barry George.

Smells. Dust, stale paint, cloth. Gas. Increasingly, the smell of gas.

The group of stagehands moved away behind the set to the side of the stage. Mike edged out of cover. He could see the prompt-corner. The stage manager stood there with folded arms, watching the action. Behind him were grouped the players who were not on. Two dressers stood apart, watching. The light from the set caught their faces. Coralie Bourne's voice sent phrases flying like birds into the auditorium.

Mike began peering at the floor. Had he kicked some gas fitting adrift? The call-boy passed him, stared at him over his shoulder and went down the passage, tapping. "Five minutes to the curtain, please. Five minutes." The actor with the elderly makeup followed the call-boy out. "God, what a stink of gas," he whispered. "Chronic, ain't it?" said the call-boy. They

stared at Mike and then crossed to the waiting group. The man said something to the stage manager who tipped his head up, sniffing. He made an
impatient gesture and turned back to the prompt-box, reaching over the
prompter's head. A bell rang somewhere up in the flies and Mike saw a
stagehand climb to the curtain platform.

The little group near the prompt corner was agitated. They looked back
towards the passage entrance. The call-boy nodded and came running back.
He knocked on the first door on the right. *"Mr. Cumberland! Mr. Cumberland!* You're on for the call." He rattled the door handle. *"Mr. Cumberland!
You're on."*

Mike ran into the passage. The call-boy coughed retchingly and jerked
his hand at the door. "Gas!" he said. "Gas!"

"Break it in."

"I'll get Mr. Reynolds."

He was gone. It was a narrow passage. From halfway across the opposite
room Mike took a run, head down, shoulder forward, at the door. It gave a
little and a sickening increase in the smell caught him in the lungs. A vast
storm of noise had broken out and as he took another run he thought: "It's
hailing outside."

"Just a minute if *you* please, sir."

It was a stagehand. He'd got a hammer and screwdriver. He wedged the
point of the screwdriver between the lock and the doorpost, drove it home
and wrenched. The screws squeaked, the wood splintered and gas poured
into the passage. "No winders," coughed the stagehand.

Mike wound Alleyn's scarf over his mouth and nose. Half-forgotten
instructions from antigas drill occurred to him. The room looked queer but
he could see the man slumped down in the chair quite clearly. He stooped
low and ran in.

He was knocking against things as he backed out, lugging the dead
weight. His arms tingled. A high insistent voice hummed in his brain. He
floated a short distance and came to earth on a concrete floor among several
pairs of legs. A long way off, someone said loudly: "I can only thank you
for being so kind to what I know, too well, is a very imperfect play." Then
the sound of hail began again. There was a heavenly stream of clear air
flowing into his mouth and nostrils. "I could eat it," he thought and sat up.

The telephone rang. "Suppose," Mrs. Alleyn suggested, "that this time
you ignore it."

"It might be the Yard," Alleyn said, and answered it.

"Is that Chief Detective-Inspector Alleyn's flat? I'm speaking from the
Jupiter Theatre. I've rung up to say that the Chief Inspector is here and that
he's had a slight mishap. He's all right, but I think it might be as well for
someone to drive him home. No need to worry."

"What sort of mishap?" Alleyn asked.

"Er—well—er, he's been a bit gassed."

"Gassed! All right. Thanks, I'll come."

"What a bore for you, darling," said Mrs. Alleyn. "What sort of case is it? Suicide?"

"Masquerading within the meaning of the act, by the sound of it. Mike's in trouble."

"What trouble, for Heaven's sake?"

"Got himself gassed. He's all right. Good-night, darling. Don't wait up."

When he reached the theatre, the front of the house was in darkness. He made his way down the side alley to the stage-door where he was held up.

"Yard," he said, and produced his official card.

" 'Ere," said the stage-doorkeeper. " 'ow many more of you?"

"The man inside was working for me," said Alleyn and walked in. The doorkeeper followed, protesting.

To the right of the entrance was a large scenic dock from which the double doors had been rolled back. Here Mike was sitting in an armchair, very white about the lips. Three men and two women, all with painted faces, stood near him and behind them a group of stagehands with Reynolds, the stage manager, and, apart from these, three men in evening dress. The men looked woodenly shocked. The women had been weeping.

"I'm most frightfully sorry, sir," Mike said. "I've tried to explain. This," he added generally, "is Inspector Alleyn."

"I can't understand all this," said the oldest of the men in evening dress irritably. He turned on the doorkeeper. "You said—"

"I seen 'is card—"

"I know," said Mike, "but you see—"

"This is Lord Michael Lamprey," Alleyn said. "A recruit to the Police Department. What's happened here?"

"Doctor Rankin, would you—?"

The second of the men in evening dress came forward. "All right, Gosset. It's a bad business, Inspector. I've just been saying the police would have to be informed. If you'll come with me—"

Alleyn followed him through a door onto the stage proper. It was dimly lit. A trestle table had been set up in the centre and on it, covered with a sheet, was an unmistakable shape. The smell of gas, strong everywhere, hung heavily about the table.

"Who is it?"

"Canning Cumberland. He'd locked the door of his dressing room. There's a gas fire. Your young friend dragged him out, very pluckily, but it was no go. I was in front. Gosset, the manager, had asked me to supper. It's a perfectly clear case of suicide as you'll see."

"I'd better look at the room. Anybody been in?"

"God, no. It was a job to clear it. They turned the gas off at the main. There's no window. They had to open the double doors at the back of the stage and a small outside door at the end of the passage. It may be possible to get in now."

He led the way to the dressing-room passage. "Pretty thick, still," he said. "It's the first room on the right. They burst the lock. You'd better keep down near the floor."

The powerful lights over the mirror were on and the room still had its look of occupation. The gas fire was against the left hand wall. Alleyn squatted down by it. The tap was still turned on, its face lying parallel with the floor. The top of the heater, the tap itself, and the carpet near it, were covered with a creamish powder. On the end of the dressing-table shelf nearest to the stove was a box of this powder. Further along the shelf, greasepaints were set out in a row beneath the mirror. Then came a wash basin and in front of this an over-turned chair. Alleyn could see the track of heels, across the pile of the carpet, to the door immediately opposite. Beside the wash basin was a quart bottle of whiskey, three parts empty, and a tumbler. Alleyn had had about enough and returned to the passage.

"Perfectly clear," the hovering doctor said again, "isn't it?"

"I'll see the other rooms, I think."

The one next to Cumberland's was like his in reverse, but smaller. The heater was back to back with Cumberland's. The dressing-shelf was set out with much the same assortment of greasepaints. The tap of this heater, too, was turned on. It was of precisely the same make as the other and Alleyn, less embarrassed here by fumes, was able to make a longer examination. It was a common enough type of gas fire. The lead-in was from a pipe through a flexible metallic tube with a rubber connection. There were two taps, one in the pipe and one at the junction of the tube with the heater itself. Alleyn disconnected the tube and examined the connection. It was perfectly sound, a close fit and stained red at the end. Alleyn noticed a wiry thread of some reddish stuff resembling packing that still clung to it. The nozzle and tap were brass, the tap pulling over when it was turned on, to lie in a parallel plane with the floor. No powder had been scattered about here.

He glanced round the room, returned to the door and read the card: "Mr. Barry George."

The doctor followed him into the rooms opposite these, on the left-hand side of the passage. They were a repetition in design of the two he had already seen but were hung with women's clothes and had a more elaborate assortment of grease paint and cosmetics.

There was a mass of flowers in the star-room. Alleyn read the cards. One in particular caught his eye: "From Anthony Gill to say a most inadequate 'thank you' for the great idea." A vase of red roses stood before the mirror: "To your greatest triumph, Coralie darling. C.C." In Miss Gay's room there were only two bouquets, one from the management and one "from Anthony, with love."

Again in each room he pulled off the lead-in to the heater and looked at the connection.

"All right, aren't they?" said the doctor.

"Quite all right. Tight fit. Good solid grey rubber."

"Well, then—"

Next on the left was an unused room, and opposite it, "Mr. H. J. Bannington." Neither of these rooms had gas fires. Mr. Bannington's dressing-table was littered with the usual array of greasepaint, the materials for his beard, a number of telegrams and letters, and several bills.

"About the body," the doctor began.

"We'll get a mortuary van from the Yard."

"But— Surely in a case of suicide—"

"I don't think this is suicide."

"But, good God!— D'you mean there's been an accident?"

"No accident," said Alleyn.

At midnight, the dressing-room lights in the Jupiter Theatre were brilliant, and men were busy there with the tools of their trade. A constable stood at the stage-door and a van waited in the yard. The front of the house was dimly lit and there, among the shrouded stalls, sat Coralie Bourne, Basil Gosset, H. J. Bannington, Dendra Gay, Anthony Gill, Reynolds, Katie the dresser, and the call-boy. A constable sat behind them and another stood by the doors into the foyer. They stared across the backs of seats at the fire curtain. Spirals of smoke rose from their cigarettes and about their feet were discarded programs. "Basil Gosset presents I CAN FIND MY WAY OUT by Anthony Gill."

In the manager's office Alleyn said: "You're sure of your facts, Mike?"

"Yes, sir. Honestly. I was right up against the entrance into the passage. They didn't see me because I was in the shadow. It was very dark off-stage."

"You'll have to swear to it."

"I know."

"Good. All right, Thompson. Miss Gay and Mr. Gosset may go home. Ask Miss Bourne to come in."

When Sergeant Thompson had gone Mike said: "I haven't had a chance to say I know I've made a perfect fool of myself. Using your card and everything."

"Irresponsible gaiety doesn't go down very well in the service, Mike. You behaved like a clown."

"I *am* a fool," said Mike wretchedly.

The red beard was lying in front of Alleyn on Gosset's desk. He picked it up and held it out. "Put it on," he said.

"She might do another faint."

"I think not. Now the hat: yes—yes, I see. Come in."

Sergeant Thompson showed Coralie Bourne in and then sat at the end of the desk with his notebook.

Tears had traced their course through the powder on her face, carrying black cosmetic with them and leaving the greasepaint shining like snail-tracks. She stood near the doorway looking dully at Michael. "Is he back in England?" she said. "Did he tell you to do this?" She made an impatient movement. "Do take it off," she said, "it's a very bad beard. If Cann had only looked—" Her lips trembled. "Who told you to do it?"

"Nobody," Mike stammered, pocketing the beard. "I mean—As a matter of fact, Tony Gill—"

"*Tony?* But *he* didn't know. Tony wouldn't do it. Unless—"

"Unless?" Alleyn said.

She said frowning: "Tony didn't want Cann to play the part that way. He was furious."

"He says it was his dress for the Chelsea Arts Ball," Mike mumbled. "I brought it here. I just thought I'd put it on—it was idiotic, I know—for fun. I'd no idea you and Mr. Cumberland would mind."

"Ask Mr. Gill to come in," Alleyn said.

Anthony was white and seemed bewildered and helpless. "I've told Mike," he said. "It was my dress for the ball. They sent it round from the costume-hiring place this afternoon but I forgot it. Dendra reminded me and rang up the Delivery people—or Mike, as it turns out—in the interval."

"Why," Alleyn asked, "did you choose that particular disguise?"

"I didn't. I didn't know what to wear and I was too rattled to think. They said they were hiring things for themselves and would get something for me. They said we'd all be characters out of a Russian melodrama."

"Who said this?"

"Well—well, it was Barry George, actually."

"*Barry,*" Coralie Bourne said. "*It was Barry.*"

"I don't understand," Anthony said. "Why should a fancy dress upset everybody?"

"It happened," Alleyn said, "to be a replica of the dress usually worn by Miss Bourne's husband who also had a red beard. That was it, wasn't it, Miss Bourne? I remember seeing him—"

"Oh, yes," she said, "you would. He was known to the police." Suddenly she broke down completely. She was in an armchair near the desk but out of the range of its shaded lamp. She twisted and writhed, beating her hand against the padded arm of the chair. Sergeant Thompson sat with his head bent and his hand over his notes. Mike, after an agonized glance at Alleyn, turned his back. Anthony Gill leant over her: "Don't," he said violently. "Don't! For God's sake, stop."

She twisted away from him and gripping the edge of the desk, began to speak to Alleyn; little by little gaining mastery of herself. "I want to tell you. I want you to understand. Listen." Her husband had been fantastically cruel, she said. "It was a kind of slavery." But when she sued for divorce he brought evidence of adultery with Cumberland. They had thought he knew nothing. "There was an abominable scene. He told us he was going away. He said he'd keep track of us and if I tried again for divorce, he'd come home. He was very friendly with Barry in those days." He had left behind him the first draft of a play he had meant to write for her and Cumberland. It had a wonderful scene for them. "And now you will never have it," he had said, "because there is no other playwright who could make this play for you but I." He was, she said, a melodramatic man but he was never ridiculous. He returned to the Ukraine where he was born and they had heard no more of him. In a little while she would have been able to presume death. But years of waiting did not agree with Canning Cumberland. He drank consistently and at his worst used to imagine her husband was about to return. "He was really terrified of Ben," she said. "He seemed like a creature in a nightmare."

Anthony Gill said: "This play—was it—?"

"Yes. There was an extraordinary similarity between your play and his. I saw at once that Ben's central scene would enormously strengthen your piece. Cann didn't want me to give it to you. Barry knew. He said: 'Why not?' He wanted Cann's part and was furious when he didn't get it. So you see, when he suggested you should dress and make-up like Ben—" She turned to Alleyn. "You see?"

"What did Cumberland do when he saw you?" Alleyn asked Mike.

"He made a queer movement with his hands as if—well, as if he expected me to go for him. Then he just bolted into his room."

"He thought Ben had come back," she said.

"Were you alone at any time after you fainted?" Alleyn asked.

"I? No. No, I wasn't. Katie took me into my dressing room and stayed with me until I went on for the last scene."

"One other question. Can you, by any chance, remember if the heater in your room behaved at all oddly?"

She looked wearily at him. "Yes, it did give a sort of plop, I think. It made me jump. I was nervy."

"You went straight from your room to the stage?"

"Yes. With Katie. I wanted to go to Cann. I tried the door when we came out. It was locked. He said: 'Don't come in.' I said: 'It's all right. It wasn't Ben,' and went on to the stage."

"I heard Miss Bourne," Mike said.

"He must have made up his mind by then. He was terribly drunk when he played his last scene." She pushed her hair back from her forehead. "May I go?" she asked Alleyn.

"I've sent for a taxi. Mr. Gill, will you see if it's there? In the meantime, Miss Bourne, would you like to wait in the foyer?"

"May I take Katie home with me?"

"Certainly. Thompson will find her. Is there anyone else we can get?"

"No, thank you. Just old Katie."

Alleyn opened the door for her and watched her walk into the foyer. "Check up with the dresser, Thompson," he murmured, "and get Mr. H. J. Bannington."

He saw Coralie Bourne sit on the lower step of the dress-circle stairway and lean her head against the wall. Nearby, on a gilt easel, a huge photograph of Canning Cumberland smiled handsomely at her.

H. J. Bannington looked pretty ghastly. He had rubbed his hand across his face and smeared his makeup. Florid red paint from his lips had stained the crêpe hair that had been gummed on and shaped into a beard. His monocle was still in his left eye and gave him an extraordinarily rakish look. "See here," he complained, "I've about *had* this party. When do we go home?"

Alleyn uttered placatory phrases and got him to sit down. He checked over H.J.'s movements after Cumberland left the stage and found that his account tallied with Mike's. He asked if H.J. had visited any of the other dressing rooms and was told acidly that H.J. knew his place in the company. "I remained in my unheated and squalid kennel, thank you very much."

"Do you know if Mr. Barry George followed your example?"

"Couldn't say, old boy. He didn't come near *me.*"

"Have you any theories at all about this unhappy business, Mr. Bannington?"

"Do you mean, why did Cann do it? Well, speak no ill of the dead, but I'd have thought it was pretty obvious he was morbid-drunk. Tight as an owl when we finished the second act. Ask the great Mr. Barry George. Cann took the big scene away from Barry with both hands and left him looking pathetic. All wrong artistically, but that's how Cann was in his cups." H.J.'s wicked little eyes narrowed. "The great Mr. George," he said, "must be feeling very unpleasant by now. You might say he'd got a suicide on his mind, mightn't you? Or don't you know about that?"

"It was not suicide."

The glass dropped from H.J.'s eye. "God!" he said. "God, I told Bob Reynolds! I told him the whole plant wanted overhauling."

"The gas plant, you mean?"

"Certainly. I was in the gas business years ago. Might say I'm in it still with a difference, ha-ha!"

"Ha-ha!" Alleyn agreed politely. He leaned forward. "Look here," he said: "We can't dig up a gas man at this time of night and may very likely need an expert opinion. You can help us."

"Well, old boy, I was rather pining for a spot of shut-eye. But, of course—"

"I shan't keep you very long."

"God, I hope not!" said H.J. earnestly.

Barry George had been made up pale for the last act. Colorless lips and shadows under his cheek bones and eyes had skilfully underlined his character as a repatriated but broken prisoner-of-war. Now, in the glare of the office lamp, he looked like a grossly exaggerated figure of mourning. He began at once to tell Alleyn how grieved and horrified he was. Everybody, he said, had their faults, and poor old Cann was no exception but wasn't it terrible to think what could happen to a man who let himself go downhill? He, Barry George, was abnormally sensitive and he didn't think he'd ever really get over the awful shock this had been to him. What, he wondered, could be at the bottom of it? Why had poor old Cann decided to end it all?

"Miss Bourne's theory," Alleyn began. Mr. George laughed. "Coralie?" he said. "So she's got a theory! Oh, well. Never mind."

"Her theory is this. Cumberland saw a man whom he mistook for her husband and, having a morbid dread of his return, drank the greater part of a bottle of whiskey and gassed himself. The clothes and beard that deceived him had, I understand, been ordered by you for Mr. Anthony Gill."

This statement produced startling results. Barry George broke into a spate of expostulation and apology. There had been no thought in his mind of resurrecting poor old Ben, who was no doubt dead but had been, mind you, in many ways one of the best. They were all to go to the Ball as exaggerated characters from melodrama. Not for the world— He gesticulated and protested. A line of sweat broke out along the margin of his hair. "I don't know what you're getting at," he shouted. "What are you suggesting?"

"I'm suggesting, among other things, that Cumberland was murdered."

"You're mad! He'd locked himself in. They had to break down the door. There's no window. You're crazy!"

"Don't," Alleyn said wearily, "let us have any nonsense about sealed rooms. Now, Mr. George, you knew Benjamin Vlasnoff pretty well. Are you going to tell us that when you suggested Mr. Gill should wear a coat with a fur collar, a black sombrero, black gloves and a red beard, it never occurred to you that his appearance might be a shock to Miss Bourne and to Cumberland?"

"I wasn't the only one," he blustered. "H.J. knew. And if it had scared him off, *she* wouldn't have been so sorry. She'd had about enough of him. Anyway if this is murder, the costume's got nothing to do with it."

"That," Alleyn said, getting up, "is what we hope to find out."

In Barry George's room, Detective-Sergeant Bailey, a fingerprint expert, stood by the gas heater. Sergeant Gibson, a police photographer, and a uniformed constable were near the door. In the centre of the room stood Barry George, looking from one man to another and picking at his lips.

"I don't know why he wants me to watch all this," he said. "I'm exhausted. I'm emotionally used up. What's he doing? Where is he?"

Alleyn was next door in Cumberland's dressing-room, with H.J., Mike and Sergeant Thompson. It was pretty clear now of fumes and the gas fire was burning comfortably. Sergeant Thompson sprawled in the armchair near the heater, his head sunk and his eyes shut.

"This is the theory, Mr. Bannington," Alleyn said. "You and Cumberland have made your final exits; Miss Bourne and Mr. George and Miss Gay are all on the stage. Lord Michael is standing just outside the entrance to the passage. The dressers and stage-staff are watching the play from the side. Cumberland has locked himself in this room. There he is, dead drunk and sound asleep. The gas fire is burning, full pressure. Earlier in the evening he powdered himself and a thick layer of the powder lies undisturbed on the tap. Now."

He tapped on the wall.

The fire blew out with a sharp explosion. This was followed by the hiss of escaping gas. Alleyn turned the taps off. "You see," he said, "I've left an excellent print on the powdered surface. Now, come next door."

Next door, Barry George appealed to him stammering: "But I didn't know. I don't know anything about it. I don't *know.*"

"Just show Mr. Bannington, will you, Bailey?"

Bailey knelt down. The lead-in was disconnected from the tap on the heater. He turned on the tap in the pipe and blew down the tube.

"An air lock, you see. It works perfectly."

H.J. was staring at Barry George. "But I don't know about gas, H.J. H.J., tell them—"

"One moment." Alleyn removed the towels that had been spread over the dressing-shelf, revealing a sheet of clean paper on which lay the rubber push-on connection.

"Will you take this lens, Bannington, and look at it. You'll see that it's stained a florid red. It's a very slight stain but it's unmistakably grease-paint."

And just above the stain you'll see a wiry hair. Rather like some sort of packing material, but it's not that. It's crêpe hair, isn't it?"

The lens wavered above the paper.

"Let me hold it for you," Alleyn said. He put his hand over H.J.'s shoulder and, with a swift movement, plucked a tuft from his false moustache and dropped it on the paper. "Identical, you see. Ginger. It seems to be stuck to the connection with spirit gum."

The lens fell. H.J. twisted round, faced Alleyn for a second, and then struck him full in the face. He was a small man but it took three of them to hold him.

"In a way, sir, it's handy when they have a smack at you," said Detective-Sergeant Thompson half an hour later. "You can pull them in nice and straightforward without any 'will you come to the station and make a statement' business."

"Quite," said Alleyn, nursing his jaw.

Mike said: "He must have gone to the room after Barry George and Miss Bourne were called."

"That's it. He had to be quick. The call-boy would be round in a minute and he had to be back in his own room."

"But look here—what about motive?"

"That, my good Mike, is precisely why, at half-past one in the morning, we're still in this miserable theatre. You're getting a view of the duller aspect of homicide. Want to go home?"

"No. Give me another job."

"Very well. About ten feet from the prompt-entrance, there's a sort of garbage tin. Go through it."

At seventeen minutes to two, when the dressing rooms and passage had been combed clean and Alleyn had called a spell, Mike came to him with filthy hands. "Eureka," he said, "I hope."

They all went into Bannington's room. Alleyn spread out on the dressing-table the fragments of paper that Mike had given him.

"They'd been pushed down to the bottom of the tin," Mike said.

Alleyn moved the fragments about. Thompson whistled through his teeth. Bailey and Gibson mumbled together.

"There you are," Alleyn said at last.

They collected round him. The letter that H. J. Bannington had opened at this same table six hours and forty-five minutes earlier, was pieced together like a jigsaw puzzle.

"Dear H.J.

Having seen the monthly statement of my account, I called at my bank this morning and was shown a check that is undoubtedly a forgery.

Your histrionic versatility, my dear H.J., is only equalled by your audacity as a calligraphist. But fame has its disadvantages. The teller recognized you. I propose to take action."

"Unsigned," said Bailey.

"Look at the card on the red roses in Miss Bourne's room, signed C.C. It's a very distinctive hand." Alleyn turned to Mike. "Do you still want to be a policeman?"

"Yes."

"Lord help you. Come and talk to me at the office tomorrow."

"Thank you, sir."

They went out, leaving a constable on duty. It was a cold morning. Mike looked up at the facade of the Jupiter. He could just make out the shape of the neon sign: I CAN FIND MY WAY OUT *by Anthony Gill.*

THE FOURTH DEGREE

by HUGH PENTECOST

"I would stand over the crib and look down at him," Harvey said, "and I would think how easy it would be to turn him over on his stomach and press his tiny face into the pillow until—until he was dead."

The room was dark except for the faint reflection from a street lamp outside. The reflection showed the outline of Paul Harvey sitting on the edge of a couch, his head buried in his hands.

"Go on, Mr. Harvey." It was a colorless voice that came from some invisible recess of the room. Harvey had spoken of an impulse to murder, but the voice reacted to it as unemotionally as if Harvey had been reading a want-ad in the newspaper.

Harvey turned his head from side to side. "I can't make it come together in the right order," he said. "It—it's all jumbled up."

"That doesn't matter," the voice said. "It's my job to put it together. Just go on, Mr. Harvey. You were talking about the impulse to smother your infant son."

"It was when that got bad that I left Ellen," Harvey said.

"Ellen?"

"My wife," Harvey said. "I haven't told you about her yet, have I? I left her and turned to Ruby. It was the only place I had to turn." He twisted his body as though he were suffering from some physical agony. "Ruby was my secretary at Verne Steiger's. She's a strange girl—not like Ellen, or Lilli. Not like anyone I ever cared for before. We don't have the same tastes, but —well, I knew it would never happen with her. I was positive of that."

" 'It' would never happen?" the voice asked.

"The same old thing," Harvey said. "Just the way it happened at Steiger's. I was head of the packaging department there. Do you know about Verne Steiger? She's the outstanding woman industrial designer in America. Very smart, very high-pressure. We were doing a tremendous business in my department—packages and labels for liquor, for perfumes, for drugs of all kinds, for foods and jewelry. I had twenty designers working under me. Then—it happened. Just as it's always happened."

The distant wail of an ambulance siren crept in and out of the dark room.

"Verne called me into her office one day. There was a man there. He was tall and sleek in a pin-stripe suit with padded shoulders. He looked like the vice-president of an advertising agency. Verne introduced me. She said the work was piling up. That I was doing a fine job, but the work was piling up. So, she said, she had decided to hire an assistant for me. Oh, it sounded plausible enough. But I knew. She had heard that I'd left Ellen. She'd heard about Ruby. This was her way of kissing me off. In a few weeks or a few months this 'vice-president' would have my job. I wasn't going to wait for that, you understand. I wasn't going to let it happen again. So—so I resigned." He was silent, except for his labored breathing.

"Didn't Verne Steiger try to persuade you to stay?" the voice asked.

"Oh, yes, she tried," Harvey said, bitterly. "She pretended that I was indispensable. But I knew. I knew this 'vice-president' was going to destroy my position, just as someone has always destroyed my position. Just as David destroyed it."

"David is the boy—your son?" the voice asked.

Harvey nodded. "I met Ellen in my senior year in college. She was—she was wonderful. The minute I saw her, I knew there'd never be anyone else for me. She had yellow hair—a little like Lilli's—and a lovely warm smile. Even the first time I talked to her I knew she understood me—that she understood how much I needed her. I'd decided to go into industrial designing even then. Ellen studied art. We both liked music—the same kind of music. We didn't have to amuse each other. We didn't even have to talk. We just knew about each other, that's all—and gave to each other.

"We were married, as soon as I'd graduated. There was some money— from Lilli, you understand. I got a job with Verne Steiger almost at once. We took a little house in the suburbs and I commuted to town. We were happy—so damned happy!" Harvey's voice broke. Then he drew a deep breath and went on.

"Very soon Ellen told me we were going to have a child. I could see how happy she was. She seemed to shine with it. I could feel the love pouring out of her to me. It was a wonderful period. I did so well at my job I was made head of the department. I had an office and a secretary of my own—Ruby!" He stopped again, and when he went on, the quality of his voice was dead.

"The child was born," he said. He suddenly beat one fist into the palm of his other hand. "It was a boy. We called him David. That day, *that very day*, I knew it had happened again. I'd lost Ellen. It was not *us* any more. She talked endlessly about David. She took care of him. It seemed as though we were never alone. At night she slept lightly, always listening for some sound from David in the next room. David was her life now. David!

David!—Well, I began drinking. I couldn't stand it. I began missing my regular train. I didn't want to get home till David was asleep. But when I *did* get home she'd make me go in and look at him. I'd stand there, looking down at the crib, and thinking how easy it would be to steal in there during the night and turn him over and hold his face down against the pillow so he couldn't cry—so he couldn't make a sound. Hold him there until—" There was a long silence. "So I left Ellen. It had happened again. Just as it always happened. Just as it happened with Lilli."

"Who was Lilli?" the voice asked, casually, out of the darkness.

"Lilli? Why, Lilli was my mother," Harvey said, as though everyone should have known that.

"Ah, yes. Go on, Mr. Harvey."

"I never knew my father," Harvey said. "He was killed in the First World War. Lilli brought me up. We lived in the country. It's funny, but I can only remember her now in a long white evening dress, bending over my bed—close to me, her warmth near my face—the special fragrance that was hers. We did everything together. She used to read to me. We used to walk in the woods. We were never separated. I loved her—*so much!* Then —then *he* came." The last sentence was spoken with explosive violence.

"Go on," the voice said, calmly.

"His name was Daniel Steele. He was a lawyer connected with a firm that handled the small estate my father'd left Lilli. He'd known my father overseas. He was a big man, with a homely face and a kind smile. I—I actually liked him at first. But he began coming often and I knew from his attitude toward Lilli that it wasn't business. Suddenly he was taking a lot of her time. Well, he came to spend the Labor Day weekend with us. I remember Lilli coming upstairs to kiss me good-night. Oh, she was very affectionate, very loving, but she seemed far away. She seemed nervous and excited. And she went downstairs where *he* was waiting for her. I could hear their voices downstairs, but I couldn't hear what they were saying. I was shut out—shut out as though I didn't belong at all!

"Suddenly it seemed to me I had to know what they were saying. I had to! I crept out of bed to the head of the stairs. I sat there, hugging the newel post, listening. *He* was talking! He was telling her that she should send me away to school. He was telling her that she was spoiling me, that I had to learn to stand on my own feet. He said boarding school would be good for me—that I should be separated from her so that I could learn to be an individual. Lilli sounded unhappy. She told him it would break my heart to be sent away. She knew! But he said I'd thank her for it later. And then—then she agreed." Harvey's voice sank so low it was almost inaudible. "I couldn't stand any more. I slipped back to my room—into bed. My world had come to an end. I rolled over on my stomach and sank my teeth into the pillow. I didn't want them to hear me crying."

"And did you go to boarding school?" the voice asked.

"Oh, yes, I went," Harvey said. "Lilli and Daniel Steele took me there. They were going to be married the next day and go on a honeymoon in the Caribbean. I hated it at school. I couldn't seem to get adjusted. All I could think of was *them*—together. Then—when I'd been there about three weeks, the headmaster sent for me. I knew I hadn't been doing well. But—but he didn't scold me. He—he seemed very upset. Finally, he showed me a newspaper that was lying on his desk. I read the headlines. AIRLINER CRASHES. PLANE STRIKES ALLEGHENY MOUNTAIN TOP. NO SURVIVORS. Right under the headlines was a little box containing a list of the known dead. The names seemed to jump out of the page at me. 'Mr. and Mrs. Daniel Steele.'" Suddenly Harvey's voice rose, harshly. "He had taken Lilli away from me. Taken her away forever!"

The voice was silent, waiting.

"So you see," Harvey said, after a while, "it's always happened. First *he* took Lilli away from me. Then David separated me from Ellen. Then the man at Verne Steiger's. And now—and now—"

"Did you murder Edgar Fremont?" the voice asked, as offhandedly as if he were inquiring about the correct time.

"No! *No!*" Harvey cried. Then his voice broke. "I—I don't think so."

"Tell me about Fremont."

"He—he was an egghead," Harvey said.

"A what?"

"An egghead. That—that's a phrase of Ruby's. She always says she's not interested in Arrow-collar men. Interesting-looking men, queer-looking men are her dish. She calls them eggheads. It's just a phrase."

"I see."

"When—when I left Verne Steiger's I decided to free-lance. I—I came here to live with Ruby in this apartment. It's her apartment, you understand. We—we don't have much in common in the way of pleasures, but we both like to drink in odd places—little bars along Third Avenue. One night, in one of those places, Fremont came in and sat down near us. He was short, with almost no neck, and very broad shoulders. It made his head look large for the rest of him. He looked kind of lonely and depressed. Ruby always likes to talk to strangers and we struck up a conversation. Fremont was shy at first, but finally he got talking. He was a writer, he said. He was writing a novel, and doing odd jobs to eat on while he worked at it. He didn't know many people. He didn't have any friends. Ruby and I felt sorry for him. We asked him to come around to see us—any time, we said.

"Well, he came—often. I liked him. He talked my language about books and art and music. We used to argue about things until Ruby got bored. She—she didn't have a feeling for things like that. So, Fremont used to eat with us often—and drop in to see us without waiting for an invitation. Then—then I began to notice. It—it was happening again. I could see that Ruby was falling for him. I had a quarrel with her about it—and others followed. I started to drink pretty heavily. Today was the pay-off. We had a terrible brawl. She—she told me to get out of here and not come back! I —I wasn't surprised, in a way. As I've told you, it always happens."

"But you did come back," the voice said. "You did come back here tonight."

"Not to the apartment," Harvey said. "Not till the police brought me up. You see—I was very drunk. I'd been drinking in a place down the street for hours. I was sitting in a little booth all by myself when, suddenly, Fremont was there. He slid into the seat opposite me. Things were all kind of blurred. He looked like a—like a monstrous little gargoyle sitting there.

" 'I've been looking for you everywhere,' he said to me.

" 'Go away,' I said.

" 'You've got to snap out of this,' he said. 'You're killing yourself, Paul. Ruby isn't worth it.'

" 'That's a funny thing for you to say,' I said.

" 'What do you mean, Paul?' he asked.

" 'I mean *you're* the reason Ruby and I have quarreled. There's no use pretending, Fremont. You're in love with her and you've taken her away from me.'

" 'In love with her!' I remember he started laughing. It sounded crazy. 'Ruby has nothing for me, Paul. Nothing! She has nothing for you, only you won't recognize it. You're killing yourself over a cheap little tart who'll leave you the minute she's bled you dry.'

" 'You can't talk that way about Ruby,' I said. But I wanted to believe he felt that way, do you understand? I wanted to believe it, because then— well, then it might not happen again, the way it always had.

"He stayed with me quite a while, telling me that I'd be better off without Ruby. It—it sounded just like Daniel Steele telling Lilli I'd be better off at school. Better off—with separation and death to follow. Finally, he left me. Then—then I got to thinking. Maybe he just wanted to make sure I wasn't seeing Ruby. Maybe he was going to see Ruby now, being certain I wasn't there. I had to know. I *had* to know. So I got out of there. I—I was drunker than I realized."

Again he paused to take a deep breath. "So—so I came over here to see. This—this old brownstone has a fire-escape leading down into a backyard. I guess you know that. I—I thought I'd go into the backyard and up the fire escape. So I went around the back way and into the yard. I—I was stumbling around there in the dark when suddenly there were lights everywhere, and policemen, and they dragged me up here and—and Fremont was lying there on the floor with—with his face shot off. And they showed me my gun. *My* gun!"

"Your gun," the voice said. "And mud on the fire escape from the backyard. And mud on your shoes from the backyard. Are you sure you didn't come up here?"

"I *was* sure," Harvey said, "before the police worked on me. I was sure. But I was very drunk. And—and maybe I forgot. I know about those things, doctor. I know sometimes, in a situation like this, you draw a blank. Maybe I drew a blank. Is—is that what you think?"

"No," the voice said.

There was the sound of a clicking light switch and the room was flooded with light. It revealed Paul Harvey, slender, dark, his wavy hair damp with perspiration, his brown eyes hollow, haunted. The voice also took shape. The shape was that of a small gray man, an anonymous-looking gray man. No one would ever have turned to look at him on the street. There was nothing about him to arouse interest. He was just small, and gray, and neutral.

The gray man looked around the room, his eyes mild and thoughtful. It was a room that would have had no charm for a man of taste, a man such as Paul Harvey appeared to be. There was a daybed on one side of the room, stacked high with pale pink and green satin cushions. There was a goldfish bowl on a stand by the window with a waving green plant that grew under the water, and two sullen fish. There was a whatnot in one corner laden with souvenirs—souvenirs from Coney Island and Broadway shooting galleries and Third Avenue junk shops. On the wall there were cheaply framed photographs of vacation incidents, intimate yet meaningless to a stranger. There was a reproduction of that tired Maxfield Parrish of the nude boy in a swing against the background of an unreal sky. On the mantelpiece was a stuffed toy panda, ten-cent-store variety, staring out at the room with shoe-button eyes.

The rug was a faded pink broadloom, except in the corner by the front door where there was a dark, irregular stain where Edgar Fremont had bled and died.

The gray man walked over to an inner door which led to the kitchen and bedroom. He opened the door.

"All right, Lieutenant," he said.

Three men came out of the bedroom: Lieutenant Mason of Homicide and two uniformed policemen. Mason was one of the department's bright young men—college degree, good clothes. He looked like a business executive.

"All right, boys, you can take him downtown," Mason said.

The two policemen moved in on either side of Paul Harvey and helped him to his feet.

"Just a minute," Harvey said. "Can I see her for a moment, Lieutenant?"

"Not now," Mason said.

"But I—"

"Not now!"

The policemen led Harvey out of the room. The sound of their feet on the stairs was plainly audible. The little gray man was standing by the window, looking down at the street.

"Well, Dr. Smith?" Mason asked, when they were alone.

Dr. Smith sighed. "God, what children suffer without their parents ever knowing!" he said.

Mason smiled to himself. He'd worked with Dr. John Smith before. He knew you didn't come at things directly with him. Mason remembered his first reaction to the little gray man; that he was the only person who could sign a hotel register 'John Smith' and be believed! Mason also knew how deceptive Dr. Smith's appearance was. Let the police give a crook a thorough going-over with all the approved third-degree methods and fail, and then Dr. Smith would be called in. The motives for murder, he claimed, were to be found, not in bank balances or vaults, not in apparent jealousies or greed, but in the dark and inaccessible corridors of the mind. Searching those corridors, battling with words and ideas, Dr. Smith called "The Fourth Degree."

"I never get to talk to anyone," Dr. Smith said, turning from the window, "till you and your boys have reduced him to a state of abject terror, Mason. Some day you may wake up to the fact that the psychiatrist should be called in first, not last!"

"I just work here," Mason said, grinning. "What do you think about Harvey, Doctor?"

"What I think isn't evidence," Dr. Smith said. "And evidence is all you're concerned with."

"We've got plenty of evidence," Mason said. "We have the note Ruby Lewis left for Harvey before she went out to the Island for the weekend. Here, you haven't actually seen it." Mason took a letter from his pocket and handed it to Smith. The doctor slid on a pair of heavy, bone-rimmed spectacles.

"Paul:" the note began,

I have had enough of your accusations and crazy jealousy of Edgar. I am going away for the weekend to the Island—The Lambert House. I expect you to have all your things moved out when I get back. This is final. Ruby

"The motive is clear," Mason said. "Harvey was crazy-jealous of Edgar Fremont. Fremont came up here and as he walked in the front door Harvey let him have it. Then he went down the fire escape to the backyard where we found him—*and* the gun. His gun! Motive, opportunity, weapon."

"I understand there were no fingerprints on the gun?" Dr. Smith said.

"Naturally—he wiped them off," Mason said.

"Unnaturally," the doctor muttered to himself. "He wiped his fingerprints off the gun, so he wouldn't be caught—and then he waited in the backyard for fifteen minutes while neighbors called the police and they came here with sirens screaming, went upstairs, found the body, and finally —God knows how long afterwards—went down in the yard and found Harvey still waiting for them."

"He was drunk," Mason said. "He didn't know what he was doing."

"But he knew enough to wipe his fingerprints off the gun?"

Mason shrugged. "Everybody knows enough to do that."

The doctor shrugged. "Physical evidence is your department, Mason," he said. "You wouldn't have called me in unless there were some doubts in your mind."

Mason gave the little gray man a wry smile. "I felt sorry for Harvey," he said. "Can you beat that? I felt sorry for him."

"There's no reason to be ashamed of a decent human emotion," Dr. Smith said.

"All the evidence indicates that Harvey set a deliberate trap for Fremont. That he invited him here, laid in wait for him, and shot him when he arrived. That's first-degree murder and it means the chair. But somehow— well, of course if he were a mental case—"

"He isn't—in the legal sense," Dr. Smith said:

"Then that's that," Mason said, and sighed.

"Harvey's a man who has been living under the terrific pressures produced by a childhood trauma," Dr. Smith said. "It has influenced every relationship and every major crisis of his life."

"And finally drove him to murder," Mason said.

"I'm not sure at all. Mason, you look for patterns on the surface—clues, fingerprints, alibis. I look for internal patterns. Harvey's is clear. Every time he's been confronted with a certain kind of situation—one in which it seemed that some woman who was close and dear to him was about to be stolen away by someone else—he reacted in exactly the same way. He ran! Now, if Harvey killed Fremont it means that pattern, which he has followed all his life, was suddenly altered. From all we know about him he should have run this time. But if he killed Fremont, he upset his whole behavior pattern. Why? *Why?*"

"I suppose there came a point when he just blew his top," Mason said.

"We have no right to suppose," Dr. Smith said. "At least, I have to know to be satisfied. Tell me something about the girl, Ruby Lewis."

"Not much to tell," Mason said. "She isn't your type—or mine! Or

Harvey's for that matter. She's like this room—a sort of brightly tinted Easter egg in a ten-cent store. But she's in the clear. She was at the Lambert Inn all evening—thirty miles from here."

"I'd like to talk to her," Dr. Smith said. "Maybe she can tell us something about Harvey that will explain what we don't quite understand at the moment."

"No reason why you shouldn't," Mason said. "She's in the bedroom. Perhaps you'd better see her there. She has a natural reluctance to come in here. We showed her Fremont before we cleaned up the place. It was pretty rough."

"Let's get it over with," Dr. Smith said.

Mason started toward the door of the bedroom. "She's got a friend with her. Fellow named George Lambert who owns the hotel where she was staying. He drove her into town."

The bedroom was almost dark. The only light came from a dim, shaded lamp on the bedside table. It showed Ruby Lewis stretched out on the bed, dabbing at her eyes with a lace-edged handkerchief. There was an almost overpowering scent of perfume in the room. Ruby had flaxen-colored hair done in a feather cut that gave it the look of a curly halo—an artificial halo. Her complexion was peach ice cream. Her figure made it quite understandable why men should be instantly interested.

A man came over to stand in the circle of light from the lamp. He was tall and handsome in a sleek way. His clothes were a little too sharp, and he wore a checkered vest such as horsemen sometimes wear in the field.

Mason introduced Dr. Smith to Ruby and George Lambert.

"I've heard about you, Doc," Lambert said. "The Madden case. I knew Senator Madden's son. You pulled him out of quite a hole."

"You own the Lambert House where Miss Lewis was staying tonight?" asked Dr. Smith.

"That's right, Doc. And that's only the beginning. I'm planning a chain of hotels."

"Dr. Smith wants to ask a few questions," Mason said. Obviously he was annoyed by Lambert's breezy manner toward the doctor.

"Sure, sure," Lambert said. "Ruby and I got nothing to hide. Our alibis stand up, don't they, Inspector?"

"Lieutenant," Mason said, sharply. "Yes, they stand up, Mr. Lambert."

With a cheerful smile which indicated he was ready for anything, Lambert turned to where Dr. Smith had been standing. Dr. Smith wasn't there. He had melted somewhere into the shadows of the room.

"I think Dr. Smith wants to hear your story, Miss Lewis," Mason said.

Ruby lifted the lace handkerchief to her eyes. "It's awful," she said. "To think that if I'd called a doctor for Paul long ago this might not have happened."

Her voice was disillusioning. It sent the curve of her charm dipping sharply downward. It was flat, complaining.

"There's no doubt in your mind that Harvey killed Fremont?" Dr. Smith's voice came from a dark corner of the room.

"He was insanely jealous," Ruby said. "He was jealous of all men but he was insanely jealous of Edgar."

"You wouldn't believe it, just meeting him," George Lambert said. "He seemed like such a quiet guy."

"You broke off with Harvey today, didn't you, Miss Lewis?"

"It was final today," she said. "But it's been coming for a long time. We had a stinker of a quarrel last night about Edgar. This morning, after Paul went to his studio to work, I thought it all over. I decided that was that."

"So you left the note for him and went down to Mr. Lambert's hotel?"

"I had to get hold of my nerves," Ruby said. "George had told me to come any time I wanted."

"Did anyone else have a key to your apartment besides Harvey?"

Ruby pushed herself up on her elbows and peered into the dark. "What kind of a girl do you think I am?" she demanded, indignantly.

"I have no idea, Miss Lewis," the doctor said. "That's why I asked."

"I was strictly on the level with Paul!" she said. "But he was insanely jealous, just the same."

"So you said. You went out to the Lambert House by train?"

"Do I look like I owned a Rolls Royce?" Ruby said, still angry. She lowered herself to the pillows again. "Will they electrocute him or just put him away somewhere?"

Mason answered that one. "It was clearly a premeditated crime. That means the chair."

"For someone," said the colorless voice from the corner of the room.

Ruby sat bolt upright on the bed. "You mean you don't think it was Paul? Why, they caught him here—it was his gun—he was insanely jealous of Edgar. He—"

"It's just that I have to make the internal facts fit the external facts," Dr. Smith said. "I'd like to know whatever you can tell me about Edgar Fremont, Miss Lewis."

Ruby's voice took on a peculiarly harsh quality. "He was going places," she said. "Everyone said he was going to be a really important writer. He just sold his book to one of those book clubs—and Hollywood. He was going to be rich and famous."

"He didn't like you, did he, Miss Lewis?"

"You wouldn't think that if you heard the way he tried to break things up between me and Paul. He was always trying to break things up between me and Paul."

"He wanted you for himself?"

"Why would he try to break things up between me and Paul if he didn't?"

"There could be other reasons."

"Look, Doc, take it easy," George Lambert said. "Ruby don't have to take that kind of a going-over from no one. What other reasons could the guy have?"

"Maybe he liked Harvey," Dr. Smith said. "Maybe he thought it would be good for Harvey if he went back to his wife and child."

"There wasn't anything stopping Paul, if that was what he wanted," Ruby said. "Paul didn't want anything but me. He said over and over he'd never let me go."

"He threatened you?"

"He acted crazy. He said he couldn't stand it if anything happened between us. He acted like it was a matter of life and death."

"It turned out to be a matter of life and death, didn't it?" the doctor said, quietly. "Were you afraid of him?"

"I tell you, he acted crazy!" Ruby said.

"Of course she was afraid of him," George Lambert broke in. "She told me about it one weekend when they were at my place. I told her she could call on me any time Harvey got out of line."

"If I hadn't known I could call on George I'd have been half out of my mind," Ruby said. She looked up at Lambert who was fingering the edge of his gaudy vest.

"What attracted you to Paul Harvey in the first place?" Dr. Smith asked.

"I was his secretary. Everyone said he was going places. He was one of the best designers in the business. I figured he'd become a partner of Verne Steiger's."

"But you stayed with him after he left Steiger's?"

"Well, I didn't think he was going to just quit and drink himself to death. I figured he'd start a business of his own."

"So you only stayed with him because you thought he had a successful future?"

"Is there anything wrong with that?" Ruby demanded. "A woman has a right to expect something from a man, doesn't she?"

"And if he doesn't produce it?"

"You have to look out for yourself," Ruby said. "That's why I finally broke off with him."

"I thought it was because you were afraid of him."

"That, too. He acted crazy about Fremont, I keep telling you."

"And there was no reason for his acting that way because Fremont didn't want you," Dr. Smith said.

"That stuck-up jerk!" Ruby said. "He didn't think I was good enough for him—or Paul either!"

There was a long silence and then the voice came from the corner of the room once more. "What are your plans now, Miss Lewis?"

"Plans?"

"Your affair with Harvey is over. What now?"

"I don't know that's any of your business!" Ruby said.

"It's nothing to be ashamed of, baby," George Lambert said. He turned toward the direction of the voice. "Ruby and I are going to be married, Doc. It's time she had some of the things out of life she wants."

"It might be rather costly for you, Mr. Lambert."

"Nothing's too good for Ruby," Lambert said.

The doctor came out of the darkness and stood in the circle of light, looking down at Ruby. "A perfect epitaph for Miss Lewis, I should say."

"Now look, Doc—" Lambert's voice was angry.

Dr. Smith ignored him. "I have the feeling Miss Lewis usually gets what she wants. Of course she failed once."

Ruby sat up. "I don't like the way you talk to me," she said. She looked at Mason. "Do I have to stand for these cracks, Lieutenant?"

"She missed out on Hollywood and the glamorous position of being a successful author's wife. You wanted Fremont pretty badly, didn't you, Miss Lewis, and he laughed at you."

George Lambert took a step forward and dropped his big hand on Dr. Smith's shoulder. "That'll be about all from you, Doc," he said.

"Oh, I'm quite through," Dr. Smith said. "But I don't imagine you'll sleep very well at night, Lambert—after you're married."

"What do you mean?"

"Well, if the chain of hotels is a little slow in coming about—"

"What do you mean?"

"Miss Lewis might be disappointed."

"So?"

"She doesn't like to be disappointed, Mr. Lambert. Harvey disappointed her, and he's in a very bad spot. Fremont disappointed her, and he's dead. It seems to be extremely unhealthy to disappoint Miss Lewis."

Ruby's voice rose shrilly. "Make him stop talking that way, Lieutenant! I'll sue him! He's got no right to talk that way. I'll—"

"Alibis are not my province," Dr. Smith said, his gray eyes fixed steadily on George Lambert. "I don't know what's wrong with Miss Lewis's alibi, Lambert. But I do know I wouldn't be in your shoes for a million dollars. As a psychiatrist I know that people are driven by repetitive compulsions they can't control. Harvey was a man who always ran away from disaster—before it happened! He actually made it happen by running away. He ran away from the danger of Fremont by drinking."

"What's all that long-haired talk got to do with me?" Ruby demanded.

"Your pattern is more aggressive, Miss Lewis. You want money and position, and you keep after it—first an important designer, then an important writer, now a chain of hotels. What next, Miss Lewis? And how will you get rid of Lambert when the time comes to move on and up?"

Lambert moistened his lips. "Get *rid* of me?"

"I hope for your sake the chain of hotels is a pretty sure thing," the doctor said, "and that it makes you a great deal of money. Otherwise—"

Ruby sat up on the bed, shrieking. "Get that filthy old jerk out of here! Get him out of here! Get him out!"

"We're going, Miss Lewis," Dr. Smith said. He turned to Lambert once more. "Good luck to you, Mr. Lambert. I have a feeling you're going to need it. Come, Mason."

"Wait!" Lambert said and his voice shook. "You—you think she killed Fremont and—and threw the blame on Harvey?"

"I think it's within the framework of her pattern, Mr. Lambert. I think she is capable of it. But—well, she has an alibi. So, of course—"

Beads of sweat glittered on Lambert's forehead. "Lieutenant," he said to Mason, "I—I think I'd like to alter my original statement."

A torrent of screaming abuse came flooding out of Ruby's twisted red mouth. Lambert backed slowly away from the bed toward the door.

" '. . . it isn't that I lied, you understand,' " Mason read aloud from the typewritten pages of George Lambert's new statement, " 'it's just that I didn't tell you everything. Ruby did arrive in the late afternoon and she went to her room, and she was there when you phoned at midnight. What I didn't tell was that she asked to borrow my car so she could go to the movies in town. I let her take the car and I didn't think anything of it until I was driving her to New York after your call. Then she said, 'George, maybe it would be easier for me if you didn't tell the police I went to the movies.' I asked her why, and she said everyone connected with Harvey would be under suspicion and if I didn't tell about her going to the movies she'd have a perfect alibi, and she wouldn't be bothered by the cops. I didn't see any harm in that because I knew—that is, I *thought* I knew—that she was in the clear. I still think she is, but I thought you ought to have all the facts.' "

Dr. Smith was standing by the windows in Mason's office, looking down at the street where the first early morning traffic was beginning to roll.

"There's not much doubt about it," Mason said. "She still contends she went to the movies—a double feature. But she's got an extraordinary lack of memory about those two pictures. The three hours involved was ample time for her to drive to New York, kill Fremont, and get back to the Lambert House without rousing suspicion. She probably had a date with Fremont . . . and he kept it because he wanted to help Harvey. But there's one thing that bothers me, doctor. Why? She didn't have to kill Fremont to get rid of him. He wasn't in her way."

"I'm bad on quotations, particularly corny ones," the doctor said. "But there's something somewhere about the anger of a woman scorned—Fremont had rejected her. Harvey had failed her and would probably make any new relationship extremely difficult. It was a perfect scheme for paying off the one and getting rid of the other."

Mason nodded. "What made you think Lambert would break?"

Dr. Smith turned away from the window. There was a faint smile on his lips. "That checkered vest," he said. "That vest, Mason, matched Ruby Lewis's living room, with the toy panda and the goldfish. They went together like ham and eggs. It occurred to me, without knowing much about Lambert beyond a surface character reading, that he and Ruby were birds of a feather. I was pretty certain Lambert would be much more interested in himself than in any woman, no matter how attractive. He was the male counterpart of Ruby, selfish, greedy, self-centered."

"What made you think Ruby's alibi was phony?" Mason asked.

"It's just the different points of view from which we work, Mason," Dr. Smith said. "You accept the outward physical facts as unassailable, and you make the internal facts fit them. My approach is just the reverse. I believe the internal facts are unassailable. The internal truth about Harvey made me certain he would run, not kill. That left Ruby or Lambert, both of whom were quite capable of killing. Ruby seemed the most likely to me because she had the most to gain—revenge for a jilting and a failure, a chain of hotels, and a man of her own kind."

"So much for scientific crime investigation," Mason said, dryly.

"You think the study of crippled personalities isn't a science?" Dr. Smith asked.

Mason pushed back his chair and stood up. "God forbid I should make such a claim," he said. He punched out his cigarette in the ashtray on the desk. "I'd like to ask you one more favor, doctor."

"Yes?"

"I'd like you to go with me while I break the news to Paul Harvey that he's free," Mason said. "He's had a pretty rough time. He has a wife and a child and a real talent, and I think there must be some way we could help him to rehabilitate himself."

"Of course I'll go with you," Dr. Smith said. "It's time Harvey stopped being afraid of ghosts."

"And that," Mason said, "holds for most of us."

MIDNIGHT ADVENTURE

by MICHAEL ARLEN

Now it is told in London how on one winter's night not long ago a gentleman who was walking from Grosvenor Square down Carlos Place was accosted by a lady in a peculiar manner and with curious results.

Earlier that same evening two gentlemen of correct appearance might have been observed dining together at a quiet corner table in the restaurant of a London hotel which is famous for the distinction of its guests. Our two friends, one lined and gray-haired, the other younger and lean and uncommonly handsome in a saturnine way, appeared to be absorbed in conversation.

The younger gentleman talked the least and, as was only proper, listened attentively to his gray-haired companion. This was not surprising, since the father was telling his son in the most urgent terms that only a rich marriage could appease the ferocity of their overdraft at the bank.

In days gone by, when the last King of Navarre strode into history as Henri IV, first and finest of the Bourbon Kings of France, the mountainous half of Navarre became, owing to reasons we cannot go into now, the Duchy of Suiza. The Dukes of Suiza were royal in that pathetically half-starved way which is disparagingly known as "minor." For several centuries the Duchy of Suiza was respected, or perhaps overlooked, as an independent kingdom, and eventually forgotten.

The two gentlemen at dinner were Carlos XXVII, Duke of Suiza, and his only son, Prince Rudolf. But, as the worldly father pointed out to his worldly son, high titles like Duke and Prince without the cash to support them added up to so much spinach put before a starving man.

"In short," said Duke Carlos, who liked to speak the English he had picked up from the American visitors who had thronged the Casinos of his duchy before his exile, "we are bust wide open, boy—unless you shake the Christmas tree to some effect."

Rudolf sipped his champagne with an air of saturnine fatality. "Our reputation," said he, "is enough to wither even the stoutest Christmas tree as we approach."

"You must find some sweet young innocent, Rudolf. Or haven't I already heard something about you and the American heiress, Baba Carstairs? I can only hope, my friend, that you are impressing the girl as being a romantic person—for you can *look* extremely romantic, particularly when you are telling lies."

Prince Rudolf finished the champagne in his glass. "Dear father," said he at last, "have you ever been in love?"

Duke Carlos looked at his son with pity.

"Frequently," said he. "Why, did you think you had invented love?"

"Perhaps," said the young man moodily, "I could suggest some badly needed improvements on it."

"So you are going to tell me that you are still crazy about that Follies girl you met last year in Paris?"

"No, not last year, but ten years ago, and not a Follies girl, but a girl. But perhaps it would be better for men like us not even to think about her."

"You look so romantic when you speak of her, Rudolf, that I feel sure you told her many lies. Forget her, boy. Remember our traditions. Remember our name. Remember our overdraft. In short, remember Miss Carstairs."

Now, it is of this Prince Rudolf it is told that, as later that night he walked moodily to his modest lodgings in the sulky shadows behind the clubs of Piccadilly, he was accosted by a lady in a peculiar manner.

He saw a car, long and dark, of sober elegance. It passed close by him, as such cars do, with no more sound than a flick of a cat's whiskers. A few yards ahead, it stopped.

As Rudolf walked past, his moody gaze ahead, he was thinking how much better it would be for that pretty, nice, empty-headed little millionairess Baba Carstairs if a selfish brute like himself left her alone. He liked her very well, of course. But it would not have occurred to him to marry her if she had been poor.

It was at that moment that a corner of his eye was caught by something strange and bright in the cold night. It was a hand and arm alight with jewelry against the black background of the car.

"Can I drop you?" said a low voice.

Rudolf, who had been very well brought up, as regards superficial manners anyway, took off his hat to the brilliant arm, observing at the same time that the hand was slender and young and cool, like the voice.

"You are very kind," said he. "But I have only a short way to go."

"There is nothing to fear," said the cool voice.

The correct and incurious profile of the elderly chauffeur at the wheel betrayed nothing but the propriety of his employer. Rudolf, stepping closer to the open window, caught a glimpse of the lady's face within the shadows

—and was lightly touched by a faint perfume that reminded him so poignantly of a past enchantment that for an instant he walked again in a garden with a slight fair girl.

Telling himself that he was a fool, he swiftly opened the door and climbed within.

"Thank you," said the lady, "for being both brave and polite."

Prince Rudolf smiled. "I fancy it is neither courage nor politeness that inspires men to do what beautiful women ask them."

He found the lady examining him with the utmost gravity.

"Height, five-eleven," he said, "hair, black; eyes, brown; one small mole on left cheek; self-confident manner; no distinctive peculiarities. . . ."

Her faint smile did not touch the gravity of her eyes, of which he had already formed a very favorable opinion. They were direct and blue, of a brilliant darkness, like the blue sea whipped by wind. The lady's hair, too, was maybe as you like it, fair and curly, but without frivolity. Rudolf, experienced in petty encounters, saw at once that only some great urgency had forced this lady to address a stranger, for she could not be corrupted by small desires.

"And I?" she said.

He noticed, but without surprise, that the car was moving. It was agreeable to find that he was not so tired of the world as he had fancied he was.

"And I, sir?" she said. "How would you describe the stranger who has kidnapped you?"

"I like you," said Prince Rudolf.

"Dear me," said the lady, "you *are* quick."

"That's me all over," said Rudolf. "The minute I set eyes on you, I said to myself, there's a woman I like a lot."

"I hadn't any idea," said the lady, "that conversation with a stranger could be made so easy as you make it."

"You are not a stranger. I recognized you right away."

"Me? You recognized me?"

"Of course. You have never heard the old chestnut about the woman whom a man always meets too late?"

"Too late? Dear me, for what?"

"For his peace of mind, since she is usually already married."

"Since I am single, sir, your peace of mind is safe. But thank you for saying nice things about my appearance."

"Not only your appearance, madam. I have also taken a big liking to your character."

"Then you are a clairvoyant?"

"A connoisseur—a student of dreams."

"Dreams? Were we talking of dreams?"

"No, but we are going to. When men dream," said Prince Rudolf, "of that kind of happiness which is too often forbidden them owing to having married in haste, or some other silly reason, their dreams are inspired by thoughts of the perfect companion. It is not necessary to shut my eyes to describe her. She must be exquisite, of course, but without the trivial emphasis that merely smart women lay on the small fashions of the moment. Her beauty should wear a certain gravity, for does she not understand much and forgive everything, particularly the greed and the follies of men? She must be wise, naturally, but not too wise never to make a mistake, never to take a risk, never to sigh for romance, never to hurt herself. She will always do her utmost not to hurt anybody else, and at all difficult times she will take refuge in laughing at herself, for above everything she is gifted with the good manners of the heart."

"Dear me," she said, "I never knew that the dreams of men were so informed by kindness. Your reputation, Prince Rudolf, scarcely prepares a listener for such sentiments."

"Madam, in your company I had permitted myself for one moment to forget all but the little that is best in me. But now that you have reminded me of my ordinary self I must admit that I should like nothing so much as to kiss you and damn the consequences."

"That rebuke," she said, "was well deserved. For no one could have been more polite than you. You have not yet asked me how I knew you, where we are going, or who I am. I recognized you from your photographs. I followed you from the restaurant where you dined. We are going to my house, which is here in Belgrave Square. My name is no matter. And I am going to ask you, sir, to do me a service. You see, I make no excuses. My behavior is too outrageous for excuses to have any value. If you wish, you may say good night now, my car will take you home, and I shall be the richer for having enjoyed an instructive conversation with a man of the world."

Undeterred by her gravity, Rudolf laughed outright. For many months he had not felt so light-hearted.

"Miss X," said he, "it was you who spoke of my reputation. So, if you think you can get rid of me so easily, you're crazy."

Her level eyes searched his face. He was sobered by the profound contempt that seemed to add a dark light to their dark brilliance. He would have noticed this contempt before had he not been so engaged, as was his way, in trying to make an impression on a beautiful woman.

"You are afraid of nothing, Prince Rudolf?"

They were on the pavement now, before the house, and he glanced at the dark imposing building.

"Of a great many things," he said, "but of no possible hurt that could come to me from you."

"Perhaps," she said, "you are wrong there."

An elderly manservant let them in. Rudolf, divesting himself of his overcoat in the large hall, had time to realize the substantial wealth of his surroundings. From above the great fireplace, in which the ashes of a log fire glowed dimly, one of Van Dyck's cavaliers thoughtfully measured the world, while on another wall was the dark and sour visage of a Rembrandt.

Then he was shown into a long paneled library. It was dimly lit, and in front of the fireplace at the far end stood the strange lady and a tall, fair, red-complexioned bull of a man of about his own age.

"This is my brother," said the lady, "Mr. Geraldine. I am Iris Geraldine."

Mr. Geraldine's brick-red complexion sharpened by contrast the paleness of his cold blue eyes. He made no attempt to conceal the hostility with which he measured the faintly smiling face of his guest.

"So now you realize," he said, "why I told my sister not to give you her name, for had you known it you certainly would not have come."

"You misjudge me, Mr. Geraldine. For the sake of a woman like your sister I should willingly risk much more than a disagreeable encounter with a man like her brother. Now what is it you want with me?"

"Surely, Prince Rudolf, you can easily guess what I——"

"Wait," said Rudolf sharply. "Before we go any further you will be so good as to ask me to sit down. I thank you. Then you will invite me to have a drink. Thank you. I prefer brandy."

Mr. Geraldine's handsome brick-red face broke into a fighting grin. You could see at once that he had good hands with a horse, that dogs would come to his whistle, and that he could both give and take a kick in the pants.

"Iris," he turned to his sister, "perhaps you had better leave Prince Rudolf and me together."

Miss Geraldine had not yet glanced at her kidnapped guest. She sat, somewhat stiffly, in a high Queen Anne chair, her eyes lost in the leaping colors of the bright fire.

"I am here," said Prince Rudolf, "at Miss Geraldine's express invitation, and I am enjoying her company very much. I hope you will stay with us, Miss Geraldine. No doubt your brother is a splendid fellow, but he is not half so pretty to look at as you are."

She held her small head very still and erect, and he was conscious that she would much prefer to ignore his presence. She spoke to the fire, in her low cool voice, as though she was thinking out loud.

"I do not like," she said, "to see any man humiliated, no matter how much he may deserve it."

"I'll risk that," said Rudolf. "Go ahead, Mr. Geraldine. As you said, I know you are the chairman of the great and famous private bank of Geraldine Brothers, and that you are the trustee of the estate of Miss Carstairs."

"Not only her trustee, Prince, but also her late father's most intimate friend. She told me no later than this afternoon that she had made up her mind to marry you."

"She ought to have told me first," said Prince Rudolf, "but her decision makes me so happy that I must forgive her. Thank you for your congratulations, Mr. Geraldine."

"Hers is a great fortune," said Mr. Geraldine dryly.

"So my father has told me every day for weeks. He will be very pleased about this, as he has been so hard up lately. How agreeable it is to meet nice young girls like Miss Carstairs who think nothing of bringing a little sunshine into the lives of tired old men like my father. When I tell him tomorrow, he will be very touched."

"He won't," Mr. Geraldine said, "because you won't."

Prince Rudolf's attention appeared at that moment to be engaged in an exhaustive study of Iris Geraldine's profile, and that he thought very highly of it was obvious from his expression.

"I won't . . . what?" he said absently.

"You won't tell your father you are going to marry Miss Carstairs, Prince, because you are not going to."

"All complaints on that head," said Rudolf, "should be addressed to Miss Carstairs in person. It is her life. It is her money. It is to be her marriage. And I am her choice."

"A girl so young," said Mr. Geraldine, "does not always know what is best for her. I cannot forbid Baba to marry you, because she is of age. I can't persuade her not to by telling her that you, in spite of your great name, are a well-known waster and adventurer, that you are notorious both for your affairs with women and for your dexterity in getting your bills paid, because she dismisses all such facts as reflections on a misunderstood, handsome, and romantic prince."

"And quite right too. That ought to teach you, Mr. Geraldine, not to go about putting nasty thoughts into young girls' heads. Just because nobody has ever thought you romantic since you were a little boy in velvet pants, why be jealous of me?"

"I am never jealous," said Mr. Geraldine, "of a crook."

"Am I to understand, Mr. Geraldine, that you have just called me a crook?"

"You are. I have."

"In that case," said Prince Rudolf, rising from his chair, "I must have another brandy. You have interested me greatly, Mr. Geraldine. Won't you please develop your theory?"

"It is not a theory, Prince, but a fact. But I had much rather not elaborate it—and I won't, if you promise not to see Miss Carstairs again."

"But that would never do, Mr. Geraldine. The poor girl would be very upset. My poor father would be very disappointed. And my poor creditors would be very angry."

"Very well," said Mr. Geraldine grimly. "On the formal announcement of your engagement to Miss Carstairs I shall notify the proper authorities that I have in my possession a check drawn in your favor by a Mr. John Anderson and cashed by you, which I have every reason to suspect is a forgery."

"But why suspect?" said Prince Rudolf. "You know it's a forgery."

"So you admit forging Anderson's signature to a check for £1,000?"

Prince Rudolf glanced aside at Iris Geraldine—and instantly found, to his surprise and consternation, that something inside him was beating painfully. He could not immediately put this curious phenomenon down to a disturbance of his heart-action, since he had for some years regarded his heart as a leathery veteran, dingily and immovably fixed within a dark cloud of cigarette smoke. But he was a reasonable man and had to face the fact that here the old veteran was, thumping like a boy's just because a fair young woman with level eyes was regarding him gravely and impersonally, as a scientist might regard a maggot.

"Mr. Geraldine," he said at last, and his voice for the first time was without any mockery at all, "when John Anderson died last week, did you not, as his executor, find any note among his papers referring to me?"

"I did not."

"I think you did. I think you have that note in your possession. John Anderson was a gambler, and like nearly all gamblers he was a very honest man. Do you still say that he left no letter in his handwriting with reference to me?"

"I have already said so, Prince Rudolf."

"Then I should like to put it on record, Mr. Geraldine, that you are a liar. This may be due to the fact that you were badly brought up, but the fact remains that you are a liar. A year ago John Anderson bet me a hundred pounds that I could not forge his signature and get away with it without suspicion. It was to be for a check of a thousand pounds merely so that the signature should be scrutinized carefully at the bank. I succeeded, returned the thousand pounds in cash to Anderson, who gave me the bet I had won and also a receipt for the sum of the forged check. I have that receipt. Among his papers you have already found a letter signed by him telling the circumstances of the forged check."

"Prince Rudolf," said Mr. Geraldine, "of course I am very glad that you have John Anderson's receipt. When you come to be examined by the police on the matter of Anderson's forged signature that receipt will no doubt form the pivot of your defense. It might even win you acquittal, and probably will, but in the absence of any letter from John Anderson among his effects exonerating you of all blame, I am afraid that a great deal of doubt will exist in the public mind as to whether you are, or are not, a common swindler. I have not yet found that letter among Anderson's effects. If and when I do, I shall of course be delighted to let you know."

"Thank you very much, Mr. Geraldine. In return I can only say that if I was a cannibal I should simply have to drown you in Worcester sauce before being able to eat you. So I am to understand that unless I give up Miss Carstairs you will make it very unpleasant indeed for me?"

"I prefer to say, Prince, that unless you agree to give up this misguided girl, I shall have to do my best to show her what sort of a man you really are. As you know, by her father's will she comes into her estate on the day she marries. And she told me today that it was her fixed intention, as she is very rich and you are poor, to settle on you a very considerable sum of money which would ensure you a comfortable income for life."

"I wish," sighed Rudolf, "that my father could hear you say that. His enthusiasm would be quite touching."

"I fear he will be disappointed, Prince. But not to depress you both too much, and since after all you are being forced to give up a considerable fortune, I am prepared here and now to write you a check for £4,000. I shall send it to you on the day that Miss Carstairs tells me that she has decided not to marry you."

"Dear me," said Rudolf, "I see that I must have another brandy. Thank you, Mr. Geraldine. Your brandy is superb. Did you say four thousand pounds?"

"I did—merely, you understand, as a small consolation——"

"Nonsense, my dear fellow—it's a big consolation. After all, are there many men whose charms could be valued at four thousand pounds? I fear you are a flatterer, Mr. Geraldine."

The banker's handsome red face was, for a man making a contemptuous offer, curiously eager, and Rudolf regarded him thoughtfully.

"Then you accept, Prince? You will agree to leave Miss Carstairs alone?"

But Rudolf's attention appeared now to be engaged in yet another careful examination of Miss Geraldine's cold profile.

"I note with regret," he said, "that Miss Geraldine's disapproval of me has increased to such an extent that, were she not a lady, she would express it in such old-fashioned terms as swindler, gigolo, and cad."

"Cad," said Iris Geraldine, "is an unpleasant word. But very descriptive. I should prefer you, Prince, to address yourself only to my brother. I am here merely as a witness to a business arrangement."

"Not at all," said Rudolf, with sudden sharpness. "It is a romantic ar-rangement."

Astonished, they stared at him. He was smiling in his saturnine way. Mr. Geraldine glanced at his sister, and laughed. It was the kind of laugh for which a small chap would have been knocked down, but he was a bull of a man.

"These fellows," said he, "can make anything seem romantic."

"What fellows, Mr. Geraldine?"

"Romantic fellows, Prince—romantic wasters."

"Well, I can promise you that your sister will find what I am going to say a good deal more romantic than you will. I am going to tell you a story."

"Not to me," said Miss Geraldine with spirit. "I am going to bed."

"This story, Miss Geraldine," said Rudolf slowly, "is about your sister."

They stared at him across an appalled silence. But his dark eyes saw only Iris Geraldine's still white face, at last turned full to his.

"You knew her?" she sighed.

"But for her," said Prince Rudolf, "I should not be here tonight."

"Fantastic nonsense!" said Geraldine harshly. "Diana died more than ten years ago."

"Ten years, three months and five days ago, my friend. I came into your car, Miss Geraldine, only because I recognized the faint scent you are wearing. It is made by an obscure perfumer in Paris, and I gave her first bottle to Diana. Then for sentimental reasons I paid my friend Louvois, the perfumer, enough money to buy the rights of the scent outright—that is, so that no one but Diana Geraldine should ever use it. I was a rich man then, you understand. Louvois, for as long as he was in business, was to send her one bottle every six months at this address.

"A year or so after she was killed in that motor accident near Fontainbleau, Louvois wrote to me enclosing a letter that he had received from England. The letter was from a girls' school near Ascot, and was written by a schoolgirl to the effect that the duty-paid scent from Paris which had been delivered to Miss Geraldine was obviously for her elder sister, who was dead, but could it please go on being sent to the address in Belgrave Square so that she could use it when she was grown up in memory of her dear sister, and it was signed 'Iris Geraldine.'

"So you will see why I so willingly came with you when you invited me. I told you, didn't I, that you weren't a stranger?"

"Diana," said Iris Geraldine, so dimly that she was scarcely audible, "was the loveliest elder sister a little girl could have. I was fourteen when she died, and as our father and mother had died so long before, she was everything in the world—all heroines in one—to me. And so I clung to the sweet dry perfume which, so she once told her little sister, a fairytale prince had given her to use forever and ever."

"Well," said Mr. Geraldine bitterly, "there's damn little of the fairytale about the Prince now."

Rudolf smiled. "That's true enough, dear me. But you must remember I was only twenty-three then—and Diana was twenty. Young people, Mr. Geraldine, are sometimes very serious indeed about such trivialities as being in love."

"Now that you have hurt Iris," said her brother harshly, "by bringing up memories of her sister, may I ask what was your point in doing so?"

"He has not hurt me," said Iris. Her eyes were hidden. Her voice came from behind an invisible curtain. "You didn't intend to, did you, Prince?"

"Indirectly, my dear, I fear I must—that is, through this brother of yours. Mr. Geraldine, I told you about Diana because she used to speak of you, her elder brother and the head of the family. You will no doubt already have remarked that I don't like you. This is not due wholly to your manner, which would make an unfavorable impression even on a drunken sailor. It is because Diana did not like you, as you of course know.

"That you are a bully goes without saying. But being a bully is not a crime—indeed it is sometimes an asset. One moment, Mr. Geraldine. I know also that in spite of your very respectable front as a great banker, you are an unscrupulous speculator. Diana—aged twenty to your twenty-five— guessed your true character.

"Now I am going to make the deduction that as Miss Carstairs's trustee you have gambled with part of her funds and that in the recent Wall Street crash you have lost heavily. Wait. On her marriage you will have to show her accounts to her lawyers, with the result that you will find yourself in the dock. That is why you do not want her to marry until you can regain your losses.

"This is all guesswork, you will say, and no doubt you will tell me I am wrong. But on one point I can ease your mind. I am not going to marry Miss Carstairs.

"That is not because I wish to save you, but because I have fallen in love tonight for the second time in my life, though I fear the lady does not approve of me at all. I can only hope to win her approval in time.

"But that is another story. Tomorrow I shall advise Miss Carstairs to ask her lawyers to look into——"

Mr. Geraldine chewed his cigar. His cold eyes were thoughtful, but there was a grin on his handsome red face. This grin had no doubt been put there by an ancestor who had been caught red-handed while committing robbery under arms and had known that the game was over.

"Iris," he said, "somebody ought to have warned me about the intelligence of princes. I begin to see now how even the shrewdest bankers have been persuaded to lend them money."

"My father, Mr. Geraldine, who has had more than sixty years' experience of owing money to the shrewdest bankers in London and New York, says that times are not what they were."

Mr. Geraldine smiled across at him. His eyes were cold and watchful.

"Prince Rudolf, I shall not like standing in the dock charged with having misappropriated my client's funds."

Rudolf nodded sympathetically. "Nor should I. Taking other people's money is nice work, if you can get away with it. Given a bad character— like yours and my father's—it's all a matter of luck."

"Then I am sorry that you are not your father, Prince. If you were, I should offer you £10,000 at the end of six months merely for keeping your mouth shut during that time. But as you are not, I fear I shall have to do something drastic, like shooting myself. But I don't like the idea at all."

Rudolf nodded sympathetically. "Yes, there is a degree of emphasis about suicide which is always disagreeable to a thoughtful mind. I shouldn't commit suicide, Mr. Geraldine. It will probably embarrass more people than it will please."

"But, my dear Prince, what else can I do? Miss Carstairs has never liked me, anyway. And when tomorrow you tell her of your suspicions, she will be only too eager to consult her lawyers."

Rudolf turned to Miss Geraldine. "What do you think of all this, Iris?"

"I think," she said very gravely, "that my brother has been playing with fire for a long time and that he has at last burned his hands. I think that tonight will mark a change for the better in him."

"Then you don't think he will shoot himself?"

She smiled unsteadily. "You are a pair of cruel babies, aren't you?"

"Mr. Geraldine," said Rudolf, "did you hear that? You are a cruel baby."

"You too," said Mr. Geraldine. "Have another brandy."

"Thank you. Then, Iris, you think I ought not to tell Miss Carstairs?"

"I can promise you," said Geraldine, "that her capital will be intact within six months. Also many innocent people will suffer loss if this comes to a head now. Later on, they won't."

"But I am lunching with the girl tomorrow," said Prince Rudolf, "and I might possibly blurt out something."

"You can put off the lunch," said Iris coldly.

"But I hate lunching alone, Iris. Here is an idea. Will you lunch with me?"

"I am already engaged."

Rudolf turned to Geraldine. "There you are, my friend. I've done my best. She doesn't like me. She won't lunch with me. I fear you will have to commit suicide, after all."

"Nonsense, Iris," said her brother. "Of course you can lunch with him."

"But I don't want to," said Iris.

"She doesn't like me," said Rudolf helplessly. "Give it up, Geraldine."

"I do like you," said Iris stormily. "It's only that you talk such nonsense so plausibly that I daren't trust myself alone with you."

"That's splendid," said Rudolf. "Unfortunately, we shall be lunching in a public place, and I shan't be able to do very much."

"But you can always talk," said Iris.

"I shall. I shall propose marriage."

"I shall refuse."

"Naturally. Then I shall point out that you lack foresight. For if you had foresight you would know that it is sheer waste of time to go on refusing a man whom you are going to accept in the end."

"Very well," said Iris, "I lack foresight."

"Mr. Geraldine," said Prince Rudolf, "we have been forgetting my father. Some time ago you called me a crook——"

"That was politics, Prince. Anderson had told me the real story."

"Politics cost money, Mr. Geraldine. In payment for your politics you will be so good as to earn my father's undying gratitude by sending him tomorrow the sum of £4,000 in notes from an Anonymous Admirer. This gift will give him great pleasure both financially and morally, since he has never had any admirers, anonymous or otherwise. Good night, Mr. Geraldine. Your servant, Iris. I shall call for you at one tomorrow."

The two men shook hands. This was a quiet and thoughtful ceremony, which they appeared to enjoy.

Iris, with a sudden high color, walked to the door and out into the hall. Prince Rudolf found her there, and she walked with him towards the front hall. Very lightly she touched his arm.

"Thank you for not ruining my brother. That was because of Diana?"

"Because of Diana and Iris," he said. "Because of enchantment and gentleness. Because I am a lucky man to have found out tonight that, even in this world, they never die."

He stooped to kiss her hand, and as he did so a flutter of lips just touched his forehead.

"Dear me," she whispered, "who would have thought you were such a darling!"

A STUDY IN WHITE

by NICHOLAS BLAKE

"Seasonable weather for the time of year," remarked the Expansive Man in a voice succulent as the breast of a roast goose.

The Deep Chap, sitting next to him in the railway compartment, glanced out at the snow, swarming and swirling past the windowpane. He replied:

"You really like it? Oh, well, it's an ill blizzard that blows nobody no good. Depends what you mean by seasonable, though. Statistics for the last fifty years would show——"

"Name of Joad, sir?" asked the Expansive Man, treating the compartment to a wholesale wink.

"No, Stansfield, Henry Stansfield." The Deep Chap, a ruddy-faced man who sat with hands firmly planted on the knees of his brown tweed suit, might have been a prosperous farmer but for the long, steady, meditative scrutiny which he now bent upon each of his fellow travelers in turn.

What he saw was not particularly rewarding. On the opposite seat, from left to right, were a Forward Piece, who had taken the Expansive Man's wink wholly to herself and contrived to wriggle her tight skirt farther up from her knee; a dessicated, sandy, lawyerish little man who fumed and fussed like an angry kettle, consulting every five minutes his gold watch, then shaking out his *Times* with the crackle of a legal parchment; and a Flash Card, dressed up to the nines of spivdom, with the bold yet uneasy stare of the young delinquent.

"Mine's Percy Dukes," said the Expansive Man. "P.D. to my friends. General Dealer. At your service. Well, we'll be across the border in an hour and a half, and then hey for the bluebells of bonny Scotland!"

"Bluebells in January? You're hopeful," remarked the Forward Piece.

"Are you Scots, master?" asked the Comfortable Body sitting on Stansfield's left.

"English outside"—Percy Dukes patted the front of his gray suit, slid a flask from its hip pocket, and took a swig—"and Scotch within." His loud laugh, or the blizzard, shook the railway carriage. The Forward Piece giggled.

"You'll need that if we run into a drift and get stuck for the night," said Henry Stansfield.

"Name of Jonah, sir?" The compartment reverberated again.

"I do not apprehend such an eventuality," said the Fusspot. "The station-master at Lancaster assured me that the train would get through. We are scandalously late already, though." Once again the gold watch was consulted.

"It's a curious thing," remarked the Deep Chap meditatively, "the way we imagine we can make Time amble withal or gallop withal, just by keeping an eye on the hands of a watch. You travel frequently by this train, Mr.——?"

"Kilmington. Arthur J. Kilmington. No, I've only used it once before." The Fusspot spoke in a dry Edinburgh accent.

"Ah, yes, that would have been on the 17th of last month. I remember seeing you on it."

"No, sir, you are mistaken. It was the 20th." Mr. Kilmington's thin mouth snapped tight again, like a rubber band round a sheaf of legal documents.

"The 20th? Indeed? That was the day of the train robbery. A big haul they got, it seems. Off this very train. It was carrying some of the extra Christmas mail. Bags just disappeared, somewhere between Lancaster and Carlisle."

"Och, deary me," sighed the Comfortable Body. "I don't know what we're coming to, really, nowadays."

"We're coming to the scene of the crime, ma'am," said the expansive Mr. Dukes. The train, almost deadbeat, was panting up the last pitch towards Shap Summit.

"I didn't see anything in the papers about where the robbery took place," Henry Stansfield murmured. Dukes fastened a somewhat bleary eye upon him.

"You read all the newspapers?"

"Yes."

The atmosphere in the compartment had grown suddenly tense. Only the Flash Card, idly examining his fingernails, seemed unaffected by it.

"Which paper did you see it in?" pursued Stansfield.

"I didn't." Dukes tapped Stansfield on the knee. "But I can use my loaf. Stands to reason. You want to tip a mailbag out of a train—get me? Train must be moving slowly, or the bag'll burst when it hits the ground. Only one place between Lancaster and Carlisle where you'd *know* the train would be crawling. Shap Bank. And it goes slowest on the last bit of the bank, just about where we are now. Follow?"

Henry Stansfield nodded.

"O.K. But you'd be balmy to tip it off just anywhere on this Godforsaken moorland," went on Mr. Dukes. "Now, if you'd traveled this line as much as I have, you'd have noticed it goes over a bridge about a mile short of the summit. Under the bridge runs a road: a nice, lonely road, see? The only road hereabouts that touches the railway. You tip out the bag there. Your chums collect it, run down the embankment, dump it in the car they've got waiting by the bridge, and Bob's your uncle!"

"You oughta been a detective, mister," exclaimed the Forward Piece languishingly.

Mr. Dukes inserted his thumbs in his armpits, looking gratified. "Maybe I am," he said with a wheezy laugh. "And maybe I'm just little old P.D., who knows how to use his loaf."

"Och, well now, the things people will do?" said the Comfortable Body. "There's a terrible lot of dishonesty today."

The Flash Card glanced up contemptuously from his fingernails. Mr. Kilmington was heard to mutter that the system of surveillance on railways was disgraceful, and the Guard of the train should have been severely censured.

"The Guard can't be everywhere," said Stansfield. "Presumably he has to patrol the train from time to time, and——"

"Let him do so, then, and not lock himself up in his van and go to sleep," interrupted Mr. Kilmington, somewhat unreasonably.

"Are you speaking from personal experience, sir?" asked Stansfield.

The Flash Card lifted up his voice and said, in a Charing-Cross-Road American accent, "Hey, fellas! If the gang was gonna tip out the mailbags by the bridge, like this guy says—what I mean is, how could they rely on the Guard being out of his van just at that point?" He hitched up the trousers of his loud check suit.

"You've got something there," said Percy Dukes. "What I reckon is, there must have been two accomplices on the train—one to get the Guard out of his van on some pretext, and the other to chuck off the bags." He turned to Mr. Kilmington. "You were saying something about the Guard locking himself up in his van. Now if I was of a suspicious turn of mind, if I was little old Sherlock H. in person"—he bestowed another prodigious wink upon Kilmington's fellow-travelers—"I'd begin to wonder about you, sir. You were traveling on this train when the robbery took place. You went to the Guard's van. You *say* you found him asleep. You didn't by any chance call the Guard out, so as to——?"

"Your suggestion is outrageous! I advise you to be very careful, sir, very careful indeed," enunciated Mr. Kilmington, his precise voice crackling with indignation, "or you may find you have said something actionable. I would have you know that, when I——"

But what he would have them know was to remain undivulged. The train, which for some little time had been running cautiously down from

Shap Summit, suddenly began to chatter and shudder, like a fever patient in high delirium, as the vacuum brakes were applied: then, with the dull impact of a fist driving into a feather pillow, the engine buried itself in a drift which had gathered just beyond the bend of a deep cutting.

It was just five minutes past seven.

"What's this?" asked the Forward Piece, rather shrilly, as a hysterical outburst of huffing and puffing came from the engine.

"Run into a drift, I reckon."

"He's trying to back us out. No good. The wheels are slipping every time. What a lark!" Percy Dukes had his head out of the window on the lee side of the train. "Coom to Coomberland for your winter sports!"

"Guard! Guard, I say!" called Mr. Kilmington. But the blue-clad figure, after one glance into the compartment, hurried on his way up the corridor. "Really! I *shall* report that man."

Henry Stansfield, going out into the corridor, opened a window. Though the coach was theoretically sheltered by the cutting on this windward side, the blizzard stunned his face like a knuckleduster of ice. He joined the herd of passengers who had climbed down and were stumbling towards the engine. As they reached it, the Guard emerged from the cab: no cause for alarm, he said; if they couldn't get through, there'd be a relief engine sent down to take the train back to Penrith; he was just off to set fog-signals on the line behind them.

The driver renewed his attempts to back the train out. But what with its weight, the up-gradient in its rear, the icy rails, and the clinging grip of the drift on the engine, he could not budge her.

"We'll have to dig out the bogeys, mate," he said to his fireman. "Fetch them shovels from the forward van. It'll keep the perishers from freezing, anyhow." He jerked his finger at the knot of passengers who, lit up by the glare of the furnace, were capering and beating their arms like savages amid the swirling snow-wreaths.

Percy Dukes, who had now joined them, quickly established himself as the life and soul of the party, referring to the grimy-faced fireman as "Snowball," adjuring his companions to "Dig for Victory," affecting to spy the approach of a herd of St. Bernards, each with a keg of brandy slung round its neck. But after ten minutes of hard digging, when the leading wheels of the bogey were cleared, it could be seen that they had been derailed by their impact with the drift.

"That's torn it, Charlie. You'll have to walk back to the box and get 'em to telephone through for help," said the driver.

"*If* the wires aren't down already," replied the fireman lugubriously. "It's above a mile to that box, and uphill. Who d'you think I am. Captain Scott?"

"You'll have the wind behind you, mate, anyhow. So long."

A buzz of dismay had risen from the passengers at this. One or two, who began to get querulous, were silenced by the driver's offering to take them anywhere they liked if they would just lift his engine back onto the metals first. When the rest had dispersed to their carriages, Henry Stansfield asked the driver's permission to go up into the cab for a few minutes and dry his coat.

"You're welcome." The driver snorted: "Would you believe it? 'Must get to Glasgow tonight.' Damn ridiculous! Now Bert—that's my Guard—it's different for him: he's entitled to fret a bit. Missus been very poorly. Thought she was going to peg out before Christmas; but he got the best surgeon in Glasgow to operate on her, and she's mending now, he says. He reckons to look in every night at the nursing home, when he goes off work."

Stansfield chatted with the man for five minutes. Then the Guard returned, blowing upon his hands—a smallish, leathery-faced chap, with an anxious look in his eye.

"We'll not get through tonight, Bert. Charlie told you?"

"Aye. I doubt some of the passengers are going to create a rumpus," said the Guard dolefully.

Henry Stansfield went back to his compartment. It was stuffy, but with a sinister hint of chilliness, too: he wondered how long the steam heating would last: depended upon the amount of water in the engine boiler, he supposed. Among the wide variety of fates he had imagined for himself, freezing to death in an English train was not included.

Arthur J. Kilmington fidgeted more than ever. When the Guard came along the corridor, he asked him where the nearest village was, saying he must get a telephone call through to Edinburgh—most urgent appointment —must let his client know, if he was going to miss it. The Guard said there was a village two miles to the northeast; you could see the lights from the top of the cutting; but he warned Mr. Kilmington against trying to get there in the teeth of this blizzard—better wait for the relief engine, which should reach them before 9 p.m.

Silence fell upon the compartment for a while; the incredulous silence of civilized people who find themselves in the predicament of castaways. Then the expansive Mr. Dukes proposed that, since they were to be stuck here for an hour or two, they should get acquainted. The Comfortable Body now introduced herself as Mrs. Grant, the Forward Piece as Inez Blake; the Flash Card, with the overnegligent air of one handing a dud half-crown over a counter, gave his name as Macdonald—I. Macdonald.

The talk reverted to the train robbery and the criminals who had perpetrated it.

"They must be awfu' clever," remarked Mrs. Grant, in her singsong Lowland accent.

"No criminals are clever, ma'am," said Stansfield quietly. His ruminative eye passed, without haste, from Macdonald to Dukes. "Neither the small fry nor the big operators. They're pretty well subhuman, the whole lot of 'em. A dash of cunning, a thick streak of cowardice, and the rest is made up of stupidity and boastfulness. They're too stupid for anything but crime, and so riddled with inferiority that they always give themselves away, sooner or later, by boasting about their crimes. They like to think of themselves as the wide boys, but they're as narrow as starved eels—why, they haven't even the wits to alter their professional methods: that's how the police pick 'em up."

"I entirely agree, sir," Mr. Kilmington snapped. "In my profession I see a good deal of the criminal classes. And I flatter myself none of them has ever got the better of me. They're transparent, sir, transparent."

"No doubt you gentlemen are right," said Percy Dukes comfortably. "But the police haven't picked up the chaps who did this train robbery yet."

"They will. And the Countess of Axminister's emerald bracelet. Bet the gang didn't reckon to find that in the mailbag. Worth all of £25,000."

Percy Dukes' mouth fell open. The Flash Card whistled. Overcome, either by the stuffiness of the carriage or the thought of £25,000-worth of emeralds, Inez Blake gave a little moan and fainted all over Mr. Kilmington's lap.

"Really! Upon my soul! My dear young lady!" exclaimed that worthy. There was a flutter of solicitude, shared by all except the cold-eyed young Macdonald who, after stooping over her a moment, his back to the others, said, "Here you—stop pawing the young lady and let her stretch out on the seat. Yes, I'm talking to you, Kilmington."

"How dare you! This is an outrage!" The little man stood up so abruptly that the girl was almost rolled onto the floor. "I was merely trying to—"

"I know your sort. Nasty old men. Now, keep your hands off her. I'm telling you."

In the shocked silence that ensued, Kilmington gobbled speechlessly at Macdonald for a moment; then, seeing razors in the youth's cold-steel eye, snatched his black hat and briefcase from the rack and bolted out of the compartment. Henry Stansfield made as if to stop him, then changed his mind. Mrs. Grant followed the little man out, returning presently, her handkerchief soaked in water, to dab Miss Blake's forehead. The time was just 8:30.

When things were restored to normal, Mr. Dukes turned to Stansfield. "You were saying this necklace of—who was it?—the Countess of Axminster, it's worth £25,000? Fancy sending a thing of that value through the post! Are you sure of it?"

"The value? Oh, yes." Henry Stansfield spoke out of the corner of his mouth, in the manner of a stupid man imparting a confidence. "Don't let this go any further. But I've a friend who works in the Cosmopolitan—the company where it's insured. That's another thing that didn't get into the papers. Silly woman. She wanted it for some big family-do in Scotland at Christmas, forgot to bring it with her, and wrote home for it to be posted to her in a registered packet."

"£25,000," said Percy Dukes thoughtfully. "Well, stone me down!"

"Yes. Some people don't know when they're lucky, do they?"

Duke's fat face wobbled on his shoulders like a globe of lard. Young Macdonald polished his nails. Inez Blake read her magazine. After a while Percy Dukes remarked that the blizzard was slackening; he'd take an airing and see if there was any sign of the relief engine yet. He left the compartment.

At the window the snowflakes danced in their tens now, not their thousands. The time was 8:55. Shortly afterwards Inez Blake went out; and ten minutes later Mrs. Grant remarked to Stansfield that it had stopped snowing altogether. Neither Inez nor Dukes had returned when, at 9:30, Henry Stansfield decided to ask what had happened about the relief. The Guard was not in his van, which adjoined Stansfield's coach, towards the rear of the train. So he turned back, walked up the corridor to the front coach, clambered out, and hailed the engine cab.

"She must have been held up," said the Guard, leaning out. "Charlie here got through from the box, and they promised her by nine o'clock. But it'll no' be long now, sir."

"Have you seen anything of a Mr. Kilmington—small, sandy chap— black hat and overcoat, blue suit—was in my compartment? I've walked right up the train and he doesn't seem to be on it."

The Guard pondered a moment. "Och aye, you wee fellow? Him that asked me about telephoning from the village. Aye, he's awa' then."

"He did set off to walk there, you mean?"

"Nae doot he did, if he's no' on the train. He spoke to me again—juist on nine, it'd be—and said he was awa' if the relief didna turn up in five minutes."

"You've not seen him since?"

"No, sir. I've been talking to my mates here this half-hour, ever syne the wee fellow spoke to me."

Henry Stansfield walked thoughtfully back down the permanent way. When he had passed out of the glare shed by the carriage lights on the snow, he switched on his electric torch. Just beyond the last coach the eastern wall of the cutting sloped sharply down and merged into moorland level with the track. Although the snow had stopped altogether, an icy wind from the northeast still blew, raking and numbing his face. Twenty yards farther on his torch lit up a track, already half filled in with snow, made by several pairs of feet, pointing away over the moor, towards the northeast. Several passengers, it seemed, had set off for the village, whose lights twinkled like frost in the far distance. Stansfield was about to follow this track when he heard footsteps scrunching the snow farther up the line. He switched off the torch; at once it was as if a sack had been thrown over his head, so close and blinding was the darkness. The steps came nearer. Stansfield switched on his torch, at the last minute, pinpointing the squat figure of Percy Dukes. The man gave a muffled oath.

"What the devil! Here, what's the idea, keeping me waiting half an hour in that blasted——?"

"Have you seen Kilmington?"

"Oh, it's you. No, how the hell should I have seen him? Isn't he on the train? I've just been walking up the line, to look for the relief. No sign yet. Damn parky, it is—I'm moving on."

Presently Stansfield moved on, too, but along the track towards the village. The circle of his torchlight wavered and bounced on the deep snow. The wind, right in his teeth, was killing. No wonder, he thought, as after a few hundred yards he approached the end of the trail, those passengers turned back. Then he realized they had not all turned back. What he had supposed to be a hummock of snow bearing a crude resemblance to a recumbent human figure, he now saw to be a human figure covered with snow. He scraped some of the snow off it, turned it gently over on its back.

Arthur J. Kilmington would fuss no more in this world. His briefcase was buried beneath him: his black hat was lying where it had fallen, lightly covered with snow, near the head. There seemed, to Stansfield's cursory examination, no mark of violence on him. But the eyeballs stared, the face was suffused with a pinkish-blue color. So men look who have been strangled, thought Stansfield, or asphyxiated. Quickly he knelt down again, shining his torch in the dead face. A qualm of horror shook him. Mr. Kilmington's nostrils were caked thick with snow, which had frozen solid in them, and snow had been rammed tight into his mouth also.

And here he would have stayed, reflected Stansfield, in this desolate spot, for days or weeks, perhaps, if the snow lay or deepened. And when the thaw at last came (as it did that year, in fact, only after two months), the snow would thaw out from his mouth and nostrils, too, and there would be no vestige of murder left—only the corpse of an impatient little lawyer who had tried to walk to the village in a blizzard and died for his pains. It might even be that no one would ask how such a precise, pernickety little chap had ventured the two-mile walk in these shoes and without a torch to light his way through the pitchy blackness; for Stansfield, going through the man's pockets, had found the following articles—and nothing more: pocketbook, fountain pen, handkerchief, cigarette case, gold lighter, two letters, and some loose change.

Stansfield started to return for help. But only twenty yards back he noticed another trail of footprints, leading off the main track to the left. This trail seemed a fresher one—the snow lay less thickly in the indentations—and to have been made by one pair of feet only. He followed it up, walking beside it. Whoever made this track had walked in a slight right-handed curve back to the railway line, joining it about one hundred and fifty yards up the line from where the main trail came out. At this point there was a platelayers' shack. Finding the door unlocked, Stansfield entered. There was nothing inside but a coke-brazier, stone cold, and a smell of cigar smoke. . . .

Half an hour later, Stansfield returned to his compartment. In the meanwhile, he had helped the train crew to carry back the body of Kilmington, which was now locked in the Guard's van. He had also made an interesting discovery as to Kilmington's movements. It was to be presumed that, after the altercation with Macdonald, and the brief conversation already reported by the Guard, the lawyer must have gone to sit in another compartment. The last coach, to the rear of the Guard's van, was a first-class one, almost empty. But in one of its compartments Stansfield found a passenger asleep. He woke him up, gave a description of Kilmington, and asked if he had seen him earlier.

The passenger grumpily informed Stansfield that a smallish man, in a dark overcoat, with the trousers of a blue suit showing beneath it, had come to the door and had a word with him. No, the passenger had not noticed his face particularly, because he'd been very drowsy himself, and besides, the chap had politely taken off his black Homburg hat to address him, and the hat screened as much of the head as was not cut off from his view by the top of the door. No, the chap had not come into his compartment: he had just stood outside, inquired the time (the passenger had looked at his watch and told him it was 8:50); then the chap had said that, if the relief didn't turn up by nine, he intended to walk to the nearest village.

Stansfield had then walked along to the engine cab. The Guard, whom he found there, told him that he'd gone up the track about 8:45 to meet the fireman on his way back from the signal-box. He had gone as far as the place where he'd put down his fog-signals earlier; here, just before nine, he and the fireman met, as the latter corroborated. Returning to the train, the Guard had climbed into the last coach, noticed Kilmington sitting alone in a first-class apartment (it was then that the lawyer announced to the Guard his intention of walking if the relief engine had not arrived within five minutes). The Guard then got out of the train again, and proceeded down the track to talk to his mates in the engine cab.

This evidence would seem to point incontrovertibly at Kilmington's having been murdered shortly after 9 p.m., Stansfield reflected as he went back to his own compartment. His fellow passengers were all present now.

"Well, did you find him?" asked Percy Dukes.

"Kilmington? Oh, yes, I found him. In the snow over there. He was dead."

Inez Blake gave a little, affected scream. The permanent sneer was wiped, as if by magic, off young Macdonald's face, which turned a sickly white. Mr. Dukes sucked in his fat lips.

"The puir wee man," said Mrs. Grant. "He tried to walk it then? Died of exposure, was it?"

"No," announced Stansfield flatly, "he was murdered."

This time, Inez Blake screamed in earnest; and, like an echo, a hooting shriek came from far up the line: the relief engine was approaching at last.

"The police will be awaiting us back at Penrith, so we'd better all have our stories ready." Stansfield turned to Percy Dukes. "You, for instance, sir. Where were you between 8:55, when you left the carriage, and 9:35 when I met you returning? Are you sure you didn't see Kilmington?"

Dukes, expansive no longer, his piggy eyes sunk deep in the fat of his face, asked Stansfield who the hell he thought he was.

"I am an inquiry agent, employed by the Cosmopolitan Insurance Company. Before that, I was a Detective Inspector in the C.I.D. Here is my card."

Dukes barely glanced at it. "That's all right, old man. Only wanted to make sure. Can't trust anyone nowadays." His voice had taken on the ingratiating, oleaginous heartiness of the small businessman trying to clinch a deal with a bigger one. "Just went for a stroll, y'know—stretch the old legs. Didn't see a soul."

"Who were you expecting to see? Didn't you wait for someone in the platelayers' shack along there, and smoke a cigar while you were waiting? Who did you mistake me for when you said, 'What's the idea, keeping me waiting half an hour?'"

"Here, draw it mild, old man." Percy Dukes sounded injured. "I certainly looked in at the huts: smoked a cigar for a bit. Then I toddled back to the train, and met up with your good self on the way. I didn't make no appointment to meet—"

"Oo! Well I *must* say," interrupted Miss Blake virtuously. She could hardly wait to tell Stansfield that, on leaving the compartment shortly after Dukes, she'd overheard voices on the track below the lavatory window. "I recognized this gentleman's voice," she went on, tossing her head at Dukes. "He said something like: 'You're going to help us again, chum, so you'd better get used to the idea. You're in it up to the neck—can't back out now.' And another voice, sort of mumbling, might have been Mr. Kilmington's—I dunno—sounded Scotch anyway—said, 'All right. Meet you in five minutes: platelayers' hut a few hundred yards up the line. Talk it over.'"

"And what did you do then, young lady?" asked Stansfield.

"I happened to meet a gentleman friend, farther up the train, and sat with him for a bit."

"Is that so?" remarked Macdonald menacingly. "Why, you four-flushing little—!"

"Shut up!" commanded Stansfield.

"Honest I did," the girl said, ignoring Macdonald. "I'll introduce you to him, if you like. He'll tell you I was with him for, oh, half an hour or more."

"And what about Mr. Macdonald?"

"I'm not talking," said the youth sullenly.

"Mr. Macdonald isn't talking. Mrs. Grant?"

"I've been in this compartment ever since, sir."

"Ever since—?"

"Since I went out to damp my hankie for this young lady, when she'd fainted. Mr. Kilmington was just before me, you'll mind. I saw him go through into the Guard's van."

"Did you hear him say anything about walking to the village?"

"No, sir. He just hurried into the van, and then there was some havers about its no' being lockit this time, and how he was going to report the Guard for it."

"I see. And you've been sitting here with Mr. Macdonald all the time?"

"Yes, sir. Except for ten minutes or so he was out of the compartment, just after you'd left."

"What did you go out for?" Stansfield asked the young man.

"Just taking the air, brother."

"You weren't taking Mr. Kilmington's gold watch, as well as the air, by any chance?" Stansfield's keen eyes were fastened like a hook into Macdonald's, whose insolent expression visibly crumbled beneath them.

"I don't know what you mean," he tried to bluster. "You can't do this to me."

"I mean that a man has been murdered, and when the police search you, they will find his gold watch in your possession. Won't look too healthy for you, my young friend."

"Naow! Give us a chance! It was only a joke, see?" The wretched Macdonald was whining now, in his native cockney. "He got me riled— the stuck-up way he said nobody'd ever got the better of him. So I thought I'd just show him—I'd have given it back, straight I would, only I couldn't find him afterwards. It was just a joke, I tell you. Anyway, it was Inez who lifted the ticker."

"You dirty little rotter!" screeched the girl.

"Shut up, both of you. You can explain your joke to the Penrith police. Let's hope they don't die of laughing."

At this moment the train gave a lurch, and started back up the gradient. It halted at the signal-box, for Stansfield to telephone to Penrith, then clattered south again.

On Penrith platform Stansfield was met by an Inspector and a Sergeant of the County Constabulary, with the Police Surgeon. Then, after a brief pause in the Guard's van, where the Police Surgeon drew aside the Guard's black off-duty overcoat that had been laid over the body, and began his preliminary examination, they marched along to Stansfield's compartment. The Guard who, at his request, had locked this as the train was drawing up at the platform and was keeping an eye on its occupants, now unlocked it. The Inspector entered.

His first action was to search Macdonald. Finding the watch concealed on his person, he then charged Macdonald and Inez Blake with the theft. The Inspector next proceeded to make an arrest on the charge of wilful murder. . . .

Whom did the Inspector arrest for the murder of Arthur J. Kilmington?

You have been given no less than eight clues by the author; these eight clues should tell you, by logical deduction, not only the identity of the murderer but also the motive of the crime and the method by which it was committed.

Thus, Nicholas Blake returns to the great 'tec tradition, the pure, unadulterated detective story—the great 'tec tradition of Poe, Gaboriau, Collins, Doyle, Zangwill, Futrelle, Freeman, Chesterton, Post, Bramah, Crofts, Christie, Bailey, Sayers, MacDonald, Berkeley, Biggers, Van Dine, Allingham, Hammett, Carr, Simenon, Gardner, Stout, and so many others. And thus, his story, in the great tradition of 'tec titles, might have been called: "A Study in White; or, The Sign of Eight."

We urge you to accept the author's challenge before going further, and when you have interpreted the eight clues compare your solution with Mr. Blake's.

Solution to

A STUDY IN WHITE

by NICHOLAS BLAKE

The Inspector arrested the Guard for the wilful murder of Arthur J. Kilmington.

Kilmington's pocket had been picked by Inez Blake, when she pretended to faint at 8:25, and his gold watch was at once passed by her to her accomplice, Macdonald. Now Kilmington was constantly consulting his watch. It is inconceivable, if he was not killed till after 9 p.m., that he should not have missed the watch and made a scene. This point was clinched by the first-class passenger who had said that a man, answering to the description of Kilmington, had asked him the time at 8:50: if it had really been Kilmington, he would certainly, before inquiring the time of anyone else, have first tried to consult his own watch, found it gone, and reported the theft. The fact that Kilmington neither reported the loss to the Guard, nor returned to his original compartment to look for the watch, proves he must have been murdered *before he became aware of the loss*— i.e., shortly after he left the compartment at 8:27. But the Guard claimed to have spoken to Kilmington at 9 p.m. Therefore the Guard was lying. And why should he lie, except to create an alibi for himself? This is Clue Number One.

The Guard claimed to have talked with Kilmington at 9 p.m. Now, at 8:55 the blizzard had diminished to a light snowfall, which soon afterwards ceased. When Stansfield discovered the body, it was buried under snow. Therefore Kilmington must have been murdered *while the blizzard was still raging*—i.e., some time before 9 p.m. Therefore the Guard was lying when he said Kilmington was alive at 9 p.m. This is Clue Number Two.

Henry Stansfield, who was investigating on behalf of the Cosmopolitan Insurance Company the loss of the Countess of Axminster's emeralds, reconstructed the crime as follows:

Motive: The Guard's wife had been gravely ill before Christmas: then, just about the time of the train robbery, he had got her the best surgeon in Glasgow and put her in a nursing home (evidence of engine-driver: Clue

Number Three). A Guard's pay does not usually run to such expensive treatment: it seemed likely, therefore, that the man, driven desperate by his wife's need, had agreed to take part in the robbery in return for a substantial bribe. What part did he play? During the investigation the Guard had stated that he had left his van for five minutes, while the train was climbing the last section of Shap Bank, and on his return found the mailbags missing. But Kilmington, who was traveling on this train, had found the Guard's van locked at this point, and now (evidence of Mrs. Grant: Clue Number Four) declared his intention of reporting the Guard. The latter knew that Kilmington's report would contradict his own evidence and thus convict him of complicity in the crime, since he had locked the van for a few minutes to throw out the mailbags himself, and pretended to Kilmington that he had been asleep (evidence of Kilmington himself) when the latter knocked at the door. So Kilmington had to be silenced.

Stansfield already had Percy Dukes under suspicion as the organizer of the robbery. During the journey Dukes gave himself away three times. First, although it had not been mentioned in the papers, he betrayed knowledge of the point on the line where the bags had been thrown out. Second, though the loss of the emeralds had been also kept out of the press, Dukes knew it was an emerald *necklace* which had been stolen: Stansfield had laid a trap for him by calling it a bracelet, but later in conversation Dukes referred to the "necklace." Third, his great discomposure at the (false) statement by Stansfield that the emeralds were worth £25,000 was the reaction of a criminal who believes he has been badly gypped by the fence to whom he has sold them. Dukes was now planning a second train robbery, and meant to compel the Guard to act as accomplice again. Inez Blake's evidence (Clue Number Five) of hearing him say, "You're going to help us again, chum," etc., clearly pointed to the Guard's complicity in the previous robbery: it was almost certainly the Guard to whom she had heard Dukes say this, for only a railway servant would have known about the existence of a platelayers' hut up the line, and made an appointment to meet Dukes there; moreover, if Dukes had talked about his plans for the next robbery, on the train itself, to anyone *but* a railway servant suspicion would have been incurred should they have been seen talking together.

Method: At 8:27 Kilmington goes into the Guard's van. He threatens to report the Guard, though he is quite unaware of the dire consequences this would entail for the latter. The Guard, probably on the pretext of showing him the route to the village, gets Kilmington out of the train, walks him away from the lighted area, stuns him (the bruise was a light one and did not reveal itself in Stansfield's brief examination of the body), carries him to the spot where Stansfield found the body, packs mouth and nostrils tight with snow. Then, instead of leaving well alone, the Guard decides to create an alibi for himself. He takes his victim's hat, returns to train, puts on his own dark, off-duty overcoat, finds a solitary passenger asleep, masquerades as Kilmington inquiring the time, and strengthens the impression by saying he'd walk to the village if the relief engine did not turn up in five minutes, then returns to the body and throws down the hat beside it (Stansfield found the hat only lightly covered with snow, as compared with the body: Clue Number Six). Moreover, the passenger noticed that the inquirer was wearing blue trousers (Clue Number Seven). The Guard's regulation suit was blue; but Duke's suit was gray, and Macdonald's a loud check—therefore, the masquerader could not have been either of them.

The time is now 8:55. The Guard decides to reinforce his alibi by going to intercept the returning fireman. He takes a short cut from the body to the platelayers' hut. The track he now makes, compared with the beaten trail towards the village, is much more lightly filled in with snow when Stansfield finds it (Clue Number Eight): therefore, it must have been made some time after the murder, and could not incriminate Percy Dukes. The Guard meets the fireman just after 8:55. They walk back to the train. The Guard is taken aside by Dukes, who has gone out for his "airing," and the conversation overheard by Inez Blake takes place. The Guard tells Dukes he will meet him presently in the platelayers' hut: this is aimed to incriminate Dukes, should the murder by any chance be discovered, for Dukes would find it difficult to explain why he should have sat alone in a cold hut for half an hour just around the time when Kilmington was presumably murdered only one hundred and fifty yards away. The Guard now goes along to the engine and stays there chatting with the crew for some forty minutes. His alibi is thus established for the period from 8:55 to 9:40 p.m. His plan might well have succeeded, but for three unlucky factors he could not possibly have taken into account—Stansfield's presence on the train, the blizzard stopping soon after 9 p.m., and the theft of Arthur J. Kilmington's watch.

THE PHANTOM GUEST

by FREDERICK IRVING ANDERSON

At midnight the snowstorm flattened out before the driving wind like a mechanical jack rabbit; the blasts rattled their whips on the fluttering shutters, twitched the rusty old tollgate bell on its frozen gimbals until it gave whimpering tongue, roused groans from the stiff limbs of bare trees. It was what they called a milk storm; it was twenty below zero—too cold to snow! All traffic had ceased; only the caterpillar plow swung back and forth through the white night like a sluggish shuttle—a ghostly crunching behemoth breathing fantastic breaths of snow that swirled against the street lamps and turned them into gaudy sundogs. Inside, the radiators bubbled placidly, and the old cat stretched its seven-toed paws in sleepy content.

It was no night for transients to come ringing the bell of the big front door of the Crossings House; nevertheless Elam, mine host, creature of habit that he was, looked up as the old clock tolled the hour and arose to greet, politely to register and to room several purely imaginary personages who, since landlords first hung up the bush, had been arriving at this witching hour craving hypothetical hospitality. Snow nor sleet nor rain nor wind nor dark deterred them. They were known in the trade as phantom guests. They always registered at the very top of the page; their ethereal presence exorcized the ghosts of emptiness. They were as necessary to the proper conduct of a good hotel, as, say, cyanide for the silver, or—or roach food.

First Elam closed up tight—even the cat hole in the woodshed. He put out the lights and the radio and the night latch. He listened at the stairwell in that last wary pause of a prudent landlord. Under the green-shaded desk lamp he turned the register to a new page, and at the top he wrote in an ornate Spencerian hand (with many curves and flourishes—such a hand as one could procure until quite recently at county fairs and cattle drawings on elegant private calling cards, interspersed with billing doves, smiling cupids and bleeding hearts) the new day, and the new date, Friday, the seventeenth of January. From a secret case he took four pens of different habits, four vials of ink of different hues; and without hesitation he registered and roomed four phantom guests. They were as follows:

Horace Manton, Harwinton, Conn.	E	18
J. H. Boles, Slocum, Mass.	E	27
Enid Wallins, N.Y.C.	E	7
Herbert Huffer, New Haven	E	10

Jim the Penman himself couldn't have done better. Elam carefully put away the tools of his guile; and, for verisimilitude, he left a call for the Wallins woman—she always took the seven o'clock train. Thus, having made oblation to the superstition of his flesh-and-blood patrons, he crept away to his apartment behind the stairs. Without arousing his cherubic wife, who slept in the full glare of a shaded lamp, he took off his shoes and put them away in a dated paper sack. This was his sole extravagance, he had a pair of shoes for every day in the month. He crept into bed, thinking of his son who was away at school, and so pleasant were his thoughts he couldn't have told where thoughts ceased and dreams began.

The front door bell rang at two o'clock. As his perspicacious toes found waiting slippers he wondered with a shiver if this were some suicide coming to claim that last divine unction which landlords have to sell. Wrapping his robe about him he went out, and rubbed the frost from the door pane. No, there were two of them. A car stood rammed into the rampart of snow at the curb. Two men stood over it. It steamed like a huge kettle. The car was freezing to death; rigor mortis would soon set in. The night had turned out ironically fine. Elam pulled the latch, pulled on a light, went back of the desk; he turned the register about, one hand on the hinge of the book—some fools will actually shut the book on registering, little suspecting that thereby someone will die in the house that day. It was precaution to put a toe on the police alarm, and to finger the butt of the .45 under the counter. The two men came in, stamping off the snow, rubbing their hands, shaking themselves like dogs as they got out of their coats. They shivered in the delicious warmth of the interior. One was short and heavy, the other was tall and slender. They wore clothes much too good for them.

"Dicks—body-snatchers," thought Elam. He had owned seventeen saloons in New York and he remembered this breed. They all aspired to a queer sartorial elegance.

"We got to get that car under cover," said the short fat man.

"The snowplow will bury it by morning," said Elam. "That's the best we can do for you."

"Oh, one of those wise hicks, eh?" said the fat man. "Well, maybe you're right. How long you been here waiting for us, old man?"

"One hundred and thirty-five years," said Elam.

"I'm glad you stayed on," said the other. "We sure need succor. What's the chance for a good room? Almost perfect?"

"What's the chance for a long stiff drink?" put in the tall one.

"It's a dry house," said Elam.

Whatever repercussion might have followed on the heels of this sad news was squelched by a truly astounding occurrence. Enid Wallins, one of Elam's most faithful and reliable phantom guests, who had been checking in ethereally for more than six years at the top of the page, chose this moment to come to life. The heavy-set man was registering as Matt Glennon, N.Y.C., when his eyes strayed to the signatures above his, and he gasped hoarsely, "Hey, Tony! Look!" Tony looked, stared with an almost cataleptic rigidity.

"Enid Wallins!" he shrilled, his eyes all but popping out of his head. "Here! Well, I'm damned! There goes our meal ticket!"

They looked at each other stupidly. Glennon was the first to come to. He turned fiercely on Elam.

"Is she in the house now?" he demanded.

"She hasn't checked out yet," said Elam weakly.

"Is she alive?" cried Tony.

Elam stared at him in amazement.

"We'll rout her out and see!" announced Tony.

"You'll rout nobody out!" said Elam.

"You're talking to the law!" snarled Glennon. With a flip he tossed a tiny badge on the counter. District Attorney's Office, New York County. Elam wetted his lips. The straightest way was the easiest. He was about to say:

"Gentlemen, do not needlessly excite yourselves. In the hotel business we have to contend with the silly superstitions of our patrons. One of them is their dislike to stop in an empty house, to register at the top of an empty page. So we always start our clean pages with dummy names. Enid Wallins is one of our dummy names. I've used it again and again. I don't know a person of that name. So far as I know, there is no such person. She is a myth, a fancy, a subterfuge, a—a phantom guest—"

But he never said it. The lean silky Tony suddenly shot out his long thin arms; his crushing fingers choked the words in Elam's throat. With a lunge across the desk, he drove Elam's head against the wall behind with a dull thud. But Elam's ready hand came away with the villainous .45; and the next instant Tony was back on his heels, hands high in air, staring into an unwavering muzzle. Elam twisted his tortured neck, wheezing.

"Getting tough, eh?" he gasped. "Softening me up, huh? Keep your hands up, both of you."

"We're the law," protested Glennon weakly.

"Not on this side of the state line!" muttered Elam, caressing the lump on the back of his head. "One more crack out of either of you and you'll sleep in an igloo. Now what's it all about?"

"It's all right—it's all right," urged Glennon placatingly. "Maybe Tony was a bit rough. But who wouldn't be? Listen. We'll put our cards on the table. Put up that gun. Nobody is going to hurt you."

"You ain't," said Elam. He lowered the gun, but kept his guard. He seethed with rage. He knew this breed. Except for that handy gun, this pair would have given him the works, softened him for questioning. "Now, what's it all about?" he said. "Who is this woman you're looking for? And what do you want her for?"

Tony took down his hands slowly, still eyeing the gun.

"She's the corpus delicti in a big-time murder," he said. "We been looking for the remains for eight months. This is bad news for somebody. Isn't there some way I can get a long drink, old man?"

"Well, this one ain't dead by a long shot," said Elam. "Maybe she comes to life again, huh?" he added sarcastically.

"Maybe she ain't so dead," said Glennon. "All we know is she's gone, without a trace. And now she bobs up and hits us in the face. Can't we get a drink? What does this one look like?"

"It's a dry house," said Elam absently. He was thinking fast. His head ached, the bump was as big as an egg; he was not of a mind to call himself a liar for this pair of strongarm johnnies. "Just a mix-up of names," he said easily.

"No," said Glennon. "Odd name. What does she look like?"

As the years had gone by, Elam had actually invented case histories for several of the older customers among his phantom guests. He had embellished the picture of this Enid Wallins in his mind's eye. He had put the name together from two residential hills in town, Eno and Wallins. He pictured her as an interesting, difficult woman with a past.

"What does she look like?" persisted Glennon.

"Classy!" said Elam. "About thirty. Blonde. Swell dresser—in a sort of horsy way."

"Horsy?" The two dicks spoke in unison.

Elam thrilled at the swift look passed. If it is true as the philosophers say that an idea cannot exist without a mind to exist in, then she surely was now alive, because they believed and were dismayed. He lowered his voice.

"We're talking too loud," he said. "She's sleeping right above here." They stared upwards, rapt, at the floor register giving to the room above. "I think she raises hunters on a farm in Vermont. She breaks her journey here." He was lying easily now, savoring the morsels.

"Oh, she's been here before?" This from Glennon, who was shaking his head and muttering to himself. Elam shivered, he was getting in deep, he was nailing it down harder with every spurt of his imagination. Morning was coming, he'd have to think it over.

"Yes, two-three times a year," he said. "She's been coming—oh, say, five or six years."

Their voices were low now, in conspirators' whispers, which somehow increased their sense of her nearness.

"When was she here last?" asked Glennon.

Elam took down one of the old registers for last fall and turned the pages.

"Here we are," he said. "October 13. Checked in late. Checked out for the seven o'clock train in the morning."

There she was indeed, in the same signature, that fetching two-story handwriting. The two dicks studied it in a daze.

"How's she come?" asked Glennon, eyeing Elam sharply. "By car?"

"That's what she always does," said Elam glibly. "Motors this far—sends the man on with the car—and takes the parlor car to town in the morning." He whistled audibly in relief. He had been wondering how he could account for her presence, without a car in the shed. The two dicks compared the signatures sullenly.

"I'd give a sawbuck for a shot!" sighed Tony. In his momentary elation Elam softened. He held up a warning finger and stealthily opened the grandfather's clock behind the desk. To their surprise, he took off the weight, a very quart of a weight. His clever wife had located every cache about the house but this one. He could afford to celebrate a little. He drew the plug and poured out three ample shots. They toasted the overhead register in silence.

"Go to bed," whispered Elam, as he restored the march of time. "I'll call you in time in the morning."

When he had roomed them on tiptoe, he returned to the office and stood holding his aching head in his hands. He interrupted the march of time several times, resetting the clock slyly after each pause. What a devil of a mess that lump on his head—and their eager gullibility—had lured him into! They'd turn him up a liar at dawn. And Enid—Enid, the interesting, the difficult woman with a history would cease to exist, go out of his life forever.

The habit of mundane things put him into his boots, cap, mittens, put the snow shovel into his hands; and he slipped out into the glistening cold to shovel a path to the curb—before people came to trample it, with the day. The frozen car that had started all this mischief lay under a kopje of snow. The street flowed by, smooth and clean, between high ramparts. The state roads were wide open! She could get away, she could go anywhere! She must flee, escape, before dawn!

"I'll have to think this out," he said hazily. He went in and put out the lights again, and crawled away to bed, to think. But not to his cherubic wife. He went up to Number Seven, and crawled into Enid's bed, and lay there open-eyed. He got up and went to the rummage closet for supplies. One could start a museum out of the odds and ends hotel guests leave behind in twenty years. He selected a torn stocking—oh, so thin and fine! A ball of a kerchief. A glove of unusual pattern—he had always wondered about the hand that glove fitted. A powder pad, a lipstick, and some note paper as thick as vellum. He planted these articles in strategic suggestive points about the room. Then he took Enid's pen, and in her swagger two-story handwriting, he filled one page:

—acable enemies, like poets—and wasps—sting once, and die, in our regard; but you, dear friend, are of tomorrow, and tomorrow and tomor—

He tore this fragmentary epistle into small bits and dropped them into the wastebasket. He crept away to his bed behind the stairs, where his cherubic wife still slept the sleep of the just under the shaded rays of her lamp.

II

"I know the house," said Parr, the police deputy, taking his chilly eye off poor Tony for the moment, and nodding to his privileged friend, Oliver Armiston, who had just come in. "That's where J. P. Morgan used to go for blueberry pie. That's where they hid Lefty Linkowitz, the bail-bond tycoon, when he was hot. It isn't far from Three Corners, where a good man can commit perjury in three states at once, if he's got three legs to stand on. Now what are you going to do for a meal ticket, Tony?"

The unhappy Tony had been sent over as the bearer of ill tidings from the Prosecutor's office, and for the last half-hour he had been on the carpet, and wishing he was under it. Mr. Parr's last question was purely rhetorical. He continued:

"I suppose this young and beauteous female with a Park Avenue air walked off among the snow drifts on her high heels without arousing any undue curiosity in the main street?"

Tony wrung his sleek hands. She was gone, indubitably gone, just as she had come—without the shadow of a shade of circumstance attending her departure. She had not left by the morning train as was her invariable custom. The public taxis were still fast in the grip of that terrible frost. Matt had stayed behind with the car and would leave no stone unturned. The roads were all open, she could go, go anywhere.

"On foot?" asked the deputy.

Tony wrung his hands again.

"On wings. On skis? How?" No answer.

"Did you see any mortal manifestation of the lady, except her signature on the register?" pursued Parr. "No, you hit the hay. Was she actually there in the flesh, Tony? Or was it just a ghost?"

Tony crossed himself hurriedly. Oh, she was there! One felt a living presence—he relived the moment when the three of them solemnly raised their glasses and toasted that hot-air hole in the ceiling.

"That one is a tough fellow!" he cried. "Oh, if I have him across the state line some day! He talked up through that hole for her to hear."

"Did anyone in the house besides this obliging landlord with the .45 set eyes on this female?" asked Parr.

Tony said, "No, she come after midnight—she go—phut!—before day, like that!"

"And she'd been there before?"

"Yes, yes, sir! Last night. Last October!" cried Tony. He was on more solid ground now. "Five times, ten times. We go back in the old registers. She come and go. Always in this Number Seven—with the hot-air pipe in the floor."

Tony had the dates of these earthly manifestations of the lady of the two-story handwriting. Her first appearance was April 22, 1932.

"That was a few days after rigor mortis set in," said Parr, studying the schedule. With a curt nod he dismissed Tony. As the sad fellow shut the door with the polite caution of the misunderstood, Parr turned with a wry smile to Armiston, his friend and occasional collaborator in those misty upper reaches of crime where gumshoe work must call in fantasy for help.

"The missing bride," he said sententiously. "She disappeared at the altar six years ago. Her husband took another woman on the honeymoon with him, and has been living with her as his wife ever since. We've been quietly looking for the remains, for the past eight months."

"Murder?"

"That's the idea we were playing with," said the deputy. "And this pair of subpoena servers blunder into her in a blizzard last night—and off she goes hopping across the snow like a scared rabbit."

"Ah, the case of the reanimated corpse," said Oliver. "Are these the mortal remains?"

He turned to the exhibits from Number Seven on the desk. The fragmentary letter had been lovingly pieced together by Tony. Oliver shook his head. The paper was hardly boudoir stationery; it was too ostentatious, as heavy as vellum—of the sort bankers affected in the later days of the lamented New Era. But he nodded approvingly over the script. It had dash, élan, a certain powerful grace. "That is a beautiful pen," he said. "I'd like to own it. Odd," he added, "the impression one gets from a fragment. I knew a woman who could have written that hand. I'm thinking of a society woman of several years ago. Tragic, fascinating creature, with tears in her voice. Perfect poise, always sure of herself—and always losing. Towards the end she went on the stage, in one of Shaw's plays. She made a great hit. Finally she killed herself. She could have used that pen. Let's see what she's got to say."

He read the few lines of the broken sentence. Proust, with a dash of Hugh Walpole. It is a terrible responsibility, being a bestseller. So many weeping women borrow your thoughts to trim their sails. He took up the fragment of the stocking. It was gossamer sheer, of the stuff that spiders spin. Some women would wear such a stocking once, maybe twice. You can buy them for, say, $25 the pair, in those coy little shops in the side streets just off the Avenue, shops that cater to lovers who require something very special. The balled-up handkerchief was an airy figment of lace, so delicately true and wistfully fine that it suggested the patient shuttles of novices in a quiet cloister where time is counted on beads. The glove was from the Rue de la Paix. A lipstick, but no rouge. She probably had big round eyes and affected a dead-pan white, thought Oliver.

"You're in sporting high life, Parr," said Oliver. "Can't you see her?"

"That stuff would go over big with a jury," said the man-hunter, smiling.

"Because it's circumstantial, Parr," said Oliver. "So much more forceful than direct evidence. It flatters us, permits us to show how clever we are. Note how the fragment makes the whole picture. Now, if she had left a hairpin—or a broken corset string—or a cotton stocking—!" Armiston grimaced. "Parr, was this stuff planted for you to find?"

The deputy massaged his chin thoughtfully.

"I haven't taken this thing very seriously," he began. "It's the District Attorney's hunch. He's been nosing around—and he comes over here occasionally for moral support. There is no accuser, no corpse; dozens of people ought to suspect—but apparently there is no suspicion. What's the motive? Why should a man go to the risk of publicly marrying a woman before he murders her? We might admit he plans to get rid of her, or else he wouldn't have had the other woman in readiness to take her place." Parr paused, frowning.

"But now that the corpse turns up alive and well," put in Oliver, "a change comes o'er the spirit of your dreams."

"Yes," said Parr. "Was this stuff planted for us to find? It would make a very pretty case, Oliver, if it was—right down your alley. Let us say that he actually got away with murder, and the substitution of a bride. He goes a step farther. He plants another woman on this hotel register, in the image of the murdered bride. Maybe this is the perfect crime you parlor criminologists talk about, Oliver. Let us say that we were expected to stumble on this lady eventually. Okay, that's fine." Parr shook his head. "But not now. They couldn't have foreseen last night's occurrence. That was pure happenstance."

"I suppose it would be too crude to suggest coincidence of names?"

"Then why should she cut and run like a scared rabbit?" said Parr. Elam would have been pleased to eavesdrop through some convenient ceiling hole on the lucubrations of the great Mr. Parr. His Enid was very very much alive, and deeply involved. "Besides, it was an odd name—improbable."

"There is no such word as improbable, Parr," said Oliver. "Probability thins out, yes, approaches zero—but never actually touches zero. It's mathematical. Let a monkey hit a typewriter at random through eternity, and eventually he will write all the sonnets. That's how some people explain Shakespeare. Does the description tally?"

"We've got a vague description of the bride—a black-haired madonna, with big eyes and white skin," said Parr.

"That's the picture I get," said Oliver.

"So does the landlord," said Parr. "He doesn't know much about her. He thinks she is horsy, doggy—has a horse farm up in Vermont some place."

"What is the name?" asked Oliver.

"Enid Wallins," said the deputy, as softly as a gunman pressing a trigger. He covertly watched for the effect. Oliver exploded.

"Enid Wallins!" he ejaculated.

"Just a minute," said Parr. "You're going to tell me you saw her and her husband dining at Chaffard's last night."

"I did!" cried Armiston. "Gregory Wallins, the gentleman jockey—"

"Friend of yours?" inquired the deputy.

"Well, I— No, you've got to smell of horse liniment to get into that crowd," said Oliver. "But I've known of them for years. Why, Parr," he cried, rising, "I was in Bermuda when they came there honeymooning."

"Was the bride a black-haired madonna?"

"She was a tall willowy blonde," said Oliver.

"There you are," said the man-hunter complacently. "We can prove that three days before he sailed on this honeymoon with your blonde he married a brunette."

"It can't be done!" cried Armiston testily. "This Gregory Wallins—he is a waster and a rotter and a drunk, yes. But he comes of good people. He is Master of the Hounds at Cowdrey's. You can't flaunt an irregular female before them for years and get away with it."

"No," said Parr. "You can't. Would you say they were listed in the Register of the Élite?"

"Undoubtedly. The Wallinses always have been."

Parr shook his head slowly.

"Not Gregory," he said. "They dropped his name six years ago."

This brought Oliver up short.

"The devil you say!" he muttered. He took down the book of the social elect. The Gregory Wallinses were not there! This was unanswerable. Next to being posted at a club, there is no blow so devastating to the socially ambitious as being dropped from this sacred index of who's who in Society. New names are admitted grudgingly. Occasionally an old one is dropped out, with a dull thud. Some mysterious *arbiter elegantiarum* turns down his thumb. Why? One might as well try to tap a confessional. Oliver took to pacing the room, pulling at his single white lock.

"Even so, Parr," he said, coming to a stop, "where does it get you? A white-slave case. You talk hypothetical murder. And in the same breath you tell me she has come back. You're a meddling old woman."

"You can't lay this baby on my doorstep," laughed the deputy. "It's the District Attorney's hunch."

"Where did he get it?"

"That's a funny story, too," said Parr. "If you were Gregory Wallins, and wanted to marry secretly, how would you go about it, in this age of candid cameras and tabloids?"

"Rather difficult. He's in the rotogravures a good deal."

"How would a Gretna Green do?" asked Parr. "One of those cut-rate marrying Squires who camp along the state line—who line up elopers Saturday nights, and put them through the hopper in jig time. No questions asked. Most of the couples are from the Connecticut mill towns. They are not news any more. Ever hear of Squire Markum?"

Who had not heard of the Marrying Squire of Ageton? He had a sign on his little shack reading "Cut-Rate Marriages. Unconditional Guarantee." For years he had been good for a laugh in the news, with the freak biota of Winsted, Conn., and the low-reading thermometer of Owl's Head, N.Y.

"There you are," said the deputy. "Your friend Gregory looks like a stable-boy. He would have passed unnoticed with the run-of-the-mill—but the damned fool had to fee the Squire with a hundred-dollar bill, instead of the usual two-spot. Even then it would have been all right, but a few days later the candid-camera boys caught the bridal pair sailing for Bermuda. A tall willowy blonde, in place of the brunette. The Squire saw the photograph and worried over it. He stands back of his guarantee, and frowns on substitutes."

"The story grows less screwy," admitted Oliver.

"For some mysterious reason, after that the Wallinses dropped out of Society news," said Parr. "Somebody knew something. Well, the Squire forgot about them." Parr smiled over the devious ways of the public prints. "But about a year ago, the Wallinses began to come back," he continued. "He got to be Master of Hounds at Cowdrey's. You know there's nothing like a horse and a five-bar gate to dump a man back into the rotogravures. And Greg broke a collarbone now and then, which was news, with action pictures. Well, the Squire woke up again, and came to town and told about the substitute bride. The District Attorney bit—and he's been nosing around ever since. It was two of his bright young flatfoots who turned up the madonna last night in the snowstorm."

At this fitting juncture the door opened and Morel, Parr's handsome young shadow, ushered in a huge waddling gibbous personage of watery eye and lugubrious mien, dressed for winter in the hills. It, of course, was old Squire Markum himself.

"Well, well!" cried Parr, springing up with outstretched hand. "How's the matrimonial market this morning, Squire?"

"Seasonal," intoned the Squire. He turned a beetling brow on Oliver. "Seasonal," he repeated. "The young man's fancy is a little torpid just now." He sat down heavily, mopping his brow. The steam heat of these parts was working its way with him.

"This is Mr. Armiston, the celebrated parlor criminologist," said Parr. "I took the liberty of calling him in as a consultant. I suppose you have heard that the—ah—the lady of the first instance has come back to life?"

The Squire nodded his head slowly.

"Very unfortunate," he rumbled. There was a pause. He looked from Oliver to Parr. "This gentleman is one of us?" he said cautiously.

"He is two of us," said Parr. "Speak freely. What is so unfortunate?"

"I'm afraid I have annoyed the District Attorney," said the Squire sadly. "Something I did last night, with the purest intentions. He told me to give you this, and confess." He struggled to extricate some bulky object caught in a torn pocket.

"Confess? To what?" said Parr.

"He called it blackmail," intoned the old man lugubriously. He lifted his innocent gaze to Parr. At last the bulky object broke free, and he bent forward and laid it on the desk. It was a lump, almost a sodden lump, of money, bills. The bills were pressed into a fat brick held together by a gridiron of rubber bands.

"One thousand dollars, in fives and tens," rumbled the Squire sepulchrally. "Mr. Gregory Wallins was kind enough to give it to me."

There was a deep silence. Deputy Parr arose thoughtfully and wandered over to his pipe rack, a thing he rarely consulted. He selected a pipe with some circumspection, filled it, lighted it, musingly savored the first puff; then he came back and sat down.

"Are you ready now?" asked the Squire. Parr nodded. "I'm like that," said the Squire. "I can't think unless I smoke." He fished out a pipe and a bag of cigar clippings; when he was loaded Parr held the match.

"I met him last night," said Squire Markum sadly. "Quite unexpectedly —to him. In a restaurant. Grand place! He had a lady with him. Beautiful blonde lady! I've seen her pictures in the Sunday papers." The Squire struck another light. "He didn't know me, I guess. Most of them don't. I told him who I was. I said: 'Sir, I trust you still take pleasure in what I did for you.' "

Parr polished the bowl of his brier on a sleeve; Oliver nervously twiddled his stick.

"He didn't say," said the Squire, shaking his head. "I think maybe he didn't like my clothes. You know we dress for winter where I come from. I said: 'Sir, I am raising funds for a boys' camp. I'm putting you down for one thousand dollars.' Well, he thought it over for some time. I said: 'Sir, if convenient, I'd like it in fives and tens, without any consecutive serial numbers.' " There was a long pause.

"Well," went on the Squire, studying Parr with his sad-dog look, "after a long time, he got up, and excused himself to the lady—she didn't seem to be very well. He led me down the aisle to the front door and took me outside. He said, 'Good night. I'll meet you at the Grand Central at eleven in the morning.' "

"And he met you?" This from Parr.

"Yes!" said the Squire, with a surprised look.

"With the money?"

"Yes, oh yes," said the Squire. "He was nice to me. He bought me a ticket, and put me on my train—and waited till it pulled out. I got off at 125th street and came back."

Parr rang a bell, and when Morel came in he said:

"Put two good men on Wallins and the blonde. You and Pelts follow along behind and see what you can see."

"There's one thing I forgot," said Squire Markum, feeling for a match. "I told him I'd come in again, and let him know how things are going. He said: 'No; I'll come up to see you.' I said: 'That's fine, if you don't wait too long.' "

III

These people are always amply documented, accounted for. That is one of the rules of the game. In the so-called rotogravure section of Society the scrutiny is less strict. But the Wallins family were of Washington Square, where the old Directory began in recounting the glories that were Knickerbocker New York. Oliver knew several of the bright young men concerned with the publication of the current Register, and for a moment he speculated on just what chance he might have of finding out what somebody knew down there. Probably nobody knew anything, excepting the grand panjandrum himself—and nobody would admit knowing who he was. In the few instances Oliver knew of noble names being dropped into the dust bin of social oblivion, the best guess was always a déclassé marriage. You can't have thoroughbreds without registered sires and dams.

"However," mused Armiston, "she's not his wife. She is merely a white slave, operating under the Mann Act."

So he put aside the tall willowy blonde for the time being, as merely a confederate who had turned a little sick when the Squire said he would like it in fives and tens with no consecutive serial numbers.

That brought up the madonna for scrutiny.

That marriage was amply documented. The civil authorities, including the cut-rate Squire, would see to that. The gentleman jockey's license was in order, filled in and signed by himself in all verity. But the lady! She wore a broken collarbone at that altar (so a notation by the town clerk recited); and the clerk courteously filled in her license for her and she signed it—with her mark! That broken collarbone was plausible enough. Those people, the horsy set—if she was horsy—collect broken collarbones as service stripes; they even quote sporty pars for certain jumps. She was set forth there, with a vast air of candor, as Enid Wolfert, 22 years old, of— Shanghai, China.

"You can perjure yourself to your heart's content on a marriage license, but perjury doesn't dissolve the holy bonds of wedlock," said Oliver to himself. Shanghai was certainly far enough away to discourage meddling curiosity, should any arise. Then Oliver happened to think of his friend Facey, who was in town. Facey had been everywhere, on government service, especially in China. He ran him down at the club.

"Facey," he said. "You've been everywhere, you know everybody in China." (It is a fact, China is a very small place indeed among whites.) "Who," he asked, "is, or was, Enid Wolfert?"

"I knew of an Enid Wolfert in Shanghai" replied the gaunt horse-faced intelligence officer promptly. "She was an 'American woman.' "

"Naturally, she was an American woman," said Oliver.

"No," said Facey. "Not naturally. Artificially, yes."

"And so, what?"

"I'm using the term 'American woman' in its Chinese sense," said the paradoxical person. "I believe her real name was Enid Wolfert. But she didn't use it. She was Dewy Plum Blossom—or Swaying Marsh Lily— something like that." He looked at Oliver curiously, and Armiston, for his part, stared startled. "Is she a friend of yours?" asked Facey.

"An 'American woman'? What do you mean?" demanded Oliver.

"It's an old Chinese usage," said Facey. "It's not very complimentary to us. In fact, when Secretary Taft was in Shanghai years ago, on that famous world cruise of his, he heard it used, and he protested so indignantly that I believe some official effort was made to suppress its use—in the delicate significance the Chinese are masters of."

"You mean a dissolute woman—a Shanghai Lil?" cried Armiston.

"Why, yes, in a way," said Facey. "Of a sheltered type. Of a type we don't know over here at all. The consort of a Chinese gentleman. Oh, don't raise your hands in pious horror! If you ever knew a Chinese gentleman, you'd think twice about your own culture. What about her?" he asked abruptly.

Facey was, of course, one of them—indeed, as Parr might have put it, two of them. Oliver told him the story.

"It's quite possible," said Facey. "Gregory Wallins was over there five or six years ago—raising hell, as usual." He told Armiston a good deal about this particular American woman. The story could be epitomized in one phrase—in Chinese it was *Mei Kuo Nu Jen,* pronounced May Gwaw Noo Run—American woman. The usage dated back to the days of Salem clippers.

The usual imperturbable Parr tossed away his stogey and filled a pipe and smoked it, when Oliver recited the fruits of this interview with the intelligence official.

"Wallins has been a mark for women all his life," said the deputy—he knew more about New York's first families than many a society doctor.

Passing over, for the time being, the now somewhat enfeebled hypothetical murder of the American woman, Armiston examined the available evidence of what he called her neo-mundane existence. She seemed amply supplied with funds. He was thinking of that atrociously expensive stocking, the convent kerchief, and the custom glove. She had a horse farm in Vermont, and she was in the habit of sending her man on with the car, and taking the parlor-car train to town in the morning. Parr's minions combed the records. A woman of her type, who raised hunters in Vermont, and kept a man and a car should be amply documented. But she was not. Nothing was found. Parr passed this off as insignificant.

"She may run her farm under a stable name," he said. "And she may have her car and chauffeur on hire—many rich people do, to outwit the fake-accident lawyers."

The Pullman porter who served buffet breakfast on that early train remembered several women who might fit the description, such as it was.

"It is a savory morsel for gossip, Parr," said Oliver, finally. "But, is it cricket?"

"You mean, is it proper police inquiry?" said Parr. "No," he said, flatly. "Nevertheless, I'm looking it over."

"I'll trail along," said Oliver. "Let's try a new tack. Why did the gentleman jockey give up the thousand bucks so easily? Why did the willowy blonde get sick when that old reprobate Squire told them he'd like it in fives and tens?"

"They are living in sin, my boy," said the deputy smiling.

"But they are pretty firmly established in their position," objected Oliver. "It takes more than a cock-and-bull story told by your cut-rate Squire to upset them. You started out with what we parlor criminologists call a perfect crime. The murderer makes his kill. The murderer feels safe—but as an added precaution, he plants a dummy to appear ghostily about the country. If he is ever actually accused, he doesn't have to produce her in person. He can always summon Elam as a witness. All he needs is a reasonable doubt. It's a good set up! Elam!" Oliver paused on the name, in a moment of illogical prescience. (They say logic is only practised 100 percent in lunatic asylums.) "Maybe Elam is a holy liar? Who is Elam?"

"A wise bird," said Parr. "His father ran the Grand Dominion Hotel in Fulton Street in this city for forty years."

"I remember his English mutton chops!" sighed Oliver.

"With pickled walnuts!" muttered Parr hungrily.

"Parr," cried Oliver, "either Gregory Wallins knows of this mysterious hotel guest—or he doesn't."

" 'Doesn't?' " said the man-hunter sharply.

"Maybe he doesn't," said Oliver. "Play with that idea for a minute."

Parr whistled. "Damn!" he said. "That's pretty, eh!"

"How would it be to dump her into his lap, and see how he reacts?" proposed Armiston.

Parr touched a bell. Morel, his handsome shadow, appeared. Morel didn't look like a cop, the underworld didn't know him as a cop. He never made an arrest—but he was always around, in what Parr called his dress-suit cases.

"You are a society reporter, Morel," said Parr. "Pick out some good names on the register of the Crossings House for the past week or so. I want a paragraph in the society columns of the *Tribune* and *Times* reading: 'Among the notables registered at the Crossings House, Greenwood's, for the skiing during the past week were Enid Wallins, so-and-so, so-and-so, and so on. Mix them up."

"Would you hold off a day or two?" suddenly asked Oliver. "I'd like to run up there and try a little shee-ing myself—or maybe shee-joring. I'm not too old for that."

Oliver was for the most part a side-lines sportsman, although he could still do fancy work in a pistol gallery. The dernier cri of the sports shop windows daunted him, and he compromised on an old Norfolk, of his student days, a cap with a feather in it, and woolly golf hose. He passed up the lusty turmoil of the snow train for the peace and plenty of his own air-conditioned coupé; and in the steely blue of a winter twilight he presented himself at the Crossings House.

"I've come for some blueberry pie," he said to Elam. "What are the prospects for a choice room? Not quite perfect, I see." There was a goodly muster of autographs on the day's register, as varied as an awkward squad.

Skis and poles leaned in sociable groups against the walls of the corridor, and hobnailed boots foregathered in dark corners. "Might I see the room?" he asked; and when Elam frowned, he added quickly: "I don't steal towels or electric light bulbs." Elam didn't like to show rooms—some people not only looked under his beds but in them. So he showed Armiston the noisiest room in the house, Number Seven, right over the office and told him to take it or leave it. Oliver was delighted.

"Why, there's an old friend of mine!" cried Oliver, stopping before a framed photograph. "The Baron! That brings back the days in the old Grand Dominion. Oh, for one of his English mutton chops!"

"That's my father," said Elam. He eyed Oliver suspiciously. Many people claimed friendship with that famous old restaurateur. "What did he serve with that mutton chop?" he asked slyly.

"A pickled walnut!" cried Oliver.

Elam thrust out his hand. There was something masonic in the clasp.

"Remember Katie's?" he said, his eyes glowing.

"And White's?" countered Oliver.

"And downtown Delmonico's?"

"And Grandpa Mouquin's?"

The ice was broken, crushed; it was merely a matter of proper credentials —that pickled walnut did the trick. This fellow wouldn't pull his .45 on him, thought Oliver. He and Elam had something to talk about that might lead to anything, anything.

The smoky talk of telemark and Christiania turns, passmark, gelaendesprung, and slaloms in the lounging room tapered off towards midnight, and the woolly yodellers of the ski-fraternity clumped their noisy way to bed. Oliver settled down to a dip into an old copy of *Midshipman Easy;* and Elam mopped up. After a time Elam came out with a basket filled with ancient menus. Here was treasure trove. He and Oliver hungrily read the tale of those gustatory days when a man let out his belt before he summoned his waiter; when snipe and quail and grouse, terrapin, mallard and teal, leg of real mutton and broiled venison-liver awaited all comers in Fulton Street.

Oliver brought down his flask to spice the recollections. They talked of Fatty Bliss, Diamond Jim Brady, Old Man Greenhut; of Larry Jerome, Doctor Parkhurst and Brian G. Hughes; of Joe Vendig, Kid Levine, and Alec Williams. Elam revealed the secret of his grandfather clock.

"We didn't tell those old waiters what we were going to eat," said Oliver. "They told us, and we ate it."

"Our customers used to look in over the swing doors at our free lunch before they'd come in," said Elam.

"What was your first job in the hotel business?"

"First, I was a cash boy in A. T. Stewart's," said Elam. "Only gentlemen's sons need apply. I was promoted to the cashier's office for my handwriting."

He took up a pen and wrote rapidly in the elegant hand of long ago, with fat curves, flourishes, and shadings.

"My first job in the hotel business was to register and room the phantom guests," said Elam.

"Eh? Phantom guests?"

"Sure," said Elam. "The signatures on the few three-four lines of the register. They're always dummies. One of the superstitions of the hotel business is never to start off a day with an empty house. That was the first job my father gave me, registering the dummy names. Let me show you."

This was a trade secret, as inviolable as a magician's clove hitch. But this was the witching hour; the phantom guests themselves were about to arrive; and this fellow knew the Baron and his pickled walnuts. Elam produced his pen case and inks; and he wrote rapidly a dozen signatures—and no two of them seemed to have been written by the same hand or pen.

The amazed Armiston let his eye run down the list:

Amos Corning
Horace Manton
J. H. Boles
Enid Wallins

Oliver's mouth fell open. He stared, dumbstruck.

"I'm good, eh?" cried Elam, delighted with the very obvious effect his art made on his drinking companion.

"Incredible!" gasped Oliver. "Enid Wallins." Her autograph, with its dash, its élan, its powerful grace—her signature stared him in the face! *She was a phantom guest,* a dummy, a figment of the imagination, a sop to superstition. *Then it was murder.*

IV

The room was huge and sumptuous, its furniture arranged in several coteries. There were sporting prints on the walls, also some rare bronzes, one a Rodin; also other bronzes not so rare, of proud hunters, a huntsman with dogs. Everything suggested horse; you could almost smell saddle leather. Gregory Wallins sat deep in a chair, his morning paper trailing from one hand, the other hand tipping an untasted drink. He had been sitting thus minutes on end. Balzac in one of his old stories had an artist with the power to paint an inanimate object so as to draw all eyes to it, in amazement, horror, loathing. That artist might have drawn this trailing newspaper; no one could have looked in on the scene and seen it without a sense of foreboding. After a time a clock, with a pawing hunter atop, struck the hour. Wallins arose and went down the corridor to his wife's room and entered. She too was seated, with a trailing paper beside her. She did not look up as he entered; but when he sat down, after a time she looked at his paper, and then at him.

A paragraph in the Society notes read, under Greenwood's dateline:

"Among the notables registered at the Crossings House for the ski running this week are Trotter Mason, the Sailing Fosters, Enid Wallins, Foster Stowe—"

Some random noise in the street broke the spell.

"Where is Greenwood's?" she asked, wetting her lips.

"In the Connecticut highlands," he said. "Up under the state line." He drained his glass.

"You'd better go slow with that stuff, now, hadn't you?" she cautioned. She asked quietly: "Do you think it possible?"

He shook his head. "No."

"You mean you are not sure? Think! Think!" she cried. "Be sure of something, now."

"That blackmailer, the Squire, knows something," he muttered. "Maybe he thinks he can bay me out from cover. I'll have to go see."

"What am I to know?" she asked.

"Nothing," he said, rising. "I've gone to the Coast on business."

Five minutes later he was in his car driving north. Two good men followed close behind.

Down in Centre Street Deputy Parr was speaking into his phone to the Greenwood's police. The action would be out of his bailiwick. An affair for the local constabulary. Parr would provide the assisting cast, with guest stars. Pelts, a wry little fellow, one of Parr's prize men, was the bell boy; Morel was the head waiter. Pin Point Annie, whom the deputy had rescued, a brand from the burning, when she was a cigarette girl, was the lay figure.

"You're not coming to the party?" said Parr to Oliver. Armiston shook his head. He liked crime in the abstract, academic; he didn't mind sitting in conference, twiddling his stick and pulling at his single white lock, the while he put forward this and that as a suggestion—like dumping a poor dumb ghost into the lap of its destroyer. But to be in at the kill, to see the illusion torn aside, to hear the trap fall—it wasn't pretty.

When Gregory Wallins registered himself as "Lon Fetty," Elam said: "Front! Show this gentleman to Number Six."

Wallins had himself well in hand. He scanned the register, turned the pages: "Enid Wallins." There it was! He wished he could remember her writing. He couldn't even remember having seen it. But there it was! With a snap he shut the book and turned away. His liquor steeled him.

"You fool!" cried the outraged Elam. "What did you do that for?"

"What?" Wallins leered drunkenly.

"Shut the book."

"Well, what of it?"

"It means a death in the house!" cried Elam nervously. He had known it to happen; even now, with the house full of police, when he was supposed to hold himself in hand, he was white with anger. Wallins moved on, grinning to himself.

"What's this next room?" demanded Wallins, as Pelts, the bell boy, unstrapped the bags. Pelts went over to him and whispered.

"Classy dame! Big eyes, white face, blue-black hair. Too swell to come down to her meals."

"What's her name?"

"I'll find out, sir."

"Anybody else on this corridor?"

"No, sir. It's away from the rest of the house."

"You can fetch my supper up here," said Gregory. "Get me some liquor." He gave Pelts a ten dollar bill; this was his besetting sin, this contemptuous giving to underlings. Pelts was hanging up the things from the bags, feeling for guns, shells. There were none; but in the ulster there was a .25, with a silencer. Pelts deftly extracted the loaded cylinder and palmed it. Passing out, the bell boy went to the rummage closet, where Pin Point Annie looked up, wide-eyed, at his entrance.

"These are for you, sister," said Pelts, extracting the bullets. "They got your name on them."

When he brought up the supper—and the liquor—he set out the things, held Gregory's chair for him, gave him his napkin.

"It's an Enid Wallins, sir," he whispered. "From China, I think—she's got some Chinese junk for jewelry, sir."

A shiver went through Gregory Wallins.

"Damn this ice-box climate!" he snarled. "Get me some more heat, and leave me alone." Pelts opened the radiator. He slyly slipped back the revolver cylinder, now loaded with blanks.

The illusion was perfect. As Oliver had said, when he looked at that lacy stocking, the kerchief, and the glove, it takes only the fragment to make the whole picture, in a mind keyed to imaginings. A woman who wore Chinese junk for jewelry!

Up to this moment it had been touch and go. The signature had been the rub—Parr had cast his all on that. A dozen unseen eyes had watched Gregory as he scanned that phantom autograph on the register, with its two-story handwriting, its dash, its élan, its powerful grace. They had won.

"Well," said Pin Point Annie, when they gave her her cue, "a girl's got to eat. I'll see you in Berlin."

She crept into Enid's bed, drew the clothes up about her, lay there waiting; the moon was high and cast deep shadows. Downstairs the revelry of the skiers gradually died; steps stumbled on stairs, the lights went out one by one; the house slept.

It was two o'clock when that shriek came, a muffled cry trailing off into nothingness; then a pleading, "Gregory! No! No!"

Then a soft *phut*—a muffled report hardly more than the slap of a stave on deep snow.

Morel the head waiter, and Pelts, the bell boy, broke in on the instant. Gregory Wallins was still staring at the object on the couch across the room in the moonlight, swaying drunkenly as he stared. The two men pinioned him with a skill beyond that of menials. The dishevelled Elam came in as they pushed the limp Gregory out into the hall.

"What the hell's going on here?" Elam cried hoarsely, in keeping with his instructions.

"Did he get her? Look and see," directed Morel quietly.

From the room came Elam's voice: "Y-yes. I—I'm afraid so."

"Call your police quietly," said Morel. Lock-steps stumbled off down the stairs. Pin Point Annie sat up, yawning, stretching. She pushed aside her robe and took off a fireman's asbestos vest. "Just in case of fire," she said, to the empty room.

"I suppose every man justifies himself in his own heart for everything he does," said Deputy Parr, settling himself in his favorite elbow chair by Oliver's desk.

"Does Gregory Wallins?"

"Absolutely," said Parr. "The astonishing fact is, this rounder is help-lessly in love, for the first time in his life—with his willowy blonde. She came out of Russia. He's been true to her, after his fashion. But when he was in Shanghai, the other woman, this 'American woman,' begged him to fetch her back to the States with him. He did it. But when he got her here and said 'good-bye' she said 'Oh, no! I'm a white slave now.' He took it to be the usual shake-down, and offered her money. She said, 'Oh, no. Marry me.' He was on the point of marrying the other woman, the blonde."

Parr looked up, spread his hands.

"Well, he married the 'American woman,' " said he grimly. "He lured her back in the woods, to the Squire's cut-rate shack, on some cock-and-bull story or other—then he drowned her in the Beaverkill—or thought he did—and went off on the honeymoon with the substitute bride."

"Wait a minute, Parr," said Oliver. "You say he thought he drowned her. Doesn't he actually know yet that he succeeded?"

Parr shook his head. "No," he said, "he still thinks that she somehow got out of the water and escaped."

"Then what have you got on him?" cried Oliver. "You've established no corpus delicti for that crime. Are you proposing to charge him with assault with intent to kill, with blank cartridges, in that fake scene in your hotel room?"

"We've got his signed confession," said the deputy complacently. "And we've established the corpus delicti."

"What!"

"The Beaverkill police turned up with a story of an unidentified drowning at that time," said Parr, smiling at Oliver's astonishment. "They've got photographs—and her effects. And she had a broken collar bone!"

Oliver stared, dumbstruck. Then that broken collar-bone wasn't a fake.

"It was just one of the little 'ifs' that spoil the 'perfect crime' that you parlor criminologists talk about," said Parr. "There is always an if. If she hadn't broken her collar bone—If Gregory hadn't tipped the Squire with a hundred-dollar bill, instead of a two-spot—If the District Attorney's bright young men hadn't roughed up Elam and made him mad—" he paused, eyeing Oliver. "Wait till the poor devil wakes up and discovers that his crime was perfect in the first place—*if* he had had sense enough to leave it alone!"

The Fifties

AS SIMPLE AS ABC
by *ELLERY QUEEN*

This is a very old story as Queen stories go. It happened in Ellery's salad days, when he was tossing his talents about like a Sunday chef, and a redheaded girl named Nikki Porter had just attached herself to his type-writer. But it has not staled, this story; it has an unwithering flavor which those who partook of it relish to this day. There are gourmets in America whose taste buds leap at any concoction dated 1861–1865. To such, the mere recitation of ingredients like Bloody Angle, Minié balls, Little Mac, *Tenting Tonight,* the brand of General Grant's whiskey, not to mention Father Abraham, is sufficient to start the passionate flow of juices. These are the misty-hearted to whom the Civil War is "the War" and the blue-gray armies rather more than men. Romantics, if you will; garnishers of history. But it is they who pace the lonely sentrypost by the night Potomac, they who hear the creaking of the ammunition wagons, the snap of campfires, the scream of the thin gray line and the long groan of the battlefield. They personally flee the burning hell of the Wilderness as the dead rise and twist in the flames; under lanterns, in the flickering mud, they stoop compassion-ately with the surgeons over quivering heaps. It is they who keep the little flags flying and the ivy ever green on the graves of the old men.

Ellery is of this company, and that is why he regards the case of the old men of Jacksburg, Pennsylvania, with particular affection.

Ellery and Nikki came upon the village of Jacksburg as people often come upon the best things, unpropitiously. They had been driving back to New York from Washington, where Ellery had done some sleuthing among the stacks of the Library of Congress. Perhaps the sight of the Potomac, Arlington's eternal geometry, Lincoln frozen in giant sadness, brought its weight to bear upon Ellery's decision to veer towards Gettysburg, where murder had been national. And Nikki had never been there, and May was coming to its end. There was a climate of sentiment.

They crossed the Maryland-Pennsylvania line and spent timeless hours wandering over Culp's Hill and Seminary Ridge and Little Round Top and Spangler's Spring among the watchful monuments. It is a place of everlasting life, where Pickett and Jeb Stuart keep charging to the sight of those with eyes to see, where the blood spills fresh if colorlessly, and the highpitched tones of a tall and ugly man still ring out over the graves. When they left, Ellery and Nikki were in a mood of wonder, unconscious of time or place, oblivious to the darkening sky and the direction in which the nose of the Duesenberg pointed. So in time they were disagreeably awakened by the alarm clock of nature. The sky had opened on their heads, drenching them to the skin instantly. From the horizon behind them Gettysburg was a battlefield again, sending great flashes of fire through the darkness to the din of celestial cannon. Ellery stopped the car and put the top up, but the mood was drowned when he discovered that something ultimate had happened to the ignition system. They were marooned in a faraway land, Nikki moaned.

"We can't go on in these wet clothes, Ellery!"

"Do you suggest that we stay here in them? I'll get this crackerbox started if . . ." But at that moment the watery lights of a house wavered on somewhere ahead, and Ellery became cheerful again.

"At least we'll find out where we are and how far it is to where we ought to be. Who knows? There may even be a garage."

It was a little white house on a little swampy road marked off by a little stone fence covered with rambler rose vines, and the man who opened the door to the dripping wayfarers was little, too, little and weatherskinned and callused, with eyes that seemed to have roots in the stones and springs of the Pennsylvania countryside. They smiled hospitably, but the smile became concern when he saw how wet they were.

"Won't take no for an answer," he said in a remarkably deep voice, and he chuckled. "That's doctor's orders, though I expect you didn't see my shingle—mostly overgrown with ivy. Got a change of clothing?"

"Oh, yes!" said Nikki abjectly.

Ellery, being a man, hesitated. The house looked neat and clean, there was an enticing fire, and the rain at their backs was coming down with a roar. "Well, thank you . . . but if I might use your phone to call a garage—"

"You just give me the keys to your car trunk."

"But we can't turn your home into a tourist house—"

"It's that, too, when the good Lord sends a wanderer my way. Now see here, this storm's going to keep up most of the night and the roads hereabout get mighty soupy." The little man was bustling into waterproofs and overshoes. "I'll get Lew Bagley over at the garage to pick up your car, but for now let's have those keys."

So an hour later, while the elements warred outside, they were toasting safely in a pleasant little parlor, full of Dr. Martin Strong's homemade poppy-seed twists, scrapple, and coffee. The doctor, who lived alone, was his own cook. He was also, he said with a chuckle, mayor of the village of Jacksburg, and its chief of police.

"Lot of us in the village run double harness. Bill Yoder of the hardware store's our undertaker. Lew Bagley's also the fire chief. Ed MacShane—"

"Jacksburger-of-all-trades you may be, Dr. Strong," said Ellery, "but to me you'll always be primarily the Good Samaritan."

"Hallelujah," said Nikki.

"And make it Doc," said their host. "Why, it's just selfishness on my part, Mr. Queen. We're off the beaten track here, and you do get a hankering for a new face. I guess I know every dimple and wen on the five hundred and thirty-four in Jacksburg."

"I don't suppose your police chiefship keeps you very busy."

Doc Strong laughed. "Not any. Though last year—" His eyes puckered and he got up to poke the fire. "Did you say, Miss Porter, that Mr. Queen is sort of a detective?"

"Sort of a!" began Nikki. "Why, Dr. Strong, he's solved some simply unbeliev—"

"My father is an inspector in the New York police department," interrupted Ellery, curbing his new secretary's enthusiasm with an iron glance. "I stick my nose into a case once in a while. What about last year, Doc?"

"What put me in mind of it," said Jacksburg's mayor thoughtfully, "was your saying you'd been to Gettysburg today. And also you being interested in crimes . . ." Dr. Strong said abruptly, "I'm a fool, but I'm worried."

"Worried about what?"

"Well . . . Memorial Day's tomorrow, and for the first time in my life I'm not looking forward to it. Jacksburg makes quite a fuss about Memorial Day. It's not every village can brag about three living veterans of the Civil War."

"Three!" exclaimed Nikki.

"Gives you an idea what the Jacksburg doctoring business is like," grinned Doc Strong. "We run to pioneer-type women and longevity . . . I ought to have said we *had* three Civil War veterans—Caleb Atwell, ninety-seven, of the Atwell family, there are dozens of 'em in the county; Zach Bigelow, ninety-five, who lives with his grandson Andy and Andy's wife and seven kids; and Abner Chase, ninety-four, Cissy Chase's great-grandpa. This year we're down to two. Caleb Atwell died last Memorial Day."

"A,B,C," murmured Ellery.

"What's that?"

"I have a bookkeeper's mind, Doc. Atwell, Bigelow, and Chase. Call it a spur-of-the-moment mnemonic system. A died last Memorial Day. Is that why you're not looking forward to this one? B following A sort of thing?"

"Didn't it always?" said Doc Strong with defiance. "Though I'm afraid it ain't—isn't as simple as all that. Maybe I better tell you how Caleb Atwell died . . . Every year Caleb, Zach, and Abner have been the star performers of our Memorial Day exercises, which are held at the old burying ground on the Hookerstown road. The oldest—"

"That would be A. Caleb Atwell."

"That's right. As the oldest, Caleb always blew taps on a cracked old bugle that came from their volunteer regiment. And Zach Bigelow, as the next oldest to Caleb Atwell, he'd be the standard bearer, and Ab Chase, as the next-next oldest, he'd lay the wreath on the memorial monument in the burying ground.

"Well, last Memorial Day, while Zach was holding the regimental colors and Ab the wreath, Caleb blew taps the way he'd been doing nigh onto twenty times before. All of a sudden, in the middle of a high note, Caleb keeled over. Dropped in his tracks. Deader than church on Monday."

"Strained himself," said Nikki sympathetically. "But what a poetic way for a Civil War veteran to die."

Doc Strong regarded her oddly. "Maybe," he said. "If you like that kind of poetry." He kicked a log, sending red sparks flying.

"But surely, Doc," said Ellery with a smile, for he was young in those days, "surely you can't have been suspicious about the death of a man of ninety-seven?"

"Maybe I was," muttered their host. "Maybe I was because it so happened I'd given old Caleb a thorough physical check-up only the day before he died. I'd have staked my medical license he'd live to break a hundred and then some. Healthiest old copperhead I ever knew. Copperhead! I'm blaspheming the dead. Caleb lost an eye at Second Bull Run . . . I know—I'm senile. That's what I've been telling myself."

"Just what was it you suspected, Doc?" Ellery forbore to smile now, but only because of Dr. Strong's evident distress.

"Didn't know what to suspect," said the country doctor shortly. "Fooled around with the notion of an autopsy, but the Atwells wouldn't hear of it. Said I was a blame jackass to think a man of ninety-seven would die of anything but old age. I found myself agreeing with 'em. The upshot was we buried Caleb whole."

"But, Doc, at that age the human economy can go to pieces without warning like the one-hoss shay. You must have had another reason for uneasiness. A motive you knew about?"

"Well . . . maybe."

"He was a rich man," said Nikki.

"He didn't have a pot he could call his own," said Doc Strong. "But somebody stood to gain by his death just the same. That is, if the old yarn's true . . . You see, there's been kind of a legend in Jacksburg about those three old fellows, Mr. Queen. I first heard it when I was running around barefoot with my tail hanging out. Folks said then, and they're still saying it, that back in '65 Caleb and Zach and Ab, who were in the same company, found some sort of treasure."

"Treasure . . ." Nikki began to cough.

"Treasure," repeated Doc Strong doggedly. "Fetched it home to Jacksburg with them, the story goes, hid it, and swore they'd never tell a living soul where it was buried. Now there's lots of tales like that came out of the War—" he fixed Nikki with a stern and glittering eye "—and most folks either cough or go into hysterics, but there's something about this one I've always half-believed. So I'm senile on two counts. Just the same, I'll breathe a lot easier when tomorrow's ceremonies are over and Zach Bigelow lays Caleb Atwell's bugle away till next year. As the oldest survivor Zach does the tootling tomorrow."

"They hid the treasure and kept it hidden for considerably over half a century?" Ellery was smiling again. "Doesn't strike me as a very sensible thing to do with a treasure, Doc. It's only sensible if the treasure is imaginary. Then you don't have to produce it."

"The story goes," mumbled Jacksburg's mayor, "that they'd sworn an oath—"

"Not to touch any of it until they all died but one," said Ellery, laughing outright now. "Last-survivor-takes-all Department. Doc, that's the way most of these fairy tales go." Ellery rose, yawning. "I think I hear the featherbed in that other guest room calling. Nikki, your eyeballs are hanging out. Take my advice, Doc, and follow suit. You haven't a thing to worry about but keeping the kids quiet tomorrow while you read the Gettysburg Address!"

As it turned out, the night shared prominently in Doc Martin Strong's Memorial Day responsibilities. Ellery and Nikki awakened to a splendid world, risen from its night's ablutions with a shining eye and a scrubbed look; and they went downstairs within seconds of each other to find the mayor of Jacksburg puttering about the kitchen.

"Morning, morning," said Doc Strong, welcoming but abstracted. "Just fixing things for your breakfast before catching an hour's nap."

"You lamb," said Nikki. "But what a shame, Doctor. Didn't you sleep well last night?"

"Didn't sleep at all. Tossed around a bit and just as I was dropping off my phone rings and it's Cissy Chase. Emergency sick call."

"Cissy Chase." Ellery looked at their host. "Wasn't Chase the name you mentioned last night—?"

"Old Abner Chase's great-granddaughter. That's right, Mr. Queen. Cissy's an orphan and Ab's only kin. She's kept house for the old fellow and taken care of him since she was ten." Doc Strong's shoulders sloped.

Ellery said peculiarly: "It was old Abner . . . ?"

"I was up with Ab all night. This morning, at six thirty, he passed away."

"On Memorial Day!" Nikki sounded like a little girl in her first experience with a fact of life.

There was a silence, fretted by the sizzling of Doc Strong's bacon.

Ellery said at last, "What did Abner Chase die of?"

"Apoplexy."

"A stroke?"

Doc Strong looked at him. He seemed angry. But then he shook his head. "I'm no Mayo brother, Mr. Queen, and I suppose there's a lot about the practice of medicine I'll never get to learn, but I do know a cerebral hemorrhage when I see one, and that's what Ab Chase died of. In a man of ninety-four, that's as close to natural death as you can come . . . No, there wasn't any funny business in this one."

"Except," mumbled Ellery, "that—again—it happened on Memorial Day."

"Man's a contrary animal. Tell him lies and he swallows 'em whole. Give him the truth and he gags on it. Maybe the Almighty gets tired of His thankless job every once in an eon and cuts loose with a little joke." But Doc Strong said it as if he were addressing, not them, but himself. "Any special way you like your eggs?"

"Leave the eggs to me, Doctor," Nikki said firmly. "You go on up those stairs and get some sleep."

"Reckon I better if I'm to do my usual dignified job today," said the mayor of Jacksburg with a sigh. "Though Abner Chase's death is going to make the proceedings solemner than ordinary. Bill Yoder says he's not going to be false to an ancient and honorable profession by doing a hurry-up job undertaking Ab, and maybe that's just as well. If we added the Chase funeral to today's program, even old Abe's immortal words would find it hard to compete! By the way, Mr. Queen, I talked to Lew Bagley this morning and he'll have your car ready in an hour. Special service, seeing you're guests of the mayor." Doc Strong chuckled. "When you planning to leave?"

"I *was* intending . . ." Ellery stopped with a frown. Nikki regarded him with a sniffish look. She had already learned to detect the significance of certain signs peculiar to the Queen physiognomy. "I wonder," murmured Ellery, "how Zach Bigelow's going to take the news."

"He's already taken it, Mr. Queen. Stopped in at Andy Bigelow's place on my way home. Kind of a detour, but I figured I'd better break the news to Zach early as possible."

"Poor thing," said Nikki. "I wonder how it feels to learn you're the only one left." She broke an egg.

"Can't say Zach carried on about it," said Doc Strong dryly. "About all he said, as I recall, was: 'Doggone it, now who's goin' to lay the wreath after I toot the bugle!' I guess when you reach the age of ninety-five, death don't mean what it does to young squirts of sixty-three like me. What time'd you say you were leaving, Mr. Queen?"

"Nikki," muttered Ellery, "are we in any particular hurry?"

"I don't know. Are we?"

"Besides, it wouldn't be patriotic. Doc, do you suppose Jacksburg would mind if a couple of New York Yanks invited themselves to your Memorial Day exercises?"

The business district of Jacksburg consisted of a single paved street bounded at one end by the sightless eye of a broken traffic signal and at the other by the twin gas pumps before Lew Bagley's garage. In between, some stores in need of paint sunned themselves, enjoying the holiday. Red, white, and blue streamers crisscrossed the thoroughfare overhead. A few seedy frame houses, each decorated with an American flag, flanked the main street at both ends.

Ellery and Nikki found the Chase house exactly where Doc Strong had said it would be—just around the corner from Bagley's garage, between the ivy-hidden church and the firehouse of the Jacksburg Volunteer Pump and Hose Company No. 1. But the mayor's directions were a superfluity; it was the only house with a crowded porch.

A heavy-shouldered young girl in a black Sunday dress sat in a rocker, the center of the crowd. Her nose was as red as her big hands, but she was trying to smile at the cheerful words of sympathy winged at her from all sides.

"Thanks, Mis' Plumm . . . That's right, Mr. Schmidt, I know . . . But he was such a spry old soul, Emerson, I can't believe . . ."

"Miss Cissy Chase?"

Had the voice been that of a Confederate spy, a deeper silence could not have drowned the noise. Jacksburg eyes examined Ellery and Nikki with cold curiosity, and feet shuffled.

"My name is Queen and this is Miss Porter. We're attending the Jacksburg Memorial Day exercises as guests of Mayor Strong—" a warming murmur, like a zephyr, passed over the porch "—and he asked us to wait here for him. I'm sorry about your great-grandfather."

"You must have been very proud of him," said Nikki.

"Thank you, I was. It was so sudden— Won't you set? I mean—Do come into the house. Great-grandpa's not here . . . he's over at Bill Yoder's . . ."

The girl was flustered and began to cry, and Nikki took her arm and led her into the house. Ellery lingered a moment to exchange appropriate remarks with the neighbors who, while no longer cold, were still curious; and then he followed. It was a dreary little house, with a dark and musty-smelling parlor.

"Now, now, this is no time for fussing—may I call you Cissy?" Nikki was saying soothingly. "Besides, you're better off away from all those folks. Why, Ellery, she's only a child!"

And a very plain child, Ellery thought, with a pinched face and empty eyes.

"I understand the parade to the burying ground is going to form outside your house, Cissy," he said. "By the way, have Andrew Bigelow and his grandfather Zach arrived yet?"

"Oh, I don't know," said Cissy Chase dully. "It's all like such a dream, seems like."

"Of course it does. And you're left alone. Haven't you any family at all, Cissy?"

"No."

"Isn't there some young man—?"

Cissy shook her head bitterly. "Who'd marry me? This is the only decent dress I got, and it's four years old. We lived on great-grandpa's pension and what I could earn hiring out by the day. Which ain't much, nor often. Now . . ."

"I'm sure you'll find something to do," said Nikki, very heartily.

"In Jacksburg?"

Nikki was silent.

"Cissy." Ellery spoke casually, and she did not even look up. "Doc Strong mentioned something about a treasure. Do you know anything about it?"

"Oh, that." Cissy shrugged. "Just what great-grandpa told me, and he hardly ever told the same story twice. But near as I was ever able to make out, one time during the War him and Caleb Atwell and Zach Bigelow got separated from the army—scouting, or foraging, or something. It was down South somewhere, and they spent the night in an old empty mansion that was half-burned down. Next morning they went through the ruins to see what they could pick up, and buried in the cellar they found the treasure. A big fortune in money, great-grandpa said. They were afraid to take it with them, so they buried it in the same place in the cellar and made a map of the location and after the War they went back, the three of 'em, and dug it up again. Then they made the pact."

"Oh, yes," said Ellery. "The pact."

"Swore they'd hold onto the treasure till only one of them remained alive, I don't know why, then the last one was to get it all. Leastways, that's how great-grandpa told it."

"Did he ever say how much of a fortune it was?"

Cissy laughed. "Couple of hundred thousand dollars. I ain't saying great-grandpa was cracked, but you know how an old man gets."

"Did he ever give you a hint as to where he and Caleb and Zach hid the money after they got it back North?"

"No, he'd just slap his knee and wink at me."

"Maybe," said Ellery suddenly, "maybe there's something to that yarn after all."

Nikki stared. "But Ellery, you said—! Cissy, did you hear that?"

But Cissy only drooped. "If there is, it's all Zach Bigelow's now."

Then Doc Strong came in, fresh as a daisy in a pressed blue suit and a stiff collar and a bow tie, and a great many other people came in, too. Ellery and Nikki surrendered Cissy Chase to Jacksburg.

"If there's anything to the story," Nikki whispered to Ellery, "and if Mayor Strong is right, then that old scoundrel Bigelow's been murdering his friends to get the money!"

"After all these years, Nikki? At the age of ninety-five?" Ellery shook his head.

"But then what—?"

"I don't know." And Ellery fell silent. But his glance went to Doc Strong and waited; and when the little mayor happened to look their way, Ellery caught his eye and took him aside and whispered in his ear. . . .

The procession—nearly every car in Jacksburg, Doc Strong announced proudly, over a hundred of them—got under way at exactly two o'clock.

Nikki had been embarrassed but not surprised to find herself being handed into the leading car, an old but brightly polished touring job contributed for the occasion by Lew Bagley; and the moment Nikki spied the ancient, doddering head under the Union army hat in the front seat she detected the fine Italian whisper of her employer. Zach Bigelow held his papery frame fiercely if shakily erect between the driver and a powerful red-necked man with a brutal face who, Nikki surmised, was the old man's grandson, Andy Bigelow. Nikki looked back, peering around the flapping folds of the flag stuck in the corner of the car. Cissy Chase was in the second car in a black veil, weeping on a stout woman's shoulder. So the female Yankee from New York sat back between Ellery and Mayor Strong, against the bank of flowers in which the flag was set, and glared at the necks of the two Bigelows, having long since taken sides in this matter. And when Doc Strong made the introductions, Nikki barely nodded to Jacksburg's sole survivor of the Grand Army of the Republic, and then only in acknowledgment of his historic importance.

Ellery, however, was all deference and cordiality, even to the brute grandson. He leaned forward.

"How do I address your grandfather, Mr. Bigelow?"

"Gramp's a general," said Andy Bigelow loudly. "Ain't you, Gramp?" He beamed at the ancient, but Zach Bigelow was staring proudly ahead, holding fast to something in a rotted musette bag on his lap. "Went through the War a private," the grandson confided, "but he don't like to talk about that."

"General Bigelow—"

"That's his deaf ear," said the grandson. "Try the other one."

"General Bigelow!"

"Hey?" The old man turned his trembling head, glaring. "Speak up, bub. Ye're mumblin'."

"General Bigelow," shouted Ellery, "now that all the money is yours, what will you do with it?"

"Hey? Money?"

"The treasure, Gramp," roared Andy Bigelow. "They've even heard about it in New York. What you goin' to do with it, he wants to know?"

"Does, does he?" Old Zach sounded grimly amused. "Can't talk, Andy. Hurts m' neck."

"How much does it amount to, General?" cried Ellery.

Old Zach eyed him. "Mighty nosy, ain't ye?" Then he cackled. "Last time we counted it—Caleb, Ab, and me—came to nigh on a million dollars. Yes, sir, one million dollars." The old man's left eye, startlingly, drooped. "Goin' to be a big surprise to the smart-alecks and the doubtin' Thomases. You wait an' see."

"According to Cissy," Nikki murmured to Doc Strong, "Abner Chase said it was only two hundred thousand."

"Zach makes it more every time he talks about it," said the mayor.

"I heard ye, Martin Strong!" yelled Zach Bigelow, swiveling his twig of a neck so suddenly that Nikki winced, expecting it to snap. "You wait! I'll show ye, ye durn whippersnapper, who's a lot o' wind!"

"Now, Zach," said Doc Strong pacifyingly. "Save your wind for that bugle."

Zach Bigelow cackled and clutched the musette bag in his lap, glaring ahead in triumph, as if he had scored a great victory.

Ellery said no more. Oddly, he kept staring not at old Zach but at Andy Bigelow, who sat beside his grandfather grinning at invisible audiences along the empty countryside as if he, too, had won—or was on his way to winning—a triumph.

The sun was hot. Men shucked their coats and women fanned themselves with handkerchiefs.

"It is for us the living, rather, to be dedicated . . ."

Children dodged among the graves, pursued by shushing mothers. On most of the graves were fresh flowers.

"*. . . that from these honored dead . . .*"

Little American flags protruded from the graves, too.

"*. . . gave the last full measure of devotion . . .*"

Doc Martin Strong's voice was deep and sure, not at all like the voice of that tall ugly man, who had spoken the same words apologetically.

"*. . . that these dead shall not have died in vain . . .*"

Doc was standing on the pedestal of the Civil War Monument, which was decorated with flags and bunting and faced the weathered stone ranks like a commander in full-dress.

"*. . . that this nation, under God . . .*"

A color guard of the American Legion, Jacksburg Post, stood at attention between the mayor and the people. A file of Legionnaires carrying old Sharps rifles faced the graves.

"*. . . and that government of the people . . .*"

Beside the mayor, disdaining the wrestler's shoulder of his simian grandson, stood General Zach Bigelow. Straight as the barrel of a Sharps, musette bag held tightly.

"*. . . shall not perish from the earth.*"

The old man nodded impatiently. He began to fumble with the bag.

"*Comp'ny! Present—arms!*"

"Go ahead, Gramp!" Andy Bigelow bellowed.

The old man muttered. He was having difficulty extricating the bugle from the bag.

"Here, lemme give ye a hand!"

"Let the old man alone, Andy," said the mayor of Jacksburg quietly. "We're in no hurry."

Finally the bugle was free. It was an old army bugle, as old as Zach Bigelow, dented and scarred.

The old man raised it to his lips.

Now his hands were not shaking.

Now even the children were quiet.

And the old man began to play taps.

It could hardly have been called playing. He blew, and out of the bugle's bell came cracked sounds. And sometimes he blew and no sounds came out at all. Then the veins of his neck swelled and his face turned to burning bark. Or he sucked at the mouthpiece, in and out, to clear it of his spittle. But still he blew, and the trees in the burying ground nodded in the warm breeze, and the people stood at attention, listening, as if the butchery of sound were sweet music.

And then, suddenly, the butchery faltered. Old Zach Bigelow stood with bulging eyes. The bugle fell to the pedestal with a tinny clatter.

For an instant everything seemed to stop—the slight movements of the children, the breathing of the people.

Then into the vacuum rushed a murmur of horror, and Nikki unbeliev-ingly opened the eyes which she had shut to glimpse the last of Jacksburg's G.A.R. veterans crumpling to the feet of Doc Strong and Andy Bige-low. . . .

"You were right the first time, Doc," Ellery said.

They were in Andy Bigelow's house, where old Zach's body had been taken from the cemetery. The house was full of chittering women and scampering children, but in this room there were only a few, and they talked in low tones. The old man was laid out on a settee with a patchwork quilt over him. Doc Strong sat in a rocker beside the body.

"It's my fault," he mumbled. "I didn't examine Caleb's mouth last year. I didn't examine the mouthpiece of the bugle. It's my fault."

Ellery soothed him. "It's not an easy poison to spot, Doc, as you know. And after all, the whole thing was so ludicrous. You'd have caught it in autopsy, but the Atwells laughed you out of it."

"They're all gone. All three." Doc Strong looked up fiercely. "Who poisoned that bugle?"

"God Almighty, don't look at me," said Andy Bigelow. "Anybody could of, Doc."

"Anybody, Andy?" the mayor cried. "When Caleb Atwell died, Zach took the bugle and it's been in this house for a year!"

"Anybody could of," said Bigelow stubbornly. "The bugle was hangin' over the fireplace and anybody could of snuck in durin' the night . . . Anyway, it wasn't here before old Caleb died; *he* had it up to last Memorial Day. Who poisoned it in *his* house?"

"We won't get anywhere on this tack, Doc," Ellery murmured. "Bige-low. Did your grandfather ever let on where that Civil War treasure is?"

"Suppose he did." The man licked his lips, blinking, as if he had been surprised into the half-admission. "What's it to you?"

"That money is behind the murders, Bigelow."

"Don't know nothin' about that. Anyway, nobody's got no right to that money but me." Andy Bigelow spread his thick chest. "When Ab Chase died, Gramp was the last survivor. That money was Zach Bigelow's. I'm his next o' kin, so now it's mine!"

"You know where it's hid, Andy." Doc was on his feet, eyes glittering.

"I ain't talkin'. Git outen my house!"

"I'm the law in Jacksburg, too, Andy," Doc said softly. "This is a murder case. Where's that money?"

Bigelow laughed.

"You didn't know, Bigelow, did you?" said Ellery.

"Course not." He laughed again. "See, Doc? He's on your side, and he says I don't know, too."

"That is," said Ellery, "until a few minutes ago."

Bigelow's grin faded. "What are ye talkin' about?"

"Zach Bigelow wrote a message this morning, immediately after Doc Strong told him about Abner Chase's death."

Bigelow's face went ashen.

"And your grandfather sealed the message in an envelope—"

"Who told ye that?" yelled Bigelow.

"One of your children. And the first thing you did when we got home from the burying ground with your grandfather's corpse was to sneak up to the old man's bedroom. Hand it over."

Bigelow made two fists. Then he laughed again. "All right, I'll let ye see it. Hell, I'll let ye dig the money up for me! Why not? It's mine by law. Here, read it. See? He wrote my name on the envelope!"

And so he had. And the message in the envelope was also written in ink, in the same wavering hand:

"Dere Andy now that Ab Chase is ded to—if sumthin happins to me you wil find the money we been keepin all these long yeres in a iron box *in the coffin wich we beried Caleb Atwell in.* I leave it all to you my beluved grandson cuz you been sech a good grandson to me. Yours truly Zach Bigelow."

"In Caleb's coffin," choked Doc Strong.

Ellery's face was impassive. "How soon can you get an exhumation order, Doc?"

"Right now," exclaimed Doc. "I'm also deputy coroner of this district!"

And they took some men and they went back to the old burying ground, and in the darkening day they dug up the remains of Caleb Atwell and they opened the casket and found, on the corpse's knees, a flattish box of iron with a hasp but no lock. And while two strong men held Andy Bigelow to keep him from hurling himself at the crumbling coffin, Doctor-Mayor-Chief-of-Police-Deputy-Coroner Martin Strong held his breath and raised the lid of the box.

And it was crammed to the brim with moldy bills.

In Confederate money.

No one said anything for some time, not even Andy Bigelow.

Then Ellery said, "It stood to reason. They found it buried in the cellar of an old Southern mansion—would it be Northern greenbacks? When they dug it up again after the War and brought it up to Jacksburg they probably had some faint hope that it might have some value. When they realized it was worthless, they decided to have some fun with it. This has been a private joke of those three old rascals since, roughly, 1865. When Caleb died last Memorial Day, Abner and Zach probably decided that, as the first of the trio to go, Caleb ought to have the honor of being custodian of their Confederate treasure in perpetuity. So one of them managed to slip the iron box into the coffin before the lid was screwed on. Zach's note bequeathing his 'fortune' to his 'beloved grandson'—in view of what I've seen of his beloved grandson today—was the old fellow's final joke."

Everybody chuckled; but the corpse stared mirthlessly and the silence fell again, to be broken by a weak curse from Andy Bigelow, and Doc Strong's puzzled: "But, Mr. Queen, that doesn't explain the murders."

"Well, now, Doc, it does," said Ellery; and then he said in a very different tone: "Suppose we put old Caleb back the way we found him, for your re-exhumation later for autopsy, Doc—and then we'll close the book on your Memorial Day murders."

Ellery closed the book in town, in the dusk, on the porch of Cissy Chase's house, which was central and convenient for everybody. Ellery and Nikki and Doc Strong and Cissy and Andy Bigelow—still clutching the iron box dazedly—were on the porch, and Lew Bagley and Bill Yoder and everyone else in Jacksburg, it seemed, stood about on the lawn and side-walk, listening. And there was a touch of sadness to the soft twilight air, for something vital and exciting in the life of the village had come to an end.

"There's no trick to this," began Ellery, "and no joke, either, even though the men who were murdered were so old that death had grown tired waiting for them. The answer is as simple as the initials of their last names. Who knew that the supposed fortune was in Confederate money and therefore worthless? Only the three old men. One or another of the three would hardly have planned the deaths of the other two for possession of some scraps of valueless paper. So the murderer has to be someone who believed the fortune was legitimate and who—since until today there was no clue to the money's hiding place—knew he could claim it legally.

"Now, of course, that last-survivor-take-all business was pure moon-shine, invented by Caleb, Zach, and Abner for their own amusement and the mystification of the community. But the would-be murderer didn't know that. The would-be murderer went on the assumption that the *whole* story was true, or he wouldn't have planned murder in the first place.

"Who would be able to claim the fortune legally if the last of the three old men—the survivor who presumably came into possession of the fortune on the deaths of the other two—died in his turn?"

"Last survivor's heir," said Doc Strong, and he rose.

"And who is the last survivor's heir?"

"*Zach Bigelow's grandson, Andy.*" And the little mayor of Jacksburg stared hard at Bigelow, and a grumbling sound came from the people below, and Bigelow shrank against the wall behind Cissy, as if to seek her protection. But Cissy moved away.

"You thought the fortune was real," Cissy said scornfully, "so you killed Caleb Atwell and my great-grandpa so your grandfather'd be the last survivor so you could kill him and get the fortune."

"That's it, Ellery," cried Nikki.

"Unfortunately, Nikki, that's not it at all. You all refer to Zach Bigelow as the last survivor—"

"Well, he was," said Nikki.

"How could he not be?" said Doc Strong. "Caleb and Abner died first—"

"Literally, that's true," said Ellery, "but what you've all forgotten is that Zach Bigelow was the last survivor *only by accident.* When Abner Chase died early this morning, was it through poisoning, or some other violent means? No, Doc, you were absolutely positive he'd died of a simple cerebral hemorrhage—not by violence, but a natural death. Don't you see that if Abner Chase hadn't died a natural death early this morning, *he'd still be alive this evening?* Zach Bigelow would have put that bugle to his lips this afternoon, just as he did, just as Caleb Atwell did a year ago . . . *and at this moment Abner Chase would have been the last survivor.*

"And who was Abner Chase's only living heir, the girl who would have fallen heir to Abner's 'fortune' when, in time, or through her assistance, he joined his cronies in the great bivouac on the other side?

"You lied to me, Cissy," said Ellery to the shrinking girl in his grip, as a horror very like the horror of the burying ground in the afternoon came over the crowd of mesmerized Jacksburgers. "You pretended you didn't believe the story of the fortune. But that was only after your great-grandfather had inconsiderately died of a stroke just a few hours before old Zach would have died of poisoning, and you couldn't inherit that great, great fortune, anyway!"

MONEY TO BURN

by MARGERY ALLINGHAM

Did you ever see a man set light to money? Real money: using it as a spill to light a cigarette, just to show off? I have. And that's why, when you used the word "psychologist" just now, a little fish leaped in my stomach and my throat felt suddenly tight. Perhaps you think I'm too squeamish. I wonder.

I was born in this street. When I was a girl I went to school just round the corner and later on, after I'd served my apprenticeship in the big dress houses here and in France, I took over the lease of this old house and turned it into the smart little gown shop you see now. It was when I came back to go into business for myself that I saw the change in Louise.

When we went to school together she was something of a beauty, with streaming yellow hair and the cockney child's ferocious, knowing grin. All the kids used to tease her because she was better-looking than we were. The street was just the same then as it is now. Adelaide Street, Soho: shabby and untidy, and yet romantic, with every other doorway in its straggling length leading to a restaurant of some sort. You can eat in every language of the world here. Some places are as expensive as the Ritz and others are as cheap as Louise's papa's Le Coq au Vin, with its one dining room and its single palm in the white-washed tub outside.

Louise had an infant sister and a father who could hardly speak English but who looked at one with proud foreign eyes from under arched brows. I was hardly aware that she had a mother until a day when that gray woman emerged from the cellar under the restaurant to put her foot down and Louise, instead of coming with me into the enchantment of the workshops, had to go down into the kitchens of Le Coq au Vin.

For a long time we used to exchange birthday cards, and then even that contact dropped; but somehow I never forgot Louise and when I came back to the street I was glad to see the name Frosné still under the sign of Le Coq au Vin. The place looked much brighter than I remembered it and appeared to be doing fair business. Certainly it no longer suffered so much by comparison with the expensive Glass Mountain which Adelbert kept opposite. There is no restaurant bearing that name in this street now, nor is there a restaurateur called Adelbert, but diners-out of a few years ago may remember him—if not for his food, at least for his conceit and the two rolls of white fat which were his eyelids.

I went in to see Louise as soon as I had a moment to spare. It was a shock, for I hardly recognized her; but she knew me at once and came out from behind the cashier's desk to give me a welcome which was pathetic. It was like seeing thin ice cracking all over her face—as if by taking her unawares I'd torn aside a barrier.

I heard all the news in the first ten minutes. Both the old people were dead. The mother had gone first but the old man had not followed her for some years after, and in the meantime Louise had carried everything including his vagaries on her shoulders. But she did not complain. Things were a bit easier now. Violetta, the little sister, had a young man who was proving his worth by working there for a pittance, learning the business.

It was a success story of a sort, but I thought Louise had paid pretty dearly for it. She was a year younger than I was, yet she looked as if life had already burned out over her, leaving her hard and polished like a bone in the sun. The gold had gone out of her hair and even her thick lashes looked bleached and tow-colored. There was something else there, too: something hunted which I did not understand at all.

I soon fell into the habit of going in to have supper with her once a week and at these little meals she used to talk. It was evident that she never opened her lips on any personal matter to anyone else; but for some reason she trusted me. Even so it took me months to find out what was the matter with her. When it came out, it was obvious.

Le Coq au Vin had a debt hanging over it. In Mama Frosné's time the family had never owed a penny, but in the year or so between her death and his own, Papa Frosné had somehow contrived not only to borrow the best part of four thousand pounds from Adelbert of the Glass Mountain but to lose every cent of it in half a dozen senile little schemes.

Louise was paying it back in five-hundred-pound installments. As she first told me about it, I happened to glance into her eyes and in them I saw one sort of hell. It has always seemed to me that there are people who can stand Debt in the same way that some men can stand Drink. It may undermine their constitutions but it does not make them openly shabby. Yet to the others, Debt does something unspeakable. The Devil was certainly having his money's worth out of Louise.

I did not argue with her, of course. It was not my place. I sat there registering sympathy until she surprised me by saying suddenly:

"It's not so much the work and the worry, nor even the skimping, that I really hate so much. It's the awful ceremony when I have to pay him. I dread that."

"You're too sensitive," I told her. "Once you have the money in the bank, you can put a check in an envelope, send it to him, and then forget about it, can't you?"

She glanced at me with an odd expression in her eyes; they were almost lead-colored between the bleached lashes.

"You don't know Adelbert," she said. "He's a queer bit of work. I have to pay him in cash and he likes to make a regular little performance of it. He comes here by appointment, has a drink, and likes to have Violetta as a witness by way of audience. If I don't show I'm a bit upset, he goes right on talking until I do. Calls himself a psychologist—says he knows everything I'm thinking."

"That's not what I'd call him," I said. I was disgusted. I hate that sort of thing.

Louise hesitated. "I have watched him burn most of the money just for the effect," she admitted. "There, in front of me."

I felt my eyebrows rising up into my hair. "You can't mean it!" I exclaimed. "The man's not right in the head."

She sighed and I looked at her sharply.

"Why, he's twenty years older than you are, Louise," I began. "Surely there wasn't ever anything between you? You know . . . anything like *that?*"

"No. No, there wasn't, Ellie, honestly." I believed her—she was quite frank about it and obviously as puzzled as I was. "He did speak to Papa once about me when I was a kid. Asked for me formally, you know, as they still did round here at that time. I never heard what the old man said but he never minced words, did he? All I can remember is that I was kept downstairs out of sight for a bit and after that Mama treated me as if I'd been up to something; but I hadn't even spoken to the man—he wasn't a person a young girl *would* notice, was he? That was years ago, though. I suppose Adelbert could have remembered it all that time—but it's not reasonable, is it?"

"That's the one thing it certainly isn't," I told her. "Next time *I'll* be the witness."

"Adelbert would enjoy that," Louise said grimly. "I don't know that I won't hold you to it. You ought to see him!"

We let the subject drop, but I couldn't get it out of my mind. I could see them both from behind the curtains in my shop window and it seemed that whenever I looked out, there was the tight-lipped silent woman, scraping every farthing, and there was the fat man watching her from his doorway across the street, a secret satisfaction on his sallow face.

In the end it got on my nerves and when that happens I have to talk—I can't help it.

There was no one in the street I dared to gossip with, but I did mention the tale to a customer. She was a woman named Mrs. Marten whom I'd particularly liked ever since she'd come in to inquire after the first dress I ever put in my shop window. I made most of her clothes and she had recommended me to one or two ladies in the district where she lived, which was up at Hampstead, nice and far away from Soho. I was fitting her one day when she happened to say something about men and the things they'll stoop to if their pride has been hurt, and before I'd realized what I was doing I'd come out with the story Louise had told me. I didn't mention names, of course, but I may have conveyed that it was all taking place in this street. Mrs. Marten was a nice, gentle little soul with a sweet face, and she was shocked.

"But how awful," she kept saying, "how perfectly awful! To burn the money in front of her after she's worked so hard for it. He must be quite insane. And dangerous."

"Oh, well," I said hastily, "it's his money by the time he does that, and I don't suppose he destroys much of it. Only enough to upset my friend." I was sorry I'd spoken. I hadn't expected Mrs. Marten to be quite so horrified. "It just shows you how other people live." I finished and hoped she'd drop the subject. She didn't, however. The idea seemed to fascinate her even more than it had me. I couldn't get her to leave it alone and she chattered about it all throughout the fitting. Then, just as she was putting on her hat to leave, she suddenly said, "Miss Kaye, I've just had a thought. My brother-in-law is Assistant Commissioner at Scotland Yard. He might be able to think of some way of stopping that dreadful man from torturing that poor little woman you told me about. Shall I mention it to him?"

"Oh, no! Please don't!" I exclaimed. "She'd never forgive me. There's nothing the police could do to help her. I do hope you'll forgive me for saying so, Madam, but I do hope you won't do anything of the sort."

She seemed rather hurt, but she gave me her word. I had no faith in it, naturally. Once a woman has considered talking about a thing, it's as good as done. I was quite upset for a day or two because the last thing I wanted was to get involved; but nothing happened and I'd just started to breathe easily again when I had to go down to Vaughan's, the big wholesale trimmings house at the back of Regent's Street. I was coming out with my parcels when a man came up to me. I knew he was a detective: he was the type, with a very short haircut, a brown raincoat, and that look of being in a settled job and yet not in anything particular. He asked me to come along to his office and I couldn't refuse. I realized he'd been following me until I was far enough away from Adelaide Street where no one would have noticed him approach me.

He took me to his superior who was quite a nice old boy in his way—on nobody's side but his own, as is the way with the police; but I got the impression that he was on the level, which is more than some people are.

He introduced himself as Detective Inspector Cumberland, made me sit down, and sent out for a cup of tea for me. Then he asked me about Louise.

I got into a panic because when you're in business in Adelaide Street, you're in business, and the last thing you can afford to do is get into trouble with your neighbors. I denied everything, of course, insisting that I hardly knew the woman.

Cumberland wouldn't have that. I must say he knew how to handle me. He kept me going over and over my own affairs until I was thankful to speak about anything else. In the end I gave way because, after all, nobody was doing anything criminal as far as I could see. I told him all I knew, letting him draw it out bit by bit, and when I'd finished he laughed at me, peering at me with little bright eyes under brows which were as thick as silver fox fur.

"Well," he said, "there's nothing so terrible in all that, is there?"

"No," I said sulkily. He made me feel like a fool.

He sighed and leaned back in his chair.

"You run away and forget this little interview," he told me. "But just so that you don't start imagining things, let me point out something to you. The police are in business too, in a way. In their own business, that is, and when an officer in my position gets an inquiry from higher up he's got to investigate it, hasn't he? He may well think that the crime of destroying currency—'defacing the coin of the realm,' we call it—is not very serious compared with some of the things he's got to deal with; but all the same if he's asked about it he's got to make some sort of move and send in some sort of report. Then it can all be . . . er . . . filed and forgotten, can't it?"

"Yes," I agreed, very relieved. "Yes, I suppose it can."

They showed me out and that seemed to be the end of it. I'd had my lesson though, and I never opened my lips again on the subject to anybody. It quite put me off Louise and for a time I avoided her. I made excuses and didn't go in to eat with her. However, I could still see her through the window—see her sitting at the cashier's desk; and I could still see Adelbert peering at her from his doorway.

For a month or two everything went on quietly. Then I heard that Violetta's boy had got tired of the restaurant business and had taken a job up North. He had given the girl the chance of marrying and going with him, and they'd gone almost without saying good-bye. I was sorry for Louise, being left alone that way; so I had to go and see her.

She was taking it very well—actually she was pretty lucky, for she had got a new waiter almost at once and her number one girl in the kitchen had stood by her and they managed very well. Louise was very lonely though, so I drifted back into the habit of going in there for a meal once a week. I paid, of course, but she used to come and have hers with me.

I kept her off the subject of Adelbert, but one day near the midsummer's quarter day she referred to him outright and asked me straight if I remembered my promise to be witness on the next pay day. Since Violetta was gone, she'd mentioned me to Adelbert, and he'd seemed pleased.

Well, I couldn't get out of it without hurting her feelings and since nothing seemed to turn on it I agreed. I don't pretend I wasn't curious: it was a love affair without, so far as I could see, any love at all.

The time for payment was fixed for half an hour after closing time on Midsummer's Day, and when I slipped down the street to the corner the blinds of Le Coq au Vin were closed and the door shut. The new waiter was taking a breath of air on the basement steps and he let me in through the kitchens. I went up the dark service stairs and found the two of them already sitting there, waiting for me.

The dining room was dark except for a single shaded bulb over the alcove table where they sat and I had a good look at them as I came down the room. They made an extraordinary pair.

I don't know if you've seen one of those fat little Chinese gods whom people keep on their mantel shelves to bring them luck? They are all supposed to be laughing but some only pretend and the folds of their china faces are stiff and merciless for all the upward lines. Adelbert reminded me of one of those. He always wore a black dinner jacket for work, but it was very thin and very loose. It came into my mind that when he took it off it must have hung like a gown. He was sitting swathed in it, looking squat and flabby against the white paneling of the wall.

Louise, on the other hand, in her black dress and tight woolen cardigan, was as spare and hard as a withered branch. Just for an instant I realized how furious she must make him. There was nothing yielding or shrinking about her. She wasn't giving any more than she was forced to—not an inch. I never saw anything so unbending in my life. She stood up to him all the time.

There was a bottle of Dubonnet on the table and they each had a small glass. When I appeared, Louise poured one for me.

The whole performance was very formal. Although they'd both lived in London all their lives, the French blood in both of them was very apparent. They each shook hands with me and Adelbert kicked the chair out for me if he only made a pretense of rising.

Louise had the big bank envelope in her black bag which she nursed as if it was a pet, and as soon as I'd taken a sip of my drink she produced the envelope and pushed it across the table to the man.

"Five hundred," she said. "The receipt is in there, already made out. Perhaps you'd sign it, please."

There was not a word out of place, you see, but you could have cut the atmosphere with a knife. She hated him and he was getting his due and nothing else.

He sat looking at her for a moment with a steady, fishy gaze; he seemed to be waiting for something—just a flicker of regret or resentment, I suppose. But he got nothing, and presently he took the envelope between his sausage fingers and thumbed it open. The five crisp green packages fell out on the white tablecloth. I looked at them with interest, as one does at money. It wasn't a fortune, of course; but to people like myself and Louise, who have to earn every cent the hard way, it was a tidy sum that represented hours of toil and scheming and self-privation.

I didn't like the way the man's fingers played over it and the sneaking spark of sympathy I'd begun to feel for him died abruptly. I knew then that if he'd had his way and married her when she was little more than a child all those years ago, he would have treated her abominably. He was a cruel beast; it took him that way.

I glanced at Louise and saw that she was unmoved. She just sat there with her hands folded, waiting for her receipt.

Adelbert began to count the money. I've always admired the way tellers in banks handle notes, but the way Adelbert did it opened my eyes. He went through them the way a gambler goes through a pack of cards—as if each individual note were alive and part of his hand. He loved the stuff, you could see it.

"All correct," he said at last, and put the bundles in his inside pocket. Then he signed the receipt and handed it to her. Louise took it and put it in her bag. I assumed that was the end of it and wondered what all the fuss was about. I raised my glass to Louise, who acknowledged it, and was getting up when Adelbert stopped me.

"Wait," he said. "We must have a cigarette and perhaps another little glass—if Louise can afford it."

He smiled but she didn't. She poured him another glass and sat there stolidly waiting for him to drink it. He was in no hurry. Presently he took the money out again and laid a fat hand over it as he passed his cigarette case round. I took a cigarette, Louise didn't. There was one of those metal match stands on the table and he bent forward. I moved too, expecting him to give me a light; but he laughed and drew back.

"This gives it a better flavor," he said, and, peeling off one note from the top wad, he lit it and offered me the flame. I had guessed what was coming, so I didn't show any surprise. If Louise could keep a poker face, so could I. I watched the banknote burn out, and then he took another and lit that.

Having failed to move us, he started to talk. He spoke quite normally about the restaurant business—how hard times were and what a lot of work it meant getting up at dawn to go to the market with the chef and how customers liked to keep one up late at night, talking and dawdling as if there was never going to be a tomorrow. It was all directed at Louise, rubbing it in, holding her nose down to exactly what he was doing. But she remained perfectly impassive, her eyes dark like lead, her mouth hard.

When that failed, he got more personal. He said he remembered us both when we were girls and how work and worry had changed us. I was nettled, but not too upset, for it soon became quite obvious that he did not remember me at all. With Louise it was different: he remembered her—every detail—and with something added.

"Your hair was like gold," he said, "and your eyes were blue as glass and you had a little soft wide mouth which was so gay. Where is it now, eh? Here." He patted the money, the old brute. "All here, Louise. I am a psychologist, I see these things. And what is it worth to me? Nothing. Exactly nothing."

He was turning me cold. I stared at him fascinated and saw him suddenly take up a whole package of money and fluff it out until it looked like a lettuce. Louise neither blinked nor spoke. She sat looking at him as if he was nothing, a passerby in the street. No one at all. I'd turned my head to glance at her and missed seeing him strike another match—so when he lit the crisp leaves it took me completely off guard.

"Look out!" I said involuntarily. "Mind what you're doing!"

He laughed like a wicked child, triumphant and delighted. "What about you, Louise? What do you say?"

She continued to look bored and they sat there facing one another squarely. Meantime, of course, the money was blazing.

The whole thing meant nothing to me; perhaps that is why it was my control which snapped.

Anyway, I knocked the cash out of his hand. With a sudden movement I sent the whole hundred notes flying out of his grasp. All over the place they went—on the floor, the table, everywhere. The room was alight with blazing banknotes.

He went after them like a lunatic—you wouldn't have thought a man that fat could have moved so fast.

It was the one that laddered my stocking which gave the game away. A spark burned the nylon and as I felt it, I looked down and snatched the charred note, holding it up to the light. We all saw the flaw in it at the same moment. The ink had run and there was a great streak through the middle, like the veining in a marble slab.

There was a long silence and the first sound came not from us but from the service door. It opened and the new waiter, looking quite different now that he'd changed his coat for one with a policeman's badge on it, came down the room followed by Inspector Cumberland.

They went up to Adelbert and the younger, heavier man put a hand on his shoulder. Cumberland ignored everything but the money. He stamped out the smouldering flames and gathered up the remains and the four untouched wads on the table. Then he smiled briefly.

"Got you, Adelbert. With it on you. We've been wondering who was passing slush in this street and when it came to our ears that someone was burning cash we thought we ought to look into it."

I was still only half comprehending and I held out the note we'd been staring at.

"There's something wrong with this one," I said stupidly.

He took it from me and grunted.

"There's something wrong with all these, my dear. Miss Frosné's money is safe in his pocket where you saw him put it. These are some of the gang's failures. Every maker of counterfeit money has them—as a rule they never leave the printing room. This one in particular is a shocker. I wonder he risked it even for burning. You didn't like wasting it, I suppose, Adelbert. What a careful soul you are."

"How did you find out?" Louise looked from them to me.

Cumberland saved me.

"A policeman, too, Madam," he said, laughing, "can be a psychologist."

THE GENTLEST OF
THE BROTHERS
by DAVID ALEXANDER

Kevin McCarty was a lay brother at the seminary, happily pruning rose-bushes in the institution's gardens, when word arrived that his young sister, Rose Kathleen, had died by her own hand with mortal sin upon her soul. The death alone was a tragic thing, but even more terrible were the letter and package that Kevin McCarty received on the first day of the laying-out. The letter and package were addressed by Rose Kathleen's own hand, the same hand that had lifted the deadly poison to her pretty mouth.

Poor Kevin read the letter over many times and it was a long and shocking message his sister had written down and mailed, along with the package, just before she took her life. Kevin had believed that Rose Kathleen, the last relative he had in all the world since his mother's death, was an actress in the theater. He did not quite approve of her occupation, but after all it was honest work and she was young and radiant and a pretty thing to see, and there was no real harm in letting people look at her there behind the footlights, for no one was ever hurt by looking upon radiance and beauty. But Rose Kathleen had not really been an actress, it seemed. She had been a "dancer." The quotation marks were her own. She had appeared in specialty numbers at Rory O'Bannon's night club called The Fig Leaf and her letter said that "dancers" there hardly danced at all but stood with blue light on them and bared their bodies before the drunken customers. Also, after hours, the "dancers" were forced to entertain the customers who had the wherewithal to pay them for their favors. Rose Kathleen had done it all because in some unaccountable way she had fallen in love with Rory O'Bannon.

Kevin McCarty knew Rory O'Bannon all too well. He had grown up on the same twisting street in Greenwich Village with him. Even as a youth Rory had been a bully, an oversized lad with a wild light in his eyes and a tangled mop of red, curly hair. When they were kids, Kevin McCarty would never fight back when Rory O'Bannon attacked him. This was not because Kevin was frail and undersized and often sickly. He had courage enough. But he could not stand violence and it was impossible for him to strike a blow that might hurt a living thing. That is why he had sought the peace and spiritual life that the brotherhood offered.

The crooked bone in Kevin's thin nose was the result of a beating Rory O'Bannon had given him for no reason at all one day when he was walking home from St. Ignatius's Parochial School. Sometimes, when the weather changed, Kevin's left arm pained him. Long ago Rory O'Bannon had twisted the arm behind his back and when Kevin had refused to say his mother was a word that the bully tried to make him say, the arm had snapped.

Kevin McCarty was not so far removed from the world outside the stone walls of the seminary that he did not read the newspapers and occasionally listen to the radio. He knew what Rory O'Bannon had become. The police had arrested Rory many times and crime commissions had questioned him as often, but only once had he been sent to jail. That time they had found a deadly weapon on his person. They said that Rory O'Bannon was a right bower of Martello, who headed the Syndicate, and that he dealt in such unsavory commodities as narcotics and prostitution. But when they questioned him, Rory stood on his constitutional rights and refused to answer, or stated he was a good citizen because he paid his taxes, and all they had against him, really, was that he owned a night club of questionable repute.

The undressing in blue light and the entertaining of Rory's customers after hours were not the worst things Rose Kathleen told of in her letter. She had lived with Rory O'Bannon for a while, it seemed, in the way that only a wife should live with a man. When Rory had grown tired of her, she had taken to the drugs her mobster peddled. Soon she was not even fit to earn her living as a "dancer." She had to have the stuff, she said, so she sold the only thing she had to sell to get it. Finally she could stand the life she led no longer and had drunk the poison, and thus had added another sin to her poor young soul that had so many scars already.

In the package that came with the letter Kevin found a diary written in his little sister's childish scrawl. She had kept it while she lived with Rory O'Bannon and she had listed names and dates and places concerning the sale of narcotics and other illegal transactions. The name of Martello appeared in the diary many times. Rose Kathleen had thought the information in the little book might enable Kevin to see that Rory O'Bannon and his dynasty of corruption were destroyed.

After Rose Kathleen's funeral, Kevin McCarty appeared before Father Francis, the seminary's rector, and told him of the contents of the letter and the diary. Father Francis had known Kevin's family and the neighborhood in which they lived for many years. He said, "You must send the letter and the diary to Danny Meighan, my son. He grew up next door to you and he was your boyhood friend. I think he loved your little sister, too. Danny is a detective now, you know."

Kevin McCarty shook his head. "I will see Danny, Father. That much I intend. But Danny cannot make Rory O'Bannon die for his sins, and die he must. It is I who must see that Rory O'Bannon dies. It is that I have come to tell you, Father. I must renounce my vows and go back into the world."

The old priest gazed unbelievingly at the frail young man whose pale skin never seemed to brown under the sun of the gardens. "Your vows . . ." the old priest said.

"The Jesuit vows of obedience and poverty," Kevin McCarty replied. "I am poor enough in both wealth and resource, Father. And I am obedient in a way you can never understand. I am obedient to the thing within me that says Rory O'Bannon must die."

"The devil's counsel," Father Francis said.

"I freely confess it is the devil and not Our Blessed Saviour that has possessed me," Kevin McCarty answered. "But to see that Rory O'Bannon dies is my mission and I cannot shirk it. I do not wish to blaspheme, Father, but I say that some men are too vile and evil for the Lord in His kindness and forgiveness to contend with. The devil is the only match for the likes of Rory O'Bannon."

"My son," said Father Francis, "your shock and grief are great and your mind is unhinged. Do you realize that you are telling me, in effect, that you plan to murder Rory O'Bannon?"

"Rory O'Bannon must die," Kevin McCarty repeated stubbornly.

The old priest shook his head and smiled. "No, my son," he said. "I do not fear for you. You are the gentlest of all the brothers. You are one of the gentlest men who has walked the earth since our Saviour died upon the Cross. I have no fear for you, I say. This mood will pass. You could not kill. You could not inflict hurt upon any living thing. Go, if you must, but I will make no report to the Father Provincial as yet. I have abiding faith you will return."

"I am going out into the world again, Father," Kevin McCarty said. "Rory O'Bannon must die, and I am the one who must see to it."

Kevin McCarty left the seminary wearing wrinkled, outmoded clothes and carrying as luggage only the letter and the diary.

His most urgent problem was to find a temporary means of earning his food and lodging while he set about his more important business. He was almost completely naïve, so the problem did not worry him at all. When he was a boy he had delivered groceries for his father's friends, the Gilberto brothers, and later he had clerked in their delicatessen store on Bleecker

Street. He would simply go to the Gilbertos and ask for his old job back again. He needed very little in the way of money.

He found the old store the same as it had always been, long and narrow and darkish and redolent of aging cheese and spicy peppers. The Gilbertos —Jacomo, Harry, and Charley—were the same, too, only older. They were garrulous, kindly, devoted to their business. The deer head was still hanging there upon the wall. All the Gilbertos were hunters. Kevin's father had sometimes accompanied them on hunting trips to upstate New York and New Jersey and as far away as Canada. The oldest brother, Jacomo, had shot the deer whose head hung on the wall. It was dusty and mangy-looking now and one of the antlers had been broken somehow. The deer's head with the accusing glass eyes had always sickened Kevin McCarty.

The three Gilberto brothers greeted Kevin effusively. At first they could not believe he had given up the religious life or that he really wanted his old job back. When they were convinced, they gave him a job as clerk readily enough, apologizing for the salary they could afford to pay. "We are growing old, the three of us," said Charley. "The hours are long. We can use a little help."

Kevin found a furnished one-room flat almost directly across the street from the store. The room was on the second-floor, in the front of the house, and he could sit by the window and watch the trucks and cars and pushcarts and the milling Irish and Italians on the street. In the distance he could see the old church where he had made his first communion.

It took him a week or so to orient himself and to formulate his plan for the killing of Rory O'Bannon.

The Gilberto brothers agreed that Kevin should open the store each morning at 8 and they gave him a key. At 10, Jacomo came in to help, then later Harry arrived, and finally Charley, who kept the store open until 10 at night. Kevin left at 5 as a rule, but if there was a rush, he often stayed on until well past dinner time. He ate at neighborhood hash counters and was never entirely conscious of what food he had ordered. Sometimes he forgot to eat at all and would be surprised when he awakened in the middle of the night with hunger pangs in his stomach.

He called the Mercer Street Station and found that Detective Danny Meighan was working the 4 to midnight shift that week. One evening he dropped around to see his friend. Danny took him to a little private office off the detective squad room where they could be alone.

They exchanged reminiscences of their boyhood on the Greenwich Village streets and in the paved playground behind St. Ignatius's School. Finally they spoke of Rose Kathleen, whom Danny Meighan had loved when he was very young, and, inevitably, of Rory O'Bannon.

"I knew she had taken up with him while you were away with the Fathers," Danny said. "I tried to stop her in my blundering, stupid way, but it did no good, no good at all. I thought of writing to you, but I doubted it would help and I was afraid it would only worry you, spoil the quiet and holy life you led. When young girls get like that there's no accounting for it. It's a certain kind of craziness, I guess. I see a lot just like her in my job. The worse the man is, the tighter hold he seems to get over young girls like Rose Kathleen."

Kevin McCarty said, "Suppose, just suppose now, Danny, that a young girl who went with a man like Rory O'Bannon kept a diary. Suppose she named names and listed places where drugs were sold and unlawful things were done. If the police had such a document, could they take action?"

Danny Meighan's eyes narrowed. "Are you trying to tell me, Kevin-boy, that your sister left such a diary?"

"Now, now, Danny," Kevin McCarty answered. "It's a game of just-suppose, like we used to play when we were kids. You were brought up by the Jesuits yourself. You should know their propensity for arguing and speculating upon abstract propositions."

"Abstract, is it?" asked the young detective. "Well, Kevin-boy, if you've got evidence of the sort that's concrete and not abstract, you'd best give it to the police without further argument or speculation about abstractions."

Kevin shook his head. "The man of action," he said. "Tell me, now. If I gave you such a little book, what would happen, Danny?"

"The police would investigate all the persons named and raid all the addresses mentioned. Given sufficient grounds, they would make arrests."

"And what would happen to the men after they were arrested?"

"They would go to trial, of course. The diary you mention might prove valuable as substantiating evidence."

"What would be their punishment?"

Danny Meighan chuckled. "None of your Jesuit tricks," he warned. "If they were guilty and the police case was presented properly, the jury would convict and the judge would sentence them."

"What would be the sentence?" the frail man persisted.

The detective shrugged. "Who knows? Ten years, perhaps. More likely five."

Kevin McCarty said, "It's not enough. Rory O'Bannon is our own age, about. He'd still be young enough when he got out of prison to ruin more young girls, to sell more narcotics to high school kids. A man like Rory O'Bannon should be condemned to die."

Danny Meighan was startled. "You say that?" he asked. "A gentle soul like you who would never hurt a fly? But you're right, of course, and I agree entirely. There have been several bills drawn up to make the sale of narcotics a capital crime carrying the death penalty, but none of them has passed."

Kevin McCarty rose. "It's been good to see you," he said. "I'm sorry to have taken up your time with suppositional matters. But Rory O'Bannon must die. I'm determined that he must."

The detective looked even more amazed.

"Wait, now, my gentle friend," he said. "Are you telling me that you'll take the law in your own two hands and go gunning for O'Bannon your own self? I must warn you, then, that the killing of even a louse-bit rat like Rory would be murder under the law."

Kevin McCarty nodded. His face was very serious. "I know," he answered. "If I stumble across something less—abstract—I may call upon you again, Danny."

"Do that," said Danny Meighan. "And be careful, Kevin-lad. The likes of Rory O'Bannon are a bit too tough for Jesuit brothers who grow flowers and ponder on abstractions."

Kevin McCarty was no detective but he had little trouble in finding Rory O'Bannon's address. During the crime investigations the papers had made much of Rory's fancy penthouse on the park. For two nights after work Kevin watched the apartment entrance from a park bench, feeding crumbs to the pigeons from a bag he had brought along, but he failed to see anyone who resembled Rory in the slightest. On the third night he left the store earlier and took up his post before he ate his dinner. His vigil was rewarded. A bulky man with a brash face and unruly red hair fringing the hatbrim of his homburg swaggered out of the glass and chromium entrance of the apartment building, flanked on each side by blank-faced men whose shoulders were ridiculously padded and whose hats appeared a size too large. The three entered a waiting limousine as black and shiny as a hearse. Kevin had not seen Rory since the young bully had gone away to reform school, but he had no trouble recognizing him. The papers had been filled with O'Bannon's pictures. Rory had grown much taller and his middle had widened to a paunch, but the wild, cruel look on his face was just the same as always. For a solid week of nights Kevin watched and fed the pigeons. Each night Rory and the blank-faced men and the big car that looked like a hearse appeared. Rory's routine seemed as well established as any respectable citizen's. His schedule varied only by minutes from night to night.

Kevin McCarty felt no qualms about ending his evening watch. The pigeons were plump to the point of exploding, for many others fed them, too. Kevin McCarty knew where to find Rory O'Bannon when he wanted him.

On the second Sabbath after his return to the world of noise and haste and evil men, Kevin took a bus to the quiet village on the Hudson where the seminary was located. Priests are ordinary men, and like ordinary men, they have their hobbies. Father Francis's hobby was photography. He had a camera with a variety of lenses and filters and he had fitted out a large closet as a darkroom. He had filled albums with his photographs of the fathers and the seminarians and the brothers at their work and studies and devotions. He had taken a great fancy to the gentle brother, Kevin Mc-Carty, and had taught him the elements of such matters as shutter-speeds and f-stops.

Father Francis was overjoyed on that sunny Sabbath afternoon when Kevin McCarty walked into his study that was filled with bright plaster saints who brooded on dark rows of books. He thought a prodigal brother had returned and although he doubted his ability to find a fatted calf on such short notice, he was fully prepared to open the best tinned delicacies in the seminary kitchen in celebration. When he found that Kevin had not returned to the fold for good, but only came to borrow his camera and use his darkroom, Father Francis's lined face fell.

"And what of your crazy fixation about this O'Bannon?" he asked.

"I've seen him several times but only from a distance," Kevin replied evasively.

The mystified old man granted Kevin permission to use his photographic equipment, although he felt a strange premonition that the camera and developers might be used for Satan's work.

Kevin had brought the diary along with him. He photographed several pages that he had marked in advance. He developed the negatives and hung the prints up on a rack to dry before Father Francis's small electric fan.

While he was waiting for the prints to dry he had a glass of wine with the old man and told him of the Gilberto brothers and their kindness and of Danny Meighan. He avoided mentioning the prints he had made or his dead sister or Rory O'Bannon. Later, when the prints were dry, he put them in an envelope, pocketed the envelope, and bade the old priest fare-well.

Father Francis pressed Kevin's arm. "My son," he said, "leave God's work to God. I have made no report of you to the Father Provincial as yet."

"Rory O'Bannon is not God's work, Father," Kevin McCarty answered.

For the next two days, Kevin McCarty did little but tend the counter of the store and eat food when he was hungry and sit by the window in his room and compose a letter in his head. When the letter was finally composed to his satisfaction, he put the words upon a piece of paper.

Dear Rory:

You may remember me from our youth or because of my late sister, Rose Kathleen, God rest her soul. I am writing you because Rose Kathleen kept a diary which is now in my possession. I enclose photostats of certain pages from the little book. You will note that your name and the name of Mr. Martello and others are mentioned frequently.

I have not decided just what should be done with this little book. I suppose it is my duty to give it to the authorities. But before I do so I would like to talk to you. If you wish to discuss this matter before I go to the police you must follow my instructions to the letter.

You will come to the room on the second floor front of the house at the address I write below at exactly 3:15 o'clock next Sunday afternoon. You will come alone. I can watch the street from my window and if there are others with you, they will not be admitted to the house. Nor will you be admitted at any time except 3:15 exactly on Sunday afternoon.

You may fear a trap, of course. I tell you that you will find me quite alone and you may remember that I am neither large nor strong. I don't believe that I need warn you to come unarmed. If you fear a trap it would be foolish to supply the police with evidence against you, wouldn't it?

If you do not arrive at 3:15 exactly next Sunday afternoon, I will go directly to the police and the diary will be in their hands by 3:30. If this occurs, you and Mr. Martello and the others will doubtless be arrested and I will make a point of seeing that Mr. Martello knows you could have prevented his arrest by merely talking to me.

Kevin McCarty

Kevin mailed the letter and the enclosures. He stopped at a small shop on Bleecker Street and had duplicates made of the keys to his front door and his room. Then he walked to Mercer Street and mounted the stairs to the detective squad room.

When he and Danny were closeted in the little office again, Kevin said, "Danny, my boy, I've progressed from the abstract to the concrete. If you do exactly as I say you may be able to arrest Rory O'Bannon, with ample evidence of his guilt, next Sunday afternoon." He handed the duplicate keys to the detective. "At 3:30 next Sunday afternoon come to this address." He wrote the address of his house upon a slip of paper and handed it to Danny Meighan. "Use the thick key to open the front door. Walk up one flight of stairs. Then left to the room at the front. Open that door with the thin key. That's all you have to do. But if you value your badge and maybe a promotion, be there at 3:30 on the dot, not a minute early or a minute late."

Danny Meighan protested loudly. He demanded to know what Kevin McCarty was up to and he warned him that Rory O'Bannon was dangerous as a rattlesnake.

Kevin silenced him. "You play my way," he said, "or I call the whole game off."

The gentle brother's next problem was obtaining a gun. He had little knowledge of such matters, but he thought you had to have some kind of permit to purchase firearms. He could think of no good reason he might give the authorities for wanting a license for a gun. The simplest thing was to use one of the hunting rifles the Gilbertos kept racked in a storage closet in the back room of the delicatessen. Acquiring the rifle posed a moral problem. Kevin McCarty had no difficulty at all, in his simple way, in determining right from wrong. But determining between two sins was a different matter. In the end, he decided that lying might be less grievous than stealing. One morning, before the other Gilbertos arrived at the store, Kevin approached Jacomo, the eldest of the brothers. He believed Jacomo would prove the most credulous of the three.

"Mr. Jacomo," he said, and he realized how false his voice must sound, "a friend has asked me to go hunting in the woods next Sunday. I wonder if you would lend me one of your fine guns."

Jacomo was not so credulous. He glared at Kevin and twirled his fierce mustachio. "You! Go hunting! Why, I remember when your father wanted to teach you to shoot when you were a boy. You'd not do so much as wing a rabbit with a BB shot. I think it's bigger game than squirrels and rabbits you want my rifle for, and I refuse." The old man twirled his mustache indignantly. "Besides," he added, "you have no hunting license."

Later in the day Jacomo took his clerk aside. "I did not mean to be so rude," he said. "Take my advice, for I am old and I knew your father, rest his soul. You are not a man who's made for violence. Leave punishment to God and the police."

So the Gilbertos had known about his sister and Rory O'Bannon, too. Everyone had known, it seemed—everyone but Kevin McCarty. He had been too busy with the flowers at the seminary.

In the end he was forced to commit two sins. He had already lied. Now he must steal.

On Friday of that week, two days after he had mailed the letter, Kevin glanced out the window of the store and saw two men eyeing the house where he lived. The shoulders of the men's suits were padded ridiculously and their hats were a size too large. The limousine that was as big and black as a hearse was not in sight, nor was Rory O'Bannon. The two blank-faced men walked down the street to a corner tavern. Presently they returned and entered Gilberto's delicatessen. They must have talked to the bartender who had grown up with Kevin. They walked straight up to him. Kevin was making a "hero" sandwich—a whole small loaf of Italian bread sliced down the middle and stuffed with spiced meat and cheese—for a neighborhood workman. When the two men saw how small and meek Kevin was, they exchanged glances and almost broke out laughing. Kevin finished the sandwich and looked inquiringly at the two blank-faced men as if he had never seen them before.

"Gimme one of them," the first man said, pointing to the bulky sandwich.

"Make it two," said the second man.

Kevin made the sandwiches, then said, "Mustard?"

"Yeah, mustard," said one blank-faced man.

"That's right," said the other.

"Bottla pop," said one.

"Make it two," said the other.

None of the Gilbertos was near. Kevin opened pop bottles on the counter. One blank-faced man pulled out a clasp knife, snapped it open, held Kevin with his eyes. He halved the sandwich with his knife, saying, "Your name McCarty?"

"It is that," Kevin answered.

The blank-faced man said, "You're gonna have a visitor Sunday. At 3:15. Be nice to him. Give him what he wants. We'll be right outside."

The blank-faced man laid the knife on the counter with the blade unsheathed. The two men with padded shoulders ate their sandwiches and drank their pop. They stared at Kevin as they ate and drank. They finished and put a bill upon the counter. One man clasped and pocketed the knife. He pushed a half-dollar tip toward Kevin.

"Be nice," he said again.

The two men with the padded shoulders and the hats a size too large left without looking back.

Kevin McCarty did not see Rory's bodyguards again that day or on Saturday.

The day that Kevin had dedicated to what he called the devil's work was a Sabbath shining with God's bright sun. Bleecker Street was festive with small Italian girls in starched and frilly dresses who clutched bouquets of white and pink rosebuds. They were starry-eyed after their first communion.

At noon Kevin crossed the street to the delicatessen store and opened the big door with his key. He nodded to several loungers in the street. The loungers knew he worked at the store—they would think nothing of his entering at a time the delicatessen was supposed to be closed. Kevin went at once to the back room and turned on a dim bulb. He secured a screwdriver from the Gilbertos' tool chest. The door to the closet where the guns were kept was fastened by a padlock that fitted two rings screwed into the wall and door. In five minutes Kevin had removed one of the rings and the door creaked open. Kevin McCarty had never pulled a trigger but he knew something about firearms. His father, hoping to interest his son in the sport of hunting, had made Kevin clean his rifles. Kevin liked the weight and balance of a Marlin rifle. He removed it from the rack and loaded it with the proper ammunition. He did not feel too guilty about taking the rifle. It would be returned when the thing was done. He could not return the ammunition, of course. Once a bullet is fired it is of no further use. He had taken only one bullet, because that was all he would need.

Kevin took his sister's diary from his pocket and placed it in the space the Marlin had occupied. It was a safe enough hiding place.

He tore a long piece of wide, brown butcher's paper from a roll in the store. He wrapped the rifle into a shapeless package and wound heavy string around it. He screwed back the ring, to which the padlock was still attached, into the wall and returned to his room with the shapeless package tucked under his arm.

Kevin unwrapped the rifle, then stuffed the paper and string into a tin wastebasket that had Easter lilies painted on it. He leaned the loaded rifle against the window, behind the drapes. He took a Bible from the table and sat down in the chair by the window. It was just 12:30.

At ten minutes after 3, Kevin glanced at the loud-ticking alarm clock on the table. He placed the Bible in his lap, shifted slightly in his chair, and gazed out the window. He saw a limousine as big and black as a hearse approaching. The car passed under Kevin's window very slowly. He could see a blurred face pressed against the window of the car.

The car moved on to the corner and was steered into a parking space. Three men got out. One was Rory O'Bannon. The other two wore suits with padded shoulders and hats a size too large. Kevin smiled. Rory was afraid to come alone. "We'll be right outside," one of the men had said. Now the two men seemed to be arguing with Rory. At length one returned to the car. The other walked briskly down the street and took up a post outside Gilberto's Delicatessen. Rory O'Bannon crossed to Kevin's side of the street. When he reached the house, he examined the number on the door. The bell buzzed in Kevin's room. It was exactly 3:15. Kevin placed the Bible on the table, then pressed the plunger that released the front door latch. He glanced out the window to make sure that only Rory entered. He opened the door of his room slightly and left it ajar. He returned to the chair by the window. He could feel the rifle through the drapes. The stairs groaned under Rory's weight.

Then there was a soft tapping on the door.

"Come in, Rory. I'm quite alone."

Rory O'Bannon's big frame filled the doorway. The wild eyes darted suspiciously about the little room. The big man crossed to Kevin's chair in three strides. He grabbed Kevin under the arms and pulled him up roughly. Without saying a word, he tapped Kevin's pockets and armpits. He shoved Kevin back into the chair, jerked open the door of the closet, and peered inside. He even looked under the bed. At last he was satisfied. He looked speculatively at Kevin McCarty, gave a short, unpleasant laugh, seated himself on the edge of a chair, and said, "You got the diary? What's the deal?"

"I don't have the diary here," Kevin answered. "It's hidden in a place known only to myself. There's a way you can prevent me taking it to the police. Let's understand each other, Rory. You once tried beating me to make me say a thing I didn't want to say. That didn't work. I know your men are downstairs. You can't kidnap me, though—Bleecker is a crowded street. You could never get away with dragging me to that big car of yours."

"How much you want?" asked Rory. "Wait. I got something to tell you first. It ain't worth much. It ain't worth much because your little sister was a hophead and a tramp. A judge or jury won't believe much of what a hophead and a tramp writes down. But it might cause a little trouble. Martello don't like trouble. He'll pay a little just to save him trouble."

Kevin McCarty stole a glance at the clock. 3:23. Seven minutes more. Maybe he had timed it wrong. Maybe he should have allowed only ten minutes instead of fifteen. He pretended to think over the sum he should ask. The clock ticked loudly but all too slowly.

Finally, he said, "I don't want money, Rory. I took the Jesuit vow of poverty once. I only want to prove a theory. The Jesuits are great ones for proving theories, Rory."

The clock ticked. 3:25. Five minutes more.

"Quit the double-talk," said Rory angrily. "Whatcha trying to prove?"

"I've always had a theory you were yellow, Rory. I want to prove it."

Rory O'Bannon's face went crimson. He rose from his chair, advanced a step toward the frail, calm man. Kevin McCarty hadn't risen from the chair. But a rifle had suddenly appeared in his hands. The rifle was pointed directly at Rory O'Bannon.

3:26.

"Don't come any closer, Rory," Kevin McCarty warned. "The rifle's loaded. Sit down in the chair."

Rory sat. "You double-crossing rat," he said.

Kevin McCarty said, "No, Rory. You'll get your chance, just as I promised. I think you're yellow. I don't think you have the guts to kill a man. I want to prove you haven't."

3:27.

Kevin McCarty glanced out the window. The big, black car was still parked down the street. The blank-faced man was standing intent, motionless, across the street. Then Kevin saw Danny Meighan approaching. He was walking at a pace that was maddeningly slow.

"In just a minute I'm going to walk out that door, Rory," Kevin McCarty said. "I'm going to get the diary and go straight to the police. There's only one way you can stop me. You can kill me."

"You've flipped your lid," said Rory. "Listen, I'll pay, see? I'll pay plenty. You can give it to the church."

Danny Meighan was in front of the house now. He was consulting a slip of paper to confirm the address. He was mounting the stoop. Kevin Mc-Carty rose. He crossed the room. He stood by the door. Below, he heard steps mounting the stairs. He tossed the rifle into Rory O'Bannon's lap. He said, "It's on safety. Snap back that little knob on the right to take it off. I'm leaving, Rory. This is your last chance." He touched the doorknob. "Shoot me now, Rory, or I go to the cops. Be sure you kill me—or I'll talk and tell them where to find the diary."

Rory raised the rifle, complete amazement on his face.

A man, walking cautiously, was coming down the hall.

"Good-bye, Rory O'Bannon," said Kevin McCarty, turning the knob.

The small room was filled with sudden sound.

Kevin McCarty crumpled to the floor.

The gentlest of the brothers lived for just 60 tickings of the clock. But he lived long enough.

He lived long enough to hear the door fly open and to see Danny Meighan standing there with a revolver in his hand. He lived long enough to hear the futile trigger-click of the now empty rifle, to hear the rifle drop to the floor, and to hear Rory's squeal, "Don't shoot! Don't shoot me, copper!"

He lived just long enough to know that Rory O'Bannon would surely die in the electric chair for the murder of Kevin McCarty.

ONE-WAY STREET

by *ANTHONY ARMSTRONG*

If it hadn't been for little Mr. Harold Bent being apparently oblivious of the fact that the Trafalgar Square traffic went one way round only, the body of James Wellson would have been discovered five minutes later than it was. It would also have been discovered half a mile away from where it was. And even an extra five minutes and an extra half-mile can, of course, be extremely useful to a murderer, particularly in London.

It happened like this:

Released by the traffic lights, George Travers, taxi driver, swung his cab round the southeast corner of Trafalgar Square and, mingling with the Whitehall stream in the usual crisscross, dodge-as-dodge-can, made for the Pall Mall destination of his fare. As was his custom in all such traffic maelstroms, he kept up under his breath a running fire of malediction against vehicles cutting across him, vehicles which objected to his cutting across them, and above all pedestrians who seemed sublimely unconscious of the fact that vehicles even existed.

As a general rule, his widely aimed obloquy was automatic and largely unnecessary, but suddenly it seemed for once justified. For as he reached the next corner a man, the above-mentioned Mr. Harold Bent, stepped off the central pavement and, narrowly missing a couple of cars, started across in front of George's taxi with his head turned the other way.

George immediately and indignantly squeezed his horn bulb to produce the two cracked and protesting squawks which should freeze the other to startled immobility while he rattled past; but for once it did not work. Instead of stopping in his tracks the pedestrian leaped wildly forward.

George swung his wheel with a blistering oath—too late. The taxi's wing caught the other above the left knee. His hat went flying in one direction, while the mackintosh he had been carrying spreadeagled itself in another, frightening the life out of George, who momentarily thought it was the body.

"——! First—accident in eighteen—years!" he ejaculated, scared and furious, as his taxi screeched to a standstill within a few yards. Next minute, however, he realized to his relief that the pedestrian, instead of lying bleeding to death in the road, had already scrambled up from the greasy wood paving and, having received his hat from one bystander and his coat from another, was limping angrily towards him. George's relief, however, was almost at once swallowed up in a vast indignation, for the other's furiously expressed idea seemed to be that it was all George's fault for driving on the wrong side of the road.

"Wrong side of the road!" he spluttered. "In Trafalgar Square there's only one—side of the road. Why, you . . ."

But Mr. Harold Bent was not listening to him. He was now appealing vigorously to bystanders. "Might have killed me! I was looking to my right, wasn't I?"

"Didn't see nothing," cautiously replied a large, stolid man.

"Only saw you on the ground," said a little man with a muffler, also keeping out of the witness-box.

Baffled, the victim opened the taxi door and applied to the fare, ignoring both George's rumbling blasphemies and the petulant honking of a No. 11 bus behind.

"Look, sir!" he began. "You saw it all and . . ." He broke off and turned round. "Here!" he said abruptly to George. "What's up with your passenger? He's ill or something."

The gathering crowd surged forward to peer inside at the hunched figure of a fattish, dark young man, who had fallen forward off the seat and was now collapsed on the floor.

"Thrown forward and stunned 'is-self!" volunteered the large stolid man, knowledgeably inactive.

"Attack o' powmain poisoning?" suggested the man with the muffler hopefully, also doing nothing at all about it.

"Maybe he's only fainted from shock," put in Mr. Harold Bent crisply. "Loosen his collar or something. . . ."

But by then a policeman had plowed through the crowd and taken charge. He gently lifted the inert figure back on to the seat; then turned. "Any one of you people a doctor, please?"

"Any doctor here?" spread outwards like a ripple. A moment later a tall, black-coated figure materialized in the little open space round the door. He knelt in the cab, made a brief examination, then said to the constable in an undertone: "This man is dead!"

"Cor!" said P. C. Robinson, startled out of his stolidity for a moment. "Hrm! I mean, shock o' the accident, sir? Or hit his head on . . ."

"No," replied the doctor, still in the same low, serious tones. "As far as I can see he's been stabbed—there's the hilt of a dagger under the right arm. . . ."

*   *   *

A week had passed and two men sat in armchairs in a small, neatly furnished suburban parlor. Pipes were going and a quart bottle of beer stood half-empty between them. An air of relaxation and contentment hung over the scene, in spite of the fact that the younger man, Inspector Painton, looked worried.

"I'm not happy about it, Dad," he said, chewing on his pipestem. "Here's this chap, James Wellson, stabbed to death about midday in the busiest part of London, a quarter of a mile from Scotland Yard, and we're still just about where we came in."

Ex-Superintendent Painton, a large man who seemed to be built on the lines of a floating dock, grinned over all his chins. "And though, as old Osborn said, you're one of our most promising young Detective-Inspectors, you nevertheless want to talk it out, as usual, with your old father who's now on the shelf."

"Why you ever retired I . . ."

His father waved him to silence.

"Let's talk it over by all means. It does this so-called clear-thinking brain of mine good to tackle a murder problem again—so get going. I've followed fairly closely all that's got into the papers, of course."

His son's face brightened a little and he took some papers from his pocket. "Good. Now, as I expect you know, the taxi driver's statement—without the blasphemy, which cuts it down by 40 percent—is that he was hailed about noon outside a pub near Oxford Circus by the murdered man. He didn't notice the man's companion particularly at that time—he had his back to him and got in quickly—except that he was short and wore a light raincoat, but no hat. Wellson—that's the murdered man—gave the directions—a destination in Pall Mall—but told the driver that his friend wanted to get off first at the southeast corner of Trafalgar Square. So he drives down Regent Street and Haymarket, and turns left for Trafalgar Square, but just as he gets to the near end of the National Gallery the murderer raps on the glass and wants to get out. He's told that this is the northwest corner, the southeast is at Charing Cross, diagonally opposite. He retorts that this is the corner he meant, and out he gets."

"So this is the first time the taxi driver hears his voice? Don't mind my interrupting, boy: I'm just getting the picture."

"That's O.K. . . . Yes, and he says he had a husky voice, as though he had a very bad throat. It's the first time, too, he sees his face and notices he has a small black mustache. Also he's wearing brown gloves."

"So you found no helpful fingerprints on the door handle, hilt of weapon, or elsewhere?"

"Quite right. Well, he tells the driver to carry on to Pall Mall, calls out 'So long' to his companion inside . . ."

"Who didn't answer, of course?"

"No. For by then obviously he was already dead, but probably propped up in the corner to look natural."

The elder man refilled his glass and then stretched his enormous body out more comfortably, as if to give his mind more scope. "What's your idea, son, about why he got out at that particular place?"

"Because he'd done the job."

Here his father nodded slowly to himself three or four times.

"He didn't want to stick around with the body any longer than he had to. He was right, too; because in point of fact it was only a few minutes afterwards that Wellson's body was prematurely discovered through a quite unforeseen accident. Not that it helps. Our murderer, a small man with a mustache—certainly shaved off by now—and a husky voice, probably a disguised one, is at large in London and we've no clue at all."

"What about the weapon?"

"No help. One of those thin, steel, paper knives, such as might have been bought anywhere, and sharpened to a keen point. Used with skill, of course."

The ex-Superintendent grunted, busied himself with refilling his pipe, then asked: "No clues from the Wellson end of the business?"

"Nope. The taxi's destination was only the corner of Pall Mall and St. James's Street—nothing to pick up there—while at the Oxford Circus pub all we've got is a barman who thinks he remembers him and that he was having a drink with a short man. But the place was very full and he was too busy to notice much. He says, however, that this other fellow, whoever he was, had no mustache, hadn't got a raincoat, and anyway, Wellson left the pub alone."

"What about Wellson's background?"

"Not much to find out. He was unmarried and lived in rooms in Hampstead. Out all day—worked in an engineering firm. Lots of pub friends, but no definite enemies at this time. Unfortunately for us, though, he had too many potential enemies from the past."

"Meaning?"

"Well, he was a nasty bit of work—been reserved all the war on a sort of traveling inspector's job and specialized in playing about with wives in the various towns he visited, generally those whose husbands were away in the Services. Almost any wronged husband, therefore, may have had it in for him—*when* he discovered, which may not have been till he came home, some good while after Wellson's association ceased. Naturally it's almost impossible to check up on all these women—different towns over five years or so—particularly when he no doubt kept his affairs as secret as possible."

"Hmf!" went the elder man, in a baffled sort of way, and drank some beer. "You *have* got something to chew on, Jack, haven't you?"

"And even that motive's only guesswork—though I've checked Wellson's background pretty carefully and can't find another as likely."

"It's probably the right one. As a starting point, let's assume it is. O.K.? . . . Right! The murderer has only recently discovered that Wellson was his wife's seducer at some time or another, and is all out for the biggest sort of revenge. Now what? Did Wellson know who he was?"

"No," said the Inspector definitely. "Or he'd have avoided him for a cert. *Yet* he knew him sufficiently well to give him a lift in his cab some distance out of his direct route to Pall Mall. So it wasn't a chance taxi-sharing."

"Good point," agreed his father.

"So the other must have deliberately scraped up an acquaintance—object: murder. But"—and his face clouded—"*why* is it that we can't pick up any hint of their having been seen together at any time prior to the murder. We know all Wellson's haunts."

"Ah!" Ex-Superintendent Painton swallowed some more beer "This at last is where I think," he announced portentously, and closed his eyes. . . .

After ten minutes he opened them and emptied his glass. "I'm getting something, Jack," he said. "Hrm! You've made two false assumptions. . . ."

"Hey, steady, Dad!" cried the other, nettled. "You make me sound like a dumb flattie, not C.I.D."

"When you've been as long in the game as I have," began his father. "However . . . you assumed, correctly, that the murderer adopted a false voice to deceive the taxi driver. But in the same breath, my boy, you assumed that his appearance—i.e. the mustache—was *real*. Why shouldn't that have been false too? In other words, though most criminals commit a crime and then 'disappear' by altering their appearance, may we not have one here who changed his appearance solely for the crime? In other words, the murderer, as seen by the only witness, not only 'disappeared' after the crime, but never existed before it."

Jack Painton was forced to admit his father had got something there. "Which accounts for our finding no trace of Wellson ever being associated with a man with a mustache. . . . Wait! But surely the murderer wouldn't have suddenly put on a mustache to go in a taxi with a fellow who knew him otherwise?"

The elder man smiled tolerantly. "Oh, he didn't do that till after he'd killed him. In the taxi. Nor did he use his disguised voice till afterwards either. Remember, he got in quickly and the driver never heard him speak or saw his face till he . . ."

"I get it," said his son, with a touch of annoyance. "What you mean is that the man we've got to find is a chap associated with Wellson before his death, who wasn't disguising his voice nor wearing a false mustache. Easy!"

"No need to be sarcastic, Jack. At least we know he's short—he can hardly have cut his legs down for the job—and"—he puffed complacently —"wasn't a short man talking to Wellson in that Oxford Circus pub?"

"Ye-es. But he hadn't a raincoat, and he didn't leave with Wellson."

"Be your age, Jack! We're obviously dealing with a clever man. The pub was crowded and you don't notice everything in a crowd. Why shouldn't he have had his raincoat on a seat where the barman couldn't see it, and then put it on and left quickly when the fellow wasn't looking—but in plenty of time to catch his victim before he got a taxi? It's a hundred to one against his finding one waiting outside."

Inspector Painton considered a moment, then his face brightened. "You know, Dad, I believe that may be about the size of it. That brain of yours is still pretty clear. I'll get round to the pub myself first thing tomorrow, as a further check. . . . By the way, didn't you say I'd made another false assumption?"

"Oh, yes. You assumed that the murderer got out at that corner of Trafalgar Square because he'd just done the job. It doesn't ring true to me."

"Why not? What's on that clear-thinking mind of yours now?"

"I don't know," said the ex-Superintendent simply. "Give me time. And get me another bottle of beer. Don't bother about my mind yet: I've got a big frame to support."

After a long draught and five minutes' silence with closed eyes, he again stirred ponderously to life. "Yes," he said. "Yes."

"Spill it, you old has-been," grinned his son.

"Here's the fallacy. It wouldn't take long to do the job, and the natural thing would have been to ask to be stopped anywhere he fancied on the direct route to Pall Mall. But he wants a corner of Trafalgar Square which is out of the way. Why? And he makes a mistake in the corner. Now! *Was* it a mistake?"

"Why not? Not everyone's certain of north and south and so on in London."

"All the same, supposing he *had* correctly specified the corner he wanted at the start. It's only a quarter of a minute's walk from the bottom of Haymarket. The obvious thing, therefore, would be to drop him there, and the taxi could at once turn right and go along Pall Mall. But, asking for the S.E. corner means it's got to go all round two sides of the Square to drop him and then come back along the third side, because Trafalgar Square is one-way. It looks, in fact, as though he wanted it to go right round and yet wanted to get . . . By God!" He heaved his vast bulk almost upright. "What a stroke of genius!"

"What is? What?" His son jumped to his feet in his excitement. "Do you think you've got it?"

"It's all Scotland Yard to a pick-pocket I have," he rumbled in heavy triumph. "This murderer is a very bold man—killing a chap in a taxi in broad daylight proves it—but, if my theory is right, his next move tops even that for audacity. Listen! He's forseen that we might get on to his disguise and start looking for him as the real person, who existed before and after. So, ignoring what we could find out about him before, he's taken terrific care not to be suspected *after*."

"How?"

"Who of the persons actually connected with the case do you suspect least?"

Jack Painton thought. "Myself," he said, with a smile, "if that's what you mean?"

"That's right. Go on!"

"Well, the taxi driver, the doctor, P. C. Robinson, who discovered the body, the . . ."

"*Did* the P. C. discover it?"

"Oh, no. The little bloke—what's his name, Harold Bent, who was run over, of course. . . ."

"And *there* you have him," chuckled his father. "Who *could* suspect the man who, by entire accident, discovered the body in front of a score of witnesses and was nearly killed himself into the bargain?"

"Well, I'm . . . but how?"

"Listen!" He spoke in short, triumphant chuckling bursts. "He was the short bloke in the pub: he nips out, putting his raincoat on, and gets his lift, concealing his face from the driver. Does the job. Then putting his mustache and false voice on, he gets out as soon as he has committed the taxi to going round three sides of Trafalgar Square. As it drives on, raincoat off, gloves off, mustache off, and hat on, taken from raincoat pocket. Then he nips down the fourth side of the square in plenty of time to involve himself in a deliberate accident with the taxi he's just left. He has only 50 yards to go, while the taxi has three sides of the square to do, to say nothing of a probable hold-up at one or other of the traffic lights. He waits; along it comes; he starts to cross the road. Remember, the driver said that, instead of stopping short at the horn, he seemed to jump forward. *He* didn't mind risking a broken leg—all the better proof of innocence. In short, your star witness is also your murderer."

He coughed, finished his beer, and said solemnly: "Very good deduction by one of our most promising young Detective-Inspectors. You'll get full marks for it."

Jack Painton rang his father up next morning. "You're right, Dad, as usual, all along," he said. "Harold Bent's wife lived in a North country town where Wellson was in 1944. He seduced her while Bent was a P.O.W. in Burma, and she later on committed suicide in remorse, leaving a letter for her husband. After getting back, Bent spent a year trying to trace the man and only recently got on to him. Then he worked this dodge."

"Have you pulled him in, poor devil?"

"Er—no. And in a way I'm glad not to have had to do it. . . . You see, Dad, Fate's taken a hand in a queer way. Bent got run over yesterday in— of all places—Trafalgar Square, and died this morning. . . ."

MURDER AT THE DOG SHOW
by MIGNON G. EBERHART

The P.A. system warbled, Dr. Marrer—Dr. Marrem—Dr. Richard Marr-rry, through the hospital corridors; I translated it to Dr. Richard Marly and went to the charge desk where I was referred to a telephone. It was Jean calling. "Richard—I was shot at just now in the park."

"That's funny. It sounded as if you said somebody shot at you."

"I did. In the park. But I think he was aiming at Skipper. I had him out for an airing. And you know the finals in the show are tonight—"

"Who shot at you?"

"I don't know. I couldn't see, there was shrubbery. I ran to the avenue, dragging Skipper, and got a taxi. I think somebody is trying to keep Skipper out of the show."

"Call the police—"

"What could I tell them?" she asked reasonably. "Richard, will you come to the show and—well, keep an eye on things? I'll leave a ticket at the box office for you."

There had been a slight coolness between us, owing to the Dog Show and to Jean's kind but firm observations that my own dog, Butch, a Kerry Blue terrier, was not likely ever to take any ribbons.

"You can get somebody else to fault him," she had said mysteriously; but in her opinion Butch's legs were too much or too little like stove pipes and his coat was too black or too blue—in short, he was not a show dog. Jean confidently expected that Skipper, the Kerry Blue she had trained, would walk away with Best in Show.

Right now I swallowed my pride and said I would be there. Jean hung up, and I finished my round of patients as hurriedly as I could and drove home.

Jean was not the type to get the wind up over nothing. On the other hand, a murderous attack on Jean—or on Skipper—seemed very unlikely.

Dogs had brought us together and had very nearly separated us. She had come to me as a patient following a battle between one of the dogs she was training and a beloved old cat; as sometimes happens with a peacemaker,

Jean had received the only wounds. Perhaps I prolonged the treatment; in any event we began to see each other frequently. Her father had died when she was a child and had left Jean and her mother with little money. Jean's only talent, she told me, was a kind of understanding and love for cats, dogs, and all small creatures. As she grew older, this talent turned into a profession: she and her mother started a small kennel at their country cottage. They prospered moderately at first, and more noticeably after Jean had undertaken the training of dogs, as well as their handling in various dog shows. She had the infinite patience required and Skipper was the first dog she had trained and steered successfully through the requisite shows and ribbons to what promised to be a peak of his, and Jean's, career. If he won Best in Show tonight it would be a very bright feather in Jean's little professional cap, for the Heather Dog Show was one of the big, important shows of the year.

Skipper, I knew, belonged to a Mrs. Florrie Carrister who lived in the country near Jean and was in affluent circumstances; she was divorced from her husband Reginald Carrister, a stockbroker in the city, who had inherited considerable fortune. Beyond that—and the fact that Jean considered Skipper a far finer dog than my own Butch—I knew nothing of Skipper, and certainly nothing that could account for anyone taking a pot shot at Jean—or at Skipper. While I could believe that rivalries in a dog show do become fervent, still I did not believe that any rival dog owner would go to such lengths.

Arriving at my apartment I told Suki, who cooks, valets, and answers the telephone for me, where I was going, patted Butch consolingly, told him he was better than any dog at the show, and departed again, this time for the Armory where the dog show was being held.

The whole vicinity of the Armory was a bedlam—taxis arriving, taxis departing, the flash of photographers' bulbs as jeweled and furred ladies and their escorts (or a dog, groomed to the last hair and led along as carefully as if it were the Bank of England on a leash) passed through the foyer. My ticket was waiting for me at the box office and I entered the Armory which I found jammed, confirming my suspicion that all the world loves a dog.

I bought a program. An usher directed me and I went upstairs and came out in a box. It was an end box, a choice one, and sparsely occupied. Two women sat in the front row talking with remarkable volubility and watching some dogs marching sedately around the ring; a man sat in the front row too but at the other end of the box, next to the wall, and leaned intently over the railing.

One of the women in the front row turned, saw me, broke off her flood of talk, and spoke to me. "Dr. Marly? I'm Mrs. Carrister. Jean asked me to leave a ticket for you." She was a large woman, with heavy shoulders that slumped down shapelessly in her seat. The woman in the aisle seat turned and she introduced us. "Miss Runcewell—Dr. Marly. You know—Jean's friend." Mrs. Carrister turned back to me. "I bought Skipper from Miss Runcewell's kennels when he was only six weeks old."

Miss Runcewell, very doggy in a tweed suit and leather hat and gloves, looked modest and Mrs. Carrister glanced back to the ring. "Oh, there's Jean!"

I sat down two rows behind them and watched Jean. She was worth watching—tall and slim and pretty with her short dark hair and level blue eyes; she was wearing a blue skirt, a neatly tailored white coat, and a red scarf, and was putting a lovely blue merle Collie through his paces deftly and precisely. But I didn't see how I was going to keep an eye on things as Jean had so confidently asked me to do. There was too much and at the same time too little to keep an eye on.

So I shifted to the dogs entering the ring and going through their prescribed routine, and decided that in the full view of so many thousands of people nothing in the way of violence was likely to happen. The two women ahead of me talked steadily—indeed, Mrs. Carrister never stopped. The man at the end of the box also watched the dogs. After the second event Miss Runcewell left the box and came back with two orange drinks, one of which she gave to Mrs. Carrister. And just before the next event a man came down the steps, took a seat in the row below and in front of me, and touched Mrs. Carrister on the shoulder. "Hello, Florrie," he said amiably.

He was handsome, as she certainly was not, in his mid-forties, and very elegantly turned out. She turned and said, "Oh, Reginald." Miss Runcewell turned and said how-do-you-do and Mrs. Carrister introduced me. "This is Dr. Marly—my former husband, Mr. Carrister."

We nodded. Mrs. Carrister said, "The Field Trials are coming up. Everything is right on time tonight because the show is on television." She turned absorbedly back to watch the ring and resume the steady talk to which Miss Runcewell contributed only rarely. Mr. Carrister folded his coat over his knees and I felt a twinge of uneasiness. Field Trials—or as the program more accurately put it, Gun Dogs in Action—that meant guns, didn't it?

Jean, however, would not be showing in the Field Trials. And, really, nothing *could* happen. Corn shocks and brush began to move into the ring. It was like Birnam Wood moving upon high Dunsinane Hill except that the corn shocks and brush were mounted on wood and carried by attendants who placed them at strategic intervals over the green ground-cloth. A brace of setters turned up, straining at a leash held by a man in a hunter's red shirt, a gun was fired, and the so-called "Field Trials" began. The gun shot was obviously a blank.

I leaned back and before I knew it was caught up in the color and drama and magnificent performance of the hunting dogs. Even Mrs. Carrister stopped talking and if Mr. Carrister ahead of me moved at all I was not aware of it. It was indeed so stunning a show that nobody in the box said a word when it ended.

The man at the end of the box rose and avoided Mrs. Carrister's bulk between him and the aisle by neatly stepping back over the rows of seats and out of the box. His face seemed suddenly but vaguely familiar to me, yet something about him seemed wrong and unfamiliar. His clothes? But he wore an ordinary dark coat and hat. He vanished at once, attendants appeared and cleared the ring, and I decided I must have seen him sometime, at the hospital.

The show went smoothly on and all at once I became aware of a kind of tension in the air. Mrs. Carrister seemed to have slumped down even more absorbedly in her seat, Miss Runcewell sat upright even more rigidly, and Mr. Carrister said over his shoulder, "It's coming up now. The Best in Show."

My own pulse quickened. I leaned forward to watch the dogs enter the ring which they shortly did, stepping very proudly, every one of them, and then Jean entered with Skipper. I had to admit that he was a beautiful dog, moving with incredible grace and ease, his square muzzle lifted so he could watch Jean for commands. Mr. Carrister turned briefly to me again. "It's amazing what Jean has done with that dog. A Kerry Blue is not easy to train—unless you use a two-by-four."

"You are quite mistaken," I said. "My own Kerry Blue understands everything."

He gave me an indulgent smile. "Look at Skipper stand like that! What he really wants to do is take on the lot of them and have a rousing good fight."

It is true there was a kind of quivering intensity about the Kerry Blue. It is also true that a magnificent Doberman was eyeing a Chesapeake next to him in a deeply brooding manner. Jean leaned over to make some invisible adjustment to the Kerry Blue's whiskers—and did not so much as count her fingers afterward which, in view of Skipper's extremely adequate teeth, astounded me—and the judging began with a long, slow parade around the ring. It was about then that I became aware of a curious mass murmur rising in the Armory. And then I saw it.

Now I am reliably informed that this cannot happen at any dog show; I can only say that it did happen. Another Kerry Blue, unattended by a handler, had mysteriously joined the parade and was marching jauntily along. He was perhaps darker than Skipper, perhaps not as stylish and certainly a little shaggy, but full of *joie de vivre*. I rose in sudden panic. It was my own dog—Butch!

Did he really understand everything? Was he determined to enter the show and compete with Skipper? In that dazed second it seemed possible.

But then he found Jean and leaped on her with glee. Skipper rightly resented this and leaped on Butch, a liberty not wisely taken. Butch has a generous nature—until he is annoyed. In the fraction of a second wild contagion blazed around the ring. I had a flashing vision of the Doberman's handler, who imprudently clung to the Doberman's leash, being dragged across the floor. The Armory rose like a tidal wave and roared. Handlers and judges ran and shouted, whistles blew, some cops came at the double from the main entrance under the correct impression that a riot had broken out, Miss Runcewell jumped up and made for the stairs, and I ran after her.

She knew the way, so she had the best of it through passages that echoed with a truly Gargantuan dog fight to the runway that led to the ring. It was a photo finish, however, for I was frightened. While Butch is remarkably intelligent he could not have induced a taxi driver to bring him to the Armory. And his entrance at that time was not an accident. Once at the runway Miss Runcewell dove into the ring.

I was blocked by a frenzied attendant who was wielding a broom over a Coonhound's back with no perceptible effect. I felt a sharp nip on my ankle, detached a tiny pug who was merely a victim of the contagion and desisted quite amiably, and was seized by Suki, in a dashing Homburg. He also had a walking stick and a wild gleam in his eyes. "I only did what you told me to do! Somebody phoned and said you wanted me to bring Butch to this runway, at exactly this time, and just let him off the leash and—ahhh—" Then Suki dashed into the fray himself, his Oriental calm completely deserting him. His hat flew off, and with his walking stick he flailed at every moving object around him including one of the judges who forgot himself and flailed back—striking, as it happened, one of the handlers who absently struck back also, but instead got a policeman squarely on the chin. This second chain reaction might have gone on and on had not the policeman collared me but then released me with a sharp cry and turned to disengage himself from a large and determined Chow.

Suddenly, magically, people and dogs began to sort themselves out. I do not say that order was instantly restored but it is a fact that judges and handlers of dogs are made of stern stuff. Dogs began to be pulled out of the melee; a doctor and some girls in Red Cross uniform set up a hasty emergency table at the edge of the ring. Their first customer was the policeman who had collared me and he had some difficulty rolling up his trouser leg but valiantly refused to remove his trousers.

I emerged at what was still the focus of a certain amount of activity just as Suki, Jean, Miss Runcewell, and a number of other people succeeded in separating Butch and Skipper. The dogs, surprisingly, took a long look at each other and while I cannot say they exchanged a mutual wink they did look all at once mightily pleased with themselves. Jean's cheeks were pink but she gave me a reassuring wave. Somebody shouted, "Get that dog out of here," and Suki and I complied—although with some difficulty—since Butch obviously wished to remain. However, we finally got him to the runway, put his leash on him, and I told Suki to take him home. Butch gave me a deeply reproachful look but disappeared in Suki's wake and by that time—incredibly!—every dog in the ring was back at his place and looking extremely and mysteriously smug.

A loudspeaker announced in shocked tones that the judging would be resumed, and I made for Mrs. Carrister's box. Once there I paused, panted, and looked around. Little had changed in the box. Miss Runcewell was perched, also panting, on the arm of a seat in the last row. Mr. Carrister was standing, looking down at the ring. Mrs. Carrister was slumped even further down in the first row. The fourth occupant of the box had not returned. The Armory still seethed with a sort of uninhibited joy, but suddenly became quiet as the judging began once more. Jean looked up to find me and I waved encouragement—and then saw her eyes travel downward.

I moved without knowing it. Jean was still staring, her face white and fixed, when I reached Mrs. Carrister's side and saw what Jean had observed from the ring. Mrs. Carrister was still slumped down—too far down.

She was dead.

Suddenly Mr. Carrister and Miss Runcewell were beside me. We all saw the dreadful blotch of wet redness on Mrs. Carrister's white blouse, under her suit jacket. And in a moment I knew that there was nothing I could do for her. I sent Carrister for the police. Mainly, just then, I was afraid of starting a mass panic. I remember telling Miss Runcewell to shut up and that she gulped and did so. I was dimly aware that the judging was proceeding; I had a glimpse of Jean, white but controlled, taking Skipper through his paces. Then a group of policemen arrived and made a blue wall around the box.

One of them said the lady had been stabbed. They tried to find the knife and couldn't, as applause suddenly roared through the Armory, flashbulbs popped, and there was Jean taking the trophy. So Skipper had won Best in Show, Mrs. Carrister had been murdered—and I knew who had murdered her.

But I didn't know how to prove it.

Some time later the situation remained much the same and Jean and I were permitted to gather up Skipper, who was yawning almost as cavernously as the by then empty Armory, and we took a taxi to my apartment. Jean thought it was all over and told me I was wonderful—which was very nice except that the investigation had barely begun and I knew it. The police were still casting about with antennae in the hope of picking up a lead. And the police have remarkably sensitive antennae.

The knife had not been found and it was the considered opinion of a police matron who had retired briefly with Jean and Miss Runcewell, and of the sergeant who had searched me and Mr. Carrister, that none of us had it. There was some muttered talk about the angle of the knife wound from which I gathered that anyone in the box could have killed Mrs. Carrister.

Nevertheless, a few facts did emerge. No one knew, or admitted knowing, the identity of the fourth occupant of the box and all I could say was that his face had seemed familiar to me, but not his clothing—which quite comprehensibly drew skeptical looks from the police.

Mr. Carrister protested that he was on good terms with his former wife, denied killing her, but admitted frankly that he paid her an extremely large alimony. He admitted with equal frankness that he—and only he—had not left the box at any time.

Jean's story of having been shot at in the park elicited the facts that both Miss Runcewell and Mr. Carrister owned guns and that neither of them had an alibi for the time when Jean had given Skipper his run in the park— but then neither of them had a conceivable motive for taking a pot shot at Jean, or at Skipper.

I brought up the problem of Butch's little frolic in the ring and the mysterious telephone call that had led to it, but the lieutenant in charge merely gave me a long look and said something about practical jokes and that young people would be young people. Since I could not possibly prove anything at all, I repressed a desire to tell him that doctors who wish to rise in their profession do not make a hobby of provoking dog fights. It was shortly after that Jean and I were permitted—I do not say asked—to leave.

Suki had heard the news over the radio and was waiting for us, with hot milk and sandwiches for Jean and a highball which he slid into my thankful hand. There was a moment of tension when the two dogs met but now, strangely enough, they seemed to regard each other as old and tried friends. Suki's fuller report of the telephone message was not illuminating. He could not be sure whether it was a woman, or a man imitating a woman's voice. "But orders are orders, Doctor," he said. "I took Butch to the side-street entrance and then to the runway, at exactly eleven o'clock as I was told to do, and just—well, let him off the leash. Nobody stopped me. When Butch saw all those dogs—" He shrugged fatalistically.

I reflected that anyone who had a program for the show knew that the final event was scheduled for eleven—which would include some thousands of people. I did not know what to do and Jean's eyes were clearly expecting something in the nature of a full-fledged miracle. So I told Suki to get my revolver.

I felt it was rather impressive; Jean's eyes widened. But Suki said with insufferable calm that he thought I might require it and pulled it from his pocket. "Load it," I said, trying to regain lost ground.

"Oh, I've already done that, Doctor," and he put the revolver on the desk beside me.

But Jean's eyes still demanded action of some sort and indeed a few questions seemed indicated. I said, "Jean, did Mrs. Carrister ever talk of her husband?"

"Oh, yes. She talked about everything really. She talked all the time. I got so I didn't really listen. But honestly, there wasn't a thing that could be —evidence. She was on good terms with him. And with Miss Runcewell, too. They drove up to my kennels often to see how Skipper was shaping up. Mrs. Carrister had her heart set on Skipper winning. She was going to start a kennel of her own, if he won."

"Mrs. Carrister? Did her husband or Miss Runcewell know of this?"

"I don't know about her husband. But she often spoke of it to Miss Runcewell. You see, if Skipper won the big championship, he'd be—he is —a very valuable dog. The fees as sire alone would be considerable."

"So she would then be a rival—at least, a competitor—of Miss Runcewell's."

"Oh, Miss Runcewell didn't mind. I heard her say something about Mrs. Carrister taking over her kennels. So I think she intends to go out of business. I suppose she was going to sell out to Mrs. Carrister."

After a moment I said, "Did they ever ask questions about—say, me? Or Butch?"

"Oh, yes. They asked all sorts of questions. I told them about Butch and —well, that he isn't a show dog. But he is sweet." Butch heard his name and put his great head on Jean's knee with infuriating complacence. Butch is many things—but he is not sweet.

The telephone rang and I picked it up. "Doctor," said a voice with a heavy French accent. "This is Henri."

"Henri," I said, and light broke upon me. "Henri! You were in the box tonight!"

A flood of English and French burst upon my ear. "My heart, she is not so good. *Le docteur* say no excitement. *Il faut que je parts toute de suite—*"

"Why did you part—I mean, leave?"

He told me at some length. "Thank you," I said at last. "No, I'm sure the police will understand. Give me your telephone number."

He did and I hung up. Jean's eyes were round with questions. I said, "That was Henri. He is headwaiter at—" and I named a famous restaurant downtown. "Mrs. Carrister gave him a ticket to her box for the show tonight. He left after the Field Trials."

I went to my bedroom for my book of special telephone numbers. It seemed to me that there was now enough evidence on which to proceed, so

I started to dial the number of a former patient of mine who is a high official in the police department when—if I may speak frankly—all hell broke loose in the front hall.

I felt for my gun, remembered that it was still on my desk, and ran for the hall amid an ear-splitting tumult of barks. Mr. Carrister was just disappearing into my study, Suki and Jean were tugging at Butch, and Miss Runcewell was efficiently scooping up Skipper's leash. Since the dogs were merely in high spirits and meant nothing really serious in the way of mayhem, we soon assembled in the study where we found Mr. Carrister crouching on top of my desk looking extremely indignant.

Miss Runcewell said, "I was worried about you, Jean. You were not at your hotel, so we thought you might be here," and she held a firm grip on Skipper's leash.

Mr. Carrister eyed Butch coldly and said, "I'll put it to you frankly, Doctor. You were in the box tonight. If you have any idea at all about the murder I want to know what it is."

"Why, certainly," I said. "I'll call the police at once and ask them to make the arrest."

His eyes bulged, Jean gave me an admiring glance, and I picked up the telephone and dialed.

"Hello—" my official friend said sleepily.

"This is Doctor Marly. You may send the police to my house to arrest the person who murdered Mrs. Carrister . . . Yes, I have proof."

Something moved behind me. The dogs burst out in full cry, I seized my gun, and my friend on the phone cried out, "Where's the dog fight?"

"Hurry," I shouted and dropped the telephone but unfortunately dropped my gun at the same time.

Miss Runcewell was already at the front door. So it was the dogs that backed Miss Runcewell into the coat closet, assisted in a hurly-burly way by the rest of us. Suki then neatly locked the door of the closet. Mr. Carrister glanced at Butch, took to the top of the desk again, and said, "Do you mean *she* murdered Florrie? But why?"

"Because you were going to be in the box tonight and Miss Runcewell knew it. She also knew that you had an excellent reason for killing your wife."

Mr. Carrister said, "Huh?"

"It was a pattern of diversionary tactics," I explained. "Your wife appears to have been an exceedingly talkative woman." Carrister nodded unhappily. "I feel sure that Miss Runcewell was told of your expected presence in the box. Certainly at some time she was told of me and my dog. She shot at Jean—not to hurt Jean or Skipper—but merely to induce Jean to ask me to come to the Armory tonight. Then later, on the excuse of getting orange drinks, she left the box and phoned Suki, telling him to bring my dog to the Armory—"

"But he's the dog that started the fight!"

"That was exactly Miss Runcewell's intention. The police would believe that Mrs. Carrister was murdered while everyone's attention was diverted by the—er—confusion attending Butch's entrance in the ring. She saw to it that she was well away from the box during that time. You remained, as she hoped, in the box and consequently became a choice suspect. But your wife was actually murdered during the Field Trials. That's why the police could not find the knife. It was tossed down into the nearest corn shock and carried off when the attendants cleared the ring."

"But how do you know that?"

"Henri—a friend of mine—was in the box. He left after the Field Trials, stepping over the seats behind him rather than disturb Mrs. Carrister to get to the aisle. As you know, we were in an end box. He told me a short time ago that he saw the knife flung down into the corn shock."

"But *why* did she kill my wife?" said Mr. Carrister.

There was clearly only one explanation. I said, "I think you'll find that Mrs. Carrister has loaned Miss Runcewell enough money to keep her kennels going. Possibly the understanding was supposed to be a friendly one and Miss Runcewell did not, in writing, use her kennels as collateral. But Mrs. Carrister was intending to take over Miss Runcewell's kennels and means of livelihood—and Miss Runcewell knew that. She kept up a pretense of friendliness, until the time came when Mrs. Carrister decided to act. Then Miss Runcewell acted first."

Jean linked her arm in mine. "But, Richard, I know that you knew who killed her even *before* Henri phoned! How did you know?"

"Oh," I said. "That. Well—it was during the Field Trials that *both women stopped talking*—Mrs. Carrister for an obvious reason, Miss Runcewell because she knew Mrs. Carrister was dead."

That night Mr. Carrister, handsomely in one way but regrettably in another, presented Skipper to Jean.

After he had gone Jean looked thoughtfully at the two dogs. "They do seem friendly," she said.

Friendly, yes. But two Kerry Blues in the same household? "Butch," I said finally, "may not be a show dog but—"

"But he's your dog," Jean smiled, "and he *is* sweet."

ALWAYS TRUST A COP

by OCTAVUS ROY COHEN

The voice at the other end of the telephone said, "I'm talking from the Los Angeles airport," but to Johnny Norton it didn't seem that way. The voice was coming to him across six thousand miles of ocean, from a steaming island in the South Pacific. He'd last heard that voice a half-dozen years ago, at night, in a foxhole. It had said:

"What's eatin' on you, Johnny? How come you ain't sayin' nothin'?"

The voice on the telephone said, "What's eatin' on you? How come you ain't sayin' nothin'?"

Johnny pulled himself together. He said, "Tex Graham!" and the voice answered, "Of course it's Tex! Who else would it be?"

"Well, listen, fella. After all this time . . ."

"Didn't I promise you'd see me after we got off that stinkin' island? How are you, you old so-and-so?" Except that Tex didn't say so-and-so. He used good, old-fashioned, affectionate Marine talk.

"I'm fine, Tex. You?"

"Right side up is all. How's tricks? You married or something?"

"Yeh. Been married six months. Living in Hollywood."

"I know. Found your name in the phone book. Solid citizen, huh? Whatcha doin' for a livin'?"

"I got a pretty good job."

"Well knock off. I'm shovin' off at 2 A.M. You got a car?"

"A sort of one."

"Hop in it. Bring the old lady. We'll have dinner together and shoot the breeze. How long it take you to make it here?"

"Forty minutes maybe."

"I'll be waitin' in the American Airlines Building. Jeez! kid, it'll be good to see you. Specially without them Japs gettin' in our hair."

Johnny Norton hung up the telephone. He was a big blond kid, 28 years old, weighing around 180. He stood with his back against the wall, staring at his wife, Mary, who was also blond and whose eyes were the same color blue as his. Johnny said, "That was Tex Graham."

"No!"

"Yeh. He's at the airport. Invited us for dinner: you and me both."

She moved close to him and put one hand on his arm. "Gee! I'm sorry, Johnny," and he said, "I got to do it, honey. I'm a cop."

Yes, he was a cop. She thought he was the handsomest cop in Los Angeles. Funny, the thrill she got out of his blue uniform with the big gold-and-silver badge, the black Sam Browne belt, and the precisely creased blue shirt. She looked him over now and said, "Where's your gun?"

"Left it with Eddie Morgan. He's putting on a new pair of grips for me. He'll have it fixed by roll call tomorrow morning." Then he caught a question in her eyes, and said, "It's not that kind of a deal, honey. Tex doesn't know I'm a cop. I'll put on civilian clothes."

"It's not going to be easy, is it, Johnny?"

"You can say that again."

"You have to go?"

"Sure. It's been set up a long time. It's my job to finger him for the FBI."

"Why?" she asked. "If they have his picture?"

"Because the boys in the local office don't know him. He may have changed since the picture was taken: deliberately or otherwise. But he couldn't be so much changed that I wouldn't recognize him."

She was sorry for Johnny. This was a tough assignment. He'd never told her much about the war, but everything he'd told her—every experience— had featured Tex Graham. She watched him dial a number.

"FBI? . . . Connor there? . . . Hilton? . . . Can you reach either of 'em? . . . Sure, it's important . . . This is Officer Norton, Hollywood Division . . . Somebody they want is in town . . . No, I'll be gone . . . Tell them to call the Lieutenant. I'll tell him the score."

He called the Station, got the Lieutenant:

"Johnny Norton talking, Lieutenant. Remember that Tex Graham deal the FBI was talking to us about?"

"The guy you was in the Marines with? The one they want for murder and robbery in Oklahoma?"

"Yeh. Well, he's here. Just till 2 A.M. Connor and Hilton, the two FBI special agents: I just called them. They're out. They want this pinch in a big way. I left word for them to give you a buzz as soon as they showed up."

"What's the scoop, Johnny?"

"I'm meeting Tex right away at the International airport. American Airlines Building. He invited Mary and me for dinner, so if we ain't in that shack, maybe we'll be eating on the Flight Deck. If anything slips, I'll phone you."

"Want us to send out a couple of detectives?"

"Handle it your own way, Lieutenant. But it's FBI's baby. I'll be in civvies."

"Keep your guard up."

"Hell! Lieutenant, I'm not in on this. Like I said, it's all FBI. All they wanted was for me to let them know if he ever got in touch with me, then to help identify him. What they do when they pick him up is their business. I'm not sticking my chin out."

The Lieutenant said okay, and Johnny hung up. He took off his uniform and arranged it meticulously on a hanger in the closet of the tiny apartment. He put on a sports shirt, a pair of slacks, and a Hollywood coat. He changed from black shoes to brown. He looked at Mary, tried to smile, and gave it up as a bad job.

She understood. She always understood how Johnny felt about things. She said, "That's why I'm going with you."

"You'll do nothing of the kind."

She came close to him and took his hands in hers. "The reason I'm going," she said, "is because when it's all over you're going to be feeling pretty low."

He was grateful and said so. It wasn't as though there would be danger. It was an FBI show exclusively. She said, "Don't let it get you down, Johnny. What you've got to do isn't easy, but it's your job."

"I know. But I still wish the guy had gone somewhere else. The FBI set up deals like this every place in the country where Tex had a pal. What hurts is . . . well, dammit! I love the guy."

"He's a murderer, isn't he?"

"Yeh. Sure. But that ain't how I remember him . . ."

No, it wasn't. He remembered boot camp, and rigorous training in Panama. Then the islands. Good times and bad times. He remembered Tex Graham as the toughest Marine in a tough outfit. He'd been flattered to be Tex's closest friend.

Tex had been a killer, even in the Marines. But you judged things by different standards then. It was your job to kill, provided you yourself wanted to live. In one or two places, it had been a little war. Even on Tarawa it had seemed little because he and Tex had usually been on patrol, isolated from the main show. A guy was on his own then. Just him and his buddy and the few others that made up the patrol. You did what you had to do, and tried not to think about it afterward.

It hadn't taken Tex long to learn his way around. He said he'd always had it tough, he didn't mind a little thing like a war. The jungle—well, he didn't like that so much, but he got used to it. Pretty soon he was teaching Johnny and the other men in the platoon. They made him corporal, and would have busted him except that he was too valuable on patrol. What he went after, he got.

He and Johnny were always close. They did a lot of talking, when they had time. It was funny about that: Johnny knew which side was up, but Tex's slant on things—once in a while that got him. He tried to shrug it off, to sell himself the idea that Tex was kidding. But he knew it was on the level, really. He had reason to know . . .

Driving out to the airport, Johnny briefed his young wife on the situation. He said they'd taken Tex off Tarawa on a stretcher, and that was the last he'd seen of the guy. Hadn't even heard from him until just now. But *about* him: that was different.

Johnny didn't know for sure whether Tex had always had a bad streak . . . you couldn't tell when there was a war on. But he certainly had gone bad since VJ day. Half a dozen deals, winding up with bank robbery and murder in Oklahoma. That was when FBI got into the case. They'd checked Tex up one side and down the other. They had made contact with everybody they heard about who'd ever been buddies with the guy: Johnny included. Some day, somewhere, they figured Tex might get in touch with one of 'em. They had read the cards right, obviously, because that's what Tex had done.

"Just one thing I'm worried about, Johnny," she said. "Are you sure he doesn't know you're a policeman?"

"Yeh. If he'd known, he'd never have called me."

The set-up seemed fantastic to her. That her Johnny and this Tex Graham had been close friends seemed incredible: one innately decent, the other plumb bad; one proud to be a cop, hating crime and criminals, the other snatching whatever he wanted at the point of a gun.

Well, what Johnny had to do was simple enough: Just meet Tex and keep him occupied until FBI showed up. Then point him out. It was a job Johnny hated, but there was nothing he could do about it. When you're a cop you don't debate letting a murderer get away, even if he is your friend. Sure, you hate to snag him, or even to help; you wish it was somebody else doing it. But when there isn't anyone else, you just go ahead and obey orders.

It was after dark when they reached the airport. Johnny voiced one last word of warning. He said, "Play it smooth, honey. Tex is sharp. Don't give him any hint you're expecting something to happen."

"Will there be trouble, Johnny?"

"Not a chance. Tex won't know these guys. They'll close in on him from both sides before he knows what's happening." He took one hand from the steering wheel and closed it reassuringly over hers. "I wouldn't let you be leading with your chin: you know that."

She said, Yes, she knew—but that didn't keep her from being worried. Not the physical danger: she accepted his word that there wasn't any, but she knew he was having a bad time, that he'd give plenty not to be mixed up in it.

There were a lot of lights at the airport. They found a parking place, and started walking. They passed TWA and United and Western and Pan-American and walked into American Airlines. It was a rather small building, with counters and clerks and porters and a newsstand, and speakers that murmured at you from the wall announcing plane departures and arrivals, summoning passengers who hadn't checked their tickets or had their luggage weighed.

They walked inside. A man got up from a leather-cushioned chair and bore down on them. He was about 30 years old, and approximately Johnny's size and build. He had black eyes and hair, and he looked as though he'd be able to handle himself anywhere.

He grabbed Johnny and started pumping his hand. He called him a lot of names and said profane things, affectionately. Then he turned around and looked at Mary, and Johnny said, "This is the old lady, Tex."

Tex stuck out a big, hard hand. He said he was pleased to meet her, and how did she ever come to pick a no-good so-and-so like Johnny Norton. He had a soft Texas drawl, and he was so unsuspecting and so delighted at meeting his wartime buddy again that Mary felt sorry for him.

Tex started telling her things about Johnny. He was a great ribber. He told about dames, and put it on so thick she knew he was kidding. Meanwhile, she saw Johnny glancing at the door, watching for the FBI agents who were to make the pinch.

"How's about some chow?" inquired Johnny. "You hungry?"

"When'd you ever see me when I wasn't?"

"They got a good restaurant right here."

"Hell," said Tex. "I been livin' in restaurants, 'specially airport ones. What about letting the Missus fix me up some home cooking: I ain't pulling out until two in the morning."

That was what Tex said, but Johnny knew that what he meant was something far deeper than that.

Tex had been on the lam for a long time. He was wanted. He never knew where or when they might close in on him, and the prospect of spending several hours in a public place was bound to make him nervous. Of course, Johnny preferred to remain right where he was, and so he tried to stall. He said, "Well gee! Tex—Mary hadn't figured on doing any cooking tonight."

Tex grinned at her. "Not even for an old friend of your husband's?" and Mary said, sure, she'd be glad to fix a dinner for him. Tex was enthusiastic. Like a kid. He said it'd be swell to relax in Johnny's home, to eat Johnny's wife's cooking, to spend a few hours chewing the fat.

Mary saw that her husband didn't like the way things were going. She knew he was mentally bawling out the Lieutenant for not having kept hard after the FBI, that he was sore at the FBI for not being at the airport. She was afraid Johnny would give himself away, and so she took the reins in her own hands. She said they'd drive back together and that she'd stop at a market and buy some beer and stuff. Johnny caught what she had in mind, and he went along with it.

Driving in, she marveled at their man-talk. Funny how the tiniest detail of their service days together seemed important. They laughed about things that didn't seem very funny to her, and she was shrewd enough to realize that what they were laughing about were the parts they both knew but weren't saying.

They approached a market that was still open and she told Johnny to stop there. She said, pointedly, "You and Tex stay in the car. I'll only be a few minutes."

She made sure they weren't following her before going to a telephone booth at the rear of the market. She called the Hollywood Station and got the Lieutenant. She identified herself, and asked what had gone wrong.

The Lieutenant said, "That's what I'm asking you, Mrs. Norton. I just got a call from those FBI boys at the airport wanting to know where you are."

She told him where they were, and explained that they'd had to play things Tex Graham's way to keep him from suspecting that anything was wrong. Besides, Johnny wasn't armed, and undoubtedly Tex was. She said they were headed home, and that she was going to cook dinner, and then they'd spend the evening until it was time for Tex to go back to the airport.

"I'll get right in touch with them Special Agents," promised the Lieutenant. "They'll probably stake your apartment house, after you get home."

"You know which apartment it is?"

"No. We just got the address."

"It's the first floor, north side of the building. We're the rear apartment. There's a front one, and two just like them on the south side. Same arrangement on the second floor." She lowered her voice. "Will there be trouble?"

"Not where you'll be, there won't. We'll probably send a few of our dicks to assist FBI. They'll stake the building on all four sides. Don't you worry: they won't come busting in. They wouldn't take that chance—shooting it out in a small apartment where there's a woman and a policeman."

"How will they get him?"

"When he goes out. And look, Mrs. Norton—there'll be a man in back of the building. How about making an excuse to step outside: you know, empty the garbage or something? You can give him the setup."

She said, "I've got a disposal unit. If I can think of any other excuse I'll . . ."

"Right. But play it cagey. This Graham is bad medicine."

She hung up, bought some beer, a loaf of bread, and a few other things she didn't need, so as to have enough packages to make her long absence look plausible. As she got in the car, taking the window seat, she caught an inquiring glance from her husband, and gave him an almost imperceptible nod in answer. They backed out of the parking space and started for home.

She'd almost told the Lieutenant she was scared. Thinking it over now, she realized that she was more worried than frightened: worried chiefly because she knew something had to happen, but she didn't know when or where or how. She kept reminding herself that this man whose big body was wedged against hers was a killer, and, what was more, the minute he was caught, his own life was forfeit. She was afraid of the unknown, afraid that her husband might make some betraying move. And she had one fear which was greater than either of those: *she was afraid of the detectives who would be watching their apartment.*

Johnny Norton worked in uniform, and he hadn't been at the Hollywood Station long. He knew a lot of the men downstairs, but he'd told her often that he seldom got to meet detectives. They didn't have much contact with each other, the detectives and the uniformed men. The few times he'd had to go upstairs with suspects or reports, it had been to talk to the day commander, and Johnny had always been in uniform.

There was another angle, too. Johnny worked days. The few detectives he knew—and who knew him—also worked that watch. They changed watch at 5 P.M. , and the men that came on after that were strangers to him and he to them.

No, the night-watch detectives wouldn't know him. The FBI men would, because they'd talked to him about this deal. But two Special Agents couldn't be on four sides of the building at the same time. And if trouble started, there was danger that one of the cops might not know which was Tex Graham and which was Johnny Norton.

They got home, left the car parked at the curb, and went inside. Johnny snapped on the light, and Tex said, "Nice apartment. We never had it so good in the Islands, did we, Johnny?" and Johnny said, No, they never had. He motioned Tex to their best easy chair, shoved some cigarettes at him and told him to make himself at home.

Mary took the men's hats and coats and hung them in the hall closet near the bedroom. She went into the kitchen and started fixing dinner. She could hear them talking. It was the same old theme: the war, the experiences they had shared. Tex lighted a fresh cigarette. "What a life that was," he said. "Nobody gave a hoot for nothin' except gettin' outa there. Didn't care whether school kept or not. When I got hit on Tarawa, it was like gettin' a vacation ticket."

"What'd they do with you?"

"Fixed me up fine after they got to me. I had a bad five hours, though, lyin' there expecting the Nips to pick me up. They didn't like Marines."

"I'll say they didn't."

"Anyway, our gang found me. They shot me full of something and I woke up in a field hospital. Next thing I knew, I was at Base. Then on board ship. Then at General in Australia. Was that a soft touch!" Tex grinned at Johnny. "You never got a scratch, did you?"

"Nah. But what was left of the boys sure missed you. The patrol never was the same."

Mary listened with half an ear. She went ahead with dinner: pork chops, baked beans, a can of asparagus, rolls, coffee, a simple salad. She took three apple turnovers out of the freezing compartment and let them sit a while, preparatory to heating them for dessert.

She wanted to go outside, to talk to whoever was stationed there. But she was afraid. Tex was keen. He might think it was funny, might follow to see what was happening. All she could manage was to get to the back window and peep through a corner of the shade over the sink. Half-concealed in the shadows, she saw a man with a shotgun. FBI or cop, she didn't know. But they were there. Front, back, and sides. No chance for Tex to get away. They'd snag him or shoot him. Either way, with the raps he had hanging over him, he was as good as dead. It didn't check with the laughter she heard coming from the other room.

What they were laughing about, she didn't know; but it must have been some intimate experience, because they'd been discussing it in whispers. There was that service side of Johnny's life, chunks of it she'd never know. It occurred to her that this could have been a wonderful evening for Johnny if his friend had been other than what he was.

Dinner was okay. It was ten o'clock before she'd finished with the dishes and joined them in the living room. There hadn't been a sound from outside.

She could see the strain in Johnny's eyes. She didn't know much, but she knew a lot more than Johnny did, and he must be worried plenty. Some of the time, it seemed as though he wasn't listening to what Tex was saying. Occasionally he looked at her, but she didn't dare to flash him any signal, even of reassurance. All she could do was to smile and give the impression that things were under control.

Time was working against them. The hands of the mantel clock were creeping forward, closer and closer to the moment when Tex would say he had to leave. That was what frightened her. It was the minutes beyond that when the play would pass into other hands. She had quit being sorry for Tex. All she could think of now was her worry about Johnny.

Sooner or later there would be fireworks. There had to be. And when they started, Johnny would be just fool enough to move in on Tex, unarmed. Duty. Johnny was too acutely aware of his responsibilities as a policeman. And she knew he'd do whatever he could to protect her when the trouble started. . . .

Tex got up and stepped into the hall. She saw him open the closet door. He fumbled in his topcoat pocket and came back with a fresh pack of cigarettes.

Tex grinned at them and went to the north window. He pulled back the shade a fraction of an inch and looked out. He said, "Nice view you got," and walked back to his chair.

He sat down, opened his pack of cigarettes, and lighted one. Then he reached under his coat and took out an army .45. He looked straight at Johnny and said quietly, "You're a cop, aren't you, kid?"

Johnny pretended surprise and asked him what gave him such an idea.

"When I got my cigarettes just now. Your uniform is in that closet."

Johnny tried to grin. "Is it so bad to be a cop?" he asked.

"Yeh." Tex's voice was flat. "Especially when there's other cops outside. I saw two of them through that window. One has a shotgun. You knew, didn't you, Johnny?"

Johnny said, Yes, he knew, and the best thing Tex could do would be to give himself up. This was a hell of a note Johnny said, putting an old friend on the spot.

Tex said, "A guy plays 'em as he sees 'em, Johnny. It looks kinda lousy to me, but then I ain't at home on your side of the fence."

Johnny choked up. He asked why Tex had been such a fool as to get in touch with him. "They figured you would if you ever came through L.A. They had the deal all set up."

"How many men outside?"

"I don't know."

Mary said, "Too many for you to have a chance, Tex."

He shook his head. "A guy's always got a chance as long as he's breathing. You know what they want me for?"

Johnny said, Yes, robbery and murder.

"So I'm cooked." Tex was silent for quite a while. "If they was figurin' to bust in, they'd have done it long ago. That means I'm safe as long as I stay here."

Johnny said that was the way it was.

"But I can't stick here forever. I gotta make a pitch."

"It won't get you anywhere, Tex."

"Being picked up wouldn't be healthy, either, Johnny. Remember that deal on one of them little islands, the first time we was on patrol together? Wasn't much chance there, it looked like. But we shot our way out, didn't we?"

"Some of us did."

"You know, that was the night I took a liking to you. Hell, we'd had fun training and in Panama and all that stuff, but that night you came through. I'll bet you're one hell of a swell cop."

There wasn't anything Johnny could say to that. After about a half-minute Tex looked Mary's way and asked a question. "You do any telephoning when you was in that market?"

She nodded.

"What'd they tell you?"

"Just that they would stake the apartment."

He said, "Where's your gun, Johnny?"

Johnny explained he didn't have it: he'd left it with a guy to have a new pair of grips put on.

"You're as crazy as I am—tying up with me without a gun."

Johnny explained he hadn't known about that when he left the Station. It wasn't until he got home that the telephone call came in.

"How did you figure to take me?"

"I didn't. Two FBI agents were supposed to be at the airport. I stalled as long as I could, waiting for them to show up. When they didn't . . . hell, Tex, you ain't any dummy. I had to follow your lead or you'd have figured something was wrong."

"I would at that." He did some more thinking. "You got to get me out of here, Johnny."

"That ain't possible."

"It's got to be. I don't know the layout here. You do. There's got to be some sort of an exit they ain't got covered."

"Not a chance, Tex. You know those guys outside wouldn't overlook something like that."

"Keep thinkin', kid. It'd be a lot healthier if you come up with an idea. What I mean is, I ain't gonna take this sittin' down."

"What can you do?"

Tex looked embarrassed. "I hate to get your wife mixed up in this, Johnny, but there's no other way."

"Meaning . . . ?"

"Well, they haven't come in yet because of her. So they wouldn't take any chances of shootin' her no matter what happened. Pretty soon I'm going out. I'm taking her with me. First move anybody makes, I'll shoot her. I ain't kiddin', Johnny."

No, he wasn't kidding. He'd do just that, because it was the only thing he could do. Tex said to Mary, "Look at it from my angle . . ."

She said she was, but did he think he could bring himself to shoot a woman?

"Sure. Why not? If it's my only chance? You got to believe me, Mary."

Johnny told her he believed Tex. He went on, "But, look—what would that give you? A little breather maybe. Sooner or later they'd snag you."

"Later. That's better than now. And look, kid: don't you start something on account you're scared about her. I'd hate to let you have it, but that's the way it would be."

"I know. Only thing is, Tex, I still don't think it would work. Honest, I don't. There's only one thing I can think of."

"What?"

"Let me talk to one of the boys outside. Or send word through the Station. They'd call it off."

"But they'd still tail me, wouldn't they?"

"Yeh, I guess so."

Mary looked from one to the other. Couple of old friends talking quietly, dispassionately. It was difficult to convince herself that her life was in danger; that, in the long run, Tex didn't have a chance; that Johnny was in the middle. It didn't seem any more real than when they'd been kidding about things that had happened on the other side of the world.

She said, with surprising calm: "We're stymied all around, aren't we, Tex? The men outside won't do anything so long as we're together in here. They can stake the place indefinitely. We can't just sit here that long."

"We won't. Like I said, you and I will walk out together. We'll walk real close, and I'll have my gun on you. They won't shoot. They won't even close in on us."

Johnny said, "I've thought of a dozen schemes, Tex—all tricks. But you'd know they were tricks."

Tex nodded. "You got me pegged, all right. You know, it's funny—you getting me into this thing, and me not being sore."

Johnny said he was thinking of Mary, nobody else.

"That's what I figure. You'd take a chance with yourself, but not with her. She's a swell gal, Johnny. Ain't many guys got it so lucky."

The clock was still moving. Time was closing in on them. Tex leaned back in his chair without relaxing his vigilance. Looked like he didn't want to talk, so they both kept quiet, too. Their eyes met and Mary smiled ever so slightly. It wasn't that she felt like smiling, but she wanted Johnny to know that she wasn't afraid.

But she was afraid. Terribly afraid. She'd been afraid all evening, ever since they left the airport, ever since she'd glanced through the window and seen the detective with the shotgun. She'd known then that the chips were down.

Five minutes passed. Tex said softly, "You'll level with me, won't you, Johnny?"

"Sure. On account of Mary."

"Those guys outside are detectives, aren't they?"

"Yes."

"You're uniform. How many detectives do you know?"

"Mighty few."

"How many know you?"

"Even less than that. And none of the boys on the night watch."

"We're going to walk around the apartment, Johnny. You're gonna peek out, real careful. Tell me whether you know the men on this side and in back."

Johnny got up. So did Mary. Tex kept close to them, his gun handy. Johnny did what he was told, and then they were back in the living room. Johnny said, "I don't know any of the three guys I could see."

"Better be sure, Johnny. If what I got in mind goes wrong, Mary's the one who takes it."

"That's straight, Tex. Of course, I don't know who's in front or on the other side. If the FBI men are there, I know 'em, and they know me."

Tex did a lot more thinking. He said, softly, "It could work, Johnny. It sure could."

Johnny waited.

"Remember in the Marines we used to wear each other's clothes once in a while?"

"What about it?"

"What's to say we couldn't do it again?"

Johnny said he didn't see what Tex was driving at.

"This. Suppose I put on your uniform. I take Mary and we slip out the back door. I make believe I'm you, and Mary plays up to me. If the men back there don't know you, they won't know there's been a switch. If you've fooled me, I'll use Mary to protect myself when the shootin' starts. So you'd better be sure."

Johnny said thoughtfully, "Maybe you got something, Tex. But not enough."

"What's wrong with it?"

"You tell the dicks out back that you're me. Why should they fall for it?"

"Because they don't know what's been going on in here. Because they don't know I got wise to your being a cop. It won't look unnatural to them like it does to us. I'll say you're just about to leave by the front door, and that Mary and I got to go back in. They'll believe me, thinking I'm you. They'll move around the house to tip the others off. Mary and I will go on through to the next street."

"And then?"

"I'll snag a car. Any driver will stop if a cop tells him to. I'll make the guy drive where I want. What do you think of it, kid?"

Johnny said that the first part of it sounded reasonable, but that business about the car . . . hell, in a few minutes a wail would go out to follow any car with a civilian driver and a cop and a girl in back.

"They won't see us, once we get in the car," explained Tex. "Mary and I will get down on the floor, keep out of sight. She won't make a move, and neither will the guy driving the car. I'll see to that."

"You won't . . ." Johnny looked beseechingly at Mary.

"Her? Not unless she forces it. Hell, fella, I like her. She's a good kid. Now, what else is wrong with my ideas?"

Johnny said, "You walk out with Mary. You got a gun on her. That wouldn't look so good."

"It won't be on her, kid. I'll have it ready, is all. I'm you, see? We walk right up to the two detectives and start talkin'. I say you went to the bathroom or something, but they better move fast." He shrugged. "So it ain't perfect—I'll give you that. But it's the best I can think of. And I can't just sit here."

Johnny looked miserable. He looked at his wife and said he guessed it had to be that way. He said, "Don't try anything funny, sweetheart. I know Tex. He'll really do what he says."

She said she understood that. But she was worried about Johnny. Tex asked why.

"Because the detectives don't know him," she said sharply. "After we're gone, Johnny will go out. They'll think he's you. They might shoot."

Johnny said, "I'll stay right here, honey. I'll telephone the station and give 'em the score. By the time they get word back here, you'll be on your way."

Tex nodded approvingly. "Give it as long as you can, kid. You got Mary to think of."

Tex changed clothes. The uniform was a pretty good fit, considering. He slipped his service revolver into Johnny's empty holster. He said, "Never thought I'd see myself rigged up like this."

Johnny said, "You'd better let me take another look out the back window, just to be sure."

Tex stood very close to him. Johnny took his time: he had to be sure, and eventually he was. The two dicks out back, he'd seen them around the second floor of the Station, but he didn't even know their names. He told that to Tex.

They looked at each other. Johnny said, "Take care of Mary, will you?"

"Sure."

She smiled at her husband. "Everything will be all right," she said.

Johnny went back into the living room. Tex said something to Mary.

Then he opened the door, and they stepped into the night. The door closed behind them.

Johnny stood motionless: tense, nervous, waiting. The play had been taken away from him now. Nothing for him to do but stand there and worry about his wife.

For what seemed an eternity there was silence. Then he heard harsh voices and the sound of a scuffle. That was what he'd been waiting for. He ran across the kitchen, flung open the back door, and went outside. A flashlight blinded him. A voice he didn't know came from a man he couldn't see. It said, "Hold it, fella." He froze.

Then someone came to him out of the darkness, and Mary's arms were around his neck. She was crying. She said, "Johnny darling . . . Johnny darling . . ." over and over again.

The flashlight went off. He held Mary tight and stroked her head gently. He saw seven or eight men milling around, then three of them took shape and walked over to him. A man said, "Is this Tex Graham?"

Johnny said, Yes, it was Tex Graham. He could see better now. He could see that they had Tex's hands handcuffed behind his back.

Tex said, "I didn't think you'd take that chance with Mary, kid."

Johnny didn't say anything.

"I figured you was telling the truth when you said you didn't know the two guys staked out in back."

"I was," said Johnny.

"Don't give me that. We walked up to this lad here. I started my spiel. So what happens? Before I can move, he's on me. He's got my gun hand and he's saying something to the other guy. They get me all wrapped up. It wouldn't of happened that quick if they hadn't known you."

Johnny said, "I leveled with you, Tex. But still I figured this would happen."

CHALLENGE TO THE READER: *How did Johnny know that the detectives wouldn't be fooled by Tex dressed in Johnny's uniform? Why did Johnny figure Tex would be nabbed and Mary would be safe?*

Tex said he didn't understand.

Johnny said, "When you suggested wearing my uniform, I pretended to oppose it. But from the beginning, I expected this to happen."

"But why, kid? *Why?*"

"Because of something you yourself said, Tex. You said the guys outside wouldn't know what had been happening in this apartment. Right. But what was the most important thing they wouldn't know? That you had found out I'm a cop. So when someone in uniform came through that back door, I figured they'd know right away it wasn't me. *They'd never believe that I changed from civvies to a uniform right in front of a man wanted by the FBI who didn't know I was a policeman!"*

THE WITHERED HEART

by JEAN POTTS

At the sound of the car turning into the driveway, Voss was instantly, thoroughly, awake. Not even a split second of fuzziness. His mind clicked at once into precise, unhurried action, just as it had last night. He sat up on the edge of his bed—Myrtle's, of course, was empty—and reached for his watch. It was only a quarter to eight. Already? he thought, as the car stopped in the driveway. He had not expected anyone quite so soon. Not that it mattered; he was ready any time.

He waited for the next sound, which would be someone knocking on the screen door of the veranda. The bedroom seemed to wait too, breathlessly quiet, except for the whir of the electric fan, tirelessly churning up the sluggish air. The heat—the relentless South American heat—shoved in past the flimsy slats of the window blinds. Even now, in the early morning, there was no escape from its pounding glare. He ought to be used to it; he had been here long enough. More than ten years stagnating in this unspeakable climate, in this forsaken backwater where nothing ever happened except the heat. . . .

There. Someone was knocking. In his pajama pants and scuffs, Voss shuffled out to the veranda. Frank Dallas—good old Frank—was waiting at the screen door, peering in through the swarming purple bougainvillea. He looked fresh and hearty. His white linen suit had not yet had time to wilt; his thinning hair still showed the marks of a damp comb.

"Rise and shine, you lazy bum! Top of the morning to you!"

Was there perhaps a hollow ring in Frank's voice? Voss could detect none. Nor any trace of trouble in Frank's open, beaming face. Relax, he told himself; it's too soon—he's come for some other reason.

"Hi. What's the idea, rousing the citizenry at this hour . . ." Yawning, Voss unhooked the screen door. "What the hell hour is it, anyway?"

"Quarter of eight. Time you were up. Look, Voss—" Frank lowered his voice to a conspiratorial whisper—"Myrtle's gone, isn't she?"

"Sure." He said it automatically, without hesitation. "She's gone up to her sister's for a couple of days. Left early, before six this morning."

"Yeah. She told me she was planning to. That's why I figured it was safe to stop by. I've got this letter that Enid wanted me to give you. She was all upset yesterday, poor kid, resigning the way she did. Well, it kind of threw me too. Anyway, this letter, I promised to see that you got it . . ."

Poor old Frank had never gotten over being nervous about his role as go-between. He was as jittery—and, Voss supposed, as secretly thrilled—today as he had been six months ago, when Voss and Enid started their clandestine affair. Happily married himself, Frank had the romantic, inquisitive disposition of a maiden aunt. Besides, as American consul, he was Enid's boss. Very natural, very convenient for him to get into the act. Fun for everybody. Great fun at first. Lately—well, it was oversimplification to say that Enid was too serious, too impetuous, too intense. Those were the very qualities in her that made this affair different from the others, that made Enid herself such an irresistible magnet to Voss. Only he couldn't respond to them any more. He did not want to be a philanderer; he wanted to be a true, star-crossed lover—and he had lost the power. It was as if Myrtle had withered his heart.

This envelope in his hand, addressed in Enid's headlong writing—her farewell note, or so she must have thought when she wrote it—even this could not penetrate his benumbed and crippled soul. To be losing, through his own inertia, a love like Enid's, and to feel nothing more than a kind of guilty weariness . . .

He had felt something more last night, all right. Sudden and vivid as lightning, Myrtle's face flashed into his mind. Alive with malice, as it had been last night—the vulgar, coarse, knowing face of his wife. "So your girlfriend's leaving," she had said. "I hear she's resigned. My, my, I never thought you'd let this one get away . . ."

Gloating over her own handiwork—because it *was* her doing; the deadly years of being married to Myrtle had very nearly destroyed in him the capacity for feeling anything. Very nearly. But not quite; last night proved that. Hate was left. And if he could hate, he could also love. So Enid need not be lost, after all.

It was going to take time for the numbness to wear off. Voss was still stunned by the impact of release—which, considering everything, was really very fortunate. This morning, if ever in his life, he needed a mind uncluttered by emotion—a mind as cool and accurate as a machine.

"You're all right, aren't you, old man?" Frank was asking anxiously.

"I'll be all right." He paused, conscious of his own pathos as he placed Enid's letter, tenderly, on the wicker table. "It's just that—well, I guess you know how I feel about Enid."

"I know. It's rugged."

Frank was brimming with sympathy. It would be unkind—more than that, it would be indiscreet—to deny him the chance to spill over. "Have a cup of coffee with me," said Voss. "We'll have to make it ourselves. Myrtle always gives the maid time off when she's going to be away. I'd rather eat at the club than up here alone. The maid's a lousy cook, anyway, but we're lucky to get anybody to come this far out." Their house was set off by itself, on the outermost fringe of the American colony. What a break that had turned out to be, last night!

Voss felt a spasm of nervous excitement, rather like stage fright, as he led the way to the kitchen. Here was where it had happened, right here by the sink . . . Another break—the tiles had been a cinch to clean. But might there be some telltale sign?

There was none. Not the smallest. He breathed easy again.

Back on the veranda, with the coffee tray between them, Frank launched into earnest, incoherent speech. The way he looked at it, it was just one of those things. Not that it was any of his business. But look at it one way, and it was the best thing all around—for Enid to pull out, that is. She was really too young for Voss, so she'd get over it. And there was this much about it, a man just couldn't walk out on a wife like Myrtle, not if he had any conscience.

"No," agreed Voss with a wan smile. "I couldn't walk out on Myrtle." But not on account of his conscience, he added to himself. He thought about last night, probing for some tiny qualm, some flicker of remorse. There was none. This extraordinary lack of any kind of feeling . . .

"Myrtle's a good egg, too, you know." Frank took out his handkerchief and mopped his moist red brow. "I've always liked Myrtle."

Oh, sure! Myrtle was more fun than a barrel of monkeys. Everybody said so. The life of every party. Suddenly the memory of the endless chain of parties, monotonous, almost identical, pressed down on Voss like a physical weight. He used to sit and drink steadily, with every nerve stretched rigid in protest against Myrtle's raucous voice, against the flushed, blowzy looseness of her face. For some reason—maybe because it was her lushness and vivacity that had attracted him in the beginning—her antics had a kind of excruciating fascination for Voss. Your wife, he used to tell himself; look at her, listen to her—she's all yours.

"What I say is," Frank floundered on, "when two people have made a go of it like you and Myrtle for this many years, why, they can't just throw it away at the drop of a hat. Myrtle doesn't know, does she?"

Unprepared for this particular question, Voss hesitated. But it took him only a moment to see the danger in assuring Frank—as he would like to have done—that of course Myrtle did not know. Only a romantic innocent like Frank could imagine that the affair had been a secret; in all likelihood Myrtle herself had unloaded to everybody she knew. Much better to play it safe, just in case the question should arise later. "She probably suspects," he said slowly. "But I don't think she has any idea that it's serious. You know how it is in a place like this—flirtations going on all the time."

"Sure. I know," said Frank, very much the man of the world. "Well, one thing, with her away for a couple of days, you'll have a chance to kind of pull yourself together. She couldn't have picked a better time."

"She certainly couldn't," said Voss sincerely. As Frank stood up to leave, he added, once more conscious of his own pathos, "Many thanks for bringing me the letter, Frank. And for the moral support."

Things couldn't have gone more swimmingly, he was thinking. With his mind clicking away in this admirable, mechanical way, there was no reason why he shouldn't breeze through the rest of the morning without turning a hair. All it took was careful planning and a cool head. He had the cool head, all right. And—thanks to Myrtle—the withered heart that would nevertheless come back to life, all in good time.

It was at this self-congratulatory moment that Frank dropped his bomb. Casually; as an afterthought, a final pleasantry that occurred to him when he was halfway out to his car. "I suppose Myrtle took Pepper with her, didn't she?" he called back. "Of course. I never knew her to go half a block without that dog."

Voss himself remained intact. The world around him reeled, and then, with a stately, slow-motion effect, it shattered. Except for Frank, who still waited out there, smiling expectantly.

"Oh, yes." Voss's voice rang, remote and dreamy, in his own ears. "Of course she took Pepper. Myrtle never goes anywhere without Pepper."

"In his traveling case, I suppose? Only dog in the country with his own specially built traveling compartment." Another cheery wave, and Frank was gone.

It was incredible. Only gradually was Voss able to grasp the magnitude of his blunder, the treachery of his own mind, seemingly so faultless in its operation, which had remembered every other detail and had forgotten—of all the ignominious, obvious things—Pepper.

For Pepper and Myrtle were devoted to each other. She referred to herself as his "Muvver." He was a small, beagle-type dog, a cheerful extrovert whose devotion to Myrtle did not prevent him from indulging in an occasional night out, and he had chosen last night for one of these escapades.

Voss closed his eyes. The veranda seemed to echo, as it had last evening, with Myrtle's strident summons: "Here, Peppy, Peppy!" But they had waited in vain for the sound of Pepper tearing through the shrubbery and up the driveway, for his joyful voice proclaiming that he was home. Ordinarily, Myrtle would have kept on calling, at intervals, until Pepper showed up—as he always did, sooner or later—looking ashamed and proud in equal parts. Ordinarily, it wouldn't have mattered that he was still not back.

But there was nothing ordinary about last night and this morning. That was just the point: Voss had to make this extraordinary, deranged, secret stretch of time *seem* ordinary. He had to. And it was impossible, because all his calculations had been made minus Pepper.

A current of panic ran through him. He willed himself to stand still and think. Now was no time to lose his head, or to dissolve in futile self-recrimination. He must think, the way he had thought last night, with that beautiful, unhurried precision. . . .

Pepper at large, perhaps galloping around the neighborhood calling attention to himself, was a shocking hazard. But to call the little beast would only advertise more fatally the fact that he was not where he ought to be, and furthermore that Voss knew it.

There was nothing to do, then, but wait.

He rubbed his clammy hands against his pajama pants. His knees threatened to buckle under him. But it was somehow unthinkable to sit down. He stood in the middle of the veranda, staring at the screen door, where the bougainvillea climbed, trying to get in. It was the personification of Myrtle, that burgeoning vine. Its harsh purplish flowers were her color, and the way it swarmed over everything, its boundless vulgarity—it was Myrtle to the life.

There was nothing to do but wait. . . .

Then all at once Pepper was there. He barked, in an apologetic way, as if he were anxious to make clear that he was only suggesting—but no means demanding—that he be let in. And when Voss tottered to the screen and opened it, the dog swaggered in with an uneasy attempt at bravado.

Trembling all over, Voss collapsed in one of the wicker chairs. He could hear the little dog clicking off in search of a more demonstrative welcome. And in spite of all he could do, memory re-enacted for him last night's whole flawless (almost) project, after— Well, just after. It had seemed to work itself out with such magical accuracy. First of all, the heaven-sent circumstances of Myrtle's visit to her sister, who lived (bless her heart) in an inland town, the road to which was infrequently traveled, curving, and in spots precipitous. Ideal for Voss's purposes. Who was likely to be abroad at three thirty in the morning to see him, either when he left the house—with Myrtle's body and the bicycle bundled in the back seat of her car—or when he returned, alone on the bicycle?

The answer was, no one. He had had the whole moonless, empty world to himself; he had managed the crash—like everything else—with dream-like precision.

And when Myrtle's body and her car were found smashed to bits at the bottom of the gorge, who was going to pry too much? Accidents happened all the time, and Myrtle was a notoriously rash driver.

He had thought of everything, including Myrtle's suitcase which, obligingly enough, she had already packed, and the new hat she had bought for her trip. It had a red veil, not quite the same shade as the flower trimming. Trust Myrtle. He had been very proud of remembering about the hat.

Only he had forgotten Pepper. She never went anywhere without him; she would as soon set out stark naked as without Pepper. She did not trust him to ride on the seat beside her; the possibility that something in the passing scene might prove too much for his inquiring temperament terrified her. So she had had a special traveling case built for him. The case, with Pepper inside, was placed on the floor of the front seat, during even the shortest trips.

When not in use, the case was stored in a corner of the garage. That was where it was now, along with Voss's own car, the one he used to drive back and forth to work. If only, last night, he had happened to glance in that particular corner. . . . He must get rid of it. And he must get rid of Pepper.

At least Pepper was here, under his control, no longer prancing around in public. Perhaps he had already been noticed? Perhaps, Voss answered himself grimly. In which case it would simply be his word against someone else's. All right, his word. But there was no way whatever to account for a hale and hearty Pepper here in the house, or for the telltale case, sitting undamaged in the garage. Voss recalled his own remote voice, replying to Frank: "Oh, yes. Of course she took Pepper." That was his story, and to make it stick, both Pepper and the traveling case ought to be in the car at the bottom of the gorge.

Well, he could get them there. He had his own car. He saw, with a flash of excitement and renewed hope, that there was time, that he still had a chance. A much chancier chance than the one he had taken last night, when no one had been around to notice his coming and going. It was broad daylight now. Even so, he would be safe enough, once he (and Pepper and the case) got on the road that led to the gorge. Getting there was the tricky part; to reach the turn-off he would have to drive through one stretch of the American colony—dark and silent last night, but buzzing with activity now that morning was here. Someone would be sure to see him. Not that that was necessarily fatal. The point was that someone would be sure to hear Pepper, who invariably barked his head off the minute he was put in his case, and kept it up until he reached his destination. No, it was a risk that simply could not be taken. Pepper must be disposed of, silenced forever, before he set off on his final trip.

How to do it? This was the problem, stripped to its basic bones. As if on cue, Pepper appeared in the doorway between the veranda and the living room. His expression was one of friendly inquiry. If this turned out to be a game of hide-and-seek, his manner seemed to convey, then they could count on him; he was always ready for fun and games; if, on the other hand, his favorite human being had actually gone away and left him—

Well, Pepper was no dog to brood. You would never catch him stretched out on somebody's grave, or refusing to eat and moping himself away to a shadow. Love came easy to this small, sturdy, lively little creature.

Voss eyed him, and Pepper, mistaking speculation for interest, trotted over, all sociability. My God, thought Voss, he'd even get attached to *me*, given time. Which of course was precisely what Pepper was not going to be given. He did not know this, however. He did not know that Voss's heart had all but withered, that he was not yet capable of the tiniest flicker of sympathy for any living thing. In cheerful ignorance, the dog sat down beside Voss's feet—tentatively, with his tail thumping and his spotted head cocked upward. He seemed to be smiling.

"Go away," said Voss coldly.

Pepper could take a hint; still smiling amiably, he ambled over to the living-room door.

A gun would be the easiest way. One neat shot—it would sound like a car back-firing, in case anyone happened to hear it—and a quick, unobtrusive burial. No problem there, with a body as small as Pepper's. But Voss did not own a gun.

Well, there was gas. Except that there wasn't. Everything here was electric.

Where did you stab a dog? That is . . . Voss glanced toward the door, where Pepper sat, alert for the smallest sign of encouragement. His anatomy must be roughly like that of a human being. But somehow his front legs became, in Voss's mind, a hopeless complication. Pepper wasn't large, but he was strong and wiry. And he loved life; he would hang on to it with all his might.

Voss turned away from Pepper's trustful gaze, and, as he turned, his eye fell on the bougainvillea. One strand had thrust its way inside the screen door, probably when he let Pepper in; it swung there, searching for a toehold. He went over, shoved it out savagely, and hooked the screen door against it.

From time to time Pepper left his post to make another fruitless tour of the house. After each trip he looked a little less debonair, a little more anxious. Now he pattered over to Voss's side and uttered a series of barks. Not loud, but insistent.

He would have to be kept quiet until the method of permanent disposal had been decided upon. Food would do it. Voss stood up. Here at least was something he could handle. And anyway, Pepper, being condemned, was entitled to a hearty breakfast. The dog bustled out to the kitchen ahead of Voss, all eagerness and good humor again.

The business of opening a can of dog food and filling Pepper's water bowl was calming. But Voss was startled to see that it was now nine thirty; he should have been at the office an hour ago. He phoned at once, with the first excuse that occurred to him.

His secretary, a flip type, said sure, she understood about his headache, and had he tried tomato juice? Or a hair of the dog?

He had a perilous impulse to laugh and laugh. "I'll see you after lunch," he said icily, and hung up.

Meanwhile Pepper, full of peace and breakfast, had retired to his favorite spot under the dining-room table for a nap. His round stomach rose and fell rhythmically. Now and then his forehead puckered, or his paws flicked busily, in pursuit of a dream-rabbit. Watching him, Voss felt a drowsiness, almost like hypnosis, creeping over him.

The jangling of the telephone jerked him to his feet, wild-eyed and suddenly drenched in cold sweat. After three rings, however, he had collected his wits and was able to answer in a normal, deliberate voice.

"Is that you, Voss? Is something wrong? Why aren't you at the office?" Myrtle's sister sounded flurried. But then she always did.

She always interrupted, too. He had barely begun to explain about his headache when she broke in. "But, Voss, what I called about—what's happened to Myrtle? I thought she was going to get an early start, I've been expecting her for hours."

"You mean she's not there yet?" He paused, just long enough. "But I don't understand it. She left here before six—"

"Before six! But it's ten thirty now, and it's only a three-hour drive—at the very most!"

"I know," he said, aware that the slight edge of irritation in his voice was a convincing touch: worry often made people snappish. "She certainly should be there by now. I don't understand it. I'd better— What had I better do? I can check with—"

"Now keep calm. There must be some simple explanation."

"I don't know what," he said bleakly. "Thank God you called me. I'll get in touch with Frank Dallas right away. He'll know what to do. In the meantime, if you hear anything—"

"I will. Of course I'll call you." Her voice quavered.

This was according to schedule. He had expected the call from Myrtle's sister; the only change was that his next move—to report his problem to good old Frank—must now be delayed until Pepper was dead and at the bottom of the gorge.

Pepper strolled in, pausing at the doorway to yawn luxuriously and stretch each leg in turn. The sight of him chilled Voss; he had a moment's sharp, appalling view not only of his own peril but of his own irresponsibility in the face of it. How could he have let so much of the morning slip by in weak hesitation? What kind of tricks was his mind playing on him, that he could draw an easy breath with Pepper still here to blow his story to smithereens?

It's Pepper or me, he thought. Life or death. Dog eat dog.

In a frenzy now that time was so short, he rushed to the sideboard in the dining room and snatched the carving knife from the drawer. Pepper capered at his heels, making little jumps toward his knee. How easy it would be to grab him by his muzzle, force his head back, and, quickly, with one stroke of the knife . . .

Only not in here. In the kitchen. Tiles, instead of rush matting.

But at that moment it came—the phone call that exploded what was left of his original carefully planned schedule. It was Frank, and his voice was even heartier than usual, in a transparent effort to hide his concern. "Look, Voss, I just had a long-distance call from Myrtle's sister. Seems Myrtle hasn't shown up yet . . ."

Damn the woman, damn her! But damn himself, too, for not foreseeing that she would jump the gun and call Frank herself, instead of leaving it to him. He made a desperate snatch to salvage what little he could. "I know. I've been trying to get you, but your line was busy."

"Now don't get in a sweat, Voss. Like I told her sister, there are any number of simple explanations. Pepper might have gotten car-sick. He does sometimes, you know. I'll get right on it and call you the minute we've found out."

Abandon the idea of getting Pepper and the traveling case out to the gorge. Scrap it—there was no time. There was just time, now, to kill him, hide his body and the case temporarily, and hope that his absence in the wreckage might at first be overlooked. Then later . . .

It came to him then—the best way, the obvious method that he should have thought of right away. He could put Pepper to sleep, the way a veterinary would. Giddy with relief, Voss hurried into the bathroom and flung open the door of the medicine chest. Both he and Myrtle had prescriptions for sleeping pills. A handful of those . . .

There was one lonesome capsule rattling around in his own prescription bottle. Myrtle had evidently packed hers. They were nowhere to be found. It was hopeless, but he could not bring himself to stop searching. Not until the phone rang.

This time Frank's voice, drained of its usual heartiness, was all hushed gravity. "Voss, I'm afraid you've got to prepare yourself for some bad news . . . There's been an accident, a bad one . . . I'll be with you in ten minutes, old man."

Ten minutes, and Pepper still here to give the lie to the whole "accident" story. For his presence would surprise Frank. It would set him to wondering, set him to investigating what wouldn't bear investigating. Pepper stood at Voss's knee, the question—"What can I do for you, sir?"—on the tip of his cordial pink tongue.

"You can die," whispered Voss.

Ten minutes left—probably only nine by now. Voss cast an agonized glance around the room, with its jumble of tawdry color and design, its clutter of Myrtle's gimcracks.

The paperweight was right there on the table beside him. Heavy; a solid, ugly chunk of onyx that fitted suggestively in his hand. One stunning blow aimed at the brown spot between Pepper's ears, and the rest would be easy.

Clasping the paperweight, Voss sat down and patted his lap invitingly. "Here, Peppy," he said.

Pepper leaped up at once; he was used to being held and petted. Snuggling the little dog's head in the crook of his left arm, Voss slowly raised the paperweight, poised it, focusing eye, hand, and will for the one smashing blow.

But he could not bring himself to do it. Now, at this untimely, this fatal, moment, he felt his withered heart stir and come to life—as it should have done for Enid.

His arm sagged; the paperweight thudded to the floor. He grabbed Pepper's warm, sturdy body between his two hands and glared down into the trustful eyes. He did not really like the foolish, friendly creature any more than he ever had. But it was as if he were holding here, in Pepper's compact person, an engine of life. It set up in him a responsive current, melting away the numbness, throbbing all through him in a triumphant flood of warmth.

Yes, triumphant—although he was lost and he knew it, although he could hear the sound of Frank's car already turning into the driveway.

His hands tightened convulsively on Pepper, who had heard too, and was struggling to free himself. Then Voss gave a helpless laugh—or maybe it was a sob—and let go.

Bursting with his tidings of welcome, Pepper rushed out to the veranda. After a moment Voss followed him to the screen door and waited there—waited for Frank.

THE GIRL WHO MARRIED
A MONSTER

by *ANTHONY BOUCHER*

There seemed from the start to be an atmosphere of pressured haste about the whole affair. The wedding date was set even before the formal announcement of the engagement; Doreen was so *very* insistent that Marie must come at once to Hollywood to serve as maid of honor; the engagement party was already getting under way when Marie arrived at the house; and she had barely had time for the fastest of showers and a change of clothes when she was standing beside Cousin Doreen and being introduced to the murderer.

Not that she knew it for certain at that moment. Then—with one of Doreen's friends adlibbing a be bop wedding march on the piano and another trying to fit limerick lyrics to it and all the others saying *"Darling . . . !"* and "But *my* agent says . . ." and "The liquor flows like glue around here" and *"Live TV?* But my dear, how quaintly *historical!"*—then it was only a matter of some forgotten little-girl memory trying to stir at the back of her mind and some very active big-girl instincts stirring in front. Later, with the aid of the man in gray and his strange friend with the invisible fly, it was to be terrifyingly positive. Now, it was vague and indefinable, and perhaps all the more terrifying for being so.

Marie had been prepared to dislike him. Doreen was only a year older than she (which was 27) and looked a year younger; there was something obscene about the idea of her marrying a man in his fifties. Marie was prepared for something out of Peter Arno, and for a moment it was a relief to find him so ordinary-looking—just another man, like the corner grocer . . . or no, more like the druggist, the nice one that was a bishop in the Latter Day Saints. For a moment after that it was a pleasant surprise to find that he was easy, affable, even charming in a way you didn't expect of ordinary elderly men. He was asking all about her family (which was of course Doreen's, too) and about Utah and how was Salt Lake nowadays, and all the time he made you feel that he was asking about these subjects only because they were connected with *you.*

In these first few moments the Hollywood party seemed to vanish and it was almost as if she was still back in Salt Lake and it was perfectly understandable that Doreen should marry him no matter how old he was—and no matter how hard a little-girl memory tried to place the name LUTHER PEABODY (in very black type) and the photograph (much younger) that had gone with it.

At this point Doreen had said, "Luther, be nice to Marie, huh? I have to make like a hostess," and disappeared. Marie was alone with Luther Peabody, the party whirling around them like a montage gone mad. It wasn't quite what he said or where he touched her as he casually steered her toward the bar, though the words were deliberately suggestive and it was not a touch commonly bestowed by a bridegroom upon the maid of honor. It was more that the voice was too soft and the fingers were too soft and the eyes—the eyes that fixed her, and her alone, as if only they were in the room—the eyes were much too hard.

The little-girl memory was still a fragment; but whatever it was, it reinforced this sudden adult recognition of peril. Without conscious thought Marie found that she had evaded Peabody, slipped behind two men arguing about guild jurisdiction in TV, and lost herself in a deep chair in an obscure corner.

Her whole body was trembling, as if it had been, in some curiously public way, outraged. And she was thinking that by contrast, a Peter Arno Lecher-of-Great-Wealth would make a clean and welcome cousin-in-law.

It was in the corner that the man in gray found her.

"You're Doreen's cousin Marie," he stated. "My name's MacDonald. You don't have a drink. Or rather," he added, "you didn't have one." And he passed her one of the two martinis he was holding.

She managed, by an active miracle, not to spill any; but she still needed two sips before she could properly arrange her face into the right smile and say, "Thank you, sir."

"Good," he said. "I wasn't sure about plying you. One never knows with girls from Salt Lake."

"Oh, but I'm not a saint."

"Who is? Thank God."

"I mean" (the smile came more easily now) "I'm not a Mormon. Doreen isn't, either. Our fathers came to Salt Lake when they were both widowers, with us squalling on their hands. They married Utah girls, and all this enormous Mormon family you read about in Doreen's publicity is just step-family."

"Remind Doreen some time," he said dryly. "She's never disbelieved a word of her publicity. Including" (his eyes wandered about the brawling room) "the word 'starlet.' How long does one go on being a starlet? Is it semipermanent, like being a Young Democrat? They're still dunning me for dues when I should be putting the money into a hair-restorer."

"Oh, but *you* are young!" she reacted hastily. She'd never have said so ordinarily—he must be in his late thirties. But she had stopped shaking and he was comfortable and reassuring and not at all like a middle-aged fragment of memory with soft fingers and eyes from hell.

Mac-what'sit seemed almost to read her thoughts. He looked across to the bar, where Luther Peabody was being charming to some columnist's third assistant leg-woman. "You just got in, didn't you?" he asked.

"Yes," Marie said uneasily. "It's all been done in such a rush. . . ."

"And you'd just as soon get out again." It wasn't a question. "I have a car. . . ."

"And that," said MacDonald, "is Catalina."

They were parked on a bluff in Palos Verdes. It was almost sunset.

"There's something so wonderful," Marie said softly, "about being on a high place and looking at something new. The this-is-the-place feeling."

"Kingdoms of the world . . ." MacDonald muttered. "You see, I knew Doreen when she first came here. Met her through a radio-actress friend of mine." His voice hardened oddly.

"Were you . . . ?" But Marie didn't finish the sentence. They had come almost close enough for such a question, but not quite.

". . . in love with Doreen?" MacDonald laughed. "Good Lord, no. No, I was thinking of the girl who introduced us. One of my best friends killed her."

Suddenly the photograph and the black type were very clear, and Marie knew the story that went with them.

MacDonald did not miss her sudden start. He eyed her speculatively. "That's why I recognized you—because I knew Doreen way back when. You don't look anything alike now, but back before she got the starlet treatment . . . And she had the same this-is-the-place look."

"And now . . ." Marie said.

"And now," MacDonald repeated. After a moment of silence he said, "Look. You'd better tell me about it, hadn't you? It's something you can't say to Doreen, and it isn't doing you any good bottled up."

Marie, almost to her own surprise, nodded. "Another martini first."

The seaside bar was small and almost deserted and exactly suited to letting one's hair down. "Not that it isn't as down as it can go, literally," Marie tried to smile.

"And very nice, too. Major difference between you and Doreen-that-was. Hers was always straight."

"I think she won't have it waved because she won't admit she's always been jealous of mine. No, that's catty and I shouldn't; but I think it *is* the only thing in me Doreen's ever envied. And it's your fault. I only said it because you're so easy to talk to."

"Occupational disease," said the man whose occupation she didn't know.

The drinks came and the waiter went and Marie tried to find the words for the thing that frightened her. "You see," she said, "I . . . know what it means to love the wrong man. Not just the wrong man, but a man who's *wrong*. I was a secretary at the radiation lab up at Berkeley and there was this research-worker. . . . You'd know his name; it's been in headlines. He was—it's a melodramatic word, but it's true—he was a traitor, and I was in love with him for months and never dreamed what he was like inside. I even wanted to defend him and stand by him, but then after he was convicted he took the mask off and for the first time . . . Anyway, that's why I went back to Utah. And why I know how Doreen can love this man and yet not know him . . . and why I have to *do* something.

"It isn't just 'woman's intuition,' or the fact that no man would ever see his eyes get like that or feel his fingers go softer than flesh. It's what I've remembered. It must be a long time ago, maybe fifteen years. I think I was in junior high. But there was this big case up in Portland or Seattle or some place. He was a . . . a Bluebeard, and this was the umpteenth wife he'd killed. It was all over the papers; everybody talked about it. And when you said something about a murder, I remembered it all and I could see the papers. It was the same name and the same face."

Now it was out, and she finished her martini in one gulp.

MacDonald showed no surprise. "That isn't," he said levelly, "the one I was thinking of. Maybe because we were obviously in junior high at different times. Funny how murder fascinates kids. I'll never forget Winnie Ruth Judd in 1931, even if I didn't understand half of it. And the one I'm remembering was a little before that, around '29. Right here in L. A. Same name, same face."

"But it can't be the same. Twice? He'd have been gassed the first time."

"Hanged, back then. But he must have been acquitted, both here and in Portland or wherever. Our innocent childish souls remember the grue, but not the trial."

"But they wouldn't acquit him twice, would they?"

"My dear girl, if you want statistics on the acquittal of murderers, even mass repeaters . . . You see, you came to a man in the right business."

Maybe it was the martini. Suddenly she felt that everything was going to be all right. This quiet man in gray would know what to do.

"Formally," he went on, "it's Lieutenant MacDonald, L.A.P.D., Homicide. I don't claim to bat a thousand, but that friend who killed the radio actress is in San Quentin now, doing life. All the information I can find on

Luther Peabody, officially and unofficially, is yours to lay before Doreen. And no matter how much in love she is, it should be hard for her to keep her eyes shut."

"Lieutenant MacDonald, I love you," said Marie. "And you'll check your files right away and let me know?"

"Files?" said MacDonald. "Of course. And," he added with deliberate mystification, "I think I have another source that's even better."

"I'm damned if I see why," Doreen objected petulantly, "you had to run off from the party like that yesterday. It was one wingding of a party and after all as maid of honor you're part of the engagement. Besides, Luther was hurt. He liked you, and you didn't give him any chance to show it."

Marie pulled on a stocking and concentrated on straightening its seam. "Are you really in love with Luther?" she asked.

"I guess so. I like him. He's fun. Even on his feet. Oh—! Want to finish zipping this for me? It always sticks . . . What's the matter? Did I shock ums?"

"Well, I hadn't thought . . . I mean, he's so . . ."

"Old? Listen, darling, there's no substitute for experience. If you knew some of these young Hollywood glamor-boys . . ."

"Doreen . . ." The zipping task over, Marie was concentrating on the other stocking.

"Mmmm?"

"Maybe I shouldn't have as just a house guest, but I asked a friend to drop in for a cocktail."

"Oh? I was kind of hoping you and Luther and I could settle down for the afternoon and make up for yesterday. Who is he?"

"That nice MacDonald man I met at the party."

"Mac? Is that whom you ran away with? He's okay, I guess . . . if you like serious-minded cops. You two can have fun disapproving of me. Doreen Arlen, Girl Failure."

"Oh, Doreen, is it that bad?"

"No, don't mind me. I've got a deal cooking at CBS, and there's one of the independents that— Is that Luther already? How's my face? Quick!"

But it wasn't Luther Peabody. It was Lieutenant Donald MacDonald, and he said, "Hi, Doreen. I hope it isn't an imposition; I brought another guest."

Doreen shrugged. "Why doesn't somebody tell me—?" Then she broke off. She and Marie found themselves involuntarily staring at MacDonald's companion.

He was a small man, almost inhumanly thin. He might have been any age from 40 to 60, and he would probably go on looking much the same until he was 80. The first thing that struck Marie was the dead whiteness of his skin—almost like the skin of a subterranean cave-dweller, or of a corpse. Then she saw the brilliant blue of his eyes, and an odd hint of so much behind the blue that she knew—despite the abnormal pallor, despite the skeletal thinness—this man was, in some way of his own, intensely alive.

"Miss Doreen Arlen," MacDonald said, "Miss Marie Arlen, may I present Mr. Noble?"

"Any friend of Mac's and stuff," said Doreen. "Come on in. Luther isn't here yet; you want to tend bar, Mac?"

And somehow they were all in the living room and MacDonald was mixing drinks and it was a party and MacDonald's Mr. Noble still hadn't said a word. Not until MacDonald was arguing with Doreen about fetching another tray of ice cubes ("The key to a martini is a pitcher *full* of ice"), did Mr. Noble lean toward Marie and say, "Right."

"I beg your pardon?"

"You were." And Mr. Noble was silent again until MacDonald brought around the tray of drinks, when he shook his head and said, "Sherry?"

"Sure," said Doreen. "There's sherry in the kitchen. Nothing special, mostly for cooking, but—"

"Okay," said Mr. Noble.

MacDonald whispered to Doreen as she left, and she returned with a water glass, the sherry bottle, and a puzzled but resolute hostess look. Marie watched Mr. Noble's white hand fill the water glass. *"You were right."* What did he know? Why had MacDonald brought him?

The doorbell rang again, and this time it was Luther. He kissed Doreen, a little less casually than one usually kisses a fiancée before strangers, and then he was moving in on Marie with a cousinly gleam. *If he tries to kiss me . . . ,* she thought in sudden terror.

And Mr. Noble looked up from his water glass of sherry to say flatly, "Peabody."

Luther Peabody looked expectantly at Doreen. He started to say "Introduce me, dar—" and then he looked at Mr. Noble again. Lieutenant MacDonald had retired to the bar. He was smiling. Peabody stared at the bony white face as if trying to clothe it with flesh and color.

"Lieutenant Noble," he said suddenly. It was not the voice with which he spoke to women.

"Ex," said Mr. Noble. "Out of the profession now. But not you, eh, Peabody? Still in the same line of work?"

"Doreen!" Luther Peabody's voice had regained its vigor, and a new dignity as well. "What is the meaning of this—this absurd confrontation scene? It's true that many years ago Lieutenant Noble, presumably in order to advance his own police career, chose to hound me as a murderer because of the accidental death of my first wife. It's a matter of public record that I was acquitted. I stand proved innocent by the courts. Why should this tragedy of my youth—?"

Marie could hardly believe it, but she would have sworn that Doreen was on the verge of laughter. Mr. Noble kept looking at Luther, but his bright blue eyes glazed over as though something was going on behind them. "Phoenix," he said. "1932. Same 'accident'—fall from stepladder. Same double-indemnity policy. Not enough evidence. No indictment."

"You see?" Peabody protested. "Another unfortunate—"

"Santa Fe. 1935. Same accident. Same policy. Acquitted. Seattle. 1938." He nodded toward Marie. "Same accident. No policy. Didn't need it; family fortune. Three trials. Three hung juries. State dropped the case. Long gap; Seattle very profitable. Butte. 1945. Same accident. Woman lived. Refused to prosecute, but got divorce. Las Vegas. 1949. Acquitted."

"You left out the funny one, Nick," MacDonald contributed. "Berkeley, 1947. Convicted, served 60 days for molesting. He went and clipped a hunk of hair off a woman he was a-courting, and she didn't like it."

"Fernandez," said Mr. Noble obscurely.

"I trust you appreciate the allusion, Mr. Peabody? Your colleague Raymond Fernandez, New York's 1949 Lonely Hearts killer, who also liked hair. He used it for sympathetic magic, but fetishism may have entered in. Which is it with you, incidentally? Some of the other victims showed signs of amateur barbering."

"Are you comparing *me,* sir, to such a brute as Fernandez?"

"On second thought," MacDonald mused quietly, "I withdraw the fetichism with him; brutes are more direct. Magic was undoubtedly his dominant motive. Now your true fetichist is usually to all appearances a fine plausible citizen. You'll agree, Nick, that we've insulted Mr. Peabody needlessly? He and Fernandez have markedly different attitudes toward hair, if not toward . . ." He left the sentence incomplete.

Marie held her breath, watching Doreen. Her cousin was still looking at Luther Peabody—not with fear and hatred, not with inextinguishable love, but now quite unmistakably with repressed laughter.

"Lieutenant MacDonald!" Luther exploded with seemly rage. "Your excolleague may well be irresponsible and I suspect that he is more than a little drunk" (Mr. Noble calmly refilled his water glass) "but you're an officer of the law. You know that the law has no charges to bring against me and that your imputations are slanderous. This is not my house. It's my fiancée's. I'll leave it to her to order you and your sherry-tippling friend from the premises."

Now Doreen's laughter burst out, clear and ringing. *"Dar*ling! You're so cute when you're stuffy."

She was the only unamazed person in the room.

"Look, Mac," she went on. "I've known this all along. I remember the news stories and the pictures. That's why I first went out with Luther. I thought it'd be fun to see what a real, live, unconvicted professional Bluebeard was like. Then I got to know him, and I like him, and he doesn't need to do any explaining to me. He's going to tell me they *were* all accidents and that he's a persecuted victim of fate—and he doesn't need to, because I'm saying it first and I'm saying it to you, Mac, and to you, Mr. Noble. And I'm not ordering anybody out of any doors, but . . . do you really think there's much point in staying?"

"But why, Doreen? For heaven's sake, *why?* "

The girls were going to bed early. Even Luther Peabody had seemed disconcerted by Doreen's reaction and had left soon after. ("I want to be alone, my dear, with this precious trust you have placed in my hands.")

"I told you, darling. I like him. Maybe I even believe him."

"But you *can't!* It can't all be just innocent coincidence. It piles up too much. And that funny thing about the hair . . ."

"That," Doreen admitted, patting her long straight hair, "might give a girl to think. But honest, he hasn't made any passes at my hair. No fetichism about *him.* "

Marie picked up the small book from the night table. It was a WAC textbook on judo for women. "So you believe him?"

"All right, so there's a 5 percent chance I'm wrong. A girl should be able to defend herself, I always say. If she wants to."

"Is that it? You *don't* want to? Are things so bad you're deliberately looking for . . . ?"

Doreen lit a cigarette. "I'm sorry. I don't need your wholesome Utah sympathy, thank you kindly. Doreen can look out for herself. And I'm *not* deliberately plunging to my death. Now will you go to sleep or am I going to have to go out and see what twenty-year-old wonders the TV's offering tonight?"

"May I ask you one question, Doreen?"

"Make it a bargain. One apiece. Something I want to say to you, too . . . You first."

"Has he . . . has he talked to you about insurance?"

"Of course. It's sensible, isn't it? He's better off than you seem to think, you know, and I'm young and healthy so the premiums are low. He's paid the first premium on a policy for me. One hundred grand. And now that your worst fears are confirmed—"

"Oh, Doreen! How *can* you?"

"I've a favor to ask of you. Don't go back to the seagulls and the Tabernacle yet. Stick around a while. We'll find you a job if you want; I've got contacts."

"Then you *do* think you need somebody to—"

"I said I believed him, didn't I? It's just . . . Well . . . Oh, skip it! Go home if you want to. Go marry a Fundamentalist and run off to the Arizona Strip. Luther marries 'em only one at a time—and when he marries me, he's going to stay married."

"I'll stay. Of course I'll stay, Doreen. But oh . . . You're not just my cousin. You've always been my best friend. And now . . . I just don't understand you at all."

"That is news?" Doreen asked, and switched off the light.

It was a small tasteful wedding, held in the Sma' Kirk O' the Braes, and chiefly distinguished by the fact that the maid of honor never met the eyes of the bridegroom.

Throughout the service Marie could not help thinking of what marriage meant to her, or rather what she hoped it might mean. And here were Doreen and Luther . . .

"Why? *Why?* " She was almost in tears as MacDonald helped her into his car after the bridal couple had left for a Palm Springs weekend.

"We're going," MacDonald said, "to see the best man on *Whys* in L.A. You've met him, though it wasn't one of his more brilliant appearances. That's the second time Luther Peabody's bested him, and if I thought Nick was capable of such a human reaction, I'd say it rankles."

"Who *is* he, Mac? That whole scene was so strange . . ."

As they drove to downtown Los Angeles, MacDonald sketched a little of the career of Nicholas Joffe Noble, ex-Lieutenant, L.A.P.D. How the brightest Homicide man in Los Angeles had been framed to take the rap for a crooked Captain under investigation; how the sudden loss of job and reputation at the beginning of the depression had meant no money for an operation for his wife; how her death had broken him until he wound up on Skid Row living on sherry . . . and puzzles.

"Ten years ago," MacDonald said, "on my first case, one of the old-line Homicide boys steered me to him. Called him the Screwball Division, L.A.P.D. If a case makes no sense at all—and Lord knows that one didn't! —feed the facts to Nick Noble. His eyes sort of glaze over and something goes *tick* inside . . . and then the facts make a pattern.

"I've told him a lot about Doreen. He's been looking up some more stuff on Peabody, especially the Seattle case. Way I see it, we've got two problems here: Why is Doreen deliberately marrying a presumable mass murderer, and how in God's name are we going to prevent another 'accident'? And if those questions have an answer, we'll find it in the Chula Negra café, third booth on the left."

The little Mexican café was on North Main Street, near the new Federal Building, and the old Plaza and the medium-new Union Station, and the old Mexican Church and the new freeway which had brought them downtown. It had a new jukebox with some very old records and cheap new sherry in cracked old glasses.

In the third booth on the left the white little man sat, a half-full glass before him. He said "Mac" to MacDonald and "Miss Arlen" to Marie and then he brushed his white hand across his sharp-pointed white nose. "Fly," he said. "Stays there."

There was no fly. Marie looked down, embarrassed, and said, "Lieutenant MacDonald thought maybe you could—"

"Heard Mac's story," Mr. Noble interrupted. "Need yours. Talk."

And while MacDonald beckoned the plump young Mexican waitress and ordered more sherry, Marie talked. When she had finished, she watched the bright blue eyes expectantly. But they didn't glaze. Instead Mr. Noble shook his head, half in annoyance, half perhaps to dislodge the persistent if invisible fly.

"Not enough," he said. "No pattern."

"A whodunit's one thing," said MacDonald. "This is a *why*dunit. Why should a girl deliberately marry a Bluebeard? F. Tennyson Jesse works out quite an elaborate and convincing theory of murderees, people who deliberately invite being murdered."

"But Doreen isn't at all like that!" Marie protested.

"I know. Miss Jesse'd agree; Doreen doesn't fit the type. Some women want morbid sensation and pick out low, often strange kinds of men."

Marie said hesitantly: "You read about people being hypnotized. Luther does have such queer eyes—"

"Tabloid stuff," said Noble. "She knows what she's doing. Not enough. No pattern." He emptied his glass.

"And there's no official action we can take to protect her," said MacDonald. "That's the frustrating part. We can't go spending the taxpayer's money without a complaint. The insurance company's just as helpless. Dan Rafetti from Southwest National was in to see me today. He wanted some notes on Peabody to show Southwest's lawyers, but he wasn't hopeful. They can't dictate the policyholder's choice of beneficiary. All they can do is stop payment—when it's too late."

Slowly Marie rose from the table. "It was very nice of you to bring me here, Mr. MacDonald." She hoped her voice seemed under control. "And it was very silly of me to think you and your friend could pass a miracle. I did think you, at least, as an officer, might protect her."

"Wait a minute, Marie!" MacDonald was on his feet, too.

"It's all right, Mr. MacDonald. I can get home. At least if—*when* Doreen gets back from Palm Springs, I'll be there to—"

"You?" Noble's voice was sharp and dry. "You staying there with them? After marriage?"

"Why, yes. Doreen asked me to."

"Tell," he commanded.

Hesitantly she sat down and told. The blue eyes faded and thought seemed to recede behind them. Suddenly he nodded and said to MacDonald, "Recap M. O."

"Peabody's *modus operandi?* It's stayed the same as in your case. Apparently a mild dose of sleeping pills, then when the woman's unconscious a sharp blow to the base of the skull with the edge of the hand. Defense is always a broken neck by accident while under the influence of a slight self-administered overdose: Almost impossible to disprove."

The eyes glazed again. When their light returned it was almost painfully bright. "Pattern clear," he said. "Obvious *why*. But proof . . . Now listen. Both of you."

The cute plump waitress refilled the water glass uninstructed.

Doreen and Luther had been back from Palm Springs for two days now, and the honeymoon was figuratively as well as literally over.

How could she go on living here? Marie thought. Even to save Doreen. But Mac and Nick Noble said it would be only a matter of days . . . Marie squirmed back into the corner where Mac had first found her and tried to cut herself off from the quarrel that raged.

"But it's only plain damn common horse sense, Luther!" Doreen was screaming. "We have the good luck that Marie's going around with a cop and he lets slip that they're reopening that Seattle case. Are you just going to sit around and wait for them to extradite you?"

Luther Peabody's tone was too imperturbable to be called a shout, but it matched Doreen's in volume. "The Seattle D. A. would be an idiot to reopen the case. I was acquitted—"

"You weren't! They were hung juries. They can try you again and I won't let them!"

"Very well. I wasn't acquitted. But I was released three times. They can't convict me. I'm comfortable here, thank you, and I'm staying."

"I *won't* be the wife of a man on trial for murder! We'll go some place—any place—slip away—use another name for just a little while—just to let it get cold again—"

"My dear Doreen, I am staying."

"And I know why, too! That filthy-rich tin heiress from Bolivia we met at Palm Springs! I see myself getting you out of town while she's here. You'd sooner stay and be indicted or extradited or whatever it is and have all the scandal! What about my career?"

"You won't mind, my dear, if I ask, 'What career?' "

And after that, Marie thought wryly, it began to get nasty. And the plan wasn't working. The Seattle rumor was supposed to make Luther eager to get out, put time-pressure on him. Mac was taking a week's vacation, switching schedules with some other Lieutenant, so that he could act privately. He and a detective he'd hired were taking turns watching the house. And if Marie observed the faintest sign of anything wrong, she was to make a signal . . . What was the signal? She was so sleepy . . .

The newlyweds had stormed off to separate rooms. They had even stopped shouting across the house to each other. She was so sleepy, but it was so much trouble to get to her bed . . .

Marie managed to dig her fingers into her thigh so viciously that her eyes opened. "The faintest sign of anything wrong . . ." Of course. The first thing he'd do would be to drug the watchdog. He'd brought her the cup of cocoa Doreen had fixed. She had to make the signal . . . the signal . . .

She would be black-and-blue for weeks, but she kept digging into her thigh. Doreen insisted on keeping the Venetian blinds throughout the house with their slats slanted *up,* so sunlight couldn't come through to fade the carpeting. If MacDonald saw any window with the slats slanting *down* . . .

She heard the gratifying rattle of the shifting vanes as her hand slipped loosely from the cord and her eyes closed.

"You was supposed to relieve me an hour ago," said the man from the O'Breen Agency reproachfully.

"I know," MacDonald snapped. "I'm on vacation, but that doesn't stop a Homicide Captain from calling me down to Headquarters for more details on a report I filed last month.— What's that!"

"Yeah, I was just gonna tell you, Lieutenant. That blind switched damn near an hour ago. I didn't phone because I figured you was on your way here, and you don't see me risking my license trying to break in—"

But MacDonald was already at the door. He had no more authority to break in than the operative; but he had self-confidence, a marked lack of desire to warn the murderer by ringing a bell, and a lock-gun. The operative followed hesitantly at his heels. They both stopped short at the archway from hall to living room.

With the blinds as Doreen liked them, the room would have been dark, but the moon shone down through the reversed slats of the warning-blind onto the body. It was chicly dressed, as any starlet should be, in a fur-trimmed dressing gown. Its face was painted to starlet-mannequin perfection and the moon gleamed back from a starlet's overpainted fingernails. But one item differed from starlet standards: the coiffure.

The hair was so close-cropped that the head seemed almost bald.

MacDonald had switched the lights on and was bending over the body. "She's breathing!" he yelled. "We got a break! Phone—" And in a moment he was through to Homicide, arranging for official reinforcements, an immediate ambulance, and the nearest patrol car in the meantime.

He set back the phone and looked up at a strange tableau. In the front arch stood the private operative, gun drawn, face questioning. In the other arch, leading to the bedrooms, stood Luther Peabody, staring at the unconscious girl on the floor.

"All right, lover-boy," MacDonald began, not unglad that his position was, at the moment, unofficial. "My man has you covered. You're not trying a thing—not any more. And before the regulars get here, you're going to tell me a few fascinating items—starting with 'Where's Marie?' "

"I don't understand," Peabody faltered. "I heard all this noise . . ." His eyes never left the body.

MacDonald hesitated. The man worried him. He *did* look as if he had just awakened from a sound sleep. And what was stranger: the gaze he fixed on the body seemed (unless he were the world's leading non-professional actor) to be one of absolute incredulous surprise.

Then a moan came from the floor that sounded almost like words, almost like "Did I . . ." MacDonald knelt and bent closer, still eying Peabody. "Did I . . . did I fix the slats right, Mac?" said the preposterous starlet-lips.

"Marie!" MacDonald gasped. "Then who—" Abruptly he rose as he saw a uniformed patrol-car man looming behind the operative. "MacDonald, Homicide," he said, moving forward with his open wallet extended. "The girl's alive—ambulance on the way."

The patrol-car man said, "We spotted a dame high-tailing it away from here, took a chance on picking her up. Bring her in, Clarence!"

And 200 pounds of Clarence brought in a scratching, biting fury who was unmistakably Doreen Arlen Peabody.

"Didn't mean to be cryptic. Honest," said Nick Noble, brushing away the fly. "Thought you saw pattern. Seattle time-pressure wouldn't pressure Peabody. Be *less* apt to act when under observation. *Would* pressure Doreen. Had to act while she still had him around."

"The hospital says Marie'll be out tomorrow. Nothing serious. Doreen was a failure even at learning judo blows out of handbooks. But if I'm going to shine as Marie's savior, I'd better at least get completely straight what the devil happened. Want to help me sort it out?"

"No sorting. Straight pattern. Clear as soon as I knew Marie was staying on with them. Then all fell into place: Only possible *why*. Failure. Insurance. Family. Judo. Hair. Above all, hair."

"OK. Let *me* try. Doreen's not talking. We're going to have to release her anyway. You can't charge attempted murder when the victim won't make a complaint; and Marie says think what it'd do to the family in Utah."

"Step-family," said Nick Noble.

"Yes, that's a key point. With all Doreen's publicity, you think of this vast Family; but Marie's her only blood relative. That made the whole scheme possible. And the most cold-blooded—But let me try to reconstruct:

"Doreen meets Peabody. She remembers a little, checks up and learns more. Maybe she thinks, 'He can't get away with it forever'—and from that comes the thought: 'If any murder happens with him around, he's *it*.' "

"*Why*," said Nick Noble.

"Exactly. The only possible *why* for deliberately marrying a mass murderer: to have the perfect scapegoat for the murder you're about to commit. She brings her cousin out here. They used to look a lot alike; really the main differences, speech and action aside, are Doreen's elaborate starlet makeup and Marie's wavy hair. So Doreen insures herself for an enormous amount, or maybe just lets Peabody do it, if that's what *he* has in mind. But Doreen's not worrying— She'll kill Marie, using Peabody's M. O. and putting her own clothes and makeup on the body. There's still the hair. Well, Peabody has a psychopathic quirk about hair. He's clipped tresses from his victims before. This time she'll make it seem he's gone hog-wild and cut off too much . . . too much to tell if it was straight or wavy. Meanwhile she'll scrub her face, use the lightest makeup, wear Marie's clothes, and wave her hair. She'll be the little cousin from Utah. It's her background, too; she was once very like Marie even in actions—it'll be a simple role.

"So Peabody is convicted of the murder of his wife. Maybe even as the Utah cousin she's going to be an eyewitness. It doesn't matter whether he's gassed or found insane. In any case the insurance company won't pay *him*. Policy reverts to the estate, which consists solely of the Utah cousin, who now has a hundred grand in cash and never goes back. Perfect!"

"She thinks."

MacDonald nodded. "She thinks. . . . You know, Nick, unofficial head that you are of the Screwball Division, L.A.P.D., this was the ideally screwball case for you. Exact illustration of the difference between a professional and an amateur. If Peabody had killed Doreen, the motive and what you call the *pattern* would have been completely obvious; and yet he'd probably have executed the details so well that the worst he'd get would be another hung jury. Now Doreen had worked out the damnedest most unlikely pattern conceivable; but if (God forbid!) she'd brought off her murder, I swear she'd have gone straight to the gas chamber. Doreen wasn't really good at anything, from acting to murder. Somewhere along the line, pure ordinary police routine would've caught up with the identification—"

"Radiation Lab," said Nick Noble.

"Of course. Marie's prints would be on file if she'd worked on such a security job. Then the hair: Doreen was giving herself a quicky fingerwave when she heard me rampaging around and panicked. I suppose later she'd have had a pro job done—and that'd be one more witness. Fake identity plus good old *cui bono?* and she's done for. All thought out in advance . . . except what happens next."

"Rouse," Nick Noble agreed.

"Exactly. The English 'blazing car' murderer back around the time of Peabody's debut. Everything brilliantly worked out up through the murder . . . then chaos. Arrested the day after the killing and executed four months later. Doreen would've gone that way too. But thanks to you—"

"What now?" Nick Noble asked as Rosario brought fresh glasses.

"Damned if I know. Maybe your pattern machine can figure it. She says she's going back to Peabody if he'll have her. Says she kind of likes him. Well, Marie didn't! Marie hated him from the start—"

"—and didn't hate you?" It was the first time MacDonald had ever seen a broad grin on that thin white face. "A little like Martha, Mac," said Nick Noble. "A little."

MacDonald remembered Martha Noble's tragic operation. "Luckier," he said. "Thanks to you." He rose, embarrassed. "I'll bring Marie around tomorrow. Want you to see her while she's still all shaven and shorn. She's lovely—it's an experience. Well," he concluded, "it's been a hell of a murder case, hasn't it? The murder case with no murder and no arrest. Files closed with nobody in prison and nobody dead."

"That's bad?" Nick Noble observed to his invisible insect.

BETWEEN EIGHT AND EIGHT

by C. S. FORESTER

At last Manners was keenly interested in his game of chess. He bent forward over the board in an attitude of concentration. He wondered if his opponent would overlook the possibility of the position; that the advance of Manners's Queen's pawn one more square would not only attack a Knight but, by clearing the diagonal, would expose the King and his guard of Pawns to a formidable attack from Bishop as well as Rook and Queen. If his opponent should delay his counter-measure by as much as one single move he would be in a serious position; even if a quick mate did not ensue it would mean the loss of at least one piece.

But the man against whom Manners was playing was not of the type who overlooks things so important. After prolonged consideration he moved his Queen, and he moved her to the one square where she could wreak most destruction.

"Check," he said stolidly.

Manners stared at the board again. He had not paid enough consideration to this possibility. Now that the move was made he could see that it initiated an attack he could not stall off. The game was lost to him, inevitably and speedily. This new guard, who had been found for him by the warden of the prison in answer to his repeated irritated requests for someone who could really play chess, played much too well for him.

And as he stared at the board again, the clock of the parish church outside the prison wall struck once more.

First the four quarters, and then, with unctuous deliberation eight o'clock. Manners's heart throbbed painfully. Where would he be when that clock struck eight again? Manners knew; at least he knew where his limp body would be. He was filled with pettish rage about that clock. Surely the church authorities ought to stop the striking mechanism when they knew that a man lay in the condemned cell within such easy earshot of it.

He rose to his feet and turned away from the chessboard.

"I don't want to play any more," he said, and he knew as he said it that the tone of his voice was that of a spoiled child.

"All right," said the stolid guard. He displayed no annoyance at being thus deprived of a well-earned victory. He spoke indulgently. He could not be exacting with a man who had only twelve hours to live.

"What about a hand of crib?" asked the other guard, the lively one.

"To hell with you and your crib," said Manners, pacing about the cell.

The two guards exchanged glances. They had been expecting this. Manners had stood the strain of the three weeks of waiting well enough up to the present. That it had been a strain was obvious, for Manners's stubbly hair, once chestnut brown, was now white, had turned white in three weeks. But that was the only sign he had shown of the strain until now, until he began pacing round the cell, seven strides up, five across, seven down. Up—across—down—across, with his thoughts racing infinitely faster, but with as little chance of reaching a definite end. Up—across—down—across. The guards were only human after all. That restless pacing began to work on their nerves.

"What about the chaplain?" asked the lively guard. "Would you like to see him now?"

"To hell with the chaplain, too," said Manners, pacing on round the cell. The dreadful throbbing of his heart made his speech blurred and indistinct.

The guards reconciled themselves to the man's caged movements. Guards in a condemned cell, who spend every minute of a man's last three weeks on earth in the closest possible contact with him, must reconcile themselves to much.

But there came a blessed distraction. There was a jingling of keys outside; the door opened to admit the Warden, and then slammed to behind him. He was a man of slight, short figure, like Manners himself, dressed in a finely cut brown suit. Manners hated him; he had a long thin pink nose and a Hapsburg lip like the King of Spain's. Everyone was conscious of a momentary tension on the Warden's entrance, in case, just in case, he bore news of a reprieve. But one glance at his face was sufficient to determine that he did not.

"Well," said the Warden, "how's the chess going this time?"

"Rotten," said Manners, and turned his back. The Warden took the opportunity to ask the guards a question by means of a raised eyebrow; the guards replied in the negative with a shake of the head. Manners had neither offered to confess nor asked for the ministrations of the chaplain.

"Sorry about that," said the Warden to Manners. "What was the matter?"

"Matter?" said Manners, in a cracked hysterical voice. "Matter? Why—why—"

He did not finish his sentence. There is hardly any need for a man who is to be hanged in the morning to explain why he cannot play chess well. The sound of the church clock striking the half-hour came in through the bars of the cell window to accentuate the point.

"Well, what about seeing the chaplain instead?" asked the Warden coaxingly. He spoke as one would to a fretful child, just as the guards had done. Manners eyed the Warden. That coaxing, indulgent tone maddened him. He had heard nothing else for three weeks. And not even to satisfy the consciences of the Warden, and of the hangman, too, for the matter of that, would he be seduced into making a confession.

"I don't want to," he said sullenly.

With all the weight and majesty of the law turned upon him he could still be a rebel.

"Oh, come," said the Warden. "That's hardly fair on us, is it? Just think—"

The thin pink nose fairly quivered with his earnestness as he pleaded for a confession. He mouthed out platitudes that Manners hardly heard; his attention was curiously distracted by that Hapsburg lip. But the Warden went on pleading, and Manners began to feel himself weaken. Three weeks in a condemned cell are bad for a man's strength of will. He felt himself being driven into a confession, and he did not want to confess. Especially he did not want to give any cause for satisfaction to the Warden. And the Warden went on talking, and Manners stared fascinated at that long Hapsburg lip.

"You see what I mean?" said the Warden.

"Oh, shut up," said Manners, and his irritation burst all bounds.

With a single stride forward he brought himself within effective range. As he came forward his right fist came up in an uppercut into which was compressed all the baffled rage which seethed within him. His fist landed on that long chin with a hard, clean smack which echoed sharply round the cell, and the Warden fell to the floor utterly stunned. Not for nothing had Manners been an amateur boxer of repute.

" 'Ere, I say," said the lively guard.

Both he and his stolid partner were on their feet in an instant. They sprang at Manners. The lively guard gripped him round the waist; the stolid guard tried to pinion his arms.

But Manners was too strong for them. Rage and desperation gave him a lunatic's strength. There was plenty of muscle in his slight form. He tore his arms free. One hand gripped the stolid guard by the back of the neck; the other arm held the lively guard pinioned. One fierce mad wrench achieved its object. The head of the stolid guard crashed against the head of the lively guard with a noise like two wooden boxes struck together. That one blow might have been sufficient, but Manners was too insane to check himself. He brought those unresisting heads together again and again, until his strength ebbed from him and he let the two limp forms fall to the ground.

Manners staggered back across the cell and surveyed the wreck he had made. The whole affair had only lasted a few seconds; and perhaps it was not more than two or three more before Manners recovered himself sufficiently to think clearly. Even then his first thought was that he was at last alone, comparatively speaking, for the first time for three weeks; that he could kill himself now and cheat the law if he wanted to—the very thing those two guards had been intended, all those three weeks, to prevent.

A slight movement of the Warden's unconscious body recalled him to action. A man cleanly knocked out, like the Warden, does not take long to recover. For a single split second Manners debated the point; whether he should give himself the not-very-satisfactory satisfaction of cheating the law, or whether he should make a wild attempt to escape.

The chances against escape were still enormous, he knew, but there was a chance, which was more than there had been five minutes ago. With a great effort he steadied himself, although he could not make his hands stop shaking—his heart was beating so fast that he trembled in every joint. But he thought clearly and fast; he was a born plotter and intriguer.

He bent over the Warden, and as the latter's mouth opened to utter the first groan of returning consciousness, he crammed his handkerchief in. Whipping the coarse cover from the long pillow of his bed he wound it round and round the Warden's head. He was about to bind the Warden's arms when he remembered and he tore off the Warden's coat and waistcoat first; it would have been impossible to have done this after tying the man's wrists together, and moreover he was now able to use his suspenders for the purpose.

Now that the Warden was bound, gagged, and helpless, Manners could spare time to attend to the guards; but a moment's examination assured him there was no need.

The two unfortunate men were still unconscious, and likely to remain so. They might even die. Manners neither knew nor cared. He dragged off the Warden's shoes and trousers, and, moving deftly despite his trembling fingers, he dressed himself in the neat brown suit thus put at his disposal. Already the Warden was writhing a little over the floor, but he could make no sound, and it would be some time before he could get to his feet with his arms tied behind him.

In the Warden's pocket he found many things which would be useful. Money—a handful of loose change and a pound or two in notes in the pocketbook. And keys—half a dozen on a ring. The largest, Manners guessed, was the passkey to the cell door. Then there were two Yale keys. For a second Manners stood fingering these, deep in thought. But he had no time to spare. He must do his thinking while in action.

He had to brace himself again to open the cell door; every one of his actions after that must be made without a trace of hesitation. The big key opened the door; of course it would. He stepped out into the corridor with his heart pounding against his ribs. His mind was racing through a long series of mazed recollections. He tried to remember the entrance to the prison; he had seen it several times; when they had taken him out to his trial and when they had brought him back to die.

He had gone more than once to the chapel—he had gone there that very morning (today was Sunday) with a guard at each side of him. Most of all was he trying to remember one certain door in the wall of the long corridor in which he found himself. It was a door rather different from the cell and chapel doors. Once, as he was being led past it, the Warden had come through it, alone, shutting it behind him. It was the door into his private apartments, Manners was sure.

As he walked down the corridor he tried to call up before his mind's eye what he remembered of that door. He could remember the color of it; he could remember the brass knob. With a huge effort he assured himself that he had noticed the tiny brass plate which surrounded the small Yale keyhole. Another huge effort assured him that the keyhole was on the left-hand side of the door—it would never do to hesitate in front of it.

One of the two Yale keys in his pocket would open it; he could not tell which. It would be a frightful risk to fumble, but it was a risk he must take. After all, it was an even chance. He put his hand in his pocket and gripped one of the keys ready. He thought, as he did so, that probably his life depended upon which key of those two chance guided into his fingers.

With such feverish rapidity had his mind worked that he had not taken more than half a dozen strides yet.

He was in the well-remembered long corridor badly lit with a series of electric bulbs at intervals along the wall. It was the ground floor, and the cell from which he had emerged was at the far end, convenient to the execution shed and the yard where he had walked for exercise, a guard on each side of him. But Manners was walking in the opposite direction, towards the entrance hall and the Warden's door.

Far down, at the very end, a guard sat on a chair looking towards him. But he was a long way off; Manners had much the same figure as the Warden's, and he wore the Warden's clothes. And the guard never thought for one moment that the man who was to die tomorrow at eight would be loose in the corridor and walking with a firm step towards him. And the light cast by the unshaded electric bulbs was harsh and deceptive.

Manners walked down towards him, past three empty cells, past the chapel doors. He stopped at the right moment outside the Warden's door. At the same instant he brought the key from his pocket and thrust it into the keyhole. For a heart-rending tenth of a second it would not turn. Then it yielded, and the door opened, and Manners stepped inside and closed the door quietly behind him.

He had never before been where he found himself now. It was a flagged hall with several doors. He flung an agonized glance round the place; his thumping heart leaped more painfully than ever when he caught sight of what was clearly the door into the street at the other end.

Even then he restrained himself sufficiently to look round for a hat and overcoat. But a woman's voice came from behind one of the doors.

"Is that you, George?"

There was no time to lose. He tiptoed across the hall, opened the front door, and passed through it into darkness and freedom, and shut it after him. It was raining terribly, and a cold wind blew, but he must not wait. He ran down the stone steps, and out through the gate to the pavement, where he hurried along, head down, shoulders bent.

There were few people about in such vile weather, and Manners regretted that he had not found a hat and overcoat—his lack of them would call attention to himself. Even as he reached this conclusion, catastrophe ensued. Fate, which had guided him well so far, ordained that it should be beside a street lamp that he should encounter a policeman.

The policeman, his cape glittering with moisture in the lamplight, looked curiously at the coatless figure hurrying by; Manners looked furtively from the corner of his eye at the policeman. He saw the policeman start with incredulous surprise at the first recognition, saw him hesitate, saw him decide, heard his voice calling him back.

Manners broke into a run. Five seconds later he heard the policeman's whistle blow. He ran madly, desperately. Behind him he still heard that remorseless whistle; the policeman, hampered with cape and greatcoat, could not hope to catch him on foot.

The prison entrance stood back from a main road—not so well lighted as usual, this being Sunday—and at the first opportunity Manners turned aside and plunged into a side street; racing down that, he turned corner after corner, his lungs bursting, his heart pounding.

It was a chase like those in a nightmare. Whistles seemed to be blowing everywhere. Once someone tried to seize him, but he tore himself free and pounded on. Luckily there were few people about in those quiet suburban by-streets in that awful weather. Stealing a glance over his shoulder he saw the lights of a motor car in pursuit—the headlights, dazzlingly bright, held him in their beam. He flung himself round another corner, and, with a mad, colossal effort, he leaped in his stride over the hedge and railings of a suburban front garden. Crouching behind the hedge in the pelting rain he saw the car tear past him; then he heard many running feet and voices.

"No 'at," panted someone to someone else as they ran by.

"No 'at? We'll find 'im all right."

Still Manners crouched in the garden; from the lighted, curtained windows behind him came music and laughter. The Sunday evening party in that little suburban house had remained unconscious of the mad pursuit outside.

Long after the last sound of pursuit had died away Manners rose stiffly to his feet. He was shuddering now with cold, and he was drenched with rain and sweat.

But the wait had given him time to plan his next move. He must find shelter and concealment. No hotel, no lodging-house, would offer him those without suspicion, dripping with wet as he was, without luggage, and (he strongly suspected) muddy with crouching in the mould of the front garden.

His wife? She would have gone away for certain, he knew not whither. Nor was he sure she would shelter him; on the contrary, he was nearly sure she would not. And now that the police knew of his escape the first place in which they would seek him would be at his wife's. There he could not go.

He decided almost automatically where he would seek refuge. He would go to Ethel's. The police had no knowledge of any connection between him and Ethel; nothing had come out about her at his trial—although, God knew, enough women had been dragged into that business. Manners, the born intriguer, had seen to it, from long before he was guilty of murder, that no one knew of their friendship, and he could rely upon Ethel not having made public her relationship with Manners, the murderer.

Ethel lived alone in rooms; Ethel had loved him—the first was a subtle result of the second. At Ethel's he would find rest and concealment. Extraordinarily fatigued, he began to walk stiffly through the remorseless rain to where Ethel lived.

He had now only a slight idea of where he was, because the prison was in a suburb with which he had but small acquaintance. But the suburb in which Ethel lived was on the same side of the river. He could probably make his way to it by keeping to the by-streets and steering in a general way eastwards. He was wet through, and excitement and his mad run had made him very tired—the three weeks of agony he had borne since his appeal was dismissed had not helped to keep him fit. But there was no chance of relaxation; not, that is to say, until he reached Ethel's.

Every footstep he heard struck terror into him; every other second he peered anxiously about for the menacing approach of a policeman. Time and time again he turned about in his tracks and made his way round some other corner because he saw people or policemen approaching him. The delays were irritating, but he could not risk passing people in the street, not at this late hour, hatless and coatless and muddy in the pelting rain.

He had to nerve himself to a fierce effort to cross the radial main roads as he encountered them, one after the other. His poor heart flogged away at his ribs; just that was enough to tire anyone, let alone this continual nervous strain and this walking—walking—walking through the dark streets and the pitiless rain. By now he could feel no emotion save that of fear. He felt neither elation nor hope.

He never thought once of the excited headlines which were being drawn up in a thousand newspaper offices, proclaiming his escape, and admitting that he was the first man in England to escape from the condemned cell since Jack Sheppard. All he could do was to tramp onwards, shaken by his pounding heart, peering continually about him.

It was a long, long walk to cross from West to East, but at last he began to reach a neighborhood which was familiar to him, and then he turned another corner and found himself in the suburban street where Ethel had her rooms. He reached the house and turned into the front yard, shutting the gate very, very quietly after him.

There he had to stop for a while, forcing his numbed brain to think clearly. He could not knock at the door. There could be no surer way of attracting attention to himself than by knocking at four in the morning at the door of an apartment house. Besides, it would not be Ethel who opened it.

He crept to the ground-floor front window and stared into the darkness there. Long and anxious peering at the shadowy shapes within assured him at last that the furniture there was familiar to him. Ethel still lived there; this was her sitting-room.

Her bedroom was the corresponding room at the back of the house— Manners knew that well; he knew, too, how the windows opened into the backyard. The house was semi-detached. He tried the side gate—so softly— but it was locked. Once more he nerved himself for an effort.

He stood and listened lest he could detect through the monotonous downpour of the rain the stealthy tread of a policeman's rubber-soled boot. He could hear nothing; bracing himself once more, he stretched his stiff limbs in a wild leap for the top of the gate. His fingers clutched it; then, with an effort which brought the sweat pouring from him in rivers, he dragged himself to the top, sprang over, and lowered himself to the ground on the other side.

He tiptoed down the dark passage to the back of the house. He had reached at last shelter and protection. Turning the corner, he crept into the yard, crept up to the window, and tapped at the pane. He leaned forward in utter exhaustion against the sill.

Ethel was in bed. She might even be said to be dozing. Hour after hour of that dreadful night she had turned back and forward in her bed. She had turned on the light and tried to read; dropping the book restlessly, she had turned off the light and tried to sleep unavailingly. She could not tear her thoughts away from the man who had to die next morning, the man in whose arms she had lain, who had wooed her with honey-sweet words.

Despite the coldness of the night her bed became fever-hot to her. The town-hall clock in the main road, tolling out remorselessly each passing quarter of an hour, sickened her each time she heard it. Not that she loved the man now. The reports of the trial had told her much about him that she had not known—not merely that he was a murderer (that she might have borne with) but that he was a married man and that there were other women in his life, so that she knew him now for the liar and cheat that he was and she hated him for it. But even that did not help her to sleep when she knew that at eight o'clock guards' arms would grasp the waist she had clasped, as they dragged him from the cell, and the hangman's rope would bruise and tear the neck she had kissed.

And yet, towards morning, she fell into a fevered, troubled doze, from which something roused her with a dreadful start. Someone was tapping on the pane of the window. She sat up in panic. Again there came the tapping at the window. Ethel was a brave woman; she flung off the bedclothes, snatched her flashlight, and approached the pane.

A shadowy shape was visible through the glass. Then she pressed the switch and saw the face. For a second she actually did not recognize him, for his hair was white now, and his face was marked with awful anxiety; he was so different from the dapper, self-confident Mr. Manners she had known. She stared dumbly at the vision.

Grimy, bloody hands pressed against the glass. The sagging mouth opened and shut, and the hands made pitiful gestures to her. She understood. She pushed up the sash quietly, and shrank back to the farther end of the room; the beam of the flashlight shone steadily on him.

Slowly, with infinite weariness, Manners hauled himself over the sill and half fell into the room; but he roused himself to close the window behind him before he turned and faced her.

"What do you want?" murmured Ethel; she spoke instinctively in a whisper.

Manners's answer was half a groan.

"Ethel!" he said, staggering blindly towards her.

But Ethel only shrank away.

"Keep back!" she said, and Manners stood still, drooping. Fatigue and anxiety had nearly done their work. But one last effort of the failing consciousness, one last flash of the intriguer's brain, told Manners what he had been fool enough to forget before. The old spell which had bound Ethel to him, which had made her subservient, had lost its power now.

Disappointment and dismay came to help fatigue and anxiety. His heart nearly failed him as he stood there, knees sagging, swaying on his feet.

"So you were married all the time?" said Ethel, bitterly.

Manners could only mumble unintelligibly in reply.

"Then, why don't you go to your wife for help?" asked Ethel. She hated him at that moment, hated him with an intensity which shook her as though in the grip of ague. But her hatred was not great enough to give her the strength to utter the scream which would bring her help and which would result in the arrival of brutal men, who would drag Manners away to the scaffold.

The bitter hostility in her tone completed the work which fatigue and anxiety had begun. Manners uttered a little moan and fell forward on his face, a senseless, motionless lump.

For a long time Ethel could only stand and gaze at him as he lay in the circle of light thrown by the flash. It was the striking of the town-hall clock which roused her. It struck the four quarters and then six o'clock. That reminder of the passage of time called her back to her senses.

She had no notion of how Manners had escaped, but she could picture the fevered search that was happening in the world outside. She could not think what to do; for the matter of that, she grimly realized, she did not know what she wanted to do. She could not bring herself to give Manners up, at the same time she did not want to be the instrument to save him. And her practical sense told her that it would be impossible for her to keep him concealed here in her rooms.

It was not until some time later that she realized that she was shuddering with cold. She dressed herself in the darkness, creeping quietly about the room. The usual early morning noises reached her from the outside.

Then she felt a sudden panic; perhaps the police had traced Manners here; they might already be quietly surrounding the house. She must go and see. She must get into the open to think. And when Manners recovered he would need food. Bread she could buy at the grocer's round the corner, who opened early; tea she would be able to make him over her gas ring here. She realized sadly that however much she hated Manners she could not deny him food. She put on her hat and her coat, and stooped over Manner's prostrate body.

"Dick," she whispered, but Manners did not answer. She shook him, but he made no movement. His clothes were wringing wet—a little pool of water had drained from them onto the floor. But his heart was still beating.

Ethel snatched the blankets from the bed and spread them over him. Then, very quietly, she opened the door, and, as a measure of precaution, she locked it after her. She crept out to the front door, unbolted it, and passed out into the street.

Her voice and her touch had done something towards rousing Manners. Some kind of consciousness began to creep back into his brain as he lay there on the floor. He was in a burning fever; already he was plunged into the semidelirium of pneumonia. And in this delirium all accurate memory of the events of the previous evening was expunged. He had some confused recollection of a fight in his cell, of a wild flight through darkened streets, with remorseless pursuit hard at his heels. What Manners could remember of the night before was no more than he could remember of other nights. And then with a sudden start, with a hideous realization which set the fevered blood pulsing hot under his skin, he remembered that he was to die today. He remembered turning sharply round yesterday afternoon in his cell to see a strange face peering through the grating of the door—the hangman come to look at him, to observe his neck and guess his weight so that he might calculate what drop to allow.

Manners moaned again; the faintest of lights that winter morning was beginning to creep in through the windows. Then he heard the clock strike; four quarters and then—and then—seven o'clock. This was the hour when they would rouse him to make a pretense at breakfast before they dragged him out to the shed in the yard which he had observed when taking exercise. He heard the rattle of a key in the lock; it would be the Warden coming in. For a moment he tried to struggle, but his frantically beating heart could stand the strain no longer.

Ethel, entering, found her problem solved for her.

KNOWING WHAT I KNOW NOW
by BARRY PEROWNE

A porter gave me a hand to lift the trunk into the luggage van. It was an ordinary brown trunk, fibre with wooden battens, like a million others. It was heavy.

"Blimey, what you got in here?" said the porter. "A body?"

I managed a laugh of sorts, and I hoped it sounded all right to him. It had a queer ring in my own ears. But he didn't seem to notice anything.

The trunk bore a label with the name *Frank Venhold,* an address, and the direction *Passenger to London.* Name and address were both fake, and *Passenger to Hell* would have been a truer direction. I had no intention of going all the way to London with that trunk. I never wanted to see it again.

I tipped the porter, and—the luggage van being placed about the middle of the train—walked along the platform toward the rear. The doors of the coaches stood open. There were the usual good-bye groups talking at the doors, the usual station smells, the usual hollow, reverberant station noises. All was as usual, yet all seemed to me subtly different. I felt as though I were walking along the bed of a chasm, with strange echoes beating back at me from soaring rock walls that inclined toward each other. But when, instinctively, I glanced up, there were only spiderwork girders supporting the station roof of dingy glass spattered with rain.

I turned the collar of my trench coat higher, jerked my hatbrim lower over my eyes. I kept a sharp watch on the station entrances. I felt cold to the marrow. My teeth wanted to chatter; my jaws ached from the tension of keeping them clamped. I was poised for a sudden pouring in at any second of burly figures in policeman's blue. I stood outside the door of a coach, my hands clenched hard, deep in my pockets. The station clock looked like a white, enigmatic moon. Its hands seemed painted on it, fixed in an eternal immobility, which it seemed to impose over the whole station. So that, as I looked at the clock face, the people around me, glimpsed out of the corners of my eyes, seemed arrested in mid-stride, held motionless, struck still as headstones. Until the slight, visible jerk of the minute hand broke the spell, loosed the bustle around me, a hiss of released steam, the hollow slam of a door.

Along the platform a guard came walking, whistle between his teeth, holding a green flag furled in one hand, consulting a watch he held in the other. I turned and stepped into the corridor of the train. The compartment before me held three middle-aged women and a small boy with his head in a comic book. I sat down in a corner seat on the corridor side, facing forward, my back to the luggage van with the trunk in it. A jerk and a clanking ran through the train from coach to coach, like a scale played on a cracked xylophone, and the platform sights began to slide away. The dirty glass roof went from overhead, letting in the gray, watery daylight of late afternoon. The train gathered speed and I felt the trunk following me.

I had to force myself to sit there, staring from the window. The gloomy suburbs of the midland town died among green, flat meadows, swollen brown brooks with humped bridges, and lines of leaning willow trees.

We were on our way, the trunk and I. So far, so good. I needed a cigarette badly, but I was afraid to take my hands out of my pockets; I knew they'd shake, and I was afraid the women or the kid would notice.

Then I heard compartment doors being slid open, one after another, all along the coach, and coming closer. It sounded to me as though somebody was being looked for, and I held my breath, strained my ears, trying to hear what was going on above the metallic *tat-tat-tat-too, tat-tat-tat-too* of the train. Suddenly a white-jacketed steward appeared in the corridor. He slid back the door of the compartment, put in his head.

"First dinner now being served," he said. "Take your places for dinner, please."

His call went on along the train, and I breathed again. Two of the women got up and left the compartment, turning to the right along the corridor. I had to have that cigarette. The kid was looking at me unwinkingly over the top of his comic. Kids sense things. I got up, stepped into the corridor, slid the door shut, lighted a cigarette. Twilight mist had quenched meadows and willows. The lights had come on. People squeezed past me along the corridor, going to dinner. It occurred to me that they must have to pass through the luggage van to get to the dining car. If so, I might have a look at the trunk, just make sure it was all right so far. I didn't want anything to happen prematurely.

People had stopped squeezing past me, but I waited till the steward had returned, on his way to the dining car, then I turned and followed him. Three coaches along, I came to the luggage van. I stopped at the edge of the slightly rocking steel footplate connecting the coaches. I peered into the van, but it was dimly lighted and I couldn't spot the trunk right off. I looked back along the corridor. No one was in sight. I stepped into the luggage van. Nobody here, either—just a smell of kippers from a stack of flat wooden crates, and some bicycles, a folding perambulator, an invalid chair, and four trunks. Two of them were exactly alike, and a moment of panic pumped the blood into my head, because I wasn't sure which was mine.

I had to stoop and glance at the label on the nearer one. The label read *G. N. Trevelyan, Passenger to London,* no address given. My trunk was right alongside. They were identical; they were like thousands and thousands of the same make. A thought came to me.

My plan had been to leave the train at Oxford, the first stop, and let the trunk labeled *Frank Venhold* go on to London, be put in the Unclaimed Luggage Office. Only, something had been nagging at the back of my mind —the thought that the porter who had helped me get the trunk into the van might be a luggage porter who traveled with the train, and he might see me leaving it at Oxford, might chase after me, shouting, "Your trunk, sir!"

Now, as I looked at this trunk labeled *G. N. Trevelyan,* I had a better idea. That label was corrugated; the gum on it must have been dry; it looked as if it might peel off easily. I tried it, and it came right off in my hand. A piston thumped in my chest. I glanced around quickly. On a small counter in a corner of the van were various pink and yellow forms, a hurricane lantern with red glass, a stack of labels, and a gluepot with a filthy brush sticking out of it.

I tell you, the thing was set up for me. *Knowing what I know now, I ask myself by what, by whom? By God? By the Devil? By Fate? By mere Chance? What is the riddle of human life? Why are we here?*

It took me thirty seconds to stick the Trevelyan label over the Venhold label, and to write a new Venhold label and stick it on the Trevelyan trunk. Then I walked back along the corridor. I hadn't really had much hope before. Now, I had hope. I was exultant. I didn't want to go back to the compartment where that wretched kid with the knowing eyes was. I looked into the other compartments I passed, but the nearest I found to an empty was one with just a girl in it. Her eyes were closed. Apparently she was asleep. I slid the door back quietly, sat down in the corner seat farthest from her. I was facing the front of the train. *Tat-tat-tat-too, tat-tat-tat-too.* I could feel the two trunks sliding along behind me through the night. But I felt better, easier. I put my hat on the rack. I undid the belt of my trench coat. I could see faintly in the window the reflection of my face against the mist and dark outside. It was a stranger's face to me—the pale, sharpish face of a man of 35, with black hair brushed back with the sheen of enamel from a high, sloping forehead.

I dropped my cigarette, trod on it, and was taking another from my packet when I felt the girl watching me. I met her eyes. They were gray, but looked dark, the pupils were so large. There was something queer about those eyes, though she was an attractive girl, with amber hair done in this short, modern way with a kind of fringe or bang, or whatever they call it. She looked pale, hunched there in her corner, her hands in the pockets of a loose, light, hip-length jacket with a high collar turned up like a frame for her head. She had neat ankles and low-heeled gray suede walking shoes, rather pretty.

I offered her a cigarette. She hesitated, her pupils contracting oddly, making her eyes look light and shallow. Then she leaned forward, took a cigarette from the packet I held out, and I noticed her hands, rather square, with long but strong fingers—imaginative hands—the nails only faintly coral-tinted. I held my lighter for her.

"Thanks," she said, and her eyes came close, looking at me, as she leaned forward to dip her cigarette in the flame.

That continual dilating and contracting of the pupils of the eyes—I had read somewhere that it is called the "hippus" and is supposed to be a sign of nervous and emotional instability. As though in confirmation of my thought, I saw her draw her shoulders together in an odd little movement, as though a kind of shudder had gone through her. I didn't like it.

"What's the matter with you?" I said. "Cold?"

"It's all right." She leaned back in her seat. "Just a goose walked over my grave."

I didn't like her saying that, either. I felt those two trunks pouring along like hounds on my heels through the mist and darkness. I didn't answer her. But she went on watching me with those witch's eyes.

"How do *you* account for that goose-over-your-grave feeling?" she said suddenly. "What's *your* theory about it?"

"I've got none," I said. "I'm not a psychiatrist."

"What are you?" she said.

I didn't like her talk. I felt those trunks sliding up closer to my back.

To shut her up—she sounded like one of these intellectual girls to me—I said, "Me? I'm a medievalist."

I couldn't tell whether she believed it, but again I saw that queer contraction and dilation of her pupils.

"Perhaps they knew more than the psychiatrists do," she said, "more of the—the essential truth, the things of—the things of the spirit—the *mysterious* things."

"Are you a student of—the mysterious things?" I said sardonically.

"I'm a student," she said, "an art student. I've just won a scholarship in London. That's where I'm going now."

An art student, I thought. Maybe that accounted both for the good hands and for the emotional instability hinted at by the curious, quite beautiful eyes. She interested me in spite of the trunks that slid along at my back.

She had a slight accent, and I said, "You aren't English, are you?"

"I grew up in Canada," she said, and again I saw that odd tightening of her shoulders, as though to a fleeting chill. "I remember once—"

She stopped. She drew deeply on her cigarette, watching the smoke drift up to the cluster of light bulbs under the bell-glass. On the rack above her head were a small, soft, green hat and a little overnight bag, faintly vibrant to the monotonous *tat-tat-tat-too* rhythm of the wheels.

"I was thinking, as you came in," she said, "of something that happened to me once in Canada. I was thinking of it because it happened so far away —thousands of miles away—and so long ago. I was thinking of it because I have this scholarship, because I'm going to London, because my real life is just beginning—because," she said, with a flash of vehemence, "I can't forget it, and I wish to heaven I could! But it's always there, following me —waiting." She looked at me with those lovely, disquieting eyes. "Have you ever had that feeling?" she said. "Surely, everyone must have had it— in some form. The feeling that something is waiting for you, something— oh, unimaginable, terrible, whether physical or psychical I don't know, but something inevitable, not to be eluded or escaped, just waiting for you, coldly and very patiently—in an appointed place?"

"Certainly, everyone's had the feeling," I said. I could feel my brow coldly damp. "You're talking of Death, a date we all have—only, we don't harp on it."

"My father called it by a different name," she said. "He called it Failure. But that isn't the answer, either. It's—" She frowned for a moment at her cigarette, then looked at me again. "It was in Canada," she said. "My father and I were living in a fair-sized town, in a rather old house, a red-brick Victorian house, on the outskirts. My father was a widower. He had a poorly paid office job, but he owned the house—on mortgage—and he rented off the upper floors as apartments. We lived below, in a kind of semibasement. He always referred to it as 'the garden apartment.' Poor darling, I loved him dearly, but I have to admit he was—ineffectual, un-lucky—oh, I don't know. Only, I used to wonder, even as a kid, why nothing ever seemed to go right for him—for us. *Little* things! You know? He tried so hard. But if he bought new furniture, for instance, it would seem to get shabby and gloomy quicker than other people's furniture. He would dig and dig in the garden, but where the neighbors' gardens were neat, with lawns and flowers, nothing ever flourished in ours but weeds. Horrible green weeds! Bad luck seemed to follow us. It seemed as though there never could be any escape from it. It was like a quagmire. I used to feel it was something to do with the house, that great, hideous barn of a house. I began to think there never could be any hope for us as long as we stayed there. I *hated* No. 15 George Street."

I wished she would stop. I didn't like this story. The train beat out its monotonous rhythm; the things on the rack vibrated. Our faces were reflected faintly in the windows against the mist and the night. I wished she would stop.

"One rainy afternoon when I was about ten years old," she said, "I walked home from school alone. That afternoon the teacher had been showing us some pictures of desert country, cactus country, dry and wide spaces full of clean, varied colors. Going home, walking home alone with my books, I was wearing rubbers, and a rubber raincoat with a hood. You know how wet rubber feels. Rain, rain, rain! I loathed it. I loathed the puddled lawns, the dripping trees, the dun sky. I loathed all wet, green, slimy things."

She dropped her cigarette, put her neat suede shoe on it. I was trying not to listen. The trunks were following me.

"I always got home before my father," she said. "There was a woman who came in to clean the place for us, leave the kitchen stove burning, everything ready for father and I to cook dinner for ourselves. I had my own key." She was biting her lower lip; her strange, shallow, changing eyes looked through me. "I didn't want to go into the house that afternoon, I hated it so much. I didn't want to set foot in it. I don't know how I made myself walk up the path and unlock that hateful old green-painted front door. It opened into a passage with coats hanging on a row of hooks to the right. On the left was the door of our living room, beyond that the door of father's bedroom. Farther on, stone steps—four stone steps—led down to a kind of flagstoned lobby, off which, on the right, opened a door to a side street. On the left, the wall of the lobby was glasspaned, like a conservatory, with a door opening into the muddy garden. Across the lobby was the kitchen."

Her breathing was quick and shallow; I could scarcely hear her voice.

"I went down the four steps into the lobby," she said, her strange eyes seeing it. "The lobby was full of gray daylight filtering through the filthy panes. I could hear the rain spattering against them. I kicked off my rubbers, as I always did, and hung up my rubber coat on a shelf, meant for flower-pots, which ran the length of the panes. I looked at the water dripping from my coat, making a pool, trickling across the flagstones. I looked out through the panes at tall sunflowers and rank stinging-nettles. The sunflowers were over, their heads hanging heavy and brown and sodden, rocking a little in the rain. The nettles were high and green, like a forest. There never were such nettles anywhere else. Their veined, hairy leaves were pressing up against the glass. They were as tall as I was. I hated to look at them. I turned to go into the kitchen."

She bit at her lips. They were pale pink where her teeth had scraped the lipstick from them. Her pupils were greatly dilated.

"The kitchen door stood open," she said. "It opened inward, to the right. The kitchen was dark except for the red glow of the coal fire through the bars of the old-fashioned stove. There was an old wicker armchair standing obliquely facing the stove, and in the chair—on the worn cushion that always had a wad of old newspapers crammed under it—was our cat. Its forepaws were folded under its chest. I could see the firelight reflected in its eyes. It seemed to be waiting. There was an old alarm clock, with a loud, tinny tick, on the shelf over the stove. I could hear the clock going tick-tick-tick, loudly and questioningly. And I couldn't move. My mouth was dry. I wanted desperately to back away, turn, run. I couldn't move. Only, I felt as though something were drawing me *forward*. But I didn't move at all. I knew that in there, in the shadows behind the open door, there was—something. I don't know. It had no shape. Only, cold came from it. It was waiting. And the clock ticked, the cat watched in the firelight, the rain spattered at the windows, the nettles pressed against the panes, the sunflowers rocked their dead, sodden heads. I don't know—I don't know—"

Suddenly she pressed her hands to her face. She cried as though her heart would break. Never had I seen or imagined such grief. The tragedy of the ages, of the unknown soul of Man and the dim beginnings of life in the swamps of the tree-ferns, was in that brief paroxysm.

"Here," I said roughly, after a minute.

She groped blindly for the handkerchief I held out to her. She wiped her eyes. She blew her nose. I could hear the shudder in her breathing. I looked toward the window, saw the ghost of my own face floating there. I thought of the trunks. I knew, now, that I shouldn't get away. I knew there was no escape for me. Anywhere. I knew they'd get me. I don't know how I knew, but I knew.

The girl spoke.

"When I came to myself," she said, "I was out in the street, in the rain, running, and had run full tilt into a man. I felt his arms go round me, and heard my father's voice, 'Why, Gina, Gina, what's this? What's the matter?' I couldn't tell him, not then. I could only say that I'd never go back into that house—never."

She was silent for a moment.

"He never made me go back," she said. "We went to a hotel for the night. I tried to tell him what had happened. He sat on the edge of my bed, listening. Did I say he was a small man? A small man, with kind eyes. He looked so tragic, so beaten, as he listened. 'Failure,' I heard him murmur— 'Failure was there.' I've thought about that so much, since. He spoke as though of some projection of himself, of some—some abstraction made carnate, waiting in the house. It was almost as though—as though he spoke of some *hump*, not on his own back, but which he feared he had prepared for mine. For me, whom he loved." She shook her head. "But that isn't the answer. I've thought so much. I've dreamed those dreadful seconds, that eternity, so many times, since—the nettles, the sunflowers, the rain, the pool dark on the flagstones, the open door, the fire red between the bars, the watching cat with the shine in its eyes—all the room, waiting for me, unchanged, and the thing waiting in the room, and the clock ticking loudly. My father died within the year. He had relations in England—in the Midlands here—and they sent for me. And I was glad as the miles became hundreds, the hundreds became thousands, between me and the waiting room. *But I know it's still there.*"

She looked at me as though asking my opinion, my help; but I had nothing to say to her. The train broke its rhythm, began to clatter over switchpoints. She glanced at my handkerchief, balled in her hand. Then she made a movement—somehow ineffectual, as her father's movements might have been, I imagined—as though to reach down her small grip from the rack, probably to take out a clean handkerchief. I rose and lifted the grip down for her.

I tell you, knowing what I know now—yet, what do I know, or any of us?—I tell you, this whole thing was set up for us. By what design of God or the Devil or Destiny or mere Chance had I chosen this girl's compartment?

As I lifted down the grip for her, I saw for the first time the label on it: *G. N. Trevelyan, Passenger to London.*

The train was slowing. Platform lights slid by, flickering, outside the misted windows. An amplified voice was intoning: "*Oxford— Oxford.* The train now arriving at Platform Four is the train to Paddington."

I muttered, "I'll be back."

But as I stepped out into the corridor, slid shut the door after me, I had no intention of going back. Oxford was where I had planned to leave the train. Yet as it pulled up with a jerk and that cracked xylophone-scale clangor, the girl was in my mind, and the trunks.

It crossed my mind that, though there was not one single Commandment that I had not broken in my futile life, all might yet be forgiven me, at the unknown end of all things, if only I changed those labels back.

I would have done it, too. I would have done it. *But I tell you, this thing was set up.* For when I rubbed the mist from the window, and stooped to peer out, the dimly lighted platform was swarming with police.

I knew who they were after, and I forgot the girl. I panicked. I hurried along the corridor to the end of the coach, where there was a door on the tracks side. The door was locked. I let down the window. There were only two policemen on the opposite platform. Chancing them, I put one foot through the open window, pulled the other foot after it, leaped from the step to the tracks. Under the loom of the train, I walked briskly toward the front, stepping from tie to tie, hoping that, if seen, I might be taken for the man with the hammer who checks on the wheels and couplings. I reached the locomotive, hissing a white cloud of steam from its belly, and glaring red from its cab, when a shout told me I'd been spotted.

I ran for it. I kept to the tracks, leaping from tie to tie. I came to an iron bridge. I knew it was the bridge over the canal. I knew Oxford; I was educated here; I might have made a different life for myself—if I'd been a different man. I'd had chances. If I'd taken them, I might never have known this hour of flight—this insane moment of clawing like an ape over the iron rim of the bridge, hanging by my hands, feeling new tar sticky under my fingers, smelling its strong, asceptic smell close to my nose. I dropped, landing on all fours on a cindered towpath.

I turned and ran.

I was a good distance away, standing—breathing hard, trying to think—between two gasometers of the Gasworks, in its galvanized iron enclosure, when I heard the train whistling. Through the mist and darkness, I saw the smokestack belching a red, pulsing glare with short, quick respirations. I heard the grind of the wheels. I saw the long line of lighted windows go by.

I knew I ought to have changed back those labels.

I kept thinking about them, about the train, about Gina Trevelyan, about what was in the luggage van. I thought Gina somehow an appealing name. I thought about her strange eyes, her good hands, the look of vulnerability about her. She seemed, alone in that compartment with the wheels going *tat-tat-tat-too,* on and on toward London, terribly solitary and defenseless to me. I thought of her as a little girl with braids, wearing rubbers, and a rubber raincoat with a hood—all sleek with rain—coming home alone from school to that great, grim, red-brick house thousands of miles away in Canada. I felt terribly sorry for her. I wanted to sit down, here in the dark, and weep for her.

Somehow, the strength had gone out from me. Guilt about those labels —not about anything I'd done before that—robbed me of the will to fight on, to live.

Knowing what I know now, I can be in two places at once. I can be me on the run and I can be Gina in the train. Take me first . . .

I found I had been walking and walking as I thought about her, and I had come to the gray stone hump of Folly Bridge. The bridge lights glimmered down on the river and on the college barges.

I went on up the lighted slope of St. Aldate's. There was nobody about —just here and there an undergraduate riding a bicycle with his gown wound about his neck like a muffler. Coming on up toward Tom Tower and Carfax, I thought of St. Ebbe's. I thought perhaps I might have a chance in that maze of ancient, squalid alleys. I took to the alleys behind Pembroke College. My mind was with Gina in the train. My own plight had become unreal to me. I knew I ought to have changed back those labels. I was afraid. I had never been so afraid. I was a fugitive in dark and misty alleys, and I was afraid of the dark.

Perhaps I wanted to be caught, rather than be alone in the dark. Anyway, I saw lights and figures and heard trumpets. I went with the figures into a plain, varnished hall, glaringly lighted with naked gasmantels. It was a Salvation Army chapel. I stood at the back of the hall, behind the rows of plain wooden chairs. The people were singing, *Onward, Christian Soldiers.* I wanted to sing with them, but I couldn't. I kept thinking of Gina, and the two trunks, and I was so sorry for her that the tears began to stream down my cheeks.

I felt a hand on my shoulder.

"All right, Caird," a voice said, "better come quietly."

I saw the faces of the congregation turn toward me, in the hard, white glare. I saw the women's faces framed in their bonnets, and the work-worn faces of the men. There was understanding in their eyes, and compassion. They were good, kind people.

I was started on my way to London, handcuffed, under escort, by the next train up. Gina's would not yet have reached Paddington. I realized that these policemen knew nothing about the trunk originally marked *Frank Venhold,* but now marked *G. N. Trevelyan.* I wanted to tell them about the trunk, in case something could be done to warn her. But since they didn't know about the trunk, there might yet be some hope for me, and I couldn't bring myself to speak the words that would hang me.

Instead I asked, "What time is it?"

They told me. I knew her train must be pulling into Paddington . . .

Knowing what I know now—the questions that I've asked and that have been answered for me—I can be with Gina. I can follow her as if she led me by the hand . . .

As her train drew into the great, dingy, echoing London terminus, Gina drew on her small, soft, green hat. Her little overnight bag lay on the seat beside her. She wondered what had happened to the man in the trench coat, the man who had not returned.

She got hold of a porter at Paddington.

"I've a trunk in the luggage van," she said. "The name's Trevelyan."

"Taking a taxi, miss?" said the porter. "All right, you go and get a place in the taxi line an' I'll bring your trunk."

He brought it, wheeling it on a trolley.

"Strike me, miss," he said, as he uptilted the trunk into the small luggage-compartment beside the taxi driver, "what you got in here? The gold reserve?"

"All my worldly belongings," said Gina. "It's my books that weigh so heavy. I'm sorry about that."

"S'all right," said the porter, strapping the trunk, upended, into place.

"Where to, miss?" said the taxi driver.

Gina told him to cruise. She wanted to find a moderate-priced hotel. She gazed from the window as the taxi left the station. The night was very misty; every light had its nimbus; muffled forms passed to and fro before the shop windows. The driver, an elbow resting on the trunk beside him, slowed down before hotel after hotel, looking round at her inquiringly.

"No," she said, shaking her head.

Either they looked too dear or too dirty. But as they passed along a narrow, quiet little street—the only shop in it a small teashop with a steamy window dimly shining through the mist—she caught a glimpse of the word *Vacancies* on a sign on some iron railings. She leaned forward quickly to tap on the glass behind the driver's head.

Gina got out, asked the driver to wait. She ran up the steps and rang the bell. After a minute, the door was opened, and an untidy, thin woman stood outlined against the dim light of a passage.

"I'm looking for lodgings," said Gina. "I wonder if you have a bed-sitting-room among your vacancies?"

The woman stood aside. "Come in. You can see what I've got."

She preceded Gina up four narrow flights of worn-carpeted stairs to a room which was an attic but fairly large and tolerably clean.

"It has a skylight," said Gina. "That's rather an advantage, because I paint. What is the rent, please?"

They arranged terms. Gina paid a week in advance, and they went downstairs.

"I've got a trunk in the taxi," said Gina. "It's rather heavy—"

The woman turned and called down some stairs, "Arthur!"

A youngish, but fat and balding man in his braces and slippers came up the stairs, grinning at Gina inanely. He and the taxi driver lifted the trunk in, dumped it down in the passage. Gina paid the driver and thanked him, and he went away. The landlady shut the front door, turned and looked at the trunk.

"Arthur'll never get that up all them stairs," she said. "You'd better keep it down in our passage and take up what you want bit by bit."

"I'll do that," said Gina.

"My name's Mrs. Coe," said the woman. "Will you be wanting anything further? Me an' Arthur goes across to the local about now."

"There's nothing I need now, thank you," said Gina.

"Then good night to you."

"Good night, Mrs. Coe."

Gina went up to her room, and, soon after, heard the front door slam . . .

Knowing what I know now, I realize that, at about this time, I was stepping

*into the neat, closed, dark-blue van—the Black Maria—which had been sent to
meet the train* . . .

The interior of the Black Maria was brightly lighted. The two policemen sat with their arms folded, watching me, but I was unaware of them. I
kept thinking of Gina and the trunk, and what might have become of her
on her first night alone in the great, grim city of London.

I kept thinking of the story she had told me—of that and of her sudden,
hopeless paroxysm of tears. I kept thinking of my wet handkerchief balled
in her hand, and of when she was a little girl with amber braids, walking
home alone from school, in rubbers and a rubber raincoat with a hood,
carrying her strapped books, on a rainy late afternoon in an unknown town
in faraway Canada. And on this ride from Paddington across London I
couldn't see from my box of a Black Maria, I understood what had happened to me, and why all the strength seemed sucked out of me into those
strange eyes of hers. I knew why I kept thinking, "If only we could have
met before . . ."

For the first time in my life, I knew I was in love—and had been in love
from the moment I had seen her cry. The realization brought me a new
fund of resolve. I knew now what I had to do.

The Black Maria pulled up in New Scotland Yard. I was taken to a room
glaring with light high up in that grim, turreted building overlooking the
Embankment. There was a lean, tight-lipped, gray-haired man sitting beside
the desk.

I stood there, handcuffed to the policeman, before the desk, and said,
"I'm going to confess. I'm doing it for the sake of somebody else. Before I
begin, put out a call for a taxi driver—she'd certainly take a taxi—who
picked up a girl in a small, green hat and a hip-length checked jacket with a
high collar. She got off the earlier train at Paddington."

The man at the desk looked at me steadily. I knew my face was working.

"Any other details, Caird?"

I heard a voice speaking that seemed not to be mine. It sounded like a
voice ringing far off in a chasm of green crystal cliffs.

"Yes," said the voice. "Her name's G. N. Trevelyan and she had a large
brown trunk in the luggage van."

"There's something in the trunk for her to fear, Caird?" said the man at
the desk.

"Yes," I said, "something in the trunk."

I saw the man at the desk reach for the telephone, and I heard a spatter of
rain at the window looking out on the Thames.

*I tell you, this whole thing was designed. It was prepared for us. Knowing
what I know now, I say that every step— Even the rain. Take this rain that
came* . . .

Gina must have been sitting on the bed in her room. She was sitting on the bed, looking round at her first room in London. An uninspiring room, but she imagined it with her canvases hung on the walls, with a studio easel in it, with shelves put up for all her art books. With its skylight, she could make it look something like a studio.

She realized that she was hungry. She hadn't dined on the train. Halfway up this street, she remembered, she had noticed a tea shop. It might still be open. She jumped up. Leaving her hat and grip on the bed, she descended the narrow, dimly lighted stairs. She didn't touch the banisters; she didn't like old houses, didn't like the feel of them.

The house was dead quiet.

She slammed the door behind her. The mist-touch was laid on her brow and lips and hair. She walked fast.

The tea shop, still open, was an arty-crafty little place. She was served coffee and poached eggs by a faded gentlewoman. Gina ate hungrily. She was lighting a cigarette when the gentlewoman apologetically presented the bill.

"We're just closing, madam. I'm sorry."

Gina paid the bill. She opened the door. It had suddenly begun to rain. She hesitated. Her jacket was very light. The tea shop was midway up the street; the lodging-house was near the end, the last house but one, on the left. The rain seemed to have settled in. She couldn't stand in this doorway all night. She thrust her hands into the pockets of her jacket, ducked her head, and walked as fast as she could.

The lights were shining much more clearly now . . .

This was when the police call went out for a taxi driver who had driven from Paddington, to a place unknown, with a girl in a green hat, with a large, brown trunk. In that glaring room in Scotland Yard, I was making a statement, a confession of murder, which was to put the rope round my neck. But as the rain beat across the Thames and ran wet on the window, it was of Gina that I was thinking. . . .

She was drenched when she hurried up the steps, put her key in the lock of the door. She went in, closed the door behind her. She pushed a hand up into her wet hair, gave it a little, quick shake. The light in the narrow passage burned dimly. There was a row of hooks on the right wall, with coats hanging on them. She looked down at herself ruefully. She was soaked to the skin. She had no change of clothes in her overnight bag, up in her room.

She glanced round for the trunk, now, but it was gone; Arthur must have shifted it below. She moved to the head of the short flight of stairs leading to the landlady's quarters.

She called, "Mrs. Coe?"—and listened. "Mrs. Coe?" she called again.

All was still in the house. There was only the sound of the rain.

She could see her trunk, down there in the flagstoned passage. The trunk stood half in light, half in shadow—a very ordinary trunk, hundreds of thousands like it. She took from her pocket the two cheap little keys tied together with a bit of string. She started down the stairs.

The stairs were of stone. There were four of them. Four stairs? She hesitated, looking at the trunk, a pace or two from her. Out of the shadows came the ticking of a clock.

I was thinking of a little girl in rubbers and a rubber coat with a hood, coming home from school through the rain to the enigma of a dark house and a waiting room. But that was in Canada, thousands of miles away . . .

Louder and louder ticked the clock from the darkness, and she could hear the rain spattering on glass somewhere to her left. There was creeping over her a feeling she had known before—in a single memory and many dreams. A feeling of something waiting for her. It had no shape. Only cold came from it. She fought against the feeling. She looked down at the trunk. Rain or something had trickled from it to form a small, dark pool, dimly visible on the flagstones.

In sudden haste, she forced herself to stoop, unlock the trunk.

She threw back the lid, and the cold was released. Wave after wave of cold passed over her. She stared down, backing away, a hand at her mouth. She was backing into the darkness. She wheeled round, as though to run— and there before her, through a door standing half-open, she saw the red glow of a fire between the bars of a kitchen stove. She saw an old wicker chair obliquely facing the stove, and in the chair a cat with its forepaws tucked under its chest, the firelight glinting in its intent eyes. The unseen clock was ticking loudly, questioningly. The rain spattered on glass to her left, and she knew that the wet, hairy leaves of stinging-nettles were there, pressed to the glass, and that the huge, dead, sodden heads of tall sunflowers rocked and nodded in the rain.

All was in waiting . . .

When the call came in, I was signing my statement. I sat with the pen in my hand, listening to the gray-haired, grim man at the desk speaking into the telephone . . .

He finished giving instructions. He was about to hang up when I stopped him. "Wait!"

He glanced at me.

I asked certain questions. He relayed them into the telephone. He repeated the answers to me. I sat with my head in my hands, thinking of Gina, with her strange eyes. Thinking how different things might have been for us— *But I tell you this whole thing was set up for us . . .*

The man at the desk said, "All right, Caird—now, what was the point of those questions you asked? The kitchen, the fire, the cat, the chair, the clock, the garden, the sunflowers, the nettles—these are common to most neglected houses anywhere in England."

"Not only in England," I thought.

I didn't say it. I looked at the keen, rational man, there at his desk, lighting his pipe. What was the good of talking to him of God or the Devil or Destiny or even mere Chance? He only knew the Law—and "facts."

But the address was a fact—the address I had heard him mention on the telephone—that was a fact. What made her go, with that trunk, to that house where she saw the sign saying *Vacancies* in the mist?

"Gina, my poor darling—"

Yet, if I hadn't changed the labels on the trunks—

I don't know. Would it have made any difference? I don't know anything. Did *I* kill her? Or what? She knows, now, the address of the house in the London mist. It was No. 15 George Street.

The Sixties

CHANGE OF CLIMATE

by URSULA CURTISS

"One lam chop," wrote Chloe Carpenter in her diary on an evening in late June—at nine years of age she had, and would have all her life, a natural talent for misspelling—"one baked potatoe, some string beans, a pice of apple pie." She studied the last item and then, because caret marks were still in her future and this was to be a very exact account, she crossed it out and wrote, "a small pice of apple pie."

Hester Carpenter had no idea that her daughter was keeping this meticulous record of Hester's food intake—fortunately; it would have made her self-conscious to the point of being unable to eat at all. But Tom Carpenter knew about it, and was both touched and approving. It seemed to him the day-by-day log of a miracle, although that was the very word he was supposed to avoid.

"Oh, she'll do better in the Southwest, no doubt about it," the doctor had said two months ago in Massachusetts. "In fact, to put it baldly, I doubt very seriously if she'd survive another winter here. But I have to warn you, Tom—after the first dramatic improvement there still may be difficulties. Chances are she'll acquire new allergies, and then there's always the existing damage. You mustn't expect a miracle."

Hester had never been really strong—it was her look of almost luminous fragility which had first caught Tom's eye; but she had not developed asthma until a year after their marriage. Or perhaps it had been there for some time, masquerading as frequent attacks of bronchitis and a faint but noticeable shortness of breath after activities like climbing stairs. In any case, the asthma had become sharply worse after Chloe's birth. At first there were seasons of the year when Hester was entirely free of it; gradually these periods shortened, and pneumonia began to make its appearance.

They saw a parade of specialists—bald and conservative, young and daring, whose advice, with minor differences, came to much the same thing in the end: avoid the known allergens—among them, cat dander; pursue a dust-free routine in the house; and "learn to live with your illness."

Surprisingly enough, until Chloe was seven years old, they managed the last instruction almost as easily as the first two. Hester was determined not to become a professional invalid, or to make a martyr of her husband and a slave of her small daughter; and for a long time she succeeded. She hoarded her strength in unobtrusive ways; on bad days, when the sound of her breathing was like a loud and steady filing, she retired to piled pillows behind her bedroom door.

She had grown up in the small town of Falcon, Massachusetts, and Tom did not have to worry about her being lonely while he was at his office and Chloe at school. Girls she had known since high school dropped in, and neighbors made morning visits for coffee, usually bringing along a sumptuous homemade pastry at which Hester could only nibble. Chloe, arriving home at three o'clock, leaped enthusiastically into her role of "housewoman"—"Housewife, do you suppose she means?" Hester asked Tom, laughing—and polished everything that could possibly be polished: vases, candlesticks, tabletops.

As a result, the little house glowed more than the prescribed dust-free routine demanded; it held a concert of personalities as undivided as a clover. Hale and hearty visitors went away with an illogical feeling of envy; they said, "There's nothing like trouble to bind a family together," but they knew it was more than that.

When Chloe was almost eight, Hester had her first bad attack of pneumonia. Six months later she had another and worse one, shrouded in an oxygen tent while Tom spent two tormented nights at her bedside and the nurses smiled at him with terrifying cheerfulness.

He made the decision then, knowing that it meant giving up the well-paid job which had enabled him to meet the medical bills; giving up their home and their friends. Although it was not really a decision at all in the sense of choosing between alternatives, because it was clear now that there was no alternative. While Hester convalesced, much more slowly than ever before, he quietly organized the move to the Southwest.

June turned and became July. Hester had gained six pounds, and her pearly skin was acquiring a faint tan. The one unfortunate side effect from the change of climate—sinus trouble, which the doctor assured them could be alleviated by drops—seemed a small price to pay.

Chloe had been her mother's anxious companion for too long to let go all at once, but little by little, as Hester grew stronger, Chloe explored a world strange to eastern eyes—a world with fleet little blue lizards, roadrunners, and even, in their landlord's back field, an aristocratic but friendly horse that came promptly up to the fence for the carrot or apple she brought. In spite of the wanderings which seemed to her boundless, but were actually contained in less than a half acre, Chloe was always in the driveway to greet Tom when he got home from work.

She was there on a late afternoon in mid-July, wiry, sunburnt, and clearly bursting with something. When Tom asked his ritual, "What did you do today?" she said excitedly, "Oh, Daddy, I helped Mrs. Whitman tear up all her flowers. Look!"

Tom did not merely look; he gaped, appalled. Mrs. Whitman was the other tenant of the duplex apartment, a pleasant gray-haired woman whose chief preoccupation seemed to be the deep brilliant border that edged her little lawn on three sides. The border was now bare drying earth, the flowers themselves a heap of ruffled and shriveling color piled up outside the gate.

To Tom, for just a flash, the child looking up at him seemed to have the wanton triumph of a small boy standing with his slingshot near a shattered greenhouse—and then Chloe was saying defensively, "The flowers, I don't know which ones, made Mother sneeze and her eyes puff up, so Mrs. Whitman *said* to."

Hester was tranquilly regretful. "It's too bad about Mrs. Whitman's garden, isn't it? I felt awful, telling her about the doctor's orders—you know, to sit out in the sun for a little while every day—but she understood perfectly; in fact, she couldn't have been nicer. I came right in and baked her a batch of brownies."

Tom, remembering the weeks of Mrs. Whitman's assiduous weeding, cultivating, watering, sent a look of wonderment at his wife's back. Did Hester possibly think that a confection hastily whipped up in the kitchen—? No, of course she didn't; she had simply made a small token apology in the only way she could on the spur of the moment.

. . . But, he thought later that night while Hester slept, her breath quiet and even, she had been mistaken in thinking that Mrs. Whitman had "understood perfectly." That brutal heap of uprooted flowers, piled there openly by someone who loved them, was a statement of cold anger only emphasized by the invitation to the complainant's child to come and help with the carnage.

It was too bad in every sense, because Tom had hoped that Hester, so used to the daily companionship of other women, would start making friends in the neighborhood. His last waking reflection, still troubled, was that it might not be a bad idea to have Chloe, an avid car washer, surprise Mrs. Whitman tomorrow or the next day by scrubbing her little cherry red Volkswagen . . .

When Tom hinted worriedly to Hester about her possible loneliness, she denied it cheerfully. Her friends back East had been marvelous, and of course she missed them; but it was a positive luxury now to be able to do, unassisted, so many of the domestic things they had helped her with before.

And of course—here she glanced around vaguely—she had Chloe for company.

But this, although it was not borne in on Tom immediately, was less and less the case . . .

The doctor was enormously pleased with Hester's progress, and she apparently took this as carte blanche because, by the time August had arrived, she was seldom still. Wearing Bermuda shorts, a thing she could not have done before because of the sticklike thinness of her legs, Hester took down and washed and rehung the venetian blinds; she carried out the scatter rugs to air. She also washed the windows, inside and out, scoured the oven, and began on the paintwork. If the apartment did not have the warm glow of the little house back East, it was at least very shiny.

Tom did not find it surprising, in view of Hester's steady gain, that Chloe had stopped keeping her diary; the last entry, for July 26th, was: "Steak, asparagis, mashed potatoes, vinila ice cream." He now had a small but annoying problem of his own: his sinuses had evidently become affected by the dry heat and at night, frequently, his forehead felt bound with iron. Hester's wonder-working nose drops, trickling bitterly down the back of his throat no matter how carefully he administered them, did not seem to help.

One night in mid-August, when he was cautiously congratulating himself on feeling fine, the tense pain came creeping back at the dinner table. Maybe a storm approaching, thought Tom; the sky looked thunderous and he had sensed electricity in the air ever since his return home from work. Well, they needed the rain—

"Eat your dinner!" said Hester in a voice that made Tom's fork jump in his hand. He glanced at her astoundedly—she had delivered the words like a cuff; but her attention was on Chloe, fair head bent, hands in her lap although they were having roast chicken, which she loved.

"Eat your dinner," repeated Hester more quietly and perhaps more dangerously. The storm which Tom had thought so innocently to be in the upper elements was closer, and he was so bewildered that he could only stare.

"I'm not hungry," said Chloe, the corners of her mouth beginning to waver helplessly. "I feel sick."

"Very well, then, you're excused," said Hester evenly, and held herself remorselessly still and attentive while the child pushed back her chair, dropped her napkin, bumped her head on the table in the course of retrieving it, and then fled.

The door of her bedroom closed. Hester sprinkled salt and said calmly to Tom, "You look tired—was it a rough day?"

"Not bad," said Tom distractedly, putting down his own napkin and starting to rise. This was like a dream, in which elk went by in Easter bonnets and nobody thought it odd at all. "I'll go see what's the matter with—"

"Chloe is sulking because that foolish horse is gone," said Hester casually, and proceeded to tell him.

Tom had been aware of the affection between Chloe and the horse in the next field, and knew that the landlord let her mount occasionally and go for blissful ambles. As the horse was trained to halt the instant the weight in the saddle began to slip, it had seemed the most innocent of diversions. What Tom hadn't known—"I hate being such a constant nuisance to everybody"—was that Hester reacted badly to close contact with horses, and had begun to wheeze when Chloe came in from her rides.

She had, she said, forbidden Chloe to ride the horse, but at every opportunity the child had slipped over to the fence to caress the whiteblazed face and brush the dark-gold mane dedicatedly. "—which came to pretty much the same thing," said Hester ruefully. "Mr. Lacey saw the problem right away, and said his son would be delighted to keep the horse at his place—it doesn't get enough exercise here anyway. Somehow, I expected Chloe to understand."

Or understand *perfectly,* like Mrs. Whitman with her flowers? Tom was shocked at this disloyal thought—they were here after all for Hester's health, and allergies were not to be played around with; but his forehead now felt sealed with pain. When he had eaten what he could of his dinner he picked up Chloe's untouched plate. "I think I'll bring this in to her now."

Hester's eyebrows rose, but all she said was, "If you think it's wise."

Chloe got over the horse, as Hester had sensibly predicted she would, and settled herself to the serious business of making friends in the neighborhood before the opening of school. This was not the automatic process of a child who had been constantly with other children, but an almost adult approach. As a result, she was home at noontime for a sandwich and milk, usually with a standoffish and staring little girl in tow.

Tom took his headaches to a doctor, was informed that his sinuses were as clear as a bell, and, although he kept it from Hester so that she would not worry, he began to take the tranquilizers the doctor prescribed.

Hester bloomed, even in the scorching heat. Her delicate tan had turned brown, and she was strong and rangy. She was busy making new curtains, busy registering Chloe for school, busy waxing the floors, relining the kitchen shelves, taking down and washing the ceiling light fixtures. She had grown used to, as Tom and Chloe had, her own newly nasal voice, although she would say irritably now and then, "I sound exactly like a duck."

Although it was only the end of August, the annual weather prophets were out in force. Tom and Hester, who could seldom find any news of Massachusetts in the local papers, nevertheless learned with guilty pleasure that an early and very hard winter was predicted for the East.

(But how warm and snug the little house in Massachusetts had been, with Hester on the couch in a pretty housecoat, Chloe bustling importantly in the kitchen, Tom peacefully reading the evening paper while the wind raged outside and the fire simmered and snapped on the hearth. Lamplight over everything, and a perfect security that had nothing to do with locks or bolts or storm windows.)

We are all happy, Tom informed himself, swallowing his white pill; the pity is that we didn't do this sooner.

School was to begin on August 29th. On the 27th, coming home with the commissioned notebooks and pencils and lunch box, Tom saw that Chloe had washed Mrs. Whitman's car again; the little red Volkswagen was dripping and flashing in the sun. And there was, mystifyingly, a cat fight in progress somewhere close by. Of all the things Hester couldn't have near her . . . How could a cat have gotten—?

He was alarmedly out of his car and inside the gate when the menacing shrills became distinguishable words instead of rising and falling howls. "— *so* nice of you to be sweet and considerate with the neighbors," shrieked the cat voice. "Never mind me, *I* don't count. But how many times have I told you about those filthy sneakers? And look at those shorts. You've been in the wading pool with those dreadful children, haven't you, Miss? I said, *Haven't you, Miss?*"

There was an odd sound then, not a response from Chloe but still a sound. Tom's stupefied eye caught a lunge past the screen door; his ear heard a panting, "There you stay!" and then a sharp bang.

The bang seemed to split the frontal bones of his head. Standing paralyzed on the path, at once incredulous and certain, he realized that this strident plunging creature in Bermuda shorts was his gentle luminous Hester, this contemptible "Miss" his skinny worshipful child.

He made himself go in. Hester was washing lettuce at the sink, her hands unsteady. There was no sign of Chloe. Tom said with a weariness he did not know he had accumulated, "What's the matter?" and Hester whirled.

"You'll have to talk to that child, Tom." *That child.* "She's always been spoiled, but now she's completely out of hand."

Spoiled. The nine-year-old who by now was an expert at doing dishes, ironing her own clothes, compiling bizarrely spelled shopping lists, and trudging faithfully around supermarkets . . . "What's she done?"

"Disobeyed me, deliberately. There are some very dubious-looking children up the street who have a wading pool, and I told Chloe that she was not to go there."

"Hester, this was a hot afternoon—"

"That's not the point. The point is that I told her not to," said Hester, spacing the last five words almost softly. By contrast, pots and their lids leaped into a clattering frenzy under her hands when she turned to the stove, and the glance she flung at Tom was razorish with—was it anger? Or some perverse excitement? Something, at any rate, that changed her into the kind of woman you saw dragging a small sobbing child ruthlessly by the hand, jerking all the harder when the child stumbled.

"I think we'd better get it clear here and now that I won't stand for this kind of behavior," the stranger at the stove was saying in her nasal and driving voice. "If you don't punish her, I will."

There were still a few shafts of late sunlight in Chloe's prim little room. She lay on her bed with her back to the door, not so much crying as shuddering, taking convulsive breaths which she buried fiercely in the pillow. Tom sat down on the bed and turned her gently to face him; he had to glance away quickly for a moment, feeling his own throat prickle at the dull red mark on her cheek.

That was the curious sound he had heard. From outside.

He had meant to tell Chloe quietly and reasonably that she could not disobey her mother, making it—because he realized suddenly that in the past week or so they had understood each other very well indeed—more of a father-to-daughter warning than a parental thunderbolt. But the reasonable words would not come; so he simply sat there, stroking the tumbled hair away from her forehead and talking about small detached things until she was able to heave a very deep breath with only the barest tremor.

She said, "Mother doesn't like being better, does she."

It was neither a question nor an accusation. It was an observation delivered with adult despair, and it encompassed much more than a hard humiliating slap. It took in the last—three weeks, four? Tom could not be sure, in his shock at the nakedness of the words, any more than a man could be sure when, after living with an obscure pain that frightened him, he was asked by the doctor who put an exact finger on the source, "How long have you had this?"

He didn't—at the moment he couldn't—answer his child. He gave her forehead a final pat and walked to the window, where he gazed out blindly into the coming dusk.

Was it possible? Could Hester have acquired the last allergy of all, and be no more able to assimilate health than cat dander? Were there personalities who could not thrive, or thrive sanely, on physical well-being?

It was appalling to think so, but it was less spine-touching than the notion that this personality had dwelt inside Hester all along, and had simply never been well enough to come out before. How, in that case, it must have raged and struggled against the tranquillity and binding love in the little Massachusetts house . . .

Tom's shoulder muscles gave a quick cold ripple as he shook that off and went back to the first possibility. If their past happiness even in the face of illness had been so present in his mind, how much more so must it have been in Hester's? Certainly she had never consciously liked being a semi-invalid, but—the stream of solicitous friends dropping in, the cheerful little gifts of a crocheted bed jacket or a homemade coffee cake, the momentous gaining or losing of half a pound—and, yes, the attention.

Chloe had been her devoted shadow, but now, like any other healthy nine-year-old, Chloe roamed and played. And Hester had flung herself into frenetic activity, perhaps battling unconsciously with this terrible new allergy, before it began to win.

Tom had never asked, but he was coldly sure now that Chloe had admired and helped in Mrs. Whitman's garden. She had worshipped the friendly horse. She had set about making friends, to prepare herself for entering a strange school, and been invited to wade in a back-yard pool. The sacrifices to Hester had not been voluntary, or even appeasing, but they had certainly been made.

And yet . . . Hester will be as upset as I am, said Tom to himself.

Hester was not. Told falsely that Chloe was asleep, she said with an edge, "Funny how easily she falls asleep on nights when we have meat loaf," and attacked her own dinner with zest. It was very good meat loaf, and a few small bites of it settled in Tom's stomach like the best cement; Chloe's vacant place at the table, and the silence from her room, pressed upward against his ribs.

Although Hester said nothing further about punishing Chloe, her face was curiously set, and when she asked Tom after the dishes were done, "Aren't you going to take your usual walk?" he manufactured a yawn and said, "Too tired."

He was, of course, not worried about any small personal action which might be taken in his absence down the long driveway. Certainly not. He was simply—tired.

He lay awake all night—not like someone with merely restless intervals, but literally all night. Once he got up quietly to look in at and cover Chloe; for the rest, he listened to his wife's deep untroubled breathing and studied a number of scenes which unwound like tape against the black ceiling.

In the morning he said cheerfully to Chloe, "Come on, I'll buy you a new dress for school," and to Hester, "They're having some kind of executive session at the office and I don't have to be in until eleven."

Surely Hester did not look somehow impotent as they left?

"Daddy," said Chloe hesitantly in the car—she was pleating the fabric of her skirt incessantly, a new and disturbing habit—"won't Mother be mad because she didn't come too?"

"She's got a million things to do," Tom said airily, and bore her off to the back-to-school department of a downtown store. He found a reliable-looking saleswoman to whom he gave vague suggestions about a dress, and told Chloe firmly to wait for him there.

There were public phone booths on the first floor, and from one of these Tom sent himself an urgent telegram signed with the name of his former employer in Massachusetts; he would be home to open it when it arrived, so that no question would be raised as to its place of origin. To make doubly sure, he instructed the operator to have the message delivered; there would be no one at that telephone all day, he said.

From the phone booth, because it was somehow of immense importance that Chloe should not even uncomprehendingly hear what he was going to say, he proceeded to the railroad station. Judging by a few banners strung about it was "Sunshine Appreciation Week," which was just chasing out "Eat More Cottage Cheese Week." When he asked the pretty clerk at a ticket window for two and a half fares to Falcon, Massachusetts, she said with arch reproachfulness, "Oh, surely that's round trip, sir?"

The buoyancy assumed for Chloe's sake had left him. Perhaps as a result of his sleepless night his ears resounded queerly with the doctor's voice: "To put it baldly, I doubt very seriously . . ." and the prediction of the weather prophets.

There was nothing momentous in the glance he sent through the ticket window. To the pretty clerk, who remembered him for approximately a minute afterward, he was just an ordinary, pleasant-looking man; fair, thirty-fivish, rather tired, with lines around his mouth. There was certainly no special inflection in his voice when he said, as though arousing himself from a dream, "No—that will be one way."

EDITORS' NOTE: *In addition to the killer and the victim, there are three major factors in every murder situation: motive, opportunity, and means. In most cases, real or fictional, the means is "ordinary"—gun, knife, bludgeon, poison, and so on. Now think of Ursula Curtiss' "Change of Climate" from the standpoint of means: to the best of our recollection, Ursula Curtiss has come up with a new means of murder—or, if it is not new, surely one of the most unusual on record . . .*

LIFE IN OUR TIME
by ROBERT BLOCH

When Harry's time capsule arrived, Jill made him put it in the guest house.

All it was, it turned out, was a big metal box with a cover that could be sealed tight and soldered so that the air couldn't get at what was inside. Jill was really quite disappointed with it.

But then she was quite disappointed with Harry, too—Professor Harrison Cramer, B.A., B.S., M.A., Ph.D. Half the alphabet wasted on a big nothing. At those flaky faculty cocktail parties, people were always telling her, "It must be wonderful to be married to a brilliant man like your husband." Brother, if they only knew!

It wasn't just that Harry was 15 years older than she was. After all, look at Rex Harrison and Richard Burton and Cary Grant and Lawrence Olivier. But Harry wasn't the movie-star type—definitely not! Not even the mad-scientist type, like Vincent Price in those crazy "campy" pictures. He was nothing—just a big nothing.

Of course, Jill got the message long before she married him. But he did have that imposing house and all that loot he'd inherited from his mother. Jill figured on making a few changes, and she actually did manage to redo the house so that it looked halfway presentable, with the help of that *fagilleh* interior decorator. But she couldn't redo Harry. Maybe *he* needed an interior decorator to work on him, too; *she* certainly couldn't change him.

And outside of what she managed to squeeze out of him for the redecorating, Jill hadn't been able to get her hands on any of the loot, either. Harry wasn't interested in entertaining or going out or taking cruises, and whenever she mentioned a sable jacket he mumbled something under his breath about "conspicuous consumption"—whatever that was! He didn't like modern art or the theater, he didn't drink or smoke—why, he didn't even watch TV. And he wore flannel pajamas in bed. *All* the time.

After a couple of months Jill was ready to climb the walls. Then she began thinking about Reno, and that's where Rick came in. Rick was her attorney—at least, that's the way it started out to be, but Rick had other ideas. Particularly for those long afternoons when Harry was lecturing at seminars or whatever he did over there at the University.

Pretty soon Jill forgot about Reno; Rick was all for one of those quickie divorces you can get down in Mexico. He was sure he could make it stick and still see to it that she got her fifty-fifty share under the community property laws, and without any waiting. It could all be done in 24 hours, with no hassle; they'd take off together, just like eloping. Bang, you're divorced; bang, you're remarried; and then, bang, bang, bang—

So all Jill had to worry about was finding the right time. And even that was no problem, after Harry told her about the time capsule.

"I'm to be in full charge of the project," he said. "Complete authority to choose what will be representative of our present culture. Quite a responsibility, my dear—but I welcome the challenge."

"So what's a time capsule?" Jill wanted to know.

Harry went into a long routine and she didn't really listen, just enough to get the general idea. The thing was, Harry had to pick out all kinds of junk to be sealed up in this gizmo so that sometime—10,000 years from now, maybe—somebody would come along and dig it up and open it and be able to tell what kind of civilization we had. Big deal! But from the way Harry went on, you'd think he'd just won the Grand Prix or something.

"We're going to put the capsule in the foundation of the new Humanities Building," he told her.

"What are humanities?" Jill asked, but Harry just gave her one of those *Good-lord-how-can-you-be-so-stupid?* looks that always seemed to start their quarrels; and they would have had a fight then and there, too, only he added something about how the dedication ceremonies for the new building would take place on May 1st, and he'd have to hurry to get everything arranged for the big day. Including writing his dedicatory address.

May 1st was all Jill needed to hear. That was on a Friday, and if Harry was going to be tied up making a speech at the dedication, it would be an A-OK time to make that little flight across the border. So she managed to call Rick and tell him and he said yeah, sure, perfect.

"It's only ten days from now," Jill reminded Rick. "We've got a lot to do."

She didn't know it, but it turned out she wasn't kidding. She had more to do than she thought, because all at once Harry was *interested* in her. *Really* interested.

"You've got to help me," he said that night at dinner. "I want to rely on your taste. Of course, I've got some choices of my own in mind, but I want *you* to suggest items to go into the capsule."

At first Jill thought he was putting her on, but he really meant it. "This project is going to be honest. The usual ploy is pure exhibitionism—

samples of the 'best' of everything, plus descriptive data which is really just a pat on the back for the *status quo ante*. Well, that's not for me. I'd like to include material that's self-explanatory, not self-congratulatory. Not art and facts—but artifacts."

Harry lost her there, until he said, "Everything preserved will be a clue to our contemporary social attitudes. Not what we *pretend* to admire, but what the majority actually *believes in* and *enjoys*. And that's where you come in, my dear. You represent the majority."

Jill began to dig it, then. "You mean like TV and pop records?"

"Exactly. What's that album you like so much? The one with the four hermaphrodites on the liner?"

"Who?"

"Excuse me—it's purportedly a singing group, isn't it?"

"Oh, you're talking about the Poodles!" Jill went and got the album, which was called *The Poodles Bark Again*. The sound really turned her on, but she had always thought Harry hated it. And now he was coming on all smiles.

"Great!" he said. "This definitely goes in."

"But—"

"Don't worry, I'll buy you another." He took the album and put it on his desk. "Now, you mentioned something about television. What's your favorite program?"

When she saw that he was really serious, she began telling him about "Anywhere, U.S.A." What it was, it was about life in a small town, just an ordinary suburb like, but the people were great. There was this couple with the two kids, one boy and one girl, sort of an average family, you might say, only he was kind of playing around with a divorcee who ran a *discothetique* or whatever they call them, and she had a yen for her psychiatrist—he wasn't really *her* psychiatrist, he was analyzing one of the kids, the one who had set fire to the high school gymnasium, not the girl—she was afraid her parents would find out about her affair with the vice-principal who was really an enemy agent only she didn't know it yet, and her real boy friend, the one who had the brain operation, had a "thing" about his mother, so—

It got kind of complicated, but Harry kept asking her to tell him more, and pretty soon he was smiling and nodding. "Wonderful! We'll have to see if we can get films of a typical week's episodes."

"You mean you really want something like that?"

"Of course. Wouldn't you say this show faithfully captured the lives of American citizens today?"

She had to agree he was right. Also about some of the things he was going to put into the capsule to show the way people lived nowadays—like tranquilizers and pep pills and income tax forms and a map of the freeway-expressway-turnpike system. He had a lot of numbers, too, for Zip Code and digit dialing, and Social Security, and the ones the computers punched out on insurance and charge-account and utility bills.

But what he really wanted was ideas for more stuff, and in the next couple of days he kept leaning on her. He got hold of her souvenir from Shady Lawn Cemetery—it was a plastic walnut that opened up, called "Shady Lawn in a Nutshell." Inside were twelve tiny color prints showing all the tourist attractions of the place, and you could mail the whole thing to your friends back home. Harry put this in the time capsule, wrapping it up in something he told her was an actuarial table on the incidence of coronary occlusion among middle-aged, middle-class males. Like heart attacks, that is.

"What's that you're reading?" he asked. And the next thing she knew, he had her copy of the latest Steve Slash paperback—the one where Steve is sent on this top-secret mission to keep peace in Port Said, and right after he kills these five guys with the portable flame thrower concealed in his judo belt, he's getting ready to play beddy-bye with Yasmina, who's really another secret agent with radioactive fingernails—

And that's as far as she'd got when he grabbed the book. It was getting so she couldn't keep anything out of his eager little hands.

"What's that you're cooking?" he wanted to know. And there went the TV dinner—frozen crêpes suzettes and all. To say nothing of the Plain Jane Instant Borscht.

"Where's that photo you had of your brother?" It was a real nothing picture of Stud, just him wearing that beatnik beard of his and standing by his motorcycle on the day he passed his initiation into Hell's Angels. But Harry put *that* in, too. Jill didn't think it was very nice of Harry, seeing as how he clipped it to another photo of some guys taking the Ku Klux Klan oath.

But right now the main thing was to keep Harry happy. That's what Rick said when she clued him in on what was going on.

"Cooperate, baby," he told her. "It's a real kinky kick, but it keeps him out of our hair. We got plans to make, tickets to buy, packing and like that there."

The trouble was, Jill ran out of ideas. She explained this to Rick but he just laughed.

"I'll give you some," he said, "and you can feed 'em to him. He's a real way-out kid, that husband of yours—I know just what he wants."

The funny part of it was that Rick did know. He was really kind of a brain himself, but not in a kooky way like Harry. So she listened to what he suggested and told Harry when she got home.

"How about a sample of the Theater of the Absurd?" she asked. Harry looked at her over the top of his glasses, and for a minute she thought she'd really thrown him, but then he grinned and got excited.

"Perfect!" he said. "Any suggestions?"

"Well, I was reading a review about this new play everybody's talking about—it's about this guy who thinks he's having a baby so he goes to an abortionist, only I guess the abortionist is supposed to be somebody mystical or something, and it all takes place in a greenhouse—"

"Delightful!" Harry was off and running. "I'll pick up a copy of the book. Anything else?"

Thank God that Rick had coached her. So she said what about a recording of one of those concerts where they use a "prepared" piano that makes noises like screeching brakes, or sometimes no sound at all. And Harry liked that. He also liked the idea about a sample of Pop Art—maybe a big blowup of a newspaper ad about "That Tired Feeling" or maybe "Psoriasis."

The next day she suggested a tape of a "Happening" which was the real thing, because it took place in some private sanatorium for disturbed patients, and Harry got really enthusiastic about this idea.

And the next day she came up with that new foreign movie with the long title she couldn't pronounce. Rick gave her the dope on it—some far-out thing by a Yugoslavian director she never heard of, about a man making a movie about a man making a movie, only you never could be quite sure, in the movie, whether the scene was supposed to be a part of the movie or the movie was a part of what was really happening, *if* it did happen.

Harry went for this, too. In a big way.

"You're wonderful," he said. "Truthfully, I never expected this of you."

Jill just gave him her extra-special smile and went on her merry way. It wasn't hard, because he had to go running around town trying to dig up books and films and recordings of all the stuff he had on his list. Which was just how Rick said it would be, leaving everything clear for them to shop and set up their last-minute plans.

"I won't get our tickets until the day before we leave," Rick told her. "We don't want to tip off anything. The way I figure it, Harry'll be moving the capsule over to where they're holding the ceremonies the next morning, so you'll get a chance to pack while he's out of the way." Rick was really something, the way he had it all worked out.

And that's the way it went. The day before the ceremony, Harry was busy in the guesthouse all afternoon, packing his goodies in the time capsule. Just like a dopey squirrel burying nuts. Only even dopey squirrels don't put stuff away for another squirrel to dig up 10,000 years from now.

Harry hadn't even had time to look at her the past two days, but this didn't bother Jill any. Along about suppertime she went out to call him, but he said he wasn't hungry and besides he had to run over and arrange for the trucking company to come and haul the capsule over to the foundation site.

They'd dug a big hole there for tomorrow morning, and he was going to take the capsule to it and stand guard over it until it was time for the dedication ceremonies.

That was even better news than Jill had hoped for, so as soon as Harry left for the trucking company she phoned Rick and gave him the word. He said he'd be right over with the tickets.

So of course Jill had to get dressed. She put on her girdle and the fancy bra and her high heels; then she went in the bathroom and used her depilatory and touched up her hair where the rinse was fading, and put on her eyelashes and brushed her teeth, and attached those new fingernails after she got her makeup on and the perfume.

When she looked at the results in the mirror she was really proud of herself; for the first time in months she felt like her real self again. And from now on it would always be this way—with Rick.

There was a good moment with Rick there in the bedroom after he came in, but of course Harry *would* drive up right then—she heard the car out front and broke the clinch just in time, telling Rick to sneak out the back way. Harry would be busy with the truckers for at least a couple of minutes.

Jill forced herself to wait in the bedroom until she was sure the coast was clear. She kept looking out the window but it was too dark now to see anything. Since there wasn't any noise, she figured Harry must have taken the truckers into the guesthouse.

And that's where she finally went.

Only the truckers weren't there. Just Harry.

"I told them to wait until first thing in the morning," he said. "Changed my mind when I realized how damp it was—no sense my spending the night shivering outside in the cold. Besides, I haven't sealed the capsule yet —remembered a couple of things I wanted to add."

He took a little bottle out of his pocket and carried it over to the time capsule. "This goes in too. Carefully labeled, of course, so they can analyze it."

"The bottle's empty," Jill said.

Harry shook his head. "Not at all. It contains smog. That's right—smog, from the freeway. I want posterity to know everything about us, right down to the poisonous air in which our contemporary culture breathed its last."

He dropped the bottle into the capsule, then picked up something else from the table next to it. Jill noticed he had a soldering outfit there to seal the lid, ready to plug in after he'd used a pump to suck all the air out. He'd explained about the capsule being airtight, soundproof, duralumin-sheathed, but that didn't interest her now. She kept looking at what he held in his hand.

It was one of those electric carving knives, complete with battery. "Another Twentieth Century artifact," he said. "Another gadget symbol of our decadence. An electric knife—just the thing for Mom when she carves the fast-frozen, precooked Thanksgiving turkey while she and Dad count all their shiny, synthetic, plastic blessings."

He waved the knife.

"They'll understand," he told her. "Those people in the future will understand it all. They'll know what life was like in our time—how we drained Walden Pond and refilled it with blood, sweat, and tears."

Jill moved a little closer, staring at the knife. "The blade's rusty."

Harry shook his head. "That's not rust," he said.

Jill kept it cool. She kept it right up until the moment she looked over the edge of the big metal box, looked down into it, and saw Rick lying there. Rick was stretched out, and the red was oozing down over the books and records and photos and tapes.

"I was waiting for him when he sneaked out the back of the house," Harry said.

"Then you knew—all along—"

"For quite a while," Harry said. "Long enough to figure things out and make my plans."

"What plans?"

Harry just shrugged. And raised the knife.

A moment later the time capsule received the final specimen of life in the Twentieth Century.

THE SPECIAL GIFT
by CELIA FREMLIN

Eileen glanced disconsolately at the little group cowering round the fire in her big, cold sitting room. Only five of them tonight. It was the weather, of course, that was keeping most of the members away; not everyone was willing to battle through wind and sleet just for the pleasure of reading aloud to one another their amateur attempts at writing, and receiving some equally amateur criticism.

Still, thought Eileen, drawing her cardigan more tightly about her, it was a pity; these meetings weren't nearly so much fun with only a few. A crowd might have made it seem a bit warmer, too.

"Well, do you think we ought to begin, Mr. Wilberforce?" she said, sitting down on the big horsehair ottoman next to the secretary.

Mr. Wilberforce, a plump, important-looking man in his fifties, glanced at the clock, rubbing his pink hands together.

"Only twenty past," he said. "Better give them a *few* more minutes. The snow, you know—buses—"

"*I* think we should start," piped up old Mrs. Peterkin, peering out like a little aggrieved mouse from the depths of the fur coat she had refused to take off. "We've got a lot to get through this evening. I've brought one of my little tales of unrequited love, if you'd care to hear it. And I'm sure Miss Williams here"—she indicated a pleasant, vacantly smiling girl on her right —"I'm sure Miss Williams has brought us another chapter of her psychological novel. And Mr. Walters"—the pale young man lowered his eyelashes self-consciously—"we hope Mr. Walters is going to read us another of his Ballads of the Seasons. It'll be summer this time, won't it, Mr. Walters?"

"Yes, it will be summer," agreed Mr. Walters, speaking rapidly and staring at the carpet. "But not summer in the *conventional* sense, you understand. Now, *my* interpretation of summer—"

A sharp, imperative ring at the front door brought Eileen to her feet, and she hurried eagerly out of the room. One more makes six, she was thinking, that's not too bad; all the same, I wish I hadn't made all those cheese sandwiches . . .

A gust of wind and snow swirled into her face as she opened the front door, and the little dark man seemed almost to be blown in by it, so slight and thin in his dark coat.

"You haven't been to these meetings before, have you?" Eileen was beginning—and then stopped, for in the dimness of the hall the stranger seemed to be staring at her with a delighted recognition.

"We—we *haven't* met before, have we?" she went on awkwardly; and the little man seemed to rouse himself.

"Why—er—no," he said hastily, shaking the snow from his boots onto the doormat. "No, indeed, I assure you! I just—well, I had a feeling—"

Again he stared at her with that odd look of recognition in his eyes; and for some reason Eileen began to feel uncomfortable; for some reason she became very eager to escape the piercing gaze of this stranger in the dimly lit hall.

"Come along and meet the others," she said nervously, and led him briskly into the sitting room.

"Fitzroy is my name," the dark man introduced himself. *"Alan* Fitzroy."

He glanced round the company with dark, sparkling eyes, and there was a little stir of interest. Not that anybody had ever heard of him, but something in the way he spoke made them feel that perhaps they *ought* to have heard of him. Perhaps, each of them was thinking, perhaps this at last is the real writer I have always hoped would turn up! The *real* writer who not only gets his own work published, but who will be able to tell me how to get *mine* published; who will recognize it as the fine work it really is . . .

With such thoughts behind them, five pairs of eyes followed the little man as he moved toward the fire; eager hands drew up a comfortable armchair for him; eager voices plied him with questions.

But Alan Fitzroy was not very communicative. No, he didn't know any of the members of this group. No (modestly) he didn't write much—well, not *very* much. No, he hadn't brought anything to read—well, not really—anyway, let everyone else read something first, *please!*

And so the meeting began. Alan Fitzroy sat motionless, his eyes closed. To everyone's disappointment he took no part in the comments and criticisms that followed each reading, and it was only when he was asked for *his* contribution that he roused himself.

"Well," he admitted, "I *have* brought a little thing. Actually, it's part of a larger work. I'm writing my autobiography, you see."

He looked round the room expectantly, and there was an almost audible sigh of disappointment. This, somehow, didn't sound like a real writer; it sounded much more like an ordinary member of the group. However—

"I want you to understand," the stranger continued, "that the whole object of my book is to bring the reader into real contact with my ego—to draw him, or her, into the life of my mind in a way which I believe has never been done before . . ."

As he spoke, he fixed his brilliant eyes on Eileen's face, and again she felt a little flicker of uneasiness—or was it even fear? Quite irrational, anyway, she assured herself; there couldn't possibly be a more harmless little man; and she settled herself to listen as he began to read from a thick, dog-eared manuscript.

"The self-doubt and self-awareness of any repressed, frustrated childhood . . ."

The voice went on and on. At intervals Eileen glanced at the clock. She hoped that Mr. Fitzroy wouldn't be offended if she went out and made the tea before he had finished. She hoped, too, that he hadn't noticed that Mrs. Peterkin was asleep inside her fur coat and might at any moment begin to snore.

Mr. Wilberforce, at Eileen's side, was fiercely making notes on the back of one of his own manuscripts. No doubt he was building up a pungent criticism of the weary verbiage through which this poor little man was plowing.

"Go easy with him!" whispered Eileen softly; somehow it seemed very important to her that nothing should be said to upset the newcomer. "Remember he's new." But Mr. Wilberforce only nodded his head irritably and went on writing.

Wasn't it *ever* coming to an end? But listen! At last! Those, surely, must be the concluding sentences:

"To point the significance of these psychodynamic disturbances to my infantile ego, I must relate a nocturnal hallucination from which I used to suffer. Or, in common parlance, a dream. I dreamed I was walking along a passage, a long stone passage, my feet clanging as I went, as if I were wearing boots of steel or armor or something like that. At the end of the passage I knew I should find my cradle—the cradle I'd had as a baby—and I should have to get into it and lie down. And I knew that as I lay there, I would see a face slowly rising over the side of the cradle, and the face would be mad. I never knew what would happen next, because I always woke up—in fact, I always woke up before I had even reached the end of the passage."

Abruptly the little man laid down his manuscript. He looked round triumphantly, and there was a little embarrassed silence, broken by a snore from Mrs. Peterkin.

"Well," said Eileen at last, wondering how to avoid hurting the little man's feelings. "It's a very *profound* piece of work, of course—"

"But it's too *long!*" exploded Mr. Wilberforce. "And too self-centered, too self-pitying! You've used the word 'I' eighty-seven times in the first six pages! I was counting!"

Alan Fitzroy turned on him indignantly.

"But I *have* to use the word 'I'! The whole book is about myself—I told you! The idea is to get the reader involved with *me*— to bring him right into my very mind, if you understand me—"

"I understand you perfectly," said Mr. Wilberforce heavily, ignoring Eileen's nudges. "The idea is far from being a novel one. But if you will allow me to say so, I think you are deceiving yourself. You speak of bringing the reader right into your mind, and in fact you don't even interest him. The whole thing is too wordy, too abstract. There's nothing in it to grip the attention."

The little man flushed angrily.

"Nothing to grip the attention?" he cried. "What about that dream, eh? Doesn't *that* grip your attention? Doesn't it?"

"Frankly, no," answered Mr. Wilberforce. "It's simply an account of a childish nightmare such as all of us have had at one time or another. I appreciate that it may have frightened you as a child, but believe me, it won't frighten anyone else!"

The little man was trembling with rage now.

"It *will* frighten people!" he almost screamed. "It *will!* I have a special gift for this sort of thing, I *know* I have! Let me tell you, a person once died of fright from hearing that dream!"

There was an awkward little silence. No one knew what to say to that absurd boast. Eileen got hastily to her feet.

"I think we all need a cup of tea!" she said, loudly and brightly, and escaped from the room. As she hurried down the passage to the kitchen, she became aware that Audrey Williams, the young psychological novelist, was following her.

"Thought I might help you, dear," explained Audrey, and added, as she piled cups and saucers onto a tray, "Whoever is that pompous little ass, do you suppose?"

"I can't think," said Eileen. "I felt rather sorry for him, really. He must have worked terribly hard on all that stuff, you know. He had chapters and chapters of it written."

"You're telling me!" giggled Audrey. "I thought at one point that he was proposing to read the whole lot! I nearly died . . ." Her voice trailed away, and both women were aware of Alan Fitzroy standing silently in the doorway.

"Funny you should say that," he said, looking straight at Audrey. "And you?" he went on, turning to Eileen. "Did *you* nearly die, too?"

Eileen flushed. No wonder the poor little chap was bitter! It was shameful of Mr. Wilberforce to have laced into a newcomer like that!

She said gently, "Don't take too much notice of Mr. Wilberforce. He's a very stern critic. He's like that to all of us sometimes, isn't he, Audrey?'

Audrey Williams nodded dumbly; and Alan Fitzroy spoke again, addressing himself to Eileen.

"And what did *you* think of my little effort? I sense a certain sympathy in you. Were you impressed by my dream?"

"Why—yes—" lied Eileen nervously, searching for words. "I thought it was quite—well, quite unusual. If you'd brought it in a bit *sooner,* though, instead of quite so much theory in the beginning—"

"But I *do* bring it in sooner!" exclaimed the little man eagerly—he seemed to have quite recovered his temper. "I bring it in all through the book—just as it has come to me at intervals all through my life. But the reader doesn't know why I keep repeating it until the last episode! Don't you think that's a good idea? Keeping him in suspense, that kind of thing?"

He glanced with pathetic eagerness from one to the other of the two women; and Eileen, anxious to show the poor fellow a little encouragement, paused in fanning biscuits on a plate to say, "Do tell us: what *is* the last episode?"

"Oh, well, you see, it was like this. This dream used to worry me, it really did. I'm not a nervous man—that is to say, my *type* of nerves, as I explain in—"

Hastily Eileen brought him back to the point.

"But the dream?" she said, counting out teaspoons onto the tray, and Alan Fitzroy continued, "Yes, yes. The dream. What worried me, you see, was that each time I dreamed it I got a *little* farther down the passage toward the cradle, where I knew I would have to lie down and see the Face. In the end I was so worried about it that I told my wife. 'If only you could be with me, my dear,' I said—just in fun, you understand—'Then I wouldn't be so scared.'

"Well, that very night I dreamed it again, and, believe it or not, she *was* there! She was walking along in front of me, wearing her old dark dressing gown. She was a big woman, my wife—a big strong woman, and she quite blocked my view of the cradle—the cradle where I knew the madness would begin. So I felt quite safe. I didn't mind the dream a bit. And when I woke up—"

The little man looked eagerly from Eileen to Audrey, like a conjuror bringing off a successful trick. "When I woke up, what do you think my wife told me?"

"Why, that she'd had the dream too, of course!" said Audrey promptly —wasn't that the obvious climax to the tale?

But Alan Fitzroy shook his head. "No," he said. "No, that didn't come till later. No, she told me that as she lay there, her head near to mine, she heard what she thought was my watch ticking under my pillow. But a funny, metallic tick, she said—like a far-off clanging of armor, or of steel boots. And then she knew that it didn't come from under the pillow but from inside my head. It was my boots clanging in my dream, you see, and she'd heard them."

Eileen and Audrey had drawn close together. Eileen's voice trembled a little.

"I think we ought to take the tea in—," she began; but the little man laid his hand on her arm beseechingly.

"Just one moment more!" he begged. "Just a few more words! After that, whenever I dreamed that dream, my wife would hear the clanging in my head, louder each night, until at last *she* had the dream, too! The clanging somehow forced her to go to sleep, she told me, though she tried hard to stay awake—and there she was, she said, right in my dream, walking down the passage in front of me, hearing my boots clanging behind her. What do you think of that?"

Eileen had recovered herself. Of course, this was just a piece of fiction on which he wanted her opinion. Mr. Wilberforce's crushing comments on the autobiography had stung him into trying to enliven it.

"Well," she said consideringly. "I suppose you could work that up into something quite dramatic. But however would you end it?"

"The way it *did* end, of course!" said the little man sharply. "It ended with my wife actually getting into the cradle. Naturally. It was *my* dream, wasn't it, and I *made* it end that way. Though there were one or two terrible struggles first. I told you, my wife was a big strong woman."

"And—and what happens to her in it?" asked Eileen. "Does she see the face? And does she tell you afterwards what it was like?"

"Oh, no!" said the little man, sounding surprised. "Of course not. She couldn't *tell* me any more after she'd got into the cradle. Naturally. She wasn't dead, but she was an imbecile by then. I found her in bed in the morning, all curled up as she would have to be to fit into this little cradle, and she could no longer talk. Naturally. That *would* be the effect of looking at the Face."

Eileen and Audrey glanced at each other. Each noticed that the other had gone rather white; but the little man went cheerfully on, apparently unaware of their dismay.

"They took her away, of course, and put her into some sort of home. But it was all right—I knew I was safe now, because if *she* was in the cradle, then of course *I* couldn't be, could I? Every time I had the dream there she was, filling up the whole cradle in her dark dressing gown so that I couldn't even see it. I felt wonderfully safe for months.

"Until, one night, she wasn't there any more. That was terrible for me. I knew then she must be dead—and sure enough the next day I had word from the Home that this was the case. But come—" he seemed suddenly to rouse himself—"I mustn't keep you ladies from your tea—allow me!" And taking one of the two trays he hurried off to the sitting room.

Eileen and Audrey had only one thought—to get back to their companions. Hastily they loaded the other tray and a few moments later they were in the sitting room.

To their surprise Alan Fitzroy was no longer there.

"Oh, he left as soon as he'd brought the tray in," explained Mr. Wilberforce. "Said he had to catch a train to Guildford, or somewhere. Asked me to apologize to you—why, what's the matter with you?"

Eileen recounted briefly the story that Alan Fitzroy had told them in the kitchen, and Mr. Wilberforce looked grave.

"Fellow must be crazy!" he said. "I *thought* he looked funny. Wouldn't have let him go if I'd known. Should have kept him, and rung the police."

"Oh, I'm only too thankful he *has* gone!" said Eileen. "I don't want a fuss. Besides, he must have meant it as fiction—though even so, he must be a *bit* abnormal to try—"

"Abnormal? Of *course* he was abnormal!" interrupted old Mrs. Peterkin. "I could see *that* the very first moment! 'That's an Egalomaniac!' I said to myself—"

"Egomaniac," corrected Audrey Williams, who was well up in the jargon needed for her novel. "Or do you mean megalomaniac—?"

The chatter went on, and the clink of teacups, and Eileen felt more and more thankful that the strange little man had gone. Suppose he had been the *last* to go instead of the first? She couldn't very well have forced him out—

Eleven o'clock now. One by one the members left, and finally Eileen was alone.

"I must get all this cleared up," she thought, glancing wearily round the untidy room; and she began to move about collecting ashtrays and dirty cups. As she passed the ottoman she noticed that Mr. Wilberforce had left his gloves there; and so she was not surprised when a moment later the front doorbell rang urgently.

But it was not Mr. Wilberforce. The little dark figure had slipped past her into the hall before she had properly taken in what was happening.

She gave a little gasp of horror—and then recovered herself. After all, he seemed a very innocuous little man, standing there under the hall light and asking if he could look at a timetable. He had missed his last train, he said, but maybe—on the other line—perhaps a connection at Croydon—if he might just study the timetable a moment?

Eileen had no alternative but to lead him into the sitting room and hand him the ABC. He settled himself in the armchair with it and was soon thumbing through its pages with apparent concentration. Eileen went on with her tidying, trying to appear quite unperturbed. After all, she was saying to herself, what can he *do*? I'm twice his size, a big strong woman—

Where had she heard that phrase before? The words echoed in her head —"My wife . . . a big strong woman."

It was then that she noticed how quiet everything was. The rustling of the pages of the ABC had ceased; and when she looked across at him, Eileen saw that Alan Fitzroy was asleep. His head was leaning back against the chair, his mouth was open, and his face was rather white.

"He looks queer!" she thought, stepping closer. "I think perhaps I *will* ring the police. Luckily the phone's in the kitchen, not in here, so it won't wake him—"

And then she heard the noise. At first she thought it was a clicking in his throat, the prelude to a snore. But no, it wasn't a click; it was a tiny clanking noise—distant—metallic—inside his head.

Eileen did not stop to put down the tray she was carrying. The telephone! The telephone! That was the only idea in her mind as she hurried through the door and started for the kitchen.

But how loud the clanking sound had grown! It seemed to be following her out of the room—along the passage—clank—*clank*— CLANK—

And where *was* the kitchen? How had this passage grown so long? And why were the walls of stone, and the floor too—stone that echoed to the clanking footsteps behind her—

She could not look behind. She could only hurry on, and on and on, down the echoing passage, until in front of her she saw the end. The delicate muslin frills, stirred ever so slightly by an unseen breath. The lacy pillow, white and waiting. The coverlet, just recently turned back, in readiness, by an unseen hand.

With a strength she never knew she possessed, Eileen made herself stand still.

"It's a dream, it's a dream!" she told herself. "If I won't go with it, I'll wake up! I *won't* go with it! I won't! I won't! I *won't!*"

The clanking feet behind came nearer. Hands were pushing—pushing—fighting with her, and Eileen fought back—with that dim, strengthless fighting of dreams, which yet somehow takes all a person's strength and more—I won't! gasped Eileen silently. I won't, I won't, I *won't!*

A crash seemed to split her eardrums, and she found she could open her eyes. She opened them on her own kitchen, on the tray of crockery lying smashed at her feet. Sweat was running down her face, and tears of relief came into her eyes.

A dream, of course! A sleepwalking dream brought on by that awful little man, and perhaps by overtiredness. Why, it must have been part of the dream that he ever came back to ask for a timetable at all! Light-hearted in her relief, Eileen hurried back to the sitting room.

No. That at least hadn't been a dream. But Alan Fitzroy was no longer sitting upright in his chair. He was sprawled on the floor as if he had been struck down in a violent fight, and blood was trickling from his head where it had struck the fireplace fender in his fall.

For one insane moment Eileen thought of that dream struggle at the edge of the cradle—*one* of them had had to fall—and then, collecting her wits, she rushed to telephone the doctor . . .

The doctor felt the little man's pulse, his heart; then he shook his head. "Not a hope, I'm afraid," he said. "You'll have to phone the police, my dear, and get them to find out where he comes from and everything. You go and phone them now, while I attend to the poor fellow."

But why was Eileen still standing there, motionless?

"Go on—phone!" said the doctor irritably. It was bad enough to be called out to a fatal heart attack at this time of night, without a hysterical woman delaying things. "Go on, the telephone!"

As if in a trance, Eileen moved toward the door—along the passage toward the kitchen. After all, perhaps it had been the doctor's watch chain making that tiny clanking noise. Yes, he must still be rattling his watch chain now—louder—*louder*—LOUDER—

A NEAT AND TIDY JOB

by GEORGE HARMON COXE

Her name was Mary Heath and she stood five-foot-three in the medium heels she wore when she was on duty. She weighed one hundred and eight, her hair was shiny black, her eyes were deep blue, and her firmly rounded chin suggested she had been endowed with a full quota of spunk.

Her domain during working hours was the first car in the three-bank elevator system of the Caswell Building; and because she was young—just past nineteen—and friendly, she was a favorite with most of the tenants. They liked her cheerfulness and their kidding was basically well mannered and gentle. The fresh ones saved their more suggestive comments for Ethel and Loretta in the adjoining cars, for though they were not much older than Mary they were married and somewhat more experienced in parrying conversational liberties.

In the months she had been running the first car her passion for neatness had become well-known to the regulars. She could not control the transients but the others avoided spilling ashes on the carpet of her car. If they lit a cigarette they carried the paper match outside before discarding it, and if they forgot and opened a pack in her car they remembered not to drop the cellophane top.

This passion for tidiness was simply a facet of her personality, as much a part of her as her honesty and friendliness. She was fastidious about her appearance and somehow looked a little smarter in her gray-blue uniform than Ethel with her full-blown figure or Loretta with her tinted blond hair. Since Mary always kept her tiny apartment spic and span she saw no reason why this cage, which was actually her business office five days a week, should not be equally neat and tidy. At least, that was how she explained it when Ethel discovered that Mary kept a small whisk broom tucked behind the collapsible seat in her car. If she wanted to stop the empty car between floors on occasion and sweep the carpet, why should anyone object?

Mary's insistence on neatness came up for the umpteenth time at exactly five minutes after three one Friday afternoon in June when Harry Gilmore came into the foyer of the Caswell Building and headed for her empty car.

Harry was a maintenance man and had the title of Assistant Engineer. He wore his customary soiled coveralls and had a handful of tools in his left fist, a cigarette in his mouth.

"How about a ride, baby?" he said. "I've got some plumbing to do on the fourth."

Mary cocked one eye at the wall clock and saw that she had four minutes before she had to go up to the eighth floor and pick up Stan Norton; she cocked the other at the half-inch ash that hung from Gilmore's dangling cigarette.

"Sure, Harry," she said. "Just knock that ash off first, please."

Harry grinned. He removed the cigarette, studied it, then flicked off the ash with an elaborate gesture.

"Okay, Grandma," he said, still grinning. "But what are you going to do when you get married? I mean—if your husband smokes? You going to make him give up the filthy weed?"

"Certainly not. He can smoke as much as he wants to."

"Maybe in a corner of the kitchen with his face to the wall?"

Mary found herself smiling back at him. He had that effect on her and she remembered the speculation he had caused in her when he had come to work one morning about six months ago. For Harry was handsome in a black-browed, curly-headed way; he had a brash and conceited manner but he also had a quick and knowing smile, and his glance was bold, his manner assured.

Mary had felt his appeal, but she kept this to herself until, a few days later, he had had some repair work to do on her elevator. When he finished, there were grease stains on her carpet—pieces of dirt and oily lint had dropped down from the open ceiling hatch and been ground under foot. When she saw the damage she was too upset to control her indignation. She spoke with such spirit that Harry could only stare at her, then retreat fast. It had taken the cleaning woman two nights to get rid of the stains and Mary had even complained to George Allen, the engineer, who, while sympathizing with her complaint, said that elevators were always greasy and that Harry's problem had not been an easy one.

She had almost forgotten the incident when Harry appeared that afternoon just as she was ready to leave the building. When he apologized for dirtying her car and asked if she would let him take her out to dinner to prove he was forgiven, she had no impulse to refuse.

She had gone out with him three times afterward but had not liked his friends, his attitude, or his tactics in a taxi, and when he saw she meant it the invitations stopped. Even so, their relationship had remained friendly. He still joked with her and she knew that he liked her, but by then Stan Norton had become more attentive and she was glad she had sense enough to encourage him—Stan with his slow smile and serious manner, but with a solid dependability that would be more rewarding in the years to come.

But she could still laugh with Harry and she did so now.

"My husband," she said with amiable dignity, "can smoke wherever and whenever he likes. There will be plenty of ashtrays and I'm sure he will be thoughtful enough to use them."

The buxom Ethel, who had just discharged a load of passengers, had overheard the exchange and quickly took advantage of the opportunity.

"Come on, Harry," she said. "I'll give you a ride. You can put your ashes on my carpet any time . . . Besides," she added, "Mary has to carry the mail in a couple of minutes."

Harry accepted without further hesitation. "Right, baby." He waved his cigarette at Mary and grinned again. "And let that be a lesson to you, Grandma."

Ethel's reference to the mail reminded Mary of her weekly task—a task that always made her a little nervous. She let the door close partway and Cliff Forbes, who was the starter when he was not relieving one of the girls at lunch time or for a coffee break, came over to help her.

For the next minute or so he stood beside her in front of the partly open door and directed the incoming traffic to the other two cars. Then they both watched the plate-glass panel which formed one wall of the lobby and looked directly into the City Bank and Trust Company which had its main entrance on the corner.

This weekly routine on the payroll for the Tracy Company had been worked out over a period of time and was as foolproof as it could be made. At ten every Friday morning Stan Norton came down to the bank with a brown-leather valise to collect the currency which had been put up in the proper denominations. Ed Ewald, the bank guard, took a minute from his regular duties to accompany Stan across the lobby to the elevator where Mary made a nonstop run to the eighth floor. There were only two establishments here, one half the space occupied by the Tracy Construction Company and the other half by a girls' secretarial school. During the day the payroll would be made up in individual envelopes and then, shortly after the bank closed, the second half of the operation would begin.

At three o'clock Ed Ewald locked the bank doors from the inside and then changed into street clothes. Now, at ten minutes after three, Mary saw him coming toward the desk in the lobby with his hat and coat on. He nodded to her, picked up the telephone, and dialed the number of the Tracy Company to tell them that he would be ready. When he hung up, he gave a small wave of his hand and Cliff Forbes said, "Okay, Mary," and stepped away from the door.

When it clicked into place, the car started up and the nervousness which had been stirring inside her began to assert itself. She was not worried that anything might happen here—there would be no stops for the elevator, either up or down. As for Ed Ewald, he was a retired policeman who added to his regular income by guarding Stan on his weekly trip. When Stan reached the lobby Ed would fall in beside him, one hand on the gun in his pocket. They would take a taxicab for a ten minute ride to the construction project near the river, deliver the valise, and be back in less than a half-hour.

Stan had assured her many times that there was nothing to fear, but she could not ignore the possibility that something could go wrong. That was why she dreaded Fridays and why she could never feel relaxed until Stan and Ed Ewald were safely back in the Caswell Building.

Mary's car came to a gentle stop. The door slid back—and then she saw him.

He must have been standing close to the door because he was inside before she could move, and in that first terrifying instant she was so shocked that she only knew that he was a man, that he had an ugly short-barreled revolver in his hand, and that his head was covered with a large, brown-paper bag.

She felt the gun jab into her side as he stood beside her. The two eye-holes that had been cut in the bag only added to the grotesqueness of his appearance. She caught a brief glimpse of the eyes but they were in shadow and had no form, color, or shape. The voice that lashed out at her was muffled and distorted.

"Don't move—not a muscle! Make one sound and you're dead."

She could not have moved or cried out had her life depended on it. Her throat was closed, her muscles paralyzed.

"Stick your head out a little," the voice commanded. "Pretend you're watching for him. When you see him, smile."

She did so and now she saw the door down the hall open. Mr. O'Connor, the Tracy office manager, stepped out, glanced up and down. When he moved aside, Stan Norton passed in front of him and then he was walking toward her, the slow smile beginning to work on his angular face.

The gunman had heard the office door and the approaching steps, and the muzzle of the gun dug harder into her side. This time it hurt, but she did not cry out. She saw Stan's smile expand, heard him say, "Hi, sweetheart. Right on the button."

He started to step into the car before he saw the hooded figure, and then it was too late. After that, things happened so fast and were over so quickly that all her mind could retain were fleeting impressions.

She saw the sudden widening of Stan's startled gaze. She saw the color drain from his stricken face. Then he was inside the car and the valise had been snatched from his nerveless fingers. A hand reached out to spin him about so that he faced the elevator door and the gun was withdrawn from her side and jammed against Stan's spine.

"*Seven!* Get moving!"

Somehow she managed to push the correct button. The door closed and they moved down one flight and stopped again. As the door opened, a hand was planted against Stan's back and he was propelled violently into the corridor. She felt herself being jerked away from the controls. Before she could get her balance, she went spinning through the door, her shoes skidding on the waxed composition floor. By the time she could recover her balance and glance round, the elevator door had closed automatically.

The corridor was suddenly quiet and empty and when she glanced at Stan he was already moving. His face was stony, his jaw tight, and he did not stop to ask if she was all right or if she had been hurt.

"Find a phone!" he said. "Quick. Get the police!"

She understood him but in that first instant, not knowing why he should be running toward the fire door, she started after him. When he hit the heavy steel panel at the end of the corridor she realized that he was going to use the stairs and try to head off the gunman in the lobby. She also realized that with his long legs he might be able to do just that. The thought frightened her because she knew the man who had taken the valise still had the gun.

"*No, Stan! Please*—"

They were on the landing between floors when he wheeled on her and grabbed her shoulders. He shook her once, hard, and there was a desperate look in his eyes.

"The phone!" he said harshly. "Hurry!"

He was on his way down then, taking the steps in great leaps that covered three at a time and now the urgency made itself felt and she began running up the stairs. Then, because it seemed the quickest way, she scrambled out on the eighth floor and ran to the door of the Tracy Company.

She was not sure what she said. It exasperated her that she had to repeat her words to make the startled receptionist understand. Then, as the girl began to dial, the door opened at one side and Mr. O'Connor stepped from his office. She turned on him, the words tumbling out, and when Mr. O'Connor understood he wasted no time. He snapped a question at the operator to make sure she had the police on the line, then he took Mary by the arm and hurried her into the hall.

The next few minutes were a hectic period of frustration and confusion for Mary Heath. The first thing she saw when they stepped out on the lobby floor was Stan talking excitedly to Ed Ewald, and an odd sense of relief flowed through her when she realized that he was all right. She noticed next that the door of her elevator was closed and as she glanced at the signal panel on the wall, the light in the first column told her that the

car had been stopped at the second floor. She heard Mr. O'Connor tell
Ewald to check anyone leaving the building until the police arrived and
then he ran into the second car, followed by Stan.

No one asked Mary to go with them, but she did anyway. Ethel, who
had been watching mutely, had sense enough not to ask questions and Mr.
O'Connor spoke only once.

"Did you bring anyone down from the second floor in the last couple of
minutes?"

"No, sir."

When they found Mary's car empty, Stan wheeled and ran toward the
fire door. Mr. O'Connor yelled to ask where he was going, and Stan called
back over his shoulder.

"The basement. If he didn't come into the lobby he could have gone all
the way down."

Mr. O'Connor blew out his breath. He looked at Mary.

"I guess there's nothing more we can do here," he said. "Might as well
go back to my office and wait for the police."

Sergeant Cheney, who arrived three or four minutes after the two uniformed men from the radio squad car, took charge of the investigation. He
spent most of his time in Mr. O'Connor's office, talking to people and
getting reports from the detectives who were doing the legwork. He was
still in the office two hours later, and so was Mary.

She was the only one who had not left the room at one time or another,
and nothing happened that in any way had changed her first impression of
the sergeant—an impression that left her uncomfortable and afraid. In his
forties, she thought, with a suggestion of gray in his brown hair, and an
impassive, squarish face that never smiled. His voice was level and unac-
cented but it carried a hint of suspicion, and the shrewd gray eyes seemed
not only to take in each physical detail of her appearance, but assess her
thoughts as well.

She could not tell whether he believed her story or not, and there was no
sign that he recognized Stan Norton until all the details had been brought
to light. What he said then filled Mary with a dread she had been unable to
shake. She could still see the way he had looked at Stan, could hear the
disconcerting effect of his words.

"I know you, don't I, Norton?"

"I guess you do," Stan had said.

"The Lollar job, wasn't it?"

"Yes, sir."

"Sort of looks like history repeating itself."

Mr. O'Connor, who had been listening with a mystified air, asked what
the Lollar job was and the sergeant told him. Then, with an odd sense of
despair growing in her, Mary was listening to the story of another success-

ful payroll robbery that had happened to Stan and an armed guard three years ago when he was working for another company. The fact that eventually he had been completely exonerated did not seem now to excuse his silence about the previous holdup. Mr. O'Connor said so and Stan replied that he had not thought it important.

"When I came to work for you, sir, I didn't have anything to do with the payroll."

"But later, when we decided to give you this assignment—"

"I know, sir," Stan said lamely. "I just didn't think such a thing could happen to me twice."

Mr. O'Connor had made no further comment. He had waited while Cheney questioned Ed Ewald, and George Allen, the engineer, and Harry Gilmore. He had listened to reports from the detectives who were searching the building and had been assured that everyone who had left directly after the holdup had been given a quick but thorough inspection. When it was all over Cheney voiced an opinion. He said that in his business he had come to the conclusion that the obvious solution to any crime was usually the correct one.

"What did you do with the valise, Norton? Who is in this thing with you?"

Stan protested, and so did Mary. They had told the truth. It happened exactly as they said it had and both mentioned that Stan had been empty-handed when he came out of the fire door on the lobby floor; Ed Ewald and Cliff Forbes, the starter, could also testify to that.

"Sure," Cheney had said. "But there was a window open on the second-floor landing of those fire stairs. All you had to do," he added to Stan, "was toss the bag out that window on your way down. There's a paved court out there. You can get into it, or out of it, from the back door of the Taylor Building on the next street. A guy waiting down there at the right time could pick up the bag, go through the Taylor Building, and be home free."

Mary had waited for Stan to protest again. She had expected a vehement and indignant denial; instead there was only a hopeless shake of Stan's head and a barely audible word that sounded like, "No." This attitude dismayed her but it did not prevent her from turning on Cheney, and she spoke out in her anger, her blue eyes flashing.

She admitted that whoever took the money had to time the operation precisely and be familiar with every detail of the routine. But what about some of the others? What about George Allen, the engineer, who said he was in the basement all that time, but could not prove it? What about Harry Gilmore? He was supposed to be fixing some plumbing on the fourth floor, but was he?

Cheney heard her out and was ready with answers. True, George Allen had been alone in the basement workshop but there was no money there, nor any sign of the valise—so what had happened to it? As for Harry Gilmore, he had been seen working in the fourth floor men's room by a clerk employed on that floor.

"The guy couldn't pinpoint the time," Cheney said, "but he'll swear that it was between ten and fifteen minutes after three."

Now with the office quiet and everyone gone except Cheney and his men, the sergeant sat in Mr. O'Connor's desk chair, a dead pipe in his mouth. Mary could tell that the inquisition was about over as she saw him turn to Stan.

"All right, Stanley," he said. "It's time you took a ride down to the precinct house and did some talking."

Mary, watching Stan's bony shoulders move in a faint shrug, sensed that he was deliberately avoiding her glance.

"That's all I've been doing."

"You'll talk some more. The Lieutenant will want to hear your story. He'll have some more questions. So will I. Maybe an assistant district attorney will want to get into the act. I don't know how long it will take —maybe all night. But we've got plenty of time."

Cheney stood up and sighed. "I understand you and Mary want to get married."

Stan nodded.

"You made a nice score this afternoon—nearly ten thousand bucks."

"I've told you," Stan cut in, anger finally showing in his voice.

"I know," Cheney interrupted. "But if you did I promise you'll never enjoy it. We're going to be watching you from now on. You're going to have to account for everything you spend and we'll know about every move you make. It won't be any fun—in fact, it'll be a lousy way to start a marriage . . . Let's go."

He walked to the door with Stan and spoke to one of his men; then he came back, the pipe still in his mouth, and looked at Mary.

"We'll need a statement from you too, but it can wait until morning."

"I told you the truth," Mary said woodenly.

"I'm beginning to believe you."

She wasn't sure she understood him and the faintest of hopes began to stir inside her.

"But if you believe me, you have to believe Stan."

Cheney shook his head.

"So far as *you* know, this thing happened just as you said. But there's another way you haven't thought about. Look." He leaned forward and pointed the pipestem. "Suppose a guy you never heard about—a guy who's been coached on the timing and all the details—walked in downstairs a little after three with a gun in his pocket and a folded paper bag under his coat."

He paused and put the pipe back between his teeth. "The job happens the way you said. You and Stanley get pushed off on the seventh floor. Stanley runs. You run for the telephone. This guy with the bundle rides down to the second, beats it to the fire stairs, and drops the bag out the window. He climbs up a floor or two and rides down again when he can. Who's to stop him? His hands are clean; he's got no package; he gets past the bank guard and the starter even though they search him. He goes around the block, through the Taylor Building, and—"

Mary interrupted him. She didn't like the direction Cheney's reconstruction was taking. "But how could anyone do that without Stan's help?"

"That's what I mean," Cheney said.

He did not finish. He did not have to. The meaning was perfectly clear and as they left the office and went into the hall to wait for the elevator, the thought kept penetrating Mary's consciousness with a terrible persistence. She kept thinking about that earlier robbery, and each time she thrust the thought aside by telling herself that Stan could not have planned such a thing—not the Stan she knew and loved. The sergeant *must* be wrong . . .

The elevator door slid back and when Mary stepped inside and saw the dark smudges on the carpet it was all she could do to keep from bursting into tears. Why, she asked herself, was it always like this whenever she left her car for any length of time? No one seemed to care whether it was clean and tidy and now, with the strain of the past hours working on her, she had to blink back her tears. She kept her face averted until they reached the lobby.

"I have to go back to the second floor," she said; then aware that Cheney did not understand, she added, "To the restroom to change my clothes."

The door closed again and she could not keep her eyes from the floor. The dark spots and smudges looked greasy and she wondered if the cleaning woman would be able to remove them during the night. Only once before had the carpet been so soiled and that time—

She knelt quickly as this new thought overwhelmed her. A touch of her finger told her that the smudges *were* oily, and suddenly her heart gave a little flip and she could feel an odd tension working on the emptiness inside her chest.

Something made her turn and look at a panel in the metal wall of the car. There was an almost invisible door here, its presence indicated by hairline cracks and a tiny keyhole. Its purpose was a means of escape in case the car got caught between floors. When that happened, the adjoining car could move up to the same height and, with both emergency doors open, passengers could move safely from one car to the other. There was still another way out of this car and as her glance moved to the ceiling she felt the tension grow and a new excitement plucked at her nerves.

Unaware that the car had stopped and remembering only the other time when the ceiling hatch was open and the oily pieces of dirt and lint had fallen to the floor, she reached for the round collapsible seat.

When she pulled it down from the side of the car her little whisk broom fell to the floor but this time she did not notice it. Pulling her skirts up, she got one foot on the seat and then the other, straightened up, and placed one hand flat against the metal side panel so that she could keep her balance. A flick of her finger and the little catch on the escape hatch in the ceiling clicked back and she pushed it open; then she was groping above the hatch, her probing fingers sliding over greasy metal surfaces, finally coming to an object which was definitely not metal.

She stood on tiptoe, feeling the strap of her brassiere snap as she strained to get better leverage. Her fingernails helped to draw the object a little closer and then she was pulling it, seeing the edge of the valise now in the opening and pulling still harder until it came too far, slipped from her grasp, and thumped solidly onto the carpet below.

She stepped down carefully and let the seat snap back against the elevator wall. She was still staring at the grease-stained valise when she heard a slight sound behind her. Then, as her muscles froze and she tried to turn, she heard the familiar voice.

"Well, well. So you and old Stan lifted the payroll after all?"

Harry Gilmore stood in the doorway, an odd grin on his handsome face. He looked very sharp in his blue suit with a trench coat thrown over one arm. There was also a narrowed brightness in his gaze.

"We had nothing to do with it," Mary snapped.

"Then how did you know the bag was up there?"

"I didn't." She pointed at the soiled rug. "But I remembered the last time this car was all messed up with grease and dirt was when you were up there working on the machinery with that hatch open. It gave me an idea. I don't know how you did it, Harry—that's for the police to find out—"

She stopped at a movement of his hands and then she was looking at the same revolver she had seen earlier in the afternoon. Before she could fully understand what it meant, Harry had stepped past her and tipped the hatch back into place. He picked up the valise and gestured with the gun.

"Let's go, baby."

"Go? Where?"

"To the girl's room. I'll need a little time to figure things out."

He pulled her into the hall and they walked down the corridor, turned left, and finally came to a door near the end. Mary took the key from her pocket and when the lock clicked they moved into this room which had metal lockers along one wall, a couch, three wicker chairs, a round table, and an electric grill for making coffee.

"Go ahead," Harry said. "Get on with your change."

She saw he meant it. When she realized she had no choice, she stepped over to her locker and worked the combination. She took out her gray dress and cloth coat and put them on the couch. She placed her handbag beside them. She took off her uniform jacket and tossed it aside; then, turning her back to him, she removed her blouse, gave a tug at the zipper on her skirt, and stepped out of it. For a moment only she stood in her slip but there was no room in her mind for embarrassment as she quickly pulled the dress down over her head. She wasted no time on speculation as to what might happen now, but her mind was working and she had to know how Harry had done so much alone.

"After you put Stan and me out on the seventh," she said, "you rode to the second. That gave you time enough to hide the payroll. You went to the fire stairs and made sure they were empty—Stan was probably all the way down to the first floor—and then you went back up to the fourth. When did you change your clothes?"

"There's a vacant office next to the men's john on the fourth floor. I had an old suit on under my coveralls when Ethel took me up. All I had to do in the vacant office was take off the coveralls and leave my tools."

"But that clerk who said he saw you in the men's room—"

"That was a break I hadn't counted on," Harry said. "Nobody saw me get out on the second floor or go in or out of that vacant office on the fourth. The men's room was empty and I tore up the paper bag and flushed it down the toilet. I was still working on that when this character comes in."

"And tonight you were waiting for me to leave the elevator—"

"That's right, baby, and if you hadn't been so nosey it would have been a cinch." He swore softly. "You can't open that damn hatch without some of that oily junk falling into the car, but you were the only one who noticed it."

"But all those pay envelopes?"

"That's why I brought this trench coat. It's got two pockets in it big enough to hold a crate of oranges. Now you can give me a hand."

When she turned she saw that he was inspecting her handbag. It was a large one because she carried her lunch in it every day. Harry had opened the valise and was now tucking some of the pay envelopes inside her bag. The others he distributed in the two pockets of his trench coat. Then, as she hung up her uniform in the locker, he stepped past her and put the valise at the bottom of her locker.

"That's a good place for it," he said. "When the cops find that tomorrow it should make it even tougher for your boyfriend."

"How will it?" Mary said. "I'll simply tell them the truth."

"You'll tell them nothing, baby. I've got other plans for you." He waved the gun. "Right now we're going out together. The night watchman might be down in the lobby and there could be a cop with him, but they're not going to stop us, understand? Because I'm already a two-time loser in Pennsylvania and I've gone too far with this to chicken out now. If I have to use the gun I'll do it, and if I do you're going to get it first. Understand?"

Mary was surprised to find the elevator still there until she realized that they had been gone only a few minutes. Harry Gilmore had draped the trench coat containing most of the pay envelopes over his left arm to hide the gun he was holding. He gave her a final word of caution as the car started down, but it was a phrase he had used earlier that stuck in her mind. She did not know what he meant by having plans for her, but she did understand one thing clearly: if anything did happen to her or if she did not come back, the police would find the valise in her locker and Stan would not only go to prison, he would have on his record another black mark that would remain there as long as he lived.

As they stepped from the car she saw Sergeant Cheney standing by the cigar counter talking to the night watchman and she realized this might be her one and only chance—and her last chance. But she believed what Harry Gilmore had threatened: she knew he would use the gun if he had to. She dared not make a precipitous move, but she was able surreptitiously to twist the catch on her handbag so that it snapped open.

It was the kind of bag which had two straps and when properly held they served to keep the top of it closed. Now, with the catch open, she could only hope that Cheney might catch a glimpse of what was inside. And so she moved up, her young face frozen in a half smile and all too conscious of Harry Gilmore's nearness. As they approached the cigar counter, both Cheney and Charlie Doyle, the night watchman, straightened up from the glass case.

"I thought I might give you a ride home," Cheney said.

"No, thanks, Sergeant," Mary said through stiff lips. "Harry's taking me."

"Yeah," Gilmore said. "It's no trouble."

She came to a stop as they spoke, her handbag turned toward Cheney. When nothing happened, she felt the pressure of Gilmore's arm and trench coat against her back and she started to walk again when she saw something happen to Cheney's eyes. For an instant they flicked to the handbag and seemed to fasten there. When he said, "Just a second, Mary," she made her move.

Having started to step toward the door she spun on her right foot and her arm whipped around, the bag at the end of it. She was aiming at the hand with the gun, feeling a sudden terror as she waited for a shot and finally understanding that the suddenness of her attack had startled Harry into a precious moment of inaction.

Then the bag slammed into the hidden hand and one strap broke. She heard the muffled shot that followed and saw the small pay envelopes begin to spill onto the floor. She knew she had not been hit, but when her momentum carried her against Harry he pushed her violently and she fell. She struck the marble floor on both knees, felt pain, then heard the second shot.

By the time she could get her head up and bring the scene into focus, Harry was on the floor and Cheney and the night watchman were on top of him. Suddenly Cheney had the short-barreled revolver in his hand and Charlie Doyle was jerking Harry to his feet.

Cheney was still too startled to do more than stare at her as she squirmed into a sitting position and pulled her skirt down. She was not really angry with the sergeant but reaction hit her hard and one knee was throbbing painfully. As though in protest against the hours of injustice, she spoke sharply and the words came out high-pitched.

"Now maybe you'll get it through that thick head of yours that Stan had nothing to do with the payroll robbery."

She was ashamed as soon as she said the words. Cheney came over to help her to her feet and ask her if she was all right and then she was telling him what had happened in the elevator and what she knew. It did not take long and Cheney needed no diagram. He had handcuffs on Harry Gilmore and all the pay envelopes were quickly collected and Charlie Doyle was using the telephone.

"I'm going to take this lad with me," Cheney said to her, "but there'll be a car along in a minute for you. You've had a rough day and I think you'll want to go home and maybe put some hot compresses on that knee of yours."

"And where are you taking Harry?" Mary demanded.

"To the precinct house."

"Is that where Stan is?"

"Yes."

"Then I'm going with you. If anybody's going to take me home tonight it's going to be Stan."

"All right, all right," Cheney said, and for the first time he smiled at her. It was a nice smile, genuine and sympathetic, and it changed his whole face. It seemed to Mary that for the first time he really approved of her and, thus comforted, she hitched her coat into place and patted the back of her hair. When she was ready she spoke to Charlie Doyle.

"Will you do something for me, Charlie?"

"Sure, Mary."

"Then *please* tell the cleaning woman to see if she can get those grease spots out of the carpet in my car. Right now it's a mess and I'd like it looking halfway decent in the morning when I come in."

Then, reassured by Charlie's promise, she was ready to ride with Cheney . . . to Stan.

RUN—IF YOU CAN

by CHARLOTTE ARMSTRONG

She was there, of course. She was always there. This was his home, but he never came home without finding her waiting—no matter how late.

There she was. Sitting in the stiff chair under the lamp, wearing a dark blue dress. She was his sister, his whole family, and this was his home, so he had to come here; but he stared at her hands, her splay-fingered, big-knuckled old hands, holding the Book.

"It's midnight," she said.

"I'm a big boy," he answered nastily. "I'm forty-two years old. You know that, Helen?"

He dashed across the sitting room and through the alcove to the kitchen. He found the liquor, poured a drink. The garage was locked—he had remembered to lock it.

He came back with the glass in his hand. "I need this," he whined, because he needed her. She was his sister, she was all he had. "I had a terrible scare just now. I'm pretty much shaken up. I got home all right, though. Nobody saw me."

"Somebody saw you, Walter," she said in that mad and maddening way she had, that way of being so absolutely sure.

"No, no," he said, knowing that his eyes were rolling, that he was sweating again. "Way out in the country. Not a soul around. Listen, I don't know where she came from. All of a sudden there was this little car. How could I stop? It wasn't my fault. I just couldn't stop. I did stop, afterwards." He gulped at the drink. "I don't know who she was. How could I know? I got out of there. Little bitty car, turned right over. They make them too small, too narrow . . . Listen, she was dead. There was nothing I could do for her any more—nothing."

"Alone?" his sister asked.

"Of course, alone," he said angrily. "And I got home all right, didn't I? The car's in the garage. I looked it over, as good as I could. There isn't a mark on it."

"There is a mark," his sister said.

"Quit with that stuff, will you?" he shouted. "It was an accident, I tell you! How can you stop if you're doing seventy? You don't know anything about things like that. I'm telling you, nobody saw, nobody is going to know, and you won't say anything."

"There'll be no need," she said, with the certainty that was like contempt. She had no color in her long narrow face. She never had. Even her lips had no color. Her pale hands lifted the Book. "Nothing shall be hidden," she whispered.

She drove him nuts sometimes. "I couldn't do anything for her, could I? It wasn't really my fault, was it? I'd been driving a long time and my eyes were tired. I couldn't help that, could I? It's too bad. I mean, I'm sorry. I'm upset, believe me I am. Tomorrow I'll change all the tires on the car. I'm not . . ."

Her eyes were set deep, and the eye sockets caught shadows.

"Don't talk about it," he cried, although she was not speaking. "Listen, I'm all in. I had a shock. I got to get some sleep. I had an awful shock and I'm tired. So don't talk about it."

She said nothing. But he went staggering away, off to his bedroom. He'd sleep. He'd take a pill—two of them, to make sure. She wouldn't approve. Helen didn't approve of anything. He ought to get away from her; but he couldn't get away. Curled up in his bed, he could hear her moving around the apartment, making everything neat for the night . . . and somehow he felt safe.

"You're late," she said, when he came home from work the next night and stood, tense and wary, just inside the door.

"Anybody come around? Anybody poking around the garage?"

"No."

"The bus was slower than molasses," he grumbled, and then took a few steps, on tiptoe. Which was absurd. "It's in the evening paper," he told her. "Her name was Mary Lovelace. Lovelace. Some name, eh? She was dead, all right. Some farmer found her, about four in the morning." He moistened his lips. "Hit-and-run, they say in the paper."

"Yes," said his sister, nodding agreement. "Dinner is waiting."

"There was nothing I could do, was there? I didn't see her. I couldn't stop. Didn't mean to do it. Listen, it happens every day—every day. Forget it. Get dinner on, will you?"

"As soon as you wash up, Walter," his sister said.

But at the table he kept talking and talking. "I looked at the car this morning, by daylight, and I couldn't see a thing. Nothing's dented. Didn't scrape the paint, not that I can make out. No glass broken. But I'm not going to drive it, Helen. See, they've got these police laboratories. It's spooky what they can come up with. One speck of dust, maybe, and you're a gone goose. What am I going to do with the car?"

"It doesn't matter what you do with the car," she said.

"Oh, come on," Walter shoved his chair back. "You're nuts, you know that, Helen? *You* ought to know that. I know it. So I'm taking care of this. And you're not going to open your mouth about it—not one word."

He grinned and looked sly, because he was sure. She was all he had, his whole family, and she would not betray him.

"I have prayed for you," she said.

"You'd do better to try and help me figure out how to get rid of it. Of the car, I mean. The *car.*" (Sometimes she looked so stupid!) "Say I buy four new tires. But who knows if they're checking up on sales like that? Say I have a new paint job done. Same thing—they may be checking. What I've got to do, I've got to be a little bit smarter than that, that's all."

She said nothing. She just looked at him in that stupid way.

"Also," he continued, finding some ease in voicing his anxieties, "I know better than to drive it out to the desert, or some place, and just leave it. They'd pick it up and trace it so fast . . . Well, so I can't run it off some cliff into the ocean, either. They'd find it—you can bet on it. They'd want to know how and why. So how am I going to get rid of that car?"

His sister whispered, "How are you going to get rid of your sin?"

"What sin?" he bellowed. "Sure, I broke the law. I know that. Sure, there's a law that says you've got to report a thing like that. Well, I didn't want to report it. I didn't want to be in a mess over just an accident—an unavoidable accident, I tell you! Nobody saw. Nobody knows. Nobody *will* know, if I can only get rid of the car. So that's my problem."

"Why don't you sell it?" she said in a moment.

"What will I do? Trade it in? And the cops find it on a secondhand lot? And there are records kept—damn it, you don't understand."

"I understand better than you," she sighed.

"Oh, shut up, will you? Will you, please? I'm *going* to get rid of the car and the whole mess with it. There must be a way. I'll figure out a way. I can't eat," he said. "I don't want any more dinner." He glowered at her. "Don't you get any nutty idea *you'll* go to the police."

"It won't be necessary," she said.

He flung himself up from the table. "It'll stay in the garage till Saturday. I'll do something about it on Saturday."

"You cannot—"

He interrupted viciously, "You want to bet? You want to put your money where your mouth is, just once in your life? You're getting worse all the time. You know that, Helen? I'm going to buy us a television set too."

He mumbled away into the sitting room. They didn't even have a television set. She read one Book—one Book all the time. He had to go watch television in some bar.

As soon as Walter turned the Saturday sports page, he saw the ad. Carrying the paper, he trotted to where his sister was watering her row of potted plants in the kitchen window.

"I got it," he told her. "Listen to this swap ad. Talk about perfect! This is it, Helen.

" 'Exchange: Fine view lot for late model auto. Must be in good condition for long trip. Quick deal. Phone——'

"So?" he cried. "Isn't this it? Isn't it?" She straightened her long flat back, and her thin neck lengthened. "The perfect way to get rid of the car," he cried impatiently. "I'll swap it for whatever he's got. A lot, it says here."

"A piece of land?"

"All right! I need a lot like a hole in the head. What's the difference? Here's a man, he's going on a long trip and he's going quick. So let *him* drive that car out of the state and that's the way to be rid of it."

"Do you think so?" his sister said tonelessly.

"The deal gets recorded, sure. But so what? License number, engine number, make and model, and all that. So what about it? They won't tell anything. The car itself will be gone, far away. So how will the police ever get the car into their laboratories? This is going to be the way, I tell you, and it'll work."

"There is another way," she said.

"What way?"

"Confess."

"Oh for . . . ! Listen, I could go to jail! Which I am *not.*" Walter flung himself off to the telephone.

When he hung up, he was sweating a little. But he said to his sister (to whom else could he say anything?), "Sounds good. Fellow wants me to run over to his place right away, and we can go take a look at this lot. Well, from his point of view it makes sense, you know? So I got to take the chance and drive the car. He's only two, three miles away. Then this lot is way up in the hills and who's going to be up there? Nobody's been around here yet, and it's four days. Listen, the best of it is, he wants to take off on a trip tonight! So this is really it—the way out."

His sister said nothing and he shouted to her silence. "What can happen? Nothing is going to happen. You're going to keep your mouth shut and you are the only one who knows."

"I am not the only one who knows," she said.

"God knows, eh?" snarled Walter. "You give me the creeps sometimes. You know what you are, Helen? You're superstitious, that's what you are.

You're a real nut with this stuff. You don't understand this world at all. I'm going, and I'm going to get rid of the car."

"Go with God," she said sadly.

"With or without, I'm *going,*" he shouted, sweating.

But Walter went in terror and he knew it. He backed his car out of the garage for the first time since the accident and walked all around it, convincing himself that there was absolutely no visible sign of any damage. Nothing to betray him.

Then he drove off, carefully. The sight of a prowl car drenched him in sweat, but the policemen didn't even see him.

He was peering at house numbers when a tall thin young man came walking toward him with an air of having been waiting impatiently. He said his name was Anderson. He seemed to have no time to waste and no inclination for small talk. He paid little attention to the appearance of the car, to the paint or the chrome. He did lift the hood. Then he got into the driver's seat and Walter, who kept talking nervously, got in beside him.

"I take care of a car," Walter babbled. "I believe in that. I'm not one of these people who runs a car into the ground. A car's a valuable piece of property. She runs pretty sweet, wouldn't you say?"

Anderson, testing the car's functioning, drove up into the hills along winding streets and then, above the streets, on winding roads. Then he stopped.

"This it?" Walter blinked. Oh, yes, he had better show some interest in the lot.

They got out and Walter blinked again. There was a fine view. The great basin of Los Angeles lay, wide and beautiful in spite of itself, below them. The lot was more level than most. Anderson pointed out the boundary stakes. It wasn't a bad size, either.

"That's it," said the young man with his air of impatient briskness. "I'll take the car if you'll take the lot. Is it a deal?"

Walter licked his lips. "You'll take the car," he said slowly, "and be gone. Right? But this real estate—the title check, the closing? I mean, what guarantee do I have?"

"I've got the deed in my pocket and my lawyer, with a power of attorney, can handle the details. Suppose I have him meet us right away."

"You don't . . . er . . . want to stick around, yourself till Monday?"

"No," said Anderson, and his voice was positive.

Walter glanced around the site once more. "Looks okay," he admitted. "I mean, how can it miss? Unless there's a gimmick. Eh, Mr. Anderson?"

The young man turned his back and started toward the car. "If you don't want it, say so."

"Title clear? No liens?" Walter walked after him.

"That's what I said. You know they'll search it. Well? If not, say so and I'll find another car."

"Well, I'll tell you—" Suddenly Walter recalled his prime motive. "Okay, it's a deal. Say the car is yours, the lot is mine, even swap, as of right now. Okay?"

"Okay."

In the sunlight, on the high hillside, with the wind on them, they shook hands on it.

There remained only the paperwork. Walter said, "Why don't we do this over a cup of coffee? I'll drive. There's a short cut down to my place from here. You can call your lawyer to come over to my place, can't you?" Now he was anxious to get it done with.

"Any way that's quick," Anderson said.

On the way downhill, Walter kept glancing at the face of his silent companion. "This trip," he said, "you taking off tonight?"

"Yes—right away."

"Going far?"

"As far as I can go."

Walter said no more. When they came to the apartment building in which he and Helen lived, he ran the car around the corner and into the garage, pretending that he was doing this absent-mindedly. He apologized and left the garage door open. It was safe enough. He then led his companion up the stairs.

She was there, of course. She was always there.

"This is my sister, Helen, Mr. Anderson. We've got some business," he added quickly, before she could speak. His tone told her that the business was none of hers. "Make us some coffee, will you, Helen?" He showed Anderson to the phone. While Anderson was using it, Walter followed his sister into the kitchen.

"This is it," he said, "So keep still. Swear to me, you'll keep your mouth shut."

Her pale lips parted. Her pale eyes in their deep caverns looked at him with pity. Then they closed, and her lips closed.

The two men sat down at the table in the alcove and began to produce what papers they had. Helen brought in the coffee silently. She left them and sat down in the stiff chair in the other room, and took the Book into her hands.

When there was nothing more to do until the lawyer arrived, there seemed nothing more to say. Anderson glanced at the woman in the chair, glanced at his watch. Walter began to find the silence too hard to bear. "This lawyer *is* coming, isn't he?"

"In a few minutes."

"How do I know—?" Walter began. Then he controlled himself. "Kind of in a hurry, aren't you, Mr. Anderson?" he inquired.

"I'd like to be on my way."

"Well, all we got to do is wait for this . . . er . . . friend of yours."

Walter looked up slyly from under lowered brows. He was nobody's pigeon. How did he know that the man they were waiting for was, in fact, a lawyer?

Anderson looked at his watch again. He glanced through the arch at the silent woman, stiff in the stiff chair.

Walter said, "How come you don't own a car? A young fellow like you. I was kind of wondering."

"I own a car. It's in bad shape."

"No trade-in value?"

"Not worth bothering about."

Walter twitched. After a moment he said, "How long did you say you owned that lot, Mr. Anderson?"

"I didn't say," snapped the young man. He seemed about to jump out of his skin. "A little more than a year," he answered, rather coldly.

"More coffee?" asked Walter, beginning to rise.

"No. No, thanks."

Walter sighed and began to wish that his sister would get up and come over to them and act like—well, like a woman. Chat a little, be pleasant. But she just sat there. He jerked his head to get Anderson's eye and said in a low voice, "My sister's quite a Bible reader. Kind of wrapped up in that stuff, you know?"

"I see." But the man didn't see. He wasn't even listening. He was studying his left hand that clenched and opened and clenched again, in rhythmic tension.

Walter was too nervous to remain silent. "To me," he said, "the times are modern, right? I do my best. I work for a living. I'm a businessman." He went on uncontrollably. "Looks to me, if you'd hang on to that property six months or another year you ought to turn a nice profit. Right now— you know this, don't you?—it's worth more than a second-hand car."

"We have agreed," said Anderson stiffly.

"Oh, sure. Sure, we got a deal. I'm not complaining. No offense, Mr. Anderson. But what would it hurt, for instance, if you'd take your hair down a bit. Eh? Just for the sake of my curiosity, why don't you tell me? What's the gimmick?"

"The what?"

"The hitch? What's wrong with that lot?"

Anderson started to get up.

"No, no," said Walter quickly, holding a protective hand over the papers. "The deal is set. That's what I'm saying. Just looks to me like you're on the short end. I'm wondering why, that's all."

The man stared at him stonily.

"See, it's been my experience," Walter went on, unable to restrain himself, "that people don't ever get something for nothing—not in this world, hah, hah!"

The doorbell rang.

"Get the door, will you, Helen?" Walter called. She rose. He heard a man's voice say politely, "I am looking for a Mr. Robert Anderson."

Helen said nothing.

"Oh, for . . . !" Walter stood up. "Right this way," he called out.

He felt a deep relief, but the aftertaste of his curiosity was still strong. So he looked down and said to the young man softly, "Listen, does *he* know where the body is buried? Maybe?"

Anderson's eyes flashed. He called out the lawyer's name. An older man came toward them, well-dressed, crisp and businesslike in speech and manner. It took only a few minutes more—a few signatures. Then all three rose and Walter held out the car keys.

Anderson snatched the keys and began to cross the sitting room, moving quickly. Walter shuffled fast to keep alongside. He was convinced, now, that this man was running away. But from what?

They almost collided as Anderson stopped and murmured to Helen, still sitting in her chair, "Happy to have met you."

Her pale lips did not open. Oh, she was a nut, *really,* thought her brother.

"Come on," he said crossly, "you can say good-bye to the gentleman, Helen."

"God be with you, gentleman," she said.

This was odd enough to hold Anderson for a moment, as the lawyer, briefcase in hand, joined them.

"Good-bye," he said pleasantly to Helen, and then to Walter, "Good-bye. I'll be seeing you, perhaps. Good luck with your acquisition."

Then Walter was whining at their backs—he just couldn't help it. "Look, gents, excuse me, but that lot is worth five, six thousand, if it's worth a nickel. All right. I'm stuck with it now. And that's okay. But what's the gimmick? Please?"

The lawyer said severely, "No gimmick."

"But there *has* to be a gimmick," cried Walter.

"And you have to know, don't you?" asked Anderson hoarsely.

"Don't, Bob," said the lawyer, touching his client's arm. "We're through here. Let's go."

"Now wait," said Walter frantically. "This is beginning to look pretty funny."

344

"Funny?" said Anderson. "I bought that lot to put a dream house on it for my bride. There is no bride."

"I see. I see." Walter was deflated so suddenly that he almost fell. "I'm sorry. I didn't realize it was personal. That's okay, then." He was nodding. "Yes, that's all right."

"All right?" said Anderson on a note of rising anger. "All right?"

Walter had begun to sweat. He looked behind him. His sister, with the Book in her hands, had her head high, and on her pale lips was the weird little smile—the smile that was going to drive him nuts one of these days.

"She was driving my sports car last Tuesday night," said Anderson violently, "and somebody flipped her into a ditch. So there'll be no dream house and I never want to see the site of it again. That's what's the matter with the lot."

Now Walter was not only sweating, he was shaking from head to foot.

It was the lawyer who held out his hand in farewell. Walter didn't dare touch it. "Listen. Excuse me. I'm sorry. I didn't mean anything. So long, I mean . . . Go with God," Walter bleated idiotically. A high giggle came out of him.

"Shall we go, Bob?" the lawyer said softly.

But Anderson said, "What's the matter here?"

Walter's jowls were shaking. "No, no," he said. He spread his hands. The palms were wet. "Why should there be a gimmick? Nothing's the matter here—nothing at all."

Anderson's eyes bored into Walter's, then swerved to Helen's.

"What is it?" he said to her, sharply.

But her lips were closed.

For Walter, something cracked. "You're crazy, Helen," he shrieked. "You know that? She's crazy," he sobbed to the two men. "Don't *listen* to her! *Shut your mouth!*" he howled to his silent sister.

The lawyer had dropped any intention of leaving. Anderson spoke, in the stern and quiet voice of doom. "I think you'd better tell me. What's wrong with the car? What's the gimmick?"

LINE OF COMMUNICATION
by *ANDREW GARVE*

Larry Seton watched the two men come up through the trapdoor. The thin one came first, warily, with the flick knife open and pointing. When he was clear the other followed.

The big man lowered the trapdoor, holding it with his foot while he made a looped twine handle from a spool he'd brought with him. The old rope handle had pulled out, leaving a hole, and the last time they'd come up they'd had trouble raising the trapdoor from above once it was shut.

The thin man crossed to Larry and gave him a piece of paper, a grubby envelope, and a ballpoint pen. "Okay, write," he said.

Larry wrote as instructed:

Dear Father,
   I'm sending you this note so you'll know that what the men said on the telephone was true. They're keeping me locked up in a room where no one ever comes. They say they'll kill me if they don't get the £50,000 and I think they mean it. They are going to phone you again at ten o'clock tomorrow evening. Please do as they say about the money and don't try to bring the police in. I'm in good health but rather scared. One of them has a knife. I hope I shall see you again.   Larry

He addressed the envelope and handed it back with the note and the pen. The thin man read the note and gave a satisfied grunt. The big man then raised the trapdoor with the loop he'd improvised and the two of them backed down.

"You'll soon be okay now, mate," the thin man called, as he closed the trapdoor and shot the bolt underneath.

Larry doubted it. Not that he thought his father wouldn't pay the money. The old man was rich, and he'd take the one chance that was offered, however slender it seemed. He'd hope that the kidnappers would keep their word and let Larry go when the money was paid.

But Larry knew they wouldn't. They couldn't afford to—because he knew who they were, and they knew he knew. He'd seen them at his father's factory, where they'd been working as building laborers on a plant extension until a week or two ago. He didn't know their names, but if he ever got free again he'd be able to tell the police enough to make their capture certain.

So he wouldn't be allowed to go free. Once they'd got the money, they'd kill him. Larry had read the intention in the thin man's vicious little eyes.

He gazed desperately around his prison. It was a bare loft, about twelve feet by twenty, poorly lit and black with grime. It had no exit but the trapdoor, and no windows. The sloping raftered sides met in a square of flat roof with a skylight in it that had lost all its glass—but the skylight was at least ten feet up and barred with iron rods. There was no way of escape.

No chance, either, of making a fight of it—not a successful one. Larry was sixteen and well setup—but you couldn't argue with a knife. *He* couldn't, anyway. And the kidnappers always came up together. They never gave him an even chance.

It would have been different if he had a weapon. But there wasn't anything in the loft that he could use. A few bits of glass on the damp boards beneath the skylight—but they were too small to be effective against a knife. A wooden orange crate that they'd brought up to serve as a writing table—too unwieldy to make much of a weapon.

Apart from that, they'd left him with almost nothing. A plastic cup and a plastic water container. A plastic bucket. A plastic plate which still held the remnants of his meager supper. A few candles for use at night. The spool of twine that the big man had chucked into a corner after fixing the trapdoor. And that, literally, was all.

For a moment Larry concentrated on the new object—the spool of twine. It was a big spool, machine-rolled, and the cord was strong. Could he use it? Fantastic ideas chased each other through his head. Rig up a trip line? Weave it into some kind of net? Garotte one of the men with it? Not very promising . . .

If there had been a window he might have dangled something down and tried to attract attention. But there was no window. Or if the skylight had been lower, he might have tried throwing the spool through the bars, with a message on it. He wondered if it was possible.

He put the orange crate under the skylight and climbed onto it. The box was old and frail and gave out ominous cracks. Cautiously he raised his hand. He was still short of the bars by more than two feet. And it would be difficult to throw the spool through the bars, which were only about four inches apart. And even if he got it through, it would only go straight up

and fall straight down again onto the flat roof. No good. He'd need a
rocket to get it away from the roof. . . .

A rocket! No chance of that, of course—but it started a train of
thought. . . .

He climbed down and stood considering. *Could* he? He gazed up through
the skylight. Light clouds were moving steadily across the evening sky.
Quite fast. There was plenty of wind up there—he could feel the draft
through the opening.

He looked around, appraising his resources. The twine, the bits of glass,
the wooden crate. The nylon shirt he was wearing. Yes, there was just a
chance. Anyway, what did he have to lose?

He examined the bits of glass. There was one piece with a sharp edge.
That should do. He examined the crate. The thin strips of wood that
formed its sides would probably give him what he needed. It would take
time—but he had plenty of that.

He lit a candle in the failing light and stuck it in his cup. Then he peeled
off his shirt and spread it on the floorboards. There was more than enough
material in the shirt tail, if he was careful and made no mistake. He'd better
mark it out first. But with what?

He looked about him. Dirt from the floor mixed with water? Or dirt
from the rafters? He ran a finger along one of them. It came away coated
with soot. There was so much soot that he could scrape it off into his hand.

He made a little pile of it on the floor, puddled it, and applied some to a
bit of the shirt with a sliver of wood from the crate. The mixture wasn't as
good as ink, but it left a mark. Yes, it would do.

Cautiously now, using the crate as a straight edge, he sketched his quad-
rilateral on the nylon shirt. The last time he'd done this sort of thing was
five years ago—but he hadn't forgotten the lore his father had taught him.
It wasn't the size that mattered, but the proportions—and those he remembered. The two lower sides one and a half times the upper sides. Leave
enough material for turning in and sewing. And four flaps for making
pockets to hold the struts . . . That should do it.

Cutting out the shape was a long job. The nylon was strong and
wouldn't tear easily. The piece of glass wasn't nearly as sharp as a pair of
scissors. The final result was ragged at the edges—but it would serve.

Now for the struts. Pull one of the thin battens from the box. Score
down it with the glass, half an inch from the edge. Deeper, now. Then the
other side. Now a little pressure . . . The wood split and he had his
vertical strut.

He worked quietly, methodically, intent on the job. The kidnappers had
taken his watch and he could only guess at the time. Occasionally he lit a
fresh candle from the stump of the old one.

Sewing the edges, and making the pockets for the struts, was another long job. He used a loose nail from the crate to make the holes, and twine from the spool to thread through them. He tied the struts where they crossed. Finally he stood back and examined his handicraft.

It wasn't much of a kite. All the same, if he could get it through the skylight, it should fly. When it was well up, he'd let go, and it was bound to fall soon, carrying the message he was going to write on it.

It was only when he began to think about the message that he realized he had almost no information to give. He had no idea where he was. He could remember nothing from the time he'd been knocked out till he'd come round in the loft. He thought he was in a city, because of the distant hum of traffic, but he didn't know if he was still in London.

A dirty loft at the top of a building—that was all the description he could give and that wasn't likely to bring rescue. He could say that his kidnappers had worked at the factory—but that wouldn't bring rescue either—certainly not in time. Besides, there wasn't enough room on the kite for a long message. With his improvised ink, the letters would have to be large and thick to be legible.

He pondered. There was no point in letting the kite loose without adequate directions. Better to keep it tethered, and say who had sent it up. When the wind dropped, it would fall, and someone would find it and follow the string. Yes, that was the best bet. . . .

He wrote his message with laborious care. Big letters, well blacked in. FROM LARRY SETON. Every newspaper reader would know his name by now. TELL POLICE. DON'T BREAK STRING. That should do it.

Once more he considered. Assuming the kite flew, how long a line should he give it? In a way, the shorter the better—it would be quicker and easier for the police to follow the string. But suppose it came down on a rooftop—or in a tree? It might not be found at all.

Better to let it fly high and have more than one message. Spaced along the string. Then, wherever it fell, there'd be a good chance that one of the messages would be seen. He cut out some strips of nylon and wrote the same words on each one.

Now he was ready to try the kite. He made the end of the twine fast to it and climbed again onto the orange crate. He could just manage to push the kite through the bars. It lay flat on top of them, stirring a little in the wind but not lifting enough to take off. Somehow he'd have to raise it, give it a start.

He thought for a moment, then broke another batten from the crate and set to work to cut it into strips. Four strips tied to each other with twine made a long rod. He climbed back on the crate and poked the improvised rod through the bars. At the second attempt he found the kite's balancing point and raised it on the rod. In a moment the wind caught it and it was off, straining at the twine, beautifully steady.

Larry could only guess how much twine he was letting out into the darkness above. At what he thought was a couple of hundred feet he tied on one of his strip messages. He let out more twine, then tied on another. Near the end of the string he tied a third.

Now for tethering the kite. The twine had been wound on a stout cardboard cylinder. Placed crosswise under the bars, that would do the trick. Of course, the kidnappers might notice it when they came up in the morning. But they might also notice that the twine on the spool was gone —or that the crate had been partly dismantled. The whole operation was a gamble.

With the end of the twine fast to the cylinder, Larry climbed once more onto the crate. He would have to stretch his arm to the limit to make sure the cylinder got wedged under and across the bars. Balanced on the crate, he reached for the skylight, straining, the cylinder at his fingertips. . . . Then, without warning, with a sudden splintering crash, the crate collapsed under him. As he fell, the cylinder slipped from his grasp. When he looked up from the floor, he saw that it had been drawn through the bars and had disappeared.

He put on the remnants of his shirt, and his jacket, and sank to the floor in despair. With the kite loose, the message he'd written would help no one. FROM LARRY SETON. TELL POLICE. DON'T BREAK STRING. Nobody would find him on that information. It had all been in vain.

Superintendent Grant, in charge of the Seton kidnapping case, was in his office with Larry Seton's father. He had just seen the letter that had arrived from Larry that morning. Now he and Seton were discussing what action to take. Seton, gray with anxiety and sleeplessness, wanted to pay the ransom and keep the police out of it. Grant wanted to set a trap. They were still arguing when Sergeant Ellis entered.

"This has just been brought in, sir. Found in North London—Primrose Hill."

The sergeant put a kite on the table. There was a short length of twine, about twenty feet, attached to it, with a frayed end where the string had snapped.

Grant read the message, fingered the black lettering, examined the fabric. "Could be another hoax," he said doubtfully. He'd already been led off on one false scent.

Seton shook his head. "It's genuine—I'm sure of it." His voice had an edge of excitement. "Larry and I used to make kites like this when he was a lad. We were pretty expert—and he's remembered the model. The proportions are the same, the shape's right. I'm as sure he made it as though he'd put his signature on it."

"I see." Grant grew brisk. "Where exactly was it found, Sergeant?"

"Hanging down over a window at twelve Lucy Street—a boarding house. Chap living there—name of Forbes—found it this morning and dropped it in at his local station."

"We might be able to find the rest of the string and trace it back," Seton said eagerly. "It might lead us to Larry . . ."

Grant nodded. "Let's go."

The Superintendent studied the upper part of 12 Lucy Street through binoculars. Presently he gave a grunt. "I can see it. It's hanging from the gutter—looks as though it goes over the top of the house. Let's try the next street."

They drove round and quickly picked up the trail again. From the house the string crossed the street at rooftop level. With many detours they continued to follow its route. In several places it was broken and they had to cast about for the next piece. Twice they were helped by the sight of scraps of white material attached to it.

They traced it over buildings, over the branches of a tree, across a coal yard, between two coupled coal cars on a rusty railroad track, past a group of men preparing to unload the first car, on over a factory roof. Then, when hope was rising fast, they came upon a cardboard cylinder hanging from a street light, with broken twine attached. Beyond, there was nothing.

"Larry must have let it go," Seton said, with deep dejection.

Grant nodded. "Maybe he was interrupted before he could make it fast. Bad luck. Still, we've got something to work on."

He returned to the police car and radioed urgent instructions.

It took a squad of policemen and a fire-department truck more than two hours to collect all the bits of string they could find. Each one had to be numbered and labeled and its exact position marked on a street map before removal. There were eight breaks, all of them at street crossings—caused, no doubt, by passing traffic.

Back at New Scotland Yard, Grant had the pieces of string put together and measured. Allowing for the street gaps where sections had been carried away, the total length was almost 2000 feet. The recovery data, now plotted on a big wall map, showed that the line had fallen, with much bunching and many twists and turns, in a roughly northerly direction from Lucy Street. To the point where they had found the cardboard cylinder the beeline distance was 1200 feet. Somewhere beyond that, perhaps a long way beyond, was Larry.

*   *   *

Grant said, "You're the expert, Mr. Seton. What would you expect to happen to a kite flying on a two thousand-foot string when the end was released?"

Seton shook his head. "It's hard to say. Every kite behaves differently. The strength and consistency of the wind would clearly be a big factor. The weight of the string would be another. In general, if there was a good wind I'd expect the kite to shoot up rapidly for a short distance, lifting the string with it. Then it would begin to fall, fluttering down, diving and looping, making a good deal of leeway with the wind and carrying the string with it. To find out what this kite did, one would have to fly it experimentally in exactly the same weather conditions—and that's obviously impossible."

"We don't even know when the kite was released," Sergeant Ellis said.

Grant frowned. "What time was it found?"

"One o'clock this morning, sir. That was the time Forbes arrived home from a party. He got into bed and then he heard a tapping on the window. It annoyed him, so he went to see what was causing it, found the kite dangling, and yanked it in. He didn't put on a light, so he didn't see what was written on it till this morning . . . Anyway, he was sure it was one o'clock when he found it."

"Then just before one o'clock is the latest time it could have been released," Grant said. "Now what about the earliest time?"

"Well, Forbes said it wasn't there when he left for work yesterday morning, or he'd have seen it dangling."

"So it was released some time between, say, eight o'clock yesterday morning and one o'clock this morning. Seventeen hours . . . I wonder if the Met people can help us."

Grant was on the phone for some time, making notes as the Met man talked. His expression grew gloomier as he wrote.

"Not much help, I'm afraid," he said, as he hung up. "What you might call typical English weather. The wind yesterday morning was southwesterly, force five. In the afternoon it veered through northwest to north, dropping to force three. At night a narrow ridge of high pressure crossed London and the wind was northeasterly, force two at first, increasing to force three. Then in the early morning it backed again to northwesterly, force two."

"So we're no further forward," Seton said. "The kite was obviously released when the wind was in the northern quadrant—but which bit of the quadrant, and at what force?"

"If only there was some way of narrowing down the time," Grant said. He sat silent for a while. Then a speculative look crept into his face. "Those coal cars that were being unloaded—I wonder . . ."

Once more he reached for the telephone.

*   *   *

This time, when he hung up, his expression was jubilant. "A long shot—but it worked. Those two coal cars were shunted in just after ten o'clock last night—and the string fell between them. So now we know the kite was released between ten o'clock and one. I think I'll have another word with the Met office."

He made more notes as he repeated the information for the others to hear. "Ridge of high pressure—yes. Wind northeasterly force three up to five thousand feet throughout the period . . . Wind steady, not gusty . . . Now tell me, is there any place nearby where those conditions are being repeated at this moment? . . . Ridge has moved on—I see . . . Yorkshire? What part of Yorkshire? . . . Anywhere in the East Riding. And for how long? . . . About four hours." Grant glanced at his watch. "Thanks a lot."

He hung up. "Right," he said. "Let's go to Yorkshire and fly a kite."

Just under three hours later, an Army helicopter set down the police party on a disused airfield a few miles inland from the Yorkshire coast. A cool but gentle breeze was blowing steadily from the northeast. The sky was clear.

Grant positioned his men and Seton put the kite up. It rose quickly and smoothly as the knotted twine was let out. In a few minutes Seton was left with the bare cylinder. For a moment he held on. The kite was almost stationary, a mere dot against the blue.

"Right, let her go," Grant said.

Seton released the cardboard cylinder. It shot about fifty feet into the air, then drifted away out of sight as the kite hesitated, began to dive, turned and twisted, and slowly fluttered to earth.

A distant watcher signaled where the kite had fallen and the police got to work, checking the distance from release point to impact point, and the direction. Grant noted the results in his book. The kite had fallen 2250 feet from the point of release, on a magnetic bearing of 215 degrees.

Back at the Yard in the early evening Grant drew a circle on the wall map—2250 feet from 12 Lucy Street, on the reverse compass bearing.

"Well, that should be it," he said. "Somewhere in there. Now what kind of place are we going to look for?"

"A pretty high building," Seton said. "With some sort of exit to a roof, I should think, or I can't see how Larry could have got the kite up."

"Probably not a private dwelling," Sergeant Ellis added. "Kidnappers wouldn't risk keeping anyone shut up where there were other people around—particularly after all the publicity there's been. These villains usually hide out in vacant premises—empty warehouses, garages, that sort of thing."

Grant nodded. "I was thinking the same. An industrial building of some sort. I've just had the lab report on the substance used for the message on the kite. It's soot . . . Right, let's go."

The circle, they found, enclosed an area of dingy tenement buildings, a few factories, a scrap-metal dump, and a surprising amount of waste ground. Only the occasional new housing units relieved the squalor.

Grant divided his force into groups, each with a walkie-talkie, and allotted them streets. Every building of the slightest interest was to be reported on and discussed.

Within the circle itself they found nothing. Grant widened the field of search to take in the surrounding streets. It was almost dusk when Sergeant Ellis suddenly exclaimed, "How about that, sir?"

Grant looked ahead at the building. A blackened sign on the wall read: "Oakley Furniture Company. Depository and Repairs." It was a tall building, Victorian Gothic with a kind of tower at one end.

As they drew nearer, Grant saw that it was in fact only the skeleton of a building. Fire had gutted it. Notices above the corrugated iron fence enclosing the site warned: "Danger, keep out." But not everyone had kept out, for two of the corrugated sheets had been forced apart, leaving a two-foot gap.

Cautiously Grant led the way through the gap. He saw at once that not all the building had been destroyed. At the tower end there was a flight of stone steps, intact. They climbed. Soot lay thickly everywhere—soot from the fire.

Through a broken door on the first landing they saw junk, broken furniture, black and abandoned stores. Tensley Grant pointed—to a dirty spool of twine. "Used for furniture repairs," he said softly. "This is it."

They came to a closed door. Voices were audible from inside. Superintendent Grant gently tried the door. It opened a fraction. Sergeant Ellis moved quietly up beside him.

"Right," Grant said, and they burst in. Two men were playing cards on the floor by candlelight. They sprang up.

"Okay," Grant said, "take it easy. We're the police. Where is he?"

The thin man with the vicious little eyes gave an involuntary glance upward. Seton shouted, "Larry!"—and made for the ladder.

DANGER AT DEERFAWN
by DOROTHY B. HUGHES

Dorian said, "Tomorrow we go to Deerfawn Manor."

"Not me," said Jix. Inelegantly when you figure we were in Stratford-upon-Avon, Shakespeare's home town. But then Shakespeare was a great one for the vernacular himself.

"Not me," I echoed also ungrammatically, thankful that Jix at last had taken a stand against his sister's youthful vigor. When I, an assistant-assistant professor of drama from the unsuccessful side of the family, had greedily clutched at the gift horse of a summer in England keeping an eye on my young Hunter cousins, I hadn't considered that Twenty-seven doesn't have the bottomless pit of vitality of Nineteen and Twenty-two.

"And may I ask why not?" Dorian set her elbows on the table, almost but not quite bowling over our mugs of ale. The oaken tables at The Mace and Swan, an old Tudor black-and-white, timber-and-brick pub on Sheep Street, slanted in a Cotswolds downhill.

If Dorian had her way we wouldn't miss one Roman clump of stones, one Saxon antic column, one eroded Norman tympanum, nor one field or hall where the Edwards and Henrys and Charleses might have stopped to rest their horses and yeomen in that order. She'd been mesmerized last term by a fair-haired Briton who was giving a course in English history at Miss Waverly's Finishing School for Young Ladies—now called, in reverse snobbery, Waverly Junior College.

"I'm tired," I said. "My feet hurt. Tomorrow I plan to do nothing more strenuous than recline by the banks by the Avon and commune with the swans."

"And you?" Dorian's gray eyes stoned her brother.

"I'm up to here with manor houses," murmured Jix, his eyes on the touring South Carolina girl several tables away—the one who looked like a strawberry ice-cream cone, not the one who looked like a flute.

"Then I'll go alone." It was all of eight miles to Deerfawn. But Dorian was of an age where for status a girl must have males in tow, if only a big brother and an aging cousin. "And you can forget about the Triumph."

Jix had hire-purchased a snazzy red Triumph convertible in London. The deal was one of those with the privilege of applying the payments on full purchase later. Jix wanted it for keeps. Dorian had a way with their father. But Jix had to toe the line for her support; this tour was Dorian's party, her graduation gift.

Without removing his eyes from South Carolina, Jix agreed, "Okay, okay, I'll go." If he hadn't been wearing that particularly noxious brown-and-mustard hound's-tooth jacket he'd bought in Cambridge, he'd probably have been invited South before now.

Dorian's eyes traveled thoughtfully to Brummel Coombe, two tables away. In The Mace and Swan, two tables removed was close enough for me, in an absent-minded gesture, to have hoisted the young English squire's mug as easily as my own. Ignoring the intervening table, Dorian addressed Brummel, more or less publicly, "Why don't you join us tomorrow?"

He couldn't come out with a final, "No, thank you"—he was too well-bred for that. Brummel was Upper-U, from the crown of his smooth flaxen head to his well-rubbed, handmade London shoes.

What he said was, in that inimitable, gentle British way, "Thank you very much, but I'm afraid you'd be a bit crowded." We had given him a lift from the Theatre last night; we were all stopping at The Oak and Swan, an old Tudor black-and-white, timber-and-brick Inn, likewise on Sheep Street.

"There'll be plenty of room." Dorian tried to keep her voice as quiet and unimpassioned as his but I could detect the victory in it. "Kell isn't going."

"That's right," I said to his questioning expression. "I'm going to take it easy tomorrow."

Brummel smiled on Dorian. You'd think from that smile he'd be as enchanted to go touring with her as vice versa. "If there's room—" He broke off with something like alarm. "Where's Clara?"

The flute answered him. "She said she was going down to the Sweet-potato." Because of the size of The Mace and Swan, anybody's business was everybody's.

Before her words were half piped, Brummel pushed away from his chair, and mumbling something like, "Excuse me one moment," was away.

That Brummel should be smitten with Clara was beyond comprehension. Yet never willingly did he let her out of his sight. Touring German girls we'd previously encountered were scrubbed and polished as by laundry soap and whetstone. Not Clara. Her streaky blond hair hung unwashed and uncombed, now over one shoulder, now another, and her yellow pallor was heightened by smudges of green eye-shadow and a smear of pink lipstick. The only outfit she'd ever been seen wearing was a man's black sweater which hung to her knees, and slacks which might have once been rose colored but were now a gritty red. Even Jix, who had not reached the age of discrimination if a female was under thirty, couldn't stomach careless

Clara. While Brummel, the tweed-and-flannels, best-public-school lamb, followed her as if she were Mary of the children's nursery rhyme.

"Well," Dorian breathed, as the door closed behind him.

I said callously, "Give up, Dorian, it's no good."

"And let her take over?" Sometimes in Dorian, there was resemblance to Medea. "Come on."

"Not me," Jix echoed himself. Strawberry Ice Cream was gazing at him drippingly, I thought, Tom Swiftly.

Dorian didn't wait for more palaver. I caught up with her halfway down the block. "Do you think you're being quite smart?" I asked. "You'll never get anywhere chasing after him. Men don't like it." This hadn't been true since Victorian times but we men kept saying it.

"I am not chasing after him," Dorian retorted loftily. "I merely want to tell him what time we're leaving in the morning. I don't intend to sit up swilling ale all night like you and Jix."

By then we'd reached the Sweetpotato caff, a British version of an American jukebox joint, complete with blaring Elvis Presley records. Definitely non-Tudor, it was enormously popular with Stratford's younger set and with haversack tourists. The size of the Sweetpotato made The Mace and Swan seem spacious, and the saturation point had been reached before our arrival.

Clara's tour was there in numbers, including the bearded wonder she hung on when she could escape Brummel's attention. This was a dour character whose eyeglasses were usually focused on the pen scratches he made in a small black notebook. Neither Clara nor Brummel was present.

We started back to the pub. Halfway along the block, Dorian let out a muted pang. "Look!"

Across the street, just emerging from the close of The Oak and Swan, were the elusive two. Dorian dug her talons into my arm, indicating we were to give the appearance of having sauntered out for a breath of chill, damp night air, but we were counterobserved.

"I say there, Dorian." Brummel didn't yell—English gentlemen don't yell. However, in the hush, his words were quite clear. He came slanting over, leaving Clara in the shadows of the gateway. As he fell in with us, he said, "I'm sorry I had to run out like that. I'd be delighted to go with you tomorrow." Any knucklehead not bemused by Anglophilia would know that he'd checked with Clara.

Because I was annoyed with the way he brushed off either girl at will, I spoke up. "Is Clara going to Deerfawn tomorrow too?"

"No, she's going to Leamington—" He caught his breath. "Did you say Deerfawn?" His face was a study in anxiety, apprehension, and any and all other synonyms for almost fright.

Dorian didn't notice. She was ahead, opening the door—she hadn't learned to wait for men to do the amenities. "Yes, we're doing Deerfawn Manor House in the morning. Is ten o'clock all right? We want to go on to the ruins of St. Orlgwulf's Abbey in the afternoon." Prattling, she led Brummel inside.

I don't know why I looked back toward the close. But I did. The deserted Clara was still there, an incongruously sad little ghost, clutching the shadows. Her dirt was erased by the darkness; only her pale face and hair were visible.

She wasn't my problem; Dorian was. I followed the others into the pub, shutting Clara away in the night. Jix had moved to the southern exposure in our absence. Brummel now had Jix's place and Dorian seemed to have given up the idea of retiring for the night. This made me the happy old fifth wheel. I could now go back to the Inn and get a decent night's sleep.

I was as bright at breakfast next morning as Jix was bleary. Dorian was her normal effervescent self; she didn't need sleep. We'd finished our canned fruit juice and corn flakes, our fried eggs and scarcely cooked bacon with warm tomato, our cold toast and pot of orange marmalade—the traditional English breakfast—and we were dallying over our milk-and-sugar tea when Brummel appeared in the dining room.

We exchanged good mornings and the inevitable weather data before he said shamefacedly, "I'm afraid I can't go with you today after all. Something has come up."

Dorian, after one unbelievably stricken blink, should have been recruited for the Stratford players—her consoling smile was that convincing. "I'm terribly sorry, Brummel. But if you can't, you can't. Maybe some other day."

You could tell he thought it was terribly decent of her to take it so well, and after a few more apologies, he backed away.

"Evidently Clara isn't going to the Spa today." I was sorry as soon as I'd said it. "Long as there's room, I think I'll go Deerfawning with you. I've recovered my youth."

"You can drive," Jix said morosely. He was stuck with the trip because he'd talked Strawberry Ice Cream into meeting him there. Even his cherished jacket failed to uplift him.

It was a blue-sky day, one of the few when we could let down the top of the convertible without bailing. Eight miles is longer in England than in the United States. Who wants to speed through lanes dappled darkly with tall woods, and greened with smooth meadows where the sheep graze in motionless pattern, wearing red badges on their haunches to distinguish them from the pale saffron stones? To augment our leisurely pace, whenever a crumbling rock pile appeared on the horizon we had to stop at the nearest lay-by while Dorian loped back to investigate its import.

It was, therefore, close to eleven when we reached the gatehouse of Deerfawn Manor. The gatekeeper was on hand to collect our two-and-sixes and to present us with pink admission tickets from a wheel such as we used to have in movie houses before automation. We drove on up the cobbled half mile to the courtyard in the rear of the great Georgian house.

Deerfawn was not a National Trust—it wasn't that ancient. But the handbills at the desk of The Oak and Swan had built up a pretty picture of its fine carved staircase, its priceless library, its art masterpieces, and of the marble Folly in its woods, the only remnant of the original manor not destroyed in the Civil War. The English had a Civil War too. There were also peacocks—there were always peacocks—and formal gardens. Although the information had surely been compiled by the Marquis of Deerfawn, who just as surely had opened his house to the public to help pay his taxes, it might turn out to be of more interest than some of the shabby great houses we'd seen. For one thing, there were two authenticated paintings by Rubens and six family portraits by Van Dyck.

There was the usual sign pointing to the west basement where would be found the usual tearoom and curio and postcard counter. This was our first stop—as Jix demanded, to insure his life, coffee with a lacing of aspirin. Dorian chafed and wrote two postcards to her two best friends at home, until Jix could navigate again. She then insisted that we return outdoors and make a proper entrance.

Jix said, "I'll shuck my coat and follow you." From where we'd parked the car we could look down the avenue and see if the coach tour was approaching. I wrote off Jix and his delaying tactics for the rest of the morning.

All in all, Deerfawn Manor House wasn't bad. It wasn't great like Warwick Castle—ah, Warwick! where I'd learned what the Biblical word "covet" truly means—but it wasn't impossibly tawdry like some attractions which shall remain nameless. We went unguided, yet not unobserved. There were guardians of the treasures stationed in each room to make sure filching was out of style.

It was past one o'clock when we again descended the carved staircase to the entrance hall.

"Now we'll do the gardens," Dorian announced.

"Hadn't we better have a bite to eat first?" I'd become as English as the English; despite the breakfast spread, I was ready for another meal.

"Later," Dorian stated.

The English are absolutely mad for gardens. As most of the tours this time of year were overwhelmingly composed of English-speakers, the formal layout surrounding the Manor was already overpopulated with ritual flower-print dresses and flat tweed caps.

One look and Dorian decided, "We'll come back. After we visit the Folly."

She headed for the footpath into the deep woods, just past the handmade wooden sign: *To the Folly*. Almost immediately the path became a narrow aperture leading into far deeper woods, the kind where the sun never penetrates the undergrowth of fern. The trees actually were as tall as cathedrals. Where the bark wasn't twined with ivy, it was deeply coated with lichen.

After a more than sufficient spell of stumbling and edging onward, I ventured, "I think we took the wrong path."

"How could we?" Dorian asked, but not with her usual assurance. "The sign pointed this way. You saw it."

"It could have been turned the wrong way," I suggested half-heartedly.

At that moment a strangled cry rose from somewhere in the density. Dorian bashed up quick against my quaking shoulder. And then I remembered. "Those damn peacocks!"

She managed a shaky grin and was herself again. She crashed on and before long called back to my plodding rearguard, "There's daylight ahead. This must be it."

Hopelessly, I hoped so. I was so hungry I was ready to turn poacher at sight of game. One thing came clear in our meandering: the reason Cromwell hadn't destroyed the Folly. He couldn't find it.

Ahead there was indication of a clearing of some sort. Dorian had disappeared off the path into it. I heard her cry out and I picked up speed. The cry hadn't been of delight but of disaster.

The open space was hardly bigger than a table top. Standing in it, facing each other, were Dorian and Brummel. He wasn't the young aristocrat of The Oak and Swan. He wore the leather apron and the mudsplattered boots of the Manor's outdoor staff.

His face was the color of rain and absolutely vacant of any expression. It took me that long to see what was at his feet. An oversized black sweater, dirty rose-colored pants, and flowing yellow hair. In Brummel's right hand there was a big rock. Its smooth surface was discolored.

"Oh, no," Dorian was whimpering.

My entrance released Brummel from shock. "You, too?"

Dorian also came to life. But she didn't run away. She ran toward him. "Come on. We've got to get you out of here."

He half stumbled as she tugged at him, then stoutly released himself and stood away. "Wait," he said. "I must—"

We all heard the suspicious rustle of leaves. It could have been some Cromwellian spy creeping up on us.

"One moment," Brummel whispered. He actually knelt and with quick fingers explored the crumpled body. He took something from beneath the sweater, palming the object into his apron pocket before we could see what it was. "This way," he said under his breath, absently picking up the weapon before he moved.

He set off into what looked like impenetrable forest but which shortly emerged into a path leading up a hill. Don't ask my why, like a dumb sheep, I followed a red-handed killer. Perhaps at the time it seemed better than being lost in the woods with no chocolate bar. As for Dorian, she doubtless had absolved him from guilt the moment she recognized the victim. Like most women, Dorian has a bloodthirsty streak where rivals are concerned.

When the going was easier, I suggested, "Hadn't you better get rid of that rock?" It was making me nervous.

"What rock?" he said, puzzled, and then realized he was still holding it. "Oh, the rock," he said vaguely. "Yes. Yes, I should, I presume."

He gestured us off the path, then advanced a few yards, pondered, and selected a tree no different from any other of the hundred trees in the forest. Carefully he tucked the rock under the ferns there. It didn't seem my place to point out that his fingerprints might be all over it. Possibly it wouldn't turn up for some three hundred years, and the Dorians of that day would believe the bloodstains were made in the first Danish invasion.

Brummel seemed quite relieved to be rid of it. "Come along now," he said. "We must hurry." He was leading us not back to our hillside path but through and around the woods in what seemed a circular pattern. If Dorian wasn't uneasy, I was ashamed to be. And shortly there lay the enormous Manor House below.

Brummel paused only for a few breaths, looking down on the back court where the cars and coaches were parked. In sight were only a couple of drivers having a gossip over their cigarettes. The red shine of our Triumph was like a beacon.

Brummel said to Dorian, "You and Kell won't have any difficulty getting away. Don't talk to anyone—just go."

"But you're the one who has to get away," Dorian cried out, remembering to keep it a muted cry.

He shook his head. "I can't."

Of course he couldn't: he'd have to hide the body first.

Dorian thought quickly. "We can't either. We can't go off and leave Jix without a ride."

"I'll take care of Jix! Please. Hurry."

I was the practical one. "How do we get to the car? Make like birds or toboggans?"

"I'll lead you down," Brummel said, "but once we're in the court, walk over, get in your car, and take off. Fast." He didn't wait for Dorian to give him further argument. He set off on a transverse, and somehow or other we all managed to get down to the ditch below and start clambering up its slope into the courtyard.

We almost had it made when what can only be described as a hue-and-cry began. There were uniformed attendants legging out of every door and it didn't take someone of normal I.Q. to realize that the body had been discovered.

Under his breath, Brummel muttered, "That's torn it. Come on."

We fled to the Triumph and he squeezed in without the usual preliminary of ladies first. Dorian said, "You drive, Kell," and slid in beside him. The engine caught and we were headed down the drive before anyone could stop us. Not that anyone tried.

"Take off that silly costume," Dorian ordered, "And put on Jix's coat."

Brummel ducked out of the leather apron and stuffed it under the seat while Dorian helped envelop him in Jix's coat of too many colors. As a disguise is wasn't what I'd have chosen.

I kept a nice pace to the gate, not too fast, and returned the gatehouse attendant's friendly salute. The word hadn't reached him yet.

In the lane I picked up speed. "To Stratford?"

"Yes," Brummel said.

By this time we were approaching the turn into the Stratford road—approaching it, I suddenly observed, much too rapidly. I removed my foot entirely from the gas pedal. I didn't want to compound our troubles by crashing into the police car which was blocking the intersection.

Brummel sighed and Dorian, for once, said nothing. I braked, and a young constable strolled over to my side of the car. The bobbies in their helmets and dark formal uniforms somehow look unreal in the country; they belong in London.

"Good afternoon," he said pleasantly. "You've come from Deerfawn Manor?"

There was no other place we could have come from unless we'd been haring across the meadows, and he knew it.

I said meekly, "Yes, sir."

"I'm afraid I'll have to ask you to go back."

"But why?" Dorian asked with outraged innocence.

"There's been a bit of trouble, Miss," he said. "No one is to leave until the Chief Constable arrives."

There was no point to arguing, particularly with Brummel sitting there trying to look unperturbed and, in that dreadful coat, succeeding in looking like some ghastly Teddy boy. Back we crawled to Deerfawn Manor to join the now thronged courtyard.

We didn't need a guide to identify the nationalities of the tourists. The Americans were the indignant ones, the Continentals the wary, and the British the ones who accepted matters as if nothing untoward had happened. The only exceptions were Jix and his South Carolinian babe—they didn't mind the delay a bit. I noted that all of Clara's tour were on hand, including her special boyfriend. He was trying to find the reason for this procedure in his guide book.

Brummel took off Jix's coat, placed it on the seat, and got out of the car. A member of the Manor staff was trotting toward him. He tried to cut away but the man planted himself head on. "I'm terribly sorry, your Lordship. It seems a girl's body has been found in our woods." The words came out distinctly in spite of the strong country accent.

Your Lordship. Our Brummel was the Marquis of Deerfawn! With my mouth dropped witlessly, I looked toward Dorian. Her mouth was also cavernous, but mercifully silent.

Brummel simulated astonishment. "A girl's body?"

"Yes, your Lordship." The servitor volunteered, "It would seem to be one of the trippers, sir."

"Is Colonel Whitten in charge?"

"He has been notified. He hasn't yet arrived."

Brummel gave some inaudible directions and the man took off at a brisk pace, away from the stone steps where the constabulary were gathered. Still ignoring us, Brummel strode toward them.

"Well," I uttered.

"Well what?" Dorian bristled. "Don't just stand there. Come on." She followed Brummel and I followed her.

By then he was listening with gravity to what the police had to tell him. Meantime, his eyes were searching frantically, or as near to frantically as a marquis's eyes could, the sinuous mass in the court. His frenzy changed to resignation as the police parted the crowd to permit the entrance of a large black Humber. From it dismounted what had to be Colonel Whitten, Chief Constable of the shire. His mustaches were as long as a soliloquy. But he was as deferent to Brummel as the old retainer had been.

An inspection post was being set up and the English, sure enough, formed the inevitable queue. The foreigners had no choice but to join it. When in Rome. As Dorian and I were up front, our turn came quickly. However, before I could give name, address, and passport number to the officer at the table, Brummel was saying, "These are friends of mine, Colonel Whitten. I can assure you they know nothing about this affair."

"All we know," said Dorian in a sweet, clear voice, "is that Brummel—his Lordship—couldn't possibly have killed Clara."

If she'd said she was carrying a nuclear warhead in her handbag, she couldn't have caused more consternation. I wasn't the only one whose mouth could drop witlessly—every policeman in the vicinity was doing it. Brummel looked as if he wanted to weep.

"Because," Dorian appeared not to notice any reaction, "she was already dead when he got there."

"You saw the body? You know who this girl was?" It wasn't the speechless Colonel Whitten but an intelligent looking bobby who put the question.

"Of course we knew her. She was the German girl who's been in Stratford all week."

"I can explain," Brummel said without conviction, eyeing the crowd as if trying to find an escape route through it.

"My cousin and I heard her death cry," Dorian orated melodramatically, dragging me into it, "before his Lordship found her."

The Germans who understood some English were falling to pieces. Loudly and tearfully.

"The reason he had that bloody rock—excuse me, but it was bloody—in his hands," Dorian carried on with simple devastation, "was that he knew it must be the murder weapon and he wanted to preserve the evidence for—"

At that moment I heard Jix's voice above all other sounds. A good loud indignant American voice. "What's that guy doing in my coat?"

The queue swayed in the direction of Jix's bellow. We all saw a figure in German shorts and Jix's hound's-tooth jacket racing toward the woods.

"He mustn't get away," Brummel warned as he started after him. The police followed like Keystone Cops. Need I say that I, following Dorian, brought up the usual rear?

But Jix was well ahead in the chase. It was he who brought down the man before the others caught up, and wrestled the jacket off of him.

The thief, shouting and gesticulating in outraged German, was none other than Clara's dour friend, the black-notebook writer. Brummel waited until the German gulped for breath, then said in his most quiet way, "It's no good, Lengel. And it wasn't hidden in that coat."

On the outskirts of our panting group a rather tall man in a gray suit asked calmly, "What's going on here?"

Brummel's expression melted into enormous relief. "What took you so long, Freddie?" He indicated the captive. "This is your man. He gave himself away."

The police recognized Freddie as important. They parted to let him into the inner circle.

Distaste touched Freddie's mouth as he regarded the prisoner. "He didn't get away with anything?"

"With your men on guard? Not half," Brummel assured him. "Besides, he's only an advance man, Freddie. Clara was always sure of that. She nipped the notebook, gave me the nod—" His look saddened. "Evidently he missed it before I could get to her. He got to her first."

Freddie took a step toward the struggling Lengel.

"He doesn't have it," Brummel said. "It seems these Americans—" So much for the earlier friendship he'd protested for us. "—blundered on the meeting place before he had a chance to search the body."

"You have it?" Freddie relaxed.

"I found it." Brummel couldn't resist a gibe at the German. "He thought I'd hidden it in that coat I was wearing."

"You were wearing—" Freddie's calm faltered at sight of the coat on Jix's arm.

"As a disguise," Brummel said quickly. "I wanted to get the notebook to you before it became police property. Colonel Whitten—"

Colonel Whitten hadn't made the run. He could be seen in the distance at stone-step headquarters, puffing nonchalantly on his pipe.

"He does rather talk to reporters," Brummel regretted. "I was hoping we could continue to keep our plans private."

Freddie nodded agreement. "Let me have it."

"It's wedged under the seat of their car." Brummel gave our group the faintest nod. "The little red one."

Freddie took off at a sprint. Brummel loped behind. All strangers, and that included us, were thereupon herded down the hill by the police and pointed to the Manor gates. Dorian was determined not to leave but she had stupidly destroyed whatever influence she might have had with the Marquis of Deerfawn. Without so much as a backward glance, the marquis and Freddie were now moving away from our car, the notebook retrieved.

We drove single file back to Stratford. Even Dorian had no stomach for St. Orlgwulf's Eighth Century disasters after first-hand exposure to Twentieth Century violence. She spent the remainder of the afternoon on the banks of the Avon with me, inventing one far-fetched spy thriller after another to explain what had happened. Jix was again off somewhere with his fancy jacket and southern accent.

Dorian continued to fantasticate at The Mace and Swan that night until unexpectedly Brummel appeared at our table.

"May I sit down with you?" he asked. If he hadn't, Dorian would have yanked him into the empty chair. "I do want to apologize for any inconvenience I may have caused you today."

"They were spies, weren't they?" Dorian burst out.

"Oh, no," Brummel said, for a moment giving her that faintly alarmed glance which Britons reserve for nutty Americans. "They were after the paintings."

This was the summer of increasing thievery of art masterpieces. Dorian was disappointed. The stories she'd dreamed up in her own little head were much wilder and much more exciting.

"Freddie is head of the London branch of Interpol. They had a tip that

Deerfawn was the next target. He asked me to help out. Working with Clara."

"Clara was an operative?" I goggled.

"She was good, wasn't she?" His somber face lighted. "The way she got herself up like a grisette."

"You mean—she wasn't really—," Dorian stammered.

"She was a lovely girl," Brummel said. Defendingly, not romantically. "A very clever girl. She got on the student tour that the gang was using as a cover and attached herself to Lengel." He shook his head. "We don't know if someone informed or if he suddenly realized that she wasn't as stupid as he thought her. But when she found out he was going to Deerfawn after telling her he was going to Leamington Spa, she knew she had to get the notebook as soon as she could. It has the plans for all the robbings in the Midlands. It's my fault she was killed." His emotion was too deep for display. "I didn't arrange carefully enough."

Dorian, possibly therapeutically, broke the silence. "I knew you didn't kill her."

Brummel came out of his shadows. "I'm afraid I panicked a bit when I saw you and Kell there. I'm rather new at this sort of thing. And I had to find that notebook." He turned and looked into Dorian's eyes, not half shy. "And I must say I wanted to get you away from there before you found out my connection with Deerfawn. I was afraid it might spoil things between us."

It didn't. During our last days in the Stratford country, Dorian and Brummel were as inseparable as Jix and South Carolina. This was a happy breather for me. I read Shakespeare by day and watched it by night. I'm as much of a nut on Shakespeare as Dorian is on ancient monuments. Oh, yes, the Folly sign had a habit of veering. Most people had sense enough to take the pebbled path to the right, not wander into untrammeled woods.

I also had plenty of time for thought those days. But I wasn't able to discuss certain peculiar aspects of the Deerfawn day until we were off on the road again, headed toward Shropshire. Without Jix—he would join us after Miss South Carolina moved on.

I asked Dorian flatly, "What were you trying to do to Brummel, hang him? Telling the police all that stuff."

"Of course not!" she replied with indignation. "I knew he wasn't a killer, not even when I first saw him bending over the body with that bloody rock. Before you got there. He isn't the type."

A lecture on criminal types would have made no dent at that moment. She was on her high white horse with banners flying. "But if he was guilty," she proclaimed, "I wasn't going to let him get away with doing Clara in, just because of all that bow-and-scrape-your-Lordship stuff."

For one split second I believed Dorian had recovered from Anglophilia.

And then she was blasting in my ear, "Stop the car! Stop the car!"

I wondered if in the side mirror she'd noted Brummel catching up with us a day early. No, it wasn't that. It was only another ragged clump of rocks rising out of the rolling green.

With a silent sigh I wheeled into the nearest lay-by and stopped the car.

THE MAN WHO UNDERSTOOD WOMEN

by A. H. Z. CARR

We were having lunch together, the four of us, and we started talking about women. Whately, Barker, and I agreed that Dr. Kinsey notwithstanding, women are enigmatic creatures, difficult for the male to comprehend. Whately told a story about his wife to prove it, then Barker and I told stories about our wives to prove it.

Milliken disagreed, as he always does. He is a bachelor, and he writes plays. When we told him that he did not know what he was talking about, he paid no attention.

"The trouble with you husbands," he said, "is that you allow yourselves to be bewildered by what your wives say to you. In my experience—let me finish—if a man listens to what a woman says, he's done for. But he can tell all he has to know about a woman just by looking at her."

He ignored a small crust of bread that Barker threw at him, and continued. "A woman's appearance gives her away every time. It enables you to tell what she has been doing and to predict what she will do. That is, it reveals all this to the discerning."

"Like you," said Whately, frankly sneering.

"Like me," agreed Milliken. "I suppose it's only natural that you fellows should regard women as mysterious. You're all married to wives much smarter than yourselves. But to one who observes carefully, thinks clearly, and has a reasonable amount of intuition, a woman's secret thoughts are exposed before she ever opens her mouth."

Barker said, "It's easy enough to talk."

"It isn't talk. Do you remember Kate Loring, the heroine of my last play?"

"You mean the one that closed the second week?" I said. There is no point in being subtle with Milliken.

"That has nothing to do with it. Everybody who saw the play was sure that I had known a woman like Kate Loring intimately at some time in my life. Because I understood her, felt her, I caught her essence. As a matter of fact, it wasn't the fault of the script that the play flopped. If Hogan, the producer, had only—"

"Stick to the point," said Whately, who is a lawyer.

"All right, then. Now actually, I never even met a woman like Kate Loring. But I saw her once, sitting at a distance of ten feet, in a bar. I studied her for a few minutes, and at the end of that time I knew her past, her future, her whole life, better than she knew it herself."

"Do you dare to say," Barker put in, "that you can look at *any* woman and deduce the facts of her private life just from her appearance?"

"That's what I have been telling you," Milliken said patiently. "I do not say that mine is a unique gift. With application, you could all do it. Even Bob here, if given time and help, might make a stab at it."

"Give us an example," Barker urged. "Take that woman who just came in. At the third table, with that tall man. She looks interesting. What can you tell us about her?"

For some time Milliken stared at the woman indicated. Neither she nor her escort noticed us. They were discussing the menu. Finally Milliken said, "Very well. She is a good subject—an unusual woman. I will take you step by step through the process, leaving out nothing, so you can see exactly how I do it."

He ordered another drink before going on. "That woman is intelligent and purposeful. She is unmarried. Although at one time in her life she was well off, she is now having a hard time making ends meet. A very hard time. Money, or the lack of it, has become almost an obsession with her." He held up his hand to prevent interruption.

"She is in love with that man, and he is with her. He, too, is poor. Now, at the age of thirty-three or thirty-four, she is still highly attractive. But she feels that her chances of the good life are ebbing. And she intends to marry another man, a wealthy man."

"Oh, now, really, Milliken!" exclaimed Barker.

"I've hardly begun," Milliken said. "Within the last few days she has returned from a long stay abroad. She was on the Mediterranean—probably North Africa, Algiers. The chances are that she met the man she intends to marry on that trip."

Whately caught my eye and shrugged. Milliken smiled grimly. "I see that you don't believe me. Let me tell you something else. Her true lover, the man with her now, does not yet know her intention. Soon—perhaps at this very luncheon—she will break the news to him. She will do it even at the expense of her self-respect. For money, as I have said, is now the dominating force of her life. She will sacrifice everything for financial security."

We looked at the woman, and Milliken lowered his voice. "Even now, while she laughs gaily at her companion's remarks, she is considering how best to broach the subject. If we sit here long enough we will witness high drama—the shattering of a sincere love on the shoals of poverty."

He paused for effect and breath. After a short silence Whately said flatly, "Prove it."

"I shall," said Milliken. "Take first the question of intelligence. Observe the broad, high, well-developed forehead and the alert, wide-open eyes— her whole expression, animated yet controlled. These are the universal marks of a good mind. Just as the eyebrows, the set of the mouth, and the resolute chin indicate firmness of character."

This seemed reasonable—or possible—so we said nothing.

"Glance at her hands, feet, ankles, wrists. Slender and shapely, the bones solid but unobtrusive, the limbs rounded. Note the fine texture of her hair. And then her poise, the ease of her manner, her self-assurance, her great natural dignity. These are signs of breeding which even you fellows should be able to recognize."

"There's nothing remarkable about that," Whately said. "I put her down for an intelligent, well-bred woman myself."

"Good. You're coming along," Milliken replied. "How would you deduce that her family was once well-to-do?"

"You're doing this," said Whately, a certain slyness in his tone.

Milliken smiled. "Well, then, observe her clothes. In admirable taste. Expensive. That hat, that dress, those shoes come from Paris."

"How do you know that?" I demanded.

Milliken looked pained. "Surely it is obvious." If he had added, "my dear Watson," I should have kicked him then and there—but he had sense enough to refrain. "The dress is the clue. Fabrics like that are simply not woven in this country. And then, notice the restrained fullness in the upper arm and the subtle molding of the material around the bust. Only Balenciaga or Molyneux gets that effect. As for the hat, it bears the stamp of the Faubourg St. Honoré all over it. Even our smartest shops never quite achieve the quality of excitement that is added by that twist of the crown. The shoes, too, are definitely French. American designers haven't yet adopted that two-way curve of the instep."

None of us felt qualified to argue these points. Whately said, "If her clothes come from Paris, wouldn't that signify she is well off?"

"Ha!" said Milliken. "That's just where the amateur goes wrong. Instead of studying essential details, you jump at conclusions. Of course the clothes are expensive—I said so. But—and mark this—they are far from new. Look carefully, and you can see a slight giving at the seam of the sleeve of her cloth coat. And the shoes, although elegant, are creased by use. The purse is relatively cheap and certainly outmoded. No woman would spoil the whole effect of an ensemble with such a purse if she could afford a finer one. What must we deduce therefore? When she buys clothes, she buys good ones, but she has few. Once she had money enough to indulge expensive tastes. Now, lacking money, she still tries to indulge those tastes."

"You're just guessing," Whately objected. "Her clothes don't necessarily signify her own taste. She may not have selected them herself. Somebody may have given them to her."

"Whately, you're not thinking. Look at that aristocratic, proud face. This is no lady's maid, no poor companion, no impoverished relative, to accept hand-me-downs."

"Well, maybe a man——," Whately began.

"You're suggesting that she is someone's mistress? A kept woman?"

"Why not? There are such women—or haven't you heard?"

"It is your idea that this woman would go into a shop with a man and let *him* pick out her clothes? Good heavens, is this the legal mind in action? Use your head, man! Her refusal to pluck her eyebrows, her subtle use of cosmetics—does that suggest a woman who depends on the fancy of a man for support? The kept woman invariably tries to look feminine and fascinating. She cannot resist the little superficial touches that arrest most masculine eyes—the exaggeration of curves, the vivid color. But not this woman, gentlemen. There can be absolutely no doubt that those clothes were selected by a woman of taste—selected to please herself."

Whately cleared his throat and for a moment looked combative; but he said nothing. I took up the gauntlet. "You still haven't convinced me," I said, "that she is poor. Just because she is wearing an old dress and coat at this moment—"

"There's other evidence. I call your attention to her hair where it shows under her hat. Obviously her natural shade, that brown—and not really flattering. If it were a shade lighter, a dark blond, the effect would be ravishing—and she must know it. Moreover, there's her hairdo. That bun in the back does nothing for her. She certainly would not wear it that way if she could afford a first-class hairdresser."

I had to admit that this did indeed look like drastic economy. "Even so," I contended, "that doesn't mean money is an obsession with her, as you claimed."

"Then you missed the expression on her face when that stout overdressed woman across the room came in. If you had seen our subject's lips tighten when she glanced at that mink coat, you would know what I mean when I speak of an obsession. What was she envying, if not five thousand dollars' worth of mink? Here we have a poised, controlled, proud woman. When she allows such an expression to appear on her face for such a reason, you may be sure that the longing for money has sunk deep into her heart."

"All that may be so," said Barker. "But what I want to know is how you deduced the love affair you spoke of."

Milliken nodded. "Did you get a good look at our lady's escort before he sat down? A fine-looking man. Generous, open features. Not an acquisitive nature. Look at his hands—strong, bony fingers. The hands of an artist —a musician, perhaps, or a painter. But not a 'successful' man. He is close to forty—an age when men who have achieved success wear the stamp of it. But his eyes have a worried look, and his clothes are cheap and ready-made."

"How do you know they're ready-made?" I said, thinking of my own, which were.

"The shoulders are a dead give-away. Those wrinkles at the seams— characteristic of the mass-produced suit, after it has been worn a while. That man is hard up, depend on it."

"Then what's he doing taking her to a restaurant like this?" Whately demanded.

"Ah, there is a good point. Under what conditions does a man strain his purse for a woman? He will do it if he loves her—and especially if it is their first meeting after a long separation. But did you notice that she refused a cocktail? And that he attempted to insist? The inference is clear. She likes a cocktail, he knows it, but she is sparing his pocketbook. And the meal she ordered—ravioli. Substantial and filling, but decidedly inexpensive. Isn't it obvious that he can't really afford an elaborate luncheon?"

"You said she loves him," Barker persisted. "Is that why you thought so —just because she refused a cocktail and ordered ravioli?"

Milliken shook his head. "Her eyes, Barker, her eyes. Surely you have seen love in a woman's face before. The tenderness of her smile tells us all. And he loves her, too. Twice he has surreptitiously touched her hand. He hardly takes his eyes from her face. Lovers, beyond a doubt."

"Maybe you're right," said Barker.

"Of course I'm right."

"But the other man—the rich one," Whately interjected. "Where does he come in? And how do you know she has just been abroad?"

"Start with her complexion," said Milliken. "That deep coat of tan. Where did she get it, in late November?"

"Sun lamp," I suggested.

"Nonsense. People who use sun lamps regularly have pale spots around the eyes, where they put the protective pads. Anyone can see that is no artificial tan."

"Florida?" said Barker.

"At this time of the year? Incredible. Besides, look at her gestures. She is an Anglo-Saxon type, but she uses her hands and shoulders freely. The chances are excellent that she picked up the habit of free gesticulation on the Mediterranean, as so many American women do. But that's not all. You see those two heavy silver bracelets with the exotic design?"

The woman and her companion were so absorbed in their conversation that they never noticed our surreptitious glances. "What about the bracelets?" I said.

"They are the kind of thing you get only in North Africa. The design is absolutely distinctive. And they are not cheap—not the stuff that is provided for the regular tourist trade. Those blue stones in the lower bangle are sapphires, I would swear. I have seen similar things in Marrakesh—there's a shop there that specializes in them."

"Somebody who has recently come back from there may have given them to her," Whately pointed out.

"One, perhaps," Milliken said. "But two? Besides, you will notice that the two bracelets are quite different in detail—and yet both are a perfect match for that dress. Put it all together and what do you have? For this woman to buy two such expensive pieces for herself, when she needs a new handbag, is altogether out of character. For any friend to have bought her two such carefully chosen bracelets, of the same type, is highly unlikely. Add the deep suntan—and can't you see it? She is strolling in Marrakesh, or possibly Algiers, with a friend. She sees the bracelets in a shop window, glinting in the sunlight, and stops to admire them. No woman could resist entering to inquire the price.

"Try to imagine it," Milliken went on, with the air of a visionary. "She looks at some bracelets, is tempted, but disturbed by the price. Finally she succumbs. Very well—she will buy one, the less expensive one. It will mean not buying the new handbag that she needs—but the urge is irresistible and the bracelet goes so perfectly with the dress. It is then that her friend picks up the other bracelet, the one with the sapphires, and insists on presenting her with it."

We all objected at once. "Sheer romancing," Whately growled.

"Not in the least," Milliken replied stoutly. "I admit that I have reconstructed this scene intuitively, rather than from wholly physical evidence. Still, it explains the facts—it explains them better than any other theory you can offer."

"But you're not consistent," I protested. "If this woman is poor, how could she have afforded a trip to Europe and North Africa?"

"My dear fellow," Milliken said, looking at me as if he were wearing a monocle; there are times when he imagines himself to be Lord Peter Wimsey. "Many people of small means manage to get to Europe. They save for it—or they receive a small inheritance—or they win the trip in a contest—or some wealthy aunt puts up the cash. Surely you don't expect me to give you every last detail of her finances. I will tell you, though, that she just got back."

"How do you know that?" I said.

"Again, a combination of things. The weather has been cloudy for weeks, yet her tan has not yet worn off. Even more important, look at her as she talks. The flow of her words, the animation of the man's response, the air of excitement around them. This is plainly their first meeting in a long while. But can you imagine that two people who are in love would let an unnecessary day go by before meeting? She has returned recently, very recently. She may have flown, but my guess is that she came in on the *Liberté*, which docked yesterday. Attractive women usually prefer a boat crossing."

"Still," I said, "I don't get this other man. It seems to me you have just rung him in without reason."

"A lovely woman on a trip abroad, and you do not see a man in the picture? Why, you could not keep men away from her! On a boat especially, a French boat, on her way to Paris, she would have a choice of ardent males within two days. And the man in this case is very likely a Frenchman. Here my reasoning may be a little tenuous, I admit. I judge from the quality of the sentiment in that bracelet, and the fact that it was bought in Algiers. A Frenchman might well have encouraged her to go there. I don't insist on the point, though. All I say is that there was a man, that he is wealthy, and that she has decided to marry him."

"That's all," said Whately, with heavy sarcasm.

"You doubt me? Then I take it that you did not notice the ring she wears on the third finger of her right hand. No, you cannot see it now. She has turned the stone inward. It is a beautiful cabochon emerald, which must have cost thousands. The man with her has been glancing at it curiously, even anxiously, and she has dropped her hand into her lap. She is fidgeting with the ring nervously, now."

Whately frowned. "What of it?"

"Man, man," Milliken sighed. "Don't you see? Her companion is too proud to ask her outright about the ring. But he has never seen it before. What must we conclude? She acquired the ring on the trip from which she has just returned. Where would she get it? She could not afford to buy it for herself. But it is precisely the kind of ring that a wealthy man of excellent taste would give to the woman he loves—and that a woman like her would accept only from the man she intends to marry."

"But she's wearing the ring on her right hand," Barker said.

"Just so, Barker. Ask yourself why."

When Barker looked uncertain, Milliken said, "It's because she does not wish to announce blatantly to her real lover, the man with her now, that she is engaged to marry another. She wants to tell him at the right moment, in the way that will hurt him least. That's the only reasonable explanation of her behavior."

"Then why does she wear the ring at all?" I said.

"Where are your sensibilities? She does not want to deceive this man, or to act a part. This is a fine woman, as you must realize by now. She is letting him draw his own inferences, letting him suspect the truth, so that when the denouement comes it will not be a complete shock to him. See the tenderness in her glance. There is even a little pain in her eyes when she looks away. And now, consider: what would impel her to give up the man she loves for another? We already know the answer. She needs, she craves money. That is the weak spot in an otherwise noble character. To her, happiness without money is inconceivable."

There was tremendous intensity in Milliken's manner as he spoke, and his eyes were somber. He went on, "She will tell him soon—very soon, now. Possibly after the coffee is served. She will not want to prolong the agony of his suspense, or her own self-reproaches. This is going to cost her something of her self-respect, but she cannot help it. Love with her is less important at this moment than security. That is what modern life does to people. And that, you may be sure, is what she is thinking at this moment, behind her mask of gaiety."

None of us spoke. After a moment, Milliken said, "Here we are, four total strangers to this woman. Yet, through a little observation, a little insight, we unravel the mystery of her life. We glimpse her tragedy at the very moment of its climax. We know her past and present. We can guess at her hard, brilliant, regretful future. We understand her motives and her actions; we can predict her behavior. And how have we done all this? Merely, as I maintained in the beginning, by looking at her."

"By George," said Barker. "I've got to admit—that's pretty good."

Whately said grudgingly, "I've got to admit too—you have made out a case."

"There could be something in it," I said.

Milliken glanced at his watch, then rose suddenly. "Great Scott, I've got to run. You take care of my end of the check, will you?" And he dashed off.

We did not mind. It seemed to us that he had earned his lunch. We had all learned something, and we sat silently, thinking how we might apply the lesson Milliken had taught us. If observation and analysis could enable us to penetrate the innermost secrets of our wives' hearts, the power we would gain!

We paid the check and stood up to go. As we passed the table where the couple who had occupied our minds was sitting, we heard a snatch of their conversation.

"Dickie said the cutest thing this morning after you left the house," the woman was saying. "He said, 'Mummy, why does Daddy have to go—' "

We could not hear the rest.

I looked back at the third finger of her left hand, and there was the unmistakable mark of a wedding ring, tight-fitting and long-worn. I suppose she had taken it off for some reason.

The next time Milliken has lunch with us, he pays for it. The charlatan!

REVOLVER

by *AVRAM DAVIDSON*

There was a Mr. Edward Mason who dealt in real estate. His kind of real estate consisted mainly of old brownstone houses into which Mr. Mason crammed a maximum number of tenants by turning each room into a single apartment. Legally this constituted "increasing available residence space" or some similar phrase. As a result of this deed of civic good, Mr. Mason was enabled to get tax rebates, rent increases which were geometrically rather than arithmetically calculated, and a warm glow around his heart.

Mr. Mason's tenants were a select group, hand-picked; one might say— to use a phrase favored in other facets of the real estate profession—that his holdings were "restricted." He didn't care for tenants who had steady employment. You might think this was odd of him, but that would be because you didn't know the philanthropic cast of Mr. Mason's mind. He favored the lame, the halt, and the blind; he preferred the old and the feeble; he had no scruples, far from it, against mothers without marriage licenses.

And his kindheartedness was rewarded. For, after all, employment, no matter how steady, can sometimes be terminated. And then rent cannot be paid. A landlord who can't collect rent is a landlord who can't meet his own expenses—in short, a landlord who is bound to go out of business. In which case it follows that he is a landlord who can no longer practice philanthropy.

Therefore, Mr. Mason would be obliged to evict such a tenant in order to protect his other tenants.

But, owing to his care, foresight, and selectivity, he had no such tenants. Not any more. No, sir. All his tenants at the time our account begins were in receipt of a steady income not derived from employment. Welfare checks come in regularly, and so do old-age assistance checks, state aid checks, and several other variety of checks more or less unknown to the average citizen (and may he never have to know of them from the recipients' point of view—that is our prayer for him), the average citizen whose tax dollar supplies said checks.

Then, too, people who earn their own income are inclined to take a high-handed attitude toward landlords. They seem to think that the real estate investor has nothing better to do with his income than to lavish it on fancy repairs to his property. But a tenant whose soul has been purified by long years as the recipient of public charity is a tenant who is less troublesome, whose tastes are less finicking, who is in no position to carry on about such *rerae natura* as rats, mice, roaches, crumbling plaster, leaky pipes, insufficient heat, dirt, rot, and the like.

Is it not odd, then, that after a term of years of being favored by the philanthropic attentions of Mr. Mason and similarly minded entrepreneurs, the neighborhood was said to have "gone down"? It could not really be, could it, that garbage, for instance, was collected less frequently than in other sections of town? Or that holes in streets and sidewalks were not repaired as quickly as in "better" neighborhoods? Surely it was a mere coincidence that these things were so—if, indeed, they were so at all.

And anyway, didn't the City make up for it by providing more protection? Weren't patrol cars seen on the streets thereabouts more often than elsewhere? Weren't policemen usually seen on the streets in congenial groups of three? To say nothing of plainclothesmen.

This being the case, it was disconcerting for Mr. Mason to acknowledge that crime seemed to be on the increase in the neighborhood where he practiced his multifold benevolences. But no other conclusion seemed possible. Stores were held up, apartments burglarized, cars broken into, purses snatched, people mugged—

It was almost enough to destroy one's faith in human nature.

Finally, there was no other choice but for Mr. Mason to secure a revolver, and a license for same. Being a respectable citizen, a taxpayer, and one with a legitimate reason to go armed—the necessity to protect himself and the collection of his tenants' rents—he had no difficulty in obtaining either . . .

Among Mr. Mason's tenants was a Mrs. Richards. She was quite insistent, whenever the matter was raised (though it was never raised by Mr. Mason, who was totally indifferent to such items), that "Mrs." was no mere courtesy title. She had, indeed, been married to Mr. Richards and she had a snapshot of Mr. Richards to prove it. The wedding may have occurred in North Carolina, or perhaps in South Carolina. Nor did she recall the town or county where the happy event took place: Mr. Richards (she *did* remember that his given name was Charley) had been a traveling man. Also, it was a long time ago.

Mrs. Richards may have been a bit feeble-minded, but she possessed other qualities, such as a warm, loving, and open—very open—heart. She had two children by the evanescent Mr. Richards, and two children by two other gentlemen, with whom she had been scrupulous not to commit bigamy; and was currently awaiting the birth in about six months of her fifth child, the father of whom she thought was most probably a young man named Curtis.

Current social welfare policy held that it would be destructive to the family unit to suggest that Mrs. Richards, now or at any time, place her children in a day nursery and go out and labor for her (and their) bread. Consequently, she was supplied with a monthly check made up with city, state, and federal taxes. It cannot be said that the amount of the check was lavish, but Mrs. Richards did not demand very much and was easily satisfied. She had never been trained in any craft, trade, or profession, and if anyone was crude or unkind enough to suggest that she had enough skill required to manipulate a scrub brush and bucket, she would point out that when she did this her back hurt her.

The state of the floor of her "apartment," on the day when Mr. Mason came to call, at an hour nicely calculated with reference to the mail schedule, indicated that Mrs. Richards had not risked backache lately.

After an exchange of greetings, Mr. Mason said, "If you've cashed your check, I've got the receipt made out."

"I don't believe it's come," she said placidly. This was her routine reply. It was her belief that eventually it might be believed, although it never had been; nor was it now.

"If you spend the rent money on something else," Mr. Mason said, "I'll have to go down to the Welfare and have them close your case." This was his routine reply.

Curtis, in a peremptory tone, said, "Give the man his money." The prospect of approaching fatherhood had raised in him no tender sentiment; in fact, it raised no sentiment at all other than an increasing daily restlessness and a conviction that it was time for him to move on.

Without so much as a sigh Mrs. Richards now produced an envelope from her bosom and examined it closely. "I guess maybe it might be this one," she said. "I haven't opened it."

Curtis, quite tired of every routine gambit of his lady-love, now said, quite testily, "*Give* the *man* his *money!*" He wanted cigarettes and he wanted whiskey and he knew that neither of these could be had until the check was cashed. "If I got to *hit* you—"

Mrs. Richards endorsed the check with her landlord's pen, and Mr. Mason began to count out her change. A new consideration now entered Curtis's mind—previously occupied only by the desire for cigarettes, whiskey, and moving on; it entered with such extreme suddenness that it gave him no time to reflect on it. He observed that Mr. Mason had a revolver in a shoulder holster inside his coat and he observed that Mr. Mason's wallet was quite engorged with money.

Curtis was not naturally malevolent, but he was naturally impulsive. He whipped Mr. Mason's revolver from its holster, struck Mr. Mason heavily on the side of the head with it, and seized his wallet.

Mr. Mason went down, but he went down slowly. He thought he was shouting for help, but the noise coming out of his mouth was no louder than a mew. He was on his hands and knees by the time Curtis reached the door, and then he slid to one side and lay silent.

Mrs. Richards sat for a moment in her chair. New situations were things she was not well equipped to cope with. After the sound of Curtis's feet on the stairs ceased, she continued to sit for some time, looking at Mr. Mason.

Presently a thought entered her mind. The familiar-looking piece of paper on the dirty table was a receipt for her rent. The money scattered around was the money Mr. Mason had been counting out to cash her check. His practice was to count it out twice and then deduct the amount of the rent.

Mrs. Richards slowly gathered up the money, slowly counted it, moving her lips. It was all there.

And so was the receipt.

Mrs. Richards nodded. She now had the receipt for her rent *and* the money. True, she no longer had Curtis, but, then, she knew he was bound to move along sooner or later. Men always did.

She hid the rent money in one of the holes with which the walls of the "apartment" were plentifully supplied, and then reflected on what she had better do next.

All things considered, she decided it was best to start screaming.

Curtis went down the stairs rapidly, but once in the street he had sense enough to walk at a normal pace. Running men were apt to attract the attention of the police.

Three blocks away was a saloon he favored with his trade. He entered by the back door, causing a buzzer to sound. He tried to slip quickly into the men's room, but wasn't quite quick enough to escape the attention of the bartender-proprietor, an irascible West Indian called Jumby, and no great friend of Curtis's.

"Another customer for the toilet trade," said Jumby, so loudly that he could be heard through the closed door. "I'd make more money if I gave the drinks away free and charged admission to the water closet!"

Curtis ignored this familiar complaint, and emptied the wallet of its money, dropping the empty leather case into the trash container which stood, full of used paper towels, alongside the sink. Then he left.

Police cars sped by him, their sirens screaming.

Vague thoughts of cigarettes and whiskey still floated in Curtis's mind, but the desire to move on was by now uppermost. It was with some relief, therefore, that he saw a young man sitting in an open convertible. The convertible was elegantly fitted out, and so was the young man. His name was William.

"You've been talking about going to California, William," Curtis said.

"I have *also* been talking," William said with precision, "about finding some congenial person with *money* to share the *expenses* of going to California."

Curtis said, "I hit the numbers. I got money enough to take care of all the expenses. Don't that make me congenial?"

"Very *much* so," said William, opening the door. Curtis started to slide in, but William stopped him with a long, impeccably groomed hand, which touched him lightly. "Curtis," he said in low but firm tones, "if you have something *on* you, I really must *insist* that you get *rid* of it first. Suppose I meet you here in an *hour?* That will also enable me to *pack.*"

"One hour," Curtis said.

He went into another bar, obtained cigarettes and whiskey. At the bar was a man generally, if not quite popularly, known as The Rock.

"How you doing, Rock?" Curtis inquired.

The Rock said nothing.

"Got some business to talk over with you," Curtis went on.

The Rock continued to say nothing.

"Like to take in a movie?" Curtis asked.

The Rock finished his drink, set down the glass, looked at Curtis. Curtis put down money, left the bar, The Rock behind him. He bought two tickets at the movie theater and they went in. The house was almost empty.

After a minute or two Curtis whispered, "Fifty dollars buys a gun. I got it on me."

The Rock took out a handkerchief, spread it in his lap, counted money into it, passed it to Curtis. After a moment Curtis passed the handkerchief back. The Rock soon left, but Curtis stayed on. He still had the better part of an hour to kill.

The Rock took a bus and traveled a mile. He walked a few blocks on a side street and entered a house which, like most of its fellows, bore a sign that it has been selected for something euphemistically called "Urban Renewal," and that further renting of rooms was illegal. Most of the windows were already marked with large X signs.

On the second floor The Rock disturbed a teenage boy and girl in close, though wordless, conversation. The boy looked up in some annoyance, but after a quick glance decided to say nothing. The girl clutched his arm until the intruder passed.

The door on the third floor was locked, but The Rock pushed hard, once, and it yielded. The room was ornately furnished, and the dressing table was crowded with perfumes and cosmetics and a large doll; but seated on the bed was a man.

"It ain't you," the man said. He was red-eyed drunk.

"It ain't me," The Rock agreed.

"It's Humpty Slade," said the man on the bed. *"He* don't pay for her rent. *He* don't buy her no clothes. *He* don't feed her. *I* do."

The Rock nodded his massive head.

"Everybody knows that," The Rock said. He took a handkerchief out of his pocket, laid it on the bed, opened its folds. "Seventy-five dollars," he said.

A quick turnover and a modest profit—that was The Rock's policy.

The boy and girl, now seated on the stairs, shrank to one side as he came down. They did not look up. It was not very uncomfortable there in that all but abandoned house; but it was private—as private as you can get when you have no place of your own to go.

Upstairs, on the bed, the waiting man stared at the revolver with his red, red eyes. . . .

After a while the boy and the girl sauntered down into the street and went separate ways in search of something to eat. But after supper they met again in the same hallway.

Scarcely had they taken their places when they were disturbed. A man and woman came up, talking loudly. They paused at the sight of the younger pair in the dim light of the single bulb, and for a moment the two couples looked at one another. The older woman was handsome, flamboyantly dressed and made up. Her companion was large and on the ugly side, his looks not improved by a crooked shoulder which jutted back on one side.

"What are you kids doing here?" he demanded. "Go on, get out—"

"Oh, now, Humphrey," the woman pleaded. "You leave them alone. They ain't hurting nobody."

"Okay, sugar," the big man said submissively. They continued up the stairs. The boy and girl listened as they fumbled at the door. Then the woman's voice went high and shrill with fear, screaming, *"No—no—no—"*

At the loud sound of the revolver the boy and girl leaped to their feet. Something fell past them, and landed below with a thud.

"You'd point a gun at *me?*" a man's voice growled. Then there was the noise of a blow.

"My woman—!"

"You'd take a shot at *me?*"

The sound of fist on flesh, again and again. The boy and girl crept down the stairs.

"No, Humpty, don't hit me any more! I'm sorry, Humpty! I didn't mean it! I was—oh, please, Humpty! *Please?*"

"Don't hit him any more, honey. He was drunk. Honey—"

The boy and girl stopped at the bottom floor for only a moment. Then they were gone. . . .

Curtis paused, uncertain. He was sure that it was dangerous for him to remain on the street, but he didn't know where to go. That little rat, William, had failed to reappear. There were planes flying, and trains and buses running, but even if he decided what to take he would still have to decide *which* airfield, *which* station, *which* terminal. The problems seemed to proliferate each time he thought about them.

He would have a drink to help him consider.

There wasn't really any hurry.

That dirty rat, William!

The Sepoy Lords were holding an informal meeting—a caucus, as it were.

Someone has remarked that the throne of Russia was neither hereditary, nor elective, but occupative. The same might be said of office in the Sepoy Lords.

The scene was a friendly neighborhood rooftop.

"So you think you're going to be Warlord?" a boy named Buzz demanded.

"That's right," said the one called Sonny.

The quorum, including several Sepoy Ladies, listened with interest.

"*I* don't think you're going to be Warlord," said Buzz.

"I *know* I am," said Sonny.

"What makes you so sure?" inquired Buzz.

"*This,*" Sonny said, simply, reaching into his pocket, and taking something out.

Sudden intakes of breath, eyes lighting up, members crowding around, loud comments of admiration. "Sonny got a *piece!*" "*Look* at that piece Sonny's got!"

The President of the Sepoy Lords, one Big Arthur, who had until now remained above the battle, asked, "Where'd you get it, Son'."

Sonny smirked, cocked his head. "*She* knows where I got it," he said. His girl, Myra, smiled knowingly.

Buzz said only one word, but he said it weakly. He now had no case, and he knew it.

The new Warlord sighted wickedly down the revolver. "*First* thing I'm going to do," he announced; "there's one old cat I am going to *burn.* He

said something about my old lady, and that is something I don't take from
*any*body, let alone from one of those dirty old Ermine Kings."

Diplomatically, no one commented on the personal aspect of his grievance, all being well aware how easy it was to say something about Sonny's
old lady, and being equally aware that the old lady's avenging offspring
now held a revolver in his hand. But the general aspect of the challenge was
something else.

"Those Ermine Kings better watch out, is all!" a Sepoy Lady declared.
There was a murmur of assent.

Big Arthur now deemed it time to interpose his authority. "Oh, yeah,
sure," he said. " 'They better watch out!'—how come? Because we got one
piece?"

Warlord Sonny observed a semantic inconsistency. With eyes narrowed
he said, "What do you mean, 'we'? *'We'* haven't got *any*thing. *I'm* the one
who's got the piece, and *no*body is going to tell me what to do with my
personal property—see?" He addressed this caveat to the exuberant Sepoy
Lady, but no one misunderstood him—least of all, Big Arthur.

Allowing time for the message to sink in, Sonny then said, "Big Arthur
is right. I mean, one ain't enough. We need money to get more. How? I got
a plan. Listen—"

They listened. They agreed. They laughed their satisfaction.

"Now," Sonny concluded, "let's get going."

He watched as most of them filed through the door. He started after
them, then stopped. *Was* stopped. Big Arthur seized his wrist with one hand
and grabbed the revolver with the other.

Sonny, crying, "Gimme that back!" leaped for it. But Big Arthur, taking
hold of Sonny's jacket with his free hand, slapped him—hard—back
against the door.

"You got the wrong idea, Son'," Big Arthur said. "You seem to think
that *you* are the President around here. That's *wrong*. Now, if you really
think you are man enough, you can try to get this piece away from me.
You want to try?"

For a while Sonny had been somebody. Now he was nobody again. He
knew that he would never in a million years take the revolver away from
Big Arthur, never burn that one old cat from the Ermine Kings who had
said something about his old lady. Tears of pain and humiliation welled in
his eyes.

"Cheer up," Big Arthur said. "We're going to see how your plan works
out. And it better work out *good*. Now get down those stairs with the other
members, Mr. Sonny Richards."

Head down, Sonny stumbled through the door. Myra started to slip
through after him, but Big Arthur detained her. "Not so quick, chick," he

said. "Let's move along together. You and me are going to get better acquainted." For just a second Myra hesitated. Then she giggled.

"*Much* better acquainted," Big Arthur said.

Feeling neither strain nor pain, Curtis glided out of the bar. The late afternoon spread invitingly before him. He was supposed to meet somebody and go somewhere . . . William . . .

There, slowly passing by in his fancy convertible, was the man himself. With great good humor Curtis cried, "William!" and started toward him.

William himself saw things from a different angle. Curtis, to be sure, was *rough,* but what had really set William against going to California with him was the fact that he had observed Curtis that way. He, William, wanted nothing to do at any time with people who carried guns. And, anyway, he wasn't quite ready to leave for California—something had come up.

What came up at that moment was Curtis, roaring (so it seemed) with rage, and loping forward with murder in his eye.

William gave a squeak of fright. The convertible leaped ahead, crashing into the car in front. And still Curtis came on—

Screaming, "Keep away from me, Curtis!" William jumped out of the car and started to run. Someone grabbed him. "Don't stop me—he's got a gun—Curt*is!*" he yelled.

But they wouldn't let go. It was the police, wouldn't you know it, grim-faced men in plain clothes; of all the cars to crash into—

One of them finished frisking Curtis. "Nope, no gun," he said. "This one ain't dangerous. *You.*" He turned to William. "What do you mean by saying he had a gun?"

William lost his head and started to babble, and before he could move, the men were searching *him.* And the *car.* They found his cigarette case stuffed with sticks of tea, and they found the shoebox full of it, too.

"Pot," said one of them, sniffing. "Real Mexican stuff. Convertible, hey? You won't need a convertible for a long time, fellow."

William burst into tears. The mascara ran down his face and he looked so grotesque that even the grim faces of the detectives had to relax into smiles.

"What about this one, Leo," one of them asked, jerking his thumb. "He's clean."

But Leo was dubious. "There must be some connection, or the pretty one wouldn't of been so scared," he said. A thought occurred to him. "What did he call him? What did you say his name was? Curtis?"

The other detective snapped his fingers. "Curtis. Yeah. A question, Curtis: You in the apartment of a Mrs. Selena Richards today?"

"*Never* heard of her," said Curtis, sobering rapidly. Move on, that's what he should have done—move on.

Mrs. Richards was entertaining company. The baby was awake—had been awake, in fact, since those chest-deep, ear-splitting screams earlier in the afternoon—and the girls had come home from school. She had sent them down to the store for cold cuts and sliced bread; they hadn't eaten more than half of it on the way back, and Mrs. Richards and the neighbors were dining off the other half. There was also some wine they had all chipped in to buy. Excitement didn't come very often, and it was a shame to let it go to waste.

"Didn't that man *bleed!*" a neighbor exclaimed. "All over your floor, Selena!"

"All over *his* floor, you mean—*he* owns this building."

After the whoops of laughter died down, someone thought of asking where Mrs. Richards's oldest child was.

"I don't know where Sonny is," she said, placid as ever. "He takes after his daddy. His daddy always was a traveling sort of man." She felt in her bosom for the money she had placed there—the money she had taken from the hole in the wall after the police and ambulance left. Yes, it was safely there.

All in all, she thought, it had been quite a day. Curtis gone, but he was on the point of becoming troublesome, anyway. Excitement—a *lot* of excitement. Company in, hanging on her every word. The receipt for the rent, *plus* the rent itself. Yes, a lucky day. Later on she would see what the date was, and tomorrow she would play that number.

If luck was coming to you, nothing could keep it away.

They had taken three stitches in Mr. Mason's scalp, and taped and bandaged it.

"You want us to call you a taxi?" the hospital attendant asked.

"No," Mr. Mason said. "I don't have any money to waste on taxis. The bus is still running, isn't it?"

"There's a charge of three dollars," the attendant said.

Mr. Mason snorted. "I don't have three cents. I'll have to borrow bus fare from some storekeeper, I guess. That dirty—he took everything I had. Right in broad daylight. I don't know what we pay taxes for."

"I guess we pay them to reward certain people for turning decent buildings into flophouses," the attendant said. He was old and crusty and due to retire soon, and didn't give a damn for anybody.

Mr. Mason narrowed his eyes and looked at him. "Nobody has the right to tell me what to do with my personal property," he said meanly.

The attendant shrugged. "That's your personal property, too," he said, pointing. "Take it with you; we don't want it."

It was the empty shoulder holster.

On leaving the hospital Mr. Mason headed first for a store, but not to borrow bus fare. He bought a book of blank receipts. He still had most of his rents to collect, and he intended to collect every single one of them. It hardly paid a person to be decent, these days, he reflected irritably. One thing was sure: nobody else had better tangle with him—not today.

He headed for the first house on his round, and it was there, in the hallway, that the Sepoy Lords caught up with him.

THE ETERNAL CHASE

by ANTHONY GILBERT

I don't know what to do. I don't know, and there's no one to ask. They say lightning never strikes twice in the same place, but how can you be sure? How can you be *sure?*

When I heard that The Dingle House had been rented by a widow with a little girl I was glad, because I thought now I should have someone to play with. Ours is an old household, just Grandmother and Aunt Agatha, with Uncle Ned coming down from Friday to Monday. And even he's pretty old—about 30. I share a governess with my three sisters, but they're all older and they think I'm silly.

So I waited eagerly for Grandmother to call on Mrs. Craddock. Until she did, of course, I couldn't even ask the little girl to tea. And I expected so much of the meeting.

But that, of course, was before I met Harriet.

In fact, Grandmother never did call at The Dingle House and my first meetings with Harriet were accidental. One afternoon Maryanne—she had been my nurse and had stayed on after I was nine and didn't really need a nurse any more—sent me to the mailbox with a letter she'd forgotten to give to the postman. Coming back, I saw two strangers approaching. In Hilton Abbas you know everyone whether your grandmother calls on them or not, so these had to be the mysterious Mrs. Craddock and her daughter.

It was Harriet I looked at first—and had a shock. She was shorter than I, and as elegant as her mother; they both wore clothes you wouldn't see at The Dower House even on one of Grandmother's "At Home" days; and she was striking enough to hold anyone's attention. Her skin had the soft gold of an apricot, and she had huge brown eyes and long raying lashes.

But at the very first glance I knew she would never be my playmate. Because, though she was two months younger, she wasn't a child. She was like a small adult; even her movements were smooth and controlled. I knew she would never bump into things or break them as I am always doing.

Still, as we drew close I smiled at her—to show that if Grandmother hadn't called it had nothing to do with me.

And she looked straight through me. I actually felt as though I were a ghost. In mortification, I looked at Mrs. Craddock—and got my second shock. I had heard Uncle Ned talk about the Jersey Lily, how people jumped on park benches and crowded the windows just to see her go by. The Immortal Beauty, he called her.

Well, Margaret Craddock was the same. When she caught my eye she smiled, and I just stood and gaped. It was as if someone had switched on the sun.

She didn't speak—she knew the rules of good society as well as I—and the next minute I had gone past, but not so far that I didn't hear Harriet say, "There was no need to take any notice. We don't know her."

And Mrs. Craddock's voice, as lovely as the rest of her, floated back. "I wish we did, Harriet. For your sake, I wish we did."

"I met Mrs. Craddock and her daughter," I told Maryanne when I got back. "Why won't Grandmother call on them?"

"Because!" said Maryanne, as she always did when she didn't know the answer. But later I heard her say to Jessie, the parlormaid, "But who was Mr. C? That's what I'd like to know."

I leaned over the banisters. "He's dead," I called. I supposed he'd been a very wicked man, and it was a case of touching pitch and being defiled. Only no one could really think of Mrs. Craddock as pitch.

Still Grandmother didn't pay the call, and about a month went by before I saw the Craddocks again. Maryanne had taken me to buy a pair of gloves at Robinson's—Mr. Robinson had the only draper's shop in Hilton Abbas. He used to stand in the doorway wearing a morning coat and welcoming important customers; his two daughters, Lucy and Elsie, served in the shop.

We had bought my gloves and Maryanne was whispering with Lucy at the far end of the shop when Mrs. Craddock and Harriet came in. Mrs. Craddock asked for a muff for her little girl. We all wore muffs, mostly of white rabbit fur with little black "tails," strung round our necks with a silk cord.

Elsie said they were out of white muffs, but she showed Mrs. Craddock a very pretty brown one. More serviceable than the white, Elsie said.

Harriet immediately flew into a tantrum. "I won't have a brown one," she screamed. "A horrid dirty color." And she flounced across the shop to where I was looking at some little brooches. There was one shaped like a cat that I thought very pretty.

"They're trash," said Harriet in a scornful voice. In a second she had gone back to her grown-up way of speaking. She picked up a little locket and threw that down, too. "It's not even real," she scoffed.

She was wearing a very pretty locket herself and she began to dangle it before my eyes. She must have accidentally touched a spring in it, because suddenly the chain parted and the locket fell to the ground. I stooped to pick it up. It had a little black band with three pearls in it on one side and initials—*H.W.*— on the other.

"Did it belong to your grandmother?" I said. I had one for Sundays that had been my grandmother's.

"Of course not," said Harriet, bending her head so that I could refasten the chain. "Don't pull my hair. This was given me when I was six years old."

"But it says *H.W.*," I insisted. "Your initials are *H.C.*"

"That's because my father went away," she said. I knew she meant he had died, but nobody in Hilton Abbas ever died; they passed over or passed on or were gathered by the Grim Reaper, but they all meant the same thing. "Before that I was Harriet Winter and we had a house by the sea and my grandmother had a bigger house than yours and her own carriage. I had an aunt, too," she wound up. "Aunt Grace."

"I will take the brown muff," we heard Mrs. Craddock say.

Harriet looked over her shoulder and laughed. "You will look silly with a muff that small," she said. "If you give it to me I shall never use it. I shall throw it out of the window." And she stamped her little foot.

While Elsie was packaging the muff, Mrs. Craddock turned round and said, "You are the little girl from The Dower House, aren't you?"

Maryanne must have heard her; she was buying a pair of corsets in whispers. Although everyone knew we wore underclothes it was thought more polite to pretend they didn't exist.

"Now, Miss Vicky, I've told you, don't bother people," she said. She put out her hand and I went up reluctantly and took it. Mrs. Craddock took her parcel and went out, followed by Harriet.

"She's nothing but a *baby*," I heard Harriet say scornfully. "She liked the little cat brooch."

"I know someone who needs a dose of syrup of figs," said Maryanne as we walked home. "The little lady!"

"Maryanne," I asked—I didn't really want to confide in her, but she was the only one I had, "if my father died would I have to change my name?"

"Whyever?" Maryanne exclaimed. "The funny things you say, Vicky. What put that idea into your head?"

"Harriet Craddock used to be Harriet Winter until her father passed on," I said. "She lived in a house by the sea, and she has a grandmother, too, and an aunt called Grace."

There was a minute's silence. Then Maryanne said, in a voice I didn't know, "Is that what she told you? Well, fancy me not thinking of it!"

"Not thinking of what?" I pleaded.

She gave my hand a tug and began to hurry us home. "You know what your grandmother says about repeating gossip," she warned me. "It's vulgar."

There were visitors to lunch, so I had mine in the old nursery that was now the schoolroom. I was never allowed to eat in the kitchen, which I should have liked much better. Afterward, I took my book and went into the garden. The book was dull, and I hoped Uncle Ned would bring me a new one from London, where he worked during the week.

Presently I thought I would try and find a frog in the orchard, but there weren't any, so I decided to ask Gorman, our cook, for a glass of water; even if I couldn't catch a frog I could paint a picture of one.

I skirted round the house, but when I passed the kitchen window I saw Gorman and Maryanne and Jessie and Jessie's sister, Louisa, who was the housemaid, all gathered round the table, with their heads together.

"It's as true as I stand here," said Maryanne. "She couldn't make up a story like that!"

"To think of her coming here and expecting decent people to call on her!" marveled Jessie.

"I think it's lovely," said Louisa. "A real murderer."

"She isn't," said Gorman in her flat Scottish voice. "The court said not. And the poor thing has to live somewhere."

"It's no wonder the little girl's a Tartar," contributed Maryanne. "That's what I can't forgive her, Sarah. (I'd never known Gorman's name was Sarah —I'd never thought of her as having any other name). Letting Harriet be mixed up in it."

"She *was* mixed up in it," asserted Gorman. "Well, it was her father who was poisoned."

I crouched under the sill, shaking with excitement.

"It's a wonder I didn't think of it," Maryanne mused. "Her name being Harriet, I mean—and the pictures in the paper."

Jessie said, "The paper. Let's see, it was four months ago, wasn't it? Has Mr. Coutts called lately, Cook?"

Old newspapers at The Dower House were always stored in the cellar. Every few months Mr. Coutts called for them and bought them by weight for use in his shop, and Gorman gave the money to save little Chinese girl babies who would otherwise be allowed to die.

I heard the cellar door open, so I knew Jessie was going down to look. I raised myself slightly, but I believe if I had sat on the sill none of them would have noticed me. They were too much engrossed.

When Jessie came back I heard the rustle of papers and after a longish time Louisa said, "Here we are! Here's a picture of Harriet Winter in the box."

I couldn't think what box she meant. I wondered if it could be a coffin, only it was Mr. Winter who was dead, not Harriet. They were all so busy they didn't hear Uncle Ned come in. It was earlier than usual for him and he came straight to the kitchen. He was the only member of the household who would have dared appear in the middle of an afternoon, but they would have done anything for him. It wasn't just that he was so goodlooking with his frank, blue eyes and little golden mustache; he was always the same, whatever happened, and hardly anyone is like that.

"Am I interrupting a study group?" I heard him say, and, then, "What a lovely face! I seem to have seen it—of course. But why are you digging up the Winter case? It's closed for good."

It was Maryanne who told him. "It's the new lady at The Dingle House," she said. "Her little girl spoke to Miss Vicky in Robinson's this morning."

When Uncle Ned spoke again I hardly recognized his voice. "So here we go," he said. "The eternal chase. I suppose no one will ever let her forget. Where is she, by the way? Victoria, I mean?"

"In the garden," said Maryanne.

I slipped from under the sill and crawled round the corner of the house. Then I raced down to the orchard and opened my book, waiting for his step on the path.

"Enjoying yourself?" said Uncle Ned. "Since when do you read a book upside down?"

"Did you bring me another?" I asked. "I've read this one."

"How long have you been here?" said Uncle Ned. "Now, Vicky, no lies."

"I didn't mean to listen," I burst out, wondering how Harriet would have coped with the situation. "I went to ask for some water and they were talking, and I heard Harriet's name—"

"And what did you make of it?" my uncle asked.

"That—that Mrs. Craddock poisoned her husband," I faltered.

"No. That Mrs. Craddock was cleared by a jury of poisoning her husband—cleared and sent out to be free."

"If she didn't do it," I said, "why did she have to change her name?"

"Because it's not enough to be innocent—everyone has to believe in your innocence. Do you understand?"

I nodded. "I think so. Last Christmas Aunt Agatha said I had broken the little green vase in the drawing room. And I hadn't. It must have been the wind. But she didn't believe me."

I remembered my dismay at the discovery that you could tell the truth but not be believed because you couldn't prove it. No one but myself knew I hadn't done it—and God, I amended silently. Sometimes I wondered why He didn't speak up for all the people in trouble. But that would mean perfect justice in this world, and what's a heaven for?

"Is it like that for Mrs. Craddock?" I asked.

Uncle Ned nodded. "Yes, Vicky," he said. "It's like that."

When I was crossing the hall that evening, I saw Aunt Agatha pasting long strips of newsprint onto sheets of brown paper. I didn't need to be told it was the story of Mrs. Craddock's trial. Aunt Agatha is like the beasts in the Revelations that had eyes before and behind; she couldn't have seen me, yet she called out, "I've told you before, Victoria (a sign of deep displeasure this) it's vulgar to pry."

I hurried up to bed, resolved that by hook or crook I would get hold of those sheets of brown paper and read the whole story for myself.

I had to wait more than a week. Uncle Ned had gone back to London and I was practically a prisoner in my own house. I wasn't even allowed to go to the mailbox alone.

Then one afternoon the hired carriage came round to take Grandmother and Aunt Agatha calling. I heard her say they might be a little late getting back. I supposed they thought it their duty to tell everyone about Mrs. Craddock.

By good luck (for me) Maryanne had a toothache and had to go to have a tooth pulled, Jessie and Louisa (sisters) had their half day together, and only Gorman was left in the house. I was told not to be a nuisance, but to play quietly in the garden.

As soon as I was sure the coast was clear I crept into the study. I was sure the papers would be in Uncle Ned's Wellington chest. This was locked, but I found the keys in a drawer of his desk, and there they were, pages and pages of small print, with pictures of Mrs. Craddock (whom I must learn to call Mrs. Winter) and Harriet and Mr. Winter, referred to as "the deceased."

I snatched up the bundle and fled to the attic where I knew no one would follow me. Past the roll of oilcloth where I used to hide, and the dressmaker's dummy that used to frighten me out of my wits, I flung myself on the Victorian love seat, with its padding bursting through the fading rose brocade, and started to read.

Some of the wording puzzled me and I had to go back several times to understand certain points; but this was the story I pieced together.

About ten years earlier, Margaret Craddock, then aged 18, married Charles Winter, who was a good deal older; they had one child. Harriet, whom her mother idolized, said Mr. Paull, who was someone called Counsel for the Prosecution, at her husband's expense.

About a month before his death Mr. Winter was offered and accepted a position abroad, where a child could not be taken because of the climate. He proposed to leave Harriet with his mother and his unmarried sister,

Grace. Mrs. Winter said nothing should separate her from her child. Harriet created a scene, as Maryanne would have said, declaring that if her mother went away she would drown herself. It was unfortunate, said Mr. Paull, that so much attention was given to the outbreaks of a spoiled child.

Neither side would yield. Mrs. Winter said that if her husband insisted on going overseas she would remain behind. This was the position when, about a week before his untimely death, Mr. Winter fell ill with a sort of fever. It was not denied, said Mr. Paull, that his wife nursed him with exemplary care and patience, though she refused to allow the little girl to stay with her grandmother and Aunt Grace at the Big House.

There was only one servant in the Winter house, the other having recently given notice and not been replaced, since Mr. Winter intended to close his establishment. Therefore, Mrs. Winter cooked most of the food as well as attended the sick man in the bedroom. The doctor (who also gave evidence) said the fever was running its normal course, and there was no reason to anticipate anything but a happy issue of the illness. Mr. Winter still declared his intention of closing the house and taking up his appointment abroad, and he still insisted that his wife should accompany him.

On the fatal afternoon the servant had gone out to visit her parents and, a fine morning having turned to clouds of rain, the child, Harriet, played on the square landing outside the sickroom. She was giving a doll's tea party, and this fact, irrelevant though it might sound, would be shown to be of the greatest significance.

At about four o'clock Mrs. Winter told Harriet she was going downstairs to prepare tea.

"Sit with your father until I come back," she said. "If he should ask for anything, don't cross him, as he is still very ill."

This was in direct opposition to the doctor's opinion that he was by then well on the road to recovery.

About fifteen minutes later, Mrs. Winter returned with the tea tray, and Harriet went back to her own tea party. Almost immediately, strange sounds were heard from the sickroom, groans and the noise of vomiting. Harriet remained where she was until her mother came to the door to say, "Your father has taken a turn for the worse. We must have Dr. Blair, but who is there to fetch him? Alice has gone out, and I do not like to leave you alone with him when he is so ill."

Harriet said, "I could go for the doctor," and although Mrs. Winter did not like the idea of a little girl going out alone in such weather she felt she had no choice. So she gave Harriet a note, and a little later the child was seen by her Aunt Grace, who was driving home in the family carriage.

The aunt stopped and got out to know why Harriet was wandering about alone. Harriet, who had lost her way, explained about the sudden change, and Miss Winter drove to the doctor's and accompanied both him and the child back to her brother's house.

Mrs. Winter opened the door and said, "Oh, Doctor, come at once, he seems to be sinking fast. I can't think what can have caused the change—it can't be anything he ate, since he's had nothing I haven't prepared myself."

She led the way upstairs, where the door stood open. When Mr. Winter saw his sister he said in a weak voice, "Grace, I have been poisoned."

Miss Winter wanted to stay, but the doctor turned her and Harriet out of the room while he made his examination. It told against Mrs. Winter that she had kept none of the vomited matter. Later, Grace Winter was allowed to come back and she sat by the bedside, holding her brother's hand, and asking him, "Henry, who has done this?" But he was too far gone to speak to her.

Later still, Miss Winter went home with a furious and reluctant Harriet in tow, Mrs. Winter having promised to come and fetch her first thing the next morning. The doctor stayed on at the house, and about 4:00 a.m. Henry Winter died, having drifted into a coma from which he never recovered.

The doctor, in the light of what the dead man had said, declared he could not issue a death certificate until an autopsy had been performed (I wasn't sure what this meant). Mrs. Winter wasn't allowed to go back and get Harriet as she had promised, and she sent the servant Alice with a note. There was no telephone in the house; my grandmother does not have one either, saying she had no intention of being at the beck and call of an "instrument."

Presently the police called at the Big House and asked to see Harriet. She seemed quite composed, asking, "Is he dead? Was it poison? Could it have been something in the milk?"

The police said that so far as they knew he had had no milk and then Harriet told her story. After her mother had gone downstairs her father said, "I am very thirsty. Can you give me something to drink?"

The water carafe had been taken downstairs by Mrs. Winter to be re-filled from the jug of boiled water in the kitchen. There had been a recent typhoid epidemic and all drinking water had to be boiled; so Harriet could not fill a glass from the small sink near the landing. She said she had some milk for her tea party and asked if that would do.

Her father said, "I suppose so." So Harriet poured the milk into a glass and then he said, "Give me my bottle of tablets from the medicine chest." He took one—Harriet was sure it was only one—and it made the milk fizz a little.

He handed back the glass saying, "Do not tell your mother of this—she does not like me to have tablets." And he added half to himself, "Sometimes I think she would be glad if I were dead."

The police asked Harriet, "Why did you say nothing of this before?"
Harriet said, "Because my father told me not to."
"When did you tell your mother?"
"I didn't tell her. I didn't see her again."
"Did you tell anyone?"
"There was no one to tell."
"There was your grandmother and your aunt."
"I should never tell them anything about us," Harriet retorted.

So far as I could understand it, this Mr. Paull wanted to make the jury believe that the story about the milk was just a fabrication to help Mrs. Winter, but Harriet clung to it. She had had no chance of concocting it with her mother, and no one supposed she could have invented it herself.

Since both the glass and the cups from the tea tray had been washed while Mrs. Winter was waiting for the doctor, there was nothing to show how the poison had been introduced. In addition to the tea Mr. Winter had had part of a buttered scone; other scones had been put back on the tray, but the bitten piece that he had not finished had been disposed of. Mrs. Winter said she wanted the sickroom to look tidy and she had no reason to suppose her husband's attack was anything but a natural one.

The autopsy showed that he had had some poison from a tin that had been bought to kill rats in the garden. The tin was kept on a shelf in the garden shed. The gardener, a man named Richards, told the court that he had been given the tin by Mr. Winter, from whom he took his orders. He only saw Mrs. Winter when she wanted flowers for the house. Mr. Winter did not care for cut blooms, calling them decaying vegetation. Richards said he had sometimes heard arguments about this, but about nothing else. He never came into the house, taking the flowers and vegetables to the kitchen door; if he wanted a cup of tea it was handed to him through the kitchen window by one of the servants.

When Mrs. Winter went into the box (I knew what that meant by now), they seemed to be trying to make out that she liked Richards—who was about as old as Uncle Ned, though less good-looking—better than she liked her own husband, which seemed silly, as he was only the gardener and wouldn't have any money anyway.

Then Harriet was called to the box. The Judge protested, but Mr. Leslie, the Counsel for the Defense, said she was a vital witness. I could imagine her, perfectly composed, not stammering or shuddering as I would, saying, "I don't know," and "I don't remember." She said her mother had not gone into the garden all that day; she herself had been playing on the lawn until the rain started. She had been looking out of the window while her mother got the tea and would have seen her if she had gone to the shed. No trace of wet shoes or skirt had been found, and the police could not trace any more of the poison in the house.

There was a great deal more of this—far too much for me to read; but in the end the jury decided that Mrs. Winter had not done it. They said there was insufficient evidence to show how the poison was administered. I supposed they meant he could have taken it himself.

Then there was a clipping to say that Mrs. Winter was taking her child and leaving the neighborhood for some place where she might begin life afresh. That seemed silly to me, too. You can't start life over again when you are quite old, going on 30.

My chief feeling was an overwhelming jealousy of Harriet. To be a heroine before you are even ten years old! There were pictures of her in the paper. I indulged in a daydream in which I stood in the box and gave evidence on Uncle Ned's behalf. He wouldn't be accused of murder, of course, but something nearly as bad; he might perhaps rob a bank, or people would think he had.

I became so lost in this vision that my grandmother almost caught me putting the papers back when she returned from her visits.

"What have you been doing this afternoon?" Aunt Agatha said, and I told her I had been reading. I had Uncle Ned's new book under my arm. I began to wonder if I was getting almost as cunning as Harriet.

Now I longed to meet her again, but she and her mother seemed to have gone to ground like a pair of foxes. I decided I must search her out, so one afternoon I let my ball bounce through the front gate and start running down the hill.

The Dingle House stood at the bottom and one of the reasons it was so often vacant was because it was said to be so damp. As I drew near the gate I could hear Harriet talking and I wondered who was bold enough to visit her.

Deliberately I threw my ball up in the air so that it went into her garden; when I looked over the gate I saw that her companions were imaginary. She was sitting on the lawn and the famous tea set was spread on a white cloth. When she saw me she said imperiously, "What do you want?"

"My ball came over into your garden," I said.

She seemed to think for a minute, then she said, "You'd better come in and fetch it."

I was fascinated by the tea service, which was an exact replica of a real one down to the sugar bowl and tiny spoons. Harriet, who clearly did nothing by halves, had arranged colored pebbles and leaves and bits of twigs to represent biscuits and buns.

"You can stay to tea if you like," she said carelessly. "I set a place for you anyway."

In for a penny, in for a pound, I thought. I was already in trouble just by opening the gate.

"How did you know I was coming?" I asked. "The others are rather late, aren't they?"

She gave me a look brimming with scorn. "They're here," she said. "It's not my fault if you can't see them."

She picked up the teapot and poured out a stream of invisible tea.

"Help yourself to cream," she told me, pointing to the jug.

I poured it carefully. I had never seen cream at home, though I supposed my grandmother gave it to her guests. Then I picked up the sugar bowl and shook some of the sugar into the cup. To my surprise Harriet grasped my arm.

"You're not supposed to help yourself till you're invited to," she said, and again I remembered Grandmother slapping my hand away when I helped myself uninvited to cake.

"But I take sugar," I said.

"That cup isn't for you, it's for your grandmother." Harriet pointed to a place on the grass and meekly I set the cup down.

"Now your aunt." She passed me another cup. "And Mrs. Dixon." That was the Rector's wife. "She doesn't take sugar, either."

"And Uncle Ned?" I urged.

"Oh, we don't ask men," said Harriet. "You can't, if you're ladies living alone. Besides, we don't want them."

"I always want Uncle Ned," I said, and I added cruelly, "Don't you miss your father?"

"Oh, he never played with me—he was always too busy," she replied, in the coolest voice imaginable. "Fathers don't, you know. And they travel all over the world." She fixed me with a furious golden glance. "Where's your father? Did he go away too?"

"He went to India; he has another wife now. I think of The Dower House as my home."

"So he did go away." She sounded triumphant. "I've seen your Aunt Agatha. My mother says she withered on a virgin thorn."

I wasn't sure what that meant, but it sounded unpleasant enough even for Aunt Agatha. Before I could think of a reply someone called my name and there was Uncle Ned standing at the gate.

"Your grandmother is getting anxious about you, Victoria," he said. "You should have left word that you had been invited to tea."

He bowed to Harriet and took off his hat.

"She wanted to stay," said Harriet carelessly.

I began to explain about the ball, then I saw he wasn't looking at me any longer. He was staring at the front door that had just opened. Mrs. Craddock came down the path.

"I will introduce myself if I may," he said. "I am Victoria's uncle, Edward O'Hare. Victoria forgot to tell us where she was going."

"It is a pleasure for Harriet to have a playfellow," Mrs. Craddock said. "There are not many young children here."

Harriet said furiously, "I'm nine, that's not young. And I didn't ask her, she wanted to stay, she threw her ball over the wall on purpose!"

"Then she paid us an unusual compliment," said her mother swiftly. She turned back to Uncle Ned. "I should like to ask her again, but we shall be leaving the neighborhood soon."

"I am sorry," said Uncle Ned. "They say the house—"

"Is damp. Yes. But it's not that. It is just that I never cared for industrial cities—not even Coventry."

"If there is a gate into the city there must also be a gate out of it," said my uncle.

"A secret gate," suggested Mrs. Craddock, and once more I saw that golden, life-giving smile. She should smile more often, I thought; she would light up the world.

"If you can't find the key someone else might find it for you."

"And if it only opens in one direction?"

"One could enter."

They were like two people playing tennis, hitting the ball over the net to each other, indifferent to everyone else. I did not understand what they were saying, but I listened, fascinated.

"It's a solitary place," said Mrs. Craddock.

"Surely that depends on your company. And, you know," Uncle Ned added, "it doesn't do to be swayed by the mob. That is, one doesn't have to believe all one hears."

"You're the first person to tell me that."

This exchange might have gone on endlessly—I could see neither of them remembered we were there—had not Harriet broken in to observe, "If Victoria's grandmother is worried about her, shouldn't she go home?"

"Perhaps you will change your mind, after all," Uncle Ned urged. "I'm sorry to break up your party, Harriet."

"Oh, there are plenty of people left," said Harriet in that grown-up voice she could put on so easily. She looked at me. "I told you we didn't want men. They come and spoil things and then they go away."

"What did Mrs. Craddock mean about Coventry?" I asked Uncle Ned as we went back up the hill.

"It's a place where no one speaks to anyone else."

"Then why go there?"

"You don't go, you're sent. You have no choice."

At the top of the hill Aunt Agatha was waiting. "Where have you been?" she scolded me.

"Her ball ran down the hill, so she had to retrieve it," said Uncle Ned. Not a word about Mrs. Craddock or Harriet. . . .

Suddenly I lost interest in the Craddocks. A family called Weston came to live nearby and their daughter, Cynthia, joined us for lessons. The first day we met I knew she was what I had been waiting for. Like me, she was an only child, and she understood at once my world of Make Believe.

All through those hot summer days we were inseparable. Grandmother called at once, so I was at liberty to invite Cynthia home; even Maryanne liked her. I thought of Harriet, so capricious and domineering. I still caught sight of her occasionally, so I knew they hadn't left The Dingle House yet; but she didn't matter to me anymore—or so I believed.

Then in August the Westons went away to the seashore. We never left the house—Grandmother said there was no better air in the country. I missed Cynthia dreadfully. I used to lie in the long grass in the orchard, making up stories in which I rescued her from plunging horses, charging bulls (though I was terrified of them), and boiling seas.

Aunt Agatha used to scold me. "You will ruin your eyesight and your head will poke forward if you spend all your days with your nose in a book."

Uncle Ned still came on Fridays, but even he had lost some of his glamor. I counted the days until Cynthia's return.

Then came the afternoon when my whole world blew up in my face.

Bored by my book, I looked about me for some distraction and saw a hedgehog squeezing under the fence between the garden and the wild commonland beyond. Grandmother had been asked to grant a right of way there, but she had refused, because of the gypsies who camped in the neighborhood every summer.

I went down to the wild land through the blue wooden gate of the orchard, but the hedgehog had already gone to ground. I thought I would go a little way farther and see if there were any gypsies camped among the furze bushes—they would be a pleasant change from my aunt and Maryanne. But all I saw were two people, a man and woman, walking together; and suddenly he drew her into his arms and they stood like one person.

They were Mrs. Craddock and Uncle Ned.

I don't remember if I cried out—they were too absorbed to hear me anyway; but I knew without being told that this wasn't the first time they had met here. She went to his embrace as readily as a bird to its nest. Cynthia and I had sometimes talked of love and marriage, linking the two like bacon and eggs, or bread and butter. One without the other was unthinkable, yet how could Uncle Ned even consider marrying Mrs. Craddock?

But it seemed that he did. He told Grandmother about it that same night. I had rushed indoors as soon as I could find the strength to plump in Grandmother's arms.

"What has frightened you so?" she asked. She could be surprisingly gentle at times. "You have not got a touch of the sun, I hope?"

She let me come into the drawing room and gave me the Chinese doll that Grandfather had brought back forty years ago. This was an unusual treat. I settled down behind the sofa, glad to escape Grandmother's fierce eyes. She and Aunt Agatha sat at either end of the long sofa, both embroidering an altar cloth. That was how Uncle Ned found us sometime later.

"Have you heard the latest rumor?" Aunt Agatha asked him. "They say Mrs. Craddock is leaving The Dingle House at last. I can't imagine why she stayed so long."

"You get tired of running," said Uncle Ned.

"She will be running somewhere else now," said Aunt Agatha in a satisfied tone.

"But this time she won't be alone. Or unprotected. I shall be going with her."

"You shouldn't joke about things like that," snapped Aunt Agatha. "Even to suggest bringing a low woman into the family, even to suggest it in fun—"

"Margaret is not a low woman," said Uncle Ned. "Soon she will be my wife."

My grandmother asked, "Have you taken leave of your senses? To marry a woman like that would be your ruination. Who do you suppose will bring you his business when it's known?"

"Oh, we don't propose to compromise you," said Uncle Ned. "I am accepting a position in Canada. You know how I have always wished to travel, and in a new country people have better things to do than gossip about someone who has been unfortunate."

"You don't mind that your children's mother was accused of murdering her former husband, and put on trial?"

"She was acquitted," said Uncle Ned.

"For lack of evidence."

"She was found innocent."

"No," said Grandmother. "She was not found guilty. There is a world of difference. Edward, if you do this thing we shall not speak to each other again."

"I refuse to believe you really mean that," said Uncle Ned, "but in any case I cannot give Margaret up. I love her with all my heart."

I must have made some movement then, for suddenly they recalled my presence behind the sofa. Aunt Agatha pounced on me and shook me and told me how wicked it was to eavesdrop.

"Let her alone," said Uncle Ned, as furious as she. "I should be glad to take her with us. In any case, Vicky, I hope one day not too far off you can come and pay us a visit."

But I pushed him away. "You'll belong to them," I cried. "You will forget us. And you don't *know* she didn't do it."

I thrust at him violently, then rushed out of the room.

I met Harriet in the lane some days later. Already the news was all round the village. The Dingle House had the air of a place soon to be deserted. "Why couldn't you leave him alone?" I burst out. "We were happy until you came."

"It was he who wouldn't leave us alone," she retorted. "We didn't need anyone."

"Your mother doesn't think so. I saw them together."

"She belongs to me," shrilled Harriet.

"Not any more," I said, as cruel as she. "Now he will come first."

Suddenly the fury drained out of her; she seemed miles away, although we were standing face to face.

"He had better watch out," she said. "I told you—didn't I?—that I'm a witch. When I want things to happen they happen."

"You didn't want this to happen," I taunted.

But she only laughed and went away.

That night there was a tremendous thunderstorm. I lay shivering in my bed, hating the roars and the reverberations. I thought of Harriet and her claim: "When I want things to happen they happen." What she wanted was her mother all to herself. Once before someone had tried to separate them, and he had died.

It was like a light going on in a dark room.

In that instant I knew the truth about Mr. Winter's death.

I didn't blame the police for not realizing it—who would suspect a child barely nine years old? But in my imagination I saw her deliberately pouring the milk, adding the poison—she had been playing in the garden that morning and would have seen Richards laying it out for all the rats—and who would notice the movements of a child? She must have taken the poison to use as opportunity offered, not knowing that the chance would come the same day. But intending to use it all the same, because she knew that in the end her mother would leave her—her mother's duty as a wife really gave her little choice.

I had wondered why she didn't go down and fill the glass with water in the kitchen where a supply was always kept handy, but of course the rat powder would show less in milk. And then she washed the glass so that no trace remained.

I knew, I tell you I knew—but I didn't know how to prove it. And no one would listen to me, a jealous child—I might even be whipped for suggesting such a thing.

And then I remembered the day of the tea party in the garden of The

Dingle House. The sugar bowl! That was it. The police might have searched the house for traces of poison, but they wouldn't think of a child being involved. They wouldn't know, as I knew, that Harriet had never been a child.

Now Uncle Ned had to be warned and there was not much time left; but first I must get hold of the sugar bowl. Accusation without proof would be a waste of time.

So the next day I went openly to The Dingle House. Everything had a very desolate air; pictures had been taken from the walls, and there were no carpets on the floor.

Mrs. Craddock came to meet me. Love had made her even more beautiful, though I wouldn't have believed that possible. I knew I was going to wreck that happiness: I didn't think for a moment that she might know what Harriet had done, because surely she wouldn't risk it happening a second time, not to Uncle Ned.

"I came to see Harriet," I told her.

"She has been helping me pack," said Mrs. Craddock. And she called, "Harriet, here is Victoria come to say good-bye. Or perhaps only *au revoir.*"

Harriet came slowly out and stopped halfway down the stairs. "Good-bye," she said. Her face was dark and unwelcoming.

"That's no way to say good-bye," Mrs. Craddock told her, laughing. "Come in, Victoria. You don't bring a message from your grandmother? No, I see that was a foolish question. What would you like to do while you are here?"

"I should like to play with the tea set once more," I said. "I never saw one I liked so well."

"Oh, but it's already packed," said Harriet carelessly. "You have come too late."

"We have been washing it," Mrs. Craddock said.

Harriet nodded. "Every single piece."

Her eye held mine, and I understood that she knew what I suspected and was mocking me because now I was helpless. I said, "There was sugar in the bowl," and Harriet said, "It wouldn't be much good if there wasn't."

"Why don't you give it to Victoria?" Mrs. Craddock urged. "Something to remember us by."

"Won't she remember us without that?" asked Harriet, but she went docilely enough to fetch the box in which the tea set was packed. I knew I should never play with it. I hated it; I told myself I would trample it to smithereens, but I was saved the trouble.

Mrs. Craddock was saying, "Harriet would have thought of it herself if she had been used to having a playmate," when there came a tremendous crash. We ran to the foot of the stairs and there lay the tea set, a welter of chipped and broken china, with Harriet bent over the fragments.

"Be careful," Mrs. Craddock warned. "You may cut yourself. What happened?"

"I slipped," said Harriet calmly. "I had to let the box go or I would have hurt myself."

"We will send you another, Vicky," promised her mother. "What is left of this one is only fit for the dustbin."

She fetched a brush and swept up the pieces, wrapping them in paper. I knew then that my last chance had slipped between my fingers. Now there was no proof, no proof at all.

"How about a real cup of tea?" Mrs. Craddock said when she had disposed of the parcel. "Fortunately, we still have some cake. And, Vicky, my dear, do you take sugar?"

I thought, half-dazed, "When I am quite old and write my memoirs I shall be able to say—Once I had tea with a murderer."

That was five days ago. Tomorrow Mrs. Craddock and Harriet leave for London where Uncle Ned will meet them, and Mrs. Craddock and Uncle Ned will be married, and after that it will be too late.

It is three o'clock in the morning—there are still four hours to go. God holds time in the hollow of His hand—a thousand years are but an instant in His sight—there's still time for a miracle, for a thunderstorm to bring The Dingle House crashing to the ground, smothering its occupants . . . for lightning or a fireball to devour all of them.

I sit waiting for the dawn, a pale green sky with the birds calling, then light stealing back to the world, then a sea of pale rose. It's like that poem by Robert Browning:

> *All night long I have not stirred*
> *And still God has not said a word.*

I don't know what to do.
I don't know, and there's no one to ask . . .

The Seventies

REASONS UNKNOWN

by STANLEY ELLIN

This is what happened, starting that Saturday in October.

That morning Morrison's wife needed the station wagon for the kids, so Morrison took the interstate bus into downtown Manhattan. At the terminal there, hating to travel by subway, he got into a cab. When the cabbie turned around and asked, "Where to, mister?" Morrison did a double take. "Slade?" he said. "Bill Slade?"

"You better believe it," said the cabbie. "So it's Larry Morrison. Well, what do you know."

Now, what Morrison knew was that up to two or three years ago, Slade had been—as he himself still was—one of the several thousand comfortably fixed bees hiving in the glass-and-aluminum Majestico complex in Greenbush, New Jersey. There were 80,000 Majestico employees around the world, but the Greenbush complex was the flagship of the works, the executive division. And Slade had been there a long, long time, moving up to an assistant managership on the departmental level.

Then the department was wiped out in a reorganizational crunch, and Slade, along with some others in it, had been handed his severance money and his hat. No word had come back from him after he finally sold his house and pulled out of town with his wife and kid to line up, as he put it, something good elsewhere. It was a shock to Morrison to find that the something good elsewhere meant tooling a cab around Manhattan.

He said in distress, "Jeez, I didn't know, Bill—none of the Hillcrest Road bunch had any idea—"

"That's what I was hoping for," said Slade. "It's all right, man. I always had a feeling I'd sooner or later meet up with one of the old bunch. Now that it happened, I'm just as glad it's you." A horn sounding behind the cab prompted Slade to get it moving. "Where to, Larry?"

"Columbus Circle. The Coliseum."

"Don't tell me, let me guess. The Majestico Trade Exposition. It's that time of the year, right?"

"Right," said Morrison.

"And it's good politics to show up, right? Maybe one of the brass'll take notice."

"You know how it is, Bill."

"I sure do." Slade pulled up at a red light and looked around at Morrison. "Say, you're not in any tearing hurry, are you? You could have time for a cup of coffee?"

There was a day-old stubble on Slade's face. The cap perched on the back of his graying hair was grimy and sweatstained. Morrison felt unsettled by the sight. Besides, Slade hadn't been any real friend, just a casual acquaintance living a few blocks farther up Hillcrest Road. One of the crowd on those occasional weekend hunting trips of the Hillcrest Maybe Gun and Rod Club. The "Maybe" had been inserted in jest to cover those bad hunting and fishing weekends when it temporarily became a poker club.

"Well," Morrison said, "this happens to be one of those heavy Saturdays when—"

"Look, I'll treat you to the best Danish in town. Believe me, Larry, there's some things I'd like to get off my chest."

"Oh, in that case," said Morrison.

There was a line of driverless cabs in front of a cafeteria on Eighth Avenue. Slade pulled up behind them and led the way into the cafeteria which was obviously a cabbies' hangout. They had a little wrestling match about the check at the counter, a match Slade won, and, carrying the tray with the coffee and Danish, he picked out a corner table for them.

The coffee was pretty bad, the Danish, as advertised, pretty good. Slade said through a mouthful of it, "And how is Amy?" Amy was Morrison's wife.

"Fine, fine," Morrison said heartily. "And how is Gertrude?"

"Gretchen."

"That's right. Gretchen. Stupid of me. But it's been so long, Bill—"

"It has. Almost three years. Anyhow, last I heard of her Gretchen's doing all right."

"Last you heard of her?"

"We separated a few months ago. She just couldn't hack it any more." Slade shrugged. "My fault mostly. Getting turned down for one worthwhile job after another didn't sweeten the disposition. And jockeying a cab ten, twelve hours a day doesn't add sugar to it. So she and the kid have their own little flat out in Queens, and she got herself some kind of cockamamie receptionist job with a doctor there. Helps eke out what I can give her. How's your pair, by the way? Scott and Morgan, isn't it? Big fellows now, I'll bet."

"Thirteen and ten," Morrison said. "They're fine. Fine."

"Glad to hear it. And the old neighborhood? Any changes?"

"Not really. Well, we did lose a couple of the old-timers. Mike Costanzo and Gordie McKechnie. Remember them?"

"Who could forget Mike, the world's worst poker player? But McKechnie?"

"That split-level, corner of Hillcrest and Maple. He's the one got himself so smashed that time in the duck blind that he went overboard."

"Now I remember. And that fancy shotgun of his, six feet underwater in the mud. Man, that sobered him up fast. What happened to him and Costanzo?"

"Well," Morrison said uncomfortably, "they were both in Regional Customer Services. Then somebody on the top floor got the idea that Regional and National should be tied together, and some people in both offices had to be let go. I think Mike's in Frisco now, he's got a lot of family there. Nobody's heard from Gordie. I mean—" Morrison cut it short in embarrassment.

"I know what you mean. No reason to get red in the face about it, Larry." Slade eyed Morrison steadily over his coffee cup. "Wondering what happened to me?"

"Well, to be frank—"

"Nothing like being frank. I put in two years making the rounds, lining up employment agencies, sending out enough résumés to make a ten-foot pile of paper. No dice. Ran out of unemployment insurance, cash, and credit. There it is, short and sweet."

"But why? With the record you piled up at Majestico—"

"Middle level. Not top echelon. Not decision-making stuff. Middle level, now and forever. Just like everybody else on Hillcrest Road. That's why we're on Hillcrest Road. Notice how the ones who make it to the top echelon always wind up on Greenbush Heights? And always after only three or four years? But after you're middle level fifteen years the way I was—"

Up to now Morrison had been content with his twelve years in Sales Analysis. Admittedly no ball of fire, he had put in some rough years after graduation from college—mostly as salesman on commission for some product or other—until he had landed the job at Majestico. Now he felt disoriented by what Slade was saying. And he wondered irritably why Slade had to wear that cap while he was eating. Trying to prove he was just another one of these cabbies here? He wasn't. He was a college man, had owned one of the handsomest small properties on Hillcrest Road, had been a respected member of the Majestico executive team.

Morrison said, "I still don't understand. Are you telling me there's no company around needs highly qualified people outside decision-making level? Ninety percent of what goes on anyplace is our kind of job, Bill. You know that."

"I do. But I'm forty-five years old, Larry. And you want to know what I found out? By corporation standards I died five years ago on my fortieth birthday. Died, and didn't even know it. Believe me, it wasn't easy to realize that at first. It got a lot easier after a couple of years' useless job-hunting."

Morrison was 46 and was liking this less and less. "But the spot you're in is only temporary, Bill. There's still—"

"No, no. Don't do that, Larry. None of that somewhere-over-the-rainbow line. I finally looked my situation square in the eye, I accepted it, I made the adjustment. With luck, what's in the cards for me is maybe some day owning my own cab. I buy lottery tickets, too, because after all somebody's got to win that million, right? And the odds there are just as good as my chances of ever getting behind a desk again at the kind of money Majestico was paying me." Again he was looking steadily at Morrison over his coffee cup. "That was the catch, Larry. That money they were paying me."

"They pay well, Bill. Say, is that what happened? You didn't think you were getting your price and made a fuss about it? So when the department went under you were one of the—"

"Hell, no," Slade cut in sharply. "You've got it backwards, man. They do pay well. But did it ever strike you that maybe they pay too well?"

"Too well?"

"For the kind of nine-to-five paperwork I was doing? The donkey work?"

"You were an assistant head of department, Bill."

"One of the smarter donkeys, that's all. Look, what I was delivering to the company had to be worth just so much to them. But when every year —every first week in January—there's an automatic cost-of-living increase handed me I am slowly and steadily becoming a luxury item. Consider that after fourteen-fifteen years of those jumps every year, I am making more than some of those young hotshot executives in the International Division. I am a very expensive proposition for Majestico, Larry. And replaceable by somebody fifteen years younger who'll start for a hell of a lot less."

"Now hold it. Just hold it. With the inflation the way it is, you can't really object to those cost-of-living raises."

Slade smiled thinly. "Not while I was getting them, pal. It would have meant a real scramble without them. But suppose I wanted to turn them down just to protect my job? You know that can't be done. Those raises are right there in the computer for every outfit like Majestico. But nobody in management has to like living with it. And what came to me after I was canned was that they were actually doing something about it."

"Ah, look," Morrison said heatedly. "You weren't terminated because you weren't earning your keep. There was a departmental reorganization. You were just a victim of it."

"I was. The way those Incas or Aztecs or whatever used to lay out the living sacrifice and stick the knife into him. Don't keep shaking your head, Larry. I have thought this out long and hard. There's always a reorganization going on in one of the divisions. Stick a couple of departments together, change their names, dump a few personnel who don't fit into the new table of organization.

"But the funny thing, Larry, is that the ones who usually seem to get dumped are the middle-aged, middle-level characters with a lot of seniority. The ones whose take-home pay put them right up there in the high-income brackets. Like me. My secretary lost out in that reorganization too, after eighteen years on the job. No complaints about her work. But she ran into what I did when I told them I'd be glad to take a transfer to any other department. No dice. After all, they could hire two fresh young secretaries for what they were now paying her."

"And you think this is company policy?" Morrison demanded.

"I think so. I mean, what the hell are they going to do? Come to me and say, 'Well, Slade, after fifteen years on the job you've priced yourself right out of the market, so good-bye, baby?' But those reorganizations? Beautiful. 'Too bad, Slade, but under the new structure we're going to have to lose some good men.' That's the way it was told to me, Larry. And that's what I believed until I woke up to the facts of life."

The piece of Danish in Morrison's mouth was suddenly dry and tasteless. He managed to get it down with an effort. "Bill, I don't want to say it—I hate to say it—but that whole line sounds paranoid."

"Does it? Then think it over, Larry. You still in Sales Analysis?"

"Yes."

"I figured. Now just close your eyes and make a head count of your department. Then tell me how many guys forty-five or over are in it."

Morrison did some unpalatable calculation. "Well, there's six of us. Including me."

"Out of how many?"

"Twenty-four."

"Uh-huh. Funny how the grass manages to stay so green, isn't it?"

It was funny, come to think of it. No, funny wasn't the word. Morrison said weakly, "Well, a couple of the guys wanted to move out to the Coast, and you know there's departmental transfers in and out—"

"Sure there are. But the real weeding comes when there's one of those little reorganizations. You've seen it yourself in your own department more than once. Juggle around some of those room dividers. Move some desks here and there. Change a few descriptions in the company directory. The smokescreen. But behind that smoke there's some high-priced old faithfuls getting called upstairs to be told that, well, somebody's got to go, Jack, now that things are all different, and guess whose turn it is."

Slade's voice had got loud enough to be an embarrassment. Morrison pleaded: "Can't we keep it down, Bill? Anyhow, to make villains out of everybody on the top floor—"

Slade lowered his voice, but the intensity was still there. "Who said they were villains? Hell, in their place I'd be doing the same thing. For that matter, if I was head of personnel for any big outfit, I wouldn't take anybody my age on the payroll either. Not if I wanted to keep my cushy job in personnel, I wouldn't." The wind suddenly seemed to go out of him. "Sorry, Larry. I thought I had everything under control, but when I saw you—when I saw it was one of the old Hillcrest bunch—it was too much to keep corked up. But one thing—"

"Yes?"

"I don't want anybody else back there in on this. Know what I mean?"

"Oh, sure."

"Don't just toss off the 'oh, sure' like that. This is the biggest favor you could do me—not to let anybody else in the old crowd hear about me, not even Amy. No post-mortems up and down Hillcrest for good old Bill Slade. One reason I let myself cut loose right now was because you always were a guy who liked to keep his mouth tight shut. I'm counting on you to do that for me, Larry. I want your solemn word on it."

"You've got it, Bill. You know that."

"I do. And what the hell"—Slade reached across the table and punched Morrison on the upper arm—"any time they call you in to tell you there's a reorganization of Sales Analysis coming, it could turn out you're the guy elected to be department head of the new layout. Right?"

Morrison tried to smile. "No chance of that, Bill."

"Well, always look on the bright side, Larry. As long as there is one."

Outside the Coliseum there was another of those little wrestling matches about paying the tab—Slade refusing to take anything at all for the ride, Morrison wondering, as he eyed the meter, whether sensitivity here called for a standard tip, a huge tip, or none at all—and again Slade won.

Morrison was relieved to get away from him, but, as he soon found, the relief was only temporary. It was a fine Indian summer day, but somehow the weather now seemed bleak and threatening. And doing the Majestico show, looking over the displays, passing the time of day with recognizable co-workers turned out to be a strain. It struck him that it hadn't been that atrocious cap on Slade's head that had thrown him, it had been the gray hair showing under the cap. And there was very little gray hair to be seen on those recognizable ones here at the Majestico show.

Morrison took a long time at the full-length mirror in the men's room, trying to get an objective view of himself against the background of the others thronging the place. The view he got was depressing. As far as he could see, in this company he looked every minute of his 46 years.

Back home he stuck to his word and told Amy nothing about his encounter with Slade. Any temptation to was readily suppressed by his feeling that once he told her that much he'd also find himself exposing his morbid reaction to Slade's line of thinking. And that would only lead to her being terribly understanding and sympathetic while, at the same time, she'd be moved to some heavy humor about his being such a born worrier. He was a born worrier, he was the first to acknowledge it, but he always chafed under that combination of sympathy and teasing she offered him when he confided his worries to her. They really made quite a list, renewable each morning on rising. The family's health, the condition of the house, the car, the lawn, the bank balance—the list started there and seemed to extend to infinity.

Yet, as he was also the first to acknowledge, this was largely a quirk of personality—he was, as his father had been, somewhat sobersided and humorless—and, quirks aside, life was a generally all-right proposition. As it should be when a man can lay claim to a pretty and affectionate wife, and a couple of healthy young sons, and a sound home in a well-tended neighborhood. And a good steady job to provide the wherewithal.

At least, up to now.

Morrison took a long time falling asleep that night, and at three in the morning came bolt awake with a sense of foreboding. The more he lay there trying to get back to sleep, the more oppressive grew the foreboding. At four o'clock he padded into his den and sat down at his desk to work out a precise statement of the family's balance sheet.

No surprises there, just confirmation of the foreboding. For a long time now, he and Amy had been living about one month ahead of income which, he suspected, was true of most families along Hillcrest Road. The few it wasn't true of were most likely at least a year ahead of income and sweating out the kind of indebtedness he had always carefully avoided.

But considering that his assets consisted of a home with ten years of mortgage payments yet due on it and a car with two years of payments still due, everything depended on income. The family savings account was, of course, a joke. And the other two savings accounts—one in trust for each boy to cover the necessary college educations—had become a joke as college tuition skyrocketed. And, unfortunately, neither boy showed any signs of being scholarship material.

In a nutshell, everything depended on income. This month's income. Going by Slade's experience in the job market—and Slade had been the kind of competent, hardworking nine-to-five man any company should have been glad to take on—this meant that everything depended on the job with Majestico. Everything. Morrison had always felt that landing the job in the first place was the best break of his life. Whatever vague ambitions he had in his youth were dissolved very soon after he finished college and learned that out here in the real world he rated just about average in all departments, and that his self-effacing, dogged application to his daily work was not going to have him climbing any ladders to glory.

Sitting there with those pages of arithmetic scattered around the desk, Morrison, his stomach churning, struggled with the idea that the job with Majestico was suddenly no longer a comfortable, predictable way of life but for someone his age, and with his makeup and qualifications, a dire necessity. At five o'clock, exhausted but more wide-awake than ever, he went down to the kitchen for a bottle of beer. Pills were not for him. He had always refused to take even an aspirin tablet except under extreme duress, but beer did make him sleepy, and a bottle of it on an empty stomach, he estimated, was the prescription called for in this case. It turned out that he was right about it.

In the days and weeks that followed, this became a ritual: the abrupt waking in the darkest hours of the morning, the time at his desk auditing his accounts and coming up with the same dismal results, and the bottle of beer which, more often than not, allowed for another couple of hours of troubled sleep before the alarm clock went off.

Amy, the soundest of sleepers, took no notice of this, so that was all right. And by exercising a rigid self-control he managed to keep her unaware of those ragged nerves through the daylight hours as well, although it was sometimes unbearably hard not to confide in her. Out of a strange sense of pity, he found himself more sensitive and affectionate to her than ever. High-spirited, a little scatterbrained, leading a full life of her own what with the boys, the Parent-Teachers Club, and half a dozen community activities, she took this as no less than her due.

Along the way, as an added problem, Morrison developed some physical tics which would show up when least expected. A sudden tremor of the hands, a fluttering of one eyelid which he had to learn to quickly cover up. The most grotesque tic of all, however—it really unnerved him the few times he experienced it—was a violent, uncontrollable chattering of the teeth when he had sunk to a certain point of absolute depression. This only struck him when he was at his desk during the sleepless times considering the future. At such times he had a feeling that those teeth were diabolically possessed by a will of their own, chattering away furiously as if he had just been plunged into icy water.

In the office he took refuge in the lowest of low profiles. Here the temptation was to check on what had become of various colleagues who had over the years departed from the company, but this, Morrison knew, might raise the question of why he had, out of a clear sky, brought up the subject. The subject was not a usual part of the day's conversational currency in the department. The trouble was that Greenbush was, of course, a company town, although in the most modern and pleasant way. Majestico had moved there from New York 20 years before; the town had grown around the company complex. And isolated as it was in the green heartland of New Jersey, it had only Majestico to offer. Anyone leaving the company would therefore have to sell his home, like it or not, and relocate far away. Too far, at least, to maintain old ties. It might have been a comfort, Morrison thought, to drop in on someone in his category who had been terminated by Majestico and who could give him a line on what had followed. Someone other than Slade. But there was no one like this in his book.

The one time he came near bringing his desperation to the surface was at the Thanksgiving entertainment given by the student body of the school his sons attended. The entertainment was a well-deserved success, and after it, at the buffet in the school gym, Morrison was driven to corner Frank Lassman, assistant principal of the school and master of ceremonies at the entertainment, and to come out with a thought that had been encouragingly flickering through his mind during the last few insomniac sessions.

"Great show," he told Lassman. "Fine school altogether. It showed tonight. It must be gratifying doing your kind of work."

"At times like this it is," Lassman said cheerfully. "But there are times—"

"Even so. You know, I once had ideas about going into teaching."

"Financially," said Lassman, "I suspect you did better by not going into it. It has its rewards, but the big money isn't one of them."

"Well," Morrison said very carefully, "suppose I was prepared to settle for the rewards it did offer? A man my age, say. Would there be any possibilities of getting into the school system?"

"What's your particular line? Your subject?"

"Oh, numbers. Call it arithmetic and math."

Lassman shook his head in mock reproach. "And where were you when we really needed you? Four or five years ago we were sending out search parties for anyone who could get math across to these kids. The last couple of years, what with the falling school population, we're firing, not hiring. It's the same everywhere, not that I ever thought I'd live to see the day. Empty school buildings all over the country."

"I see," said Morrison.

So the insomnia, tensions, and tics continued to worsen until suddenly one day—as if having hit bottom, there was no place for him to go but up —Morrison realized that he was coming back to normal. He began to sleep through the night, was increasingly at ease during the day, found himself cautiously looking on the bright side. He still had his job and all that went with it, that was the objective fact. He could only marvel that he had been thrown so far off balance by that chance meeting with Slade.

He had been giving himself his own bad time, letting his imagination take over as it had. The one thing he could be proud of was that where someone else might have broken down under the strain, he had battled it out all by himself and had won. He was not a man to hand himself trophies, but in this case he felt he had certainly earned one.

A few minutes before five on the first Monday in December, just when he was getting ready to pack it in for the day, Pettengill, departmental head of Sales Analysis, stopped at his desk. Pettengill, a transfer from the Cleveland office a couple of years before, was rated as a comer, slated sooner or later for the top floor. A pleasant-mannered, somewhat humorless man, he and Morrison had always got along well.

"Just had a session with the brass upstairs," he confided. "A round table with Cobb presiding." Cobb was the executive vice president in charge of Planning and Structure for the Greenbush complex. "Looks like our department faces a little reorganization. We tie in with Service Analysis and that'll make it Sales and Service Evaluation. What's the matter? Don't you feel well?"

"No, I'm all right," said Morrison.

"Looks like you could stand some fresh air. Anyhow, probably because you're senior man here, Cobb wants to see you in his office first thing tomorrow morning. Nine sharp. You know how he is about punctuality, Larry. Make sure you're on time."

"Yes," said Morrison.

He didn't sleep at all that night. The next morning, a few minutes before nine, still wearing his overcoat and with dark glasses concealing his reddened and swollen eyes, he took the elevator directly to the top floor. There, out of sight on the landing of the emergency staircase, he drew the barrel and stock of his shotgun from beneath the overcoat and assembled the gun. His pockets bulged with 12-gauge shells. He loaded one into each of the gun's twin barrels. Then concealing the assembled gun beneath the coat as well as he could, he walked across the hall into Cobb's office.

Miss Bernstein, Cobb's private secretary, acted out of sheer blind, unthinking instinct when she caught sight of the gun. She half-rose from her desk as if to bar the way to the inner office. She took the first charge square in the chest. Cobb, at his desk, caught the next in the face. Reloading, Morrison exited through the door to the executive suite where Cobb's assistants had been getting ready for the morning's work and were now in a panic at the sound of the shots.

Morrison fired both barrels one after another, hitting one man in the throat and jaw, grazing another. Reloading again, he moved like an automaton out into the corridor where a couple of security men, pistols at the ready, were coming from the staircase on the run. Morrison cut down the first one, but the other, firing wildly, managed to plant one bullet in his forehead. Morrison must have been dead, the medical examiner later reported, before he even hit the floor.

The police, faced with five dead and one wounded, put in two months on the case and could come up with absolutely no answers, no explanations at all. The best they could do in their final report was record that "the perpetrator, for reasons unknown, etc., etc."

Management, however, could and did take action. They learned that the Personnel Department psychologist who had put Morrison through the battery of personality-evaluation tests given every applicant for a job was still there with the company. Since he had transparently failed in those tests to sound out the potentially aberrant behavior of the subject, he was, despite sixteen years of otherwise acceptable service, terminated immediately.

Two weeks later, his place in Personnel was filled by a young fellow named McIntyre who, although the starting pay was a bit low, liked the looks of Greenbush and, with his wife in complete agreement, saw it as just the kind of quiet, pleasant community in which to settle down permanently.

THREE WAYS TO ROB A BANK
by HAROLD R. DANIELS

The manuscript was neatly typed. The cover letter could have been copied almost word for word from one of those "Be an Author" publications, complete with the proforma "Submitted for publication at your usual rates." Miss Edwina Martin, assistant editor of *Tales of Crime and Detection,* read it first. Two things about it caught her attention. One was the title— "Three Ways to Rob a Bank. Method 1." The other was the author's name. Nathan Waite. Miss Martin, who knew nearly every professional writer of crime fiction in the United States and had had dealings with most of them, didn't recognize the name.

The letter lacked the usual verbosity of the fledgling writer, but a paragraph toward the middle caught her eye. "You may want to change the title because what Rawlings did wasn't really robbery. In fact, it's probably legal. I am now working on a story which I will call 'Three Ways to Rob a Bank. Method 2.' I will send this to you when I finish having it retyped. Method 2 is almost certainly legal. If you want to check Method 1, I suggest that you show this to your own banker."

Rawlings, it developed, was the protagonist in the story. The story itself was crude and redundant; it failed to develop its characters and served almost solely as a vehicle to outline Method 1. The method itself had to do with the extension of credit to holders of checking accounts—one of those deals where the bank urges holders of checking accounts to write checks without having funds to back them. The bank would extend credit. No papers. No notes. (The author's distrust of this form of merchandizing emerged clearly in the story.)

Miss Martin's first impulse was to send the story back with a polite letter of rejection. (She never used the heartless printed rejection slip.) But something about the confident presentation of the method bothered her. She clipped a memorandum to the manuscript, scrawled a large question mark on it, and bucked it to the editor. It came back next day with additional scrawling: "This is an awful piece of trash but the plan sounds almost real. Why don't you check it with Frank Wordell?"

Frank Wordell was a vice-president of the bank that served Miss Martin's publisher. She made a luncheon date with him, handed him the letter and the manuscript, and started to proofread some galleys while he looked it over. She glanced up when she heard him suck in his breath. He had turned a delicate shade of greenish white.

"Would it work?" she asked.

"I'm not quite sure," the vice-president said, his voice shaking. "I'd have to get an opinion from some of the people in the Check Credit Department. But I think it would." He hesitated. "Good Lord, this could cost us millions. Listen—you weren't thinking of publishing this, were you? I mean, if it got into the hands of the public—"

Miss Martin, who had no great admiration for the banking mentality, was noncommital. "It needs work," she said. "We haven't made a decision."

The banker pushed his plate away. "And he says he's got another one. His Method Two. If it's anything like this it could ruin the entire banking business." A thought came to him. "He calls this '*Three* Ways to Rob a Bank.' That means there must be a Method Three. This is terrible! No, no, we can't let you publish this and we must see this man at once."

This was an unfortunate approach to use with Edwina Martin who reached out her hand for the letter and manuscript. "That is our decision to make," she told him coldly. It was only after he had pleaded the potential destruction of the country's economy that she let him take the papers back to the bank. He was so upset that he neglected to pay the luncheon check.

He called her several hours later. "We've held an emergency meeting," he told her. "The Check Credit people think that Method One *would* work. It might also be legal but even if it isn't it would cost us millions in lawsuits. Listen, Miss Martin, we want you to buy the story and assign the copyright to us. Would that protect us against him selling the story to someone else?"

"In its present form," she told him. "But there would be nothing to prevent him from writing another story using the same method." Remembering his failure to pay the luncheon check, she was not inclined to be especially cooperative. "And we don't buy material that we don't intend to publish."

But after an emergency confrontation between a committee of the City Banking Association, called into extraordinary session, and the publisher, it was decided to buy Nathan Waite's story and to lock the manuscript in the deepest vault of the biggest bank. In the interest of the national economy.

Economy, Miss Martin decided, was an appropriate word. During the confrontation a saurian old capitalist with a personal worth in the tens of millions brought up the subject of payment to Nathan Waite. "I suppose we must buy it," he grumbled. "What do you pay for stories of this type?"

Miss Martin, knowing the author had never been published and hence had no "name" value, suggested a figure. "Of course," she said, "since it will never be published there is no chance of foreign income or anthology fees, let alone possible movie or TV rights." (The Saurian visibly shuddered.) "So I think it would be only fair to give the author a little more than the usual figure."

The Saurian protested. "No, no. Couldn't think of it. After all, we won't ever get our money back. And we'll have to buy Method Two and Method Three. Think of that. Besides, we've still got to figure out a way to keep him from writing other stories using the same methods. The usual figure will have to do. No extras."

Since there were 30 banks in the Association and since the assessment for each would be less than $10.00 per story, Miss Martin failed to generate any deep concern for the Saurian.

That same day Miss Martin forwarded a check and a letter to Nathan Waite. The letter explained that at this time no publication date could be scheduled but that the editor was very anxious to see the stories explaining the second and third ways to rob a bank. She signed the letter with distaste. To a virgin author, she knew, the check was insignificant compared with the glory of publication. Publication that was never to be.

A week later a letter and the manuscript for "Three Ways to Rob a Bank. Method 2" arrived. The story was a disaster but again the method sounded convincing. This time it involved magnetic ink and data processing. By prearrangement Miss Martin brought it to Frank Wordell's office. He read it rapidly and shivered. "The man's a genius," he muttered. "Of course, he's had a lot of background in the field—"

"What was that? How would you know about his background?" Edwina asked.

He said in an offhand manner, "Oh, we've had him thoroughly checked out, of course. Had one of the best detective agencies in the business investigate him—ever since you showed me that first letter. Couldn't get a thing on him."

Miss Martin's voice was ominously flat. "Do you mean to tell me that you had Mr. Waite *investigated*— a man you only learned of through his correspondence with us?"

"Of course." Wordell sounded faintly surprised. "A man that has dangerous knowledge like he has. Couldn't just trust to luck that he wouldn't do something with it besides write stories. Oh, no, couldn't let it drop. He worked in a bank for years and years, you know. Small town in Connecticut. They let him go a year ago. Had to make room for the president's nephew. Gave him a pension though. Ten percent of his salary."

"Years and years, you said. How many years?"

"Oh, I don't remember. Have to look at the report. Twenty-five, I think."

"Then naturally he wouldn't hold any resentment over being let go," she said drily. She put out her hand. "Let me see his letter again."

The letter that had accompanied the second manuscript had cordially thanked the publisher for accepting the first story and for the check. One paragraph said, "I assume you checked Method 1 with your banker as I suggested. I hope you'll show him Method 2 also, just to be sure it would work. As I said in my first letter, it's almost certainly legal."

Miss Martin asked, "Is it legal?"

"Is what legal?"

"Method Two. The one you just read about."

"Put it this way. It isn't illegal. To make it illegal, every bank using data processing would have to make some major changes in its forms and procedures. It would take months and in the meantime it could cost us even more millions than Method One. This is a terrible thing, Miss Martin—a terrible thing."

Method 2 caused panic in the chambers of the City Banking Association. There was general agreement that the second story must also be bought immediately and sequestered forever. There was also general agreement that since Method 3 might be potentially even more catastrophic, there could be no more waiting for more stories from Mr. Waite. (Miss Martin, who was present, asked if the price of the second story could be raised in view of the fact that Mr. Waite was now, having received one check, a professional author. Saurian pointed out that Waite hadn't actually been published, so the extra expense was not justified.)

A plan was adopted. Miss Martin was to invite Mr. Waite to come up from Connecticut, ostensibly for an author-editor chat. Actually he would be brought before a committee chosen by the City Banking Association. "We'll have our lawyers there," Saurian said. "We'll put the fear of the Lord into him. Make him tell us about that Method Three. Pay him the price of another story if we have to. Then we'll work out some way to shut him up."

With this plan Miss Martin and her fellow editors and her publisher went along most reluctantly. She almost wished that she had simply rejected Nathan Waite's first submission. Most particularly she resented the attitude of the bankers. In their view, Nathan Waite was nothing more than a common criminal.

She called Nathan Waite at his Connecticut home and invited him to come in. The City Banking Association, she resolved to herself, would pay his expenses, whatever devious steps she might have to take to manage it.

His voice on the phone was surprisingly youthful and had only a suggestion of Yankee twang. "Guess I'm pretty lucky selling two stories one right after the other. I'm sure grateful, Miss Martin. And I'll be happy to come in and see you. I suppose you want to talk about the next one."

Her conscience nipped at her. "Well, yes, Mr. Waite. Methods One and Two were so clever that there's a lot of interest in Method Three."

"You just call me Nate, miss. Now, one thing about Method Three: there's no question about it being legal. The fact is, it's downright honest. Compared with One and Two, that is. Speaking about One and Two, did you check them with your banker? I figured you must have shown him Method One before you bought the story. I was just wondering if he was impressed by Method Two."

She said faintly, "Oh, he was impressed all right."

"Then I guess he'll be really interested in Method Three."

They concluded arrangements for his visit in two days and hung up.

He showed up at Miss Martin's office precisely on time—a small man in his fifties with glistening white hair combed in an old-fashioned part on one side. His face was tanned and made an effective backdrop for his sharp blue eyes. He bowed with a charming courtliness that made Miss Martin feel even more of a Judas. She came from behind her desk. "Mr. Waite—," she began.

"Nate."

"All right. Nate. I'm disgusted with this whole arrangement and I don't know how we let ourselves be talked into it. Nate, we didn't buy your stories to publish them. To be honest—and it's about time—the stories are awful. We bought them because the bank—the banks, I should say—asked us to. They're afraid if the stories were published, people would start actually using your methods."

He frowned. "Awful, you say. I'm disappointed to hear that. I thought the one about Method Two wasn't that bad."

She put her hand on his arm in a gesture of sympathy and looked up to see that he was grinning. "Of course they were awful," he said. "I deliberately wrote them that way. I'll bet it was almost as hard as writing good stuff. So the banks felt the methods would work, eh? I'm not surprised. I put a lot of thought into them."

"They're even more interested in Method Three," she told him. "They want to meet you this afternoon and discuss buying your next story. Actually, they want to pay you *not* to write it. Or write anything else," she added.

"It won't be any great loss to the literary world. Who will we be meeting? The City Banking Association? An old fellow who looks like a crocodile?"

Miss Edwina Martin, with the feel for a plot developed after reading thousands of detective stories, stepped back and looked at him. "You know all about this," she accused him.

He shook his head. "Not all about it. But I sort of planned it. And I felt it was working out the way I planned when they put a detective agency to work investigating me."

"They had no business doing that," she said angrily. "I want you to know that we had nothing to do with it. We didn't even know about it until afterwards. And I'm not going to the meeting with you. I wash my hands of the whole business. Let them buy your next story themselves."

"I want you to come," he said. "You just might enjoy it."

She agreed on condition that he hold out for more money than her publisher had ostensibly been paying him. "I sort of planned on charging a bit more," he told her. "I mean, seeing they're that much interested in Method Three."

At lunch he told her something of his banking career and a great deal more about his life in a small Connecticut town. This plain-speaking, simple man, she learned, was an amateur mathematician of considerable reputation. He was an authority on cybernetics and a respected astronomer.

Over coffee some of his personal philosophy emerged. "I wasn't upset when the bank let me go," he said. "Nepotism is always with us. I could have been a tycoon in a big-city bank, I suppose. But I was content to make an adequate living and it gave me time to do the things I really liked to do. I'm basically lazy. My wife died some years after we were married and there wasn't anybody to push me along harder than I wanted to go.

"Besides, there's something special about a small bank in a small town. You know everyone's problems, money and otherwise, and you can break rules now and then to help people out. The banker, in his way, is almost as important as the town doctor." He paused. "It's not like that any more. It's all regimented and computerized and dehumanized. You don't have a banker in the old sense of the word. You have a financial executive who's more and more just a part of a large corporation, answerable to a board of directors. He has to work by a strict set of rules that don't allow for any of the human factors."

Miss Martin, fascinated, signaled for more coffee.

"Like making out a deposit slip," he went on. "Used to be you walked into the bank and filled out the slip with your name and address and the amount you wanted to deposit. It made a man feel good and it was good for him. 'My name is John Doe and I earned this money and here is where I live and I want you to save this amount of money for me.' And you took it up to the cashier and passed the time of day for a minute."

Nate put sugar in his coffee. "Pretty soon there won't be any cashiers. Right now you can't fill out a deposit slip in most banks. They send you computer input cards with your name and number on them. All you fill in is the date and amount. The money they save on clerical work they spend on feeble-minded TV advertising. It was a TV ad for a bank that inspired me to write those stories."

Miss Martin smiled. "Nate, you used us." The smile faded. "But even if you hold them up for the Method Three story, it won't hurt anything but their feelings. The money won't come out of their pockets and even several thousands of dollars wouldn't mean anything to them."

He said softly, "The important thing is to make them realize that any mechanical system that man can devise, man can beat. If I can make them realize that the human element can't be discarded, I'll be satisfied. Now then, I suppose we should be getting along to the meeting."

Miss Martin, who had felt concern for Nathan Waite, felt suddenly confident. Nate could emerge as a match for a dozen Saurians.

A committee of twelve members of the City Banking Association, headed by the Saurian, and flanked by a dozen lawyers, awaited them. Nathan Waite nodded as he entered the committee room. The Saurian said, "You're Waite?"

Nate said quietly, "Mr. Waite."

A young lawyer in an impeccable gray suit spoke out. "Those stories that you wrote and that we paid for. You realize that your so-called methods are illegal?"

"Son, I helped write the banking laws for my state and I do an odd job now and then for the Federal Reserve Board. I'd be happy to talk banking law with you."

An older lawyer said sharply, "Shut up, Andy." He turned to Nate. "Mr. Waite, we don't know if your first two methods are criminal or not. We do know it could cost a great deal of money and trouble to conduct a test case and in the meantime, if either Method One or Two got into the hands of the public it would cause incalculable harm and loss. We'd like some assurance that this won't happen."

"You bought the stories describing the first two methods. I'm generally considered an honorable man. As Miss Martin here might put it, I won't use the same plots again."

Gray Suit said cynically, "Not this week, maybe. How about next week? You think you've got us over a barrel."

The older lawyer said furiously, "I told you to shut up, Andy," and turned to Nate again. "I'm Peter Hart," he said, "I apologize for my colleague. I accept the fact that you are an honorable man, Mr. Waite."

Saurian interrupted. "Never mind all that. What about Method Three—the third way to rob a bank. Is it as sneaky as the first two?"

Nate said mildly, "As I told Miss Martin, 'rob' is a misnomer. Methods One and Two are unethical, perhaps illegal, methods for getting money from a bank. Method Three is legal beyond the shadow of a doubt. You have my word for that."

Twelve bankers and twelve lawyers began talking simultaneously. Saurian quieted the furor with a lifted hand. "And you mean it will work just as well as the first two methods?"

"I'm positive of it."

"Then we'll buy it. Same price as the first two stories and you won't even have to write it. Just tell us what Method Three is. And we'll give you $500 for your promise never to write another story." Saurian sank back, overwhelmed by his own generosity. Peter Hart looked disgusted.

Nathan Waite shook his head. "I've got a piece of paper here," he said. "It was drawn up by the best contract lawyer in my state. Good friend of mine. I'll be glad to let Mr. Hart look it over. What it calls for is that your Association pay me $25,000 a year for the rest of my life and that payments be made thereafter in perpetuity to various charitable organizations to be named in my will."

Bedlam broke loose. Miss Martin felt like cheering and she caught a smile of admiration on Peter Hart's face.

Nate waited patiently for the commotion to die down. When he could be heard he said, "That's too much money to pay for just a story. So, as the contract specifies, I'll serve as consultant to the City Banking Association— call it Consultant in Human Relations. That's a nice-sounding title. Being a consultant, of course, I'll be too busy to write any more stories. That's in the contract too."

Gray Suit was on his feet, yelling for attention. "What about Method Three? Is that explained in the contract? We've got to know about Method Three!"

Nate nodded. "I'll tell you about it as soon as the contract is signed."

Peter Hart held up his hand for quiet. "If you'll wait in the anteroom, Mr. Waite, we'd like to discuss the contract among ourselves."

Nate waited with Miss Martin. "You were tremendous," she said. "Do you think they'll agree?"

"I'm sure they will. They might argue about Clause Seven—gives me the right to approve or disapprove all TV bank commercials." His eyes twinkled. "But they're so scared of Method Three I think they'll agree to even that."

Five minutes later Peter Hart called them back to face a subdued group of committee members. "We have decided that the Association badly needs a Consultant in Human Relations," he said. "Mr. Graves"—he nodded toward a deflated Saurian—"and myself have signed in behalf of the City Banking Association. By the way, the contract is beautifully drafted— there's no possibility of a legal loophole. You have only to sign it yourself."

Gray Suit was on his feet again. "Wait a minute," he shouted. "He still hasn't told us about Method Three."

Nate reached for the contract. "Oh, yes," he murmured, after he had signed it. " 'Three Ways to Rob a Bank.' Method Three. Well, it's really quite simple. *This* is Method Three."

THE PERFECT SERVANT

by *HELEN NIELSEN*

Lieutenant Brandon was trying to bridge a generation gap when the woman walked into the police station and deposited a wad of currency on the counter. The trio of teenagers he had charged with collecting hubcaps that belonged to irate citizens seemed unimpressed with the idea that they had committed theft, and then the woman, who was in her middle forties, shabbily dressed and wearing a look of quiet despair in her eyes, relinquished a cheap money clip containing the bills and said, "Please, who is the officer I see about this?"

Brandon nodded for a uniformed officer to take away the teenagers, grateful for a release from the pointless conversation, and asked the woman to state her problem.

"I was walking down the street—down Broadway," she stated, "and I saw this on the sidewalk. I picked it up. It is money."

Brandon pulled the bills out of the clip. There were three twenty-dollar bills, three tens, and two fives. "One hundred dollars," he said.

"Yes," the woman agreed. "I counted, too. That's a lot of money for someone to lose."

It was a lot of money, and the woman looked as if she had never had her hands on that much at any one time in all her life. Brandon called the desk sergeant to fill out a report and explained to the woman that the money would be held for 30 days, during which time the real owner could report his loss, describe the bills and the clip, and have the money returned, or, failing a claimant, the money would then become the property of the finder.

"Your name?" asked the sergeant.

She hesitated. "Maria," she said. "Maria Morales."

"Occupation?"

"I have no work now. When I work I am a domestic."

"Address?"

She gave the number of a cheap roominghouse in the Spanish-speaking section of town. She told them she was very poor, unemployed, and without any property of her own. When the report was offered for her signature she placed both hands on the desk. A plain gold band adorned the third finger of her left hand.

"Just sign here, Miss Morales," the sergeant said.

"Mrs. Morales," she corrected. "I am a widow."

Brandon caught the desk sergeant's eye and shook his head in wonder.

"You should get those cocky young kids back in here to see this," the sergeant suggested.

"Waste of time," Brandon answered. "They wouldn't appreciate anything this square. Don't forget now, Mrs. Morales, in thirty days you check back with us. Chances are you'll get the money—or at least a reward."

"Thank you," she said in a very soft voice, "but I would rather have a job."

A young reporter from the Tucson daily came into the station just as Maria Morales was leaving, and Brandon, the bitter taste of the cynical teenagers still in his mouth, related the incident of the honesty of Maria Morales. It was a slow day on the newsfront and when the morning papers came out, the story of the unemployed widow and the $100 was written up in a neat box on the front page.

By noon Lieutenant Brandon was flooded with calls from people who claimed the money, and also with job offers for Maria Morales. Having developed a protective interest in the widow, he took it upon himself to screen the offers and decided that the best prospect was Lyle Waverly, a bachelor and a physician with a lucrative practice among the country-club set.

Waverly needed a housekeeper he could trust. He owned a fine home in one of the better suburbs and entertained a well-heeled social set. He offered Maria a home, a good salary, and free medical care for as long as she remained in his employ.

Brandon approved the credentials and gave Waverly the woman's address, feeling the kind of inner warmth he always got from delivering Christmas parcels to the Neediest Families.

Maria Morales was extremely pleased with young Dr. Waverly. He was easy to work for. The house was large but new, and there was a gardener to help with the heavy work. She was an excellent cook but, aside from breakfast, the doctor seldom dined in. He was a busy man in more ways than one, which was only natural for one so attractive and increasingly affluent.

It soon became apparent that the doctor's love life was divided between two women: Cynthia Reardon, who was 23 and the sole heir of Josiah Reardon of Reardon Savings and Loan, and Shelley Clifford, ten years older, who had an additional handicap of being already married to Ramsey Clifford, the owner of Clifford Construction Company. Clifford was a huge burly man of 50 who had too little time to spend with a lovely wife who liked younger men.

Maria observed these things with professional silence, and long before Dr. Lyle Waverly was aware of his destiny, she knew that Cynthia had the inside track and would eventually get her man.

Life was pleasant in the Waverly house and Maria had no desire to return to the kind of employment she had recently known. She began to plot a campaign of self-preservation. When the doctor gave her an advance on her salary, she purchased fitted uniforms with caps and aprons for the frequent cocktail parties he gave for his wealthy friends and patients.

He soon learned that a caterer was no longer necessary. Maria's canapés became the envy of every hostess, and she herself became a topic of conversation not unwelcome in the tension created whenever Cynthia and Shelley were present on the same occasion. Shelley had the prior claim—a fact made obvious by the way she took over as hostess. She was the "in" woman fighting against the inevitable successor, and only Clifford's preoccupation with business could blind him to what anyone else could see. Of the two women, Maria preferred Shelley, who was no threat to her own position as mistress of the house. Shelley wanted only Lyle Waverly; Cynthia wanted his name, his life, and his home.

"Maria is a miracle," Shelley explained at the second party. "Imagine finding someone with her divine talent who is honest as well. Why, she's a perfect servant!"

"An honest woman?" Cynthia echoed. "Impossible! No woman can be honest and survive! Maria must have a few secrets."

Maria smiled blandly and continued to serve the canapés.

"I refuse to believe it!" Dr. Waverly announced. "All my life I've searched for a pure woman and this is she!"

"Perhaps you'd better marry her, darling," Shelley said. "You could do worse."

That remark was aimed at Cynthia, and Maria didn't wait to hear the reply. She returned to the kitchen and began to clean up the party debris. It was sometime later, after most of the guests had gone home and even Ramsey Clifford had taxied off to catch a late plane for a business appointment, that she heard Shelley berating Dr. Waverly for his interest in Cynthia Reardon. Maria returned to the living room to collect abandoned glasses and saw them alone.

"You needn't think I don't know what you're doing," Shelley was saying. "You needed me when you were beginning your practice—you needed my contacts and influence. Now you want a younger woman."

"Shelley, please," the doctor begged.

"No, I'm going to have my say! You want a younger and a richer woman, don't you, darling? What better catch than Josiah Reardon's sexy daughter? You'll never hold her, Lyle. She'll wear you like a pendant until she's bored with you. She's used up half a dozen handsome young men already."

"I'm not a child!" Waverly protested.

"No. You're a man and vain enough to think you can use Cynthia Reardon. I'm warning you, you'll be the one who gets used!"

"You're jealous," Waverly said.

"Of course I'm jealous. I love you, and I need you, Lyle. Now *I* need *you*—"

Maria retreated quickly to the kitchen before she was noticed. Sometime later the doctor came in carrying the glasses. All the guests were gone. He loosened his tie and drew a deep breath. "The things they don't teach you in medical school!" he sighed. "Maria, you are the only sane person on earth. You must never leave me."

"I'll fix you a hot milk," Maria said.

"Oh, no—"

"A bromide?"

"Brilliant idea. Are you sure you never worked the social route before?"

Maria's face darkened. "I worked for women," she said. "I didn't like it. They talk about you in front of others. 'You just can't trust anyone these days,' she said with savage mockery. 'They'll steal you blind and expect to get paid besides!' "

Waverly laughed. "I think I understand why honesty is so important to you. By the way, the thirty days are up. Did you ever go back to claim that hundred dollars?"

"Tomorrow," Maria said. "Tomorrow I go."

"Good! I hope it's there. If it isn't I'll give you a bonus to make up for losing it."

Maria returned to the police station the next day. Lieutenant Brandon gave her a paper to sign and then handed her the money which was still held in the money clip made of cheap metal with a silver dollar for decoration. None of the claimants could identify the exact denominations of the bills or describe the clip, so the money was now legally hers.

"How's the job?" Brandon asked.

"The best one I ever had," Maria said.

"Now, that's what I like to hear! There's some justice in the world after all."

"Yes," Maria said, and slipped the money into her handbag.

Her position at the Waverly house continued to improve. She had her own room and, with an adequate household budget, was able to buy food less fattening than the starchy diet of the poor. She soon replaced her uniforms with a smaller size and had her hair done once a month. She was beginning to feel and look more like a woman. Waverly soon took notice.

"Maria," he said, "you never told me about your husband. He was one lucky guy. What was his name?"

"Wa—" she began.

"Juan?"

She smiled softly. "Yes," she said, "his name was Juan."

"Handsome?"

"Of course!"

"And a passionate devil, I'll bet! What do you have going for you now? There must be a boyfriend somewhere."

The doctor had been drinking. He slipped a friendly arm about her shoulder.

"No boyfriend," Maria said.

"No? That's a shame! What's the matter? With legs like yours you could still do a fancy fandango. I'll bet you've done many a fancy fandango in your day."

"In my day—yes," Maria admitted.

"Then get back in circulation. Take a night off once in a while. Take tonight off. I'm going out with Miss Reardon."

"In that case, I think I should make you another bromide."

"No, you don't! I'm just a teensy-weensy bit drunk and I need much more fortification tonight. I'm going to ask Miss Reardon to marry me."

"She will accept," Maria said flatly.

"That's what I'm afraid of. You see, Maria, I've never been married. I'm afraid of marriage. I like women but I like my freedom better."

"Then why—?"

"Why marry? Because it's the thing to do. It's stabilizing. It builds character. It's what every rising young doctor should do, Maria, but I'm still scared. I don't like to be dominated."

"Then don't be dominated," Maria said. "Be the boss."

Waverly picked up his glass. "I'll drink to that," he said.

But it was Maria who feared the marriage more than Waverly. No sooner was the engagement announced than Cynthia began to reorganize the household, and Maria began to worry again about her security. Waverly caught her reading the want ads and demanded an explanation.

"What's the matter? Aren't you happy here?" he asked. "Do you want more money?"

"No," Maria said.

"Then what's wrong?"

"Things will change after you marry."

"What things? Don't you like Miss Reardon?"

"It's not what I like. It's what Miss Reardon likes."

"Stop worrying. Nobody's going to treat you the way you were treated before I found you. I like you and that's all that matters. I'll tell you something I was going to keep secret. I've had my lawyer draw up a new will—a man does that when he gets married. I've made a $5000 bequest in your behalf. Now do you feel more secure?"

Maria was reassured, but she had lived long enough to take nothing for granted except money in the bank. Dr. Waverly was impulsive and generous, but Cynthia Reardon was a spoiled, strong-willed girl and Shelley Clifford's description of her character was more accurate than anything a prospective bridegroom was likely to see. What's more, Shelley didn't give up the battle simply because the engagement was announced. The mores of Dr. Waverly's social set, Maria learned, were more liberal than her own.

Shelley immediately developed symptoms requiring the doctor's professional attention at indelicate hours—particularly when her husband was away on business. There were surreptitious calls going both ways. When Waverly finally refused to go to see Shelley again, she came to see him. Traveling over an unpaved, circuitous drive, Shelley's small imported coupe made the trip between the Clifford estate and the doctor's house with increasing frequency.

It was a shameful thing, Maria reflected, for a woman to cling so to a man. As much as she had loved her husband, she would have let him go the minute he no longer wanted her. But no matter how many women Walter might have had before their marriage, he was faithful to his vows. Walter —not Juan. Juan Morales was the name of the father Maria barely remembered. Walter Dwyer was the name of the man she had wed. But when one must work as a domestic for the Anglos, it seemed better not to let it be known that she had once been married to an Anglo, had once lived like a lady.

She had been hardly 20 when Walter married her, but Walter was a gambler and gamblers die broke. After settling with the creditors, there was nothing for the widow Dwyer to do but return to Tucson and again become Maria Morales, domestic.

She had nothing left of the past but what Walter had called her "Irish luck," but her mind was no longer servile. She saw things now with the eyes of Mrs. Walter Dwyer, and what she saw was troubling. When a woman lost at love it was the same as when a man lost at cards. If she cried, she cried alone. What she could never do was cling to anything that was finished.

If Cynthia Reardon knew what was going on, she showed no outward sign. She might even be enjoying Shelley's humiliation. If Ramsey Clifford knew what was going on, he was indifferent. Eventually Dr. Waverly had it out with Shelley in a verbal battle over the telephone. Maria didn't eavesdrop. It was impossible not to hear him shouting in his study.

"No, I won't come over tonight!" he shouted. "There's nothing wrong with you, Shelley, and I won't come over tonight or any other night! I suggest that you get another doctor. I have no time for a chronic neurotic." It was cruel, but it seemed to work. The telephone calls stopped. Two weeks before the scheduled wedding, Cynthia Reardon moved into the doctor's house and Maria's moral values were again updated. It seemed to be accepted practice in the young doctor's circle and Maria made no comment.

But her worst fears about her future status were soon confirmed. She couldn't please the new mistress who took Maria to task on the slightest provocation. The good days were finished. Cynthia was vicious. She would get whatever she wanted on her own terms either by using her sex or the lure of Josiah Reardon's wealth and prestige. If there was any doubt of who would rule the Waverly manse, it was decided the night of Josiah Reardon's prenuptial dinner party.

Once a week Dr. Waverly spent a day at the local free clinic, and, because Cynthia didn't care about these things, he sometimes talked about this work with Maria. It was the one thing of which he was genuinely proud, and because of it she was proud of him. A twelve-year-old Mexican boy had been under his care for some time. Minor surgery had been performed and confidence carefully built for the major surgery which, if successful, would restore him to a normal life. Half of the battle, Waverly assured her, was in the rapport he had established with the frightened boy. On the evening before the scheduled major surgery Reardon gave his dinner party. Maria heard the doctor try to get Cynthia to change the date.

"I have nine o'clock surgery," he said. "It's imperative that I get my rest."

"You're not the only doctor at the clinic!" Cynthia scoffed.

"But this is a special case!"

"And Daddy's dinner isn't, I suppose! Lyle, you must be mad. You know Daddy doesn't change his plans for anyone, and this is a very special occasion. You see, darling, you're the first man I've ever known that Daddy liked. He thinks you're a stabilizing influence for me. I happen to know what his wedding present is going to be. What would you think of fifteen percent of the Reardon Corporation?"

Dr. Waverly thought through a few moments of absolute silence. "You're dreaming."

"Then I must have dreamed the papers I saw Daddy's lawyer drawing up. That's what the dinner is for tonight—the presentation of the gift. Now I know you can get somebody else to take over for you tomorrow. It's not as if you had a paying patient. It's just one of those clinic cases."

Maria held her breath and said a silent prayer, but she lost. Waverly went to the dinner with Cynthia. It was almost two A.M. when he returned and, minutes later, Cynthia was at the door. Maria heard them laughing in the entry hall.

"You shouldn't have come here," Waverly said. "The old boy doesn't know we've jumped the gun, and he might not like it."

"He would loathe it—but who cares? Darling, isn't it wonderful? You see, I didn't lie to you. We've got something to celebrate."

"It's so late—"

"A little nightcap—please."

Maria, listening from the kitchen, sighed and went back to bed. In the morning she arose, made a pot of coffee, and carried it up to Waverly's room. He was asleep. Cynthia opened one eye and then threw a pillow at her.

"Nobody called you!" she whispered angrily.

"The doctor has a hospital call—"

"Cancel it! Tell them he's sick or something. Can't you see that he's asleep? If you don't call the hospital this minute, I will!"

Maria retreated from the room. She went downstairs and phoned the hospital to inform them that Dr. Waverly couldn't perform the nine o'clock operation. It was noon before the doctor came downstairs and that was just a few minutes after the hospital called to tell him that the boy had died on the operating table. It was a small event in the life of a young doctor who was slated to become the most popular society doctor in the area, but it destroyed Maria's last vision of Camelot.

She remembered that Walter, who was crude and uneducated, had once left a game during a winning streak—and that was the one thing he had taught her a gambler should never do—to donate blood to the black porter who parked his car at the casino each night. The friend who took over Walter's hand had lost everything, but that hadn't mattered because the porter lived and Walter came back as happy as a schoolboy playing hookey. And so Maria was thoroughly disenchanted with her position at the Waverly house even before the night that Shelley Clifford returned.

It was four nights before the wedding. Cynthia, tired from rehearsals of the ceremony, had gone up to bed and taken two sleeping pills. The doctor was preparing a deposit slip for the visit to the bank that he wanted Maria to make for him in the morning. Maria went to the front door when the bell rang and there was no way to keep Shelley out of the house. She had been drinking and was hysterical. One eye was blackened and she had a cut on one cheek. Her husband, she explained when Waverly hurried out of the study, had learned of their relationship and beaten her. Her story might be true or untrue, but the doctor's reaction was firm.

"You can't stay here!" he insisted.

"Just for tonight," she begged. "Ram's been drinking, too. I'm afraid to go home."

"I don't believe you," Waverly said. "Ram Clifford doesn't drink."

"He did tonight. I'm afraid, Lyle. I'm afraid he'll kill me!"

Maria watched the doctor's face. He looked as if he thought that might be a good solution. Firmly he took Shelley by the shoulders and turned her back toward the door.

"Then go to a hotel," he said.

"Why can't I stay here?"

"Because I won't let you."

Waverly was trying to keep his voice down. When Shelley noticed him glance apprehensively toward the stairs, she sensed immediately what he was trying to hide. Her eyes widened. *"She's* here, isn't she? Cynthia's *here!"* And then she laughed and pushed Waverly away from her. "You couldn't even wait for the marriage! Oh, that's beautiful! Now wouldn't old Josiah Reardon love to know about this! His daughter may be a swinger, but the old boy's a stickler for the proprieties! And there's nothing more conservative than a savings and loan corporation, darling. When they hear about this you may not get that partnership and seat on the Board of Directors."

"Get out of the house!" Waverly ordered.

"Oh, I will, I will—just as soon as I've run upstairs to check—"

She lunged past him and started to run up the stairs. Waverly was about two steps behind her when the liquor, the shock, and the injuries caught up with Shelley. She was more than halfway up the stairway when she stumbled and fell against the railing. She shrieked and grabbed at the air and then, as both Waverly and Maria watched in horror, she plummeted over the railing and fell to the marble floor of the entry hall. There was a sickening sound as her head struck the marble. She was dead when Dr. Waverly reached her.

For a few moments he was too stunned to speak. Then he turned to Maria. "You've got to help me," he said.

"What do you mean?" Maria asked.

"You saw what happened. It was an accident—she killed herself. But I can't have her found in my house like this. Can you drive a car, Maria?"

"Yes."

"Good. Cynthia's asleep. The pills I gave her will last until morning. I'll get my car out of the garage and you follow me in it. I'll take Mrs. Clifford's body in her car and leave it out on that short cut she uses."

Maria hesitated.

"Do you understand what I've said?" Waverly asked.

"I understand," Maria said, "but suppose the police come—"

"Out on that unpaved stretch? No chance. Anyway, I'll be the one taking the risk. I'll have the body with me. If you see a police car, just keep going."

"Still, there could be trouble," Maria said.

"Maria, there's no time to argue! I'm not going to hurt Mrs. Clifford—she's already dead. But I can't afford a scandal now. This is a matter of self-preservation!"

"With me, too, it is a matter of self-preservation," Maria said coldly.

It took the doctor a few seconds to understand Maria's words. He had taken her for granted too long a time to make a sudden change without a certain anguish. When he finally did understand, he asked how much self-preservation she had in mind.

"A will is risky," she said. "Wills can be changed. Five thousand dollars in cash is more reliable."

"I don't have that much money in the house," he protested.

"I'll take a check," Maria said.

Minutes later, the doctor's check tucked away in her handbag, Maria drove Waverly's sedan at a safe distance behind Mrs. Clifford's little sports car. There was no traffic at all on the narrow road. When they reached a wide shoulder forming a scenic view over a ravine, Waverly stopped the small car and parked off the roadway. Maria stopped the sedan and watched him carry Shelley Clifford's body to the edge of the shoulder and toss it into the shrubbery.

Waverly then returned to the car and emptied Shelley Clifford's handbag of all cash and credit cards. Leaving the emptied purse on the seat, and pocketing the items that a robber would steal, he then took out his pocketknife and jammed it between the treads of one rear tire, letting out the air. The scene was set: a flat tire on a seldom-used road; a passing car hailed and a grim harvest of murder and robbery.

Waverly folded his pocketknife and walked to the waiting sedan. He drove the car back to the house himself and then he and Maria scrubbed away the bloodstains on the marble entry floor.

When they had finished, Waverly said, "Nothing happened here tonight."

"Nothing," Maria agreed, "except that there's a bloodstain on your coat sleeve, Doctor. Give me the coat and I'll sponge out the stain before I go to bed."

Waverly pulled off his suit coat and gave it to her without hesitation. "Don't call me in the morning," he said. "I'm going to take a couple of sleeping pills myself."

Maria took the coat to her room but she didn't sponge out the blood. She turned off the light and tried to sleep. When that didn't work, she got up and packed her bag. In the morning, she got the doctor's bank deposit from his study, the suitcase and the stained coat from her room, and then, because the keys were still in the ignition, drove the doctor's car to the bank. Ordinarily she would have taken the bus. Today was urgent. Because she was so well known at the bank, and particularly after having made the doctor's deposit, she had no difficulty cashing the check for $5000.

On the return trip she took the unpaved short cut. No other cars passed and she reached Mrs. Clifford's abandoned coupe unseen. Drawing alongside, she tossed Dr. Waverly's coat into the front seat, and then drove on.

Both Waverly and his fiancé were still asleep when Maria returned the doctor's sedan to the garage. Then, bag in hand, she walked to the bus stop.

Shelley Clifford's body was found early in the afternoon. The story of her death was on the evening television newscasts. An apparent victim of a casual murderer, her death inspired urgent editorial demand for increased police patrols and an end to permissive education. Ramsey Clifford offered a $10,000 reward for the apprehension and conviction of her murderer. It wasn't until the third day after Shelley's body was found that Lieutenant Gannon came to Dr. Waverly's house. He carried a small bundle wrapped in brown paper.

"I've been doing some checking, Doctor," he said. "I understand that you and the late Shelley Clifford were very good friends."

"You've picked up some gossip," Waverly stated.

"I don't think so. We didn't release all the evidence we had in her death when the body was found. We needed a little time to check out something that was found in the seat of her car—" Gannon ripped open the package and held up Waverly's suit coat. "We've traced this to your tailor, Dr. Waverly, and we've matched the bloodstains to Mrs. Clifford's. Now all we want from you is an explanation of what it was doing in her car."

On the fourth day after Shelley Clifford's death a smartly dressed, middle-aged woman checked into a hotel on the Nevada side of Lake Tahoe. She signed the register as Mrs. Walter Dwyer and then took a stroll through the casino because the atmosphere of a gambling town made her feel closer to Walter. Later, upstairs in her room, she studied the Tucson newspaper she had picked up in the lobby and was amused to learn that the police of that area were conducting an intensive search for her body.

Confronted with his blood-stained jacket, Waverly had told the truth— but he wasn't believed. When it developed that his housekeeper had last been seen on the morning of Mrs. Clifford's death cashing a $5000 check at Waverly's bank, Lieutenant Gannon formed the theory that Waverly had used Maria Morales to get him some ready cash in the event the doctor was linked to Mrs. Clifford and had to leave the country, and had then disposed of the woman so she wouldn't talk.

It was all nonsense, of course, and Maria was sure that Gannon could prove nothing. No crime had been committed. The worst that could happen to Dr. Waverly was that his marriage would be called off. That was a little sad since he deserved Cynthia Reardon as much as she deserved him. The other thing that would happen—and this was the reason she had placed the doctor's coat in Mrs. Clifford's car—was that the community would be made aware of Waverly's true character. This was imperative, in Maria's mind, in view of the nature of his profession.

Mrs. Dwyer remained at the hotel for several weeks. By that time the Tucson papers no longer referred to the Shelley Clifford affair, and she could assume that it was in a state of permanent limbo with no need for her reappearance to save Waverly from a murder charge.

Before leaving the resort, Mrs. Dwyer put a down payment on a smartly furnished condominium apartment which, the salesman assured her, would bring a prime weekly rental in high season. Mrs. Dwyer explained that she traveled in her work and would occupy the apartment only a few months of the year, but that it was nice to have roots somewhere and a woman did need a good investment for her retirement years.

A few days later, a shabbily dressed woman, wearing a look of quiet despair in her eyes, entered the Tahoe bus station. She carried a cheap suitcase and a handbag containing $100 in a money clip. The bills were old —in fact, they were the same bills, in the same money clip, that Maria Morales, who was then 19 and the prettiest cocktail waitress on the Strip, saw drop from Walter Dwyer's pocket as he bent over a casino gambling table. Maria had nothing of her own but a $10 advance on her salary, and when she returned the $100 to Dwyer he was so impressed by her honesty, and other attributes, that he took her to dinner. A week later they were married and the marriage was for love—not the cheap bargain that Dr. Lyle Waverly had tried to make with Cynthia Reardon. The money and the clip had been Walter's wedding present.

"Keep it for luck," he said. "Your Irish luck" . . .

In the bus station Maria bought a ticket to Sacramento, the state capital of California. There would be many wealthy people in that area who were so nervous about their own corruption that they would be eager to hire a housekeeper honest enough to go to the police station with $100 found on the street while looking for a job.

Walter had taught her never to walk out on a winning streak.

THE MARKED MAN
by DAVID ELY

It was early evening when he entered the Park. He headed for the darkest part, away from the lamps that lighted the pathways. He didn't see any other strollers, but he hurried all the same, not wanting to take chances.

When he reached the shelter of the first trees, he stopped and looked back toward the drive, even though he knew the car was no longer there. They had driven off as soon as they'd let him out. He'd been clapped on the shoulder—like the jump sign in a plane—and one of them had said, "Good luck, Major," and then he'd stepped out, with the weight of his flying suit dragging on him.

Good luck, Major. If he did have luck, those would be the last words anyone would address to him for four weeks.

He pulled back, startled. Someone had run past him, right past him, no more than a yard away—a man or boy running hard but with light steps in the direction of Fifth Avenue.

The Major squatted; his breath came quick, his pulse beat high. That had shaken him, whatever it had been—some college kid training for track, or some fellow running for the hell of it, or maybe a purse snatcher, and in that case there might be police on the way. The police were the ones he feared the most. The Agency had cleared things with the Commissioner, and the captains of the nearest precincts had been informed, as a safeguard against publicity in the event he got caught, but of course the ordinary officer didn't know. Just one flash of a patrolman's torch could put an end to the project.

He had to avoid the lights. He'd had no idea there would be so many, not only the lamps along the pathways but also the automobile headlights on the drive that crossed the Park, and the big hotels and apartment buildings along its boundaries.

He kept moving through the trees, trying to shore up his confidence by physical activity. This first night would be the hard one. He knew that. If he managed this one, and the day to come, he'd probably be all right. He'd have to pick a hiding place that was far from where people normally went

—away from the zoo, the lake, and the playing fields. He'd rather be caught by a policeman than by kids playing ball. If one of them got a glimpse of him, they'd all come shouting and pointing. He imagined a grotesque chase—a gang of boys pursuing a man made clumsy by the pilot's suit. They'd be yelling: *His head, his head. Look at his head.*

The head—that was the Agency's guarantee of his honesty. He couldn't cheat, not with that head. When they'd told him about it, he hadn't objected. He knew they were right. The project psychologist had talked to him for a long time about it. The object was to measure the psychological stress on a man hiding in the midst of a hostile population. If they could do that, then they could build a rescue program that made sense for the one pilot in twenty who'd been shot down but not captured, and had managed to hide somewhere—in a field, a bomb-blasted ruin, an abandoned apartment, anywhere he could find.

"You'll be that twentieth pilot, Major," the psychologist had told him. "You'll make it to the Park. Then you'll have to hide until you're rescued. But remember, you're a marked man. You're isolated from the people around you by the one thing you can't change—you can't speak the language. Well, for the purposes of this test, we can simulate almost anything but that. Nothing would prevent you from hiding that flying suit and swiping the pants off some Park tramp if you had to. Then you could just stroll over to the nearest bench to spend a quiet day reading the papers with nobody the wiser, and if some policeman came up to you, you could pass the time of day with him just as nicely as you pleased."

"Oh, we know you have no such intention, Major. We know you're determined to play this thing straight. But we also know that when a man is in a stress situation, even if it's a simulated situation, he may do things he wouldn't normally do. So you understand that we've got to protect the project. We've got to give you a handicap that's roughly the equivalent of loss of language. We've got to make you conspicuous in a way that's beyond your control."

And so they'd shaved his head and stained it green, a clear fresh green, green as new-grown grass.

The Major found a crevice between two boulders at the base of a small ridge. It was just wide enough for him to squeeze his body through. He worked for several hours in there with his entrenching tool hollowing out a cavity in the earth. He had stripped off his pilot's suit and laid it on the ground to hold the dirt he dug out. When he had a load, he gathered up the suit in his arms and carried it off, shaking it, so that the dirt was distributed over a wide area. Then from one of his pockets he took a small can—dog-repellent—and sprayed his entrance carefully.

The spring night was chilly, but at least it wasn't raining. On a wet night he'd have left muddy prints and tracks all over. He was lucky, too, that it was midweek, for there'd be fewer people in the Park during the day. It was the weekends that brought the crowds, and by the weekend he'd have his place improved or would have found a better one.

The night was ending. Dawn was on its way. He watched the sky lighten, and the trees and shrubs take shape. The cold mist was drifting where the ground was low. In the distance the skyscrapers blazed with red fire as the sun struck their crowns. He edged out of the crevice to examine the entrance one last time. There were no traces of his work. The grass was flattened where he had laid the flying suit, but it would rise again, and besides, the Park was full of places where kids had played and couples had spread blankets.

Then he saw his entrenching tool lying on open ground ten feet away. He crawled over and grabbed it, scuttled back, wedged himself through and inside, and lay there, breathing hard. That was worse than carelessness, he thought. The psychologist had warned him that he'd be his own worst enemy, that there'd be times when his fear would make traps for him, that there'd be a weakness in him that couldn't take the strain. He cursed himself, and spat in the dirt. Suppose he hadn't seen that tool and had left it there? Typical, he thought bitterly. He'd always forgotten something; he'd always fallen short. He'd tried to qualify for the space program, but he'd been rejected. He hadn't quite been up to the standards.

But the project psychologist hadn't made it either, had he? The psychologist had been nosed out by psychologists who had just a little bit more on the ball. Yes, the Major thought, he and the psychologist were leftovers. They hadn't made the space team. They weren't quite good enough.

And maybe the project wasn't any better than they were. He had wondered about it already. True, it didn't look bad on paper. But suppose a man could survive undetected in the middle of Manhattan for four weeks—would that really produce much useful information for survival-and-rescue planning? Or was it just a flashy stunt dreamed up by some Operations lieutenant bucking for promotion?

Well, it wasn't his job to criticize the project. He was supposed to make it work—and he wasn't starting off very well. He hadn't made that hole long enough. He couldn't stretch out full length. Already his legs were cramping. He began massaging them. Weariness came on him, and hunger. He hadn't eaten since afternoon. He opened a can of rations, and ate with his fingers, then buried the can in the earth beside him, and put the sleeping mask on his face—it covered the mouth to muffle snoring—and settled back to wait out the day.

By nightfall he was in agony. His legs tormented him. He felt stifled by the mask. He kept falling into a dangerous kind of sleep where he twisted like an animal trying to burrow deeper, or maybe to burrow out into the air and sunlight, his traitor hands trying to rip off the mask, his legs threatening at any moment to go into a full screaming cramp.

The entire population of New York came, it seemed, to climb on his boulders and sit on the ridge above him. He heard voices, footsteps, shouts, laughter. At times unseen feet sent dirt sifting down. He cursed those who came. He feared them, he hated them. Yes, it was a definite reaction. He ought to remember to tell the psychologist. He could imagine what these people were from their voices—stupid kids and nagging mothers, and old men full of nastiness, and younger ones who had no business lounging around parks during the day. He was their prisoner. The least of them might find him, and turn him out to sunlight, like a mole. He clasped his knees tighter, and rocked his body to and fro, grinding his teeth to keep from crying out in pain and rage.

When darkness came, he stretched out at last, his head and shoulders thrust out of the hole and into the narrow space between the boulders. He slept until midnight, and woke in panic when the moon sent its light slicing through the crevice to fall on his upturned face. Then he worked, digging to make his burrow longer. After that he crawled about the area outside picking up candy wrappers, cigarette butts, and sandwich bags—why, he didn't know. Perhaps to wipe out every trace of the people who had tormented him all day.

He forced himself to walk off through the trees. He needed to stay away from his refuge until dawn. The psychologist had warned him he'd be tempted to keep too close to it for the safety it offered, until finally he might surrender to a compulsion to remain in it night and day.

He knew he would have to be careful. He was under unusual pressure: a man alone, fearing every hint of human presence—every voice, every movement, every sound—fearing the light of day most of all. True, it was a simulated situation. He could end it any time he chose. But that would be humiliating to his pride, and hurtful to his career. And he was a volunteer. He'd asked for it.

From one of his pockets he took a radio no larger than a pack of cigarettes. He could transmit three simple signals. The first meant: *I am here.* He sat at the base of a tree, holding the radio, studying the shadows that stretched toward the glow of the lamps along the pathways. At five-minute intervals he repeated: *I am here, I am here.* Somewhere someone was listening. He was in contact with another human being. But then he reasoned that the Agency would be unlikely to pay a technician to sit up night after night simply to monitor his signals. They'd have a machine record them. And the machine would answer him—yes, there it was, a return signal, barely audible.

The return signal meant: *We hear you.* He was heard, then, but only by a machine, and it wouldn't be until morning that they'd check to be sure their man in the Park had called in.

He wondered if the green head had been talked about. Probably. It was too ludicrous for the Houston people to keep quiet about. "Remember that gung-ho major who didn't make the space program? Well, guess where he is now. And guess what color his head is . . . That's right, I said his *head."*

He signaled again—*I am here*— just to hear the machine whisper back: *We hear you, we hear you.* Four weeks of this. They said they'd need that much time in a real situation, first to alert the nearest undercover agent that a flyer was down, and then to allow the agent to track down the signal, and finally, to work out a plan of escape.

He sent his second signal, a variation of the first. It meant: *I receive you.* And the machine dutifully replied: *We receive each other.* That was all. A few pulses through the ether, back and forth, meaningless to an enemy monitoring system, and then one day the *we hear you* would become more frequent, indicating that the agent was coming for him.

There was a third signal. *Emergency.* Which would mean he was sick or caught or couldn't stand it any more and was giving up.

I am here.

I receive you.

Emergency.

This was his vocabulary. This was all he had, he thought. He was just a green-headed man in a dirt-caked flying suit, sitting in a city park at night, talking without words to a machine he'd never seen.

As the days went by, he deepened his burrow, made it more comfortable, more secure, better camouflaged. By night he explored the Park, studying each unknown reach of ground with care before venturing onto it. Whenever he passed the zoo, the animals sensed him, and stirred. It occurred to him that he was like them, in a way—a creature caged, and troubled by the scent of man.

Sometimes he saw others at night. He hid from them, drawing back in the deepest shadows. He had known he wouldn't be alone. The Agency people had told him he'd find himself among the scourings of New York— the weird ones, the oddballs, the misfits, the crazy men, all roaming the Park, hunting one another down. Well, he could take care of himself. He could handle two or three of them with judo and the knife. Besides, any-body who got a look at his head would run, for he was weirder than any of them, and more alone. Except that he would have just four weeks of it, and they were trapped for life. That was a difference; quite a difference.

They were frightened; so was he. They were hungry—and he'd be hun-gry, too. He didn't have enough rations for four weeks. The people at Houston had explained that they wanted him to live off the land—in part, anyway. That meant he would have to rummage through trash baskets looking for apple cores and sandwich leavings. If he had to, he could graze on grass, wild onions, daisies, and chew the bark of saplings. With care he might be able to stretch his rations. He had spent nine days in the Park already. There were nineteen to go, then. He could calculate how much he could allow himself to eat each day.

But of course a downed pilot wouldn't know how long he'd have to hold out. And therefore he, the Major, shouldn't know, either. Surely the Agency people had thought of that. Surely they had planned something to simulate the uncertainties of a real situation.

The Major thought about that. It worried him. He wondered if the Agency people intended to lengthen the test. That must be it. Nobody would come for him on that twenty-eighth night. They'd make him sweat for a few more days, maybe as long as a week.

Or they would trick him in another way. Perhaps they had filled some of the ration cans with water, or sand. It could be that. He would go along half starving himself to maintain food discipline—and then he'd find two or three useless cans.

He hefted each can, and shook it near his ear, but there was no way of telling what was inside. He'd have to wait. He couldn't open the cans early.

They would know that these doubts would occur to him. They would know he'd worry about them. They had planned it that way. It was part of the test. The tension, the strain. On top of the loneliness, on top of the fear. They had lied to him—lied for the good of the project, of course. But it was a dirty business, lying. You told the truth to your friends. That was the rule, wasn't it? It was the enemy you lied to.

The sounding of a siren deep in the city came echoing across the Park. He glanced uneasily around in the darkness, hearing something in that distant mechanical cry that made him want to speak out—to curse, to pray, anything—just to hear his own voice. But he was afraid to speak aloud; he was afraid.

He had premonitions of deep hunger. His limbs and eyes would ache. Sometimes he would drift in the delirium of fatigue. He worried about remembering things. When he filled his canteen at the lake, had he put in the purifier? Fear nagged at his senses, sharpening some, dulling others. He lost the exact count of his days—was it sixteen, seventeen?—but he had a greater awareness of the shape and touch of things.

He lived in the dark. He never saw the sun. By day he lay in his hole, sweating in the thick air, listening drowsily to the voices of people he could not see. He dreamed of capture, of death. When night came, he crept out, his body stiff, his bones aching, to face the dangers of the darkness.

One night he saw an old man shuffling along a path some thirty yards away, and he knew what would happen even before it occurred, as though it had taken place already in his dreams. Two figures rushed out of the dark; the old man fell at once to the ground beneath their blows. They tore at his clothing, searching for something of value. The Major crouched where he was, his knife open in his hand, but he was unable to intervene. He could not jeopardize the project.

Besides, the robbers moved with the swiftness of young men. He might not be equal to them, weakened as he was. They found nothing, and in their fury they kicked their victim, and stamped on his face before they ran off. The old man might be dead or dying, and yet the Major could do nothing, and so he turned away, in a rage that he had been the one to see that attack, impotent as he was, when those who might have helped were sleeping in comfort far away—the ones for whom the Park had been created, for whom it was patrolled and kept clean, and for whose amusement the zoo beasts were caged. The body would be found in the morning, and removed. They would not know about it. The incident was too common to warrant more than a line or two in the newspapers. At noon people would be walking over the very spot.

He saw other things on other nights—a dog stoned to death; a woman raped; a cripple beaten with his own crutch; a tramp sleeping in newspapers set afire and sent dancing, dressed in flames.

His anger left him. He watched as an animal might watch, ready at any moment to retreat and hide. The daytime people had lost the attributes of humankind. They were only voices, and footsteps. He could no longer imagine their faces. The ones who appeared at night were little more than shadows; still, they seemed more real to him. He thought about them often, wondering if any of these miserable, ferocious outcasts inhabited the Park as he did, hiding by day, prowling by night. He wasn't sure; he couldn't tell. But he wanted to believe there were at least a few. It made him feel less alone.

There were heavy rains for several days. His shelter was a morass. He himself was smeared with mud. His hands were blackened now. He thought that perhaps his face, too, had changed color, for the filth and dirt of the Park had been ground into his skin. He could feel his new-grown hair and beard stubble, and he wondered what he might look like, but he could not form a satisfactory picture in his mind.

He thought the full period had elapsed, but he wasn't sure. In any case, he had mastered the test; he had survived. But his achievement wasn't much. He had got through a few weeks. Those others—the night people of the Park—they had survived years. And in all that time no one had come to save them. No one had sought to arrange their escape.

He picked up his radio, and sent the signal. *I am here, I am here.* And the answer came back as always: *We hear you, we hear you.* But now he wondered—did they really hear him, were they listening?

For a time he was ill. He didn't know for how long. He lay in his burrow shivering with fever day and night. He had difficulty remembering why he was there, and pondered the matter, puzzled, until the answer came to him—oh, yes, the project. But it seemed to him that the project was not reason enough for him to be buried this way, alone and suffering and sick. There must be another, more important reason. He could not think what it might be.

His fever slackened, but he remained hidden. He did not care to leave his refuge. The project people might be searching for him, he realized. They would come at night with dogs and flares. But if they couldn't find him? If he'd hidden himself too well? Perhaps this time he had done that absolutely first-rate piece of work he had been struggling to do all his life—and it would be the end of him. How the Agency men would grumble. How annoyed with him they'd be. They might suspect that he had sabotaged the project on purpose, vanishing into the earth like that.

Or maybe they wouldn't come at all. Maybe they wouldn't search. They hadn't looked for the others—the other men who lived underground. They hadn't cared about them. Perhaps he, too, would be abandoned.

He crawled to the lake. He was too weak to stand. At the water's edge he plunged his head down and drank at the reflected lights of the buildings as though by drinking he could extinguish them. He drank the foulness of the water that had already put poison in him, but the lights remained on the surface, and when he roiled the water with his hand, the lights raced back and forth, dancing, shaking, as if quivering with laughter.

The days were hot now, the nights humid. There was the odor of decay everywhere. The rain slid down like grease. There was no grass to eat; it had been trodden away. The bark of the young trees was denied him, for somehow he had lost his knife. He scraped with his fingernails at the saplings, pulled weeds from the earth, leaves from the shrubs.

It was clear to him now that he had misinterpreted the meaning of the test. The object wasn't survival. A man who wants to survive doesn't hide in the earth, doesn't make himself sick with loneliness and fear—no, no, a man who does that has been betrayed into doing it. *Good luck, Major.* They had sent him off to get rid of him. He wasn't quite good enough for their needs, and so they shoved him out with a Judas touch to bury himself among the other outcasts for the sake of the project, which was death.

He was expected to die. He knew that now. They did not really believe, did they, that a man shot out of the sky could be rescued? The risks were too great. No agent—if there were any agents—could be asked to undertake them. Rather, their intention was to prevent a pilot from surrendering by persuading him that all he had to do was find a hiding place and wait for a rescue that had never even been considered. It would be death that came instead.

The radio was the cleverest part of the trick. A desperate man would believe its lies right up to the end, but there was no one listening, not even a machine, for surely it was the radio itself that produced those answering responses, as if they came from far away: *We hear you.* That was the ultimate betrayal, to kill a man with hope.

He was to die, like those others who lived underground, the hopeless ones, too weak to strike out at the enemies who had promised to save them but didn't come, who gave them short rations and told them to eat grass, who'd shorn their heads to humiliate them into hiding. And the poor crippled fools, they had accepted all that, just as he had. They had been eager to make the project work—and if the daytime laughter overhead sometimes drove them to violence, all they were capable of doing was to maim and to kill one another.

The project was death. They were all to die. Very well, he thought, but let them die in the sight of their executioners, let them die in the open air, beneath the sun.

He left his refuge at noon, when the Park was crowded. The sun was blinding. At first he could hardly see the people among whom he staggered, his arms outstretched, feeling his way. He gestured impatiently at trees, bushes, rocks; he shouted for the others to come out of hiding, too. He went tottering about looking for them, commanding them to appear.

The crowds gathered to follow him, warily and at some distance until they saw how weak he was. He fell sometimes, and crawled, rose again to his feet and lurched forward, crying out a summons that went unanswered.

People came nearer; they circled around him. Boys ran up close, hooting. Women held their babies high, so they, too, could see, the young men jogged over from the playing fields, anxious to look at the green-headed man crusted with dried mud, the madman in rags, the zany, the fool howling in their midst—yes, all were eager to have a good look at him before the police arrived to bundle him away.

FLOWERS THAT BLOOM
IN THE SPRING
by JULIAN SYMONS

The outsider, Bertie Mays was fond of saying, sees most of the game. In the affair of the Purchases and the visiting cousin from South Africa he saw quite literally all of it. And the end was enigmatic and a little frightening, at least as seen through Bertie's eyes. It left him with the question whether there had been a game at all.

Bertie had retired early from his unimportant and uninteresting job in the Ministry of Welfare. He had a private income, he was unmarried, and his only extravagance was a passion for travel, so why go on working? Bertie gave up his London flat and settled down in the cottage in the Sussex countryside which he had bought years earlier as a weekend place. It was quite big enough for a bachelor, and Mrs. Last from the village came in two days a week to clean the place. Bertie himself was an excellent cook.

It was a fine day in June when he called next door to offer Sylvia Purchase a lift to the tea party at the Hall. She was certain to have been asked, and he knew she would need a lift because he had seen her husband Jimmy putting a case into the trunk of their ancient Morris. Jimmy was some sort of freelance journalist, and often went on trips, leaving Sylvia on her own. Bertie, who was flirtatious by nature, had asked if she would like him to keep her company, but she did not seem responsive to the suggestion.

Linton House, which the Purchases had rented furnished a few months earlier, was a rambling old place with oak beams and low ceilings. There was an attractive garden, some of which lay between the house and Bertie's cottage, and by jumping over the fence between them Bertie could walk across this garden. He did so that afternoon, taking a quick peek into the sitting room as he went by. He could never resist such peeks, because he always longed to know what people might be doing when they thought nobody was watching. On this occasion the sitting room was empty. He found Sylvia in the kitchen, washing dishes in a halfhearted way.

"Sylvia, you're not ready." She had on a dirty old cardigan with the buttons done up wrong. Bertie himself was, as always, dressed very suitably for the occasion in a double-breasted blue blazer with brass buttons, fawn trousers, and a neat bow tie. He always wore bow ties, which he felt gave him a touch of distinction.

"Ready for what?"

"Has the Lady of the Manor not asked you to tea?" That was his name for Lady Hussey up at the Hall.

She clapped a hand to her forehead, leaving a slight smudge. "I forgot all about it! Don't think I'll go, can't stand those bun fights."

"But I have called specially to collect you. Let me be your chauffeur. Your carriage awaits." Bertie made a sketch of a bow, and Sylvia laughed. She was a blonde in her early thirties, attractive in a slapdash sort of way.

"Bertie, you are a fool. All right, give me five minutes."

The women may call Bertie Mays a fool, Bertie thought, but how they adore him.

"Oh," Sylvia said. She was looking behind Bertie, and when he turned he saw a man standing in the shadow of the door. At first glance he thought it was Jimmy, for the man was large and square like Jimmy and had the same gingery fair coloring. But the resemblance went no further, for as the man stepped forward he saw that their features were not similar.

"This is my cousin, Alfred Wallington. He's paying us a visit from South Africa. Our next door neighbor, Bertie Mays."

"Pleased to meet you." Bertie's hand was firmly gripped. The two men went into the sitting room, and Bertie asked whether this was Mr. Wallington's first visit.

"By no means. I know England pretty well. The south, anyway."

"Ah, business doesn't take you up north?" Bertie thought of himself as a tactful but expert interrogator, and the question should have brought a response telling him Mr. Wallington's occupation. In fact, however, the other man merely said that was so.

"In the course of my work I used to correspond with several firms in Cape Town," Bertie said untruthfully. Wallington did not comment. "Is your home near there?"

"No."

The negative was so firm that it gave no room for further conversational maneuver. Bertie felt slightly cheated. If the man did not want to say where he lived in South Africa, of course he was free to say nothing, but there was a certain finesse to be observed in such matters, and a crude "no" was not at all the thing. He was able to establish at least that this was the first time Wallington had visited Linton House.

On the way up to the Hall he said to Sylvia that her cousin seemed a dour fellow.

"Alf?" Bertie winced at the abbreviation. "He's all right when you get to know him."

"He said he was often in the south. What's his particular sphere of interest?"

"I don't know. I believe he's got some sort of export business around Durban. By the way, Bertie, how did you know Jimmy was away?"

"I saw him waving good-bye to you." It would hardly do to say that he had been peeping through the curtains.

"Did you now? I was in bed when he went. You're a bit of a fibber, I'm afraid, Bertie."

"Oh, I can't remember *how* I knew." Really, it was too much to be taken up on every little point.

When they drove into the great courtyard and Sylvia got out of the car, however, he reflected that she looked very slenderly elegant, and that he was pleased to be with her. Bertie liked pretty women and they were safe with him, although he would not have thought of it that way. He might have said, rather, that he would never have compromised a lady, with the implication that all sorts of things might be said and done providing they stayed within the limits of discretion.

It occurred to him that Sylvia was hardly staying within those limits when she allowed herself to be alone at Linton House with her South African cousin. Call me old-fashioned, Bertie said to himself, but I don't like it.

The Hall was a nineteenth-century manor house and by no means, as Bertie had often said, an architectural gem, but the lawns at the back where tea was served were undoubtedly fine. Sir Reginald Hussey was a building contractor who had been knighted for some dubious service to the export drive. He was in demand for opening fêtes and fund-raising enterprises, and the Husseys entertained a selection of local people to parties of one kind or another half a dozen times a year. The parties were always done in style, and this afternoon there were maids in white caps and aprons, and a kind of majordomo who wore a frock coat and white gloves. Sir Reginald was not in evidence, but Lady Hussey presided in a regal manner.

Of course Bertie knew that it was all ridiculously vulgar and ostentatious, but still he enjoyed himself. He kissed Lady Hussey's hand and said that the scene was quite entrancing, like a Victorian period picture, and he had an interesting chat with Lucy Broadhinton, who was the widow of an Admiral. Lucy was the president and Bertie the secretary of the local historical society, and they were great friends. She told him now in the strictest secrecy about the outrageous affair Mrs. Monro was having with somebody who must be nameless, although from the details given, Bertie was quite able to guess his identity. There were other tidbits too, like the story of the scandalous misuse of the Church Fund restoration money. It was an enjoyable afternoon, and he fairly chortled about it on the way home.

"They're such snobby affairs," Sylvia said. "I don't know why I went."

"You seemed to be having a good time. I was quite jealous."

Sylvia had been at the center of a very animated circle of three or four young men. Her laughter at their jokes had positively rung out across the lawns, and Bertie had seen Lady Hussey give more than one disapproving glance in the direction of the little group. There was something undeniably attractive about Sylvia's gaiety and about the way in which she threw back her head when laughing, but her activities had a recklessness about them which was not proper for a lady.

Bertie tried to convey something of this as he drove back, but was not sure she understood what he meant. He also broached delicately the impropriety of her being alone in the house with her cousin by asking when Jimmy would be coming back. In a day or two, she said casually. He refused her invitation to come in for a drink. He had no particular wish to see Alf Wallington again.

On the following night at about midnight, when Bertie was in bed reading, he heard a car draw up next door. Doors were closed and there was the sound of voices. Just to confirm that Jimmy was back, Bertie got out of bed and lifted an edge of the curtain. A man and a woman were coming out of the garage. The woman was Sylvia. The man had his arm round her, and as Bertie watched, the man bent down and kissed her neck. Then they moved toward the front door, and the man laughed and said something. From his general build he might, seen in the dim light, have been Jimmy, but the voice had the distinctive South African accent of Wallington.

Bertie drew away from the window as though he had been scalded.

It was a feeling of moral responsibility that took him round to Linton House on the following day. To his surprise Jimmy Purchase opened the door.

"I—ah—thought you were away."

"Got back last night. What can I do for you?"

Bertie said he would like to borrow the electric hedge clippers, which he knew were in the garden shed. Jimmy led the way there and handed them over. Bertie said he had heard the car coming back at about midnight.

"Yeah." Jimmy had a deplorably Cockney voice, not at all out of the top drawer. "That was Sylvia and Alf. He took her to a dance over at Ladersham. I was too fagged out, just wanted to get my head down."

"Her cousin from South Africa?"

"Yeah, right, from the Cape. He's staying here for a bit. Plenty of room."

Was he from the Cape or from Durban? Bertie did not fail to notice the discrepancy.

Bertie's bump of curiosity was even stronger than his sense of propriety. It became important, even vital, that he should know just what was going on next door. When he returned the hedge cutters he asked them all to dinner, together with Lucy Broadhinton to make up the number. He took pains in preparing a delicious cold meal. The salmon was cooked to perfection, and the hollandaise sauce had just the right hint of something tart beneath its blandness.

The evening was not a success. Lucy had on a long dress and Bertie wore a smart velvet jacket, but Sylvia was dressed in sky-blue trousers and a vivid shirt, and the two men wore open-necked shirts and had a distinctly unkempt appearance. They had obviously been drinking before they arrived. Wallington tossed down Bertie's expensive hock as though it were water, and then said that South African wine had more flavor than that German stuff.

"You're from Durban, I believe, Mr. Wallington." Lucy fixed him with her Admiral's-lady glance. "My husband and I were there in the sixties, and thought it delightful. Do you happen to know the Morrows or the Page-Manleys? Mary Page-Manley gave such delightful parties."

Wallington looked at her from under heavy brows. "Don't know them."

"You have an export business in Durban?"

"That's right."

There was an awkward pause. Then Sylvia said, "Alf's trying to persuade us to pay him a visit out there."

"I'd like you to come out. Don't mind about him." Wallington jerked a thumb at Jimmy. "Believe me, we'd have a good time."

"I do believe you, Alf." She gave her head-back laugh, showing the fine column of her neck. "It's something we've forgotten here—how to have a good time."

Jimmy Purchase had been silent during dinner. Now he said, "People here just don't have the money. Like the song says, it's money makes the world go round."

"The trouble in Britain is that too much money has got into the wrong hands." Lucy looked round the table. Nobody seemed inclined to argue the point. "There are too many grubby little people with sticky fingers."

"I wish some of the green stuff would stick to my fingers," Jimmy said, and hiccuped. Bertie realized with horror that he was drunk. "We're broke, Sylvie, old girl."

"Oh, shut up."

"You don't believe me?" And he actually began to empty out his pockets. What appalling creatures the two men were, each as bad as the other. Bertie longed for the evening to end, and was delighted when Lucy rose to make a stately departure. He whispered an apology in the hall, but she told him not to be foolish, it had been fascinating.

When he returned, Wallington said, "What an old battleaxe. *Did you happen to know the Page-Manleys.* Didn't know they were still around, people like that."

Sylvia was looking at Bertie. "Alf, you're shocking our host."

"Sorry, man, but honest, I thought they kept her sort in museums. Stuffed."

"You mustn't say stuffed. That'll shock Bertie too."

Bertie said stiffly, "I am not in the least shocked, but I certainly regard it as the height of bad manners to criticize a guest in such a manner. Lucy is a very dear friend of mine."

Sylvia at least had some understanding of his feelings. She said sorry and smiled, so that he was at once inclined to forgive her. Then she said it was time she took her rough diamonds home.

"Thanks for the grub," Wallington said. Then he leaned across the dining table and shouted, "Wake up, man, it's tomorrow morning already." Jimmy had fallen asleep in his chair. He was hauled to his feet and supported across the garden.

Bertie called up Lucy the next morning and apologized again. She said he should think no more about it. "I didn't take to that South African feller, though. Shouldn't be surprised if he turns out to be a bad hat. And I didn't care too much for your neighbors, if you don't mind my being frank."

Bertie said of course not, although he reflected that there seemed to be a sudden spasm of frankness among his acquaintances. Mrs. Purchase, Lucy said, had a roving eye. She left it at that, and they went on to discuss the agenda for the next meeting of the historical society.

Later in the morning there was a knock on the door. Jimmy was there, hollow-eyed and slightly green. " 'Fraid we rather blotted our copybook last night. Truth is, Alf and I were fairly well loaded before we came round. Can't remember too much about it, but Syl said apologies were in order."

Bertie asked when Sylvia's cousin was leaving. Jimmy Purchase shrugged and said he didn't know. Bertie nearly said that he ought not to leave the man alone with Sylvia, but refrained. He might be inquisitive, but he was also discreet.

A couple of nights later he was doing some weeding in the garden when he heard voices raised in Linton House. One was Jimmy's, the other belonged to Sylvia. They were in the sitting room shouting at each other, not quite loudly enough for the words to be distinguishable. It was maddening not to know what was being said. Bertie moved along the fence separating the gardens, until he was as near as he could get without being seen. He was now able to hear a few phrases.

"Absolutely sick of it . . . drink because it takes my mind off . . . told you we have to wait . . ." That was Jimmy.

Then Sylvia's voice, shrill as he had never heard it, shrill and sneering. "Tell me the old, old story . . . how long do we bloody well wait then . . . you said it would be finished by now." An indistinguishable murmur from Jimmy. "None of your business," she said. More murmuring. "None of your business what I do." Murmur murmur. "You said yourself we're broke." To this there was some reply. Then she said clearly, "I shall do what I like."

"*All right,*" Jimmy said, so loudly that Bertie fairly jumped. There followed a sharp crack, which sounded like hand on flesh.

Sylvia said, "You damn—that's it, then."

Nothing more. No sound, no speech. Bertie waited five minutes and then tiptoed away, fearful of being seen. Once indoors again he felt quite shaky, and had to restore himself by a nip of brandy.

What had the conversation meant? Much of it was plain enough. Sylvia was saying that it was none of her husband's business if she carried on an affair. But what was it they had to wait for, what was it that should have been finished? A deal connected with the odious Alf? And where was Alf, who as Bertie had noticed went out into the village very little?

He slept badly, and was wakened in the middle of the night by a piercing, awful scream. He sat up in bed quivering, but the sound was not repeated. He decided that he must have been having a nightmare.

On the following day the car was not in the garage. Had Jimmy gone off again? He met Sylvia out shopping in the village, and she said that he had been called to an assignment on short notice.

"What sort of assignment?" He had asked before for the name of the paper Jimmy worked on, to be told that he was a freelance.

"A Canadian magazine. He's up in the Midlands, may be away a few days."

Should he say something about the row? But that would have been indiscreet, and in any case Sylvia had such a wild look in her eye that he did not care to ask further questions. It was on that morning that he read about the Small Bank Robbers.

The Small Bank Robbers had been news for some months. They specialized in fast well-organized raids on banks, and had carried out nearly 20 of these in the past year. Several men were involved in each raid. They were armed, and did not hesitate to use coshes or revolvers when necessary. In one bank a screaming woman customer had suffered a fractured skull when hit over the head, and in another a guard who resisted the robbers had been shot and killed.

The diminutive applied to them—small—referred to the banks they robbed, not to their own physical dimensions. A bank clerk who had

admitted giving information to the gang had asked why they were interested in his small branch bank, and had been told that they always raided
small banks because they were much more vulnerable than large ones. After
the arrest of this clerk the robbers seemed to have gone underground. There
had been no news of them for the last three weeks.

Bertie had heard about the Small Bank Robbers, but took no particular
interest in them. He was a nervous man, and did not care to read about
crime. On this morning, however, his eye was caught by the heading:
"Small Bank Robbers. The South African Connection." The story was a
feature by the paper's crime reporter, Derek Holmes. He said that Scotland
Yard knew the identities of some of the robbers, and described his own
investigations, which led to the conclusion that three or four of them were
in Spain. The article continued:

"But there is another connection, and a sinister one. The men in Spain
are small fry. My researches suggest that the heavy men who organized the
robberies, and were very ready to use violence, came from South Africa.
They provided the funds and the muscle. Several witnesses who heard the
men talking to each other or giving orders during the raids have said that
they used odd accents. This has been attributed to the sound distortion
caused by the stocking masks they wore, but two men I spoke to, both of
whom have spent time in South Africa, said that they had *no doubt the accent
was South African.*"

The writer suggested that these men were now probably back in South
Africa. But supposing that one of them was still in England, that he knew
Jimmy and Sylvia and had a hold over them? Supposing, even, that Jimmy
and Sylvia were minor members of the gang themselves? The thought made
Bertie shiver with fright and excitement. What should or could he do
about it? And where had Jimmy Purchase gone?

Again he slept badly, and when he did fall into a doze it was a short one.
He dreamed that Wallington was knocking on the door. Once inside the
house the South African drew out a huge wad of notes, said that there was
enough for everybody, and counted out bundles which he put on the table
between them with a small decisive *thwack.* A second bundle, *thwack,* and a
third, *thwack.* How many more? He tried to cry out, to protest, but the
bundles went on, *thwack, thwack, thwack . . .*

He sat up in bed, crying out something inaudible. The thin gray light of
early morning came through the curtains. There was a sound in the garden
outside, a sound regularly repeated, the *thwack* of his dream. It took him, in
his slightly dazed state, a little while to realize that if he went to the
window he might see what was causing the sound. He tiptoed across the
room and raised the curtain. He was trembling.

It was still almost dark, and whatever was happening was taking place at
the back of Linton House, so that he could not see it. But as he listened to

the regularly repeated sound, he had no doubt of its nature. Somebody was digging out there. The sound of the spade digging earth had entered his dream, and there was an occasional clink when it struck a stone. Why would somebody be digging at this time in the morning? He remembered that terrible cry on the previous night, the cry he had thought to be a dream. Supposing it had been real, who had cried out?

The digging stopped and two people spoke, although he could not hear the words or even the tones. One, light and high in pitch, was no doubt Sylvia's, but was the other voice Wallington's? And if it was, had Jimmy Purchase gone away at all?

In the half light a man and woman were briefly visible before they passed into the house. The man carried a spade, but his head was down and Bertie could not see his face, only his square bulky figure. He had little doubt that the man was Wallington.

That morning he went up to London. He had visited the city rarely since his retirement, finding that on each visit he was more worried and confused. The place seemed continually to change, so that what had been a landmark of some interest was now a kebab or hamburger restaurant. The article had appeared in the *Banner,* and their offices had moved from Fleet Street to somewhere off the Gray's Inn Road. He asked for Arnold Grayson, a deputy editor he had known slightly, to be told that Grayson had moved to another paper. He had to wait almost an hour before he was able to talk to Derek Holmes. The crime reporter remained staring at his desk while he listened to Bertie's story. During the telling of it Holmes chewed gum and said "Yup" occasionally.

"Yup," he said again at the end. "Okay, Mr. Mays. Thanks."

"What are you going to do about it?"

Holmes removed his gum and considered the question. "Know how many people been in touch about that piece, saying they've seen the robbers, their landlord's one of them, they heard two South Africans talking in a bus about how the loot should be split, et cetera? One hundred and eleven. Half of 'em are sensationalists, the other half plain crazy."

"But this is different."

"They're all different. I shouldn'ta seen you only you mentioned Arnie, and he was a good friend. But what's it amount to? Husband and wife having a shindig, husband goes off, South African cousin's digging a flowerbed—"

"At that time in the morning?"

The reporter shrugged. "People are funny."

"Have you got pictures of the South Africans you say are involved in the robberies? If I could recognize Wallington—"

Holmes put another piece of gum in his mouth, chewed on it meditatively, then produced half a dozen photographs. None of them resembled

Wallington. Holmes shuffled the pictures together and put them away. "That's it then."

"But aren't you going to come down and look into it? I tell you I believe murder has been done. Wallington is her lover. Together they have killed Purchase."

"If Wallington's lying low with his share of the loot, the last thing he'd do is get involved in this sort of caper. You know your trouble, Mr. Mays? You've got an overheated imagination."

If only he knew somebody at Scotland Yard! But there was no reason to think that they would take him any more seriously than the newspaperman had. He returned feeling both chastened and frustrated. To his surprise Sylvia got out of another carriage on the train. She greeted him cheerfully.

"Hallo, Bertie. I've just been seeing Alf off."

"Seeing Alf off?" he echoed stupidly.

"Back to South Africa. He had a letter saying they needed him back there."

"Back in Durban?"

"That's right."

"Jimmy said he was from the Cape."

"Did he? Jimmy often gets things wrong."

It was not in Bertie's nature to be anything but gallant to a lady, even one he suspected of being a partner in murder. "Now that you are a grass widow again, you must come in and have a dish of tea."

"That would be lovely."

"Tomorrow?"

"It's a date."

They had reached his cottage. She pressed two fingers to her lips, touched his cheek with them. Inside the cottage the telephone was ringing. It was Holmes.

"Mr. Mays? Thought you'd like to know. Your chum Purchase is just what he said, a freelance journalist. One or two of the boys knew him. Not too successful from what I hear."

"So you did pay some attention to what I told you!"

"Always try and check a story out. Nothing to this one, far as I can see."

"Wallington has gone back to South Africa. Suddenly, just like that."

"Has he now? Good luck to him."

Triumph was succeeded by indignation. He put down the telephone without saying good-bye.

Was it all the product of an overheated imagination? He made scones for Sylvia's visit next day and served them with his home-made blackcurrant preserve. Then he put the question that still worried him. He would have liked to introduce it delicately, but somehow didn't manage that.

"What was all that digging in the garden early the other morning?"

Sylvia looked startled, and then exclaimed as a fragment of the scone she was eating dropped onto her dress. When it had been removed she said, "Sorry you were disturbed. It was Timmy."

"Timmy?"

"Our tabby. He must have eaten something poisoned and he died. Poor Timmy. Alf dug a grave and we gave him Christian burial." With hardly a pause she went on, "We're clearing out at the end of the week."

"Leaving?" For a moment he could hardly believe it.

"Right. I'm a London girl at heart, you know, always was. The idea of coming here was that Jimmy would be able to do some writing of his own, but that never seemed to work out—he was always being called away. If I'm in London I can get a job, earn some money. Very necessary at the moment. If Alf hadn't helped out, I don't know what we'd have done. It was a crazy idea coming down here, but then we're crazy people."

And at the end of that week Sylvia went. Since the house had been rented furnished, she had only suitcases to take away. She came to say good-bye. There was no sign of Jimmy, and Bertie asked about him.

"Still up on that job. But anyway he wouldn't have wanted to come down and help, he hates things like that. Good-bye, Bertie, we'll meet again I expect." A quick kiss on the cheek and she was driving off in her rented car.

She departed leaving all sorts of questions unanswered when Bertie came to think about it, mundane ones like an address if anybody should want to get in touch with her or with Jimmy, and things he would have liked to know, such as the reason for digging the cat's grave at such an extraordinary hour. He found himself more and more suspicious of the tale she had told. The row he had overheard could perhaps be explained by lack of money, but it seemed remarkable that Jimmy Purchase had not come back.

Linton House was locked up and empty, but it was easy enough to get into the garden. The area dug up was just inside the boundary fence. It was difficult to see how much had been dug because there was a patch of earth at each side, but it looked like a large area to bury a cat.

On impulse one day, a week after Sylvia had gone, Bertie took a spade into the garden and began to dig. It proved to be quite hard work, and he went down two feet before reaching the body. It was that of a cat, one he vaguely remembered seeing in the house, but Sylvia's story of its death had been untrue. Its head was mangled, shattered by one or two heavy blows.

Bertie looked at the cat with distaste—he did not care for seeing dead things—returned it, and had just finished shoveling back the earth when he was hailed from the road. He turned, and with a sinking heart saw the local constable, P.C. Harris, standing beside his bicycle.

"Ah, it's you, Mr. Mays. I was thinking it might be somebody with burglarious intent. Somebody maybe was going to dig a tunnel to get entrance into the house. But perhaps it was your *own* house you was locked out of." P.C. Harris was well known as a local wag, and nobody laughed more loudly at his own jokes. He laughed heartily now. Bertie joined in feebly.

"But what *was* you doing digging in the next-door garden, may I ask?" What could he say? I was digging for a man, but only found a cat? Desperately Bertie said, "I'd—ah—lost something and thought it might have got in here. I was just turning the earth."

The constable shook his head. "You was trespassing, Mr. Mays. This is not your property."

"No, of course not. It won't happen again. I'd be glad if you could forget it." He approached the constable, a pound note in his hand.

"No need for that, sir, which might be construed as a bribe and hence an offense in itself. I shall not be reporting the matter on this occasion, nor inquiring further into the whys and wherefores, but would strongly advise you in future to keep within the bounds of your own property."

Pompous old fool, Bertie thought, but said that of course he would do just that. He scrambled back into his own garden, aware that he made a slightly ludicrous figure. P.C. Harris, in a stately manner, mounted his bicycle and rode away.

That was almost, but not quite, the end of the story.

Linton House was empty for a few weeks and then rented again, to a family called Hobson who had two noisy children. Bertie had as little to do with them as possible. He was very conscious of having been made to look a fool, and there was nothing he disliked more than that. He was also aware of a disinclination in himself to enter Linton House again.

In the late spring of the following year he went to Sardinia for a holiday, driving around on his own, looking at the curious nuraghi and the burial places made from gigantic blocks of stone which are called the tombs of the giants. He drove up the western coast in a leisurely way, spending long mornings and afternoons over lunches and dinners in the small towns, and then moving inland to bandit country. He was sitting nursing a drink in a square at Nuoro, which is the capital of the central province, when he heard his name called.

It was Sylvia, so brown that he hardly recognized her. "Bertie, what are you doing here?"

He said that he was on holiday, and returned the question.

"Just come down to shop. We have a house up in the hills—you must come and see it. Darling, look who's here."

A bronzed Jimmy Purchase approached across the square. Like Sylvia he seemed in fine spirits, and endorsed enthusiastically the suggestion that Bertie should come out to their house. It was a few miles from the city on the slopes of Mount Ortobene, a long low white modern house at the end of a rough road. They sat in a courtyard and ate grilled fish, and drank a hard dry local white wine.

Bertie felt his natural curiosity rising. How could he ask questions without appearing to be—well—nosy? Over coffee he said that he supposed Jimmy was out here on an assignment.

It was Sylvia who answered. "Oh, no, he's given all that up since the book was published."

"The book?"

"Show him, Jimmy." Jimmy went into the house. He returned with a book which said on the cover *My Tempestuous Life. As told by Anita Sorana to Jimmy Purchase.*

"You've heard of her?"

It would have been difficult not to have heard of Anita Sorana. She was a screen actress famous equally for her temperament, her five well-publicized marriages, and the variety of her love affairs.

"It was fantastic luck when she agreed that Jimmy should write her autobiography. It was all very hush-hush and we had to pretend that he was off on assignments when he was really with Anita."

Jimmy took it up. "Then she'd break appointments, say she wasn't in the mood to talk. A few days afterwards she'd ask to see me at a minute's notice. Then Sylvia started to play up—"

"I thought he was having an affair with her. She certainly fancied him. He swears he wasn't, but I don't know. Anyway, it was worth it." She yawned.

"The book was a success?"

Jimmy grinned, teeth very white in his brown face. "I'll say. Enough for me to shake off the dust of Fleet Street."

So the quarrel was explained, and Jimmy's sudden absences, and his failure to return. After a glass of some fiery local liqueur Bertie felt soporific, conscious that he had drunk a little more than usual. There was some other question he wanted to ask, but he did not remember it until they were driving him down the mountain, back to his hotel in Nuoro.

"How is your cousin?"

Jimmy was driving. "Cousin?"

"Mr. Wallington, Sylvia's cousin from South Africa."

Sylvia, from the back of the car, said, "Alf's dead."

"Dead!"

"In a car accident. Soon after he got back to South Africa. Wasn't it sad?"

Very few more words were spoken before they reached the hotel and said good-bye. The heat of the hotel room and the wine he had drunk made Bertie fall asleep at once. After a couple of hours he woke, sweating, and wondered if he believed what he had been told. Was it possible to make enough money from "ghosting" (he had heard that was the word) a life story to retire to Sardinia? It seemed unlikely. He lay on his back in the dark room, and it seemed to him that he saw with terrible clarity what had happened.

Wallington was one of the Small Bank Robbers, and he had come to the Purchases looking for a safe place to stay. He had his money, what Holmes had called the loot, with him, and they had decided to kill him for it. The quarrel had been about when Wallington would be killed, the sound that wakened him in the night had been Wallington's death cry.

Jimmy had merely pretended to go away that night, and had returned to help Sylvia dispose of the body. Jimmy dug the grave and they put Wallington in it. Then the cat had been killed and put into a shallow grave on top of the body. It was the killing of the cat, those savage blows on its head, that somehow horrified Bertie most.

He cut short his holiday and took the next plane back. At home he walked round to the place where he had dug up the cat. The Hobsons had put in bedding plants, and the wallflowers were flourishing. He had read somewhere that flowers always flourished over a grave.

"Not thinking of trespassing again, I hope, Mr. Mays?"

It was P.C. Harris, red-faced and jovial.

Bertie shook his head. What he had imagined in the hotel room might be true, but then again it might not. Supposing that he went to the police, supposing he was able to convince them that there was something in his story, supposing they dug up the flowerbed and found nothing but the cat? He would be the laughingstock of the neighborhood.

Bertie Mays knew that he would say nothing.

"I reckon you was feeling a little bit eccentric that night you was doing the digging," P.C. Harris said sagely.

"Yes, I think I must have been."

"They make a fine show, them wallflowers. Makes you more cheerful, seeing spring flowers."

"Yes," said Bertie Mays meekly. "They make a fine show."

A NICE PLACE TO STAY
by NEDRA TYRE

All my life I've wanted a nice place to stay. I don't mean anything grand, just a small room with the walls freshly painted and a few neat pieces of furniture and a window to catch the sun so that two or three pot plants could grow. That's what I've always dreamed of. I didn't yearn for love or money or nice clothes, though I was a pretty enough girl and pretty clothes would have made me prettier—not that I mean to brag.

Things fell on my shoulders when I was fifteen. That was when Mama took sick, and keeping house and looking after Papa and my two older brothers—and of course nursing Mama—became my responsibility. Not long after that Papa lost the farm and we moved to town. I don't like to think of the house we lived in near the C & R railroad tracks, though I guess we were lucky to have a roof over our heads—it was the worst days of the Depression and a lot of people didn't even have a roof, even one that leaked, plink, plonk; in a heavy rain there weren't enough pots and pans and vegetable bowls to set around to catch all the water.

Mama was the sick one but it was Papa who died first—living in town didn't suit him. By then my brothers had married and Mama and I moved into two back rooms that looked onto an alley and everybody's garbage cans and dump heaps. My brothers pitched in and gave me enough every month for Mama's and my barest expenses even though their wives grumbled and complained.

I tried to make Mama comfortable. I catered to her every whim and fancy. I loved her. All the same I had another reason to keep her alive as long as possible. While she breathed I knew I had a place to stay. I was terrified of what would happen to me when Mama died. I had no high school diploma and no experience at outside work and I knew my sisters-in-law wouldn't take me in or let my brothers support me once Mama was gone.

Then Mama drew her last breath with a smile of thanks on her face for what I had done.

Sure enough, Norine and Thelma, my brothers' wives, put their feet down. I was on my own from then on. So that scared feeling of wondering where I could lay my head took over in my mind and never left me.

I had some respite when Mr. Williams, a widower twenty-four years older than me, asked me to marry him. I took my vows seriously. I meant to cherish him and I did. But that house we lived in! Those walls couldn't have been dirtier if they'd been smeared with soot and the plumbing was stubborn as a mule. My left foot stayed sore from having to kick the pipe underneath the kitchen sink to get the water to run through.

Then Mr. Williams got sick and had to give up his shoe repair shop that he ran all by himself. He had a small savings account and a few of those twenty-five-dollar government bonds and drew some disability insurance until the policy ran out in something like six months.

I did everything I could to make him comfortable and keep him cheerful. Though I did all the laundry I gave him clean sheets and clean pajamas every third day and I think it was by my will power alone that I made a begonia bloom in that dark back room Mr. Williams stayed in. I even pestered his two daughters and told them they ought to send their father some get-well cards and they did once or twice. Every now and then when there were a few pennies extra I'd buy cards and scrawl signatures nobody could have read and mailed them to Mr. Williams to make him think some of his former customers were remembering him and wishing him well.

Of course when Mr. Williams died his daughters were johnny-on-the-spot to see that they got their share of the little bit that tumbledown house brought. I didn't begrudge them—I'm not one to argue with human nature.

I hate to think about all those hardships I had after Mr. Williams died. The worst of it was finding somewhere to sleep; it all boiled down to having a place to stay. Because somehow you can manage not to starve. There are garbage cans to dip into—you'd be surprised how wasteful some people are and how much good food they throw away. Or if it was right after the garbage trucks had made their collections and the cans were empty I'd go into a supermarket and pick, say, at the cherries pretending I was selecting some to buy. I didn't slip their best ones into my mouth. I'd take either those so ripe that they should have been thrown away or those that weren't ripe enough and shouldn't have been put out for people to buy. I might snitch a withered cabbage leaf or a few pieces of watercress or a few of those small round tomatoes about the size of hickory nuts—I never can remember their right name. I wouldn't make a pig of myself, just eat enough to ease my hunger. So I managed. As I say, you don't have to starve.

The only work I could get hardly ever paid me anything beyond room and board. I wasn't a practical nurse, though I knew how to take care of sick folks, and the people hiring me would say that since I didn't have the training and qualifications I couldn't expect much. All they really wanted was for someone to spend the night with Aunt Myrtle or Cousin Kate or Mama or Daddy; no actual duties were demanded of me, they said, and they really didn't think my help was worth anything except meals and a place to sleep. The arrangements were pretty makeshift. Half the time I wouldn't have a place to keep my things, not that I had any clothes to speak of, and sometimes I'd sleep on a cot in the hall outside the patient's room or on some sort of contrived bed in the patient's room.

I cherished every one of those sick people, just as I had cherished Mama and Mr. Williams. I didn't want them to die. I did everything I knew to let them know I was interested in their welfare—first for their sakes, and then for mine, so I wouldn't have to go out and find another place to stay.

Well, now, I've made out my case for the defense, a term I never thought I'd have to use personally, so now I'll make out the case for the prosecution.

I stole.

I don't like to say it, but I was a thief.

I'm not light-fingered. I didn't want a thing that belonged to anybody else. But there came a time when I felt forced to steal. I had to have some things. My shoes fell apart. I needed some stockings and underclothes. And when I'd ask a son or a daughter or a cousin or a niece for a little money for those necessities they acted as if I was trying to blackmail them. They reminded me that I wasn't qualified as a practical nurse, that I might even get into trouble with the authorities if they found I was palming myself off as a practical nurse—which I wasn't and they knew it. Anyway, they said that their terms were only bed and board.

So I began to take things—small things that had been pushed into the backs of drawers or stored high on shelves in boxes—things that hadn't been used or worn for years and probably would never be used again. I made my biggest haul at Mrs. Bick's where there was an attic full of trunks stuffed with clothes and doodads from the twenties all the way back to the nineties—uniforms, ostrich fans, Spanish shawls, beaded bags. I sneaked out a few of these at a time and every so often sold them to a place called Way Out, Hippie Clothiers.

I tried to work out the exact amount I got for selling something. Not, I know, that you can make up for theft. But, say, I got a dollar for a feather boa belonging to Mrs. Bick: well, then I'd come back and work at a job that the cleaning woman kept putting off, like waxing the hall upstairs or polishing the andirons or getting the linen closet in order.

All the same I *was* stealing—not everywhere I stayed, not even in most places, but when I had to I stole. I admit it.

But I didn't steal that silver box.

I was as innocent as a baby where that box was concerned. So when that policeman came toward me grabbing at the box I stepped aside, and maybe

I even gave him the push that sent him to his death. He had no business acting like that when that box was mine, whatever Mrs. Crowe's niece argued.

Fifty thousand nieces couldn't have made it not mine.

Anyway, the policeman was dead and though I hadn't wanted him dead I certainly hadn't wished him well. And then I got to thinking: well, I didn't steal Mrs. Crowe's box but I had stolen other things and it was the mills of God grinding exceeding fine, as I once heard a preacher say, and I was being made to pay for the transgressions that had caught up with me.

Surely I can make a little more sense out of what happened than that, though I never was exactly clear in my own mind about everything that happened.

Mrs. Crowe was the most appreciative person I ever worked for. She was bedridden and could barely move. I don't think the registered nurse on daytime duty considered it part of her job to massage Mrs. Crowe. So at night I would massage her, and that pleased and soothed her. She thanked me for every small thing I did—when I fluffed her pillow, when I'd put a few drops of perfume on her earlobes, when I'd straighten the wrinkled bedcovers.

I had a little joke. I'd pretend I could tell fortunes and I'd take Mrs. Crowe's hand and tell her she was going to have a wonderful day but she must beware of a handsome blond stranger—or some such foolishness that would make her laugh. She didn't sleep well and it seemed to give her pleasure to talk to me most of the night about her childhood or her dead husband.

She kept getting weaker and weaker and two nights before she died she said she wished she could do something for me but that when she became an invalid she had signed over everything to her niece. Anyway, Mrs. Crowe hoped I'd take her silver box. I thanked her. It pleased me that she liked me well enough to give me the box. I didn't have any real use for it. It would have made a nice trinket box, but I didn't have any trinkets. The box seemed to be Mrs. Crowe's fondest possession. She kept it on the table beside her and her eyes lighted up every time she looked at it. She might have been a little girl first seeing a brand-new baby doll early on a Christmas morning.

So when Mrs. Crowe died and the niece on whom I set eyes for the first time dismissed me, I gathered up what little I had and took the box and left. I didn't go to Mrs. Crowe's funeral. The paper said it was private and I wasn't invited. Anyway, I wouldn't have had anything suitable to wear.

I still had a few dollars left over from those things I'd sold to the hippie place called Way Out, so I paid a week's rent for a room that was the worst I'd ever stayed in.

It was freezing cold and no heat came up to the third floor where I was.

In that room with falling plaster and buckling floorboards and darting roaches, I sat wearing every stitch I owned, with a sleazy blanket and a faded quilt draped around me waiting for the heat to rise, when in swept Mrs. Crowe's niece in a fur coat and a fur hat and shiny leather boots up to her knees. Her face was beet red from anger when she started telling me that she had traced me through a private detective and I was to give her back the heirloom I had stolen.

Her statement made me forget the precious little bit I knew of the English language. I couldn't say a word, and she kept on screaming that if I returned the box immediately no criminal charge would be made against me. Then I got back my voice and I said that box was mine and that Mrs. Crowe had wanted me to have it, and she asked if I had any proof or if there were any witnesses to the gift, and I told her that when I was given a present I said thank you, that I didn't ask for proof and witnesses, and that nothing could make me part with Mrs. Crowe's box.

The niece stood there breathing hard, in and out, almost counting her breaths like somebody doing an exercise to get control of herself.

"You'll see," she yelled, and then she left.

The room was colder than ever and my teeth chattered.

Not long afterward I heard heavy steps clumping up the stairway. I realized that the niece had carried out her threat and that the police were after me.

I was panic-stricken. I chased around the room like a rat with a cat after it: Then I thought that if the police searched my room and couldn't find the box it might give me time to decide what to do. I grabbed the box out of the top dresser drawer and scurried down the back hall. I snatched the back door open. I think what I intended to do was run down the back steps and hide the box somewhere, underneath a bush or maybe in a garbage can.

Those back steps were steep and rose almost straight up for three stories and they were flimsy and covered with ice.

I started down. My right foot slipped. The handrail saved me. I clung to it with one hand and to the silver box with the other hand and picked and chose my way across the patches of ice.

When I was midway I heard my name shrieked. I looked around to see a big man leaping down the steps after me. I never saw such anger on a person's face. Then he was directly behind me and reached out to snatch the box.

I swerved to escape his grasp and he cursed me. Maybe I pushed him. I'm not sure—not really.

Anyway, he slipped and fell down and down and down, and then after all that falling he was absolutely still. The bottom step was beneath his head like a pillow and the rest of his body was spreadeagled on the brick walk.

Then almost like a pet that wants to follow its master, the silver box jumped from my hand and bounced down the steps to land beside the man's left ear.

My brain was numb. I felt paralyzed. Then I screamed.

Tenants from that house and the houses next door and across the alley pushed windows open and flung doors open to see what the commotion was about, and then some of them began to run toward the back yard. The policeman who was the dead man's partner—I guess you'd call him that—ordered them to keep away.

After a while more police came and they took the dead man's body and drove me to the station where I was locked up.

From the very beginning I didn't take to that young lawyer they assigned to me. There wasn't anything exactly that I could put my finger on. I just felt uneasy with him. His last name was Stanton. He had a first name of course, but he didn't tell me what it was; he said he wanted me to call him Bat like all his friends did.

He was always smiling and reassuring me when there wasn't anything to smile or be reassured about, and he ought to have known it all along instead of filling me with false hope.

All I could think was that I was thankful Mama and Papa and Mr. Williams were dead and that my shame wouldn't bring shame on them.

"It's going to be all right," the lawyer kept saying right up to the end, and then he claimed to be indignant when I was found guilty of resisting arrest and of manslaughter and theft or robbery—there was the biggest hullabaloo as to whether I was guilty of theft or robbery. Not that I was guilty of either, at least in this particular instance, but no one would believe me.

You would have thought it was the lawyer being sentenced instead of me, the way he carried on. He called it a terrible miscarriage of justice and said we might as well be back in the eighteenth century when they hanged children.

Well, that was an exaggeration, if ever there was one; nobody was being hung and nobody was a child. That policeman had died and I had had a part in it. Maybe I had pushed him. I couldn't be sure. In my heart I really hadn't meant him any harm. I was just scared. But he was dead all the same. And as far as stealing went, I hadn't stolen the box but I had stolen other things more than once.

And then it happened. It was a miracle. All my life I'd dreamed of a nice room of my own, a comfortable place to stay. And that's exactly what I got.

The room was on the small side but it had everything I needed in it, even a wash basin with hot and cold running water, and the walls were freshly painted, and they let me choose whether I wanted a wing chair with a chintz slipcover or a modern Danish armchair. I even got to decide what color bedspread I preferred. The window looked out on a beautiful lawn edged with shrubbery, and the matron said I'd be allowed to go to the greenhouse and select some pot plants to keep in my room. The next day I picked out a white gloxinia and some russet chrysanthemums.

I didn't mind the bars at the windows at all. Why, this day and age some of the finest mansions have barred windows to keep burglars out.

The meals—I simply couldn't believe there was such delicious food in the world. The woman who supervised their preparation had embezzled the funds of one of the largest catering companies in the state after working herself up from assistant cook to treasurer.

The other inmates were very friendly and most of them had led the most interesting lives. Some of the ladies occasionally used words that you usually see written only on fences or printed on sidewalks before the cement dries, but when they were scolded they apologized. Every now and then somebody would get angry with someone and there would be a little scratching or hair pulling, but it never got too bad. There was a choir—I can't sing but I love music—and they gave a concert every Tuesday morning at chapel, and Thursday night was movie night. There wasn't any admission charge. All you did was go in and sit down anywhere you pleased.

We all had a special job and I was assigned to the infirmary. The doctor and nurse both complimented me. The doctor said that I should have gone into professional nursing, that I gave confidence to the patients and helped them get well. I don't know about that but I've had years of practice with sick people and I like to help anybody who feels bad.

I was so happy that sometimes I couldn't sleep at night. I'd get up and click on the light and look at the furniture and the walls. It was hard to believe I had such a pleasant place to stay. I'd remember supper that night, how I'd gone back to the steam table for a second helping of asparagus with lemon and herb sauce, and I compared my plenty with those terrible times when I had slunk into supermarkets and nibbled overripe fruit and raw vegetables to ease my hunger.

Then one day here came that lawyer, not even at regular visiting hours, bouncing around congratulating me that my appeal had been upheld, or whatever the term was, and that I was as free as a bird to leave right that minute.

He told the matron she could send my belongings later and he dragged me out front where TV cameras and newspaper reporters were waiting.

As soon as the cameras began whirring and the photographers began to aim, the lawyer kissed me on the cheek and pinned a flower on me. He made a speech saying that a terrible miscarriage of justice had been rectified. He had located people who testified that Mrs. Crowe had given me the box —she had told the gardener and the cleaning woman. They hadn't wanted to testify because they didn't want to get mixed up with the police, but the lawyer had persuaded them in the cause of justice and humanity to come forward and make statements.

The lawyer had also looked into the personnel record of the dead policeman and had learned that he had been judged emotionally unfit for his job, and the psychiatrist had warned the Chief of Police that something awful might happen either to the man himself or to a suspect unless he was relieved of his duties.

All the time the lawyer was talking into the microphones he had latched onto me like I was a three year old that might run away, and I just stood and stared. Then when he had finished his speech about me the reporters told him that like his grandfather and his uncle he was sure to end up as governor but at a much earlier age.

At that the lawyer gave a big grin in front of the camera and waved good-bye and pushed me into his car.

I was terrified. The nice place I'd found to stay in wasn't mine any longer. My old nightmare was back—wondering how I could manage to eat and how much stealing I'd have to do to live from one day to the next.

The cameras and reporters had followed us.

A photographer asked me to turn down the car window beside me, and I overheard two men way in the back of the crowd talking. My ears are sharp. Papa always said I could hear thunder three states away. Above the congratulations and bubbly talk around me I heard one of those men in back say, "This is a bit too much, don't you think? Our Bat is showing himself the champion of the Senior Citizen now. He's already copped the teenyboppers and the under thirties using methods that ought to have disbarred him. He should have made the gardener and cleaning woman testify at the beginning, and from the first he should have checked into the policeman's history. There ought never to have been a case at all, much less a conviction. But Bat wouldn't have got any publicity that way. He had to do it in his own devious, spectacular fashion." The other man just kept nodding and saying after every sentence, "You're damned right."

Then we drove off and I didn't dare look behind me because I was so heartbroken over what I was leaving.

The lawyer took me to his office. He said he hoped I wouldn't mind a little excitement for the next few days. He had mapped out some public appearances for me. The next morning I was to be on an early television show. There was nothing to be worried about. He would be right beside me to help me just as he had helped me throughout my trouble. All that I had to say on the TV program was that I owed my freedom to him.

I guess I looked startled or bewildered because he hurried on to say that I hadn't been able to pay him a fee but that now I was able to pay him back

—not in money but in letting the public know about how he was the champion of the underdog.

I said I had been told that the court furnished lawyers free of charge to people who couldn't pay, and he said that was right, but his point was that I could repay him now by telling people all that he had done for me. Then he said the main thing was to talk over our next appearance on TV. He wanted to coach me in what I was going to say, but first he would go into his partner's office and tell him to take all the incoming calls and handle the rest of his appointments.

When the door closed after him I thought that he was right. I did owe my freedom to him. He was to blame for it. The smart alec. The upstart. Who asked him to butt in and snatch me out of my pretty room and the work I loved and all that delicious food?

It was the first time in my life I knew what it meant to despise someone. I hated him.

Before, when I was convicted of manslaughter, there was a lot of talk about malice aforethought and premeditated crime.

There wouldn't be any argument this time.

I hadn't wanted any harm to come to that policeman. But I did mean harm to come to this lawyer.

I grabbed up a letter opener from his desk and ran my finger along the blade and felt how sharp it was. I waited behind the door and when he walked through I gathered all my strength and stabbed him. Again and again and again.

Now I'm back where I want to be—in a nice place to stay.

PAUL BRODERICK'S MAN
by *THOMAS WALSH*

Flanagan was warned in good time. Which meant, following Paul Broderick's advice, that he was not stupid enough to retire abruptly on the pension. At such a time that action would have been markedly suspicious, and so, in its place, a police-doctor friend of Broderick's put it down that because of a bad back Captain Anthony Vincent Flanagan was granted a necessary period of sick leave.

There were no hitches or awkward moments. There never were, with Paul Broderick handling things. True enough, half a dozen men were questioned later by a Grand Jury, but they were all pretty small fish, as is usual in such matters, and in the end the investigation fizzled out with nothing changed. Captain Flanagan, of course, was unable to testify: medical reasons. The bad back confined him on strict bed rest to an upstate sanitarium, and there he remained, again on Broderick's advice, until after the election in the fall.

And after that there was nothing at all for Flanagan to worry about. He had it made. A widower with four grown children, he sold the old brick house in Bay Ridge where he had raised them all, bought himself a fine new $12,000 car, and rented a small but elegantly luxurious apartment in the East Seventies. His son Frank, the doctor, was set up in an impressive midtown office; Flanagan bought a fine new house up in Westchester, cash on the barrelhead, for his daughter Mamie and her family; and Paul Broderick, who always knew the right people, just as he had known where to locate an obliging police doctor, enrolled Flanagan's younger son Jerry in what was reputed to be the best law school in the country.

The only child for whom he was not permitted to buy anything was his other daughter Maureen. Damned queer notions of life, that one. There were times, Flanagan thought grimly, when it seemed to him that about all she was suited for was the convent.

"But I really don't want anything," she tried to excuse herself when Flanagan asked her straight out. "Jack and I have everything we need, Papa. Don't worry about us."

"Have you now?" Flanagan demanded, his lips tightening noticeably. "Well, well, well. Isn't that just wonderful? Everything you need: a satisfied woman. You don't even want a check from me, then?"

"Nothing at all, sir," the husband chimed in; the damned stick of a social worker, whatever the hell they were, up in East Harlem. "But thank you very much."

Maureen, who knew Flanagan much better than her husband did, tried to pass it off lightly.

"Now don't get all huffy," she said. "Don't be that silly, Papa. All we mean—"

"Maybe I know what you mean," Flanagan said, turning his back curtly. "So don't bother explaining yourself. Good day to you both."

Yet the incident irritated him more than was sensible on his part. He had always been an extremely practical man, with very little patience for fine, sensitive consciences; but Maureen, after all, had always been his favorite, the very image of her dead mother.

But after that day, whenever they met at Mamie's house for Sunday dinner, or at Frank's, there was nothing at all of the old closeness between them—and that was more due to Flanagan himself, he had to admit, than to Maureen. In certain matters Flanagan had long been aware that he had the pride of the devil in him.

All right, then. Why bother his head about anyone now, even Maureen? He had everything in the world. No money worries; damned good health for his age; the finest of food and drink; and a drawerful of medals and commendations for meritorious police work. There was no one who could say a word about Flanagan, at least not openly. So right after Christmas, still on sick leave, he went to Florida for the winter. Very pleasant, too. Fine sunny weather; breakfast at poolside every day—lamb chops, hashed brown potatoes, and imported Canadian ale, or grilled kidneys and one or two Bloody Marys; and in the afternoons friends to be met, his or Broderick's, at the $50 Clubhouse window in Gulfstream Park.

Yes, Maureen would learn about life one day. The answer might be that he had always made things a little too easy for her. She had never been forced to fight her way up out of the dirt the way her father had; to see when an opportunity presented itself and to have brains enough to grab hold of it. But the hurt remained in him, deep down, and when her first child was born that spring, even though she named it Anthony after him, he went to see it one day when Frank took him, but never bought it a present of any kind—not a toy, not a feeding cup, not a rattle. Flanagan had never been a forgiving man. He had been struck to the heart once, and for no reason; he did not intend to place himself in that vulnerable a position ever again.

But one night not long afterward, in a well-known Third Avenue bar, he got himself into a tussle. There was a drunk who kept pushing at him, to get his place, and when Flanagan jabbed a resentful elbow into the man's side, the drunk muttered something to the tart with him.

Flanagan did not actually hear the remark, and yet he knew what it was; there was something about the drunk's sly contemptuous smile that informed Flanagan. So he yanked the drunk around, slapped him back and forth across the mouth, and pitched him headlong into the nearest wall.

Joe Martin, Mamie's husband, was much amused by that at the next family dinner.

"You'd better watch out," he grinned, "or they'll be throwing you into the ring with Muhammed Ali one of these days. I hear you knocked out three of his teeth. What did you hit the guy for anyway, Pop? What did he say to you?"

"What could he say?" Flanagan said, with a certain cold dangerous note in his voice. "Let's have your opinion, Joe. What do you think? What would you suggest, eh?"

"Oh, who cares?" Maureen said, moving behind him and putting both hands on his shoulders; so she knew, of course, and a lot quicker than any of them. "I wouldn't pay any attention to people like that, Papa. They simply don't know what they're talking about. When are you ever going to come up to the Bronx and see the baby again?"

So he did go up there a few days later and solemnly permitted little Anthony to curl a tiny paw around big Anthony's finger. But something had changed. It was a very effortful evening both for him and for Maureen. There fell long silences, and when they talked it seemed to Flanagan it was always about something that neither of them was thinking about.

He felt unaccountably depressed when he got home, whatever the reason might have been, and decided to have a drink for himself. In the end, however, it was more than one, and he woke up at four in the morning, very drunk, and still in his clothes, sitting up in the easy chair and with the television still blaring away.

He had never been much of a drinker before. Now he was. When fall came he had got into the habit of taking his first drink of the day even before breakfast, and had to buy three or four new suits for himself. The old ones had got too small around the waist. Always a trim, leanly built man, in good hard fettle, it shocked him to discover that he had put on something like 30 pounds.

Have to do something, Flanagan decided; time to get hold of myself. He must have forgotten who he was—a police captain, a respected police captain named Anthony Vincent Flanagan. There was no one who told him what to do. He told them. Yet, if that were true, why had he avoided facing up to Paul Broderick for month after month now? He was not afraid, surely; not Captain Flanagan. Then, damn it to hell, why was he letting it go on and on?

So next morning he shaved and dressed very carefully, had nothing to drink, and took a cab downtown to Broderick's office.

And with the old iron toughness and independence stiffening his back, he was the old Flanagan that day, blunt and forceful as a rifle bullet.

"I'll tell you what I came to see you about," he announced, as soon as they had shaken hands and sat down. "I'd like my job back. I'd say it's about time, Paul. Will you see to it, then? I'm still on the sick leave, you know."

"Thought you were enjoying yourself," Broderick murmured gently, pushing his fine Cuban cigars over. "Don't know any reason why you wouldn't be. You're a very lucky man, Anthony. You're a man who started out with nothing at all and who's got himself everything in the world now. Just think it over a little. You've put your time in. Get out on the pension. What's to prevent?"

"At my age?" Flanagan demanded, sitting forward an inch. "No, no, Paul. There's a year or two yet until I hit fifty. I don't care for the job itself, you understand. It's a dog's life, and I hate it. But I want to stop this loose talk that's going around concerning me. It's getting a bit bothersome. Even my own daughter Maureen seems to think—but of course that's no matter. I just want the job again. It's all I'm fitted for. So give me the plain answer, Paul. Yes or no?"

Broderick, sitting very low in the leather desk chair, did not look at Flanagan. He looked at the long cigar in his fingers.

"Then I'm sorry," he said at last, raising world-weary and palely untouchable blue eyes. "It's no, Anthony. It has to be. You're well out of it now, and I'd say you're a lot better off that way. I managed to smooth it out for all of us, or for most of us, but it was a damned close thing. I can see no point at all in stirring it up again. There's another Grand Jury in session now and they might get just a little curious as to why your back trouble came up at such a convenient time last year—convenient for you and for me, at any rate. Why risk that? Don't you see what a fool's game it would be?"

"Yes, I do see," Flanagan heard himself gritting. "At least I see what a damned fool I was. Don't forget that I could have come back and talked about that construction contract we each had a piece of—and if I had, there was no one in God's world who could have kept even you out of the box."

"True enough," Broderick agreed, nodding tranquilly. "We'd have gone down the drain, all right, the whole shooting match—and you with us."

The flesh under Flanagan's eyes darkened. Again he leaned forward, his big fist clenching itself tightly on the desk blotter.

"I'm telling you to fix it for me!" he declared thickly. "I'm owed that! I was a damned good police officer before I ever met up with you, but you ran the whole department then from behind the curtain—and you still do. To get on in the department I had to do what you asked me—or else I had to get out. Now is that true as the Book, or isn't it?"

"As far as it goes," Broderick admitted. "But you've forgotten one thing. For what you did for me you were paid—and paid damned well. We did business for a long time, and very satisfactory business. I understand you're worth something like three-quarters of a million dollars now. A great saver on your police salary, weren't you?"

"And if I am"—but with his voice beginning to shake—"how much are you worth? With your cab companies and your plumbing supply houses and your building construction firms? And with every one of them having first say on any city contract that ever comes up? I'm not denying that I did what I did. I'd have been the fool of the world to turn my back on the thing. But—"

"Yes, you would have been," Broderick agreed calmly once more. "But remember, Anthony, you made your own decision. Nobody forced you. Think of that for a moment, and don't stand there shouting at me in my own office like a mad bull. I won't have it. You're not your own man any more, and you haven't been for a good many years. You're Paul Broderick's man, and you'll do as you're told here, as you always have. Is that quite clear now?"

"Me?" Flanagan said, on his feet suddenly and gripping the edge of the desk with both hands. "Is that it? Your man, am I? A Broderick office boy, to fetch and carry for you? Well, by God—"

He moved so abruptly that he knocked over the inkwell. Broderick clicked his tongue and rang for the girl.

"My fine rug," he mourned. "Damn it, Anthony, what the hell is the matter with you? I'll never get that spot out of it now. Come back and see me again when you've thought out this business. I'll put you down for lunch at the club next Tuesday. And then we'll—"

But Flanagan, shoving the girl to one side, had lunged out through the office doorway. Down in the street a flood of bright summer sunshine burst over him, but had he come down in the elevator moments ago or had he walked? It was impossible for him to remember. Broderick's man! Not Flanagan's man, not for years now—never Flanagan's man. But Broderick's. Was that true? Could it be true?

In the $12,000 car he sat motionless, trying to decide on the answer. Only there was a numbed thickness in his head, presenting to him not steady and consecutive reasoning, but scraps and fragments. You never knew what was really being asked of you the first time—that was one fragment. You were only a sergeant then, and a man came around to the precinct house shortly before Christmas with his overcoat pockets full of envelopes. An envelope for the sergeant, an envelope for the lieutenant, an envelope for the captain, and all with Season's Greetings from Paul Broderick. So you had taken your envelope, as the others had taken theirs, and from then on, wherever Broderick's big black Cadillac was left parked, you looked out for it.

Soon it was "Good morning, Mr. Broderick, sir," to the great man, and then it was a couple of tickets pressed into your hand for the next Yankee game at the Stadium, or the Ranger game that night at the Garden. Mr. Broderick liked your style, he said, and one day, when he noticed a dent in your old jalopy, he had one of his men take it downtown to his taxicab garage. Might as well let them hammer that dent out, you were told, only when you got the car back the next day, they had repainted the whole thing. They had also put in new slipcovers and an expensive FM radio and substituted whitewall tires. They had tuned the motor and put in new sparkplugs, a new air filter, and a new fly belt. The old jalopy ran like a charm and looked like a new car.

"Just between us," Broderick had said, "I like your style, Anthony. You've got a good level head on your shoulders, and you've done me many a favor. What's holding your name up on the lieutenants' list? I think I'd better find out about that. I'll let you know in a few days. The bill for your car? What bill? What are you talking about? Favor for favor, that's all. I've got a friend at court now, and so do you. So let's keep it that way, eh? How was the game last night?"

And it had been kept that way. After that there had always been a friend at court for Mr. Broderick in times of need, and also, since Sergeant Flanagan made lieutenant in another month, the fair exchange had been no robbery. Now and again a stock tip, always a good stock tip; later on a chance to buy in as a silent partner in one of the Broderick Construction firms a few days before it landed a $38,000,000 city contract; but never even the hint of Broderick's man, or not until today.

But today, if you had never realized it before, or had insisted stubbornly to yourself that you didn't realize it, the thing had come out in plain words, the plainest possible. Not his own man, Flanagan remembered—and not for years. Was it possible? And at last, forcing himself to look back, he saw that it was not only possible, it was true.

He drove home with that queer numbness still inside his head, parked his car in the apartment-house garage, went upstairs, and began to drink. He drank steadily for eight days, the first time in his life, and came out of it to find himself in a private hospital suffering from acute alcoholism, with Maureen crying beside him and holding his hand.

And that shamed him. When he was permitted home again, he emptied every bottle of whiskey in the place, and to get through the hours of the day in one fashion or another forced himself to take long walks, even late-at-night walks, on the many occasions when he could not sleep. Broderick's man? Never! Not if he fought it out now. There was a way back for him. He had only to find the right door, wherever it was. Now he knew. Now he could understand how true were those couple of lines from Omar Khayyam. How did they go?

"I wonder often what the Vintners buy
One half so precious as the stuff they sell."

And what had Anthony Vincent Flanagan sold? Himself? His work, his manhood, his pride, his reason for living? He knew now, and had to find the way back. There must still be a chance to start all over again for himself, to reshape his life. That was all he had left now, and it was necessary to hold fast to it. The way back existed. But where could he find it? Precisely where had he left it behind him?

He did not know. He had to search. So sometimes very late at night he walked desolate and deserted areas along the river, in the same district that Captain Flanagan had once held in the palm of his hand, with a power almost of life and death over it. The dark alleys; the gloomy warehouse walls on each side; the high coldly indifferent street lamps; the sneaking wind-driven shadows. What did Captain Flanagan expect there? What was he looking for? But still he knew, somehow or other. Patience, it came to him. He had been a man in those days and he would be again. Here was the way back—right here waiting for him. Only where and when?

On the night he found out he had stopped briefly to rest, looking out over the river, when a prowl car pulled in to the curb beside him.

"Hey, old-timer," a voice said out of the passenger side. "What are you doing in this neighborhood night after night? It's a hell of a section to get mugged in, in case you don't know. What's your name, Pop? Where do you live? Just come over here to the car now and speak up. You've got us interested. We've been watching you every night for the past week."

"Where do I live?" Flanagan repeated. "Not around here. How are you, Boudreau? How have you been, Mahoney?"

Boudreau got out of the car at that, peering more closely.

"Gee," he said then. "Captain Flanagan! But you got so old-looking—or—I mean—well, I just didn't happen to recognize you, Captain, not with your back turned. How you been, Captain? Can we give you a lift someplace? Where you headed for?"

But Captain Flanagan did not know that himself. He got into the prowl car, however, and all at once he seemed to be back in time about 20 years or more. This car might have been the same car he had known then, and it might have been a patrolman named Flanagan who was back of the steering wheel, not Harry Mahoney; just as it might have been Flanagan's partner Bert Bailey in the passenger seat, not Phil Boudreau. Flanagan and Bailey had been partners then, but there came a time when only Flanagan had come back from another spell of night duty.

They had chanced upon a liquor-store holdup in East Seventy-ninth Street. A night much like this, Flanagan remembered, with the same kind of clear lazy rain trickling down the car windows, and then, beyond it, three men suddenly bursting out of the liquor store with their guns waving. Bailey, always the quicker of them, was out at once, shouting the necessary warning; but it had been an unheeded warning, and even yet Flanagan could see the sudden tiny spurt of flame over there in the liquor-store doorway. The bullet had knocked Bailey back onto the car, spinning him around on it, and Flanagan could see again the sudden surprised look on his face, the kind of frightened and realizing half smile that had followed it. Bailey had touched himself on the chest, then looked at his hand. The smile had wavered.

"Holy God," he had said. "I'm hit bad. I feel all—they got me. I'm going, Tony. So long, fella. Tell Agnes and the kid—"

Then he had pitched forward, and a young Flanagan had been out of the car and after the three men. One he had dropped right away, with the first shot he fired; the second he had got around the street corner; and the third he had trapped in a dark alleyway.

But the alleyway had not frightened young Flanagan, nor had the bullets that had whistled out of it past his head. There was a company to which young Flanagan belonged, and so there was a thing that had to be done by him. He had not thought about it at all. He had just raced ahead, into the dark alleyway, and had done it. But of course all that was a long time ago. Oh, yes, old Flanagan remembered. Twenty years or more.

"We were talking about you the other night at the precinct," Harry Mahoney told him. "They give us a new guy that ain't too bad, but lemme tell you he ain't no Tony Flanagan, Captain. How you feeling these days? You coming back on the job soon?"

"I don't know," Flanagan replied slowly. "It's pretty hard to say, Harry. But I've been thinking, since I've got my time in—" Outside the window Bailey's terrified white face wisped away under a curl of three-in-the-morning fog, so that Flanagan could no longer see it even when he brushed mist from the glass. But it had been there, surely. Flanagan had seen it as plain as—

"Can't blame you a bit," Boudreau said. "Get the hell out of the department while you still got a lot of good years to expect, that's the way I see it. You got it made, Captain. You got everything in the world now, so why not enjoy it, huh?"

"Right on," Mahoney agreed. "But I got to take a break down at that diner, Phil. Give me a couple of minutes, huh? I'll be right back."

They swung in to the curb and Mahoney trotted off. Boudreau got out, too, yawning and stretching. Then, glancing along the other side of the street, he suddenly froze.

"Look at that car," he told Flanagan. "Over there by the loading dock, Captain. Black Dodge, isn't it?"

And it was, Flanagan could see, twisting his head around in the car to look at it.

"But I bet," Boudreau said, hurriedly checking his revolver holster, "it isn't the same license plate. Of course. They change that on every job they pull. Smart cookies, these fellas. They've been hitting the warehouses around here for the past six months. Guess I better make a quick check over there, Captain. Tell Harry, will you? He said he'd be right back."

Boudreau moved quickly and quietly off, into the deep shadows around the loading dock and the parked Dodge. Flanagan stayed where he was. He had better, something whispered to him. It would be time enough to help after Boudreau had made the identification. Now he would only be in the way. His wristwatch showed him that it was 4:25, and the street ahead shone emptily, with a black glisten of pavement, under the arc lights. Even on the elevated highway down at the end of it, only an occasional car whizzed by.

Flanagan, sitting edgily forward on the back seat, felt a sudden cold prickle along the spine. Was he afraid? Captain Flanagan? There was a company to which he belonged, as he had belonged to it more than 20 years ago outside that liquor store, so not to worry now. Still, he had to admit that he felt damned queer—a brief dryness in the throat, a slight quiver of the arm muscles, a sudden unsteadiness in the way his heart had begun to beat. What the hell bothered him? It could not be fear. It had never been that before. Then what?

He got out of the prowl car. Up on the highway a night-hawk taxi raced by, but around him all other sounds seemed to be cushioned in thick velvet. He rubbed his mouth, roughly passing the back of his hand over it three or four times, and moved ahead hurriedly to shelter himself in a garage doorway. But he was only obeying a proper caution here, that was all. Flanagan had attended to matters like this before and by God he could attend to them again!

It was annoying, however, not to be sure of what was going on. He could see no one, not even Boudreau, and not even a small telltale sound could be heard anywhere. What had happened to Harry Mahoney? Why wasn't he back yet? But trust a rotten time-serving little cringer of that type. He knew well when and where to make himself scarce. Let Flanagan and Boudreau attend to this matter. Mahoney would do the sensible thing. He would post himself down in the corner diner, safe and secure there, until he knew it was all over.

The thought of it brought up in Flanagan a wild surge of fury. Damn it, why had he met them tonight? Why had he been stupid enough to get into the car with them? Trapped now—and it might be, very soon, a bullet in the head for his pains. No matter then that Tony Flanagan had got everything in God's world for himself. Dead and destroyed here in the gutter if he so much as poked his nose out of the garage doorway. Keep it in, then. Look out for himself. Who the hell else? Where was Boudreau? What was he doing?

It was impossible to say. He must be moving along in the shadows, silently, with great care, and peering vainly for him. Flanagan became aware of a rapid and persistent tic under the lower lid of his right eye. He had his police revolver out, and it seemed to him that his hand clung to it with desperate tightness, as if his fingers had become frozen in that position, as if from the shoulder down his whole arm had become paralyzed. Sudden cold sweat broke out on his forehead and on his chest. Why?

The thing was incomprehensible. When had Tony Flanagan been afraid of anyone or anything in the world? It had to be only a stupid idea that had come into his head—that he stood all alone now, with no one to care what happened to him, because there was a company of which he was no longer a member. He felt the sweat drop into his eyes at that and shook his head savagely. Was that why, more than 20 years ago, he had been able to plunge into that dark alley after a man with a gun without even thinking about it —and why tonight he could not move even a step out of this doorway? Once there had been the fellowship of the department for him—but tonight there was not. Could that be the answer?

No, never! He had lost nothing. What he had to do here was simple enough—follow Boudreau and no matter what happened, stand shoulder to shoulder with him. But there was an open area in the street before he could reach that loading dock where the Dodge was parked, and Flanagan discovered that he could not force himself out into it. He simply could not. Twice he tried. Twice, as if by the grasp of a physical hand from behind, he was pulled back.

He lifted his head, eyes squeezed shut tightly, an agonized expression twitching the corners of his lips. But he did not try to move out into the open a third time. He felt a shudder deep inside him, and then, little by little, felt it ripple down through his whole body. He did nothing. He just waited.

"What is it?"—and Harry Mahoney's anxious voice was just beside him. "Where's Phil, Captain? What's going on?"

Flanagan, averting his face, managed to gesture with the gun—up ahead —and as he did so a door rasped open at the loading dock. No light was turned on, but four men could be seen gathered now in the loading doorway. One of them jumped down quickly and opened the car trunk. The three on the platform, deftly and rapidly, in perfect silence, passed down carton after carton. Then one by one the three men jumped down also, not bothering to close the loading door after them. But Boudreau used his head. He was one against four, so far as he knew, and it must have seemed to him that about the only chance he had was to let them get into the car before he revealed himself.

"Hold it right there!" Flanagan heard. "I got you covered. Don't start that car!"

But they did. Apparently they started it with the gas pedal down to the floor, rocketing it straight ahead, and when Boudreau ran out into the street, gun drawn, they fired at him. Yellow flares as tiny as fireflies spat at him, and Boudreau was hit. He spun around in the headlights, staggered to one side, and crashed head-on into an areaway railing.

Flanagan saw all that, felt the cold sweat once more, and stayed right where he was. Harry Mahoney did not. At the first shot he was out in the street, on one knee, firing back, and Flanagan found himself making an altogether foolish attempt to force his body back. The car rushed on drunkenly at him, windshield shattered, and for the fraction of a moment he could see the two men in the front seat and the two in the back. So they would all have been sitting ducks, in that breath of time under the street light, for Tony Flanagan who twice in earlier years had made the police rifle team.

But he did not fire at them. All he did was to fall to his knees and cross his two arms over his face. It was Harry Mahoney who never gave an inch, who fired a second time, a third time, a fourth time as the black Dodge roared by, straight across the street, and smashed into a parked truck. There was a squeal of tires, a whining of brakes, then the crash and then stinging quiet. The Dodge lay on its side. One of the doors had popped open. An arm reached out of it, groped around vaguely, and flopped back.

Harry Mahoney, letting out a long shaky breath, swung around to Flanagan.

"You all right?" he demanded. "You didn't get hit, did you?"

"No, fine," Flanagan croaked. Still on his knees, he lowered his arms dazedly and realized that he had dropped his police revolver. Mahoney retrieved it out of the gutter and ran down to check on Boudreau.

"Not too bad," he yelled back. "Just in the shoulder, Captain. But we had a pretty good ruckus there for a while, didn't we?"

Flanagan did not answer him. He was peering ahead down the long narrowing street, empty and rain-washed under the street lights, and it seemed to him that he could see a figure dwindling away down there, getting smaller and smaller, farther and farther away; a figure all by itself. It did not turn its head to him, but he knew who it was. It was Anthony Vincent Flanagan.

He pushed himself up dumbly. But that couldn't be true. He needed another chance. He wanted one! It had not been a deliberate thing. He had just failed to understand in time that the bargain with Broderick had been all or nothing. So listen up there. Please, please! There was more to his life still than walking into a dead end. There was a company that still existed and Flanagan was still a member. Even if just now he—

"Better sit down in the car," Mahoney suggested. "You look kind of shaken up, Captain. Let me give you a hand."

But Flanagan backed off at that, shaking his head quickly and thrusting out both arms. There was no room in the prowl car for Tony Flanagan, it came to him; in that company his place was now forever forfeited. A certain problem had arisen. So he turned blindly, before the others would get there, and with one arm still extended, as if groping, he lurched around the street corner.

After that he was all alone. He moved hurriedly in whatever direction the pavement took him. He knew what he had become at last. He was the ex-police captain who had got everything in the world for himself—and who, in return, had been clever enough to trade off for that nothing more vitally needful to a man than his honor.

WHEN NOTHING MATTERS
by FLORENCE V. MAYBERRY

It was a long tiring walk from the top of Mount Carmel to the shore of the sea, but Solange had taken it again, as she had for the past week, every day since Thorwald was gone. Gone. No longer her husband.

The tiring was good. She yearned for a fatigue so sodden and compelling that she would sleep, stop thinking.

She crossed the highway, stumbled over rough ground to the railroad tracks, stepped over them down to the sandy beach. She kicked off her loafers, rolled up her slacks, and let the waves lick her feet. She shaded her eyes, gazing at the water. Near the shore, the Mediterranean was a brilliant turquoise. A few meters out it deepened into dark blue, almost cobalt. In the distance a white ship, contrasting sharply against the sea, moved slantwise from the horizon toward Haifa's harbor.

Perhaps she should take a ship, go to Greece, Italy, America. Anywhere but Haifa and Israel.

She faced southward, in the direction of Tel Aviv. No ship to be seen there, only the empty horizon. "Like me. Empty. Alone with itself," Solange said aloud. Vaguely she realized that it was aloud, and vaguely she was troubled because it was. For the past week, and only for the past week, she had been holding conversations with herself. "It's because I'm alone. Alone!" she shouted at the sea. The rush and thud of the waves against the shore blotted up the sound, leaving her even more lonely.

She moved away from the soothing touch of the warm sea, rubbed the sand from her damp feet, slipped on her shoes, and continued on down the beach, past a service station, past the public beach, on and on. When she considered she was sufficiently tired she crossed the highway to a weedy space of ground where an Arab shepherd guarded a straggle of black goats and began the long slow climb up the steep height of Carmel. "Surely you'll sleep tonight," she assured herself.

Short of the mountain top she turned along a narrow slanting lane, went down a flight of stairs past terraced gardens, turned the key in the lock of her ground-floor apartment, shut the door behind her. She hesitated, not wanting to go farther into the empty room. "Empty," she said aloud. "Not even a cat or a dog or a bird. Nothing but you." She looked at herself in the hall mirror, watched her mouth twist in a grimace, its bitterness intensified by contrast with the delicate blossoms of the potted plant beneath the mirror. On impulse she picked up the plant, walked through the living room to the window area, pushed aside the glass of one window, and hurled the pot into the deep wadi below. "Nothing," she repeated.

She went to the kitchen, thinking: *boil the water, put in the filter paper, measure the coffee, pour the water, drink it and you'll feel better. Anything else, Solly—a poached egg? No? Corn flakes? Yes, corn flakes. Eat.*

"Why?" she asked.

She removed the bowl she had filled with brown flakes and the bluish Israeli milk from the table, carried it to the sink, poured its contents into the drain. She returned to the living room and lay down on the sofa, her face pressed against an embroidered Indian pillow. Its little metal mirrors scratched her cheek as though to sharpen memory of when she and Thorwald had bought the pillow covers in India, almost in the shadow of the Taj Mahal.

Almost as if she were taking it again, the long taxi drive from New Delhi to Agra ribboned through her mind. Passing crews of women in dull-colored saris as they scrabbled in dirt to build a highway, male supervisors idly watching. Past painted elephants, monkeys chattering in trees above strange long protuberances that their driver said were birds' nests, dangling from branches to protect their eggs from marauders. At Thorwald's request the taxi stopped and laughingly he pulled her toward a painted elephant, insisted she clamber onto it and have her picture taken. "You looked like a princess riding to meet your lover," he said, once they were back in the taxi.

"I am," she said confidently, snuggling close to him. "And I've met him." How long had they been married then? Six months? No, a year but it was still like a honeymoon, traveling continually to Thorwald's engineering assignments in exotic, wonderful places. That was what he liked, a constant change, and so did she as long as he was with her.

That day they had stopped at village rest stations where men charmed snakes out of baskets, where scraggly Himalayan bears danced pathetically to reedy music, where men wandered casually in and out of open-doored relief sheds. The heat throbbed over the land and crescendoed into a blinding, staggering white blaze as they walked past reflecting pools toward the scalding noon beauty of the Taj Mahal. It was so hot she thought she might faint, and she clung to Thorwald to steady herself against the swirling vertigo in her head. He hurried her forward, fleeing from the heat into the shadowed protection of the exquisite mausoleum that the Shad Jahan had built for the wife he loved so dearly.

She had gazed, fascinated, at the jeweled final token of adoration a king had given his beloved, yearning not for it but for the love that caused it. "Thorwald, if you were king and I had died, would you build me a Taj like this?"

"Of course," he said easily. "Now let's find a restaurant. I'm famished." As they walked back past the pools he added, "Jewels are easy to give when they are only promises. Even a poor man can give them."

And she had answered, "But promises like that *are* jewels."

She sat up and asked the empty room, "Are they?" She walked again to the window to distract the memory, but it would not leave. It kept reeling on, like a film, with the rest of that day's journey as they drove back to New Delhi, traveling the same road, past the same houses, trees with monkeys and birds. But the late golden sun changed the scene, made it into a new road, a new country and people. Now the village women were clean and fresh, dressed in brilliant saris, like butterflies freed from the chrysalis of the dusty morning's work. They walked gracefully beside the highway, copper pots of water balanced on their heads, calling to children, laughing with neighbors, their staccato chatter rising like fragmented music. Happy, serene, gentle.

But then, so soon after, she had become tearful, almost hysterical from the awful proof that happiness is fragile, fleeting. Ahead of them a crowd was gathered on the highway. The taxi slowed, then veered sharply to hasten past the group with its terrible center. A body's crumpled figure was flat on the road, face down, one leg askew, a jagged white bone glistening from mangled flesh and torn trousers, the road beneath him streaked red.

"Don't cry," Thorwald had soothed. "Never waste life by crying over things you can't do anything about. Where shall we have dinner tonight? At the hotel, or go adventuring?"

Her stomach had turned at the thought of food, but she forced down the repugnance. This was their continuing honeymoon, it must be kept happy, not spoiled. She leaned against him, drawing on his cool control. For yes, Thorwald was as controlled as the engineering graphs he produced for his company. She determined to learn from him, to become pragmatic, objective.

She had not learned.

"Solly, you're all emotion, no control. And I might add, that's damned wearing," he had told her a week ago. "No, I will not tell you who she is, I'll not have you messing about with some crazy, useless confrontation. It wouldn't change a thing, only make everything more difficult. I've told you before and I tell you again, don't waste strength on things you can't change. Because frankly, Solly, you haven't got what it takes to change what I'm going to do."

But she couldn't stop trying; she was driven to know about the woman who was taking Thorwald away from her. "Thorwald, what is she that I'm not? Prettier? Poised, controlled the way you want me to be? I'll change, truly I will, but don't leave me, Thorwald."

"Oh, God, not that again," he had answered. Turned his back on her. Zipped up his shaving kit, stuffed it in his travel case, snapped the case shut. Snapped her out of his life.

New York. Thorwald's head office. Sooner or later Thorwald would be intending to go to his New York office. "I'll call Simon, that's the thing to do," she said aloud. She sat again on the sofa, reached for the telephone on the low teak table beside it, slowly dialed a familiar number. A secretary in New York answered. "This is Mrs. Thorwald Jensen, calling from Israel," Solange said. "Please connect me right away with Mr. Simon, it's important."

The voice of Simon, Thorwald's chief, came over the wire as clearly as though he was on a telephone in the next apartment. "Hello, hello? Solange? Good to hear your voice. Where is Thorwald anyway, we've been expecting him every day. We need a briefing on that Negev Desert job. Here in New York? No, no sign of him, I said we're waiting for him."

"But he said New York." Her mouth was dry. "I thought . . . I haven't heard . . . where do you suppose . . ."

"Take it easy, Solange, don't go getting upset," Simon was saying. "You ought to know by now how crazy survey engineers can be. Any place they land is home and they never think anybody should be notified, especially bosses and wives. Thorwald's probably stopped off in London to catch some shows, yeah, I'd bet on London. I'll put in a call to the hotel he usually stays at, or have you called there already? No? Well, leave it to me, I'll track him down. Listen, go out on the town yourself. Where are you? Tel Aviv?"

"Haifa," she said. And for no particular reason she added, "It's a quiet town."

"Go to a movie," Simon said. "And listen, the minute I catch Thorwald I'll have him phone you."

A few more soothing words. A click. And she was alone with herself again. Thorwald call her? Never.

She lay on the sofa until the summer sky changed from afternoon brightness to twilight, to dark, and even after that for a long time. "Why not a movie?" she finally asked herself. She rose, chose a light shawl, and went outdoors. As she walked up the stone stairs, from far behind her came the ecstatic hungering cries of animals in the zoo located at the head of the wadi in Gan Ha'em, the Mothers' Park. She shivered, an unbidden primitive fear tightening the muscles of her back. She moved rapidly up the steep lane, pursued by the sounds, gasped with relief as she reached the sidewalk and saw the piercing headlights of cars speeding by.

A last faint, almost laughing howl came from the animals. Then silence. The silence and the howling told her it was too late for the movie. Each night, for what reason she did not know, the animals cried briefly, at almost ten o'clock. And again in the dark early morning before dawn. Not feeding hours surely. Perhaps a check by caretakers; it didn't matter, did it? Nothing mattered, Thorwald was gone.

Even though she decided against the movie she continued up the steeply sloping street toward Central Carmel, the clustered shopping district on the crest of Mount Carmel. There she moved among laughing, noisy groups of youth clustered in front of restaurants, ice-cream stands, fellafel counters. Although so different, yet it made her think of other crowds of youth on Shaftsbury and Piccadilly in London where she and Thorwald had strolled after the theater, window-gazing at shops she might visit the following day. Standing in front of a china shop choosing table settings she would never have. How could birds of passage possess china, or silver, having no home other than hotels, leased apartments, pensions? A few weeks here, a few months there, never a year, then off on another exciting journey, the adventure of change that Thorwald craved.

"I'll go, I'll leave Haifa, I can't stay here any longer," she told herself. Then clapped her hand over her mouth, fearful to be noticed talking to herself.

She walked swiftly back down the mountainside, running the last few steps into her apartment. She turned the key and leaned, panting, against the door.

In the night, near morning, she heard the animals cry again and she moaned as she struggled to recapture sleep. With eyes staring into the dark she tried to imagine how the woman, Thorwald's unknown love, might look. Dark hair and violet eyes, like a movie actress? No, Thorwald liked blondes; that was why she had lightened her own red-brown hair, had become a titian blonde. She fretted with the idea of perhaps getting up, turning on the light to see again how well her titian hair contrasted with sage-green eyes. "You're unreal," Thorwald had said when he first saw the change of color. "Absolutely not real, Solly, I must be imagining you. Eyes of an Egyptian cat and hair of an angel. Come here, give us a kiss."

He had loved her then. What had changed him?

Face it, be realistic: Thorwald was in love with change, always another project, another country, and now another woman. Sameness bored him. On the go, here, there, anywhere, everywhere.

"God, tell me, where is he now?"

She sat up, arms clasping her shoulders in a comforting hug. She rocked to and fro in a terrible wrestling with God, "Tell me, God, tell me!" Then fell back on the pillow, exhausted, smothered by the dark and the loneliness.

In the morning she tried to eat, couldn't, only drank coffee. She opened the utility cupboard, found the key to her storeroom, picked up a flashlight, went into the open foyer and down the basement stairs. In the storeroom she surveyed the travel cases, selected one of medium size, and carried it upstairs.

She went to the telephone and called their travel agent. "This is Mrs. Thorwald Jensen. I want to make a flight reservation."

"Shalom, shalom, Mrs. Jensen. You going to join Mr. Jensen? By the way, was he able to make his connection in Europe?"

Connection? To New York? Or to some other place where the woman would be waiting to greet him? *I never looked at his ticket. I should have looked at his ticket. I could only think that he was leaving me.*

"He hasn't cabled," she said. "But make my ticket just like Mr. Jensen's, please." *Perhaps I'll find the woman and when I do I'll—*

"Very good. When will you want to leave? And would you like me to make a hotel reservation in Mexico City? Oh, but of course, your husband will be taking care of that."

"Yes. Yes, of course." Mexico City! Then the woman would be there, otherwise Thorwald would have gone directly to New York. "And I want to leave right away, tomorrow. I'll call for the ticket this afternoon."

The arrangements finished, she went into the bedroom with the travel case. "How can I take everything?" she asked, helpless at the thought. It was a leased furnished apartment but the paintings, the books and ornaments were hers. And all the clothes she had delighted to preen herself in before Thorwald. What good had that been?

She sat on the bed beside the case, dully contemplating its limited size. She rose, took the key and flashlight again.

In the foyer that opened directly onto the terraced garden she halted abruptly, startled to see a small deer run across the flagged walkway. Its hoofs spattered on the graveled path which bordered the flower-strewn terrace. In swift succession behind the deer ran a stocky mustached man and two lean youths in work clothes. Tree branches thrashed against the building as the three vanished around the building, their pounding footsteps crescendoing into heavy thuds as they leaped down the last terrace onto the sharply descending sides of the wadi.

She hurried down the basement stairs, picked her way along the narrow hallway beside the row of storerooms to the door that opened onto the side garden. From there she went to the edge of the embankment above the wadi. Dry brush cracked in the canyonlike depths below. She saw, far down, the deer dodging among trees, leaping ahead of its pursuers. *It has run away from the zoo,* she thought, *escaped its prison. Did Thorwald do that?*

She began to tremble.

One of the youths left the group and turned back along the wadi's floor toward the zoo located at its end. She stayed to see how the search progressed, but soon the deer and the other two men vanished, concealed by brush and trees. She sat on the ground, waiting, watching. After a time the youth who had returned to the zoo came back with a second older man who carried a gun, an unusual kind of gun which she recognized from a safari trip in Africa she had taken with Thorwald. A gun to shoot tranquilizing darts.

She felt a momentary pang for the fleeing animal, then hardened against it. "It shouldn't run away, it's safer in the zoo, it's not good to run away."

She rose and went back to the storeroom. There she hesitated beside a large travel case, left it untouched, then chose a smaller one and a duffel bag.

Back upstairs the thought of the deer and the men in the wadi clung and troubled her. She went to the wide living-room window which faced the deep sprawling ravine, pushed aside the glass to let in the air, pulled a chair close, and sat down to see if the searchers would succeed. Shortly before noon one youth, carrying the tranquilizer gun, hurried up the wadi toward the zoo. Behind him, moving slowly with the weight of the sleeping beast, were the man who had brought the gun and the other youth. The first man, the one with the mustache, was not with them.

Solange stood up and went to the bedroom.

In late afternoon she decided she was finished with packing. Too bad about the paintings, the fragile ceramics. But she could return; there were months left on the lease. Only she wouldn't, not ever, never see her charming collections again; too bad, too bad, everything was too bad.

She changed clothes, walked to the shopping district. There she closed out her bank account and picked up her ticket that was made out for Mexico City. Yes, surely the woman would be there. Somehow she would find that woman. And she would kill her.

Back home she remembered that she had not eaten all day. She went to the kitchen, prepared tea and toast, thought vaguely about poaching an egg but gave up the idea. She took her tea and toast into the living room, sat before the window, nibbled and sipped as she stared into the wadi. Not seeing it, seeing only the pictures in her mind, she drifted into sleep.

The excited wailing of the zoo animals awakened her in the night. She switched on the light, looked at her watch. Ten o'clock. Why did the animals cry at this hour? Were they lonely? Was the deer awake too? Or perhaps it was dead, never to join again in the nightly excitement of the animals.

She telephoned a taxi company, made arrangements to be picked up early in the morning. Then she bathed, carefully made up her face, blotting out the dark circles under her eyes, outlining her lips, filling between the lines with provocative color. She assessed the mouth Thorwald had kissed so many times. The vulnerable mouth of a baby, he had said, tantalizing with the cat eyes and the angelic hair. *Thorwald, how could you have left me?* Briefly the eyes in the mirror flamed, then became shuttered.

When she finished dressing she did not lie down but sat in the chair waiting for morning.

Before dawn she carried the two cases up the steep lane to the sidewalk, tucked them against shrubbery, and returned for the duffel bag. Back again in the open entranceway she hesitated uncertainly, looked down the basement stairs, waited, thinking. Then she returned to the apartment and found the storage-room key.

When she came back up the basement stairs she was carrying the large travel case. She took both it and the duffel bag up to the street to wait for the taxi.

At Lod Airport she joined the passenger queue going through security check. When her turn came she lifted the smaller cases to the checking table. *Did you pack these yourself, did anyone give you anything to carry, did anyone other than yourself have access to these, give you any gifts to transport?* Yes, no, no, no. The girl security officer expertly prodded and lifted clothing, felt inside shoes, tested bottles, finally closed the cases.

"You have another case, Madam. Please lift it to the table."

Solange lifted the large case. "Open it, please." She did. The girl's voice sharpened. "Are you certain you packed this case yourself?"

"Yes."

"But these are men's clothes. Is your husband with you?"

Involuntarily Solange started to look behind her, caught herself. "No. They are my husband's clothes. He left earlier. I'm taking this case to him."

The girl hesitated, then systematically lifted out the clothes, searching pockets, unrolling socks, unzipping the shaving kit, squeezing the shaving-cream tube, turning the razor's handle. Finally she said, "It is all right. Thank you."

Solange went to the ticket check-in station, paid the excess-baggage charge, went upstairs, through customs and the body-and-hand-luggage search. Inside the departure lounge she bought the English-language newspaper, then wandered unseeing past jewelry and souvenir displays to the exit gate. Almost time, almost time to leave Israel, almost time . . .

Her flight was announced and she filed down to the bus, onto the plane, found her seat beside the window. Opened the newspaper. Breath whistled through clenched teeth with her sharp intake of air. Even though the headlines were small, the article sprang at her from the middle of the front page. *Body of American Oil Official Found on Mount Carmel.*

The deer had found him. Staggered by the dart it had floundered into the brush and fallen almost on the body mutilated by wild animals almost beyond recognition. Except for the airline ticket, found in the torn and scattered clothing and finally pieced together, it would have been difficult to identify the man. But when all the ticket fragments were rejoined, there it was: Thorwald Jensen, destination New York via Mexico City.

The plane taxied slowly to the runway. Its engines revved, then quieted as a white car sped toward it. Two men got out of the car, motioned authoritatively at a truck which hurried forward. Workmen leaped from it, rolled mobile stairs against the airliner's side. A stewardess unlocked the exit door.

She waited, hands gripped together, eyes closed as scenes of that last night with Thorwald skimmed through her mind. The frightening, furtive struggle to push and pull Thorwald down the basement stairs, past the storerooms, into the garden. Then along the garden path, rolling him down the wadi's sharp incline, every cracking twig an alarm, every lighted window discovery.

The exit door opened and the two men entered the plane. As they started down the aisle she rehearsed in her mind what she would tell them. The truth, only the truth. *He was straightening his tie before the bathroom mirror. I came behind him, begging him again not to leave me. He smiled and shook his head, not even bothering to answer, as though what I said had no importance, merely a whim to be smiled at. I already had the knife, held behind me. I struck. Hard. It was terrible. Awful. I begged him to come alive. But he couldn't. I knew that, and I was terrified. So I took him into the wadi.*

As the men stopped in the aisle beside her row she stood up, almost in welcome.

THIS IS DEATH

by DONALD E. WESTLAKE

It's hard not to believe in ghosts when you are one. I hanged myself in a fit of truculence—stronger than pique, but not so dignified as despair—and regretted it before the thing was well begun. The instant I kicked the chair away I wanted it back, but gravity was turning my former wish to its present command; the chair would not right itself from where it lay on the floor, and my 193 pounds would not cease to urge downward from the rope thick around my neck.

There was pain, of course, quite horrible pain centered in my throat, but the most astounding thing was the way my cheeks seemed to swell. I could barely see over their round red hills, my eyes staring in agony at the door, *willing* someone to come in and rescue me, though I knew there was no one in the house, and in any event the door was carefully locked. My kicking legs caused me to twist and turn, so that sometimes I faced the door and sometimes the window, and my shivering hands struggled with the rope so deep in my flesh I could barely find it and most certainly could not pull it loose.

I was frantic and terrified, yet at the same time my brain possessed a cold corner of aloof observation. I seemed now to be everywhere in the room at once, within my writhing body but also without, seeing my frenzied spasms, the thick rope, the heavy beam, the mismatched pair of lit bedside lamps throwing my convulsive double shadow on the walls, the closed locked door, the white-curtained window with its shade drawn all the way down. *This is death,* I thought, and I no longer wanted it, now that the choice was gone forever.

My name is—was—Edward Thornburn, and my dates are 1938–1977. I killed myself just a month before my fortieth birthday, though I don't believe the well-known pangs of that milestone had much if anything to do with my action. I blame it all (as I blamed most of the errors and failures of my life) on my sterility. Had I been able to father children my marriage would have remained strong, Emily would not have been unfaithful to me, and I would not have taken my own life in a final fit of truculence.

The setting was the guestroom of our house in Barnstaple, Connecticut, and the time was just after seven p.m.; deep twilight, at this time of year. I had come home from the office—I was a realtor, a fairly lucrative occupation in Connecticut, though my income had been falling off recently—shortly before six, to find the note on the kitchen table: "Antiquing with Greg. Afraid you'll have to make your own dinner. Sorry. Love, Emily."

Greg was the one; Emily's lover. He owned an antique shop out on the main road toward New York, and Emily filled a part of her days as his ill-paid assistant. I knew what they did together in the back of the shop on those long midweek afternoons when there were no tourists, no antique collectors to disturb them. I knew, and I'd known for more than three years, but I had never decided how to deal with my knowledge. The fact was, I blamed myself, and therefore I had no way to *behave* if the ugly subject were ever to come into the open.

So I remained silent, but not content. I was discontent, unhappy, angry, resentful—truculent.

I'd tried to kill myself before. At first with the car, by steering it into an oncoming truck (I swerved at the last second, amid howling horns) and by driving it off a cliff into the Connecticut River (I slammed on the brakes at the very brink, and sat covered in perspiration for half an hour before backing away) and finally by stopping athwart one of the few level crossings left in this neighborhood. But no train came for 20 minutes, and my truculence wore off, and I drove home.

Later I tried to slit my wrists, but found it impossible to push sharp metal into my own skin. Impossible. The vision of my naked wrist and that shining steel so close together washed my truculence completely out of my mind. Until the next time.

With the rope; and then I succeeded. Oh, totally, oh, fully I succeeded. My legs kicked at air, my fingernails clawed at my throat, my bulging eyes stared out over my swollen purple cheeks, my tongue thickened and grew bulbous in my mouth, my body jigged and jangled like a toy at the end of a string, and the pain was excruciating, horrible, not to be endured. I can't endure it, I thought, it can't be endured. Much worse than knife slashings was the knotted strangled pain in my throat, and my head ballooned with pain, pressure outward, my face turning black, my eyes no longer human, the pressure in my head building and building as though I would explode. Endless horrible pain, not to be endured, but going on and on.

My legs kicked more feebly. My arms sagged, my hands dropped to my sides, my fingers twitched uselessly against my sopping trouser legs, my head hung at an angle from the rope, I turned more slowly in the air, like a broken windchime on a breezeless day. The pains lessened, in my throat and head, but never entirely stopped.

And now I saw that my distended eyes had become lusterless, gray. The moisture had dried on the eyeballs, they were as dead as stones. And yet I could see them, my own eyes, and when I widened my vision I could see my entire body, turning, hanging, no longer twitching, and with horror I realized I was dead.

But *present*. Dead, but still present, with the scraping ache still in my throat and the bulging pressure still in my head. Present, but no longer in that used-up clay, that hanging meat; I was suffused through the room, like indirect lighting, everywhere present but without a source. What happens now? I wondered, dulled by fear and strangeness and the continuing pains, and I waited, like a hovering mist, for whatever would happen next.

But nothing happened. I waited; the body became utterly still; the double shadow on the wall showed no vibration; the bedside lamps continued to burn; the door remained shut and the window shade drawn; and nothing happened.

What *now?* I craved to scream the question aloud, but I could not. My throat ached, but I had no throat. My mouth burned, but I had no mouth. Every final strain and struggle of my body remained imprinted in my mind, but I had no body and no brain and no *self,* no substance. No power to speak, no power to move myself, no power to *re*move myself from this room and this suspended corpse. I could only wait here, and wonder, and go on waiting.

There was a digital clock on the dresser opposite the bed, and when it first occurred to me to look at it the numbers were 7:21—perhaps twenty minutes after I'd kicked the chair away, perhaps fifteen minutes since I'd died. Shouldn't something happen, shouldn't some *change* take place?

The clock read 9:11 when I heard Emily's Volkswagen drive around to the back of the house. I had left no note, having nothing I wanted to say to anyone and in any event believing my own dead body would be eloquent enough, but I hadn't thought I would be *present* when Emily found me. I was justified in my action, however much I now regretted having taken it, I was justified, I knew I was justified, but I didn't want to see her face when she came through that door. She had wronged me, she was the cause of it, she would have to know that as well as I, but I didn't want to see her face.

The pains increased, in what had been my throat, in what had been my head. I heard the back door slam, far away downstairs, and I stirred like air currents in the room, but I didn't leave. I couldn't leave.

"Ed? Ed? It's me, hon!"

I know it's you. I must go away now, I can't stay here, I must go away. Is there a God? Is this my soul, this hovering presence? *Hell* would be better than this, take me away to Hell or wherever I'm to go, don't leave me here!

She came up the stairs, calling again, walking past the closed guestroom door. I heard her go into our bedroom, heard her call my name, heard the beginnings of apprehension in her voice. She went by again, out there in the hall, went downstairs, became quiet.

What was she doing? Searching for a note perhaps, some message from me. Looking out the window, seeing again my Chevrolet, knowing I must be home. Moving through the rooms of this old house, the original structure a barn nearly 200 years old, converted by some previous owner just after the Second World War, bought by me twelve years ago, furnished by Emily—and Greg—from their interminable, damnable, awful antiques. Shaker furniture, Colonial furniture, hooked rugs and quilts, the old yellow pine tables, the faint sense always of being in some slightly shabby minor museum, this house that I had bought but never loved. I'd bought it for Emily, I did everything for Emily, because I knew I could never do the one thing for Emily that mattered. I could never give her a child.

She was good about it, of course. Emily *is* good, I never blamed her, never completely blamed *her* instead of myself. In the early days of our marriage she made a few wistful references, but I suppose she saw the effect they had on me, and for a long time she has said nothing. But I have known.

The beam from which I had hanged myself was a part of the original building, a thick hand-hewed length of aged timber eleven inches square, chevroned with the marks of the hatchet that had shaped it. A strong beam, it would support my weight forever. It would support my weight until I was found and cut down. Until I was found.

The clock read 9:23 and Emily had been in the house twelve minutes when she came upstairs again, her steps quick and light on the old wood, approaching, pausing, stopping. "Ed?"

The doorknob turned.

The door was locked, of course, with the key on the inside. She'd have to break it down, have to call someone else to break it down, perhaps she wouldn't be the one to find me after all. Hope rose in me, and the pains receded.

"Ed? Are you in there?" She knocked at the door, rattled the knob, called my name several times more, then abruptly turned and ran away downstairs again, and after a moment I heard her voice, murmuring and unclear. She had called someone, on the phone.

Greg, I thought, and the throat-rasp filled me, and I wanted this to be the end. I wanted to be taken away, dead body and living soul, taken away. I wanted everything to be finished.

She stayed downstairs, waiting for him, and I stayed upstairs, waiting for them both. Perhaps she already knew what she'd find up here, and that's why she waited below.

I didn't mind about Greg, about being present when he came in. I didn't mind about *him*. It was Emily I minded.

The clock read 9:44 when I heard tires on the gravel at the side of the house. He entered, I heard them talking down there, the deeper male voice slow and reassuring, the lighter female voice quick and frightened, and then they came up together, neither speaking. The doorknob turned, jiggled, rattled, and Greg's voice called, "Ed?"

After a little silence Emily said, "He wouldn't— He wouldn't *do* anything, would he?"

"Do anything?" Greg sounded almost annoyed at the question. "What do you mean, do anything?"

"He's been so depressed, he's— Ed!" And forcibly the door was rattled, the door was shaken in its frame.

"Emily, don't. Take it easy."

"I shouldn't have called you," she said. "Ed, *please!*"

"Why not? For heaven's sake, Emily—"

"Ed, *please* come out, don't scare me like this!"

"Why *shouldn't* you call me, Emily?"

"Ed isn't stupid, Greg. He's—"

There was then a brief silence, pregnant with the hint of murmuring. They thought me still alive in here, they didn't want me to hear Emily say, "He *knows,* Greg, he knows about us."

The murmurings sifted and shifted, and then Greg spoke loudly, "That's ridiculous. Ed? Come out, Ed, let's talk this over." And the doorknob rattled and clattered, and he sounded annoyed when he said, "We must get in, that's all. Is there another key?"

"I think all the locks up here are the same. Just a minute."

They were. A simple skeleton key would open any interior door in the house. I waited, listening, knowing Emily had gone off to find another key, knowing they would soon come in together, and I felt such terror and revulsion for Emily's entrance that I could feel myself shimmer in the room, like a reflection in a warped mirror. Oh, can I at least stop seeing? In life I had eyes, but also eyelids, I could shut out the intolerable, but now I was only a presence, a total presence, I *could not* stop my awareness.

The rasp of key in lock was like rough metal edges in my throat; my memory of a throat. The pain flared in me, and through it I heard Emily asking what was wrong, and Greg answering, "The key's in it, on the other side."

"Oh, dear God! Oh, Greg, what has he done?"

"We'll have to take the door off its hinges," he told her. "Call Tony. Tell him to bring the toolbox."

"Can't you push the key through?"

Of course he could, but he said, quite determinedly, "Go *on,* Emily," and I realized then he had no intention of taking the door down. He simply wanted her away when the door was first opened. Oh, very good, *very* good!

"All right," she said doubtfully, and I heard her go away to phone Tony. A beetle-browed young man with great masses of black hair and an olive complexion, Tony lived in Greg's house and was a kind of handyman. He did work around the house and was also (according to Emily) very good at restoration of antique furniture; stripping paint, reassembling broken parts, that sort of thing.

There was now a renewed scraping and rasping at the lock, as Greg struggled to get the door open before Emily's return. I found myself feeling unexpected warmth and liking toward Greg. He wasn't a bad person; an opportunist with my wife, but not in general a bad person. Would he marry her now? They could live in this house, he'd had more to do with its furnishing than I. Or would this room hold too grim a memory, would Emily have to sell the house, live elsewhere? She might have to sell at a low price; as a realtor, I knew the difficulty in selling a house where a suicide has taken place. No matter how much they may joke about it, people are still afraid of the supernatural. Many of them would believe this room was haunted.

It was then I finally realized the room *was* haunted. With me! *I'm a ghost,* I thought, thinking the word for the first time, in utter blank astonishment. I'm a ghost.

Oh, how dismal! To hover here, to be a boneless fleshless aching *presence* here, to be a kind of ectoplasmic mildew seeping through the days and nights, alone, unending, a stupid pain-racked misery-filled observer of the comings and goings of strangers—she *would* sell the house, she'd have to, I was sure of that. Was this my punishment? The punishment of the suicide, the solitary hell of him who takes his own life. To remain forever a sentient nothing, bound by a force greater than gravity itself to the place of one's finish.

I was distracted from this misery by a sudden agitation in the key on this side of the lock. I saw it quiver and jiggle like something alive, and then it popped out—it seemed to *leap* out, itself a suicide leaping from a cliff—and clattered to the floor, and an instant later the door was pushed open and Greg's ashen face stared at my own purple face, and after the astonishment and horror, his expression shifted to revulsion—and contempt?—and he backed out, slamming the door. Once more the key turned in the lock, and I heard him hurry away downstairs.

The clock read 9:58. *Now* he was telling her. *Now* he was giving her a drink to calm her. *Now* he was phoning the police. *Now* he was talking to her about whether or not to admit their affair to the police; what would they decide?

"Noooooooooo!"

The clock read 10:07. What had taken so long? Hadn't he even called the police yet?

She was coming up the stairs, stumbling and rushing, she was pounding on the door, screaming my name. I shrank into the corners of the room, I *felt* the thuds of her fists against the door, I cowered from her. She can't come in, dear God don't let her in! I don't care what she's done, I don't care about anything, just don't let her see me! *Don't let me see her!*

Greg joined her. She screamed at him, he persuaded her, she raved, he argued, she demanded, he denied. "Give me the key. Give me the key."

Surely he'll hold out, surely he'll take her away, surely he's stronger, more forceful.

He gave her the key.

No. *This* cannot be endured. *This* is the horror beyond all else. She came in, she walked into the room, and the sound she made will always live inside me. That cry wasn't human; it was the howl of every creature that has ever despaired. *Now* I know what despair is, and why I called my own state mere truculence.

Now that it was too late, Greg tried to restrain her, tried to hold her shoulders and draw her from the room, but she pulled away and crossed the room toward . . . not toward *me*. I was everywhere in the room, driven by pain and remorse, and Emily walked toward the carcass. She looked at it almost tenderly, she even reached up and touched its swollen cheek. "Oh, Ed," she murmured.

The pains were as violent now as in the moments before my death. The slashing torment in my throat, the awful distension in my head, they made me squirm in agony all over again; but I *could not* feel her hand on my cheek.

Greg followed her, touched her shoulder again, spoke her name, and immediately her face dissolved, she cried out once more and wrapped her arms around the corpse's legs and clung to it, weeping and gasping and uttering words too quick and broken to understand. Thank *God* they were too quick and broken to understand!

Greg, that fool, did finally force her away, though he had great trouble breaking her clasp on the body. But he succeeded, and pulled her out of the room, and slammed the door, and for a little while the body swayed and turned, until it became still once more.

That was the worst. Nothing could be worse than that. The long days and nights here—how long must a stupid creature like myself *haunt* his death-place before release?—would be horrible, I knew that, but not so bad as this. Emily would survive, would sell the house, would slowly forget. (Even I would slowly forget.) She and Greg could marry. She was only 36, she could still be a mother.

For the rest of the night I heard her wailing, elsewhere in the house. The police did come at last, and a pair of grim silent white-coated men from the morgue entered the room to cut me—it—down. They bundled it like a broken toy into a large oval wicker basket with long wooden handles, and they carried it away.

I had thought I might be forced to stay with the body, I had feared the possibility of being buried with it, of spending eternity as a thinking nothingness in the black dark of a casket, but the body left the room and I remained behind.

A doctor was called. When the body was carried away the room door was left open, and now I could plainly hear the voices from downstairs. Tony was among them now, his characteristic surly monosyllable occasionally rumbling, but the main thing for a while was the doctor. He was trying to give Emily a sedative, but she kept wailing, she kept speaking high hurried frantic sentences as though she had too little time to say it all. "I did it!" she cried, over and over. "I did it! I'm to blame!"

Yes. That was the reaction I'd wanted, and expected, and here it was, and it was horrible. Everything I had desired in the last moments of my life had been granted to me, and they were all ghastly beyond belief. I *didn't* want to die! I *didn't* want to give Emily such misery! And more than all the rest I didn't want to be here, seeing and hearing it all.

They did quiet her at last, and then a policeman in a rumpled blue suit came into the room with Greg, and listened while Greg described everything that had happened. While Greg talked, the policeman rather grumpily stared at the remaining length of rope still knotted around the beam, and when Greg had finished the policeman said, "You're a close friend of his?"

"More of his wife. She works for me. I own The Bibelot, an antique shop out on the New York road."

"Mm. Why on earth did you let her in here?"

Greg smiled; a sheepish embarrassed expression. "She's stronger than I am," he said. "A more forceful personality. That's always been true."

It was with some surprise I realized it *was* true. Greg was something of a weakling, and Emily was very strong. (*I* had been something of a weakling, hadn't I? Emily was the strongest of us all.)

The policeman was saying, "Any idea why he'd do it?"

"I think he suspected his wife was having an affair with me." Clearly Greg had rehearsed this sentence, he'd much earlier come to the decision to say it and had braced himself for the moment. He blinked all the way through the statement, as though standing in a harsh glare.

The policeman gave him a quick shrewd look. "Were you?"

"Yes."

"She was getting a divorce?"

"No. She doesn't love me, she loved her husband."

"Then why sleep around?"

"Emily wasn't sleeping *around*," Greg said, showing offense only with that emphasized word. "From time to time, and not very often, she was sleeping with me."

"Why?"

"For comfort." Greg too looked at the rope around the beam, as though it had become me and he was awkward speaking in its presence. "Ed wasn't an easy man to get along with," he said carefully. "He was moody. It was getting worse."

"Cheerful people don't kill themselves," the policeman said.

"Exactly. Ed was depressed most of the time, obscurely angry now and then. It was affecting his business, costing him clients. He made Emily miserable but she wouldn't leave him, she loved him. I don't know what she'll do now."

"You two won't marry?"

"Oh, no." Greg smiled, a bit sadly. "Do you think we murdered him, made it look like suicide so we could marry?"

"Not at all," the policeman said. "But what's the problem? You already married?"

"I am homosexual."

The policeman was no more astonished than I. He said, "I don't get it."

"I live with my friend; that young man downstairs. I am—capable—of a wider range, but my preferences are set. I am very fond of Emily, I felt sorry for her, the life she had with Ed. I told you our physical relationship was infrequent. And often not very successful."

Oh, Emily. Oh, poor Emily.

The policeman said, "Did Thornburn know you were, uh, that way?"

"I have no idea. I don't make a public point of it."

"All right." The policeman gave one more half-angry look around the room, then said, "Let's go."

They left. The door remained open, and I heard them continue to talk as they went downstairs, first the policeman asking, "Is there somebody to stay the night? Mrs. Thornburn shouldn't be alone."

"She has relatives in Great Barrington. I phoned them earlier. Somebody should be arriving within the hour."

"You'll stay until then? The doctor says she'll probably sleep, but just in case—"

"Of course."

That was all I heard. Male voices murmured a while longer from below, and then stopped. I heard cars drive away.

How complicated men and women are. How stupid are simple actions. I had never understood anyone, least of all myself.

The room was visited once more that night, by Greg, shortly after the police left. He entered, looking as offended and repelled as though the body were still here, stood the chair up on its legs, climbed on it, and with some difficulty untied the remnant of rope. This he stuffed partway into his pocket as he stepped down again to the floor, then returned the chair to its usual spot in the corner of the room, picked the key off the floor and put it in the lock, switched off both bedside lamps and left the room, shutting the door behind him.

Now I was in darkness, except for the faint line of light under the door, and the illuminated numerals of the clock. How long one minute is! That clock was my enemy, it dragged out every minute, it paused and waited and paused and waited till I could stand it no more, and then it waited longer, and *then* the next number dropped into place. Sixty times an hour, hour after hour, all night long. I couldn't stand one night of this, how could I stand eternity?

And how could I stand the torment and torture inside my brain? That was much worse now than the physical pain, which never entirely left me. I had been right about Emily and Greg, but at the same time I had been hopelessly brainlessly wrong. I had been right about my life, but wrong; right about my death, but wrong. How *much* I wanted to make amends, and how impossible it was to do anything any more, anything at all. My actions had all tended to this, and ended with this: black remorse, the most dreadful pain of all.

I had all night to think, and to feel the pains, and to wait without knowing what I was waiting for or when—or if—my waiting would ever end. Faintly I heard the arrival of Emily's sister and brother-in-law, the murmured conversation, then the departure of Tony and Greg. Not long afterward the guestroom door opened, but almost immediately closed again, no one having entered, and a bit after that the hall light went out, and now only the illuminated clock broke the darkness.

When next would I see Emily? Would she ever enter this room again? It wouldn't be as horrible as the first time, but it would surely be horror enough.

Dawn grayed the window shade, and gradually the room appeared out of the darkness, dim and silent and morose. Apparently it was a sunless day, which never got very bright. The day went on and on, featureless, each protracted minute marked by the clock. At times I dreaded someone's entering this room, at other times I prayed for something, anything—even the presence of Emily herself—to break this unending boring *absence*. But the day went on with no event, no sound, no activity anywhere—they must be keeping Emily sedated through this first day—and it wasn't until twilight, with the digital clock reading 6:52, that the door again opened and a person entered.

At first I didn't recognize him. An angry-looking man, blunt and determined, he came in with quick ragged steps, switched on both bedside lamps, then shut the door with rather more force than necessary, and turned the key in the lock. Truculent, his manner was, and when he turned from the door I saw with incredulity that he was *me*. Me! I wasn't dead, I was alive! But how could that be?

And what was that he was carrying? He picked up the chair from the corner, carried it to the middle of the room, stood on it—

No! No!

He tied the rope around the beam. The noose was already in the other end, which he slipped over his head and tightened around his neck.

Good God, *don't!*

He kicked the chair away.

The instant I kicked the chair away I wanted it back, but gravity was turning my former wish to its present command; the chair would not right itself from where it lay on the floor, and my 193 pounds would not cease to urge downward from the rope thick around my neck.

There was pain, of course, quite horrible pain centered in my throat, but the most astounding thing was the way my cheeks seemed to swell. I could barely see over their round red hills, my eyes staring in agony at the door, *willing* someone to come in and rescue me, though I knew there was no one in the house, and in any event the door was carefully locked. My kicking legs caused me to twist and turn, so that sometimes I faced the door and sometimes the window, and my shivering hands struggled with the rope so deep in my flesh I could barely find it and most certainly could not pull it loose.

I was frantic and horrified, yet at the same time my brain possessed a cold corner of aloof observation. I seemed now to be everywhere in the room at once, within my writhing body but also without, seeing my frenzied spasms, the thick rope, the heavy beam, the mismatched pair of lit bedside lamps throwing my convulsive double shadow on the walls, the closed locked door, the white-curtained window with its shade drawn all the way down. *This is death*

WOODROW WILSON'S NECKTIE

by *PATRICIA HIGHSMITH*

The façade of MADAME THIBUALT'S WAXWORK HORRORS glittered and throbbed with red and yellow lights, even in the daytime. Knobs of golden balls—the yellow lights—pulsated amid the red lights, attracting the eye and holding it.

Clive Wilkes loved the place, the inside and the outside equally. Since he was a delivery boy for a grocery store, it was easy for him to say that a certain delivery had taken him longer than had been expected—he'd had to wait for Mrs. So-and-so to get home because the doorman had told him she was due back any minute, or he'd had to go five blocks to find some change because Mrs. Smith had had only a twenty-dollar bill. At these spare moments—and Clive managed one or two a week—he visited MADAME THIBAULT'S WAXWORK HORRORS.

Inside the establishment you went through a dark passage—to be put in the mood—and then you were confronted by a bloody murder scene on the left: a girl with long blond hair was sticking a knife into the neck of an old man who sat at a kitchen table eating his dinner. His dinner consisted of two wax frankfurters and wax sauerkraut. Then came the Lindbergh kidnapping scene, with Hauptmann climbing down a ladder outside a nursery window; you could see the top of the ladder out the window, and the top half of Hauptmann's figure, clutching the little boy. Also there was Marat in his bath with Charlotte nearby. And Christie with his stocking, throttling a woman.

Clive loved every tableau, and they never became stale. But he didn't look at them with the solemn, vaguely startled expression of the other people who looked at them. Clive was inclined to smile, even to laugh. They were amusing. So why not laugh?

Farther on in the museum were the torture chambers—one old, one modern, purporting to show Twentieth Century torture methods in Nazi Germany and in French Algeria. Madame Thibault—who Clive strongly suspected did not exist—kept up to date. There were the Kennedy assassination and the Tate massacre, of course, and some murder that had happened only a month ago somewhere.

Clive's first definite ambition in regard to MADAME THIBAULT'S WAXWORK HORRORS museum was to spend a night there. This he did one night, providently taking along a cheese sandwich in his pocket. It was fairly easy to accomplish. Clive knew that three people worked in the museum proper—down in the bowels, as he thought of it, though the museum was on street level—while a fourth, a plumpish middle-aged man in a nautical cap, sold tickets at a booth in front. The three who worked in the bowels were two men and a woman; the woman, also plump and with curly brown hair and glasses and about 40, took the tickets at the end of the dark corridor, where the museum proper began.

One of the inside men lectured constantly, though not more than half the people ever bothered to listen. "Here we see the fanatical expression of the true murderer, captured by the supreme wax artistry of Madame Thibault"—and so on. The other inside man had black hair and black-rimmed glasses like the woman, and he just drifted around, shooing away kids who wanted to climb into the tableaux, maybe watching for pickpockets, or maybe protecting women from unpleasant assaults in the semidarkness. Clive didn't know.

He only knew it was quite easy to slip into one of the dark corners or into a nook next to one of the Iron Molls—maybe even into one of the Iron Molls; but slender as he was, the spikes might poke into him, Clive thought, so he ruled out this idea. He had observed that people were gently urged out around 9:15 P.M., as the museum closed at 9:30 P.M. And lingering as late as possible one evening, Clive had learned that there was a sort of cloakroom for the staff behind a door in one back corner, from which direction he had also heard the sound of a toilet flushing.

So one night in November, Clive concealed himself in the shadows, which were abundant, and listened to the three people as they got ready to leave. The woman—whose name turned out to be Mildred—was lingering to take the money box from Fred, the ticket seller, and to count it and deposit it somewhere in the cloakroom. Clive was not interested in the money. He was interested only in spending a night in the place and being able to boast he had.

"Night, Mildred—see you tomorrow," called one of the men.

"Anything else to do? I'm leaving now," said Mildred. "Boy, am I tired! But I'm still going to watch Dragon Man tonight."

"Dragon Man," the other man repeated, uninterested.

Evidently the ticket seller, Fred, left from the front of the building after handing in the money box, and in fact Clive recalled seeing him close up the front once, cutting the lights from inside the entrance door, then locking the door and barring it on the outside.

Clive stood in a nook by an Iron Moll. When he heard the back door shut and the key turn in the lock, he waited for a moment in delicious silence, aloneness, and suspense, and then ventured out. He went first, on tiptoe, to the room where they kept their coats, because he had never seen it. He had brought matches—also cigarettes, though smoking was not allowed, according to several signs—and with the aid of a match he found the light switch. The room contained an old desk, four metal lockers, a tin wastebasket, an umbrella stand, and some books in a bookcase against a grimy wall that had once been white. Clive slid open a drawer and found the well-worn wooden box which he had once seen the ticket seller carrying in through the front door. The box was locked. He could walk out with the box, Clive thought, but he didn't care to, and he considered this rather decent of himself. He gave the box a wipe with the side of his hand, not forgetting the bottom where his fingertips had touched. That was funny, he thought, wiping something he wasn't going to steal.

Clive set about enjoying the night. He found the lights and put them on so that the booths with the gory tableaux were all illuminated. He was hungry, took one bite of his sandwich, then put it back in the paper napkin in his pocket. He sauntered slowly past the John F. Kennedy assassination—Mrs. Kennedy and the doctors bending anxiously over the white table on which JFK lay. This time, Hauptmann's descent of the ladder made Clive giggle. Charles Lindbergh, Jr.'s face looked so untroubled that one would think he might be sitting on the floor of his nursery, playing with blocks.

Clive swung a leg over a metal bar and climbed into the Judd-Snyder tableau. It gave him a thrill to be standing right *with* them, inches from the throttling-from-behind which the lover of the woman was administering to the husband. Clive put a hand out and touched the red-paint blood that was seeming to come from the man's throat where the cord pressed deep. Clive also touched the cool cheekbones of the victim. The popping eyes were of glass, vaguely disgusting, and Clive did not touch those.

Two hours later he was singing church hymns, *Nearer My God to Thee* and *Jesus Wants Me for a Sunbeam*. Clive didn't know all the words. And he smoked.

By two in the morning he was bored and tried to get out by both the front door and back, but couldn't—both were barred on the outside. He had thought of having a hamburger at an all-night diner between here and home. However, his enforced incarceration didn't bother him, so he finished the now-dry cheese sandwich and slept for a bit on three straight chairs which he arranged in a row. It was so uncomfortable that he knew he'd wake up in a while, which he did—at 5 A.M. He washed his face, then went for another look at the wax exhibits. This time he took a souvenir—Woodrow Wilson's necktie.

As the hour of 9:00 approached—MADAME THIBAULT'S WAXWORK HORRORS opened at 9:30 A.M.—Clive hid himself in an excellent spot, behind one of the tableaux whose backdrop was a black-and-gold Chinese screen. In front of the screen was a bed and in the bed lay a wax man with a handlebar mustache, who was supposed to have been poisoned by his wife.

The public began to trickle in shortly after 9:30 A.M., and the taller, more solemn man began to mumble his boring lecture. Clive had to wait till a few minutes past ten before he felt safe enough to mingle with the crowd and make his exit, with Woodrow Wilson's necktie rolled up in his pocket. He was a bit tired, but happy—though on second thought, who would he tell about it? Joey Vrasky, that dumb cluck who worked behind the counter at Simmons' Grocery? Hah! Why bother? Joey didn't deserve a good story. Clive was half an hour late for work.

"I'm sorry, Mr. Simmons, I overslept," Clive said hastily, but he thought quite politely, as he came into the store. There was a delivery job awaiting him. Clive took his bicycle and put the carton on a platform in front of the handlebars.

Clive lived with his mother, a thin highly strung woman who was a saleswoman in a shop that sold stockings, girdles, and underwear. Her husband had left her when Clive was nine. She had no other children. Clive had quit high school a year before graduation, to his mother's regret, and for a year he had done nothing but lie around the house or stand on street corners with his pals. But Clive had never been very chummy with any of them, for which his mother was thankful, as she considered them a worthless lot. Clive had had the delivery job at Simmons' for nearly a year now, and his mother felt that he was settling down.

When Clive came home that evening at 6:30 P.M. he had a story ready for his mother. Last night he had run into his old friend Richie, who was in the Army and home on leave, and they had sat up at Richie's house talking so late that Richie's parents had invited him to stay over, and Clive had slept on the couch. His mother accepted this explanation. She made a supper of baked beans, bacon, and eggs.

There was really no one to whom Clive felt like telling his exploit of the night. He couldn't have borne someone looking at him and saying, "Yeah? So what?" because what he had done had taken a bit of planning, even a little daring. He put Woodrow Wilson's tie among his others that hung over a string on the inside of his closet door. It was a gray silk tie, conservative and expensive-looking. Several times that day Clive imagined one of the two men in the museum, or maybe the woman named Mildred, glancing at Woodrow Wilson and exclaiming, "Hey! What happened to Woodrow Wilson's tie, I wonder?"

Each time Clive thought of this he had to duck his head to hide a smile. After twenty-four hours, however, the exploit had begun to lose its charm and excitement. Clive's excitement only rose again—and it could rise two or three times a day—whenever he cycled past the twinkling façade of MADAME THIBAULT'S WAXWORK HORRORS. His heart would give a leap, his blood would run a little faster, and he would think of all the motionless murders going on in there, and all the stupid faces of Mr. and Mrs. Johnny Q. Public gaping at them. But Clive didn't even buy another ticket—price 65 cents—to go in and look at Woodrow Wilson and see that his tie was missing and his collar button showing—his work.

Clive did get another idea one afternoon, a hilarious idea that would make the public sit up and take notice. Clive's ribs trembled with suppressed laughter as he pedaled toward Simmons', having just delivered a bag of groceries.

When should he do it? Tonight? No, best to take a day or so to plan it. It would take brains. And silence. And sure movements—all the things Clive admired.

He spent two days thinking about it. He went to his local snack bar and drank beer and played the pinball machines with his pals. The pinball machines had pulsating lights too—*More Than One Can Play* and *It's More Fun To Compete*— but Clive thought only of MADAME THIBAULT'S as he stared at the rolling, bouncing balls that mounted a score he cared nothing about. It was the same when he looked at the rainbow-colored jukebox whose blues, reds, and yellows undulated, and when he went over to drop a coin in it. He was thinking of what he was going to do in MADAME THIBAULT'S WAXWORK HORRORS.

On the second night, after a supper with his mother, Clive went to MADAME THIBAULT'S and bought a ticket. The old guy who sold tickets barely looked at people, he was so busy making change and tearing off the stubs, which was just as well. Clive went in at 9:00 P.M.

He looked at the tableaux, though they were not so fascinating to him tonight as they had been before. Woodrow Wilson's tie was still missing, as if no one had noticed it, and Clive chuckled over this. He remembered that the solemn-faced pickpocket-watcher—the drifting snoop—had been the last to leave the night Clive had stayed, so Clive assumed he had the keys, and therefore he ought to be the last to be killed.

The woman was the first. Clive hid himself beside one of the Iron Molls again, while the crowd ambled out, and when Mildred walked by him, in her hat and coat, to leave by the back door, having just said something to one of the men in the exhibition hall, Clive stepped out and wrapped an arm around her throat from behind.

She made only a small *ur-rk* sound.

Clive squeezed her throat with his hands, stopping her voice. At last she slumped, and Clive dragged her into a dark, recessed corner to the left of the cloakroom. He knocked an empty cardboard box of some kind over, but it didn't make enough noise to attract the attention of the two men.

"Mildred's gone?" one of the men asked.

"I think she's in the office."

"No, she's not." The owner of this voice had already gone into the corridor where Clive crouched over Mildred and had looked into the empty cloakroom where the light was still on. "She's left. Well, I'm calling it a day too."

Clive stepped out then and encircled this man's neck in the same manner. The job was more difficult, because the man struggled, but Clive's arm was thin and strong; he acted with swiftness and knocked the man's head against the wooden floor.

"What's going on?" The thump had brought the second man.

This time Clive tried a punch to the man's jaw, but missed and hit his neck. However, this so stunned the man—the little solemn fellow, the snoop—that a quick second blow was easy, and then Clive was able to take him by the shirtfront and bash his head against the plaster wall which was harder than the wooden floor. Then Clive made sure that all three were dead. The two men's heads were bloody. The woman was bleeding slightly from her mouth. Clive reached for the keys in the second man's pockets. They were in his left trousers pocket and with them was a penknife. Clive also took the knife.

Then the taller man moved slightly. Alarmed, Clive opened the pearl-handled penknife and plunged it into the man's throat three times.

Close call, Clive thought, as he checked again to make sure they were all dead. They most certainly were, and that was most certainly real blood, not the red paint of MADAME THIBAULT'S WAXWORK HORRORS. Clive switched on the lights for the tableaux and went into the exhibition hall for the interesting task of choosing exactly the right places for the three corpses.

The woman belonged in Marat's bath—not much doubt about that. Clive debated removing her clothing, but decided against it, simply because she would look much funnier sitting in a bath wearing a fur-trimmed coat and hat. The figure of Marat sent him off into laughter. He'd expected sticks for legs, and nothing between the legs, because you couldn't see any more of Marat than from the middle of his torso up; but Marat had no legs at all and his wax body ended just below the waist in a fat stump which was planted on a wooden platform so that it would not topple. This crazy waxwork Clive carried into the cloakroom and placed squarely in the middle of the desk. He then carried the woman—who weighed a good deal —onto the Marat scene and put her in the bath. Her hat fell off, and he pushed it on again, a bit over one eye. Her bloody mouth hung open.

Good lord, it *was* funny!

Now for the men. Obviously, the one whose throat he had knifed would look good in the place of the old man who was eating wax franks and sauerkraut, because the girl behind him was supposed to be stabbing him in the throat. This took Clive some fifteen minutes. Since the figure of the old man was in a seated position, Clive put him on the toilet off the cloakroom. It was terribly amusing to see the old man seated on the toilet, throat apparently bleeding, a knife in one hand and a fork in the other. Clive lurched against the door jamb, laughing loudly, not even caring if someone heard him, because it was so comical it was even worth getting caught for.

Next, the little snoop. Clive looked around him and his eye fell on the Woodrow Wilson scene which depicted the signing of the armistice in 1918. A wax figure sat at a huge desk signing something, and that was the logical place for a man whose head was almost split open. With some difficulty Clive got the pen out of the wax man's fingers, laid it to one side on the desk, and carried the figure—it didn't weigh much—into the cloakroom, where Clive seated him at the desk, rigid arms in an attitude of writing. Clive stuck a ballpoint pen into his right hand. Now for the last heave. Clive saw that his jacket was now quite spotted with blood and he would have to get rid of it, but so far there was no blood on his trousers.

Clive dragged the second man to the Woodrow Wilson tableau, lifted him up, and rolled him toward the desk. He got him onto the chair, but the head toppled forward onto the green-blottered desk, onto the blank wax pages, and the pen barely stood upright in the limp hand.

But it was done. Clive stood back and smiled. Then he listened. He sat down on a straight chair and rested for a few minutes, because his heart was beating fast and he suddenly realized that every muscle in his body was tired. Ah, well, he now had the keys. He could lock up, go home, and have a good night's rest, because he wanted to be ready to enjoy tomorrow.

Clive took a sweater from one of the male figures in a log-cabin tableau of some kind. He had to pull the sweater down over the feet of the waxwork to get it off, because the arms would not bend; it stretched the neck of the sweater, but he couldn't help that. Now the wax figure had a sort of bib for a shirtfront, and naked arms and chest.

Clive wadded up his jacket and went everywhere with it, erasing fingerprints from whatever he thought he had touched. He turned the lights off, made his way carefully to the back door, locked and barred it behind him, and would have left the keys in a mailbox if there had been one; but there wasn't, so he dropped the keys on the rear doorstep. In a wire rubbish basket he found some newspapers; he wrapped up his jacket in them and walked on with it until he found another wire rubbish basket, where he forced the bundle down among candy wrappers, beer cans, and other trash.

"A new sweater?" his mother asked that night.

"Richie gave it to me—for luck."

Clive slept like the dead, too tired even to laugh again at the memory of the old man sitting on the toilet.

The next morning Clive was standing across the street when the ticket seller arrived just before 9:30 A.M. By 9:35 A.M. only four people had gone in; but Clive could not wait any longer, so he crossed the street and bought a ticket. Now the ticket seller was doubling as ticket taker, and telling people, "Just go on in. Everybody's late this morning."

The ticket man stepped inside the door to put on some lights, then walked all the way into the place to put on the display lights for the tableaux, which worked from switches in the hall that led to the cloakroom. And the funny thing, to Clive who was walking behind him, was that the ticket man didn't notice anything odd, didn't even notice Mildred in her hat and coat sitting in Marat's bathtub.

The other customers so far were a man and a woman, a boy of fourteen or so in sneakers, alone apparently, and a single man. They looked expressionlessly at Mildred in the tub as if they thought it quite "normal," which would have sent Clive into paroxysms of mirth, except that his heart was thumping madly and he could hardly breathe for the suspense. Also, the man with his face in franks and sauerkraut brought no surprise either. Clive was a bit disappointed.

Two more people came in, a man and a woman.

Then at last, in front of the Woodrow Wilson tableau, there was a reaction. One of the women, clinging to her husband's arm, asked, "Was someone shot when the armistice was signed?"

"I don't know. I don't *think* so," the man replied vaguely.

Clive's laughter pressed like an explosion in his chest; he spun on his heel to control himself, and he had the feeling he knew *all* about history, and that no one else did. By now, of course, the real blood had turned to a rust color. The green blotter was now splotched, and blood had dripped down the side of the desk.

A woman on the other side of the room, where Mildred was, let out a scream.

A man laughed, but only briefly.

Suddenly everything happened. A woman shrieked, and at the same time a man yelled, "My God, it's *real!*"

Clive saw a man climbing up to investigate the corpse with his face in the frankfurters.

"The blood's *real!* It's a *dead* man!"

Another man—one of the public—slumped to the floor. He had fainted. The ticket seller came bustling in. "What's the trouble here?"

"Coupla corpses—*real* ones!"

Now the ticket seller looked at Marat's bathtub and fairly jumped into the air with surprise. "Holy Christmas! *Holy* cripes!—it's *Mildred!*"

"And this one!"

"And the one here!"

"My God, got to—got to call the police!" said the ticket seller.

One man and woman left hurriedly. But the rest lingered, shocked, fascinated.

The ticket seller had run into the cloakroom, where the telephone was, and Clive heard him yell something. He'd seen the man at the desk, of course, the wax man, and the half body of Marat on the desk.

Clive thought it was time to drift out, so he did, sidling his way through a group of people peering in the front door, perhaps intending to come in because there was no ticket seller.

That was good, Clive thought. That was all right. Not bad. Not bad at all.

He had not intended to go to work that day, but suddenly he thought it wiser to check in and ask for the day off. Mr. Simmons was of course as sour as ever when Clive said he was not feeling well, but as Clive held his stomach and appeared weak, there was little old Simmons could do. Clive left the grocery. He had brought with him all his ready cash, about $23.

Clive wanted to take a long bus ride somewhere. He realized that suspicion might fall on him, if the ticket seller remembered his coming to MADAME THIBAULT'S often, or especially if he remembered Clive being there last night; but this really had little to do with his desire to take a bus ride. His longing for a bus ride was simply, somehow, irresistible. He bought a ticket westward for $8 and change, one way. This brought him, by about 7:00 P.M., to a good-sized town in Indiana, whose name Clive paid no attention to.

The bus spilled a few passengers, Clive included, at a terminal, where there was a cafeteria and a bar. By now Clive was curious about the newspapers, so he went to the newsstand near the street door of the cafeteria. And there were the headlines:

Triple Murder in Waxworks

Mass Murder in Museum

Mystery Killer Strikes: Three Dead in Waxworks

Clive liked the last one best. He bought the three newspapers, and stood at the bar with a beer.

"This morning at 9:30 A.M., ticket man Fred J. Carmody and several of the public who had come to see Madame Thibault's Waxwork Horrors, a noted attraction of this city, were confronted by three genuine corpses among the displays. They were the bodies of Mrs. Mildred Veery, 41; George P. Hartley, 43; and Richard K. McFadden, 37, all employed at the waxworks museum. The two men were killed by concussion and stabbing, and the woman by strangulation. Police are searching for clues on the premises. The murders are believed to have taken place shortly before 10:00 P.M. last evening, when the three employees were about to leave the museum. The murderer or murderers may have been among the last patrons of the museum before closing time at 9:30 P.M. It is thought that he or they may have concealed themselves somewhere in the museum until the rest of the patrons had left. . . ."

Clive was pleased. He smiled as he sipped his beer. He hunched over the papers, as if he did not wish the rest of the world to share his pleasure, but this was not true. After a few minutes Clive stood up and looked to the right and left to see if anyone else among the men and women at the bar was also reading the story. Two men were reading newspapers, but Clive could not tell if they were reading about him, because their newspapers were folded.

Clive lit a cigarette and went through all three newspapers to see if any clue to him was mentioned. He found nothing. One paper said specifically that Fred J. Carmody had not noticed any person or persons entering the museum last evening who looked suspicious.

". . . Because of the bizarre arrangement of the victims and of the displaced wax figures in the exhibition, in whose places the victims were put, police are looking for a psychopathic killer. Residents of the area have been warned by radio and television to take special precautions on the streets and to keep their houses locked."

Clive chuckled over that one. Psychopathic killer! He was sorry about the lack of detail, the lack of humor in the three reporters' stories. They might have said something about the old guy sitting on the toilet. Or the fellow signing the armistice with the back of his head bashed in. Those were strokes of genius. Why didn't they appreciate them?

When he had finished his beer, Clive walked out onto the sidewalk. It was now dark and the streetlights were on. He enjoyed looking around in the new town, looking into shop windows. But he was aiming for a hamburger place, and he went into the first one he came to. It was a diner made up to look like a crack railway car.

Clive ordered a hamburger and a cup of coffee. Next to him were two Western-looking men in cowboy boots and rather soiled broad-brimmed hats. Was one a sheriff, Clive wondered? But they were talking, in a drawl, about acreage somewhere. Land. They were hunched over hamburgers and coffee, one so close that his elbow kept touching Clive's. Clive was reading his newspapers all over again and he had propped one against the napkin container in front of him.

One of the men asked for a napkin and disturbed Clive, but Clive smiled and said in a friendly way, "Did you read about the murders in the wax-works?"

The man looked blank for a moment, then said, "Yep, saw the headlines."

"Someone killed the three people who worked in the place. Look." There was a photograph in one of the papers, but Clive didn't much like it because it showed the corpses lined up on the floor. He would have preferred Mildred in the bathtub.

"Yeah," said the Westerner, edging away from Clive as if he didn't like him.

"The bodies were put into a few of the exhibits. Like the wax figures. They say that, but they don't show a picture of it," said Clive.

"Yeah," said the Westerner, and went on eating.

Clive felt let down and somehow insulted. His face grew a little warm as he stared back at his newspapers. In fact, anger was growing quickly inside him, making his heart go faster, as it always did when he passed MADAME THIBAULT'S WAXWORK HORRORS, though now the sensation was not at all pleasant.

Clive put on a smile, however, and turned to the man on his left again. "I mention it, because I did it. That's my work there." He gestured toward the picture of the corpses.

"Listen, boy," said the Westerner casually, "you just keep to yourself tonight. Okay? We ain't botherin' you, so don't you go botherin' us." He laughed a little, glancing at his companion.

His friend was staring at Clive, but looked away at once when Clive stared back.

This was a double rebuff, and quite enough for Clive. He got out his money and paid for his unfinished food with a dollar bill. He left the change and walked to the sliding-door exit.

"But y'know, maybe that guy ain't kiddin'," Clive heard one of the men say.

Clive turned and said, "I *ain't* kiddin'!" Then he went out into the night.

Clive slept at a Y.M.C.A. The next day he half-expected he would be picked up by a passing cop on the beat, but he wasn't. He got a lift to another town, nearer his hometown. The day's newspapers brought no mention of his name, and no mention of clues. In another café that evening, almost the identical conversation took place between Clive and a couple of fellows his own age. They didn't believe him. It was stupid of them, Clive thought, and he wondered if they were pretending? Or lying?

Clive hitched his way home and headed for the police station. He was curious as to what *they* would say. He imagined what his mother would say after he confessed. Probably the same thing she had said to her friends sometimes, or that she'd said to a policeman when he was sixteen and had stolen a car.

"Clive hasn't been the same since his father went away. I know he needs a man around the house, a man to look up to, imitate, you know. That's what people tell me. Since he was fourteen Clive's been asking me questions like, 'Who am I, anyway?' and 'Am I a person, mom?' " Clive could see and hear her in the police station.

"I have an important confession to make," Clive said to a deskman in the front.

The man's attitude was rude and suspicious, Clive thought, but he was told to walk to an office, where he spoke with a police officer who had gray hair and a fat face. Clive told his story.

"Where do you go to school, Clive?"

"I don't. I'm eighteen." Clive told him about his job at Simmons' Grocery.

"Clive, you've got troubles, but they're not the ones you're talking about," said the officer.

Clive had to wait in a room, and nearly an hour later a psychiatrist was brought in. Then his mother. Clive became more and more impatient. They didn't believe him. They were saying his was a typical case of false confession in order to draw attention to himself. His mother's repeated statements about his asking questions like "Am I a person?" and "Who am I?" only seemed to corroborate the opinions of the psychiatrist and the police.

Clive was to report somewhere twice a week for psychiatric therapy.

He fumed. He refused to go back to Simmons' Grocery, but found another delivery job, because he liked having a little money in his pocket, and he was fast on his bicycle and honest with the change.

"You haven't *found* the murderer, have you?" Clive said to the police psychiatrist. "You're all the biggest bunch of jackasses I've ever seen in my life!"

The psychiatrist said soothingly, "You'll never get anywhere talking to people like that, boy."

Clive said, "Some perfectly ordinary strangers in Indiana said, 'Maybe that guy ain't kidding.' They had more sense than *you!*"

The psychiatrist smiled.

Clive smoldered. One thing might have helped to prove his story—Woodrow Wilson's necktie, which still hung in his closet. But these dumb clucks damned well didn't deserve to see that tie. Even as he ate his suppers with his mother, went to the movies, and delivered groceries, he was planning. He'd do something more important next time—like starting a fire in the depths of a big building or planting a bomb somewhere or taking a machine gun up to some penthouse and letting 'em have it down on the street. Kill a hundred people at least, or a thousand. They'd have to come up in the building to get him. *Then* they'd know. *Then* they'd treat him like somebody who really existed, like somebody who deserved an exhibit of himself in Madame Thibault's Waxwork Horrors.

The Eighties

THE JACKAL AND THE TIGER

by MICHAEL GILBERT

On the evening of April 15th, 1944, Colonel Hubert, of Military Intelligence, said to the Director of Public Prosecutions, "The only mistake Karl made was to underestimate young Ronnie Kavanagh."

That afternoon, Karl Muller, who sometimes called himself Charles Miller, had been shot in the underground rifle range at the Tower of London, which was the place being used at that time for the execution of German spies.

"A fatal mistake," agreed the Director.

Jim Perrot, late of the Military Police, wrote to his friend, Fred Denniston:

"Dear Denny,

"Do you remember those plans we talked over so often in North Africa and Italy? Well, I've got an option on a twenty-one-year lease of a nice first-floor office in Chancery Lane. That's bang in the middle of legal London, where the legal eagles are beginning to flap their wings and sharpen their claws again. Lots of work for an Enquiry Agency and not much competition—as yet. The lease is a snip. I've commuted my pension and got me a bit of capital. I reckon we'll have to put in about £2,000 each to get going. Denny's Detectives! How about it?"

And Denny's Detectives had turned out to be a success from the start.

As Perrot had said, there was no lack of work. Much of it was divorce work, the sad byproduct of a long war. It was in connection with this branch of their activities, which neither of the partners liked, that they acquired Mr. Huffin. He was perfectly equipped for the role he had to play. He was small, mild-looking, and so insignificant that many businessmen, departing to alleged conferences in the Midlands, had failed to recognize the little man who traveled in the train with them and occupied a table in an obscure corner of their hotel dining room until he stood up in court and swore to tell the truth, the whole truth, and nothing but the truth about the lady who had shared the businessman's table, and, later, his bedroom.

Jim Perrot's job was the tracing of elusive debtors. His experience as a policeman was useful to him here. Fred Denniston, for his part, rarely left the office. His specialty was estimating the credit-worthiness of companies. He gradually became expert at reading between the lines of optimistic profit-and-loss accounts and precariously balanced balance sheets. He developed, with experience, a quite uncanny instinct for over-valued stocks and under-depreciated assets. Perrot would sometimes see him holding a suspect document delicately between his fingers and sniffing at it, as though he could detect, by smell alone, the odor of falsification.

One factor that helped them to show a steady profit was their absurdly small rent. When Perrot had described the lease as a "snip" he was not exaggerating. At the end of the war, when no one was bothered about inflation, twenty-one-year leases could be had without the periodical reviews which are commonplace today. As the end of their lease approached, the partners did become aware that they were paying a good deal less than the market rent. Indeed, they could hardly help being aware of it—their landlords, the Scotus Property Company, commented on it with increasing bitterness.

"It's no good complaining about it," said Perrot genially. "You should have thought about that when you granted the lease."

"Just you wait till the end of next year," said Scotus.

Denniston said, "I suppose we shall have to pay a bit more. Anyway, they can't turn us out. We're protected tenants."

When a friendly valuer from the other end of Chancery Lane learned what their rent was, he struggled to control his feelings. "I suppose you realize," he said, "that you're paying a pound a square foot—"

"Just about what I made it," said Denniston.

"And that the going rate in this area is between five and six pounds."

"You mean," said Perrot, "that when our lease comes to an end, we'll have to pay five times the present rent."

"Oh, at least that," said the valuer cheerfully. "But I imagine you've been putting aside a fund to meet it."

The partners looked at each other. They were well aware that they had been doing nothing of the sort.

That was the first shock.

The second shock was Perrot's death. He had been putting on weight and smoking too much, but had looked healthy enough. One afternoon he complained of not feeling well, went home early, and died that night.

Denniston had been fond of him and his first feelings were of personal loss. His next feeling was that he was going to need another partner and additional capital; and that fairly quickly.

He considered and rejected the idea of inviting Mr. Huffin to become a partner. The main drawback was that Denniston disliked him. And he was so totally negative. He crept into the office every morning on the stroke of nine and, unless he had some outside business, stayed in his room, which had been partitioned off from Denniston's, until half past five. The partition was so thin that Denniston could hear him every time he got up from his chair.

Not partner material, said Denniston to himself.

He tried advertising, but soon found that the limited number of applicants who had capital would have been unsuitable as partners, while the rather greater number who might have been acceptable as partners had no capital.

After some months of fruitless effort he realized two other things. The first was that they were losing business. Jim Perrot's clients were taking their affairs elsewhere. The second was that the day of reckoning with his landlords was looming.

It was at this point that Andrew Gurney turned up. Denniston liked him at sight. He was young. He was cheerful. He seemed anxious to learn the business. And he made a proposal.

In about a year's time, when he attained the ripe old age of twenty-five, he would be coming into a bit of capital under a family trust. By that time he would have a fair idea whether the business suited him and he suited them. All being well, he was prepared to invest that capital in the firm.

They discussed amounts and dates and came to a tentative agreement. Gurney took over Perrot's old room. Denniston breathed a sigh of relief and turned his mind to the analysis of a complex set of group accounts.

It was almost exactly a month later when Mr. Huffin knocked on his door, put his head round, blinked twice, and said, "If you're not too busy, I wonder if I might have a word with you."

"I'm doing nothing that can't wait," said Denniston.

Mr. Huffin slid into the room, advanced toward the desk, and then, as if changing his mind at the last moment, seated himself in the chair that was normally reserved for clients.

Denniston was conscious of a slight feeling of surprise. Previously when Mr. Huffin had come to see him, he had stood in front of the desk and had waited, if the discussion was likely to be lengthy, for an invitation to sit down.

He was even more surprised when Mr. Huffin spoke. He said, "You're in trouble, aren't you?"

It was not only that Mr. Huffin had omitted the "sir" which he had previously used when addressing his employer. It was more than that. There was something sharp and cold in the tone of his voice. It was like the sudden unexpected chill which announces the end of autumn and the beginning of winter.

"You haven't seen fit to take me into your confidence," Mr. Huffin continued, "but the wall between our offices is so thin that it's impossible for me not to hear every word that's said."

Denniston had recovered himself sufficiently to say, "The fact that you can overhear confidential matters doesn't entitle you to trade on them."

"When the ship's sinking," said Mr. Huffin, "etiquette has to go by the board."

This was followed by a silence which Denniston found difficult to break. In the end he said, "It's true that Mr. Perrot's death has left us in a difficult position. But as it happens, I have been able to make arrangements which should tide us over."

"You mean young Gurney? In the month he's been here, he's earned less than half you pay him. And speaking personally, I should have said that he's got no real aptitude for the work. What you need is someone without such nice manners, but with a thicker skin."

Denniston said, "Look here, Mr. Huffin—" and stopped. He was on the point of saying, "If you don't like the way I run this firm, we can do without you." But could they?

As though reading his thoughts, Mr. Huffin said, "In the old days, Mr. Perrot, you, and I earned roughly equal amounts. Recently the proportions have been slipping. Last year I brought in half our fees. At least those were the figures you gave our auditor, so I assume they're correct."

"You listened to that discussion also?"

"I felt I was an interested party."

Mr. Denniston said, "All right. I accept that your services have been valuable. If that's your point, you've made it. I imagine it's leading up to something else. You want an increase in salary?"

"Not really."

"Then perhaps you had it in mind that I should make you a partner?"

"Not exactly."

"Then—"

"My proposal was that I should take over the firm."

In the long silence that followed, Denniston found himself revising his opinion of Mr. Huffin. His surface meekness was, he realized, a piece of professional camouflage, as meaningless as the wigs of the barristers and the pin-striped trousers of the solicitors.

Mr. Huffin added, "Have you thought out what would happen if I did leave? Maybe you could make enough to cover expenses. Until your lease expires. But what then? Have you, I wonder, overlooked one point. At the conclusion of a twenty-one-year lease there is bound to be a heavy bill for dilapidations."

"Dilapidations?" said Denniston slowly. The five syllables chimed together in an ominous chord. "Surely, there's nothing much to do."

"I took the precaution of having a word with an old friend, a Mr. Ellen. He's one of the surveyors used by the Scotus Property Company. He's a leading expert in his field and his calculations are very rarely challenged by the court. Last weekend I arranged for him to make an inspection. He thought that the cost of carrying out all the necessary work in a first-class fashion would be between six and eight thousand pounds."

"For God's sake!" said Denniston. "It can't be!"

"He showed me the breakdown. It could be more."

To give himself time to think, Denniston said, after a pause, "If you have such a poor opinion of the prospects of the firm, why would you want to buy me out?"

"I'm sorry," said Mr. Huffin gently. "You've misunderstood me. I wasn't proposing to pay you anything. After all, what have you got to sell?"

It was not Denniston's habit to discuss business with his wife, but this was a crisis. He poured out the whole matter to her as soon as he got home that evening.

"And I know damned well what he'll do," he said. "As soon as he's got me out, he'll bring in some accomplice of his own. They won't stick to divorce work. That's legal, at least. The real money's in dirty work. Finding useful witnesses and bribing them to say what your client wants. Faking evidence. Fudging expert reports."

His wife said, "He seems to be prepared to pay eight thousand pounds for the privilege of doing it."

"Of course he won't: that's a put-up job between him and his old pal, Mr. Ellen, of Scotus. He'll pay a lot less and be allowed to pay it in easy installments."

"What happens if you say no?"

"I'd have to challenge the dilapidations. It'd mean going to court and that's expensive."

"If you used some of Gurney's money—" Mrs. Denniston stopped.

They were both straightforward people. Denniston put what she was thinking into words. "I can't take that boy's money and put it into a legal wrangle."

"And there's no other way of raising it?"

"None that I can think of."

"Then that's that," said his wife. "I'd say cut your losses and clear out. We're still solvent. We'll think of something to do."

It took a lot of talk to persuade him, but in the end he saw the force of her arguments. "All right," he said. "No sense in dragging it out. I'll go in tomorrow and tell Huffin he can have the firm. I'll also tell him what I think of him."

"It won't do any good."

"It'll do me a lot of good."

On the following evening, Denniston arrived back on the stroke of six. He kissed his wife and said to her, "Whatever you were thinking of cooking for supper, think again. We're going out to find the best dinner London can provide. We'll drink champagne before it, burgundy with it, and brandy after it."

His wife, who had spent the day worrying about how they were going to survive, said, "Really, Fred. Do you think we ought—"

"Certainly we ought. We're celebrating."

"Celebrating what?"

"A miracle."

It had happened at nine o'clock that morning. While Denniston was polishing up the precise terms in which he intended to say good-bye to Mr. Huffin, his secretary came into his room. She was looking ruffled. She said, "Could you be free to see Mr. Kavanagh at ten?"

Denniston looked at his diary and said, "Yes. That'll be all right. Who is Mr. Kavanagh?"

"Mr. Ronald Kavanagh," said his secretary. While he was still looking blank, she added, "Kavanagh Lewisohn and Fitch. He's the chairman."

Denniston said, "Good God!" And then, "How do you know that?"

"Before I came here, I worked in their head office."

"Do you know Mr. Kavanagh?"

His secretary said, "I was in the typing pool. I caught a glimpse of him twice in the three years I was there."

"Did he say what he wanted?"

"He wanted to see you."

"You're sure he didn't ask me to go and see him? He's coming here?"

"That's what he said."

"It must be some mistake," said Denniston.

Kavanagh Lewisohn and Fitch were so well known that people said KLF and assumed you would understand what they meant. They were one of the largest credit-sale firms in London, so large that they rarely dealt with individual customers. They sold everything from computer banks to motor cars and television sets and washing machines to middle men, who in turn sold them to retailers. If Ronald Kavanagh was really planning to visit a small firm of enquiry agents, it could hardly be in connection with business matters. It must be private trouble. Something that needed to be dealt with discreetly.

When Kavanagh arrived, he turned out, surprisingly, to be a slight, quiet, unassuming person in his early fifties. Denniston was agreeably surprised. Such managing directors of large companies as he had come across in the past had been intimidating people, assertive of their status and conscious of their financial muscle. A further surprise was that he really had come to talk business.

He said, "This is something I wanted to deal with myself. Some time ago you did credit-rating reports for us on two potential customers." He mentioned their names.

"Yes," said Denniston, wondering what had gone wrong.

"We were impressed by the thorough way you tackled them. I assume, by the way, that you did the work yourself."

Denniston nodded.

"You gave a good rating to one, although it was a new company. The other, which was older and apparently sound, you warned us against. In both cases, you were absolutely right. That's why I'm here today. Up to the present we've been getting the reports we needed from half a dozen different sources. This is now such an important part of our business that the Board has decided that it would like to concentrate it in one pair of hands. Our first idea was to offer you the work on a retainer basis. Then we had a better idea." Mr. Kavanagh smiled. "We decided to buy you. That is, of course, if you're for sale."

Denniston was incapable of speech.

"We had it in mind to purchase your business as a going concern. We would take over the premises as they stand. There is, however, one condition. It's *your* brains and *your* flair that we're buying. We should have to ask you to enter into a service contract, at a fair salary, for five years certain, with options on both sides to renew. Your existing staff, too, if they wish. But you are the one we must have."

The room, which had shown signs of revolving on its axis, slowed down. Denniston took a grip of himself. He said, "Your offer is more than fair, but there is one thing you ought to know. You spoke of taking over these premises. There is a snag—"

When he had finished, Kavanagh said, "It was good of you to tell me. It accords, if I may say so, with your reputation. We are not unacquainted with Scotus." He smiled gently. "We had some dealings with them over one of our branch offices last year. Fortunately, we have very good solicitors and excellent surveyors. The outcome was a lot happier for us than it was for them. However, in this case it doesn't arise. Our own service department will carry out such repairs and redecoration as *we* consider necessary. If Scotus object, they can take us to court. I don't think they will. They're timid folk when they're up against someone bigger than themselves."

"Like all bullies," said Denniston. As he said it, he reflected with pleasure that Mr. Huffin had undoubtedly got his ear glued to the wall.

*   *   *

It soon became apparent that Ronald Kavanagh was not a man who delegated to others things that he enjoyed doing himself.

On the morning after the deal had been signed, he limped into the room, accompanied by the head of his service department and a foreman. They inspected everything and made notes. The next morning, a gang of workmen arrived and started to turn the office upside down.

Kavanagh arrived with the workmen. He said to Denniston, "We'll start with your room. Strip and paint the whole place. They can do it in two days. What colors do you fancy?"

"Something cheerful."

"I agree. My solicitor's office looks as if it hasn't been dusted since Charles Dickens worked there. What we want is an impression of cheerful reliability. Cream paint, venetian blinds, and solid-brass light fittings. And we'll need a second desk. I propose to establish a niche here for myself. I hope you don't mind."

"I don't mind at all," said Denniston. It occurred to him that one cause of his depression had been that since Perrot's death he had really had no one to talk to. "I'll be glad of your company, though I don't suppose you'll be able to spare us a lot of time."

"It's a common fallacy," said Kavanagh, sitting on a corner of the table, swinging his damaged leg ("a relic of war service," he had explained), "widely believed, but quite untrue, that managing directors are busy men. If they are, it's a sign of incompetence. I have excellent subordinates who do the real work. All I have to do is utter occasional sounds of approval or disapproval. It's such a boring life that a new venture like this is a breath of fresh air. Oh, you want to move this table. We'd better shift into young Gurney's office.

"As I was saying," he continued when they had established themselves in Gurney's room, "I have an insatiable curiosity about the mechanics of other people's business. When we went into the secondhand car market, we took over a motor-repair outfit. I got so interested that I put on overalls and started to work there myself. The men thought it was a huge joke, but they soon got used to it. And the things I learned about faking repair bills, you wouldn't believe. Oh, sorry—I'm afraid they want to start work in here, too. Let's go to my club and get ourselves an early luncheon."

Denniston found the new regime very pleasant. Kavanagh did not, of course, spend all his time with them, but he managed to put in a full hour on most days. His method of working was to have copies made, on the modern photocopying machine which had been one of his first innovations, of all of Denniston's reports. These he would study carefully, occasionally asking for the working papers. The questions he asked were shrewd and could not be answered without thought.

"Really," he said, "we're in the same line of business. Success depends on finding out who to trust. I once turned down a prosperous-looking television wholesaler because he turned up in a Green Jackets' tie. I'm damned certain he'd never been near the Brigade. Quite the wrong shape for a Rifleman."

"Instinct, based on experience," agreed Denniston. He already felt years younger. It was not only the steady flow of new work and the certainty of getting a check at the end of each month, the whole office seemed to have changed. Even Mr. Huffin appeared to be happy. Not only had his room been repainted, it had been furnished with a new desk and a set of gleaming filing cabinets equipped with Chubb locks. These innovations seemed to have compensated him for the setback to his own plans and he went out of his way to be pleasant to Kavanagh when he encountered him.

"Slimy toad," said Denniston to his wife. "When I asked Kavanagh if he planned to keep him, he laughed and said, 'Why not? I don't much like the sort of work he's doing, but it brings in good money. As long as he keeps within the law. If you hear any complaints of sharp practice, that's another matter.'"

"Mr. Kavanagh sounds terrific."

"Terrific's not quite the right word. He's honest, sensible, and unassuming. Also, he's still a bit of a schoolboy. He likes to see the wheels go round."

"I don't believe a single word of it," said his wife.

"Well, Uncle," said Andrew Gurney. "What next?"

Kavanagh said, "Next, I think, a glass of port."

"Then it must be something damned unpleasant," said Gurney.

"Why?"

"If it wasn't, you wouldn't be wasting the Club port on me."

"You're an irreverent brat," said Kavanagh.

"When you wangled me into the firm I guessed you were up to something."

"Two large ports, please, Barker. Actually, Andrew, all I want you to do is to commit a burglary."

"I said it was going to be something unpleasant."

"But this is a very safe burglary. You're to burgle the offices of Denny's Detectives. Since the firm belongs to me, technically hardly a burglary at all, would you say?"

"Well—," said Gurney cautiously.

"I will supply you with the key of the outer door, the key of Mr. Huffin's room, and a key for each of his new filing cabinets and his desk. Mr. Huffin is a careful man. When the desk and cabinets were installed, he asked for the duplicate keys to be handed to him. Fortunately, I had a second copy made of each. Nevertheless, I was much encouraged by his request. It showed me that I might be on the right track."

"What track?"

Kavanagh took a sip of his port and said, "It's Warre '63. Don't gulp it. I suggest that you start around eleven o'clock. By that time, Chancery Lane should be deserted except for the occasional policeman. In case you should run into trouble, I'll supply you with a note stating that you are working late with my permission."

"Yes, Uncle, but—"

"When you get into Mr. Huffin's room, take all the files from his cabinets and all the papers from his desk and photograph them. Be very careful to put them back in the order you found them."

"Yes, but—"

"I don't imagine you'll be able to finish the job in one night, or even in two. When you leave, bring the photocopies round to my flat. You can use my spare room and make up for your lost nights by sleeping by day. I'll warn my housekeeper. As far as the office is concerned, you're out of town on a job for me. I think that's all quite straightforward."

"Oh, quite," said Gurney. "The only thing is you haven't told me what you're up to."

"When I've had a chance of examining Mr. Huffin's papers, I may have a clearer idea myself. As soon as I do, I'll put you in the picture."

Andrew sighed. "When do you want me to start?"

"It's Monday today. If you start tomorrow night, you should be through by the end of the week. I suggest you go home now and get a good night's rest."

As his uncle had predicted, it took Andrew exactly four nights to finish the job. If he expected something dramatic to happen, he was disappointed. For a week his uncle failed to turn up at the office.

"Our owner," said Mr. Huffin with a smirk, "seems to have lost interest in us."

Andrew smiled and agreed. He had just had an invitation to dinner at his uncle's flat in Albany and guessed that things might be moving.

During dinner, his uncle spoke only of cricket. He was a devotee of the Kent team, most of whom he seemed to know by name. After dinner, which was cooked and served by the housekeeper, they retired to the sitting room. Kavanagh said, "And how did you enjoy your experience as a burglar?"

"It was a bit creepy at first. After nightfall, Chancery Lane seems to be inhabited by howling cats."

"They're not cats. They're the spirits of disappointed litigants."

"Did I produce whatever it was you were looking for?"

"The papers from the cabinets related only to Mr. Huffin's routine work. They showed him to be a thorough, if somewhat unscrupulous operator. A model trufflehound. Ninety-nine percent of his private papers likewise. But the other one percent—two memoranda and a bundle of receipts—were worth all the rest put together. They demonstrated that Mr. Huffin has a second job. He's a moonlighter."

"He's crooked enough for anything. What's his other job? Some sort of blackmail, I suppose."

"Try not to use words loosely, Andrew. Blackmail has become a portmanteau word covering everything from illegal intimidation to the use of lawful leverage."

"I can't imagine Mr. Huffin intimidating anyone."

"Personally, probably not. But he has a partner. And that man we must now locate. Those scraps of paper are his footprints."

Andrew looked at his uncle. He knew something of the work he had done during the war, but he found it hard to visualize this mild grey-haired man pursuing, in peace, the tactics which had brought Karl Muller and others to the rifle range in the Tower. For the first time, he was striking the flint under the topsoil and it was a curiously disturbing experience. He said, "You promised—"

"Yes, I promised. So be it. Does the name David Rogerson mean anything to you?"

"I know he was one of your friends."

"More than that. During the retreat to Dunkirk, he managed to extract me from a crashed and burning lorry—which was, incidentally, full of explosives. That was when I broke my right leg in several places and contracted this limp which ended my service as an Infanteer. Which was why I went into Intelligence.

"I kept up with David after the war. Not as closely as I should have liked. He had married a particularly stupid woman. However, we met once or twice a year for lunch in the City. We were both busy. I was setting up KLF and he was climbing the ladder in Clarion Insurance. About six months ago, he asked me to lend him some money—a thousand pounds. Of course I said yes and didn't ask him what he wanted it for. But I suppose he felt he owed me some sort of explanation. When he was leaving he said, with something like a smile, 'Do you play draughts?' I said I did when I was a boy. 'Well,' he said, 'I've been huffed. By Mr. Huffin.' Those were his last words to me. The next news I had was of his death."

Gurney said, "I read about that. No one seemed to know why he did it."

"You may recall that at the inquest his wife was asked whether he had left a note. She said no. That was a lie. He did leave a note, as I discovered later. David had made me executor. My first job was to look after his wife. I soon saw that Phyllis Rogerson had one objective. To live her own life on the proceeds of some substantial insurance policies David had taken out—and to forget about him. I accepted that this was a natural reaction. Women are realists. It was when I was clearing up his papers that she told me the truth. He *had* left a letter and it was addressed to me. She said, 'I guessed it was something to do with the trouble he'd been having. I knew that if you read it all the unpleasantness would have to come out into the open, so I burnt it. I didn't even read it.' I said, 'If it was some sort of blackmailer, David won't have been his only victim. He must be caught and punished.' She wouldn't listen. I haven't spoken to her since."

"But you located Mr. Huffin."

"That wasn't difficult. The Huffin clan isn't large. A clergyman in Shropshire, a farmer in Wales, a maiden lady in Northumberland. Little Mr. Huffin of Denny's Detectives was so clearly the first choice that I had no hesitation in trying him first."

"Clearly enough for you to spend your company's money in buying the agency?"

"We were on the lookout for a good credit-rating firm. My Board was unanimous that Denniston was the man for the job. So I was able to kill two birds with one stone—always an agreeable thing to do. My first idea was to expose Huffin as a blackmailer. I felt that there would be enough evidence in his files to convict him. I was wrong. What those papers show is that a second man is involved—possibly the more important villain of the two. I see Huffin as the reconnaissance unit, the other man as the heavy brigade."

"Do you know his name?"

"The only lead I have to him is that Mr. Huffin used to communicate privately with a Mr. Angus. The address he wrote to was a small newsagent's shop in Tufnell Park, an accommodation address, no doubt. Receipts for the payments he made to the shopkeeper were among his papers. I visualize Mr. Angus calling from time to time to collect his letters. Or he may send a messenger. That is something we shall have to find out."

"And you want me to watch the shop?"

"It's kind of you to offer. But no. Here I think we want professional help. Captain Smedley will be the man for the job. You've never heard of him? He's the head of a detective agency." Rather unkindly, Kavanagh added, "A *real* detective agency, Andrew."

Captain Smedley said, "I shall need exactly a hundred, in ones and fives. That's what it will cost to buy the man in the shop. I'll pay it to him myself. He won't play silly buggers with me."

Kavanagh looked at Captain Smedley, who had a face like a hank of wire rope, and agreed that no one was likely to play silly buggers with him.

"I'll have a man outside," Smedley said. "All the shopkeeper's got to do is tip him the wink when the letter's collected. Then my man follows him back to wherever he came from."

"Might it be safer to have two men outside?"

"Safer, but more expensive."

"Expense no object."

"I see," said the Captain. He looked curiously at Mr. Kavanagh, whom he had known for some time. "All right. I'll fix it up for you."

On the Wednesday of the third week following this conversation, Kavanagh got a thick plain envelope addressed to him at his flat. It contained several pages of typescript, which he read carefully. The look on his face was partly enlightenment and partly disgust. "What a game," he said. "I wonder how they work it."

After breakfast, he spent some time in the reference section of the nearest public library browsing among Civil Service lists and copies of *Whittaker's Almanac*. Finally he found the name he wanted. Arnold Robbins. Yes, Arnold would certainly help him if the matter was put to him in the right way. But it would need devilish careful handling. "A jackal," he said, "and a tiger. Now all we need is a tethered goat to bring the tiger under the rifle. But it will have to be tethered very carefully, in exactly the right spot. The brute is a man-eater, no question."

A lady touched him on the shoulder and pointed to the notice which said SILENCE, PLEASE. He was not aware that he had spoken aloud.

During the months that followed, Kavanagh resumed his regular visits to the office in Chancery Lane, but Denniston noticed that his interest in the details of the work seemed to be slackening. He would still read the current reports and comment on them, but more of his time seemed to be spent in conversation.

In the old days, Denniston might have objected to this as being a waste of time which could better have been spent in earning profits. Now it was different. He was being paid a handsome salary, and if it pleased the owner of the firm to pass an occasional hour in gossip why should he object? Moreover, Kavanagh was an excellent talker, with a rich fund of experience in the byways of the jungle which lies between Temple Bar and Aldgate Pump. Politics, economics, finance; honesty, dishonesty, and crime. Twenty years of cut-and-thrust between armies whose soldiers wore lounge suits and carried rolled umbrellas—warfare in which victory could be more profitable and defeat more devastating than on any field of battle.

On one occasion, Kavanagh, after what must have been an unusually good luncheon, had devoted an entertaining hour to a dissertation on the tax system.

"At the height of their power and arrogance," he said, "the Church demanded one-tenth of a man's income. The government of England exacts six times as much. The pirate who sank an occasional ship, the highwayman who held up a coach, was a child compared to the modern taxman."

"You can't fight the State," said Denniston.

"It's been tried. Poujade in France. But I agree that massive tax resistance is self-defeating. Each man must fight for himself. There are lawyers and accountants who specialize in finding loopholes in the tax laws, but such success can only be temporary. As soon as a loophole is discovered, the next Finance Act shuts it up. The essentials of guerrilla warfare are concealment and agility."

Really interested now, Denniston said, "Have you discovered a practical method of sidestepping tax? I've never made excessive profits, but I do resent handing over a slab of what I've made to a government who spends most of it on vote-catching projects."

"My method isn't one which would suit everyone. Its merit is simplicity. I arrange with my Board that they will pay me only two-thirds of what I ought to be getting. The other third goes to charities nominated by me. They, of course, pay no tax. That part of it is quite legitimate. Our constitution permits gifts to charity."

"Then how—?"

"The only fact which is *not* known is that I set up and control the charities concerned. One is a local village affair. Another looks after our own employees. A third is for members of my old Regiment. I am chairman, secretary, and treasurer of all three. Some of the money is devoted to the proper objects of the charity. The balance comes back, by various routes, to me. A lovely tax-free increment."

"But," said Denniston, "surely—"

"Yes?"

"It seems too simple."

"But, I assure you, effective."

And later, to himself, Kavanagh asked, I wonder if that was too obvious. I can only wait and see.

"There's something stirring," said Captain Smedley. "My men tell me those two beauties have got a regular meeting place. Top of the Duke of York's Steps. It isn't possible to get close enough to hear what they're saying—no doubt that's why they chose it—but they're certainly worked up about something. Licking their lips, you might say."

"The bleating of the goat," said Kavanagh, "excites the tiger."

The letter which arrived at his flat a week later was in a buff envelope, typed on buff paper. It was headed *Inland Revenue Special Investigation Branch.* It said, "Our attention has been drawn by the Charity Commissioners to certain apparent discrepancies in the latest accounts submitted to them of the undermentioned charities, all of which have been signed by you as treasurer. It is for this reason that we are making a direct approach to you before any further action is considered. The charities are the Lamperdown Village Hall Trust, the City of London Fusiliers' Trust, and the KLF Employees' Special Fund. You may feel that an interview would clarify the points at issue, in which case the writer would be happy to call on you, either at your place of business or at your residence, as you may prefer."

The writer appeared to be a Mr. Wagner.

Kavanagh observed with appreciation the nicely judged mixture of official suavity and concealed threat. A queen's pawn opening.

Before answering it, he had a telephone call to make. The man he was asking for was evidently important since he had to be approached through a secretary and a personal assistant, with suitable pauses at each stage. When contact had been made, a friendly conversation ensued, conducted on christian-name terms. It concluded with Ronnie inviting Arnold to lunch at his club on the following Monday.

He then composed a brief letter to Mr. Wagner, suggesting a meeting at his flat at seven o'clock in the evening on the following Wednesday. He apologized for suggesting such a late hour, but daytime commitments made it difficult to fix anything earlier.

"I wonder if it really is a tiger," said Kavanagh, "or only a second jackal. That would be disappointing."

When he opened the door to his visitor, his fears were set at rest. Mr. Wagner was a big man, with a red-brown face. There was a tuft of sandy hair growing down each cheekbone. He had the broad, flattened nose of a pugilist. His eyes were so light as to be almost yellow and a deep fold ran down under each eye to form a fence round the corners of an unusually wide mouth. His black coat was glossy, his legs decorously striped. He was a tiger. A smooth and shining tiger.

"Come in," said Kavanagh. "I'm alone this evening. Can I get you a drink?"

"Not just now," said Mr. Wagner.

He seated himself, opened his briefcase, took out a folder of papers, and laid it on the table. This was done without a word spoken. The folder was tied with tape. Mr. Wagner's spatulate fingers toyed with the tape and finally untied it. With deliberation, he extracted a number of papers and arranged them in two neat lines. Kavanagh, who had also seated himself, seemed hypnotized by this methodical proceeding.

When everything was to his satisfaction, Mr. Wagner raised his heavy head, fixed his yellow eyes on Kavanagh, and said, "I'm afraid you're in trouble." An echo. Had not Mr. Huffin said the same thing to Fred Denniston?

"Trouble?"

"You're in trouble. You've been cheating."

Kavanagh said, "Oh!" Then, sinking a little in his chair: "You've no right to say a thing like that."

"I've every right to say it, because it's true. I've been studying the accounts of the three charities I mentioned in my letter. In particular, the accounts you submitted last month. They proved interesting indeed." The voice had become a purr. "Previously, your accounts were in such general terms that they might have meant—or concealed—anything. The latest accounts are, fortunately, much fuller and much more specific."

"Well," said Kavanagh, trying out a smile, "the Commissioners did indicate that they wanted rather more detail as to where the money went."

"Yes, Mr. Kavanagh. And where *did* it go?"

"It's—" Kavanagh waved a hand feebly toward the table. "It's all here. In the accounts."

"Then shall we look at them? These are the accounts of the Fusiliers' Trust. Previously the accounts only showed a lump sum, described as 'Grants to disabled Fusiliers and to the widows and dependents of deceased Fusiliers.'"

"Yes. Yes, that's right."

"In the latest accounts you supply a list of their names." The voice deepened even further. The purr became a growl. The tiger was ready to spring. "A very interesting list, because on reference to the Army authorities we have been unable to find any record of any of the people you mentioned as having served with the Fusiliers."

"Possibly—"

"Yes, Mr. Kavanagh?"

"Some mistake—"

"Thirty names. *All* of them fictitious?"

Kavanagh seemed incapable of speech.

"On the other hand, when we look at the KLF Fund we find that the names you have given do correspond to the names of former employees of the firm. But a further question then presents itself. Have these people in fact received the sums shown against their names? Well? Well? Nothing to say? It would be very simple to find out. A letter to each of them—"

This seemed to galvanize Kavanagh into action for the first time. He half rose in his seat and said, "No. I absolutely forbid it."

"But are you in any position to forbid it?"

Kavanagh considered this question carefully, conscious that Mr. Wagner's yellow eyes were watching him. Then he said, "It does seem that there may have been some irregularity in the presentation of these accounts. I cannot attend to all these matters myself, you understand. Income may not always go where it should. There may be some tax which ought to have been paid—"

Mr. Wagner had begun to smile. The opening of his lips displayed a formidable set of teeth.

"I had always understood," went on Kavanagh, "that in these circumstances, if the tax was paid, together with a sum by way of penalties—"

Mr. Wagner's mouth shut with a snap. He said, "Then you misunderstood the position. It is not simply a question of payment. When you sign your tax return, the form is so arranged that if you make a deliberate misstatement you can be charged before the court with perjury."

There was a long silence. Kavanagh was thinking, So this is how he does it. Poor old David. I wonder what slip-ups he made. I'm sure it was unintentional, but a charge of perjury. Good-bye to his prospects with the Clarion. And a lot of other things, too.

He said, in a voice which had become almost a bleat, "You must understand how serious that would be for me, Mr. Wagner. I'd be willing to pay any sum rather than have that happen. Is there no way—" He let the sentence tail off.

Mr. Wagner had taken a silver pencil from his pocket and seemed to be making some calculations. He said, "If, in fact, the sums of money shown as going to the beneficiaries of these three trusts ended up in your own pocket, I would estimate—a rough calculation only—that you have been obtaining at least ten thousand pounds a year free of tax. I am not aware of how long this very convenient arrangement has been going on. Five years? Possibly more? Had you declared this income, you would have paid at least thirty thousand pounds in tax."

"Exactly," said Kavanagh eagerly. "That's the point I was making. Isn't this something that could more easily be solved by a money payment? At the moment I have considerable resources. If a charge of perjury was brought, they would largely disappear. What good would that do anyone?"

Mr. Wagner appeared to consider the matter. Then he smiled. It was a terrible smile. He said, "I have some sympathy with that point of view, Mr. Kavanagh. Allow me to make a suggestion. It is a friendly suggestion and you can always refuse it. At the moment, the file is entirely under my control. The information came from a private source. It is known only to me. You follow me?"

"I think so. Yes."

Mr. Wagner leaned forward and said with great deliberation, "If you will pay me ten thousand pounds, the file will be destroyed."

"Ten thousand pounds?"

"Ten thousand pounds."

"How would the payment be made?"

"You would pay the money into an account in the name of M. Angus at the Westminster Branch of the London and Home Counties Bank."

"That should be enough for you," said Kavanagh. He was addressing the door leading into the next room, which now opened to admit Sir Arnold Robbins, the Deputy Head of Inland Revenue, and two other men.

Robbins said, "You are suspended from duty. These gentlemen are police officers. They will accompany you and will impound your passport. It will be for the Director of Public Prosecutions to decide on any further action."

Mr. Wagner was on his feet. His face was engorged. A trickle of blood ran from one nostril down his upper lip. He dashed it away with the back of his hand and said, in a voice thick with fury, "So it was a trap!"

"You must blame your accomplice for that," said Kavanagh. "He saw the writing on the wall and sold you to save his own skin. There's not much honor among thieves."

When Wagner had gone, Sir Arnold said, "I apologize for not believing you. I suppose the fact is that we give these special-investigation people too much rope. Incidentally, I've had a look at Rogerson's file. It was as you thought. A minor omission, not even his own income. Some money his wife got from Ireland. She may not even have told him about it."

"Probably not," said Kavanagh. He switched off the microphone, which connected with the next room. "We've got all this on tape if you need it."

"Good. And, by the way, I take it those donations of yours are in order?"

"Perfectly. Every penny that went into these charities has gone to the beneficiaries. I'll show you the receipts. The only thing I fudged was that list of Fusilier names. I'll have to apologize to the Charity Commissioners and send them the correct list."

As Sir Arnold was going, he said, "Why did you tell Wagner it was his accomplice who had shopped him? Was it true?"

"It was untrue," said Kavanagh. "But I thought it might have some interesting results. It's going to be very difficult to get at Mr. Huffin. He really was only the jackal. He picked up scraps of information when he was doing his job and fed them to Wagner, who moved in for the kill. Wagner will be at liberty until the Director makes up his mind. I felt we should give him a chance to ask Mr. Huffin for an explanation."

"He didn't say anything," said Captain Smedley. "He just hit him. Huffin's not a big man. It lifted him off his feet and sent him backward down the steps. Cracked his skull. Dead before he got to hospital."

"And Mr. Wagner?"

"I had a policeman standing by, like you suggested. I thought he was going to put up a fight, but he seemed dazed. When they got him to the station, he just keeled over."

"You don't mean he's dead, too?"

"No. But near enough. And if he does recover from whatever it is—a stroke of kinds—he's in every sort of trouble. A good riddance to a nasty pair."

But that was not their real epitaph. That had been spoken by Colonel Hubert on the evening of April 15th in the year 1944.

THE FIX

by ROBERT TWOHY

Stremberg got the word on the third race at Peninsula Meadows. It came from Vassily, a part-time private guard at the track who knew things. Vassily had given Stremberg three tips in the past five years and they had all paid off. Vassily wasn't a klutz or a juicehead and he knew the race game—and he liked Stremberg who had driven him for years and had done some favors for him. They weren't buddies but they could trust each other.

Vassily said that he knew the trainer of Bugle Call. Bugle had been held back his last six outings to set up a payday. The payday was today, Thursday the 9th. All the jocks were in on it. Bugle would get off at least 20 to 1. He'd run away from the field in the stretch.

Stremberg went to the Tropical Club, which on Thursday morning was pretty full of track fans having a few before taking off for the track. He had two one-dollar bills, three quarters, and two dimes in his pocket. That was all he had to his name. He wasn't working. He'd quit when the horses had come to Peninsula Meadows nearly two months ago. When Ray behind the bar put his beer in front of him Stremberg said, "Ray, you want in on a big one?"

Ray didn't look like he did. Stremberg went on talking, low, "The third is set up. I got the word."

"That a fact."

"Stake me ten and we'll split. I'll bring you back over a hundred."

Ray looked thoughtful. He stroked his thick chin. Stremberg felt hopeful.

Then Ray said, "Nah," and walked away.

Stremberg lit a cigarette. He looked along the mirror behind the bar, sizing up who was there.

Big Otto. He had the money. But Stremberg was scared of him. Otto was said to be the local syndicate man. He operated a chauffeur service, wore black suits, smoked thin cigars, and was always at the Tropical or the Moondust, drinking cola—never went near his chauffeur service. He had dark patches under tired-looking eyes that looked like he never slept, like maybe he couldn't sleep because the faces of victims and their beat-up bodies kept coming between him and sleep. Stremberg didn't want anything to do with Big Otto.

Graveyard Flo. Tall and skinny with big weird eyes who when you drove her home in the cab sat beside you and stroked your hand with her clammy claws and whispered, "Thank you for being you." Sometimes she threw a fit and went rigid and more than a few times Stremberg had carried her like a plank up the stairs to her second-floor apartment off Floribunda and her husband Curly, who was a railroad accountant with a gimpy leg, would open the door and say, "Oh, damn. Dump her on the couch," and give Stremberg five bucks over the fare.

Flo was sitting alone at a table sipping something foamy in a long-stemmed glass and looking over the daily form. It was worth a shot.

He went over to her with his beer. "How's it going, Flo?"

She looked at him with her big weird eyes.

"You, uh, see anything good going today?" He indicated the form.

She said, in a loud voice, "Do I know you?"

"Sure. Stremberg. You know, the cab driver."

"Ray, do I know this person?"

Everybody turned to look. Ah, hell, thought Stremberg, she's in one of her goofy moods.

"Quit yelling, Flo," said Ray.

"Is this the kind of place where a ratty-looking individual comes up and fersts himself off on a lady? Is that the kind of dump you run here?"

She was starting to breathe funny. Her eyes had begun to roll. She was stiffening.

Ray called, "Stremberg, get the hell away from her."

"Yeah," said Stremberg. He went back to the bar.

Ray said, "Stay away from her."

"I will."

"She's ready to throw one. She went out of here last night with a guy whose wife caught up with them in the Moondust and bopped her on the head five times with a beer glass."

Stremberg shook his head, and sipped his beer. He looked in the mirror and saw that Flo had stopped going stiff, and was quietly sipping her drink and flicking her fingernail over the form.

He said when Ray came back up the bar, "Say, Ray, are you sure—"

"I'm sure."

Tiny Jane, about 70, with a face all blown up from drinking, slid up to Stremberg. She held her little green coin purse in both spotty hands. "I heard what you said to Ray when you came in. You need backing?"

"Hello, Tiny," he said, suddenly very weary.

"You're a nice little fella." Her voice was a creaky whisper. "You ain't a bad little fella at all. I'll stake you fifty dollars."

"Fine, Tiny."

She struggled the snaps of her purse open, stuck shaky fingers in, pulled out a nickel and a penny. He took them. "Thanks, Tiny."

"I trust you. You can bring me the money tonight. Now you can buy me a drink." Her face parted in a horrible grin.

She climbed like somebody climbing a fence up on the stool next to him. Ah, hell, thought Stremberg, and felt defeated. "Ray," he said, and thumbed at Tiny.

Ray poured her a shot of brandy, water back, and took all Stremberg's money except one buck and Tiny's six cents.

Hell, he thought, I'm out $1.95 already and I still don't have any backing.

Tiny took the brandy down in one loud suck. She moaned and sighed and tears ran down her swollen cheeks that looked ready to split open and spray liquor all over the place.

Stremberg looked at the clock. Past 11:30. Some of the fans were drifting out, to get down to the track—first post, 12:30.

The guy that always wore two hats, a dark regular hat and a kind of straw hat under it, and a pair of woman's dark glasses, came up on the other side of Stremberg. He was the guy who had once been a dentist with a big practice in town, and an estate on the hill. He said, sharp and low, "I got a good one going today."

"Yeah?" said Stremberg.

"Yeah. In the sixth. Split ten and I'll bring you back over $100."

"I'm not working. I only got a buck."

"Well, give me the buck then." The dentist sounded irritated.

Stremberg heard Tiny sighing on his left. The dentist had his hand out, was jiggling his fingers, getting impatient. Stremberg got a sudden strange and sinking feeling that he had no will of his own. He gave the dentist his last buck.

"Okay." The dentist went down the bar to hit up someone else.

Stremberg shook his head. I don't even know him, he said to himself. Why the hell did I give him my last buck?

He had the impulse to go after the ex-dentist and get his buck back, but that was stupid. You don't go chasing after a guy in a bar where you're known and argue about a buck.

But now all he had left was Tiny's six cents, half a pack of butts, and about an inch of beer.

Tiny said, "I could handle another."

"I'm sorry, Tiny."

"You're *sorry!*" Her voice was thin with amazement. She shook her blown-out cheeks at him. "Ray," she shrilled. "Ray!"

Ray happened to be three feet away, drawing a beer. "Yeah, Tiny," he said, not looking up.

"Can you imagine anyone as mean as this? I sit and talk with this man and he won't even buy me a drink!"

"Yeah, Tiny." Ray looked at Stremberg and there was a twist to his lips. "It don't seem like your day."

"Not yet it don't."

Tiny said, "That's dirty pool, mister! You know what? I'm a friend of Big Otto. He's right down the bar there."

"I know."

"You could be found in the alley with big red holes in your head."

She half slid, half fell from the stool. "Don't get smart with me," she said, and departed.

Ray drew a beer and put it in front of Stremberg.

Stremberg nodded, and drank half of it.

Ray lingered. "You really got something in the third?"

"Yeah. From Vassily."

"I don't know him. Do I?"

"Prob'ly not. He don't make the bars. But he's on the inside. He knows his stuff."

Ray reached in his pocket. "Okay." He handed over a $10 bill.

"Thanks, Ray. But now I need $3.50 more."

"Why?"

"Two-fifty to get in, buck for bus fare."

"Okay," said Ray, reaching again. "But that's a loan. You owe me $3.50."

"Thanks, Ray."

"Which horse?"

The bar was emptying, nobody was near, but you don't take chances. You want to keep the odds up. Stremberg put a hand to the side of his face, just scratching his cheek if anyone on that side was watching. He said low, "Bugle Call."

Ray raised his eyebrows, pursed his lips. "What's he done?"

"Nothing—never been close. They been setting it up for today. All the jocks are in on it."

Ray shook his head. Then he said, "Well, what do *I* know? I ain't had a winner all meet."

Stremberg finished his beer and pushed back from the bar.

As he got off the stool he realized he was being stared at. He turned. Graveyard Flo was the starer.

"Wait a minute!" she yelled, and her eyes started to roll. "Ray," she screamed, "who *is* that little rat?"

Ray said, "Get out of here, Stremberg."

"I'm going." He hurried out, as Flo kept screaming.

Ten minutes later he caught the bus. It was crowded. He stood in the aisle. A man pressed against him with a hard fat stomach. The man started to look at him, and Stremberg looked away. But there was no room to look away. To his right was someone's red neck with blisters. To his left was a woman's coiled blue hair. He couldn't turn his head far enough either way to avoid the fat man's stare.

He looked down, then up. Finally there was nothing to do but look back at the man.

The eyes were glazed, yellow-green. Under them was a pitted nose and under that a mouth which, as Stremberg helplessly stared, began to curve in a smile that got wider and wider, until Stremberg got a feeling the tongue was going to come looping out, like a soft sticky pink hook, and clamp around his neck.

He shuddered, tried to close his eyes—but they wouldn't close. The guy is hypnotizing me, he thought helplessly. Now why in hell is he doing that?

Then the bus slammed to a stop and everybody staggered around and fell into each other, and the hypnotist fell and staggered like everyone else, and Stremberg was freed from his spell. He stayed behind him as they all got off and from the rear the man seemed to be just an ordinary person, just a normal sloppy fat man hurrying to the track.

Stremberg thought suddenly, I'm pretty light-headed. He couldn't remember when he'd last had a meal.

He ran the gauntlet of hot-sheet touts, shouting and snarling in their booths, paid his entrance fee, and was in under the grandstand. He stood smoking cigarettes and watching while the first two races were run, with a Daily Double payoff of $42.60. Then the morning line started flashing for the third.

He copped a look at someone's program. Bugle Call was post position 6. The morning line was 15 to 1.

Stremberg waited, jumping around, smoking more cigarettes. The tote odds were climbing. Big Otto and his henchmen, who of course knew when a fix was on, were letting this one go by. They did that a lot—they knew what they were doing. Get too greedy and jump in on every boat ride and the public starts to catch on when the price dip shows suddenly on the tote, and then everyone's jumping in and it's a messed-up situation. The syndicate knows when to lie low.

40 to 1, the tote said now. $400 to split with Ray. Stremberg tried to keep his face masklike, but realized that he was walking around in a tight

quick circle and smacking his palms together. A man and a girl were looking at him. The girl giggled.

Stremberg hit his palms together a few more times, with a serious expression on his face like someone with a circulation problem who knows what he's doing, then walked away flopping his hands like checking to be sure the blood was flowing again. He thought he had done it in a cool way but as he walked away the girl seemed to be giggling louder.

He saw it was four minutes to post and hurried to the parimutuel lineup. The flashboard on the wall showed that Bugle Call was now 50 to 1. $500 to split with Ray. The syndicate hadn't jumped in on this one, just like he'd figured they wouldn't.

He put Ray's $10 on Number 6 to win, went back outside, and stood there tense and still, watching as they loaded the horses into the starting gate. Bugle Call went in prancing. He looked fit and sharp. His jock seemed to wear a tight, knowing grin. The grin was to let those in on the fix know that everything was set, on target.

The starting bell yanged, the gates whanged open.

Bugle broke good, and hitting the first turn of the mile race the jock had him tucked in at the rail in third place, two lengths back and running low and easy. Stremberg felt the deep joy he had been waiting to feel since the meet started 51 racing days ago beginning to build inside him.

Bugle ran smooth and easy through the back stretch and around the far turn, holding fourth now, five lengths back, and came out of the turn near the middle of the track with room on the outside, in perfect position—all the jocks had done their job, all cooperating to get Bugle positioned like this. Just like Vassily had said, he was going to run away from the field, a clear sweep down the stretch. The jock got ready to unload with the whip, and the deep joy swelled in Stremberg.

Then the horse hung.

Stremberg couldn't believe it. He watched it and couldn't believe it. It was like the animal had run into an 80-mile head wind. His legs moved like each shoe weighed 35 pounds. Everyone sailed past him up the stretch.

He couldn't believe it. Everything had gone just right all the way from the start.

And the jock had had that tight little grin.

Stremberg was walking toward the exit, fingering the six cents in his pocket, when it all came clear to him.

For reasons of its own the syndicate, which hadn't got in on this one, wanted the fix off. Maybe they'd got a flash that some Congressional committee investigating rackets in sports had got wind of the Bugle Call fix and was busy rigging up evidence that would make it look like the syndicate was behind the fix. So the syndicate flashed the word to the track to the guys behind the fix to take it off, and right now—and seconds from the finish, when he was starting up the stretch, the jock got the flash from the stands: It's off, pull him.

So the jock, hip as all jocks are, did as he was ordered.

Near the exit Stremberg saw Vassily, sagging against a wall, with a kind of stunned look on his face.

Vassily didn't duck away. He looked Stremberg in the eyes and mumbled, "I sure thought I was giving you the straight goods."

"You were," said Stremberg. "You couldn't know it would get called off."

Vassily rubbed his hand over his mouth. His eyes looked kind of stunned again. Then he said, "Yeah. Right. That's something you can't figure on."

"The syndicate does what they have to do."

"Right. They do what they have to do."

Stremberg fingered the six cents in his pocket. "Got a buck I can borrow for bus fare?"

Vassily went through his pockets. He had 23 cents. "I put all I had, $27, on Bugle Call."

Stremberg churned up a smile, to let Vassily know that Stremberg knew that if Vassily had a buck he'd lend it to Stremberg. "See you around." He turned away.

Vassily said, "You want the twenty-three cents?"

"No, that's okay."

"How you going to get home?"

"I'll probably run into someone I know with a car." He said good-bye to Vassily, and went out the exit.

In the parking lot he stopped to light his last butt. He stood and smoked it, then dropped it, and started walking the four miles home.

About four o'clock he got to the room he had at Mrs. Mustie's, and was glad to see her car gone, so she couldn't hassle him about the rent being eight days late. He locked his door, took off his shoes and jacket, stretched out on the bed, and went to sleep.

He woke up to hammering on the door. It was dark outside the window. Mrs. Mustie's terrible voice yelled, "Stremberg! I know you're in there! Open the door!" She kept on hammering and yelling as he lay quiet.

Finally her husband called from downstairs, "Oh, for Pete's sake, knock it off."

"The door's locked! He's in there!"

"So he's in there. So he ain't got the dough, so he ain't answering—what's the good hollering?"

"You know what's going to happen tomorrow, Stremberg?" she yelled. "Tomorrow a padlock goes on this door!"

Stremberg waited until she had lumped away down the stairs. Then he got up and stood at the window. He hoped she'd go out again. She spent most of every day going out somewhere or coming back. In a little while her mean-looking little white car rolled away down the drive.

He got his shoes and jacket back on, and put socks, shorts, two shirts, pants, comb, toothbrush, and razor, which were all the things he had in the world except what he was wearing, in the big grocery bag he carried them in when he moved. He opened the door and called, "Mr. Mustie?"

"Yeah, Stremberg."

"I'll be going. You better take a look so she won't yell I've swiped something."

A chair wheezed and Mr. Mustie came in sight, holding his evening *Courier*. He climbed the stairs while Stremberg waited. He said, "Where you going to go?"

"I'll find a place. I'll bring her the dough when I get it."

"Yeah." Mr. Mustie looked around the room, picked up the painted china ashtray that was a nicely shaped pair of woman's hands, looked at it, looked surprised that he was looking at it, then set it down. "Okay, Stremberg. Take it easy."

"Yeah," said Stremberg.

He went downstairs and out the door.

He walked eight blocks to the Tropical. There was a good crowd. Big Otto was there, drinking cola and rolling poker dice with some guys Stremberg didn't know, at a dollar a flop. Flo was at the bar with a short punk who looked like bad news. Tiny wasn't in sight. He was glad of that.

He got a stool near the door. Ray come over. Stremberg laid the $10 win ticket on Bugle Call in front of him. "Everything was great and then the fix came off."

Ray tossed the ticket behind the bar. "You owe me $3.50."

"Right. How about a beer?"

Ray shrugged and drew one.

"Got a cigarette?"

Ray gave him one.

Stremberg sat there drinking and smoking. He looked in the mirror and saw the dentist with two hats sitting at a table with a couple of women and laughing, his mouth wide showing a few whole teeth but mostly yellow stumps. He wore the woman's dark glasses that he always wore. There was a pile of money by his hand. The three of them looked pleased with life.

The dentist raised his glass. "To Trader Jack and Vinnie Espinosa, the best damn jockey at the meet!" The women said, "Hurray!" and laughed and drank, while the dentist grinned at them with his stumps.

Stremberg called, "Ray."

Ray came over.

"Who won the sixth?"

Ray was silent. Then he walked away. He conferred with Big Otto, and came back.

"Trader Jack. Paid 60 to 1."

Stremberg went over to the dentist. "Remember me?"

"Sure. You're the cab driver."

"I split a bet with you today on Trader Jack."

"Did you?" The dark glasses caught the light and gave a sparkle. "No, not Trader Jack. Little Steamy."

Stremberg looked at the money on the table. "Little Steamy?"

"Yeah, that was my tip. He run a damn fine race, but didn't have it in the stretch."

Stremberg nodded at the money. "Didn't you win that betting on Trader Jack?"

"Yeah, I did actually. But I put your buck and another guy's dough on Little Steamy, which was my tip. Trader Jack was just a wild hunch I played because one of my ex-wives is named Jacqueline."

Stremberg nodded. What was the use?

"Have a beer," the dentist invited.

"Thanks, I got one at the bar."

"You need money or anything? You want a buck?"

"That's okay." Stremberg went back to his drink. He said to Ray, who was near, "I ought to have my butt kicked. I split a bet with him and didn't get the name of the horse."

Ray pulled his lips in and shook his head slowly, like someone looking at a pitiful specimen.

Stremberg nodded, agreeing with Ray's shake. "I just ain't been with it today."

He finished his beer, picked up his bag, and walked down the block to the hole-in-the-wall Red & Black cab office. All the cabs were off the stand. A sharp-faced old Swede lounged behind the counter.

"Hello, Oscar."

"Hello, Stremberg."

"How's it going?"

"Not too bad."

Stremberg leaned on the counter, setting his bag on it. "Got a smoke?"

Oscar gave him a cigarette. Stremberg lit it.

"Need a driver?"

Oscar looked at him a while with his pale blue eyes. "You figure to go back to work?"

"Yeah."

"Horses not treating you so good?"

Stremberg fished in his pocket and laid his six cents on the counter.

Oscar said, "You had nearly three thousand bucks when you quit. You said you was going to make a killing, you'd never drive cab again."

"I guess I did say that."

"You'll never beat the horses, Stremberg."

Stremberg didn't answer. It wasn't the time to argue about it.

Oscar smoked, and eyed him. "Okay, I'll put you back on. You ain't a drunk and you're honest, or reasonably honest, and you ain't smashed up any of my cabs. Next time you quit me though, don't bother coming back."

"Okay," said Stremberg. "Listen, Oscar, can I sleep in a cab tonight?"

"Throw you out of your room?"

"Yeah."

Oscar said, "All right." Then he reached in a pocket. "Here's three bucks. Go get yourself something to eat, you look like someone's been dug up."

"Okay."

"And clean up in the washroom before you start on shift tomorrow."

"Okay."

A man came in. "You got the racing form?"

"Sure." There was a pile on the desk behind the counter. Oscar handed one to the man and accepted a buck, which he dropped in a cigar box.

The man leaned on the counter, slit the paper open with the side of his hand, worked a cigar around in his mouth, and said, "You got anything for tomorrow?"

"I ain't a horse player," Oscar said.

The man glanced at Stremberg. "*You're* a horse player. I've seen you down at the track."

"I used to be," Stremberg said. "I gave it up."

"You're smarter than I am." The man went out.

Stremberg walked up the block past the Tropical Club toward the bowling alley where they had a lunch counter. He'd get a pack of cigarettes from the machine there, and still have enough for a burger and coffee. It had been a long time since he'd eaten.

He thought of Bugle Call, and shook his head. He didn't blame Otto, or the syndicate—they only did what they had to do. They had to protect themselves when Congressional committees got too nosey.

He took a few deep breaths of the crisp autumn night air. He glanced in a store window as he passed and was surprised how pale and seedy and caved-in he looked.

Driving cab in the winter months ain't a bad job. You can make a buck.

By the time the thoroughbreds came back in the spring, he should have a nice stake.

ONE MOMENT OF MADNESS
by EDWARD D. HOCH

The rain had stopped but the night air was still muggy with August heat. Leopold stood by the window in his pajamas, silently cursing the window air-conditioner that still hummed loudly but delivered only warm air. Across town there was a fire burning, and as he listened to the distant sound of sirens he tried to pinpoint its location. Something in the Mill Road Shopping Center, he guessed—one of the stores.

He was glad he wasn't a fireman.

For a time he watched the flames reflecting off the low clouds, casting an orange glow over one whole end of the city. He was just turning to get back into bed when the telephone rang.

"Leopold here."

"Captain, you'd better get down here." It was Fletcher's voice, talking too loud.

"What's up? Is it the fire?"

"Hank Schultz just went berserk in the squadroom and shot four people!"

"I'll be right down! You got it under control?"

"I shot Hank, Captain. There was no other way."

"All right. I'll be there in ten minutes."

He was dressed and down to his car in less than five. The highrise building where he lived was generally a fifteen-minute drive away from headquarters, but at three in the morning traffic was light. He stuck the magnetized flasher on the roof of his car and turned it on, and held his speed steady at fifty-five all the way downtown.

There were ambulances and cars all over the street in front of the aging headquarters building. He recognized a couple of reporters trying to buck the hastily erected police line. "What's up, Captain?" one of them shouted, recognizing him, but Leopold ignored him. At the moment he couldn't imagine what was up. Hank Schultz was a nine-year veteran of the Force who'd done various sorts of undercover work in addition to regular patrol duty. Though he'd never been on Leopold's Violent Crimes Squad, Leopold knew him well.

"Coming through!" a white-coated stretcher-bearer shouted, and Leopold stepped aside. The man on the stretcher, who seemed to be unconscious, was Hank Schultz. Leopold hurried up the steps to the second floor and found Lieutenant Fletcher standing in the middle of the squadroom surveying the damage. A chair was overturned and there was blood on the floor and one of the walls. The police photographer was snapping pictures of one uniformed body, but Leopold couldn't see who it was.

"How many dead?" he asked grimly.

Fletcher glanced up as if surprised that Leopold had arrived so soon. "One. Sam Bentley over there. We think he took the first shot."

Leopold had known Sergeant Bentley since the day twenty years earlier when Leopold came up from New York to join the Force in the city where he grew up. Bentley was on the Force already then. Now he was only a year from retirement. "Who else did Hank shoot?"

"Unidentified white male prisoner and the two detectives who brought him in. Sweeney and Gross. They're not bad, but the prisoner has two wounds. Hank emptied his service revolver before I could stop him."

"Is Hank alive?"

"Just barely. All four of them are at the hospital."

Leopold walked over and stared down at the body of Sam Bentley. He felt like hell. "You'd better tell me the whole thing, from the beginning." The Police Commissioner would be arriving soon and he wanted to have some answers.

"We don't know a great deal, Captain. I was in my office. Things were fairly quiet and Bentley was at his desk typing up an arrest report. A little after two-thirty Sweeney and Gross came in with their prisoner. Then Hank Schultz came in."

"Was he in uniform?"

"No, civilian clothes. I don't think he was on duty. I heard them talking but I didn't pay much attention. Sam had just gotten a report on the Crown SuperShopper fire out at the shopping center and was telling them about it. I happened to look out through my glass partition just as Hank drew the revolver from under his jacket and fired. I couldn't believe what I was seeing! But then Sam fell against the wall and went down. Hank kept firing at the others and everybody was yelling at once. I ran out of the office, drawing my gun. Sweeney and Gross were both on the floor by now, along with their prisoner—I hadn't counted the shots. Hank turned and pointed his revolver at me and—I had to shoot him, Captain! His gun was already empty but I didn't know that." Fletcher's voice was trembling.

"You had no choice," Leopold said, resting a hand on his shoulder. "I would have done the same thing."

"I was drinking coffee with him just last night—"

Others were arriving now—the Commissioner and someone from the District Attorney's office. Leopold didn't have any answers for them. He greeted them briefly and said he was on his way to the hospital.

"This will look terrible in the papers," the Commissioner said.

"It *is* terrible."

"How could a rational man just flip out like that? Could he be on drugs?"

"I'm going to find out," Leopold promised.

The Commissioner stared bleakly at the blood on the floor and the wall. It seemed to bother him more than the sight of Sam Bentley's body.

Leopold went downstairs to his car. It was a short drive to the hospital and the four wounded men were still in Emergency when he arrived. He found a doctor named Rice working with an intern over Milt Sweeney, who seemed to be the least injured of the four.

"Can I speak to him?" Leopold asked when the doctors came out of the curtained cubicle for a moment.

"As soon as we get him stitched up. He's lucky—the bullet passed through the fleshy part of his thigh."

"How are the others?"

The doctor consulted an admissions sheet. "Schultz is bad. We're preparing him for surgery now. The other officer, Gross, has an abdominal wound but I think he'll pull through. The woman is unconscious—"

"What woman?"

"Beats me. Unidentified. A woman dressed in man's clothing."

"She was brought in with the others? From Police headquarters?"

"That's right. We didn't know she was a woman at first. She's fairly young, I'd say—under thirty."

He excused himself and went back into the cubicle, and Leopold paced the floor. Perhaps Sweeney could shed some light on this craziness. He certainly hoped so.

Some minutes later the doctor emerged and motioned to Leopold. "You can have five minutes with him, no more. He's still weak from loss of blood."

Leopold nodded, pushed aside the white curtain, and went in. "Hi, Milt," he said. "How're you feeling?"

Sweeney managed a lopsided grin. "I'll live. What about the others?"

"Gross will be all right, I understand. Sam Bentley's dead."

"God!"

"I'm sorry I had to tell you like this."

"What about Schultz? I didn't see a thing after he shot my leg out from under me."

"Fletcher got him in the chest. They're taking him to the operating room now."

"Why in hell did he do it!"

Leopold sighed. "I was hoping you could tell me."

"We'd just come in with our prisoner. Sam was behind his desk talking about a fire somewhere and all of a sudden there was Hank Schultz out of nowhere, taking his gun from the belt holster under his jacket."

"What did he say?"

"Nothing I can remember. I think Bentley put out his hand to grab for the gun. Schultz shot him first and then turned on me and kept on firing. I felt a blow to my leg and just went down."

"What about the suspect you'd brought in?"

"Was he hit too?"

"Yes. But the doctor says it's a woman dressed in men's clothes."

"What?" Sweeney struggled to sit up, but winced in pain and abandoned the effort. "A *woman?*"

Leopold nodded. "What did you arrest her for?"

"Gross and I were checking the after-hours bars on Field Avenue. We were parked in front of the Old Athens when this guy—we thought it was a guy—came along and threw an empty bottle through the front window of the bar. We jumped out and grabbed him. We figured we had a drunk on our hands and we drove downtown to book him."

"Did Hank seem to know your prisoner?"

"I wouldn't know. Like I said, I didn't even see him until he was there pulling out his gun."

The doctor appeared at the curtain. "Better let him get some rest now. You can see him again in the morning."

Leopold squeezed Sweeney's shoulder. "Take it easy, Milt. I'll be back."

"Right, Captain. Find out why he did it, huh?"

"I'm trying."

Outside, Leopold asked the doctor, "How's the woman?"

"Not so good, but we think she's got a better than even chance. Any luck on identification?"

"Not a thing. Let me look at her clothes."

The doctor led him to a little cubicle and opened a garment bag bearing a numbered label and the single word UNIDENTIFIED. Leopold noticed the fresh blood around the hole in the front of the coat and shirt. Otherwise the man's suit was reasonably clean and nondescript, with a label from a cut-rate men's store downtown. "Did the clothes seem to fit her?" Leopold asked.

"I guess so, yes. But I wasn't really paying attention to their fit," Rice answered.

"I'm wondering if she bought them for herself or got them from somebody," Leopold murmured, going through the pockets. They were empty except for a handkerchief, a few coins, and a crumpled five-dollar food stamp. "Any sign of drug addiction on her?" Leopold asked.

"Not that I noticed."

A young intern poked his head in. "Dr. Rice, they're waiting for you in the operating room."

Rice told Leopold, "I'm assisting at the operation on Schultz. I have to scrub now."

"Good luck," Leopold said, meaning it.

He waited in the corridor until they wheeled Hank Schultz past him. The young detective's eyes were closed and his breathing seemed irregular. An intern with an intravenous bottle walked alongside.

Damn it, Hank, Leopold asked silently, why did you do it?

In the morning, while Fletcher dealt with the press as best he could, Leopold began the arduous task of reconstructing Hank Schultz's recent activities. He had been, Leopold learned, doing some undercover narcotics work, but his superior officer believed he'd veered away into something else.

"He was onto a new line," Lieutenant Maxwell told Leopold. "On one of his drug busts he discovered the shipment had been paid for with a hundred thousand dollars in stolen food stamps."

Food stamps.

Leopold remembered the crumpled food stamp in the unidentified woman's pocket. "When was this?"

"About two months ago. He told me he had a line on the source of the stolen stamps and asked to be taken off the narcotics angle to pursue it. I contacted the proper federal agencies and they gave me the go-ahead. In fact, Schultz was supposed to meet with a man from the Justice Department today regarding his investigation."

"It doesn't sound as if he was having emotional problems of any sort."

"No apparent ones," Maxwell agreed. "He was doing his job. I'm as dumbfounded as anyone else by what happened this morning."

"And yet something caused him to draw his revolver and shoot four people. What was it?"

"Damned if I know. In this business, sometimes the strain builds up over weeks and months until suddenly it explodes."

"I know," Leopold agreed. "But that answer won't be good enough for the Commissioner."

"What are Hank's chances of living to tell us about it?"

"He was still in the operating room when I left the hospital at four o'clock. I'm going back over there now."

*   *   *

With the coming of morning the emergency room had quieted down to its usual summer pace of children with broken arms and cut feet. Leopold asked for Dr. Rice and was directed to an office on the second floor, where he found the surgeon staring bleakly into an empty coffee cup.

"A long night?" Leopold asked.

Rice nodded. "We lost Schultz a half hour ago. He survived the surgery but died in the recovery room."

Leopold shook his head sadly. "Can I use your phone?"

"I've already called the Police Commissioner."

"I want to tell the man who shot him," Leopold said.

He dialed the squadroom number but was told Fletcher had finally gone home for some sleep. Leopold hesitated a moment and then dialed Fletcher's home number, hoping Fletcher would answer instead of his wife. He was in luck.

"Hello, Fletcher. How are you?"

"I'm exhausted, Captain. I'm going to sleep for a week."

"Hank Schultz died a half-hour ago," Leopold told him. "I thought you'd want to know."

"Thanks. I guess he's been dead for me since the minute I shot him."

"Try to get some sleep."

Leopold hung up and turned back to Dr. Rice. "How about the others?"

"Gross is coming along, and the woman is conscious now. Do you want to see her?"

"I certainly do."

Rice escorted him to a private room on the third floor. "I'll want a guard posted here," he told the doctor. "I'll arrange for it."

"Okay. You can have five minutes alone with her."

Leopold entered the room and walked over to the bed. He saw at once that the woman was awake, watching him with deep-blue eyes that he might have found attractive in other circumstances. She must have been in her late twenties. Her brown hair was cut short as a man's, but Leopold couldn't imagine that Sweeney and Gross had failed to realize she was a woman. Her high cheekbones and soft features contributed to a decidedly feminine appearance.

"I'm Captain Leopold," he told her, "investigating last night's shooting."

"I don't know what happened," she said, closing her eyes.

"Let's start with your name. Who are you and why were you dressed as a man?"

"I'm Cathy Wright. I'm an artist and I wasn't dressed as a man. I was wearing my usual clothes. They had no right to arrest me."

"You broke the window of the Old Athens with a bottle," Leopold pointed out. "And unfortunately you did it right in front of an unmarked police car."

"Whatever I did, I didn't deserve being shot."

"No," he agreed, "you didn't. The man who shot you was a detective named Hank Schultz. Does that name mean anything to you?"

"No. Should it?"

"He opened fire on you and several others without warning. I'm trying to find the reason."

"What happened to him?"

"He was shot by one of my men. He died a short time ago. But the doctor assures me you're going to be all right."

"Thanks," she said. Her eyes began to mist.

"I'll need your address for the records. I don't think you need to worry about the charges against you, though. Under the circumstances they'll probably be dropped."

She gave him an address in one of the older downtown areas, not far from where she'd been arrested. "I'd like to be alone now," she told him.

"Certainly," Leopold agreed. "But one other thing—there was a five-dollar food stamp in your pocket. Where'd you get it?"

"At the bank. Artists don't always make enough to live on."

Leopold nodded and left the room. He wasn't satisfied with the answers she'd given, but she was too weak to pursue it now. He'd come back later and maybe get some answers then. Maybe he'd find out why she seemed about to cry when he told her Hank Schultz was dead.

Detective Irving Gross was a middle-aged man with too much weight and too little hair. He'd been more seriously wounded than Sweeney. Lying flat on his back with a tube up his nose and another in his arm, he seemed wounded by more than Schultz's bullet.

"Schultz is dead," Leopold told him.

"That's no great loss, Captain. He was always an odd sort."

"In what way?"

"Oh, suspicious of everyone. Ever since his divorce a few years back after he caught his wife cheatin' he thought everybody was out to betray him or something. Beats me how Maxwell put up with him all these years."

"I never realized that. Maybe I didn't know him as well as I thought. But why'd he start shooting last night, Irving?"

"I thought maybe you came here to tell me."

"What about the suspect you and Sweeney arrested?"

"Guy broke a window with a bottle."

"It was a woman, dressed more like a man."

"Yeah? Nothing surprises me in that neighborhood."

"Did Hank Schultz see her before he started shooting?"

"Sure, he saw her. She was standing right there with us."

"In handcuffs?"

"No, we took them off when we got her inside."

"Did Schultz speak to her?"

"Not a word."

"What was your impression when you arrested her—that she was high, drunk, or what?"

"Tell you the truth, Captain, it was none of those. My impression was that he—we thought it was a he—wanted to be arrested. You know, like the guy in the O. Henry story who wanted a warm cell for the winter?"

"I know," Leopold said. "Only this is summer."

He tried not to read the newspapers that night, with their screaming black headlines about the shooting. There were big pictures of Schultz and Bentley, smaller photos of Sweeney and Gross. They didn't have a picture of Cathy Wright, but a subhead referred to her as the "mystery woman" in the case. The story was given so much play on the front page that the fire at the Crown SuperShopper had been relegated to an inside page.

Leopold stayed late at headquarters in order to see Fletcher when he came on duty. That was how he happened to be at his desk when the man from the Justice Department arrived. His name was Arnold Ellis and he was a light-skinned black man with a tiny mustache.

He smiled as he shook hands and said, "Lieutenant Maxwell said you're the one to see. I understand you're in charge of the investigation into last night's tragic events."

"I seem to be," Leopold admitted.

"I flew up from Washington this afternoon to meet with Hank Schultz. That was before I knew he'd been killed."

"Maxwell told me you were working in the same area."

The man from Washington nodded. "Stolen food stamps. It's gotten to be a major problem, especially in urban areas. The underworld uses them like money, to buy narcotics and guns and just about everything else. For all practical purposes they are money, but in most instances they're a great deal easier to steal."

"But what finally happens to all these food stamps?" Leopold asked. "At the end of the line someone must redeem them for cash, knowing they're stolen."

"That's what Schultz was working on. We believe they're funneled into large supermarkets, probably at about twenty-five to fifty cents on the dollar. The store managers are happy to pocket the profit, with very little risk."

"Supermarkets," Leopold repeated. "Did you happen to hear about our fire last night?"

"Where was that?"

"At the Crown SuperShopper. It broke out just a little while before the shooting."

"Arson?"

"I don't know," Leopold said. "But I intend to find out."

"Let me come with you. I have to do something to justify my trip up here."

Leopold picked up a copy of the arson squad's report, which showed evidence that the Crown fire was of suspicious origin. He and Arnold Ellis drove out to look at the scene, but in the darkness there was little they could do or see. "Roof caved in," Leopold observed as they walked around the ruined building. "Looks like a total loss."

"A good way to destroy the evidence," Ellis remarked.

"What evidence?"

"A hundred thousand dollars in stolen food stamps. Someone knocked over our local distribution center last month, but we kept it out of the papers. It was no big deal. The place was in a parking garage behind the federal building. Someone who knew the setup just walked in during the lunch hour and helped himself. With a duplicate key all he had to do was stay out of the sight line of one television camera and he was home free."

This brought a whistle from Leopold. "Schultz was working on it?"

Ellis nodded. "His contacts told him the stamps were being redeemed through local supermarkets. I did a computer graph on the number of redemptions per market plotted against the relative income of the surrounding neighborhoods. Crown here had too many redemptions for its area. That's why I came here to meet Schultz today. I wanted to raid the place tomorrow on the strong possibility these latest stolen stamps were on the premises. I told Schultz on the phone we'd probably go after a search warrant tomorrow."

Leopold sighed and kicked at a piece of charred wood. "The trouble is, your Hank Schultz was a tough undercover cop who got results, but I'm left with one who went berserk in the squadroom and shot four people."

"It does sound like two different men. What about the supermarket manager? His name must be in the arson-squad report."

They went back to the car and checked. The name was there—Titus Kern, with an address in one of the better suburbs. "Business must be pretty good," Leopold remarked. "Let's go see him."

Arnold Ellis hesitated. "Not me. At this point in my investigation it's probably better if we don't meet. Keep it on a local level, but find out what you can."

Leopold dropped Ellis at his hotel downtown and drove out to see Titus Kern alone. It was nearly eleven when he reached the house, and it was dark. He was about to abandon the idea till morning when a taxi turned into the street and pulled up in front of the house. A man opened the door and paid the driver. Leopold got out. "Pardon me," he called as the man headed up the walk toward the darkened house. "Mr. Kern?"

The man hesitated, perhaps fearing a robbery. "Yes?"

"Captain Leopold, police. I'd like to ask you a few questions about last night's fire."

As he came closer, Leopold saw that Titus Kern was a man in his fifties, slim and gray-haired, with a high-cheekboned face that seemed vaguely familiar. "I've had a very trying day, Captain. I'm sure you understand. My store was destroyed by fire and I've just come from visiting my daughter who is ill. I'm sure I can't tell you anything you don't already know."

"I promise it won't take more than a few minutes."

Titus Kern sighed. "Very well. You can come in for a minute."

Leopold followed him into the large colonial house and waited while he turned on a few lamps in the living room. "My wife's away," he explained. "I'm something of a bachelor these days. Please sit down."

Leopold sat opposite the piano, where a number of family portraits were on display. "You must realize that last night's fire had a suspicious origin," he began. "The arson squad found evidence of a timing device—"

"I know nothing of that. I manage the store, I don't own it. The fire causes me grief, but the corporation collects the insurance."

"It's been suggested that the fire might have been set, not to collect the insurance but to destroy evidence of a felony."

"What? What are you talking about?"

But before Leopold could reply, his eyes focused on the large middle portrait in the grouping on the piano. Suddenly he knew why Titus Kern's face was familiar. "That must be your daughter in the picture," he said. "She looks very much like you."

"I'm afraid she's a bit wild, like so many young people today."

"You said she was ill?"

"I—yes, that's correct."

"In the hospital, I imagine."

"Did I say that?"

"I met your daughter today, Mr. Kern. The picture is a very good likeness. She's using the name Cathy Wright and the newspapers call her a mystery woman."

"I told her to stop that foolishness and tell the truth."

Suddenly the pieces of the puzzle were beginning to fall into place. "What about Hank Schultz, Mr. Kern?"

"What about him? I never heard of him until he shot my daughter. And you can be sure the city's going to find itself with a very large lawsuit on its hands over this."

"How did you know it was your daughter in the hospital?"

"She telephoned me earlier this evening. I suppose she feared I'd report her missing to the police."

"Does she live here?"

"No, she has an apartment where she works as an artist. But she helps with some of my bookkeeping at the store." He glanced pointedly at his watch. "I'm very tired, and I can't see how these questions about my daughter have a bearing on the fire."

"There may be a connection between the fire and the shooting of your daughter," Leopold said. He got to his feet. "Thank you for your help, Mr. Kern."

In the morning Leopold went back to the hospital. He waited outside Cathy's door while Dr. Rice examined her. "She's coming along," the doctor said as he departed. "But try not to tire her with your questions."

Leopold went in and sat by the bed. "How are you feeling?"

"A little better than yesterday," she replied.

"I talked to your father last night."

Her face seemed to freeze. "I don't—"

"There's no point in denying your identity."

"All right, so you talked to my father. So what?"

"I thought you might have something to tell me—about yourself and Hank Schultz."

"What are you talking about?"

"It was seeing you in the squadroom that set him off, wasn't it? He knew you well enough to recognize you even in men's clothes. Your handcuffs were off and he didn't realize you'd been arrested. He thought you were there to betray him, as another woman—his wife—had once betrayed him in a different way."

She started crying then, not holding back the tears that had threatened the day before, and Leopold turned for a moment to stare out the window. He remembered how he'd seen the fire burning from the window of his bedroom, and that reminded him of why he was here. He had a job to do. Hank Schultz had forgotten about his job and that had been his fatal flaw. He turned back to the sobbing girl.

"When Schultz stumbled onto the stolen-food-stamp racket he met you, didn't he? The two of you had the last couple of months for your special form of insanity."

"It wasn't insanity! It was love!"

"Hank stole that last batch of food stamps from the federal building garage, didn't he? And you helped. He needed your help because the stamps had to be funneled through your father's store. But a man named Ellis at the Justice Department used a computer and pinpointed Crown as redeeming more than its share of stamps for the income area it was in. Ellis wanted to get a search warrant and raid the store today. The stolen stamps were there and you couldn't get them out in time, so you had to burn the place down. If your father had been involved he could have removed them, but for some reason you couldn't reach them in time."

"I'd hidden them in the storeroom," she said listlessly, wiping her eyes with a tissue, "until it was safe to turn them in to the government. I had one in my pocket because we were trying to sell them elsewhere—but everyone was scared after the robbery, especially when there was nothing in the papers about it. We didn't know what the Justice Department was up to. So the stamps were there in my father's storeroom, and then Hank heard that Ellis had pinpointed Crown and wanted a search warrant. I could get in only when the store was open, and they were doing an inventory back there. I was helpless till Friday, and that would have been too late."

"How did you manage all this without your father knowing?"

"When I was doing the bookkeeping I handled things like foodstamp redemptions. I'd been buying them from people in my neighborhood for the past two years and selling them back to the government through his store. He never asked questions. He trusted me."

"And you were willing to burn down the store rather than lose that trust." When she didn't answer he went on. "You dressed in men's clothes to disguise yourself in case you were seen planting the firebombs behind the store. Then you broke a window while a couple of plainclothes cops were watching to give yourself a perfect alibi. If the fire was ever traced to you, you could claim you were in jail when it started. Of course, the arson squad recovered the remains of the timing device so the alibi wouldn't have held water, but you didn't know that."

"I wasn't thinking straight," she admitted. "Neither was Hank."

"He certainly wasn't. He walked into the squad room night before last and saw you with Sweeney and Gross. He probably never noticed what you were wearing. He'd probably gone through the day on the edge of insanity, fearful of what Ellis might do when he arrived from Washington. Then he saw you and thought you'd betrayed him, sold him out to save your own skin. He didn't wait for words. He drew his revolver and when Sergeant Bentley made a dive for it he got the first bullet. Then he shot you twice, and Gross and Sweeney, before Lieutenant Fletcher killed him."

"One moment of madness," she said, the tears spilling over again.

"Are you willing to talk about it?" Leopold asked. "Before a grand jury?"

"It'll be rough on me, won't it?"

"Not half as rough as it was on Hank Schultz."

LOOPY

by RUTH RENDELL

At the end of the last performance, after the curtain calls, Red Riding Hood put me on a lead and with the rest of the company we went across to the pub. No one had taken makeup off or changed, there was no time for that before the George closed. I remember prancing across the road and growling at someone on a bicycle.

They loved me in the pub—well, some of them loved me. Quite a lot were embarrassed. The funny thing was that I should have been embarrassed myself if I had been one of them. I should have ignored *me* and drunk up my drink and left. Except that it is unlikely I would have been in a pub at all. Normally, I never went near such places. But inside the wolf skin it was very different, everything was different in there.

I prowled about for a while, sometimes on all-fours—though this isn't easy for us who are accustomed to the upright stance—sometimes loping, with my forepaws held close up to my chest. I went over to tables where people were sitting and snuffled my snout at their packets of crisps. If they were smoking I growled and waved my paws in air-clearing gestures. Lots of them were forthcoming, stroking me and making jokes or pretending terror at my red jaws and wicked little eyes. There was even one lady who took hold of my head and laid it in her lap.

Bounding up to the bar to collect my small dry sherry, I heard Bill Harkness (the First Woodcutter) say to Susan Hayes (Red Riding Hood's Mother): "Old Colin's really come out of his shell tonight."

And Susan, bless her, said, "He's a real actor, isn't he?"

I was one of the few members of our company who was. I expect this is always true in amateur dramatics. There are one or two real actors, people who could have made their livings on the stage if it wasn't so overcrowded a profession, and the rest who just come for the fun of it and the social side.

Did I ever consider the stage seriously? My father had been a civil servant, both my grandfathers in the ICS. As far back as I can remember it was taken for granted I should get my degree and go into the Civil Service. I never questioned it. If you have a mother like mine, one in a million, more a friend than a parent, you never feel the need to rebel. Besides, Mother gave me all the support I could have wished for in my acting. Acting as a hobby, that is. For instance, though the company made provision for hiring all the more complicated costumes for that year's Christmas pantomime, Mother made the wolf suit for me herself. It was ten times better than anything we could have hired. The head we had to buy, but the body and the limbs she made from a long-haired grey-fur fabric such as is manufactured for ladies' coats.

Moira used to say I enjoyed acting so much because it enabled me to lose myself and become, for a while, someone else. She said I disliked what I was and looked for ways of escape. A strange way to talk to the man you intend to marry! But before I approach the subject of Moira or, indeed, continue with this account, I should explain what its purpose is.

The psychiatrist attached to this place or who visits it (I'm not entirely clear which), one Dr. Vernon-Peak, has asked me to write down some of my feelings and impressions. That, I said, would only be possible in the context of a narrative. Very well, he said, he had no objection. What will become of it when finished I hardly know. Will it constitute a statement to be used in court? Or will it enter Dr. Vernon-Peak's files as another case history? It's all the same to me. I can only tell the truth.

After the George closed, then, we took off our makeup and changed and went our several ways home. Mother was waiting up for me. This was not invariably her habit. If I told her I should be late and to go to bed at her usual time she always did so. But I, quite naturally, was not averse to a welcome when I got home, particularly after a triumph like that one. Besides, I had been looking forward to telling her what an amusing time I'd had in the pub.

Our house is late-Victorian, double-fronted, of grey limestone, by no means beautiful, but a comfortable, well built place. My grandfather bought it when he retired and came home from India in 1920. Mother was ten at the time, so she has spent most of her life in that house.

Grandfather was quite a famous shot and used to go big-game hunting before that kind of thing became, and rightly so, very much frowned upon. The result was that the place was full of "trophies of the chase." While Grandfather was alive, and he lived to a great age, we had no choice but to put up with the antlers and tusks that sprouted everywhere out of the walls, the elephant's-foot umbrella stand, and the snarling maws of *tigris* and *ursa*. We had to grin and bear it, as Mother, who has a fine turn of wit, used to put it.

But when Grandfather was at last gathered to his ancestors, reverently and without the least disrespect to him, we took down all those heads and horns and packed them away in trunks. The fur rugs, however, we didn't disturb. These days they are worth a fortune and I always felt that the tiger skins scattered across the hall parquet, the snow leopard draped across the back of the sofa, and the bear into whose fur one could bury one's toes before the fire gave to the place a luxurious look. I took off my shoes and snuggled my toes in it that night.

Mother, of course, had been to see the show. She had come on the first night and seen me make my onslaught on Red Riding Hood, an attack so sudden and unexpected that the whole audience had jumped to its feet and gasped. (In our version we didn't have the wolf actually devour Red Riding Hood. Unanimously, we agreed this would hardly have been the thing at Christmas.) Mother, however, wanted to see me wearing her creation once more, so I put it on and did some prancing and growling for her benefit. Again I noticed how curiously uninhibited I became once inside the wolf skin. For instance, I bounded up to the snow leopard and began snarling at it. I boxed at its great grey-white face and made playful bites at its ears. Down on all fours I went and pounced on the bear, fighting it, actually forcing its neck within the space of my jaws.

How Mother laughed! She said it was as good as anything in the pantomime and a good deal better than anything they put on television.

"Animal crackers in my soup," she said, wiping her eyes. "There used to be a song that went like that in my youth. How did it go on? Something about lions and tigers loop the loop."

"Well, *lupus* means a wolf in Latin," I said.

"And you're certainly loopy! When you put that suit on again I shall have to say you're going all loopy again!"

When I put that suit on again? Did I intend to put it on again? I had not really thought about it. Yes, perhaps if I ever went to a fancy-dress party— a remote enough contingency. Yet what a shame it seemed to waste it, to pack it away like Grandfather's tusks and antlers after all the labor Mother had put into it. That night I hung it up in my wardrobe and I remember how strange I felt when I took it off that second time, more naked than I usually felt without my clothes, almost as if I had taken off my skin.

Life kept to the "even tenor" of its way. I felt a little flat with no rehearsals to attend and no lines to learn. Christmas came. Traditionally, Mother and I were alone on the Day itself, we would not have had it any other way, but on Boxing Day Moira arrived and Mother invited a couple of neighbors of ours in as well. At some stage, I seem to recall, Susan Hayes dropped in with her husband to wish us the compliments of the season.

Moira and I had been engaged for three years. We would have got married some time before, there was no question of our not being able to afford to marry, but a difficulty had arisen over where we should live. I think I may say in all fairness that the difficulty was entirely of Moira's making. No mother could have been more welcoming to a future daughter-in-law than mine. She actually wanted us to live with her at Simla

House—she said we must think of it as our home and of her simply as our housekeeper. But Moira wanted us to buy a place of our own, so we had reached a deadlock, an impasse.

It was unfortunate that on that Boxing Day, after the others had gone, Moira brought the subject up again. Her brother (an estate agent) had told her of a bungalow for sale halfway between Simla House and her parents' home that was what he called "a real snip." Fortunately, *I* thought, Mother managed to turn the conversation by telling us about the bungalow she and her parents had lived in in India, with its great collonaded veranda, its English flower garden, and its peepul tree. But Moira interrupted her.

"This is *our* future we're talking about, not your past. I thought Colin and I were getting married."

Mother was quite alarmed. "Aren't you? Surely Colin hasn't broken things off?"

"I suppose you don't consider the possibility *I* might break things off?"

Poor Mother couldn't help smiling at that. She smiled to cover her hurt. Moira could upset her very easily. For some reason this made Moira angry.

"I'm too old and unattractive to have any choice in the matter, is that what you mean?"

"Moira," I said.

She took no notice. "You may not realize it," she said, "but marrying me will be the making of Colin. It's what he needs to make a man of him."

It must have slipped out before Mother quite knew what she was saying. She patted Moira's knee. "I can quite see it may be a tough assignment, dear."

There was no quarrel. Mother would never have allowed herself to be drawn into that. But Moira became very huffy and said she wanted to go home, so I had to get the car out and take her.

All the way to her parents' house I had to listen to a catalogue of her wrongs at my hands and my mother's. By the time we parted I felt dispirited and nervous. I even wondered if I was doing the right thing, contemplating matrimony in the "sere and yellow leaf" of forty-two.

Mother had cleared the things away and gone to bed. I went into my bedroom and began undressing. Opening the wardrobe to hang up my tweed trousers, I caught sight of the wolf suit and on some impulse I put it on.

Once inside the wolf I felt calmer and, yes, happier. I sat down in an armchair but after a while I found it more comfortable to crouch, then lie stretched out on the floor. Lying there, basking in the warmth from the gas fire on my belly and paws, I found myself remembering tales of man's affinity with wolves, Romulus and Remus suckled by a she-wolf, the ancient myth of the werewolf, abandoned children reared by wolves even in these modern times. All this seemed to deflect my mind from the discord between Moira and my mother and I was able to go to bed reasonably happily and to sleep well.

Perhaps, then, it will not seem so very strange and wonderful that the next time I felt depressed I put the suit on again. Mother was out, so I was able to have the freedom of the whole house, not just of my room. It was dusk at four, but instead of putting the lights on I prowled about the house in the twilight, sometimes catching sight of my lean grey form in the many large mirrors Mother is so fond of. Because there was so little light and our house is crammed with bulky furniture and knickknacks, the reflection I saw looked not like a man disguised but like a real wolf that has somehow escaped and strayed into a cluttered Victorian room. Or a werewolf, that animal part of man's personality that detaches itself and wanders free while leaving behind the depleted human shape.

I crept up upon the teakwood carving of the antelope and devoured the little creature before it knew what had attacked it. I resumed my battle with the bear and we struggled in front of the fireplace, locked in a desperate hairy embrace. It was then that I heard Mother let herself in at the back door. Time had passed more quickly than I had thought. I escaped and whisked my hind paws and tail round the bend in the stairs just before she came into the hall.

Dr. Vernon-Peak seems to want to know why I began this at the age of forty-two, or rather why I had not done it before. I wish I knew. Of course, there is the simple solution that I didn't have a wolf skin before, but that is not the whole answer. Was it perhaps that until then I didn't know what my needs were, though partially I had satisfied them by playing the parts I was given in dramatic productions?

There is one other thing. I have told him that I recall, as a very young child, having a close relationship with some large animal, a dog perhaps or a pony, though a search conducted into family history by this same assiduous Vernon-Peak has yielded no evidence that we ever kept a pet. But more of this anon.

Be that as it may, once I had lived inside the wolf I felt the need to do so more and more. Erect on my hind legs, drawn up to my full height, I do not think I flatter myself unduly when I say I made a fine handsome animal. And having written that, I realize that I have not yet described the wolf suit, taking for granted, I suppose, that those who see this document will also see it. Yet this may not be the case. They have refused to let *me* see it, which makes me wonder if it has been cleaned and made presentable again or if it is still—but, no, there is no point in going into unsavory details.

I have said that the body and limbs of the suit were made of long-haired grey-fur fabric. The stuff of it was coarse, hardly an attractive material for a coat, I should have thought, but very closely similar to a wolf's pelt. Mother made the paws after the fashion of fur gloves but with the padded and stiffened fingers of a pair of leather gloves for the claws. The head we bought from a jokes-and-games shop. It had tall prick ears, small yellow eyes, and a wonderful, half open mouth—red, voracious-looking, and with a double row of white fangs. The opening for me to breathe through was just beneath the lower jaw where the head joined the powerful hairy throat.

As Spring came I would sometimes drive out into the countryside, park the car, and slip into the skin. It was far from my ambition to be seen by anyone. I sought solitude. Whether I should have cared for a "beastly" companion, that is something else again. At that time I wanted merely to wander in the woods and copses or along a hedgerow in my wolf's persona. And this I did, choosing unfrequented places, avoiding anywhere that I might come in contact with the human race.

I am trying, in writing this, to explain how I felt. Principally, I felt *not human*. And to be not human is to be without human responsibilities and human cares. Inside the wolf, I laid aside my apprehensiveness about getting married, my apprehensiveness about *not* getting married, my fear of leaving Mother on her own, my justifiable resentment at not getting the leading part in our new production. All this got left behind with the depleted sleeping man I left behind to become a happy mindless wild creature.

Our wedding had once again been postponed. The purchase of the house Moira and I had finally agreed upon fell through at the last moment. I cannot say I was altogether sorry. It was near enough to my home, in the same street in fact as Simla House, but I had begun to wonder how I would feel passing our dear old house every day knowing it was not under that familiar roof I should lay my head.

Moira was very upset.

Yet, "I won't live in the same house as your mother even for three months," she said in answer to my suggestion. "That's a certain recipe for disaster."

"Mother and Daddy lived with Mother's parents for twenty years," I said.

"Yes, and look at the result!" It was then that she made that remark about my enjoying playing parts because I disliked my real self.

There was nothing more to be said except that we must keep on house-hunting.

"We can still go to Malta, I suppose," Moira said. "We don't have to cancel that."

Perhaps, but it would be no honeymoon. Anticipating the delights of matrimony was something I had not done up till then and had no intention of doing. And I was on my guard when Moira—Mother was out at her bridge evening—insisted on going up to my bedroom with me, ostensibly to check on the shade of the suit I had bought to get married in. She said she wanted to buy me a tie. Once there, she reclined on my bed, cajoling me to come and sit beside her.

I suppose it was because I was feeling depressed that I put on the wolf skin. I took off my jacket—but nothing more, of course, in front of Moira —stepped into the wolf skin, fastened it up, and adjusted the head. She watched me. She had seen me in it when she came to the pantomime.

"Why have you put that on?"

I said nothing. What could I have said? The usual contentment filled me, though, and I found myself obeying her command, loping across to the bed where she was. It seemed to come naturally to fawn on her, to rub my great prick-eared head against her breast, to enclose her hands with my paws. All kinds of fantasies filled my wolfish mind and they were of an intense piercing sweetness. If we had been on our holiday then, I do not think moral resolutions would have held me back.

But unlike the lady in the George, Moira did not take hold of my head and lay it in her lap. She jumped up and shouted at me to stop this nonsense, stop it at once, she hated it. So I did as I was told, of course I did, and got sadly out of the skin and hung it back in the cupboard. I took Moira home. On our way we called in at her brother's and looked at fresh lists of houses.

It was on one of these that we eventually settled after another month or so of picking and choosing and stalling, and we fixed our wedding for the middle of December. During the summer the company had done *Blithe Spirit* (in which I had the meager part of Dr. Bradman, Bill Harkness being Charles Condomine) and the pantomime this year was *Cinderella* with Susan Hayes in the name part and me as the Elder of the Ugly Sisters. I had calculated I should be back from my honeymoon just in time.

No doubt I would have been. No doubt I would have married and gone away on my honeymoon and come back to play my comic part had I not agreed to go shopping with Moira on her birthday. What happened that day changed everything.

It was a Thursday evening. The stores in the West End stay open late on Thursdays. We left our offices at five, met by arrangement and together walked up Bond Street. The last thing I had in view was that we should begin bickering again, though we had seemed to do little else lately. It started with my mentioning our honeymoon. We were outside Asprey's, walking along arm-in-arm. Since our house wouldn't be ready for us to move into till the middle of January, I suggested we should go back for just two weeks to Simla House. We should be going there for Christmas in any case.

"I thought we'd decided to go to a hotel," Moira said.

"Don't you think that's rather a waste of money?"

"I think," she said in a grim sort of tone, "I think it's money we daren't not spend," and she drew her arm away from mine.

I asked her what on earth she meant.

"Once get you back there with Mummy and you'll never move."

I treated that with the contempt it deserved and said nothing. We walked along in silence. Then Moira began talking in a low monotone, using expressions from paperback psychology which I'm glad to say I have never heard from Dr. Vernon-Peak. We crossed the street and entered Selfridge's. Moira was still going on about Oedipus complexes and that nonsense about making a man of me.

"Keep your voice down," I said. "Everyone can hear you."

She shouted at me to shut up, she would say what she pleased. Well, she had repeatedly told me to be a man and to assert myself, so I did just that. I went up to one of the counters, wrote her a check for, I must admit, a good deal more than I had originally meant to give her, put it into her hands, and walked off, leaving her there.

For a while I felt not displeased with myself, but on the way home in the train depression set in. I should have liked to tell Mother about it but Mother would be out, playing bridge. So I took recourse in my other source of comfort, my wolf skin. The phone rang several times while I was gamboling about the rooms but I didn't answer it. I knew it was Moira. I was on the floor with Grandfather's stuffed eagle in my paws and my teeth in its neck when Mother walked in.

Bridge had ended early. One of the ladies had been taken ill and rushed to the hospital. I had been too intent on my task to see the light come on or hear the door. She stood there in her old fur coat, looking at me. I let the eagle fall and bowed my head—I wanted to die I was so ashamed and embarrassed. How little I really knew my mother! My dear faithful companion, my only friend! Might I not say, my other self?

She smiled. I could hardly believe it but she was smiling. It was that wonderful, conspiratorial, rather naughty smile of hers. "Hallo," she said. "Are you going all loopy?"

In a moment she was down on her knees beside me, the fur coat enveloping her, and together we worried at the eagle, engaged in battle with the bear, attacked the antelope. Together we bounded into the hall to pounce upon the sleeping tigers. Mother kept laughing (and growling too) saying, "What a relief, what a relief!" I think we embraced.

Next day when I got home she was waiting for me, transformed and ready. She had made herself an animal suit. She must have worked on it all day, out of the snow-leopard skin and a length of white-fur fabric. I could see her eyes dancing through the gap in its throat.

"You don't know how I've longed to be an animal again," she said. "I used to be animals when you were a baby. I was a dog for a long time and then I was a bear, but your father found out and he didn't like it. I had to stop."

So that was what I dimly remembered. I said she looked like the Queen of the Beasts.

"Do I, Loopy?" she said.

We had a wonderful weekend, Mother and I. Wolf and leopard, we breakfasted together that morning. Then we played. We played all over the house, sometimes fighting, sometimes dancing, hunting of course, carrying off our prey to the lairs we made for ourselves among the furniture. We went out in the car, drove into the country, and there in a wood got into our skins and for many happy hours roamed wild among the trees.

There seemed no reason, during those two days, to become human again at all, but on the Tuesday I had a rehearsal and on the Monday morning I had to go off to work. It was coming down to earth, back to what we call reality, with a nasty bang. Still, it had its amusing side too. A lady in the train trod on my toe and I had growled at her before I remembered and turned it into a cough.

All through that weekend neither of us had bothered to answer the phone. In the office I had no choice and it was there that Moira caught me. Marriage had come to seem remote, something grotesque, something that others did, not me. Animals do not marry. But that was not the sort of thing I could say to Moira. I promised to ring her. I said we must meet before the week was out.

I suppose she did tell me she'd come over on the Thursday evening and show me what she'd bought with the money I had given her. She knew Mother was always out on Thursdays. I suppose Moira did tell me and I failed to take it in. Nothing was important to me but being animals with Mother—Loopy and the Queen of the Beasts.

Each night as soon as I got home we made ourselves ready for our evening's games. How harmless it all was! How innocent! Like the gentle creatures in the dawn of the world before man came. Like the Garden of Eden after Adam and Eve had been sent away.

The lady who had been taken ill at the bridge evening had since died, so this week it was cancelled. But would Mother have gone anyway? Probably not. Our animal capers meant as much to her as they did to me, almost more perhaps, for she had denied herself so long.

We were sitting at the dining table, eating our evening meal. Mother had cooked, I recall, a rack of lamb so that we might later gnaw the bones. We never ate it, of course, and I have since wondered what became of it. But we did begin on our soup. The bread was at my end of the table, with the bread board and the long sharp knife.

Moira, when she called and I was alone, was in the habit of letting herself in by the back door. We did not hear her, neither of us heard her, though I do remember Mother's noble head lifted a fraction before Moira came in, her fangs bared and her ears pricked. Moira opened the dining-room door and walked in. I can see her now, the complacent smile on her lips fading and the scream starting to come. She was wearing what must have been my present, a full-length white sheepskin coat.

And then? This is what Dr. Vernon-Peak will particularly wish to know but what I cannot clearly remember. I remember that as the door opened I was holding the bread knife in my paws. I think I remember letting out a low growling and poising myself to spring. But what came after?

The last things I can recall before they brought me here are the blood on my fur and the two wild predatory creatures crouched on the floor over the body of the lamb.

THE PLATEAU

by CLARK HOWARD

Tank Sherman felt his daughter's hand shaking him gently. "Tank. Tank, wake up. Bruno's dead."

Tank sat up, moving his legs off the side of the cot where he had been napping, fully clothed except for his boots. Bruno? Bruno dead?

"You mean Hannah," he said, automatically reaching for his boots.

"No, Tank, I mean Bruno. Hannah's still alive. It's Bruno that died."

Tank frowned. That was not the way it was supposed to happen. He pushed first one foot, then the other, into black Atlas boots with riding heels. He had owned the boots for eighteen years, and they were as soft as glove leather. After he got them on, he sat staring at the floor, still confused. Bruno dead? How could that be? Bruno was supposed to have survived Hannah. Bruno was young; Hannah was old. And it was on Bruno that the lottery had been held.

"What happened?" he asked Delia, his daughter.

"I don't know. Doc Lewis is on his way over to check him." She crossed the little one-room cabin to the stove and turned on a burner under the coffee pot. Getting out a cup, she poured a shot of peach brandy into it. "Will they still have the hunt, do you think? Since it's Hannah and not Bruno?"

"No," Tank said emphatically, "they couldn't. Hannah's too old. It wouldn't be a hunt; it would be a target shoot."

When the coffee was ready, Delia poured it in with the brandy and brought it to him. As he sipped it, Tank studied his daughter. She had the dark hair of her mother: thick and black as a crow's wing. And the high cheekbones of her mother's people, the Shoshone. Her light halfbreed coloring and blue eyes she got from him. All her life she had called him "Tank" instead of "Daddy." At nineteen, her body was round and strong. She lived in her own mobile home down the road, and dealt blackjack for a living in an illegal game behind the Custer's Last Stand restaurant. Tank himself still lived in the cabin where Delia had been born. He had been alone for a year, since Delia left; and lonely for six years, since her mother had died of bone disease.

"Are you going down to the concession?" Delia asked.

"In a minute." He held the coffee cup with both hands, as if warming his palms, and smiled at his daughter. "Remember how your Ma used to raise hell when she caught you lacing my coffee with brandy?"

"Yes." Delia smiled back.

"She always wanted me to make something of myself, your Ma. Always wanted me to do something important. But I guess it just isn't in the cards. If Hannah had died first, like she was supposed to, why, I could have done something important for the first time in my life. Important to your Ma, at least. And to Bruno. But Bruno ups and dies first, so I'm left with nothing important to do. If your Ma was still alive, she'd swear on her medicine bag that I arranged it this way."

Shaking his head wryly, Tank drank a long swallow from his cup. At fifty, he was a rangy, well-worn man with not an ounce of fat on him. His face showed the results of a hundred fists, maybe more. Twenty years earlier he had come to town as part of a traveling boxing show, whites against Indians. Dan Sherman, his name had been, but they billed him as "Tank" because he was so tough. Tank Sherman, after the Sherman tank. A hide like armor. Took punches like Jake LaMotta. But he had taken too many by then. In their little Montana town, a Northern Cheyenne who hated whites had beaten him to a pulp, and when the outfit moved on it took the Northern Cheyenne with it and left Tank behind. Delia's mother had found him sitting behind the 7-Eleven, trying to eat some crackers and Vienna sausage he had bought with his last dollar. His lips were swollen so grotesquely he could barely chew, his eyes puffed to slits through which he could hardly see. Delia's mother took him home with her. They were never to part. Delia was their only child.

"Let's go on down to the concession," Tank said when he finished his coffee.

His cabin was on the slope of a low hill, and as Tank and Delia walked down its path they could see a small crowd already beginning to gather at the concession's corral. The concession itself was nothing more than a small barn next to the corral, with a gaudy red sign over its door which read: LAST TWO LIVING BUFFALO—ADMISSION $1. Tourists bought tickets and lined up around the corral, then the barn doors were opened and Bruno and Hannah were driven out to be viewed. They were the last two remaining buffalo in North America.

Now there was only one.

Old Doc Lewis, the reservation veterinarian from the nearby Crow agency, had just finished examining Bruno when Tank and Delia eased their way through the crowd to him.

"What killed him, Doc?" asked Tank, looking down at the great mass of animal spread out on the ground.

"Stroke," the vet said, brushing off his knees. "He was carrying too much weight. Must have been upwards of two thousand pounds."

Tank nodded. "Can't run off much fat in a corral," he observed.

Doc Lewis was making notes in a small book. "How old was he, do you know?"

"Nine," Tank said. "My wife helped deliver him." His scarred boxer's face saddened as he noticed his daughter reach out and pat the dead buffalo's massive head. Then he glanced over to a corner of the corral and saw Hannah, standing quietly, watching. Unlike Bruno, a young bull, Hannah was a cow and much older: at least thirty. She had thinner, lighter hair than most buffalo, and a triangular part of her neck and shoulder cape was almost blond, indicating the presence somewhere in her ancestry of a white buffalo. Much smaller than Bruno, she stood only five feet at her shoulders and weighed a shade over seven hundred pounds.

"I guess this means the big hunt is off, doesn't it, Doc?" Tank asked. It was the same question Delia had asked him, and Doc gave the same answer.

"Of course. There wouldn't be any sport at all going after Hannah. She's much too old."

The three of them walked over to Hannah and, as if compelled by some irresistible urge, they all patted her at once. "Well, old girl," Doc said, "you made the history books. The last North American plains buffalo."

"Maybe they'll put her on a stamp or something," said Delia.

"Maybe," Doc allowed. "They already had the buffalo on a nickel, but that was before your time."

From the barn, a pretty young woman in the tan uniform of a state park ranger walked over to them. White, educated, poised, she was everything Delia was not. "Hello, Dr. Lewis—Mr. Sherman," she said. "Hello there, Delia." She snapped a lead rein onto the collar Hannah wore. "I just got a call from headquarters to close down the concession. And to trim Hannah's hooves. Isn't it exciting?"

Doc and Tank exchanged surprised looks. "Isn't what exciting?" Doc asked, almost hesitantly. Instinctively, both he and Tank already knew what her answer would be.

"The hunt, of course. Oh, I know it won't be the same as it would have been with Bruno as the prey. But it will still be the last buffalo hunt ever. That's history in the making!"

"That," Doc rebuked, "is barbarism."

"Are you saying the hunt's still on?" Tank asked. "With Hannah as the prey?"

"Of course." She shrugged her pretty shoulders. "I mean, how else can it be? The tickets have been sold, the lottery has been held. You don't expect the state to go back on its word, do you?"

"No," Delia said, "definitely not. Never. Not the state."

"Well, there you are," the young ranger said, missing Delia's sarcasm entirely. "But, listen, they *have* changed the rules a little to make it fairer. Bruno was only going to be given a twelve-hour start, remember? Well, Hannah gets a full *twenty-four.*" She smiled, apparently delighted by the allowance.

Doc Lewis turned and walked away, thoroughly disgusted. Tank and Delia left also. Walking back up the path to Tank's cabin, Delia said, "Looks like you're getting your chance to do something important, after all."

Tank, thinking about his dead wife, nodded. "Looks like . . ."

When it had become clear that the plains buffalo had finally reached the threshold of extinction, when it was absolutely certain that no new calves would be born because the remaining cows were too old to conceive, the state had immediately done two things: penned up the few remaining members of the species and put an admission on their viewing, and devised a nationwide lottery to select the persons who would be allowed to hunt— and take the head and hide of—the last American buffalo.

Both moves proved enormously successful. The Last Remaining Buffalo concession, let by the state to one of its own departments, the Bureau of Parks, was open nine months of the year. Managed by park rangers, it operated under very low overhead and was the most profitable tourist attraction in the state. All around the corral where the buffalo were exhibited, there were coin-operated machines where for a quarter visitors could purchase cups of processed food pellets to toss into the corral for the buffalo to eat. Like peanuts to caged monkeys. Except that the buffalo refused to do tricks. Despite considerable effort in the beginning, including the use of a whip, the buffalo had remained stoic and refused to be trained. Finally, the park rangers had to resign themselves to simply leading their charges into the corral and letting them stand there while small children pelted them with synthetic food. The attraction, nevertheless, was popular.

As profitable as the concession was, however, its earnings were modest compared to the proceeds of the lottery. In a scheme devised by one of the General Accounting Office's young financial wizards, two million numbered tickets had been sold throughout the state and through the mail nationally, for five dollars a chance. The ticket supply was exhausted within a month, and the state had made a quick ten million dollars. Even people who had no interest whatever in hunting bought a ticket for investment speculation. Even before the drawing, advertisements had been run by people offering to buy a winning ticket from anyone whose number was picked.

The drawing, wherein three winners were selected, was by the use of a single, predesignated digit each day from the total shares traded on the New York Stock Exchange. The lucky ticket holders were a piano tuner from Boston, a waiter in Memphis, and a ranch hand in Nevada. The piano tuner sold his ticket for ten thousand dollars to Gregory Kingston, the actor. The waiter sold his for eighty-five hundred to bestselling author Harmon Langford. Lester Ash, the ranch hand, kept his, deciding that the head and hide would be worth far more than the ticket. He was counting on being a better hunter and shot than the actor and author were.

Within two hours of the untimely death of Bruno, the three registered owners of the winning tickets were notified to come claim their prize. Hannah, the last surviving plains buffalo, would be released fifty miles out on the prairie at noon on Friday.

At noon on Saturday, the three lottery winners would be free to hunt her.

By midnight on Thursday, Tank Sherman was ready to go. Hitched to the rear of his Ford pickup truck was a double-stall horse trailer from which he had removed the center divider, creating one large stall.

Parking the rig on the prairie some one hundred yards behind the concession corral, he and Delia slipped through the quiet night to the barn, snipped the padlock with bolt-cutters, and led Hannah out. The old buffalo cow was as docile as a rabbit and made no noise whatever as Delia fed her a handful of fresh meadow grass and Tank slipped a braided halter over her head.

After walking the buffalo aboard the trailer and quietly closing her in, Tank handed Delia an envelope. "Here's the deed to the cabin and lot. And the passbook to your ma's savings account. She had six hundred and forty dollars saved when she died; it was supposed to be yours when you were twenty-one. Oh, and the title to the pickup is there, too, just in case. Guess that's about all."

Delia got a paper bag and thermos jug from her Jeep. "Sandwiches," she said. "And coffee. With, uh—"

"Yeah." He put the bag and jug on the seat of the pickup and sniffed once as if he might be catching cold. But he wasn't catching cold. "Listen, take care of yourself, kid," he said brusquely, and started to get into the truck. Then he turned back. "Look, I know I ain't never won no Father-of-the-Year prize and I never gave you noplace to live but that cabin and I never sent you to college or nothing, but those things don't have nothing to do with caring. You understand?"

"Sure," Delia said. She shrugged. "After all, you did teach me when to fold in poker. And how to change a flat. And how to get a squirrel to eat out of my hand. Lots of girls never learn those things." She had to struggle to control her voice. She was not able to control her tears. But she knew that Tank couldn't see the tears in the darkness.

"Okay," he said. "I'll be hitting the road then."

He eased the door of the pickup shut, quietly started the engine, and slowly pulled away without headlights.

Behind him, Delia waved in the darkness and said, "Bye—Daddy."

When he reached the highway, turned on his headlights, and increased speed, Tank thought: *Okay, Rose, this is for you, honey.*

Rose was Tank's dead wife, the woman who had always wanted him to do something important. Her Shoshone name was Primrose, given to her by her father because she had been born on a day in early July when the evening primrose had just blossomed. Later, when she moved into town and took up the ways of the white woman, she shortened it to Rose.

Tank always remembered Rose as being beautiful, but she was not; she was not even pretty. Her face was very plain, her eyes set too close together, her nose too long, and one cheek was pitted with pockmarks. Only her hair, lustrous as polished onyx, could truly be called beautiful. But Tank saw so much more of her than was outside. He saw her hopes and dreams, her pride, her nakedness when they made love, her secret joys. He saw everything about her, and it was all of those things combined which made her beautiful to him.

The first time she had shown him the buffalo was three months after she had taken him to live with her, after she had nursed him back to health from the beating he had taken. They got up early one morning on Rose's day off from the sugar-beet processing plant, and in her old Jeep they drove thirty miles out onto the raw prairie. There, on an isolated meadow, was a small buffalo herd: three bulls, a cow, and six calves. They were the beginning of the last migration, when the ocean of tourists had started driving them north and west from the Black Hills.

"See how noble they look," Rose had said. "See the dignity with which they stand and observe." Her eyes had become water and she had added, "They are watching their world come to an end."

Once, Rose explained to him, there had been sixty *million* plains buffalo. Their presence on the Northern Plains had been the greatest recorded aggregation of large land animals ever known to man. To the red man of the prairie, the vast herds had been the mainstay of his economy. That single species provided food, clothing, shelter, and medicine for an entire race— the only time in history that such a natural balance between man and beast had ever been achieved.

"Then, of course, the whites came," Rose said. "At first, they killed the buffalo for meat and hides, as our people did, and that was acceptable because the herds were many. Later they killed them only for hides, leaving the carcasses to rot in the sun. Even that act, although it was without honor, could have been tolerated. But then they began killing them for what they called 'sport.' Fun. Recreation.

"They killed them first by the tens of thousands. The butcher Cody, whom they called 'Buffalo Bill,' personally recorded more than forty-two-thousand kills in one seventeen-month period. Soon they were being slaughtered with total wantonness, by the hundreds of thousands. Today there are only a few hundred left. Most of them are in the Black Hills. But they're slowly migrating back up here again."

"Why?" Tank asked, fascinated.

"They know the end is nearing for them. A species can tell when their breed is running out. Each year they see fewer and fewer calves, the herds become smaller and smaller. So they look for a place to end their line. They look for a grassy meadow unspoiled by humans. A place to lie down and die with dignity."

For all the years Tank Sherman knew and lived with the Shoshone woman Rose, she had loved the great buffalo and mourned its diminishing number. As much as Tank missed her in death, he was glad that she had not lived to see Bruno and Hannah, the last two of the breed, penned up and put on display—or known about the lottery for the privilege of hunting the survivor.

So this is for you, honey, he thought as he headed southeast with Hannah in the horse trailer. He would have about five hours' head start. Possibly two hundred-fifty miles. Maybe it would be enough.

Maybe not.

Two hours after dawn, a tall, very handsome man, livid with anger, was stalking back and forth in the empty concession corral.

"What the hell do you mean, *missing?* How can something as large as a buffalo be *missing?*" His name was Gregory Kingston. An Academy Award-winning actor, he was not acting now; he was truly incensed.

"The state guaranteed this hunt," said a second man. Smaller, plumper, not as handsome but with a good deal more bearing, this was Harmon Langford, internationally known bestselling author. Like Kingston, he was dressed in expensive hunting garb, carrying a fine, hand-tooled, engraved, foreign-made rifle. "Exactly who's in charge here?" he quietly demanded.

A third man, Lester Ash, the ranch hand from Nevada, stood back a step, not speaking, but observing everything. He wore hardy working clothes: denim, twill, roughout leather.

"Gentlemen," a Bureau of Mines spokesman pleaded, "please believe me, we're trying to get to the bottom of this as quickly as we can. All we know right now is that some person or persons apparently abducted Hannah sometime during the night. The highway patrol has been notified and a statewide search is getting underway at this very moment—"

"Why in hell would anyone want to abduct a *buffalo?*" Kingston inquired loudly of the world at large, throwing his arms up in bewilderment. Now he *was* acting.

"Oh, come, Kingston," said Harmon Langford, "we're not talking about *a* buffalo, we're talking about *this* buffalo. Unlike ourselves, there *are* those—" and here he glanced at Lester Ash "—who are interested in this animal not for sport but for profit." Lester Ash grinned but remained silent. Langford continued, "At any rate, we cannot waste time on *why*—we must concentrate on *where*. *Where* is our great, hairy prize? And how do we get to it?"

The Bureau of Parks man said, "We should be hearing from the highway patrol any time now. Every road in the state is covered."

"What do we do now?" asked Gregory Kingston, directing the question at Langford.

"We must be prepared to get to the animal as quickly as possible after it's located," the author declared. "Before some outsider decides to take an illegal shot at it. This part of the country is crawling with would-be cowboys. Pickup trucks, rifle racks in the back window, old faded Levis— that sort of thing. I'm sure there are a few of them who would like to be remembered as the man who gunned down the last buffalo."

"Like you, you mean?" Lester Ash said, speaking for the first time.

A smirk settled on Langford's lips. "Yes," he acknowledged. Adding, "And you." They locked eyes in a moment of mutual understanding and then Langford said, "What we need, of course, is fast, flexible transportation." He turned to the Parks man. "How far is the nearest helicopter service?"

"Fifty miles."

"I suggest we start at once. If we have a helicopter at our disposal by the time the buffalo is located, we can hurry there at once. I presume the state would have no objection to that?"

The Parks man shrugged. "Not so long as all three of you get an equal start. And don't shoot it from the air."

"Of course not. We aren't barbarians, after all." He looked at Kingston and Lester Ash. "Are we agreed?"

"Agreed," said the actor.

"Let's go," said Ash.

Three hours earlier, Tank had parked the pickup and trailer in a stand of elm and gone on foot deeper into the trees where Otter had his cabin. It had still been dark—the eerie void before dawn. He knocked softly at Otter's door.

"Who disturbs this weak old man at such an hour?" a voice asked from within. "Is it someone evil, come to take advantage of my helplessness?"

"Otter, it's Sherman," said Tank. "Your daughter's man before she passed."

"What is it you want?" asked Otter. "I am destitute and can offer you nothing. I have no money or other valuables. I barely exist from day to day. Why have you come to me?"

"For your wisdom, Otter. For your words."

"Perhaps I can give you that, although I am usually so weak from hunger that each breath could well be my last. How many others have you brought with you?"

Tank smiled in the darkness. "I am alone, Otter." Maybe now the old scoundrel would stop acting.

"You may enter," Otter said. "There are candles by the door."

Inside the front door, Tank lighted a candle that illuminated patches of an incredibly dirty and impoverished room. In one corner, an ancient cot with torn sagging mattress; in another, a rusted iron sink filled with dirty pots and pans; in a third, an old chifforobe with a broken door hanging loose to reveal a few articles of ragged clothing. Everywhere in between there was dirt, grime, clutter.

Tank didn't pause in the room. He lit his way directly to a door which led to a second room, and in that room he found Otter sitting up in a king-size bed, a cigar in his mouth, a bottle of whiskey at his side. As Tank closed the door behind him, the old Indian uncocked a double-barrel shotgun on the bed beside him and put it on the floor. "How are you, Soft Face?" he asked. The first time he had seen Tank, the young fighter's face had been beaten to pulp. Otter had called him "Soft Face" ever since.

"I'm okay," Tank said. "You look the same."

The old Indian shrugged. "There is no reason for something perfect to change."

Tank grinned and glanced around the room. It was a self-contained little world, holding everything Otter needed or wanted for his personal comfort. Portable air-conditioner, color television, microwave oven, upright freezer, power generator, small bathroom in one corner, indoor hot tub and jacuzzi in another. "How's the bootlegging business?" Tank asked.

"My customers are loyal. I make ends meet." Otter got out of bed and put a Hopi blanket around his shoulders. "Is my granddaughter still dealing cards in the white man's game?"

"Yes."

"Does she cheat them when the opportunity presents itself?"

"Yes, if they are tourists."

Otter nodded in approval. "That is good. Even a half-Indian should cheat the whites whenever possible." At a two-burner hotplate, Otter set water to boil. "Sit here at the table," he said, "and tell me your problem."

Tank explained to the old Indian what he had done, and why. When he got to the part about Rose and her love for the buffalo, Otter's eyes became misty. When Tank stopped talking, Otter rose, poured coffee and brandy for them, and brought it to the table. "How can I help you?" he asked.

"I need a safe place to put the old buffalo. Someplace where she can live out her days in peace without fear of being hunted and shot. Someplace where she will be able to die quietly, like your daughter Primrose would want her to die."

Otter sipped his coffee and pondered the problem. Several times he shook his head, as if first considering, then dismissing, a possibility. Finally he tapped a forefinger on the table and said, "Do you remember the place where Ditch Creek runs beside Bear Mountain?"

"In the Black Hills?" said Tank. "Where you used to take us on picnics when Delia was a little girl?"

"That's the place. There's a grassy meadow far above Ditch Creek that belongs to the few remaining people of the Deerfield tribe. It's within the Black Hills National Park, but the federal government deeded it to the Deerfields because there was no road into it and they must have figured the tourists wouldn't be able to get to it anyway. The Deerfield use it for religious ceremonies—it's sacred ground to them. The buffalo would be protected once it got there. But there are only dirt paths leading up to the meadow. I don't know if the buffalo could climb it or not."

"How high is it?" Tank asked.

"About seven thousand feet. There's a gravel road to about six thousand, but the rest of the way would be on footpaths. It would have been better if you'd stolen a mountain goat—you never were very smart, Soft Face."

"Can you draw me a map?" Tank asked.

"Of course. I am a man of many talents."

Otter got paper and pencil and from memory sketched a map and gave it to Tank. It was daylight now and the two of them walked out to the horse trailer.

Tank backed Hannah out to exercise and feed her.

"She's a fine old buffalo," Otter observed. "Only your people would think of shooting her."

"Just because they're the same color doesn't mean they're my people," Tank replied.

Tank tethered the buffalo to a tree and returned to the cabin with Otter. The old Indian cooked breakfast and they ate together. Then it was time for Tank to leave. Otter walked back to the rig and helped him load Hannah. After Tank got in and started the truck, Otter put a hand on the door.

"In each man's life, there is a plateau," he said. "Every man reaches that plateau. He may be there for a day or a year, or only for a moment. But his time there is the meaning of his life. It is the reason the Great One put him here on earth. I think, Soft Face, that your plateau might be that grassy meadow above Ditch Creek." He touched Tank's shoulder. "Go with the wind, son."

Tank swallowed dryly, nodded, and drove off.

The helicopter was flying a checkerboard search pattern two hundred miles from where the buffalo had been stolen. Harmon Langford sat next to the pilot. Gregory Kingston and Lester Ash occupied jumpseats behind them. All three men scanned the ground below with binoculars.

"This is maddening," Kingston muttered. He tapped Langford on the shoulder. "Tell me again!" he yelled through the noise of the rotor. "Why are we looking in this direction?"

The author yelled back, "The highway patrol reported that a pickup truck pulling a horse trailer filled up with gas in Dayton at four o'clock this morning! The station attendant said the animal in the trailer had a blanket over it and the man driving the truck said it was a rodeo bull! But he thinks it was our buffalo! They were headed toward Gillette! We're searching the area south of Gillette!"

The actor shrugged, as if it were all totally meaningless to him. Lester Ash leaned close to his ear and said, "Highway Patrol thinks he might be headed toward Thunder Basin! That's a big grassland area! Be a perfect place to set a buffalo loose!"

"I see!" Kingston said, smiling. "Now *that* makes sense!" He patted Ash fondly on the knee. Ash drew back suspiciously.

The helicopter continued to checkerboard, its pilot crossing out squares on a plot map on the console. They flew well into the grasslands, twenty miles deep, and began a random searching pattern, following shadows, wind movement, wild game—anything that attracted their attention. But they didn't find what they were looking for.

After an hour, the pilot advised Langford, "We'll have to land for fuel soon."

No sooner had he spoken, they received a radio message from the Parks man back at the concession. "The trailer has been sighted by a Civil Air Patrol scout plane. It's on Route 16, south of Osage, heading toward the Black Hills. It's sure to make it across the state line, so we're requesting the South Dakota state police to set up roadblocks. I'll keep you advised."

"How far is Osage?" Langford asked the pilot.

"Fifty miles, give or take."

"Can we make it?"

"Yessir, but that'll be the limit. We'll have to refuel in Osage."

"Go," Harmon Langford ordered.

*   *   *

Tank had his CB tuned to the law-enforcement band, so he heard the South Dakota state police order go out for roadblocks. They were being set up in Custer, Four Corners, and at the junction of Routes 85 and 16. Pulling onto the shoulder of the road, Tank shifted to neutral and unfolded a map he'd picked up at a service station near Sundance, where Otter lived. When he'd stopped at the station, the tarp flaps on the trailer had been down so no one could see inside. He was sure it hadn't been the station attendant who put the law on him. Probably that low-flying two-seater that had come in over him outside Osage.

Studying the map, Tank saw that the locations selected for the road-blocks gave him considerably more leeway than he had expected. Apparently they thought he was going to try to drive well into the Black Hills. He wasn't. He needed to penetrate them only a few miles before reaching a secondary road that ran north and then east to Ditch Creek. Smiling, he saw that he would reach all three roadblocks. Getting out of the truck for a moment, he lifted one of the trailer flaps and reached in to pat Hannah's thick, hairy cape.

"We're going to beat the sons of bitches, old girl," he said happily.

It hadn't occurred to him that they might use a helicopter.

At Osage, Harmon Langford conferred by telephone with the authorities responsible for the roadblock. "Of course, I very much appreciate your help in containing this man, Captain, and I assure you that when I write about this incident, you and your men will be prominently featured. Now if you'd just be good enough to keep your forces in place and let my associates and me handle it from here, I think justice will be properly served. We really don't consider this a criminal matter. It's more mischief than anything else—a nuisance, but we can handle it."

Then he talked with the pilot of the scout plane. "Are you keeping him in sight?"

"Yes, Mr. Langford. He's moving up a secondary road toward a place called Ditch Creek."

"Fine. Keep circling and don't lose him. We'll be airborne again in a few minutes and should be there shortly. Of course, I'll expect to see you after this is all over, for photographs and such. Over and out."

As Langford turned to face them, Kingston and Lester Ash saw a look of gleeful triumph on his face. Almost an evil look.

"In a very short while, gentlemen," he said, "we should be in position to take our buffalo back. I trust both of you are prepared to deal with this abductor if he resists us?"

Kingston frowned. "What do you mean?"

Langford did not answer. Instead, he picked up his rifle and jacked a round into the chamber.

Watching him, Lester Ash smiled.

Turning off the secondary road into the inclining gravel road, Tank was aware that the patrol plane was following him. But he wasn't overly concerned. The two men in the light plane couldn't get to him. There was noplace in the surrounding hills they could land. All they could do was radio his position and he was too close to his goal now for that to matter. He knew where the roadblocks were—no one from there could catch up with him. Only one obstacle remained in his way: the thousand feet of footpath from the end of the gravel road up to the meadow.

Frowning, he wondered if old Hannah was going to be able to make it. A lot would depend on how steep the trail was and what kind of footing it offered. Good dirt footing was what he hoped for—Hannah's freshly trimmed hooves would slide too much on rock.

At the end of the gravel road, Tank drove the rig as far into the trees as he could. Part of the trailer still stuck out and he knew it could be seen from the air. No matter, he thought, they can't catch us now.

"Come on, old girl," he said as he backed Hannah out of the trailer and rubbed her neck. Studying the terrain above them, he selected the least steep path he could find and gently pulled Hannah onto it. Moving about four feet ahead of her, he drew the halter rope tight and urged her forward. She stepped nimbly up the trail and followed him without resistance.

This might be easier than I thought, Tank told himself hopefully.

The helicopter rendezvoused with the scout plane an hour after Tank and Hannah began their climb.

"Where are they?" Langford asked the air-patrol pilot on the radio.

"In those trees on the side of the mountain, sir. You can't see them right now because of the overgrowth. They're probably about halfway up to that grassy meadow on the plateau there."

Langford praised the two men in the plane for exemplary work, dismissed them, and turned to the helicopter pilot. "Set down on that grassy meadow," he ordered.

"I can't do that, sir," said the pilot, who was half Nez Percé. "That's sacred land belonging to the Deerfield tribe. Outsiders aren't permitted there."

Langford shifted the barrel of his rifle until it pointed toward the pilot. "I really do want you to land," he said pointedly.

The Nez Percé smiled. "I'd be careful with that rifle if I were you, sir. Unless you or your friends know how to fly one of these babies. They go down mighty fast."

Pursing his lips, Langford shifted the barrel back. He reached into his pocket, extracted a roll of currency, and peeled off five one-hundred-dollar bills. "If you could just hover a few feet from the ground. Long enough for us to drop off."

"That," the pilot said, taking the money, "I can do."

The last few hundred feet were the worst for both the man and the buffalo. The trail, after an easy beginning, had become narrow, steep, rutted, and treacherous. Three times, Hannah's hooves slipped on loose rocks or concealed roots and she went sliding back fifteen or twenty feet, dragging Tank with her. Each time, she rolled over onto her side and mooed anxiously as dirt from above displaced and shifted down to half bury her. Each time, Tank had to stroke and soothe her, help her dig out and regain her balance and patiently urge her forward again.

Twice Tank himself slipped badly, the leather of his old boots reacting just as Hannah's hooves did to the hostile ground under them. The first time he fell, his left foot came out from under him and he pitched onto both knees, puncturing one trouser leg on a sharp rock and cutting his knee badly enough to bleed. The second time, he lost his balance completely and went plunging downhill, sliding helplessly past Hannah, his face, shirt, and boots catching the avalanche of loose dirt that followed him. He had the presence of mind to let go of the halter rope, and didn't upset Hannah with his spill, but he slid all of forty feet. When he straightened himself, he was filthy with dirt stuck to his sweaty clothes and body and his face and hands showed nicks and cuts seeping blood through the dirt. Cursing mightily, Tank clawed his way back up to where Hannah, watching him curiously, waited with infinite patience.

Late in the climb, perhaps two hundred feet from the plateau, Tank thought he heard the roar of a motor. It was hard to tell with the thick treetops insulating the ground from noise and the constant wind whipping about now that they were so high. Maybe it was that light plane coming in low to search the meadow. If so, he thought craftily, they would find nothing there.

We're beating them, Rose—Hannah and me. And it's important that we beat them. Important that we make that plateau.

They kept climbing, the man and the buffalo, struggling against the total environment around them—the height aloof above them, the ground resistant under them, the air thin and selfish, the dirt and dust, the rocks and roots. Blood and sweat burned their eyes, both of them, for Hannah now had cuts on her old face as well. Foam coated her lips, saliva and tears wet the man's cheeks.

They climbed until their muscles came close to locking, their lungs close to bursting, their hearts close to breaking. With no resource left but blind courage, they climbed.

Finally, they made it to the top and together crawled onto the edge of the grassy meadow.

The three hunters were waiting there for them.

Only when he saw the hunters did Tank Sherman realize that the motor roar he heard had not been the scout plane but a helicopter. As he and the buffalo struggled together to drag their bodies over the lip of the plateau, both had fallen onto their knees, Tank pitching forward so that he was on all fours, Hannah with her front legs bent, great head down. Both were panting, trying to suck enough oxygen out of the thin air to cool lungs that felt as if they had been singed. For one brief instant, as they knelt side by side, Tank's shoulder brushing Hannah's neck, both their heads hung, as if man and beast were one.

Then Tank looked up and saw the hunters. They stood in a row, the sun reflecting on their rifles.

"No," he said softly, shaking his head. "No," a little louder as he got to his feet. "No!" he yelled as he walked toward them.

Harmon Langford, standing in the middle, said, "Stop where you are—come any closer and we'll shoot!"

Eyes fixed like a madman, jaw clenched like a vise, his big fists closed, Tank stalked toward them. "No!" he kept shouting. "No! No! No!"

"You've been warned!" snapped Langford.

Tank kept coming.

"All right, shoot him!" Langford ordered, shouldering his own rifle and aiming.

No shots were fired. Langford lowered his rifle and looked frantically from Kingston to Lester Ash. "Shoot! Why don't you shoot?"

"Why don't you?" Lester Ash asked evenly.

Langford didn't have time to reply. Tank reached him, snatched the rifle from his hands, and hurled it away. Then he drove a crushing right fist into Langford's face, smashing his nose and lips, sending him reeling back in shock.

As Langford fell, Tank turned on Gregory Kingston. "Now just a minute," the actor pleaded, "I had no intention of shooting you—" He threw down the rifle as evidence of his sincerity, but that didn't deter Tank. The old fighter dug a solid right fist deep into Kingston's midsection and the actor folded up like a suitcase, the color draining from his face, his eyes bulging. Dropping to his knees, he pitched forward onto his face, the juicy meadow grass staining it green.

When Tank looked for the third man, he found that Lester Ash, experienced hunter that he was, had flanked his adversary and moved around behind him. It was now Tank standing on the meadow, Lester Ash facing him with his back to the sun.

"We can do it the easy way or the hard way, bud," said Lester. "Either way, that buffalo's mine."

Tank shook his head. "No." He moved toward Ash.

"I ain't no loud-mouthed writer or sissy actor, bud," the Nevadan said. "Mess with me and I'll put you in the hospital. That buff is *mine!*"

"No." Tank kept coming.

"Please yourself," Lester said disgustedly. He snapped the rifle to his shoulder and fired.

The round ripped all the way through the fleshy part of Tank's left thigh and knocked him off his feet. Instincts two decades old still lived in his mind, and as if someone were counting ten over him Tank rolled over and got back up. Clutching his thigh, he limped toward Ash.

"You're a damned fool, bud," said Lester Ash. He fired again.

The second slug tore a hole in Tank's right thigh and he was again spun to the ground. He moaned aloud, involuntarily, and sat up, one hand on each wound. Pain seared his body, hot and relentless, and he began to choke, cough, and cry. I'm done for, he thought.

Then at his feet he saw something white and yellow. Pawing the tears from his eyes, he managed to focus. It was a clump of wildflowers—white petals with yellow nectaries. Primroses.

Tank dragged himself up one last time. He started forward again, weaving and faltering like a drunk man. His eyes fixed on Lester Ash and held.

"Okay, bud," said Lester, "now you lose a kneecap—"

Before Lester could fire, Hannah charged. Massive head down, hooves almost soundless on the thick meadow grass, she was upon Lester Ash before he realized it. Catching him from the left side, her broad forehead drove into his chest, crushing his left rib cage, collapsing the lung beneath it. With his body half bent over her face, Hannah propelled him to the edge of the plateau and hurled him over the side.

Lester Ash screamed as his body ricocheted off the first three trees, then was silent for the rest of the way down.

The Deerfield tribe marshal and his deputy, who rode up to the meadow on horseback at the first sound of gunfire, secured the area and arranged for Harmon Langford and Gregory Kingston to be escorted down to the reservation boundary. They were released with a stern warning never to violate Deerfield land again. Some men with a rescue stretcher retrieved Lester Ash's body. His death was officially attributed to an accidental fall from the plateau.

A Deerfield medicine man named Alzada, who resided in a lodge back in the trees next to the meadow, was consulted by the marshal as to the disposition of the buffalo.

"If the Great One put the buffalo here," Alzada decreed, "then the buffalo must be sacred. It shall be allowed to graze on the sacred meadow until the Great One summons it back."

The marshal looked over at the edge of the meadow where Tank sat under a tree, exhausted and bleeding. "What about the man?"

"What man?" said Alzada. "I see no man. I see only a sacred buffalo, grazing contentedly. If you see something else, perhaps it is a spirit."

The marshal shook his head. "If Alzada sees nothing, then I see nothing. Only Alzada can see spirits."

The marshal and his deputy rode back down the mountain.

When they were gone, the medicine man went over and helped Tank into the trees to his lodge.

THE BUTCHERS

by PETER LOVESEY

He had passed the weekend in the cold-store of Pugh the Butcher's. It was now Monday morning. The door was still shut. He was unconcerned. Quite early on Saturday evening he had given up beating his fists on the door and screaming for help. He had soon tired of jumping and arm-swinging to keep his circulation going. He had become increasingly drowsy as his brain had succumbed to the deprivation of oxygen. He had lain on the tiled floor below the glistening carcases and by Sunday morning he had frozen to death.

On the other side of the door, Joe Wilkins filled two mugs with instant coffee. It was still only 8:00 A.M. and the shop didn't open until 8:30. He was Mr. Pugh's shop manager, forty-four, a master butcher, dark and good-looking, with an old-fashioned Clark Gable mustache and quick laughing eyes that had a way of involving everyone in the shop each time he passed a joke with a customer.

The second mug was for Frank, the apprentice butcher. Frank was eighteen and useful for heavy work. He earned extra money on Saturday nights as a bouncer in Stacey's, the disco across the street. When the deliveries came from the slaughterer's, Frank would take the sides of beef on his back as if they were pieces of polystyrene. The girls from Woolworth's next door often came into the shop on their lunch hour and asked Frank for rides on his motorbike. Frank got embarrassed when Joe Wilkins teased him about it.

Frank hung up his leather jacket and put on a clean apron. Joe was already wearing his straw boater. He watched the young man struggle awkwardly with the apron strings, tying a bow so loose it was sure to fall apart as soon as he stretched up to lift a carcase off its hook.

"Another heavy weekend, lad?"

"Not really," answered Frank, taking his coffee and slopping some on the chopping block. "Same as usual."

"That's good to hear. Looks as if we've got a busy morning ahead of us."

Frank gave a frown.

Joe snapped his fingers. "Come on, lad, what's different this morning, or haven't you noticed yet?"

Frank looked around the shop. "Meat's not out yet."

"Right. And why not?"

"Percy isn't in."

"Right again. By Jove, I was wrong about you. You ought to be on the telly with a mind as sharp as that. Why spend the rest of your life hacking pieces of meat when you could earn millions sitting in an armchair answering questions? And now for five hundred and a holiday for two in the Bahamas, Mr. Dobson. What do you think has happened to Percy?"

"Dunno," answered Frank.

"You don't know? Come on, lad. You're not trying."

"He could have fallen off his bike again."

"That's more like it," said Joe as he took his knives and cleavers from the drawer behind the counter and started sharpening them. "Get the window ready, will you?"

Frank put down his coffee and looked for the enamel trays that usually stood in the shop window.

Joe said, "You're probably right about Percy. He's too old to be in charge of a bike. Seven miles is a long way on a morning like this, with ice all the way up Bread and Cheese Hill and the motorists driving like lunatics. He was knocked in the ditch last week, poor old devil."

"Where does he put the trays?" asked Frank.

"Trays?"

"For the meat—in the window."

"Aren't they there then?" Joe put down his knife and went to look. "Well, I suppose he puts them away somewhere. By the time I arrive, they're always here. Have a look behind the deep-freeze cabinet. —Got 'em? Good. Blowed if I understand why he bothers to do that."

"Dust, I expect," said Frank.

"Quite right. Wipe them over with a cloth, lad. I used to wonder what Percy did with himself before we arrived in the morning. He's in by six, you know, regular. How about that? He must be up at five. Could you do that six mornings a week? And it gets no easier as you get older. He must be pushing seventy by now."

"What *does* he do before we get in?" asked Frank.

"Well, it's always spotless, isn't it?"

"I thought that was because he stays on of a night to clean up after we close."

"So he does—but there's always more dust by morning. Percy wipes all the surfaces clean. He puts out the trays, and the cuts from the cold-store. He hangs up the poultry and opens a tin of liver and checks everything against the price list, puts out the tags and the plastic parsley and the new-laid eggs and the packets of stuffing and bread sauce. I hope you're listening, lad, because I want all those jobs done before we open."

Frank gave another frown. "You want me to do all that?"

"Who else, lad?" said Joe in a reasonable voice. "It's obvious that Percy isn't going to make it this morning, and I've got the orders to get out."

"He hasn't had a day off since I started last year," said Frank, still unable to believe his bad luck.

"He hasn't had a day off in the twenty years I've been working here. Six in the morning till seven at night, six days a week. And what for? Boy's work. He does the work you ought to be doing, lad. No one else but Percy would stand for it. Fetching and carrying and sweeping up. Do you know, he's never once complained to me or Mr. Pugh or anyone else? You've seen him bent nearly double carrying in the carcases. A man of his age shouldn't be doing work like that. It's exploitation, that's what it is."

"Why does he do it then? He's old enough to draw his pension."

Joe shook his head. "He wouldn't be happy with his feet up. He's spent the best years of his life working in this shop. He was here before Mr. Pugh took it over. It was Slater's in those days. —Yes, Percy can tell you some tales about the old days. It means a lot to him, working in this shop."

Frank went to the cold-store to get out the small joints left over from Saturday. The cold-store consisted of two chambers, one for the chilled meat, the other for the frozen. He opened the door of the chiller and started taking out legs of lamb. He needed to hurry to fill the trays in the window by opening time.

Joe was still sharpening knives. He continued telling Frank about the injustices heaped on Percy. "He gets no recognition for all the work he puts in. Blind loyalty, I call it, but there are some that would call it plain stupidity. Do you think Mr. Pugh appreciates what Percy does? Of course he doesn't."

"He's never here, is he?" contributed Frank, who was becoming quite skillful at fueling Joe's maledictions against their employer.

"That's a fact. To be fair to Mr. Pugh, he has to look in at the market and collect the meat from the slaughterhouse, but that shouldn't take all day. It wouldn't hurt him to show his face here more often."

Frank gave a sly grin. "It might hurt someone else."

"What do you mean by that?" asked Joe, taking offense.

"Well, you and me. We don't want the boss breathing down our necks, do we?"

Joe said in a curt tone, "Speak for yourself, boy. I'm not ashamed of my work." He put down the knife he was holding and went to the window to rearrange the tray of lamb chops Frank had just put there. "Haven't you any idea how to put meat on a tray to make it look attractive?"

"I was trying to be quick."

"You can't hurry a job like this. That's why Percy starts so early. He's an artist in his way. His windows are a picture. I wonder what's happened to him."

"He could be dead."

Joe turned to look at Frank with clear disfavor. "That's a very unpleasant suggestion."

"It's a possibility. He's always falling off that old bike. Well, he could have been taken to hospital, anyway."

"Someone would have phoned by now."

"All right, perhaps he died in the night," persisted Frank. "He could be lying in his bed. He lives alone, doesn't he?"

"You're talking nonsense, lad."

"Can you think of anything better?"

"Any more lip from you, young man, and I'll see you get your cards. Get the chickens out—I'll attend to this."

"Do you mean the frozen birds, Mr. Wilkins?"

"The farm birds. I'll tell you if we need any frozen in a minute or two."

"Do you think we ought to phone the hospital, Mr. Wilkins, just in case something happened to Percy?"

"What good would that do?"

Frank took seven capons from the chiller and hung them on the rail above the window. "That's all there is," he told Joe. "Shall I get out some frozen ones?"

Joe shook his head. "It's Monday, isn't it? There isn't much call for poultry on a Monday."

"We'll need them for tomorrow. They need to thaw. We won't be getting any farm birds this week with Mr. Pugh on holiday."

Joe hesitated in his rearrangement of the window display. "You've got a point there, lad."

Frank waited.

"Yes," said Joe. "We shall want some frozen birds."

"Have you got the key?"

"The key?"

"There's a padlock on the freezer door."

Joe crossed the shop to take a look. It was a heavy padlock. It secured the hasp on the freezer door over an iron staple. He said, "Silly old beggar. What does he want to lock it for?"

"There's a lot of good meat in there," said Frank, in Percy's defense. "Have you got the key?"

Joe shook his head. "I reckon he takes it home with him."

Frank swore. "What are we going to do? We've got to get in there. It's not just the chickens. It's the New Zealand. We're right down on lamb."

"We'd better look for the key—he might leave it somewhere," said Joe, opening one of the drawers under the counter.

Their short search did not turn up the key.

"I think I could force it with that old file of yours," suggested Frank.

"No, lad, you might damage the door. You don't want to get your marching orders from Mr. Pugh. I've got one of those small hacksaws in my toolbag in the car. We can use that to cut through the padlock."

A short time later he returned with the saw. He held the padlock firm while Frank started sawing through the staple.

"All this trouble because of Percy," said Frank. "I'd like to strangle the old git."

"It might not be his fault after all," said Joe. "Mr. Pugh might have given him orders to use a padlock. He's dead scared of the boss. He does exactly what he's told, and I don't blame him. I heard Mr. Pugh laying into him on Saturday night after you left to deliver those orders. It was vicious, it really was."

Frank continued sawing. "What was it about?"

"Well, you were here when Mr. Pugh walked in out of nowhere, saying he wanted to see that things were straight before he went off for his week in Majorca—that was before you left with the orders."

"He'd just picked up his tickets from the travel agent."

"Right. You'd think he'd be on top of the world, wouldn't you, just about to push off for a week in the sun? Not Mr. Pugh. He happened to catch old Percy putting away the cuts we hadn't sold."

"There's nothing wrong with that, is there?"

"No, but Percy left the door of the chiller open while he was doing it. We all do it, but Percy got caught. You should have heard Mr. Pugh go for him, ranting and raving about the cost of running a cold chamber with employees who are so idle they let the cold air out because they can't be bothered to open and close the door a few times. He really laid it on thick. He was quoting things about cubic feet of air and thermal units as if old Percy had done it deliberately."

"Almost there," said Frank. "Mind it doesn't catch your hand."

The hacksaw blade cut cleanly through the staple.

Joe said, "Good." But he was determined to finish his story. "He told Percy he was too old for the job and he ought to retire soon. Percy started pleading with him. I tell you, Frank, I was so embarrassed I didn't want to hear any more. I left them to it and went home."

"I'll bring out those frozen birds," said Frank, slipping the padlock from the hasp.

"You'd have a job to find a meaner man than Mr. Pugh," Joe continued as Frank swung back the door of the freezer chamber. "Going on like that at an old man who's worked here all his life, and all for the sake of a few pence more on his electricity bill when we all know he makes enough profit to have holidays in Spain. —What's the matter, lad?"

Frank had uttered a strange cry as he entered the chamber.

Joe looked in and saw him standing over the huddled, hoar-white figure of a dead man. He went closer and crouched to look at the face. It was glistening with a patina of frost.

It was the face of Mr. Pugh.

Joe placed his hand on Frank's shoulder and said, "Come away, lad. There's nothing we can do."

From somewhere Joe produced a hip flask and poured some scotch for Frank as they sat in the shop and stared at the door of the freezer.

"We'll have to call the police," said Frank.

"I'll do it presently."

"He must have been trapped in there all the weekend."

"He wouldn't have known much about it," said Joe. "He must have died inside a few hours."

"How could it have happened?"

Joe stared into space and said nothing.

"There's a handle on the inside of that door," said Frank, speaking his thoughts as they rushed through the implications. "Anyone caught in there can open the door and walk out, usually. But he couldn't get out because the padlock on the outside was on. Someone must have put it there. It must have been Percy. Why would Percy do a thing like that?"

Joe gave a shrug and kept silent.

Frank supplied his own answer: "He must have panicked when he thought he would lose his job. He'd been in fear of losing it for years. He found some way of persuading Mr. Pugh to go into the freezer and then locked him inside.

"I know what he did! He told Mr. Pugh the handle on the inside was too stiff to move and he liked to leave the door open because he was scared of being trapped. Mr. Pugh said he was making excuses and stepped inside to show how easy it was to get out." Frank began to smile. "Mr. Wilkins, I think I'm going to laugh."

The tension relaxed a little.

"I'll tell you something funnier than that," said Joe. "Why do you think Percy hasn't come in this morning?"

"Well, it's obvious. He knew we'd open that door and find the body."

"Yes, but where do you think he is?"

Frank frowned and shook his head. "At home?"

Joe grinned and said, "Majorca."

"No!" Frank rocked with laughter. "The crafty old beggar!"

"When Mr. Pugh came in on Saturday he had a large brown envelope containing his travel tickets."

"I remember. I saw it. He put it on the counter by the cash register."

"Well, it isn't there now, is it?"

Frank said, "You can't help admiring the old man. He's probably sitting on the hotel terrace at this minute, ordering his breakfast and thinking of you and me finding Mr. Pugh in the freezer."

"I'd better phone the police," said Joe, getting up.

"You know, if it wasn't for that padlock on the door no one would suspect what happened," said Frank. "Mr. Pugh might have just felt ill and fainted in there. They'd call it misadventure, or something."

"And Percy would get away with it," said Joe reflectively. "It isn't as if he's a vicious murderer. He's no danger to anyone else."

"I could get rid of it," offered Frank. "I could put it in the pannier on my bike and get rid of it lunchtime."

"We'd have to stick to the same story," said Joe. "We just opened the door and found him lying there."

"It's the truth," said Frank. "We don't need to say a word about the padlock. Shall we do it? Poor old Percy—he hasn't had many breaks."

"All right," confirmed Joe. "We'll do it."

After they had shaken hands, he picked up the phone and called the police. Frank took the padlock to his motorbike in the yard at the back of the shop and secreted it under the toolbag in the pannier.

A squad car drew up outside the shop within five minutes of Joe's call. A bearded sergeant and a constable came in and Joe opened the freezer chamber and showed them Mr. Pugh's body. Frank described how he had found it, omitting to mention the padlock. Joe confirmed Frank's statement.

"So it looks as if the body's been lying in there since you closed on Saturday," said the sergeant after they had withdrawn to the warmer air of the shop. "You say that Mr. Pugh looked in late in the afternoon. What did he want?"

"He was just making sure everything was in order before he went on holiday," said Joe.

"He was off to Majorca for a week," added Frank.

"Lucky man," put in the constable.

The sergeant gave him a withering look. "Was Mr. Pugh in good health?" he asked Joe.

"I thought he looked rather off-color," answered Joe. "He drove himself hard, you know."

"He needed the holiday," said Frank, quick to see the point of what Joe was suggesting.

"Well, he didn't get it," said the sergeant. "He must have collapsed.

Heart, I expect. The doctor will tell us. There's an ambulance on the way. I suggest you keep the shop closed for a couple of hours. I shall want statements from both of you. Was there anyone else working here on Saturday?"

"Only Percy—Mr. Maddox," answered Joe. "He isn't in this morning. I believe he was going to ask Mr. Pugh for a few days off."

"I see. We'll want a statement from him. Have you got his address?"

"He told me he was hoping to go away," said Joe.

"We'll catch up with him later then. Which of you was the last to leave on Saturday?"

"That was Percy," said Joe.

"He stays behind to clear up," explained Frank.

"He puts things away, you mean?"

"That's right," said Joe. "He's getting on a bit. He's worked here for years. A bit slow now, but he likes to be useful. He puts everything away at the end of the day."

"In the freezer?"

Joe shook his head. "We don't refreeze meat. It has to be put in the chiller at the end of the day."

"So he wouldn't have opened the freezer door?"

"It's unlikely," said Joe. "If he had, he'd have found Mr. Pugh, wouldn't he?"

They took a statement from Frank. He said nothing to incriminate Percy. He simply explained how he had seen Mr. Pugh come into the shop late on Saturday afternoon shortly before he, Frank, had left to deliver the orders. As for this morning, he had opened the freezer door and found Mr. Pugh dead on the floor. The constable read the statement back and Frank signed it. "Would you like some coffee and a fresh doughnut?" he asked the policeman. "We always have a doughnut in the morning. It's my job to collect them from Jonquil's. I go on my bike and they're still warm when I get back."

"I like the sound of that," said the sergeant, putting his hand in his pocket. "How much are they?"

Frank felt an exhilarating sense of release as he wheeled his motorcycle into the street and started the engine. He rode up the hill toward the baker's, stopping a few yards short, by the place where the front of the delicatessen was being renovated. Outside was a builder's skip containing old wood and masonry. Frank took the padlock from his basket and dropped it unobtrusively into the skip. He collected the bag of doughnuts from the baker's and drove back to the shop.

An ambulance had drawn up outside. As Frank approached, one of the attendants was closing the rear door. The man walked round the side of the vehicle and got in. It moved away. The few bystanders who had collected outside the shop moved on.

When Frank went in, Joe had already made the coffee. He was talking to the police about football.

"We should have gone by now," the sergeant told Frank. "We've got both your statements and the body's been collected, but we didn't want to miss those doughnuts."

Frank handed them around.

"Still warm," said the sergeant. "I hope you observed the speed limit, lad."

Frank smiled.

The police finished their coffee and doughnuts and left the shop.

Frank heaved a huge breath of relief.

Joe took out his handkerchief and mopped his forehead. "Did you get rid of it?"

Frank nodded.

"Well done," said Joe. "Well done, Frank."

"I reckon old Percy owes us both a beer after that," said Frank.

"It's worth more than that," said Joe.

"We couldn't have turned him in," said Frank.

They opened the shop. Customers who had seen the shop closed earlier now returned in force. They all wanted to know what the police had been doing here and whether it was a body that the ambulance men had collected. Joe and Frank explained that they were unable to comment. The inquiries persisted and the queue got longer.

"If you ask me," one woman notorious for voicing her opinions said, "it was that old boy who sweeps the floor. He was far too old to be working in a shop."

"If you mean Percy Maddox, you're wrong," said the woman next in line. "There's nothing wrong with Percy. There he is coming up the street on his bike."

Joe dropped the cleaver he was using and went to the window. He was joined by Frank, who gave a low whistle of amazement.

"Crazy old man," said Joe angrily. "What does he think he's up to? He ought to be in Spain."

They watched through the window as Percy came to a halt outside the shop, dismounted, removed his cycle-clips, and wheeled his bicycle up the side passage. A moment later he appeared in the shop, a slight, bald-headed, worried-looking man in a faded grey suit. He picked his apron off the hook and started getting into it. "Morning, ladies," he said to the queue, then turned to Joe and said, "Morning, Joe. Shall I tidy up the window? It's a bit of a mess."

Joe said, "What are you doing, coming in here?"

"Sorry I'm late," said Percy. "The police kept me waiting."

"You've been to the police?" said Joe in a shrill voice. "What did you tell them?"

Frank said, "Listen, I've just thought of something. I'd better go and fetch it." He started untying his apron.

But he was slower than Joe, who was already out of his. He said, "You stay. I'll go."

While Frank was saying, "But you don't know where I put it," Joe was round the counter and out to the street.

He didn't get far. Apparently from nowhere, two policemen grabbed him. A squad car drew up and he was bundled into the back. It drove away, its blue light flashing.

"Who's next?" said Percy, who had taken Joe's place behind the counter.

An hour or so later, when there was no queue left and Frank and Percy had the shop to themselves, Frank said, "What's going to happen to Joe?"

"Plenty of questions, I should think," answered Percy. "You know about Mr. Pugh being found dead, don't you?"

"I was the one who found him."

"Well, Joe must have murdered him."

"Joe? We thought it was you."

Percy blinked. "Me, son?"

"When you didn't come in this morning, we thought you must have bunked off to Spain with that ticket Mr. Pugh left on the counter."

"But why should I want to kill Mr. Pugh after all these years?"

"Well, because of the bad time he gave you—all those long hours without a word of thanks. Exploitation, Joe called it."

"Did he, by George," said Percy with a smile.

"He said there was a bit of a scene on Saturday because you left the freezer door open. He said he felt so embarrassed he cleared off home while Mr. Pugh was still laying into you."

Percy shook his head. "Son, that isn't true. I left before Joe on Friday. Mr. Pugh had told me it might be better if I wasn't around while he did some stocktaking with Joe. We had our suspicions about Joe, you see. The books weren't right. There were big discrepancies. Mr. Pugh and I decided to check things carefully for a week and confront him with the evidence on Saturday after we closed."

Frank's eyes widened.

"Mr. Pugh and *you?*"

"Yes. You weren't to know this, and nor was Joe, but Mr. Pugh made me a partner last year, after I'd done fifty years in the shop. Nice of him, wasn't it? I told him I wouldn't ever make a manager, and I certainly didn't want to upset Joe, so we agreed to keep the partnership a secret and I carried on the same as ever, with the work I know best. But as things have turned out, with me the surviving partner, I can't keep it a secret any longer, can I? It's my shop now. I'm the boss."

Frank was shaking his head, trying to understand. "So did you put the police onto Joe?"

Percy nodded. "But I didn't mean to. I didn't know what had happened. On Sunday morning Joe drove over to see me. He told me Mr. Pugh had changed his mind about going to Spain because the auditors were coming to look at the books and he'd asked Joe to offer the ticket to me. I believed him. I thought he wanted me out of the way to spare me any unpleasantness."

"When it was really Joe who wanted you out of the way," said Frank. He recollected the events of the morning, the way Joe had tricked him into covering up the crime out of sympathy for Percy, when in reality Percy was innocent. The trick had almost succeeded too. The police had gone away convinced Mr. Pugh had died by misadventure. They hadn't suspected murder, and they certainly hadn't suspected Joe of committing it. But now he was under arrest.

"Well, if you weren't suspicious of Joe," Frank said to Percy, "why aren't you in Spain? What made you go to the police?"

Percy picked up Joe's straw boater.

"You know how it is with me, son. I haven't had a holiday in years, let alone a holiday abroad. I haven't got a passport. I dropped in at the police station to ask where I can get one, and—" He handed the boater to Frank. "I need a new manager now, don't I?"

BURNING BRIDGES
by JAMES POWELL

As soon as Barber hit the ball off the tee on the sixth hole, he suspected that Billy Hicks was no longer among the living. Barber's stance, swing, and follow-through, all the despair of the club pro, all the reason he golfed alone, had come together perfectly. The high lofting ball cleared the water trap at the end of the fairway to drop like a ripe plum onto the green. Yes, Hicks was dead. When the ball rolled toward the pin and fell into the cup, well, that was just a little something extra. Barber knew enough about golf to know a hole-in-one was luck. But that was Hicks, a great athlete and a real lucky bastard. Up till now. Barber gave a small, sad smile.

He trundled back toward the clubhouse in the gold cart without retrieving his ball. And he wouldn't mention the hole-in-one. That would only start heads shaking again. People had been doing that for as long as Barber could remember. At first they'd shaken their heads in amazement that the apple had fallen so far from the tree, that Titus Barber had sired so bland, awkward, and undriven a son. Then they tut-tutted over the wild crowd he ran with in high school. But more recently Barber had given those same heads another reason to shake, by totally confounding their early estimates of him. Ten years out of college, not only had he restructured his father's company but he'd come up with a product line that placed Barber Textiles among the country's top three producers of casual stockings for women. Looking back on it, perhaps Barber was more baffled than anyone else by the transformation. Recently he'd come to suspect what Hicks's death now seemed to confirm: that it had something to do with the Four Musketeers.

They'd been best of friends since high school—Billy Hicks, the jock of the group; Sterne, the ringleader, the brain, the one who came up with the ideas; hotshot Hagerdorn, with his bray of a laugh and a knack for organizing things; Lundeen, who, when he wasn't fighting off the girls, would do anything on a dare. And Barber. The Four Musketeers, they called themselves. All for one and one for all. Sterne picked the name, meaning it as a joke on Barber's shortcomings in the personality department. They used to call him "the little man who almost wasn't there." Barber had never minded. Alone, he'd been shy, clumsy, tongue-tied, and not so much un-popular as ignored or overlooked. But with them he'd felt full of life and purpose.

He could still remember his excitement after the prom their sophomore year when Sterne came up with the idea of burning one of the old covered bridges that still served the narrower, less-traveled roads in that corner of the county. The one they chose was a fifty-footer tucked away in a small valley. They came in one car. When the fire was going well, they drew lots and took their turns driving across the burning bridge and back again. It was a variation on the old road game called Chicken, the winner being the one who dared to make the last run. That was usually Lundeen, who never seemed to give a damn—which might have been part of his charm with women. After that, burning a covered bridge became a regular prom-night event for the Four Musketeers. And they always got away with it, although bridge number three had been a close call.

When Barber graduated from high school, his father had wanted to send him to one of the big colleges out East. In a rare show of determination, Barber insisted on joining his friends at the state college nearby. Barber didn't do very well there. He wasn't lazy, he was just a plodder. When Sterne put two ideas together, Barber could see them catch fire. When Hagerdorn talked mathematics, it made sense. And when the popular Billy Hicks introduced him around or Lundeen demonstrated the art of charming the ladies (or "wowing the dollies" as Lundeen called it), they made it look like the easiest thing in the world. But when Barber was on his own, no ideas gave off the merest spark, nothing seemed to add up, and people made him nervous—women most of all. In fact, he stood so much in awe of Lundeen's prowess with women that one time Sterne had bounced a paper-back off his head from across the room with the angry remark, "Remem-ber, even Don Juan takes off his pants one leg at a time."

But at last, college days came to an end, sending all five of the Four Musketeers on their separate ways. Sterne, who'd been active in theater on campus, traveled to Cape Cod to work as a stagehand in summer stock and later to New York, where he set about writing plays. Hagerdorn enrolled at Wharton for an MBA. Hicks, who'd been at college on a football scholar-ship, was picked up by a major professional team. Lundeen traveled south to work for an uncle who owned a share in an insurance agency. Barber returned home to Barber Textiles.

Those next few years had been the unhappiest in Barber's life. His father shunted him around from department to department to acquaint him with every aspect of the company over which he would one day preside. Barber plodded from Sales to Raw Materials, from the mill floor to Personnel, leaving many a shaking head in his wake. In his fifth year, he was assigned to the Comptroller's office, which he found slightly more congenial because the Comptroller, a relation of the family by marriage, was a plodder, too.

Then one day, out of the blue, Barber came up with a plan for restructuring the company's long-term debt that was so ingenious he couldn't at first believe the numbers. The Comptroller stared down at the calculations, drummed his fingers, and admitted he couldn't see why it wouldn't work, either. Barber gave a high-pitched laugh. Then the two men hurried off down the hall to Barber Senior. That afternoon the company learned that young Barber had been named to the newly created post of Assistant to the President in Charge of Reorganization.

The next morning Barber came down to breakfast mulling over a shakeup in mid-level management. Without looking up from his grapefruit and newspaper, his father said, "Says here a friend of yours died. That young Hagerdorn, the one with the whinny, fell down dead getting out of a cab on Wall Street. Heart attack."

Barber surprised himself by how easily he took Hagerdorn's death. He tried to mourn, but felt no real sense of loss. Strange as it seemed, Barber felt closer to Hagerdorn now than he ever had.

During the next few years, Barber made something of a name for himself in the textile industry. A profile of him in *Modern Yarn and Spindle* spoke of the "new lean look at Barber Textiles." Sterne was making the papers, too. He'd had a couple of plays produced Off Broadway, married an actress of reputation, and gotten a divorce. Meanwhile, Billy Hicks, retired from football now with a bad knee, had gone into stock-car racing. And Lundeen had arrived back in town and used an inheritance from his uncle to open up his own insurance agency. Barber and Lundeen met occasionally for lunch. Lundeen hadn't changed a bit. He always looked like he could use a good night's sleep. Barber made sure he got the Barber Textiles business. A year later, Hicks moved back to town with his wife and kids and started a small air-freight company out at the airport.

One summer Hicks rented a beach house on North Carolina's Outer Banks just above Cape Hatteras. Whenever Barber could get away, he would go down for surf-fishing. One long weekend they were joined by Lundeen and a striking redhead named Maura, who wore a big floppy hat to protect her skin from the sun. It was windy the afternoon they arrived and Maura'd had to anchor down the hat with her forearm, which was quickly the color of boiled lobster. By Saturday, she didn't venture out from under the deck umbrella. But she fell sleep in the shade on the deckchair and the sun swung around. She awoke with angry red legs, one marked with a diagonal of white skin where the other leg had crossed over it. Barber remarked to himself that that leg looked something like a candy cane or like the nearby lighthouse except that the diagonals on the light-house were black and white.

It wasn't until the fall of that year, on a chilly day with wet leaves in the gutter, that Barber remembered that candy-cane leg and the Hatteras Light and got the idea that that would make Barber Textiles a national name. Lighthouse Legs, they would call them, a line of casual stockings for women based on the unique patterns of shape and color of the coastal lighthouses. Everyone in Design thought it was a great idea.

At breakfast the next morning, Barber's father said, "It says here your friend Sterne passed away on Martha's Vineyard. 'By his own hand,' it says." Barber took the paper from his father and read Sterne's short obituary. When he came to the line that referred to the playwright as a maker of "brittle concoctions of vespine dialogue and one-dimensional characterizations," he threw the paper against the wall with an angry force that surprised him.

But he had little time to mourn Sterne. He was busy with the advertising and sales-promotion campaigns for Lighthouse Legs, which he based on a map of the country divided into "lighthouse sectors" instead of states and mock proclamations in the media of penalties for women whose stockings didn't match the nearest lighthouse. The buying public accepted the whole thing as good fun. Two television sitcoms in the same time slot worked Lighthouse Legs into their plots on the same night, a coincidence that made parallel issues of *Time* and *Newsweek*. Lighthouse Legs became the novelty sensation of the women's apparel industry that year. And after their initial popularity, they were as successful a basic in the standard wardrobe as the little black dress and the tweed skirt.

Barber Senior was so pleased with his son's performance that he retired from the company, naming Barber as his successor. At the end of his first year as president, Barber married. While he and his wife were honeymooning in Europe, Barber's father died in his sleep.

Barber met his wife Laurel in the design department at Barber Textiles, where she was attached to the Lighthouse Legs project. She was a tall, vigorous woman with frank, self-confident eyes and a restless air. She had a considerable reputation locally as an artist in her own right and was starting to attract attention on the East Coast with her "charged mobile sculptures," as she called them—like the elaborate remote-controlled construction of firecrackers, pinwheels, and screaming rockets she'd put together for the Fourth of July Statue of Liberty Centennial.

The first time Barber asked her out she refused, seeming genuinely surprised by the invitation. And she kept saying no until he decided it was hopeless. But when work threw them together again a few months later, he asked her out again, he didn't know why—perhaps because she seemed a bit down. She countered with an invitation of her own. That coming Friday there would be a show of her work at a gallery in town. Would he take her?

The gallery was bright, and crowded with people and Laurel's charged mobile sculptures. Her work was all electronically programmed now. The one she'd christened "The Answering Machine," for example, responded with raucous noises and mechanical agitation when spoken to. Another, "Twittering Pie a la Mode de Paul Klee," resembled a covered casserole with a divided lid which it fluttered while emitting peeping sounds when approached. If the intrusion persisted, squawking metal bird-heads popped out from inside and finally the lid began to flap as if struggling to make the casserole airborne. Barber thought them very clever, and he was pleased to find Lundeen there with Dixie Thomas—a town beauty, married to one of his agency's biggest clients—proud that for once he was with an attractive woman, too.

After the gallery opening, Barber took Laurel out any chance he got. He told himself that her coolness toward him would change in time. He knew she liked to live well, admired fast cars, and dreamed of leaving Barber Textiles to give all her time to her own work. He told himself he had to be careful not to overwhelm her with an offer of these things. But having given himself all this good advice, he proposed to her within two months of the gallery show. He was almost surprised when she accepted. Billy Hicks was best man at the wedding. Barber would have asked Lundeen, but he'd just run off with Dixie Thomas.

As Mrs. Barber, Laurel played the charming hostess and represented her husband on several civic committees working for good causes. She even made love to him now and then with a kind of hurried frenzy. But time worked no magic. Worse than that, by the end of the fifth year of their marriage Barber could tell that it cost his wife a great deal of effort to tolerate him at all. Unfortunately, he now loved her more than he had in the beginning. When he sold Barber Textiles to an international conglomerate, he told people he meant to read Dickens and manage his investments. But much of his reason was the desperate hope that spending more time with Laurel might turn the situation around.

Gold had come later. The truth was that Laurel complained about having him underfoot all the time. She also told him he was putting on weight. So he took up golf, playing his solitary nine holes every morning. The game gave him his first chance to think about the changes in his life brought about by the deaths of Hagerdorn and Sterne. And as he did, his mind kept returning to the words of the old policeman that night so many years before when they'd almost been caught burning down their third bridge.

Sterne had figured people would start to be on the lookout by the third prom night, so, to draw off the local fire companies, he sent in a false alarm about another covered bridge burning about twenty miles away. But while they were standing around drinking beer and waiting for the flames to get far enough along for their game, a township police car pulled up behind them. After speaking into his car radio, a fat old policeman got out and, hitching up his trousers, headed slowly over to them.

"Relax," Sterne had whispered and nodded around significantly. Barber and the others understood what he meant. They'd left everything they'd used to start the fire out there on the bridge.

"What the hell's going on here?" demanded the policeman.

"You tell us, officer," said Sterne. "We just got here." He nodded gravely at the bridge as though the fire was a terrible thing.

The old policeman looked from Sterne to the rest of them. In that moment, they all saw that the old man knew underage drinking was the most he could charge them with. They all waited solemnly for the policeman to say something. Then Hagerdorn stretched his palms out to warm them at the fire and said, "It sure takes the chill off the night." The others tried to keep a straight face, but then the laughter came—with Hagerdorn's bray leading all the rest.

The old policeman took off his hat and, holding it, wiped his brow with the crook of his arm. Barber remembered the man's face mottled by flickering flame and darkness. And he never forgot what he told them.

"You're really something," he'd said. "I expect a person'd have to roll all five of you young men together to make one passable human being."

"It just came over the radio, Mr. Barber," said Roy, the locker-room man, holding out a fresh towel and soap. "Your friend Mr. Hicks was killed in a crash out at the airport."

"Yes, I know," said Barber solemnly and headed for the showers.

As he lathered up, he told himself that the old policeman's words offered the only explanation for what had happened to him. That made "all for one" the operative part of the Four Musketeers' motto now, with Barber the "one"—the one passable human being the five of them would make if they were all rolled together. But Barber put a different spin on what the old policeman had said. He saw Sterne, Hagerdorn, and Hicks as if they were parts of himself that he'd loaned out but didn't get paid back until death took a hand in things. And when Lundeen died, he'd be paid back in full—Lundeen's attraction for women would be his. At least enough of it, Barber was sure, for him to hold onto Laurel. Provided Lundeen died soon enough. Hicks' death gave Barber the perfect opportunity to hasten that event.

Barber drove home intending to call Lundeen as soon as he got there. But when he pulled into the circular driveway, a mournful Lundeen was getting out of his car at the front door. "I think Hicks needs a sendoff," said Barber.

Lundeen understood and liked the idea. "One Musketeer's funeral pyre coming up, good buddy," he agreed.

They left the cemetery right after Billy Hicks's funeral and drove back to Barber's separately. They'd bought an old car a couple of days before and left it parked behind the house. The bridge they'd chosen spanned the hundred-foot bed of a river—a mere trickle among the boulders, for it had been unusually dry that year. The bridge would probably burn without much smoke.

Just before the bridge, a small service road angled uphill to the transmission tower of a local television station. But there wasn't any other reason for anyone to come that way except to see the covered bridge itself, the longest in the county. It had escaped the Four Musketeers in their high-school days because a retired farmer and his wife lived right across the way in a small house which, as was the local custom, had been built for them when their children took over the farm. But when the old people died some years back, the house had been sold and moved to a site closer to town. The bridge had board-and-batten walls and a pitched shingle roof. It was painted red.

Driving up onto it was like entering a long, open-ended barn. The planking gave off a low rumble beneath the tires. Halfway across, Barber and Lundeen stopped and unloaded two three-gallon cans of paint thinner, setting them up on the foot-square beams that formed the skeleton of the structure. When they'd parked the car off to the side of the road facing the bridge, they walked back to the two cans. They drenched the middle third of the bridge and gave the liquid a minute or two to soak in. Flame skated across the wood when Lundeen tossed down the torch of rolled up newspaper.

Back at the car, Lundeen reached in and pulled out a six-pack which he offered to Barber. Barber tore off the nearest can, they bumped metal and toasted Billy Hicks, then they sat on the hood of the car, watching the fire's progress.

After a bit, Lundeen said, "Billy Hicks buying the farm like that really makes a guy stop and think about back when. And whenever I do that, do you know what gets me? No offense, old buddy, but when it comes to 'back when,' I always start remembering how you were, well, such a royal nothing back in those days. Man, have you changed! You're a different guy. Hell, a couple of different guys. And me, here I am still doing business at the same old stand."

"Still wowing the dollies, you mean?" said Barber quickly, afraid for a moment that Lundeen was beginning to understand.

Sighing like a man who'd just given up trying to put something important into words, Lundeen took a swallow of beer and said quietly, "Sure, still wowing the dollies."

Barber was surprised to find he'd drunk all his own beer. He was nervous. Simple as his plan was, it was not without risk. Of course, he had Billy Hicks's luck and skill going for him. He intended to use Lundeen's daredevil recklessness to make his friend kill himself. No matter how many runs across the bridge Lundeen made, Barber would make one more, until Lundeen—who could never let himself be beaten like that—would be forced to make the fatal run.

Barber threw his empty beer can into the ditch and jumped to the ground. "Musketeers, start your engines!" he said loudly, for he had won the toss to make the first run. Lundeen got down, too, and stood watching the flames with an absent look. Barber slid behind the wheel, pulled the car back onto the road, and hit the accelerator. He'd done the thing enough times to know that the first few runs wouldn't be anything at all. But when he got there, he was surprised to see how fast the flames had spread and to feel how hot the wind was on his cheek as the car raced through the fire. He reached the other end, spun the car around with all Hicks's skill, and drove back through the flames again.

Lundeen didn't get behind the wheel right away. He stood with his hand on the doorhandle, finishing his beer. Then he looked at Barber and said, "We're getting too old for games like this. No, I mean it. Remember, it's only the two of us left now, good buddy." He got into the car. "So I don't want anything to happen to you. I want you to take care of yourself." Lundeen smiled. "Starting tomorrow." Then he hit the accelerator and rushed the bridge in a shower of gravel.

Barber watched him go with real affection. He could no more bear Lundeen ill will than he could hate his own arm or leg. I'm doing us both a favor, he was telling himself as the car reappeared through the flames, its tires smoking.

"It's going up real fast," said Lundeen. But he still insisted they have another beer. "To Hagerdorn," he named the toast.

"To Hagerdorn," Barber agreed, raising the fresh can of beer. The fire had broken out onto the roof now—the flames seemed wind-fed. As he watched, an updraft of hot air burst out through the roof, carrying burning shingles high into the air. They fluttered down into the dry riverbed like spent fireworks. Barber averted his eyes. But he could hear the flames crack and the structure hum like a pipe organ. He took a long drink and forced himself to say, "And how about you? I hear the agency's not doing well. I hear you're planning on leaving town."

"More than thinking," said Lundeen. "Leaving."

"If it's money—," offered Barber. Funny that he could mean this offer, even while trying to get Lundeen to kill himself. When Lundeen shook his head, Barber threw away the beer can and got behind the wheel. He'd meant to drag things out, but the flames were licking up above the entrance now, he couldn't wait any longer. He put his foot on the gas and the burning bridge rushed to meet him.

Half the bridge, roadbed, and walls, was burning. Barber felt the shock of the heat as the speeding car barreled into the flames. He smelled the blistering paint. A section of boards collapsed behind him as he passed. Then he was out of the flames and down onto the road again. He clenched his teeth, spun the car around, and sped right back into the flames. Halfway across the bridge, a flaming rafter fell, turning the windshield on the passenger's side into a web of shattered glass before bouncing off to the side. In the next instant, Barber was out on the road again. His whole body was shaking when he pulled himself out of the car.

"Thanks for offering the money," said Lundeen as if he'd never left. "But I can't take it. There's nothing or nobody keeping me around here." He shared the last of the beers with Barber, adding, "A change of place may change my luck." Lundeen took his beer with him into the car and looked back. "Here's to Sterne," he said with a smile. "And, listen—no matter what anybody says, remember I never meant to do you any harm."

A puzzled Barber had to fight to keep from calling him back. He watched Lundeen accelerate the blackened car into the inferno of the bridge. The roof was completely engulfed in flames now. The structure crackled and groaned. Suddenly a section of rafters collapsed onto the bridge. Barber shook his head, mourning his friend. An instant later, the car roared out of the flames, scorched and smoking, shouldering a flaming rafter aside as it came.

Lundeen was white as a ghost when he got out of the car. "There's no way you can make it," he insisted, grabbing Barber's arm when he tried to get behind the wheel. "Old Lundeen's won again, right?" But Barber cursed and pushed him aside. He got into the car and put it into reverse for a good running start. "Don't be a damn fool!" shouted Lundeen.

Gritting his teeth, Barber launched the car at the bridge. Ahead of him everything was twisting flames and falling, burning wood. The bridge roared like an animal and Barber roared right back. His anger carried him into the fire and out the other end, where a kind of calm descended on him. As he spun the car around, he knew for a certainty he was going to make it back and that Lundeen would have to make another run and be killed.

He was smiling as he drove back onto the bridge. But suddenly, just as he reached the flames, he heard a sharp bang and the engine cut out. He pumped the gas, but nothing happened. Momentum carried the car halfway out of the flames. Fighting the smoke and the heat, Barber struggled with the unfamiliar doorhandle. Beyond the windshield, beyond the flames, he saw Lundeen's horrified eyes as he dashed onto the bridge trying to get to him. Poor Lundeen, thought Barber affectionately. He understands. In that same moment Barber got the car door open.

Laurel Barber had chaired the fund-raising committee for the hospital's new surgery wing. Now, pale and wearing a small bandage on her forehead, she sat alone in its small waiting room. When the police arrived at her door, she'd expected to be told her husband was dead. Instead they'd said her husband and his friend Mr. Lundeen had been in a bad accident. Lundeen? That was when she'd fainted, striking her head on the corner of the entranceway table. But it hadn't worked out badly. She had only seemed the stricken wife.

She felt better now. The doctor had just come by to discuss her husband's condition. He was on the operating table. The doctor said the next few minutes would be critical. He said her husband wouldn't have been alive at all if the explosion hadn't blown out the side of the bridge and him after it —she could see they had little hope for his recovery. Lundeen was another matter. He'd been hit by some flying debris while trying to get to Barber. A bad concussion. Nothing worse than that. He was unconscious but all vital signs were good.

Laurel thanked the doctor. But when he'd gone, she hadn't sat back down. Instead, she went to the window and looked out across the flat roofs, with their collections of air-conditioning and heating equipment. She found it a comforting view, resembling one of her own creations.

Well, after a frightening start, it looked like everything was working out. She hadn't wanted to kill her husband. In a way, she felt grateful for the way he'd let her use him against Lundeen. God knows he never suspected anything, though he'd almost walked in on them, coming home early like that the day Hicks died. They'd been lucky Lundeen's secretary had called when the plane crash came over the radio.

Laurel would have been content to let things go on the way they'd been going since Lundeen had come back to town, but then Lundeen started up again about leaving for good to make a new start somewhere. They'd fought and broken up many a time—never over his one-night stands, she knew the way he was, but over the longer ones like that silly cow, Dixie Thomas. But this time it wasn't another woman. He simply wanted to go away, to walk out of her life. Frantic, she'd convinced herself that it was Barber who stood in the way of their happiness. With him out of the picture and with his money hers, she was sure Lundeen would stay. Or they could go off *together*. Or, if it came to that, she could follow after him.

So even before Hicks died, Laurel had been trying to come up with a way to kill her husband. When Lundeen first told her about the bridge-burning business, their stupid Musketeer funeral pyre, she'd been furious he'd risk his life like that. But all of a sudden she saw it as a tailormade opportunity. She'd made the small detonating device from leftover Statue of Liberty Centennial parts and wired it to the gas pump of the old car they were going to use. She didn't tell Lundeen. He'd never do anything to harm his good buddy Barber. In fact, her most desperate hold over him these last few months had been her threat to tell Barber about them if he ever went off without her again.

While Lundeen and her husband played out their grim little ritual, Laurel had been watching from her car on the road leading up to the television transmission tower, the remote-control detonator in her lap. Each time Lundeen drove on the bridge, she thought she'd die. But she waited. The fire had to be just right, large enough so that the car's momentum wouldn't carry her husband out of the flames. The instant after she pushed the button, she heard the fire engines. She couldn't let herself be found there. She drove back down the hill as quickly as she could and didn't even look back when she heard the explosion on the bridge.

Someone was standing in the waiting-room doorway. It was the doctor. He shook his head with regret. "I'm sorry, Mrs. Barber," he said. "There was really nothing we could do."

"I'm sure you did your best, Doctor," she said, in a meek widow's voice.

The doctor gave a small bow and looked away. "It's Mr. Lundeen's case that baffles me," he admitted. "As I told you, all the vital signs were strong."

"Lundeen?" she managed to say.

"Mr. Lundeen died without regaining consciousness," said the doctor. "A blood clot, we expect."

Laurel Barber turned ash-gray. The doctor eased her down into a chair, adding, "The intensive-care people spoke to me just as I was coming here. Funny thing about the time of death they gave me. It's the same as we recorded for your husband's death—I mean, down to the second."

A GOOD TURN

by ROBERT BARNARD

In the darkness, the young man couldn't find a bell or a knocker, so he banged with his fist on the front door. Then he leaned his head against the cool brickwork of the strange house, his stomach heaving. Inside, all was still, and he stood up and banged again. This time his fuddled brain became aware of a dim light appearing in an upstairs window, then of the window opening. It was just then that his gut began audibly churning.

"What the hell do you want?"

"Mr. Jacklin? Fred Jacklin?"

"No, it's not. What do you mean, banging on my door at this time of night?"

"It is number fifty-seven, isn't it?"

"No, it's thirty-seven. Why, you filthy young bugger—"

For his stomach had finally risen in revolt and was emptying itself over the gladioli by the front door. As more lights came on in the house, the boy fled down the path, out the front gate, and down the road.

Fifty-seven. It must be on this side of the road. His head seemed clearer now. Funny that—that clearing out your stomach like that should affect the brain. Nice houses. Bigger than your average semi. A damned sight better than Mam's back-to-back in Gateshead—all the rooms so poky, with damp on the bedroom walls, and the two of them getting under each other's feet and on each other's nerves.

Unemployment, that's what did it. Sitting around all day with no money, no hope. He'd had a friend—a nice, normal kid—who'd gone and strung himself up under the strain. In his own case, there'd just been one big, explosive row.

Number fifty-seven. That was in darkness, too. Went to bed early round these parts, didn't they? He looked at his cheap wristwatch. Half past eleven. No time. No time when you didn't have to get up early in the morning. When you didn't have to get up at all. This is a nice house, he thought. A semi, but a big, substantial one. Room to move about, be yourself, keep yourself to yourself if you wanted to. Garden could do with a bit of attention, though.

He went up the path, and in the darkness felt around the heavy wood front door till he found the bell. It played the first notes of "Home Sweet Home."

Again there was silence on the other side of the door. Well, he supposed, if you were in bed the natural thing was to hope that whoever it was would go away. He rang again. This time there were stirrings on the other side of the door—a light upstairs in the distance, then the sound of someone shuffling slowly down the stairs. The door did not open.

"Who is it?"

"Mr. Jacklin? Dad?"

"What did you say?"

"Dad? It's Steve. Your son, Steve."

There was silence on the other side of the door. Well there might be, Steve was sober enough now to realize. Then he heard the sound of bolts being drawn across. The porch light came on, but no lights inside the house. The door was opened, but only to the limits of its chain, which was left on. Dimly he perceived a face appear in the crack.

"What do you want?"

"Dad—it's Steve. I'm your son."

"So you said. Bloody funny time to pay a visit."

"I was in Birmingham. I had a row with me Mam and hitched a lift down."

"You been drinking?"

"Yes. I was a bit sloshed. I knocked on the door of number thirty-seven. But I'm all right now. I just wanted to see you."

The scrutiny continued.

"I can see your mother in you. I suppose it's all right." The figure on the other side fiddled with the chain and the door was opened. Now a light was put on in the hall. "Go through to the kitchen. We'll have a cup of tea."

As Steve went through to the kitchen and found the light switch, the hall light was extinguished. He smiled briefly. He knew North Country people, his people—they were "near." He and his mother had to be. His father originated, he knew, in Bradford. So if he was careful with electricity, it was only to be expected.

His father came into the kitchen now and pottered over to the sink, filling up a kettle and setting it down on the gas ring. When he turned, it was Steve's first view, first proper view, of him. It was something of a shock. He had known that he'd be older than his mother, but this man was about sixty, an old man. And he looked it, too, to Steve's eyes. He was wearing an old-fashioned woolly vest, buttoned at the neck, and grubby flannel trousers with braces, hastily pulled on when the doorbell rang, no doubt. His face was wrinkled, and there was a heavy stubble on chin and cheeks that suggested that his last shave had been the day before. But he was at least wide awake. There was a sharp glint in his eyes.

"So you're Steven." He seemed to have difficulty finding anything to say. Not surprising in the circumstances. "Last time I saw you, you were—how old?"

"Two. Me Mam says you left when I was just over two."

"That'd be about it. Women remember these things. What do you do, then, Steve?"

"Nothing. I'm unemployed. I've been on schemes—youth employment schemes and that. But they're all fakes—nothing comes out of them. There's nothing in Gateshead at all. Twenty-five percent out of work. It's diabolical."

"It's bad here, too. Very bad. You need to go south, the southeast. That's where the work is."

"I know."

He hadn't expected a warm invitation to make this his home, though he had wondered whether he mightn't stop here for a week or two, maybe a month—getting to know his father, helping in the garden. But the drift of the old man's remarks thoroughly chilled the impulse. There was silence again.

"How's your mother?"

"All right. We just about manage. She has a couple of cleaning jobs, but they're a bit dicey. She helps out at the corner shop if they're short-staffed now and again. We're both around the house most of the time, so we get on each other's nerves. We had a big bust-up last night."

His father screwed up his face. "Always had a temper, your mother."

"It were me as well."

"Nasty tongue with it."

"Is that why you moved out?"

It came out more baldly than he had intended. He had always had a curiosity about his father and what had happened before and after his birth, but he hadn't intended to show it by any sort of inquisition. But the old man did not seem disconcerted.

"I never moved in." A cunning smile twisted the gnarled face and Steve saw blackened stumps of teeth. "I know a trick worth two of that. Living with her would practically have been admitting the brat was mine."

"Me."

"That's right. I never lived with your mother. I just slept with her, and slipped her money now and again. She was all right. She inherited that house when your grandparents died."

"It's not a bloody stately home!"

"She was all right," repeated the old man. He poured the tea into two cups and came across to hand one to Steve. His body smelt of meanness and neglect. When Steve tasted the tea, he found it had not been sugared. Seeing a packet on the table he went over and spooned some in, then he squatted on the edge of the table, watching the old man, his father, rolling a cigarette.

"You got a dog?" he asked, fingering a dog lead that was lying on the table. "Not much of a watchdog."

"He's in the garage. He's old, and lost control of his bowels. I'm sick of clearing up his bloody messes. He's deaf, too. I'd have him put down, but it all costs money."

"Sounds like he'd be happier."

The old man shrugged. The boy felt a sudden turn in his stomach which was not due to drink.

"So when I was two you just took off down here?"

"I didn't take off. I sold the business up there and bought a business down here. What's that fancy word the Yanks use? Relocated. That's what I did—I relocated."

"You never told me Mam, though, did you?"

"Oh, she *has* fed you a line, hasn't she? Well, there was no cause to tell her. She was the girl at the counter, the girl behind the cash register, that's all *she* bloody was. Did she expect to be treated like she was co-director? It was a nice little business selling plumbers' supplies, but she was about the smallest cog in the outfit."

"You didn't tell her until it was all wrapped up, then you said she needn't bother to come in on Monday."

"Saved a bloody scene, didn't it?"

"And that was the last she saw of you."

"It was. Mind you, I sent her a bit of money from time to time—has she told you that?"

"Peanuts."

"Money doesn't grow on trees."

Steve looked around. "You seem to have done all right."

"Anyway, if I'd sent her anything big, or sent money regular, that would have been practically acknowledging you were my son. I never did that."

"I am, though?"

"Oh, aye. I can say that now you're grown up."

"Oh, yeah—marvelous! Thanks! You acknowledge me now I'm grown up and no one's going to grant a maintenance order against you."

"That's right." The old man smiled a smile of horrible complacency. "Let me give you a bit of advice, free, gratis, and for nothing, son. There's always folk out there waiting to take you for a ride. You'll never get anywhere if you sit back and let 'em. In this world, there's mugs and there's them that take advantage of the mugs. In my book, there's nothing to be said for being one of the mugs."

"I could kill you."

The words came out flatly. They sprang unbidden from disillusion, from the shattering of hopes he didn't know he had cherished, from a sudden, overpowering distaste.

The old man took no notice. He shrugged and turned to wash up his cup. "Well, that's my philosophy, like it or leave it. I didn't ask you to turn up here, and if you were expecting a tearful family reunion you were off your rocker."

Possessed by a new desire thoroughly to frighten this miserable, mean-spirited old man who was his father, Steve spelt it out, speaking low and intensely. "I could kill you. I could put that doglead round your scrawny throat and I could pull it tight and throttle you and no one in this world would care a damn that you were gone."

Still the old man was more puzzled than frightened. He stubbed out his cigarette in an overfull ashtray. "What would you do that for? I never done you no harm."

"Fathers are supposed to do their sons good." Steve reached out and took up the dog lead. "It would almost be a public service. You'd have been done away with, like that old dog that you're too mean to put out of its misery. And no one would think of coming after me, because you haven't got a son, have you? You've never been mug enough to acknowledge you've got a son."

"Don't be daft." There was a tiny quaver of fear now in the old man's voice, showing that Steve's intensity had got through to him. "Your finger-prints'd be all over this kitchen."

"I've never been in trouble with the police. My prints won't be on their files."

"You said yourself you knocked at number thirty-seven. You'll have been seen."

"I was spewing my guts up over their gladdies. They didn't see my face. And what if they had? I'm not known here, and I wouldn't be here by the time the police found you." He tested the leather leash in his strong young hands and slipped off the table he had been sitting on. "I could strangle the life out of you and you'd probably lie on this floor till your body rotted and the stink was so foul that someone outside got a whiff of it. I could snuff you out like a candle—use the life you gave me to put an end to yours."

"Why?" There was open fear now in his face as the boy took a step toward him.

"Because of the way you treated my mother. You didn't just treat her bad, you treated her mean—and you thought yourself bloody smart while you were doing it. And because of the way you treated me. You can't just bring life into the world and slope off as if it's no concern of yours."

"People are doing it all the time."

"They shouldn't." He was now very close to the man, could smell his body, smell his breath. "And because I've never existed for you, I could kill you and nobody'd be any the wiser, nobody'd come after me, and my name wouldn't even come up."

Now he was standing over him, undeniably threatening.

"You young thug! Keep away from me!"

"You're the thug. Hit and run, f——and run—it's the same principle."

"You're dirt! That's what your mother has brought up—a lump of s——!"

Possessed by he no longer knew what compulsion, to frighten or to kill, the boy suddenly put the lead over the man's head, got his ducking body firmly under his, and tightened the leather around his neck, pulling, pulling.

"Stop! You can't—!" The voice was thick, choked, almost petering out. The boy kept pulling.

"I've left you everything!"

The words got through what seemed like a blanket of blood around the boy's brain. His hands paused.

"I've left you everything! There was no one else—you're my heir! The police will be coming after you, all right!"

Steve's hands slackened—the leather relaxed its throttlehold on the old man's windpipe. As the attack faltered, his father lay there very still. Suddenly, the boy stumbled over the pathetic heap, ran through the kitchen and out to the front door. As he pulled the door to, he heard from the kitchen a hoarse, scraggly laugh.

Next day, standing on the motorway, thumbing a lift from the cars streaming north, Steve felt almost lighthearted. From time to time, he did in fact laugh. He would never know whether he had been his father's heir, but he sure as hell would not be it much longer. That was right. He had had nothing from him, wanted nothing of him. He would go back to Gateshead, make it up with his mother, then head south looking for work. He'd see if one of his mates who'd gone down to London could put him up. Failing that, he'd get a bed in a hostel. There was work, if you could keep clear of the people who wanted to get you on drugs or into prostitution. He'd survive. He had a life ahead of him.

And it would be a life unstained by—that act. He would never know whether he would have gone through with it to the end, but a terrible gut feeling told him he would have gone on pulling tighter. It was that cunning old sod that had stopped him. His father had saved him. For once in his life, he had done someone a good turn.

CLAP HANDS, THERE GOES CHARLIE

by GEORGE BAXT

At nine o'clock one Wednesday morning Alice Carruthers sat at the neatly laid table in the breakfast nook, toying with a withered piece of buttered toast. She stared into her third cup of black coffee as though it were a crystal ball, but it told her nothing she didn't already suspect. She was positive Charles, her husband, was having an affair with another woman.

She propped up her chin with the palm of her left hand and stared out the window at the East River. In the background a garbage scow drifted lazily past her line of vision; in the foreground two men were jogging side by side on the path that occasionally invited the attentions of the friendly neighborhood muggers. If she craned her neck, she could see a bit of Gracie Mansion, the mayor's residence, but to Alice it was just an ugly relic that New York should have demolished years ago.

"Clap hands, there goes Charlie." Alice smiled at the memory of her older and wiser sister Rita on that Sunday ten years ago when Alice had married Charles Carruthers. "That's a long winding trail of broken hearts he's leaving behind. How come you drew the lucky number?"

"I was hard to get," Alice remembered replying, also remembering those months before he proposed when every nerve in her body seemed to scream, "Charlie, Charlie, give me Charlie, I must have Charlie." He was so handsome. He still is, but add ten years to the portrait. Not quite six feet tall, amazingly muscular for someone in publishing who was known only to exercise with glasses containing very dry vodka martinis or very wet bloody Marys. And those blue blue eyes. Those incredible blue blue eyes against which, in Alice's prejudiced observation, Paul Newman's paled. Ten years later Charlie was still a formidable presence now much given to absence, such as like where was he last night until three a.m.? And why did he sleep in the guestroom?

Poor sister Rita. Poor dead sister Rita, "Rita," Alice had asked her during a confrontation in Rita's apartment, "have you been having an affair with Charlie?"

She remembered Rita sitting at the vanity table trying to make her sallow face healthy through the aid of any number of cosmetics. "Past tense, sweetheart. I was the penultimate fling before he married you. After me came that peculiar authoress from Canada, you know, the one with three names and one plot." Alice couldn't remember any of the three names because after two books Charlie's publishing house dropped her and she hadn't been heard from since. "Then Mother died and you decided to repatriate yourself from London," where Alice's affair with a notorious Shakespearian star had come to an end—"and Charlie's big eyes lighted you up and here you are, Mrs. Charles Carruthers."

Alice remembered Rita's eyes locking with hers in the vanity-table mirror. "My God, you haven't been married a year yet and you suspect he's cheating?" Alice nodded solemnly. Rita then shrugged, resumed applying the unbecoming shade of rouge, and said through a hollow chuckle, "Clap hands, there goes Charlie."

Five years and seven suspected extracurricular Charlie-affairs later Alice made peace with herself about Charlie. She wanted him and she got him and she would make do with what she had. In his own way Charlie loved her. He never flaunted those clandestine romances in her face and as his star ascended in the world of publishing, so did their financial status and their social rating.

They always got preferential treatment from Elaine at her celebrated Eastside watering hole, and the heads of many a maître d' in the city's most expensive restaurants seemed to barely miss scraping the floor as the toadies bowed them to a table. Charlie was now a partner in the firm of Dickens and Welles, and the authors he continued to edit were a superb Who's Who in the world of literature.

Alice sighed and glanced at her wristwatch. It was past nine a.m. Normally Charlie would be in his office by now going through the mail and dictating to his faithful and loving and unattractive secretary, Clara Kule. Then Alice had a thought: maybe Charlie had left the house before she awakened. But after only three hours of sleep? Then Alice had another thought and this one almost made the blood drain from her face. Maybe Charlie's dead.

"Clap hands, there goes Charlie."

She left the breakfast nook and went into the living room. Charlie's topcoat and his briefcase were on the divan where he had flung them when he came home. The briefcase was open and several manuscript pages had fallen on the carpet. Alice picked them up. The pages had been heavily edited. She read some of the top sheet and shook her head in disbelief. What junk. What trash. Conversations with the dead.

Charlie had explained to her months ago that he had to take on certain books he disliked but he knew the public wanted to read. He knew because smarter publishers had recognized the trend earlier and were saving themselves from bankruptcy by publishing books that boasted lurid dust jackets and screaming two-word titles such as "The Scream," "The Shriek," and one called "The Thumb," which she never had the courage to investigate.

Alice carefully replaced the manuscript pages in the briefcase and was about to enter the guest bedroom when the telephone rang. It was three more shrill rings before she intercepted the nearest extension which was on a table next to the divan.

"It's me!" trilled the gay voice at the other end. Alice recognized Minna Walsh, one of the few friends left from the "old gang," the starry-eyed aspirants to theatrical celebrity of those wonderful days (were they really?) before she became the British Shakespearian star's idiotic camp follower and trailed him to his home in London. "Can we meet a little earlier today? I've got something special on for both of us at two o'clock promptly and I'm sure it's going to be a hoot."

Minna frequently came up with "hoots." A wealthy widow, she gave up the theater when she married Herman Walsh, a successful Westchester dentist who, Minna explained when they became engaged, "Looked in my mouth and it was love at first sight."

"What kind of hoot?" asked Alice.

"I'll tell you when I see you. Right now I'll be late for the beauty parlor and they need all the time I can give them. So twelve thirty at Joe's, okay?"

"Fine by me." Alice replaced the phone on the receiver when Charlie entered from the guestroom. He was naked except for a bath towel strategically tied around his waist. His left cheek was raked with four nasty scratches. "What happened to you?" she asked even though her mouth had gone dry. Charlie continued on to the kitchen. As he went past her she heard him mutter, "Nothing serious."

"Those scratches look ugly!" she called after him. "Let me put some peroxide on them."

"I already have." He turned in the doorway of the kitchen. "Do me a favor. Call the office. Tell Clara I'm not coming in today. I'm working at home. You having your usual lunch with Minna?"

"Yes." He went into the kitchen and she dutifully went to the phone. The usual lunch with Minna. Every Wednesday. Lunch with Minna at Joe's, a theatrical hangout in the theater district, and then a matinee. The usual lunch. The usual Minna. The usual Wednesday.

"What usual Wednesday?" asked Clara at the other end of the phone.

Alice was startled. "Did I say that?"

Clara cleared her throat and said, "You said, the usual Wednesday. Maybe it's the title of a book?"

"Not that I know of."

"He's not sick or anything, is he?"

"No . . . not sick . . . or anything. He's just decided to work at home."

"Well, that's an awful lot of appointments I've got to reschedule. And Mrs. D. due at twelve is hell on wheels about punctuality. I better get on to her right away. Okay, Mrs. C., I'll take care of everything." Good old dependable Clara. Had she opted for spinsterhood because she preferred being dependable to being married? Should Alice have tested for that television series instead of marrying Charlie?

"I'd probably be a has-been by now."

"What the hell are you talking about?" She had entered the kitchen where Charlie stood at the counter drinking a cup of black coffee.

"Do you want some eggs or something? Some fresh toast?"

"Nothing, thanks."

"What's wrong?"

"For Pete's sake lay off!" He slammed the cup onto the saucer and left the kitchen. Alice knew better than to pursue and worry him. Instead, she examined both pieces of china to see if they'd been damaged, and they hadn't been. She tidied up because this was the maid's day out. She wondered about preparing some lunch for her husband. She continued wondering while she bathed, then anointed herself, carefully made up her face, and carefully chose her wardrobe.

When she was ready to leave to meet Minna, she found Charlie seated on the divan in the living room wearing slacks, sports shirt, and scuffed loafers. He was making notes in the manuscript he'd brought home the night before.

"Any good?" asked Alice.

"This?" Charlie indicated the manuscript. "Unadulterated junk."

"I read a page this morning. Some of the manuscript fell on the floor when you came home last night."

"No, I threw them on the floor. I hate this book. I hate myself for publishing it. I hate myself lately for a lot of things and I owe you a world of apologies for how badly I've been behaving lately, but now isn't the time. So you'll forgive me if I return to this pile of tripe. I'm expecting the author at twelve thirty."

Alice stared at him and then asked, "Shall I prepare some lunch? I could do a salad or something light like that."

"No, thanks. I'll phone out and have something delivered. Give my love to Minna."

"Will do." She was in the foyer when he shouted her name. She crossed back to the living room and stood in the entrance with a quizzical expression on her face.

"How's about dinner tonight? Someplace downtown for a change. Let's go to Little Italy. I've got a sudden craving for some rich Italian food."

"It's a date," she said, favoring him with what she hoped was one of her most delicious smiles.

Five minutes later, seated in the back of the taxi heading downtown, she wondered why he told her he was expecting the author of that junk at twelve thirty. Did he really consider her such a fool? Did Charlie really think she was an idiot? Didn't he realize by now she was a past master at putting two and two together?

The author of that junk about life after death was his current sweetie. It was her fingers that had raked his cheek last night. And then after they kissed and made up, he remembered that the next day was Wednesday, Alice's usual lunch day with Minna, and that the coast would be clear. How could he? She clenched her fist as she stared out the window. How could he bring her into our home? To her knowledge, he had never done that before. But today he was entertaining the author of that junk.

Alice had a feeling of déjà vu. (How had Minna once put it? "Tippecanoe and déjà vu!") Over a decade ago in London, Alice had returned to the pied-à-terre she occasionally shared with her Shakespearian superstar to find him in a compromising situation (to put it delicately) with one of the juveniles in his company. "I don't know what you're so upset about!" he had sputtered, showering spittle all over the sitting room. (His spray was almost as famous as he was. His devoted audiences were wise enough to book their seats at least five rows away from the stage apron. It remained for the tourists to sit up front and get drenched.) "I mean as an American you should quite understand what I'm up to. What do you call it there? Of course! Diversification!"

Ten minutes later, seated across from Minna at their favorite table near the bar, Minna asked, "Why so down in the mouth?" Alice told her. She could always trust Minna. Minna didn't find Charlie in the least bit sexy and said so aloud, especially when Charlie was within earshot. "That calls for some bloody Marys." Minna flagged a waiter, gave him instructions, then redirected her words at Alice. "Listen. If he's making such a thing about taking you to dinner in Little Italy tonight, then he's giving the other one her walking papers."

"You're sure?"

"Very sure. He couldn't very well do it in the office, could he, not with Clara tuning in. Obviously he let her have the bad news last night which won him his stripes." She glanced at her wristwatch. "At this very moment he's giving her the *coup de* Grace or whatever the hell her name is. Forget it. You knew what Charlie was all about when you married him. You got what you wanted and you've lived with it this long. Believe me, there's little better out there. My late darling did plenty of kadoodling of his own.

I was no fool. While he grew hot I kept my cool. Our doctor kept warning him he was overtaxing his heart, but, oh, well, he went and here I am, rich and cosy and guess where I'm taking you at two p.m. sharp."

"I give up," said Alice while the waiter served their drinks.

"We're going to a séance."

Alice roared with laughter. "Are you mad?"

"No, just looking for some fun. Don't be a spoilsport. Say you'll come with me."

"Well, of course I'm going. I wouldn't miss it for the world."

What a weird day this is, Alice suddenly realized. It's a day that's completely out of focus. It's surreal, with settings by the late Jean Cocteau.

"You've heard of Monica Duval, of course."

"Of course." Alice sipped her drink.

"She's got this marvelously bizarre studio over at Carnegie Hall."

"You've been there before?"

"For drinks. Not to a séance."

"You know this Duval woman socially?"

"Just the one time for drinks. She was at that do at the Gastons a couple of weeks ago. We were introduced, got to talking"—Minna's voice was now singsong—"realized we had some people in common, she invited me for drinks and then this morning called and invited me to the séance."

"Does she know I'm coming?"

"Oh, sure. I told her last week about our Wednesday ritual. When she invited me for lunch on Wednesday and I said, sorry not on Wednesday, because Wednesday belongs to my good old buddy Alice and me." Minna patted Alice's hand. "And we certainly are good old buddies, aren't we, darling."

"We certainly are." Alice lifted her glass in a toast. "Here's to us. The good old buddies."

At promptly two p.m., Alice and Minna arrived at Monica Duval's studio above Carnegie Hall. The door was opened by a middle-aged woman who spoke with a trace of French accent. She led them into the main room where there was a round table which accommodated six chairs. Alice counted the chairs and thought to herself, Madam Duval likes to keep her séances intimate.

There were three people already seated at the table, two middle-aged men and a dumpy woman so badly dressed she had to be uncommonly wealthy. She was obviously married to the man on her right who kept referring impatiently to a very old and very grand pocket watch. Alice and Minna took two seats and then Alice whispered to Minna, "I thought our hostess was very strict about punctuality." It was ten minutes past two.

"How did you know that?" asked Minna.

"I remember reading it someplace." Monica Duval had given interviews to the women's page editor of the *Daily News* and to a feature writer for *New York* magazine. Alice read them both. The other clients stirred as what seemed like a cyclone came hurrying into the room.

"I am so so sorry, my darlings! But I had an urgent appointment at the other side of town and traffic is horrendous when it's normal, but on a Wednesday when all those taxis are hurtling pell-mell to the theater district it is simply *incroyable,* absolutely incredible, but here I am and ready to begin!"

Alice studied the amazing woman as she greeted Minna and the three others, exchanging meaningless pleasantries with the four, as though knowing Alice would require some time to study her. Monica Duval seemed to be in her early thirties. She was of medium height, seemed beautifully proportioned, and had exquisite skin. Her eyes were a seductive sepia and she wore a plain but beautifully cut black dress with a single strand of pearls around her neck. Alice heard Minna introduce her name.

"Mrs. Carruthers," said Madam Duval with a gracious, welcoming nod of her head. "How nice to meet you."

"Thank you. I'm looking forward to this meeting."

"I'm so glad. Is there anyone in particular you'd like to reach in the afterworld?" Alice thought of all the people she couldn't get hold of in this world and wished Madam Duval could materialize an elusive plumber. "Perhaps your sister Rita?" coaxed Madam Duval.

Alice was glad her hands were clasping her purse under the table, out of sight of the others. She was positive her knuckles had gone ivory white. She managed what she hoped was a clever smile. "Did you know my sister Rita? She was a brilliant dress designer."

"I know all about your sister. Would you like me to try and contact her?"

"Yes. By all means."

Madam Duval was looking inscrutable. Her assistant, an old woman, had drawn all the curtains and there was solitary red light strategically situated over Madam Duval's head. Now Madam Duval's eyes closed as she instructed everyone to join hands, which they dutifully did. Very dramatically Madam Duval emitted a ghostly sigh as her head flew back and her mouth fell open.

Minna squeezed Alice's hand. Alice's eyes never left the medium's face. Madam Duval was making strange noises but none of them sounded like Rita. They sounded more to Alice like screechy hinges badly in need of oiling. The unpleasant noises continued and Alice, knowing her sister Rita, was positive if there was an afterlife, Rita was off somewhere having a matinee of her own with some good-looking young man.

And then a voice came from Monica Duval's mouth that made Alice's blood freeze.

"I'm sorry about tonight, honey."

Charlie!

Had Minna recognized it too? Is that why her nails were digging into Alice's palm, although Alice felt no pain?

"I'm sorry, sweetie, but it's off. I can't make dinner." Alice stared at the medium. She had to be in a genuine trance. Her body was unnaturally rigid, almost as though she had died and rigor mortis had set in. "I love you, Alice. I only loved you, Alice. I . . ."—and then Monica Duval's body went into a convulsion. Her hands flew up, her eyes opened, she lurched to her feet, and from her mouth came what Alice and Minna would always remember as a hideous ungodly screeching such as no mortal could ever have uttered.

The lights went on and Madam Duval's assistant hurried to her side. Monica Duval collapsed into her arms and with the help of one of the men the medium was led to a sofa. They stretched her out and after a moment she seemed to have fallen into a sleep deep enough to be mistaken for a coma.

Her assistant said to the clients, "You must go. Madam is not well. She hasn't been well for some time now. She shouldn't be working. Please go. I will look after her."

Minna grabbed Alice's hand and started to hurry her out of the room when the dumpy woman stepped in front of them and said to Alice, "Was that your husband?" Her eyes were like bright kindling, her voice was drenched with anxiety. "Was that your dead husband?"

"My husband is *not* dead," Alice informed her and then her hand flew to her mouth.

"What's wrong?" whispered Minna sounding like the Ghost of Christmas Past.

"Oh, my God, Minna, come home with me! Come home with me!"

"Why? What is it?"

"Hurry, Minna, hurry!"

In the taxi going uptown Minna held tightly to Alice's hand. Alice wouldn't speak. She kept shaking her head and biting her lip, and Minna was worried that the séance might have brought on a nervous breakdown. Life with Charlie was always a strain and maybe the séance was the straw that broke Alice's back. Now what the hell was Charlie doing at the séance, Minna wondered. I mean it was Rita whom Madam Duval was trying to contact—how did Charlie get into the act? Do mediums contact the living too?

The taxi pulled up in front of Alice's apartment building on East End Avenue. Alice had a five-dollar bill ready and thrust it at the driver. She and Minna hurried into the building, into the elevator, and up to the penthouse apartment.

The police were already there.

Detective Jack Becker explained that a neighbor had seen the front door to the apartment ajar, thought it strange, and entered the apartment to investigate. The neighbor, a Mr. Alfred Wayne, a retired chiropodist, found Charlie lying face down on the divan. Protruding from his back was a pair of ornamental shears that usually lay on Charlie's desk. The shears had penetrated his heart. Death must have been instantaneous.

"Clap hands," whispered Alice, and Detective Becker, startled, looked at the freshly minted widow with suspicion.

"What did you say?"

Alice repeated, "Clap hands," then added, "there goes Charlie." She turned to Detective Becker. "It's something my late sister said to me on my wedding day. Detective Becker, I think I can name my husband's murderer."

Scattered on the floor was the manuscript that Charlie Carruthers had been working on that morning. Alice knelt to gather up the pages. Detective Becker spoke to her sharply, "Please don't touch those. We haven't dusted them yet for fingerprints."

Alice got to her feet and crossed to console Minna who stood by a window sobbing. She had really liked Charlie. Alice was glad Minna had taken her to the séance. She was glad Monica Duval had phoned Minna to invite her and to be sure to bring Alice with her. That proved premeditation, as Alice explained it all to Detective Becker who at first was skeptical and then found chills going up his spine when Alice told him about Charlie's voice coming from Monica Duval's mouth.

"I have a feeling Charlie knew Monica Duval intended to kill him. I think she tried to kill him last night but did not succeed. And I think the murder was still so fresh in Monica's mind that instead of invoking the spirit of my sister Rita, she brought in poor Charlie instead. You see, Mr. Becker, those pages scattered on the floor are from a manuscript about life after death written by Monica Duval who has been having an affair with my husband." Minna kept bobbing her head up and down in agreement. "It's a terrible piece of trash, but now that she's murdered my poor Charlie, it will sell millions in hardcover and paperback, and then there are serializations and foreign editions, and it'll make a hell of a television series."

Detective Becker phoned his precinct to have them bring in Monica Duval. He seemed to be hearing some startling news from the precinct. "Are you sure it's the same woman?" Alice and Minna exchanged glances and then moved nearer to the detective. "Okay, if that's what her mother told you, we've got to take it for gospel." Was Duval's assistant her mother?

"Monica Duval confessed killing your husband to her mother shortly before she died."

"She's dead?" gasped Alice. "But . . . what happened?"

"Her mother said she thought she was having a fit. It's as though some-one was choking her to death. But she managed to say she'd killed your husband, then collapsed and died."

"Oh, God, oh, God," said Alice.

"It's just too terrible," said Minna.

"It's worse than you think," said Alice. "Because if there's an afterlife, oh, God, Minna, if there's an afterlife then they're together!"

BIG BOY, LITTLE BOY
by SIMON BRETT

Under normal circumstances he would have thrown away the letter as soon as he recognized the cramped handwriting, but Larry Renshaw was in the process of murdering his wife and needed to focus his mind on something else. So he read it.

Mario, the barman, had handed it over. Having a variety of postal addresses in pubs and bars all over London was a habit Larry had developed in less opulent days, and one that he had not attempted to break after his marriage to Lydia. The sort of letters he received had changed, though; there were fewer instructions from "business associates," fewer guilty wads of notes buying other people's extramarital secrets. Their place had been taken by confirmations of his own sexual assignations, correspondence that could, by the widest distension of the category, be classed as love letters. Marriage had not meant an end of secrets.

But it had meant an upgrading of some of the "postes restantes." Gaston's Bar in Albemarle Street was a definite advance on the Stag's Head in Kilburn. And the Saville Row suit, from which he flicked the salt shed by Mario's peanuts, was more elegant than a hotel porter's uniform. The gold identity bracelet that clinked reassuringly on his wrist was more comfortable than a handcuff—and, Larry Renshaw sincerely believed, much more his natural style.

Which was why he had to ensure that he continued to live in that style. He was nearly fifty. He resented the injustices of a world which had kept him so long from his natural milieu, and now that he had finally arrived there he had no intentions of leaving.

Nor was he going to limit his lifestyle by removing those elements—other women—of which Lydia disapproved.

Which was why, while he sipped Campari and vodka in Gaston's Bar, he was murdering his wife.

And why he read Peter Mostyn's letter to take his mind off what he was doing.

*   *   *

"—and those feelings for you haven't changed. I know over thirty years have passed, but those nights we spent together are still the memories I most treasure. I have never had any other *friends*. Nothing that has happened and no one I have met since has meant as much to me as the pleasure I got, not only from being with you, but also from being known as *yours,* from being made fun of at school as your Little Boy.

"I know it didn't mean as much to you, but I flatter myself that you felt *something* for me at the time. I remember how once we changed pyjamas and you let me sleep in yours in *your* bed all night. I've never felt closer to you than I did that night, as if I didn't just take on your clothes, but also a bit of you—as if I became you for a little while. I had never felt so happy. Because, though we always looked a little alike, though we were the same height and had the same colouring, I never had your strength of character. Just then, for a moment, I knew what it was like to be Larry Renshaw.

"It was wonderful for me to see you last week. I'm only sorry it was for such a short time. Remember, if there's ever *anything* I can do for you, you have only to ask. If you want to meet up again, do ring. I'm only over here sorting out some problem on my uncle's will and as I'm pretty hard up, I spend most of my time in my room at the hotel. But if I *am* out when you ring, they'll take a message. I'll be going back to France at the end of the week, but I'd really like to see you before then. I sometimes think I'll take my courage in both hands and come round to your flat, but I know you wouldn't really like it, particularly now you're *married to that woman*. It was quite a shock when you told me about your marriage. I had always had a secret hope that the reason you never *had* married was—"

Larry stopped reading. Not only had the mention of his marriage brought his mind back to the murder of Lydia, he also found the letter distasteful.

It wasn't being the object of a homosexual passion that worried or challenged him. He had no doubt where his own tastes lay. He didn't even think he had gone through a homosexual phase in adolescence, but he had always had a strong libido, and what other outlet was there in a boys' boarding school? All the other Big Boys had had Little Boys, so he had played the games tradition demanded. But as soon as he had been released from that particular prison, he had quickly discovered, and concentrated on, the instinctive pleasures of heterosexuality.

But Peter Mostyn hadn't changed. He'd make contact every few years, suggesting a lunch, and Larry, aware that a free meal was one he didn't have to pay for, would agree to meet. Their conversation would be stilted, spiralling round topics long dead, and Larry would finish up his brandy and leave as soon as the bill arrived. Then, within a week, one of the "poste restante" barmen would hand over a letter full of closely written obsequious gratitude and assurances of continuing devotion.

For Mostyn the dormitory grappling had obviously meant more and he had frozen like an insect in the amber of adolescence. That was what depressed Larry. He hated the past, he didn't like to think about it. For him there was always the hope of the big win just around the next corner, and he would rather concentrate on that than on the disasters behind him.

He could forget the past so easily, instinctively sloughing off the skin of one shady failure to slither out with a shining new identity ready for the next infallible scheme. This protean ability had enabled him to melt from stockbroker's clerk to Army recruit (after a few bounced cheques), from Army reject to mail-order manager (after a few missing boxes of ammunition), from mail-order manager to pimp (after a few prepaid but undelivered orders), and from pimp to hotel porter (after a police raid). And it had facilitated the latest metamorphosis, from hotel porter to Savile-Row-suited husband of a rich neurotic dipsomaniac (just before the inevitable theft inquiry). For Larry, change and hope went hand in hand.

So Peter Mostyn's devotion was an unpleasant intrusion. It suggested that, whatever his current identity, there remained in Larry an unchanging core that could still be loved. It threatened his independence in a way the love of women never had. His heterosexual affairs were all brisk and physical, soon ended, leaving in him no adverse emotion that couldn't be erased by another conquest and, in the women, undiluted resentment.

But Peter Mostyn's avowed love was something else—an unpleasant reminder of his continuing identity, almost a *memento mori*. And Peter Mostyn himself was even more of a *memento mori*.

They had met the previous week for the first time in six years. Once again, old habits had died hard, and Larry had instinctively taken the bait of a free meal in spite of his new opulence.

As soon as he saw Peter Mostyn, he knew it was a bad idea. He felt like Dorian Gray meeting his picture face to face. The Little Boy had aged so unattractively that his appearance was a challenge to Larry's vigour and smartness. After all, they were about the same age—no, hell, Mostyn was younger. At school he had been the Little Boy to Larry's Big Boy. A couple of forms behind, so a couple of years younger.

And yet to see him, you'd think he was on the verge of death. He had been ill, apparently; Larry seemed to remember his saying something over the lunch about having been ill. Perhaps that explained the long tubular crutches and the general air of debility. But it was no excuse for the teeth and the hair—the improvement of those was quite within his power. Okay, most of us lose some teeth, but that doesn't mean we have to go around with a mouth like a drawstring purse. Larry prided himself on his own false teeth. One of the first things he'd done after marrying Lydia had been to set up a series of private dental appointments and have his mouth filled with the best replacements money could buy.

And the hair. Larry was thinning a bit and would have been greying but for the discreet preparation he bought from his Jermyn Street hairdresser. But he liked to think that, even if he had been so unfortunate as to lose all his hair, he wouldn't have resorted to a toupé that looked like a small brown mammal that had been run over by a day's traffic on the M1.

And yet that was how Peter Mostyn had appeared, a hobbling creature with concave lips and hair that lacked any credibility. And, to match his physical state, he had demonstrated his emotional crippledom with the same adolescent infatuation and unwholesome self-pity, the same constant assertions that he would do anything for his friend, that he felt his own life to be without value and only likely to take on meaning if it could be used in the service of Larry Renshaw.

Larry didn't like any of it. Particularly he didn't like the constant use of the past tense, as if life from now on would be an increasingly crepuscular experience. He thought in the future tense, and of a future that was infinite now that he had Lydia's money.

Now that he had Lydia's money . . . He looked at his watch. A quarter to eight. She should be a good five hours dead. Time to put thoughts of that tired old queen Mostyn behind him and get on with the main business of the day. Time for the dutiful husband to go home and discover his wife's body. Or if he was really lucky, discover that his sister-in-law had just discovered his wife's body.

He said good-bye loudly to Mario, and made some quip about the barman's new apron. He also asked if the barroom clock was right and checked his watch against it.

After a lifetime of obscuring details of timing and squeezing alibis from forgotten minutes, it was an amusing novelty to draw attention to time. And to himself.

For the same reason, he exchanged memorable banter with the driver of the taxi he picked up in a still-light Piccadilly Circus before settling back for the journey to Abbey Road.

Now he felt supremely confident. He was following his infallible instinct. The plan was the work of a mastermind. He even had a twinge of regret to think that when he had all Lydia's money that mind would be lost to crime. But no, he didn't intend to hazard his newfound fortune by doing anything mildly risky. He needed freedom to cram into his remaining rich life what he had missed out on in poorer days.

Which was why the murder plan was so good. It contained no risk at all.

In fact, although he didn't consciously realize it at the time he had got the murder plan at the same time he had got Lydia. She had come ready-packed with her own self-destruct mechanism. The complete kit.

*　　　*　　　*

Lydia had fallen in love with Larry when he saved her life, and had married him out of gratitude.

It had happened two years previously. Larry Renshaw had been at the lowest ebb of a career that had known many freak tides. He had been working as a porter at a Park Lane hotel, whose management was beginning to suspect him of helping himself from the wallets, handbags, and jewel cases of the guests. One afternoon he had received a tipoff that they were on to him, and determined to make one last reasonable-sized haul before another sudden exit and change of identity.

Observation and staff gossip led him to use his passkey on the door of a Mrs. Lydia Phythian, a lady whose Christmas-tree appearances in the bar left no doubts about her possession of a considerable stock of jewellery, and whose consumption of gin in the same bar suggested that she might be a little careless in locking away her decorations.

So it proved. Necklaces, brooches, bracelets, and rings lay among the pill bottles on the dressing table as casually as stranded seaweed. But there was also in the room something that promised a far richer and less risky haul than a fence's grudging prices for the gems.

There was Mrs. Lydia Phythian, in the process of committing suicide.

The scene was classic to the point of being corny. An empty gin bottle clutched in the hand of the snoring figure on the bed, on the bedside table an empty pill bottle dramatically on its side, and propped against the lamp a folded sheet of crisp blue monogrammed notepaper.

The first thing Larry did was to read the note.

This was the only way out. Nobody cares whether I live or die and I don't want to go on just being a burden. I've tried, but life's too much.

It was undated. Instinctively, Larry put it in his pocket before turning his attention to the figure on the bed. She was deeply asleep, but her pulses were still strong. Remembering some movie with this scene in it, he slapped her face.

Her eyes came woozily open. "I want to die. Why shouldn't I die?"

"Because there's so much to live for," he replied, possibly remembering dialogue from the same movie.

Her eyes rolled shut again. He rang for an ambulance. Instinct told him to get an outside line and ring the Emergency Services direct; he didn't want the manager muscling in on his act.

Then, again following the pattern of the movie, he walked her sagging body up and down, keeping her semiconscious until help arrived.

Thereafter he just followed instinct. Instinct told him to accompany her in the ambulance to the hospital; instinct told him to return (out of his hotel uniform) to be there when she came round after the ministrations of the stomach pump; instinct told him to continue his visits when she was moved to the recuperative luxury of the Avenue Clinic. And instinct provided the words which assured her that there really was a lot to live for, and that it was insane for a woman as attractive as her to feel unloved, and that he at least appreciated her true worth.

So their marriage three months after she came out of the clinic was really a triumph of instinct.

A couple of days before the registry-office ceremony, Larry Renshaw had fixed to see her doctor. "I felt, you know, that I should know her medical history now that we're going to be together for life," he said in a responsible voice. "I mean, I'm not asking you to give away any professional secrets, but obviously I want to ensure that there isn't a recurrence of the appalling incident which brought us together."

"Of course." The doctor was bald, thin, and frankly sceptical. He did not seem to be taken in by Larry's performance as the concerned husband-to-be. "Well, she's a very neurotic woman, she likes to draw attention to herself. Nothing's going to change her basic character."

"I thought, being married . . ."

"She's been married a few times before, you must know that."

"Yes, of course, but she seems to have had pretty bad luck and been landed with a lot of bastards. I thought, given someone who really loves her for herself . . ."

"Oh yes, I'm sure she'd be a lot more stable, given *that*." The scepticism was now so overt as to be insulting, but Larry didn't risk righteous anger, as the doctor went on, "The trouble is, Mr. Renshaw, women as rich as Mrs. Phythian tend to meet up with rather a lot of bastards."

Larry ignored the second insult. "What I really wanted to know was—"

"What you really wanted to know," the doctor interrupted, "was whether she was likely to attempt suicide again."

Larry nodded gravely.

"Well, I can't tell you. Someone who takes as many pills and who drinks as much as she does is rarely fully rational. This wasn't her first attempt, though it was different from the others."

"How?"

"The previous ones were more obviously simply demands for attention —she made pretty sure that she'd be found before anything too serious happened. In this case—well, if you hadn't walked into the room I think she'd have gone the distance. Incidentally—"

But Larry spoke before the inevitable question about why he came to be in her room. "Were there any other differences this time?"

"Small ones. The way she crushed up all the pills into the gin before she started suggested a more positive approach. And the fact that there was no note . . ."

Larry didn't respond to the quizzical look. When he left, the doctor shook him by the hand and said with undisguised irony, "I wouldn't worry. I'm sure everything will work out *for you.*"

The insolent distrust was back in that final emphasis, but mixed in the doctor's voice with another feeling, one of relief. At least a new husband would keep Mrs. Phythian out of his surgery for a little while. There would just be a series of repeat prescriptions for tranquillisers and sleeping pills, and he could still charge her for those.

Subconsciously, Larry knew that the doctor had confirmed how easy it would be for him to murder his wife, but he didn't let himself think about it. After all, why should it be necessary?

At first it wasn't. Mrs. Lydia Phythian changed her name again—she was almost rivalling her husband in the number of identities she had taken on—and become Mrs. Lydia Renshaw. At first the marriage worked pretty well. She enjoyed kitting out her new husband and he enjoyed being taken round to expensive shops and being treated by her. He found her a surprisingly avid sexual partner and, although he couldn't have subsisted on that diet alone, secret snacks with other women kept him agreeably nourished and he began to think marriage suited him.

Certainly it brought him a lifestyle he had never before experienced. Having been brought up by parents whose middle-class insistence on putting him through minor public school had dragged their living standards down to working-class and below, and then having never been securely wealthy for more than a fortnight, he was well placed to appreciate the large flat in Abbey Road, the country house in Uckfield, and the choice of driving a Bentley or a little Mercedes.

In fact, there were only two things about his wife that annoyed him— her unwillingness to let him see other women and the restricted amount of pocket money she allowed him.

He had found ways around the second problem; in fact, he had reverted to his old ways to get round the second problem. He had started, very early in their marriage, stealing from his wife.

At first he had done it indirectly. She had trustingly put him in charge of her portfolio of investments, which made it very easy for him to cream off what he required for his day-to-day needs. However, a stormy meeting with Lydia's broker and accountant, who threatened to disclose all to their employer, persuaded him to relinquish these responsibilities.

So he started robbing his wife directly. The alcoholic haze in which she habitually moved made this fairly easy. Mislaying a ring or a small necklace, or even finding her wallet empty within a few hours of going to the bank, were common occurrences and not ones to which she liked to draw attention since they raised the question of how much her drinking affected her memory.

Larry spent a certain amount of this loot on other women, but the bulk of it he consigned to a suitcase, which every three or four weeks was moved discreetly to another Left Luggage office—premarital habits again dying hard. Over some twenty months of marriage, he had accumulated between twelve and thirteen thousand pounds, which was a comforting hedge against adversity.

But he didn't expect adversity. Or at least he didn't expect adversity until he discovered that his wife had put a private detective onto him and had compiled a dossier of a fortnight's infidelities.

It was then that he knew he had to murder her, and had to do it quickly, before the meeting with her solicitor she had mentioned when confronting him with the detective's report. Larry Renshaw had no intention of being divorced from his wife's money.

As soon as he had made the decision, the murder plan that he had shut up in the Left Luggage locker of his subconscious was revealed by a simple turn of a key. It was so simple, he glowed from the beauty of it.

He went through it again as he sat in the cab on the way to Abbey Road. The timing was perfect; there was no way it could fail.

Every three months Lydia spent four days at a health farm. The aim was not primarily to dry her out but to put a temporary brake on the runaway deterioration of her physical charms. However, the strictness of the fashionable institution chosen to take on this hopeless task meant that the visit did have the side-effect of keeping her off alcohol for its duration. The natural consequence of this was that on the afternoon of her return she would, regular as clockwork, irrigate her parched system with at least half a bottle of gin.

And that was all the plan needed. His instinct told him it couldn't fail.

He had made the preparations that morning, almost joyously. He had whistled softly as he worked. There was so little to do. Crush up the pills into the gin bottle, place the suicide note in the desk drawer, and set out to spend his day in company. No part of that day was to be unaccounted for. Gaston's Bar was only the last link in a long chain of alibi.

During the day he had probed at the plan, testing it for weaknesses, and found none.

Suppose Lydia thought the gin tasted funny? She wouldn't, in her haste. Anyway, in her descriptions of the previous attempt, she had said there was no taste. It had been, she said, just like drinking it neat and getting gently drowsier and drowsier. A quiet end. Not an unattractive one.

Suppose the police found out about the private detective and the appointment with the solicitor? Wouldn't they begin to suspect the dead woman's husband? No, if anything, that strengthened his case. Disillusioned by yet another man, depressed by the prospect of yet another divorce, she had taken the quickest way out. True, it didn't put her husband in a very good light, but Larry was not worried about that. So long as he inherited, he didn't care what people thought.

Suppose she had already made a will which disinherited him? He knew she hadn't. That was what she'd set up with the solicitor for the next day. And Larry had been present when she made her previous will that named him, her husband, as sole legatee.

No, his instinct told him nothing could go wrong . . .

He paid off the taxi driver and told him a joke he had heard in the course of the day.

He then went into their block of flats, told the porter the same joke, and asked if he could check the right time. Eight-seventeen. Never had there been a better-documented day.

As he went up in the lift, he wondered if the final refinement to the plan had happened. It wasn't essential, but it would have been nice. Lydia's sister had said she would drop round for the evening. If she could actually have discovered the body . . . Still, she was notoriously bad about time and you can't have everything. But it would be nice . . .

Everything played into his hands. On the landing he met a neighbour just about to walk his chihuahua. Larry greeted them cheerfully and checked the time. His confidence was huge. He enjoyed being a criminal mastermind.

For the benefit of the departing neighbour and because he was going to play the part to the hilt, he called out cheerily, "Good evening, darling!" as he unlocked the front door.

"Good evening, *darling*," said Lydia.

As soon as he saw her, he knew that she knew everything. She sat poised on the sofa, and on the glass coffee table in front of her were the bottle of gin and the suicide note. If they had been labelled in a courtroom, they couldn't have been more clearly marked as evidence. On a table to the side of the sofa stood a half-empty bottle of gin. The bloody, boozy bitch—she couldn't even wait until she got home, she'd taken on new supplies on the way back from the health farm.

"Well, Larry, I dare say you're surprised to see me."

"A little," he said lightly, and smiled what he had always believed to be a charming smile.

"I think I'll have quite a lot to say to my solicitor tomorrow."

He laughed lightly.

"After I've been to the police," she continued.

His next laugh was more brittle.

"Yes, Larry, there are quite a few things to talk about. For a start, I've just done an inventory of my jewellery. And do you know, I think I've suddenly realized why you appeared in my hotel room that fateful afternoon. Once a thief, always a thief. But murder—that's going up a league for you, isn't it?"

The gin hadn't got to her; she was speaking with cold coherence. Larry slowed down his mind to match her logical deliberation. He walked over to his desk in the corner by the door. When he turned round, he was holding the gun he kept in its drawer.

Lydia laughed, loudly and unattractively, as if in derision of his manhood. "Oh, come on, Larry, that's not very subtle. No, your other little scheme was quite clever, I'll give you that. But to shoot me . . . They'd never let you inherit. You aren't allowed to profit from a crime."

"I'm not going to shoot you." He moved across and pointed the gun at her head. "I'm going to make you drink from that other gin bottle."

Again he got the harsh, challenging laugh. "Oh, come on, sweetie. What kind of threat is that? There's a basic fault in your logic. You can't make people kill themselves by threatening to kill them. If you gotta go, who cares about the method? And if you intend to kill me, I'll ensure that you do it the way that gives you most trouble. Shoot away, sweetie."

Involuntarily, he lowered the arm holding the gun.

She laughed again.

"Anyway, I'm bored with this." She rose from the sofa. "I'm going to ring the police. I've had enough of being married to a criminal mastermind."

The taunt so exactly reflected his self-image that it stung like a blow. His gun arm stiffened again and he shot her in the temple as she made her way towards the telephone.

There was a lot of blood. At first he stood there mesmerized by how much blood there was, but then, as the flow stopped, his mind started to work again.

Its deliberations were not comforting. He had blown it. The best he could hope for now was escape.

Unnaturally calm, he went to the telephone. He rang Heathrow. There was a ten o'clock flight. Yes, there was a seat. He booked it.

He took the spare cash from Lydia's handbag. Under ten pounds. She hadn't been to the bank since her return from the health farm. Still, he could use a credit card to pay for the ticket.

He went into the bedroom, where her jewellery lay in its customary disarray. He reached out for a diamond choker.

But no. Supposed the Customs searched him. That was just the sort of trouble he had to avoid. For the same reason, he couldn't take the jewellery from his case in the Left Luggage office. Where was it now, anyway? Oh, no! Liverpool Street! Fumes of panic rose to his brain. There wouldn't be time. Or would there? Maybe if he just got the money from the case and—

The doorbell rang.

Oh, my God! Lydia's sister!

He grabbed a suitcase, threw in his pyjamas and a clean shirt, then rushed into the kitchen, opened the back door, and ran down the fire escape.

Peter Mostyn's cottage was in the Department of the Lot. The nearest large town was Cahors, the nearest small town was Montaigu-de-Quercy, but neither was very near. The cottage itself was small and primitive. Mostyn was not a British trendy making a fashionable home in France; he had moved there in search of obscurity and lived very cheaply, constantly calculating how many years he could remain there on the dwindling capital he had been left by a remote uncle and hoping it would last out his lifetime. He didn't have more contact with the locals than weekly shopping demanded, and both sides seemed happy with this arrangement.

Larry Renshaw arrived there on the third night after Lydia's death. He had travelled unobtrusively by local trains, thumbed lifts, and long stretches of cross-country walking, sleeping in the fields by night. He had sold his Savile Row suit for a tenth of its value in a Paris secondhand clothes shop, where he had bought a set of stained blue overalls, which made him less conspicuous tramping along the sun-baked roads of France. His passport and gold identity bracelet were secure in an inside pocket.

If there was any chase, he reckoned he was ahead of it.

It had been dark for about four hours when he reached the cottage. It was a warm summer night. The countryside was dry and brittle, needing rain. Although the occasional car had flashed past on the narrow local roads, he had not met any pedestrians.

There was a meager slice of moon which showed him enough to dash another hope. In the back of his mind had lurked the possibility that Mostyn, in spite of his constant assertions of poverty, lived in luxury and would prove as well fleshed a body as Lydia to batten on. But the crumbling exterior of the cottage told him that the long-term solution to his problems would have to lie elsewhere. The building had hardly changed at all through many generations of peasant owners.

And when Mostyn came to the door, he could have been the latest representative of that peasant dynasty. His wig was off, he wore a shapeless sort of nightshirt and clutched a candleholder out of a Dickens television serial. The toothless lips moved uneasily and in his eye was an old peasant distrust of outsiders.

That expression vanished as soon as he recognized his visitor.

"Larry. I hoped you'd come to me. I read about it in the papers. Come inside. You'll be safe here."

*   *   *

Safe he certainly was. Mostyn's limited social round meant that there was no danger of the newcomer being recognized. No danger of his even being seen. For three days the only person Larry Renshaw saw was Peter Mostyn.

And Peter Mostyn still hadn't changed at all. He remained a pathetic cripple, rendered even more pathetic by his cringing devotion. For him Renshaw's appearance was the answer to a prayer. Now at last he had the object of his affections in his own home. He was in seventh heaven.

Renshaw wasn't embarrassed by the devotion; he knew Mostyn was far too diffident to try and force unwelcome attentions on him. For a little while at least he had found sanctuary and was content for a couple of days to sit and drink his host's brandy and assess his position.

The assessment wasn't encouraging. Everything had turned sour. All the careful plans he had laid for Lydia's death now worked against him. The elaborate fixing of the time of his arrival at the flat no longer established his alibi; it now pointed the finger of murder at him. Even after he'd shot her, he might have been able to sort something out but for that bloody sister of hers ringing the bell and making him panic. Everything had turned out wrong.

On the third evening, as he sat silent at the table, savagely drinking brandy while Mostyn watched him, Renshaw shouted out against the injustice of it all. "That bloody bitch!"

"Lydia?" asked Mostyn hesitantly.

"No, you fool. Her sister. If she hadn't turned up just at that moment, I'd have got away with it. I'd have thought of something."

"At what moment?"

"Just after I'd shot Lydia. She rang the bell."

"What—about eight-thirty?"

"Yes."

Mostyn paled beneath his toupé. "That wasn't Lydia's sister."

"What? How do you know?"

"It was me." Renshaw looked at him. "It was me. I was flying back the next morning. You hadn't *rung*. I so wanted to see you before I left, so I came to the flats. I didn't *intend* to go in. But I just asked the porter if you were there and he said you'd just arrived."

"It was you! You bloody fool, why didn't you say?"

"I didn't know what had happened. I just—"

"You idiot! You bloody idiot!" The frustration of the last few days and the brandy came together in a wave of fury. Renshaw seized Mostyn by the lapels and shook him. "If I had known it was you . . . You could have saved my life! You bloody fool! You . . ."

"I didn't know, I didn't know," the Little Boy whimpered. "When there was no reply, I just went back to the hotel. Honestly, if I'd known what was happening . . . I'd do anything for you, you *know* I would. Anything . . ."

Renshaw slackened his grasp on Mostyn's lapels and returned to Mostyn's brandy.

It was the next day that he took up the offer. They sat over the debris of lunch. "Peter, you said you'd do anything for me . . ."

"Of course, and I meant it. My life hasn't been much. You're the only person that matters to me. I'd do anything for you. I'll look after you here for as long as—"

"I'm not staying here. I have to get away."

Mostyn's face betrayed his hurt. Renshaw ignored it and continued. "For that I need money."

"I've told you, you can have anything I—"

"No, I know you haven't got any money. Not real money. But I have. In the Left Luggage office at Liverpool Street Station I have over twelve thousand pounds in cash and jewellery." Renshaw looked at Mostyn with the smile he had always believed to be charming. "I want you to go to England to fetch it for me."

"What? But I'd never get it back over here."

"Yes, you would. You're the ideal smuggler. You put the stuff in your crutches. They'd never suspect someone like you."

"But I—"

Renshaw looked hurt. "You said you'd do anything for me."

"Well, I would, but—"

"You can go into Cahors tomorrow and fix the flight."

"But—but that means you'll leave me again."

"For a little while, yes. I'd come back," Renshaw lied.

"I—"

"Please do it for me." Renshaw put on an expression he knew to be vulnerable. "Please."

"All right, I will."

"Bless you, bless you. Come on, let's drink to it."

"I don't drink much. It makes me sleepy. I haven't got the head for it. I—"

"Come on, drink."

Mostyn hadn't got the head for it. As the afternoon progressed, he became more and more embarrassingly devoted. Then he fell into a comatose sleep.

The day after next, the plane ticket was on the dining-room table next to Peter Mostyn's passport. Upstairs his small case was packed ready. He was to fly from Paris in three days' time, on the Wednesday. He would be back at the cottage by the weekend with the money and jewels which would be Renshaw's lifeline.

Renshaw's confidence started to return. With money in his pocket, everything would once more become possible. Twelve thousand pounds was plenty to buy a new identity and start again. Talent like his, he knew, could not be kept down for long.

Mostyn was obviously uneasy about the task ahead of him, but he had been carefully briefed and he'd manage it all right. The Big Boy was entrusting him with a mission and the Little Boy would see that it was efficiently discharged.

A new harmony came into their relationship. Now that his escape had a date on it, Renshaw could relax and even be pleasant to his protector. Mostyn glowed with gratitude for the attention. It didn't take much to make him happy, Renshaw thought contemptuously. Once again, as he looked at the prematurely aged and crippled figure, he found it incongruous that their bodies had ever touched. Mostyn had never been other than pathetic.

Still, he was useful. And though it was making huge inroads into his carefully husbanded wealth, he kept the supply of brandy flowing. Renshaw topped up his tumbler again after lunch on the Monday afternoon. It was then that there was a knock at the door. Mostyn leapt nervously to the window to check out the visitor. When he looked back at Renshaw, his face had even less colour under its thatch. "It's a gendarme."

Moving quickly and efficiently, Larry Renshaw picked up his dirty plate, together with the brandy bottle and tumbler, and went upstairs. His bedroom window was above the sloping roof of the porch. If anyone came up, he would be able to make a quick getaway.

He heard conversation downstairs, but it was too indistinct and his knowledge of French too limited for him to understand it. Then he heard the front door shut. From his window he saw the gendarme go to his bike and cycle off towards Montaigu-de-Quercy.

He gave it five minutes and went downstairs. Peter Mostyn sat at the table, literally shaking.

"What the hell's the matter?"

"The gendarme—he asked if I'd seen you."

"So you said you hadn't."

"Yes, but . . ."

"But what? That's all there is to it, surely. There's been an Interpol alert to check out any contacts I might have abroad. They got your name from my address book back at the flat. So now the local bobby here has done his bit and will report back that you haven't seen me since last week in London. End of story. I'm glad it's happened. At least now I don't have to wait for it."

"Yes, but, Larry, look at the state I'm in."

"You'll calm down. Come on, okay, it was a shock, but you'll get over it."

"That's not what I mean. What I'm saying is, if I'm in this state now, I just won't be able to go through with what I'm supposed to be doing on Wednesday."

"Look, all you have to do is to catch a plane to London, go to the Liverpool Street Left Luggage office, get the case, go to somewhere conveniently quiet, load the stuff into your crutches, and come back here! There's no danger!"

"I can't do it, Larry. I *can't*. I'll crack up. I'll give myself away somehow. If I were like you, I could do it. You've always had a strong nerve for that sort of thing. I wish it were you who was going to do it, because I know you *could*. But I just . . ."

He petered out. Anger invaded Renshaw. "Listen, you little worm, you've got to do it! Good God, you've said enough times you'd do anything for me—and now the first time I ask for something you're bloody chicken!"

"Larry, I would do anything for you, I would. But I just don't think I *can* go through with this. I'd mess it up somehow. Honestly, Larry, if there were anything *else* I could do . . ."

"Anything else? How about getting me off the murder charge? Maybe you'd like to do that instead?" Renshaw asked with acid sarcasm.

"If I could . . . Or if I had enough money to be any use . . . Or if . . ."

"Oh, shut up, you useless little queen!" Larry Renshaw stomped savagely upstairs with the brandy bottle.

They did not speak to each other for over twenty-four hours.

But the next evening, as he lay on the bed drinking brandy, watching the declining sun tinge the scrubby oak trees of the hillside with gold, Renshaw's instinct started to take over again. It was a warm feeling. Once more he felt protected. His instinct was an Almighty Big Boy, looking after him, guiding him, showing him the way forward, as it always had done before.

After about an hour, he heard the front door and saw Mostyn setting off down the road that led to Montaigu-de-Quercy. Again. He'd been out more than once since their row. No doubt going to buy more brandy as a peace offering. Poor little sod. Renshaw chuckled to himself at the aptness of the description.

Alone in the cottage, he dozed. The bang of the door on Mostyn's return woke him. And he was not surprised to wake up with his plan of campaign worked out in every detail.

*   *   *

Peter Mostyn looked up like a mongrel fearing a kick, but Larry Renshaw smiled at him and was amused to see how gratefully the expression changed. Mostyn had all the weakness of the sort of women Renshaw had spent his life avoiding.

"Larry, look, I'm terribly sorry about yesterday afternoon. I was just a coward. Look, I really *do* want to do something for you. You know I'd give my life for you if I thought it'd be any use. It's been a pretty wasted life—I'd like it to do *something* valuable."

"But not go to London and pick up my things?" Renshaw asked lightly.

"I just don't think I *could,* Larry, I don't think I have it *in me.* But I will go to London tomorrow. There's something else I can do for you. I *can* help you. I *have* helped you already. I—"

"Never mind." Renshaw spread his hands in a magnanimous gesture of forgiveness. "Never mind. Listen, Peter," he went on intimately, "I behaved like a swine yesterday and I want to apologize. I'm sorry, this whole thing's been a dreadful strain and I just haven't been appreciating all you're doing for me. Please forgive me."

"You've been fine. I . . ." Mostyn's expression hovered between surprise and delight at his friend's change of behaviour.

"No, I've been being a swine. Peace offering." He drew his hand out of his pocket and held it towards Mostyn.

"But you don't want to give me that. It's your identity bracelet, it's got your name on. And it's gold. I mean, you'd—"

"Please . . ."

Mostyn took the bracelet and slipped it onto his thin wrist.

"Listen, Peter, I've been so confused I haven't been thinking straight. Forget the money in London. Maybe I'll get it someday, maybe I won't. The important thing is that I'm safe at the moment, with a *friend.* A very good friend. Peter, what I want to ask is—can I stay here for a bit?" He looked up humbly. "If you don't mind."

"Mind? Look, you know, Larry, I'd be delighted. *Delighted.* You don't have to ask that."

"Bless you, Peter." Renshaw spoke softly, as if choked by emotion. Then he perked up. "If that's settled then, let's drink on it."

"I won't, thank you, Larry. You know it only makes me sleepy."

"Oh, come on, Peter. If we're going to live together, we've got to learn to enjoy the same hobbies." And he filled two tumblers with brandy.

The prospect opened up by the words "live together" was too much for Mostyn. There were tears in his eyes as he drained the first drink.

It was about an hour and a half later when Renshaw judged the moment to be right. Mostyn was slurring his words and yawning, but still conscious.

His eyes focused in pleasure for a moment when Renshaw murmured, "Why don't we go upstairs?"

"Whaddya mean?"

"You know what I mean." He giggled.

"Really? Really?"

Renshaw nodded.

Mostyn rose, swaying, to his feet. "Where are my crutches?"

"They won't help you stand up straight in the state you're in." Renshaw giggled again, and Mostyn joined in. Renshaw ruffled his Little Boy's hair, and the toupé came off in his hand.

"Gimme thaback."

"When I come upstairs," Renshaw murmured softly. Then, in an even lower whisper, "Go up to my room, get my pyjamas, put them on, and get into my bed. I'll be up soon."

Mostyn smiled with fuddled pleasure and started off up the stairs. Renshaw heard the uneven footsteps in his room above, then the hobbling noises of undressing, the thump of a body hitting the bed, and soon, predictably, silence.

He sat for about a quarter of an hour finishing his drink. Then, whistling softly, he started to make his preparations.

He moved slowly, but efficiently, following the infallible dictates of his instinct. First he went into the little bathroom and shaved off his remaining hair. It took a surprisingly short time. Then he removed his false teeth and put them in a glass of water.

He went cautiously up the stairs and inched open the door of his bedroom. As expected, Mostyn lay unconscious from the unaccustomed alcohol.

Unhurriedly, Renshaw placed the glass of teeth on the bedside table. Then he changed into the clothes Mostyn had just abandoned on the floor. He went into the other bedroom, picked up the overnight case that had been packed, and returned downstairs.

He picked up the air ticket and passport, which still lay accusingly on the dining table. He put on the toupé and compared his reflection with the passport photograph. The picture was ten years old and the resemblance quite sufficient. He picked up the crutches and tried them until he could reproduce the limp that appeared in the "Special Peculiarities" section.

Then he picked up the half-full brandy bottle, another unopened one, and the candle on the table, and went upstairs.

The Little Boy lay on his Big Boy's bed, in his Big Boy's pyjamas, even wearing his Big Boy's gold identity bracelet, but was in no state to appreciate this longed-for felicity. He did not stir as his Big Boy sprinkled brandy over the bedclothes, the rush matting, and the wooden floorboards. Nor did he stir when his Big Boy set the lighted candle on the floor and watched its flames spread.

Larry Renshaw felt the usual confidence that following his instinct produced as he travelled back to London in the identity of Peter Mostyn. He even found there were compensations in being a pathetic, toothless cripple on crutches. People made way for him at the airport and helped him with his bags.

On the plane he mused comfortably about his next movements. Certainly his first port of call must be the Left Luggage office at Liverpool Street. And then probably one of the fences he already knew, to turn the jewellery into cash. Then, who could say? Possibly abroad again . . . Certainly a new identity . . .

But there was no hurry. That was the luxury his instinct had achieved for him. In Mostyn's identity he was safe for as long as he could stand being such a pathetic figure. There was no hurry.

He felt tense as he approached Passport Control at Heathrow. Not frightened—he was confident his instinct would see him through—but tense. After all, if there was a moment when his identity was most likely to be questioned, this was it. But if he was accepted here as Peter Mostyn, then he had nothing more to worry about.

It was slightly unnerving, because the Passport Officer seemed to be expecting him. "Ah, Mr. Mostyn," he said. "If you'd just take a seat here for a moment, I'll tell them you've arrived."

"But I—" No, better not to make a scene. Reserve righteous indignation for later. Must be some minor mix-up. He imagined how feebly Peter Mostyn would whine at the nuisances of bureaucracy.

He didn't have long to wait. Two men in raincoats arrived and asked him to go with them to a small room. They did not speak again until they were all seated.

"Now," said the man who seemed to be senior, "let's talk about the murder of Mrs. Lydia Renshaw."

"Mrs. Lydia Renshaw?" echoed Larry Renshaw, bemused. "But I'm Peter Mostyn."

"Yes," said the man, "we know that. There's no question about that. And that's why we want to talk to you about the murder of Mrs. Lydia Renshaw."

"But . . . why?" Larry Renshaw asked, quite as pathetically as Peter Mostyn would have done.

"Why?" The man seemed puzzled. "Well, because of your letter of confession that arrived this morning."

*   *   *

It was some time before he actually saw the document that had incriminated him, but it didn't take him long to imagine its contents:

Because of his long-standing homosexual attraction to Larry Renshaw, Peter Mostyn had gone round to see him the evening before he was due to return to his home in France. At the block of flats in Abbey Road—where he was seen by the porter—he had found, not Renshaw, but Renshaw's wife, the woman who, in his eyes, had irrevocably alienated the affections of his friend. An argument had ensued, in the course of which he had shot his rival. Larry Renshaw, returning to his flat, seeing his wife's body and guessing what had happened, had immediately set off for France in pursuit of the murderer. It was Renshaw's arrival at his home that had prompted Peter Mostyn to make a clean breast of what he had done . . .

This put Larry Renshaw in a rather difficult position. Since he was now innocent, he could in theory claim back his own identity. But he had a nasty feeling that that would raise more questions than it would answer.

His instinct, now diminished to a limping, apologetic, pathetic thing, advised him to remain as Peter Mostyn, the Little Boy who has made the supreme sacrifice to protect his Big Boy.

So it was as Peter Mostyn that he was charged with, and found guilty of, the murder of Mrs. Lydia Renshaw.

And it was as Peter Mostyn that he was later charged with, and found guilty of, the murder of Larry Renshaw.